THE DIVINE COMEDY

DANTE ALIGHIERI was born in 1265 in Florence. His family, of minor nobility, was not wealthy nor especially distinguished; his mother died when he was a child, his father before 1283. At about the age of 20 he married Gemma Donati, by whom he had three children. Little is known of Dante's formal education—it is likely to have included study with the Dominicans, the Augustinians, and the Franciscans in Florence, and at the university in Bologna. In his youth he formed a deep friendship with the poet Guido Cavalcanti, sought learning and counsel from Brunetto Latini, and associated with a number of poets, musicians, and artists of the day. To his lady Beatrice he wrote love poems in the courtly style, and after her death in 1290 composed the *Vita Nuova* in her memory. A period of dissipation following this event was concluded by a renewed dedication to the study of philosophy. In 1295 Dante entered Florentine politics. In the summer of 1300 he became one of the six governing Priors of Florence. In 1301 the political situation forced Dante and his party into exile. For the rest of his life he wandered through Italy, perhaps studied at Paris, while depending for refuge on the generosity of various nobles, performing diplomatic and legal tasks, and writing impassioned letters asking or demanding support for his ideas. He continued to write, occasionally teaching and lecturing, producing his minor works the *Convivio* and the *Monarchia*, and the *Divine Commedia*, arguably the greatest poem of the Middle Ages. At some point late in life he took asylum in Ravenna where he completed the *Commedia* and died, much honoured, in 1321.

DAVID H. HIGGINS, a graduate of King's College, Cambridge, is Head of the Department of Italian Studies at the University of Bristol. He has written *Dante and the Bible*, and numerous articles and studies on Dante and other Italian authors in language and literary journals.

C. H. SISSON was born in 1914, in Bristol, where he graduated from the School of Philosophy and English Literature. After postgraduate studies in Germany and France he entered the Ministry of Labour, where he became an Under Secretary in 1962. He served in the army during the war, mainly in India. He is married, and lives in Somerset.

Sisson is known as a poet, translator, and critic. His books include *Collected* and *Selected Poems*, translations of Catullus, Lucretius, Virgil, and Racine, volumes of critical essays, and an autobiography. In 1980 he was made an honorary D.Litt. of Bristol (*honoris causa*) for his services to poetry.

OXFORD WORLD'S CLASSICS

*For over 100 years Oxford World's Classics have brought
readers closer to the world's great literature. Now with over 700
titles—from the 4,000-year-old myths of Mesopotamia to the
twentieth century's greatest novels—the series makes available
lesser-known as well as celebrated writing.*

*The pocket-sized hardbacks of the early years contained
introductions by Virginia Woolf, T. S. Eliot, Graham Greene,
and other literary figures which enriched the experience of reading.
Today the series is recognized for its fine scholarship and
reliability in texts that span world literature, drama and poetry,
religion, philosophy and politics. Each edition includes perceptive
commentary and essential background information to meet the
changing needs of readers.*

OXFORD WORLD'S CLASSICS

DANTE ALIGHIERI

The Divine Comedy

Translated by
C. H. SISSON

With an Introduction and Notes by
DAVID H. HIGGINS

OXFORD
UNIVERSITY PRESS

OXFORD

UNIVERSITY PRESS

Great Clarendon Street, Oxford OX2 6DP

Oxford University Press is a department of the University of Oxford.
It furthers the University's objective of excellence in research, scholarship,
and education by publishing worldwide in

Oxford New York

Athens Auckland Bangkok Bogotá Buenos Aires Calcutta
Cape Town Chennai Dar es Salaam Delhi Florence Hong Kong Istanbul
Karachi Kuala Lumpur Madrid Melbourne Mexico City Mumbai
Nairobi Paris São Paulo Shanghai Singapore Taipei Tokyo Toronto Warsaw

with associated companies in Berlin Ibadan

Oxford is a registered trade mark of Oxford University Press
in the UK and in certain other countries

Published in the United States
by Oxford University Press Inc., New York

Verse translation © Charles H. Sisson 1980

Introduction, Commentary, Notes, and Bibliography © 1981 David H. Higgins
Updated 1993

First published as a World's Classics paperback 1993
Reissued as an Oxford World's Classics paperback 1998
Reissued 2008

British Library Cataloguing in Publication Data

Data available

Library of Congress Cataloging in Publication Data

Dante Alighieri, 1265–1321.
[Divina commedia. English]
The divine comedy/Dante Alighieri: translated by Charles H. Sisson;
with an introduction and notes by David H. Higgins.
p. cm.—(Oxford world's classics)
Includes bibliographical references.
I. Sisson, C. H. (Charles Hubert), 1914– . II. Higgins, David H.
III. Title. IV. Series.
PQ4315.S57 1992 92–553

ISBN 978–0–19–953564–4

18

Printed in Great Britain by
Clays Ltd, Elcograf S.p.A.

CONTENTS

THE DIVINE COMEDY

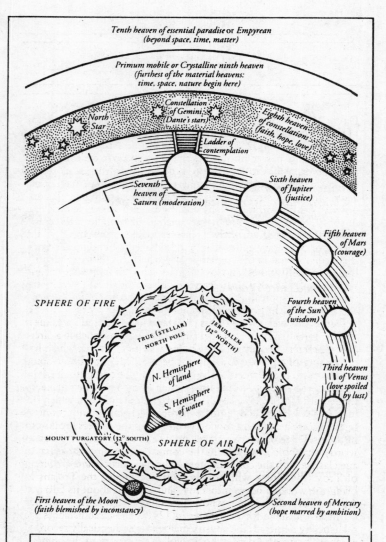

Tenth heaven of essential paradise or Empyrean
(beyond space, time, matter)

Primum mobile or Crystalline ninth heaven
(furthest of the material heavens:
time, space, nature begin here)

North
Star

Constellation
of Gemini
(Dante's stars)

Eighth heaven
of constellations
(faith, hope, love)

Ladder of
contemplation

Seventh
heaven of
Saturn (moderation)

Sixth heaven
of Jupiter
(justice)

Fifth heaven
of Mars
(courage)

SPHERE OF FIRE

TRUE (STELLAR)
NORTH POLE

JERUSALEM
(32° NORTH)

Fourth heaven
of the Sun
(wisdom)

N. Hemisphere
of land

S. Hemisphere
of water

Third heaven
of Venus
(love spoiled
by lust)

MOUNT PURGATORY (32° SOUTH)

SPHERE OF AIR

First heaven of the Moon
(faith blemished by inconstancy)

Second heaven of Mercury
(hope marred by ambition)

DANTE'S GEOCENTRIC UNIVERSE
showing also the virtues of the redeemed souls whom Dante
encounters on his journey in Paradiso

INTRODUCTION

Dante Alighieri died in Ravenna in 1321, shortly after the completion
of the *Paradiso*, the third and final canticle of *The Divine Comedy*.
Born in Florence in 1265, where he spent the first thirty-six years of
his life, Dante passed his remaining twenty years in exile, banished
for ever from his city on the grounds of fraudulent use of public
money, a charge trumped up by his political enemies. An intensely
active man, of strong convictions and outstanding intellectual
powers, his life was marked by commitment to causes, to civic life,
to study, to literature. No literary anchorite or intellectual recluse,
Dante's early and formative years especially were spent in the
forefront of literary endeavour, and in the thick of political events.
His keen interest in the contemporary world, his desire to identify
himself with his times, and his fascination for the *immediacy* of any
situation, if they led ultimately to his political downfall, were by the
same token responsible also for the genesis of *The Divine Comedy*
and in part for the power of his poetry in his major work.

Dante was well aware of his fascination and a certain weakness
for the immediate contingency, and he confesses as much in a direct
and characteristic way in *The Divine Comedy*, a work which has
the quality of a private epic and has been called, not without some
justification, the 'Danteid'. The episode is in the first canticle of the
Trilogy, the *Inferno*, in the final trench of the ten which make up
the Eighth (and next to last) Circle of Hell: the place in which the
falsifiers are punished, impersonators, alchemists and counter-
feiters. Here a common row between two of the sinners breaks out
in the presence of the two travellers, Dante and Virgil. It is a base,
wordy squabble in which (in the context of eternity) the classical
age clashes with the contemporary. The two participants are Sinon
of Troy (the Greek who treacherously persuaded the Trojans to
bring the wooden horse into Troy, and brought about its fall) and
Adam of Brescia (a coiner who achieved national notoriety and was
burnt at the stake for his crimes in 1281). The circumstances are
realistically depicted; the abusive dialogue is authentically recorded
at length between Adam, who is swollen by dropsy to the bulbous
shape of a lute, and Sinon who, conversely, is wasted with fever and
reeking with a temperature. Dante becomes wholly intent upon the
controversy, forgetful of everything else – the necessity for dispatch

to be out of the jaws of Hell, the dangers which surround him on every side, the presence of Virgil, who is impatient always of delay:

> In order to hear them I had stood stock still,
> When my master said to me: 'You are still looking!
> A little longer and I shall quarrel with you!'

Suddenly awakened from his enchantment, mortified by this rebuke from his guide and saviour, Dante is conscious that he had given way, once more, to his naturally strong curiosity for a controversial debate:

> When I heard him speaking to me in anger,
> I turned towards him and was so ashamed
> That I am so still when I think of it.

Dante's direct involvement in the contemporary scene began (if we ignore some military service in 1289) in politics, and dates from the year 1295, when he was thirty years of age, and Beatrice, the subject of much of his lyric poetry, had been dead some five years. On 1 November of that year as a White Guelf* he was elected to the special Council of the Captain of the People, in the administration of the *Comune* or Republic of Florence. A year later he found his way to the council whose task was to elect the six Priors of the city, and from 15 June to 14 August 1300, having proved himself on a local diplomatic mission, acceded himself to one of those important positions. It was as a Prior, the representative of one of the city's major guilds,† that he helped to influence the course of his city's destiny, and at the same time irrevocably moulded his own. Standing firm on behalf of the city's ancient liberties, Dante for the first time came into conflict with Pope Boniface VIII, whom he would later represent as his personal enemy. With his fellow Priors, at the head of the city's government, Dante confirmed the city's sentence against three of the Pope's Florentine agents for plotting against the State, and then refused Boniface's demand that the three offenders

*The Guelf party, supporters of the papacy, had dominated Florentine politics since 1266, when their rivals, the Ghibellines, the imperial party, had been expelled from the city. Later the Guelfs split into two factions, the Whites who wished to limit papal interference in the city's affairs, and the Blacks who sought closer political identity with papal power.

† In order to qualify for election to public offices, a recent law required any of the nobility (Dante's family belonged to the petty aristocracy of the city) to acquire membership of a guild. Dante enrolled in the Guild (*Arte*) of Physicians and Apothecaries, which incorporated also the Papermakers; as a writer this was perhaps the most appropriate guild to which Dante could belong.

should be released and their accusers sent to Rome. Frustrated by the intransigence of the *Signoria*, the Pope's legate departed Florence shortly after Dante's priorate, leaving the city's leaders under a ban of excommunication. Dante earlier incurred the Pope's displeasure by sentencing to exile some of the leaders of the two opposing factions of the ruling Guelf party who had caused bloodshed and civil strife in the city in that year. One of the leaders, Corso Donati, leader of the Black Guelfs, was the Pope's man, and a relative of Dante's wife, Gemma Donati; another, of the White Guelfs, was the great friend of Dante, Guido Cavalcanti, a brilliant man and an outstanding poet who had helped Dante in his early career as a poet, and who with him had led the important coterie of Florentine poets, the *Dolcestilnovisti* (the poets of the 'sweet new style'). In these difficult personal decisions Dante was forced to make as a civic leader, we find him already acting characteristically; none of the decisions he made here was either cautious or selfish – in fact they illustrate perfectly Dante's high-mindedness and clear sense of moral priorities, which is entirely the tone and quality of *The Divine Comedy*. The decision to oppose the Pope's political intentions the next year, by voting not to subsidise the armies of the Pope's ally Charles II of Naples, or send soldiers to swell the ranks of the papal forces, cost Dante lifelong exile and the confiscation of his wealth and property, and earned for him the promise of execution by burning should he ever fall into the hands of his fellow-citizens again.*

How much the decision cost Dante to banish a powerful kinsman of his wife and brother of a friend, as well as his intimate companion, Guido Cavalcanti, may be assessed from the record we have of Dante's high-minded, sensitive and essentially loyal nature. Having administered a direct shock to his contemporaries and friends with the unusual weapon of impartiality and probity, he received the savage riposte with philosophical fortitude, and never throughout his life regretted his action. Indeed, *The Divine Comedy* everywhere confirms Dante's decisions as having been by his own lights perfectly justifiable. Throughout the poem Boniface VIII is Dante's *bête noire*; not simply on grounds of personal animosity, but because he also represented in Dante's mind the epitome of corrupt spiritual leadership, where ambition for temporal domination eclipsed an essentially spiritual role. Canto XVI of *Purgatorio*, the central canto of the whole *Divine Comedy* (number 50 out of 100), significantly deals with the Church's

* See *Inferno* VI.64–72 and notes.

misguiding of the world: '*è giunta la spada col pastorale*' ('the sword has become joined to the shepherd's crook'). Boniface is proscribed unforgettably in *Inferno* XIX by Nicholas III, branded as "the Prince of the new Pharisees" by Guido da Montefeltro in the chasm of the crooked advisers (*Inferno* XXVII), as "the chief sinner"* by Dante in the valley of the princes in *Purgatorio* VIII, and finally castigated by Saint Peter himself in the Eighth Heaven of the Fixed Stars (*Paradiso* XXVII). As for Corso Donati, the turbulent leader of the Black Guelfs, Dante must have felt that Providence affirmed his sentence. In Purgatory, the realm of the Afterlife in which there is time and place for regret on the part of all, for private short-comings as well as political, Dante has Forese Donati pause in the execution of his penance for gluttony, and prophesy dispassion-ately his brother Corso's violent death at the hands of his enemies eight years thence (*Purgatorio* XXIV).† On the subject of Guido Cavalcanti's banishment Dante remains silent – unless *Inferno* X.61–3, an obscure tercet, may be read as an indictment of his friend's militant Guelfism.

This uncompromising attitude with regard to moral priorities is reflected also in Dante's conception of Hell. Here the novel idea of Ante-Hell is introduced, which has no precedent in either Christian or classical conceptions of the infernal realms. This region lies outside the confines of Hell proper; it is a sort of no-man's-land to which the 'luke-warm' in this life are relegated – those whose life was a compromise over important issues of all types, the 'sitters-on-the-fence', the moral cowards or neutrals: "those who lived/ Without occasion for infamy or praise" (*Inferno* III). In Dante's view they were not worthy of Hell, and even less of Heaven. The heavens rejected them because they were less than perfect; they were forbidden Hell lest the damned should feel some superiority in their presence. In Dante's view, for whom to live meant to partici-pate, "that calamitous crowd . . . never were alive". The vacillation which these *sciaurati* displayed was repugnant to Dante's whole philosophy. Reflection, the function of the *virtus intellectiva*, and free choice, mankind's highest gift, were faculties which made man

*In the Introduction, Commentary and Notes in this edition, double quotation marks indicate quotations from the translated text of *The Divine Comedy*; single quotation marks are used for quotations from any other source.
†*The Divine Comedy* was written c. 1308 to c. 1320, whereas the event it describes, Dante's journey through Hell, Purgatory and Heaven, is set in the Easter of 1300. This enables Dante to present much historical fact as prophecy.

what he was. Therefore 'renouncing the exercise of reason is renouncing existence, and so it is the same as being dead. And does not he renounce the exercise of reason who gives himself no account of the goal of his life . . . or of the path he ought to take?' (Dante, *Convivio* IV.VII.12 f.) Again, too much thought was wrong if it paralysed action. Once a line of conduct had been proposed, then to rethink could be dangerous and wrong. So Dante has Virgil rebuke him in *Purgatorio* V:

> 'Come on behind me, let those people talk:
> Stand like a solid tower which does not shake
> Its top whatever winds are blowing on it;
>
> Because the man in whom thoughts bubble up
> One after the other, goes wide of the mark,
> Because one thought weakens the force of another.'

It is precisely this aspect of Dante and his works – a concern to participate directly in the events of his time, formulate protest and register shock – that puts him in tune somewhat with our own times. Dante, the first great poet of our times, was also the first great writer whom we may term *engagé*. That is to say, he was the first creative writer of our millennium who took a notable stand with regard to the current moral, religious and political issues of his day, and whose work springs from irreconcilables, when frustration and disappointment are released in the act of creation. Indeed, it was thoroughly reprehensible in Dante's view that a person with a hold on truth should attempt to conceal it from the world, and fail to contribute to the public good:

All men whom the higher nature has imbued with a love of truth should feel impelled to work for the benefit of future generations, whom they will thereby enrich just as they themselves have been enriched by the labours of their ancestors. Let there be no doubt in the mind of the man who has benefited from the common heritage but does not trouble to contribute to the common good that he is failing sadly in his duty. (Dante, *De Monarchia* I.1)

Dante abhorred the widespread materialism, religious cynicism and political opportunism that disfigured his world. His tirades of wrath are memorable against dilatory emperors of the Holy Roman Empire such as Albert of Austria and Rudolph of Hapsburg; against the malpractices of the popes such as Boniface VIII, instrumental in Dante's expulsion from Florence, or Clement V the "lawless shepherd" who not only removed the papal seat from

Rome to Avignon in 1309 causing schism in the Church, but in 1312 betrayed the cause of Emperor Henry VII of Luxembourg, on whom Dante had pinned such hopes for the radical reform of Church and Empire. He unleashes in his poetry passionate denunciations of whole cities like spendthrift and foolhardy Siena, ambitious and treacherous Pisa, or corrupt and self-deceiving Florence – outbursts made all the more poignant by his underlying affection for his native city, or *patria* as he termed it. He fulminates against whole regions of Italy, as against the Romagna and Tuscany in *Purgatorio* XIV, and directs wholesale invective against Italy, disunited and ungovernable, as in *Purgatorio* VI:

> O enslaved Italy, a place of grief,
> A ship without a master in a great storm,
> Not mistress of provinces, but a brothel!

There follows upon this a reproachful apostrophe to the contemporary emperor of the Holy Roman Empire, Albert of Austria, with its four injunctions hammered out at the beginning of four successive tercets: to come himself and examine the ruinous state of Italy with its party factions, civil wars and family vendettas (already epitomised by the legendary dispute between the Montagues and Capulets):

> Come and see, you who are negligent,
> Montagues and Capulets, Monaldi and Filippeschi:
> One lot already grieving, the other in fear.

> Come, you are cruel, come and see the distress
> Of your noble families, and cleanse their rottenness,
> And you will see how dark Santafior is.

> Come and see your Rome, which is in tears,
> Widowed and alone, and calls day and night:
> 'My Caesar, why do you not bear me company?'

> Come and see how the people love one another!

And Dante continues in the same indignant vein for several tercets more, returning with bitterness and disillusion to the reproach once more of his own city Florence, which he loved as a patriot but which he knew too well as a former citizen. The passion which moves Dante is recognisable today, in spite of the lapse of centuries. It is akin to that of some modern writers, though hardly of the same class, for Dante castigates the whole of medieval Europe, the already ancient and declining civilisation of medieval Christendom, and burns with a purer flame perhaps than that of our modern writers. Dante was indeed a writer of literature of protest, but he does not descend to iconoclasm, moralising or priggishness. His humility in the face of his *positive* message which he felt to be greater than himself, the mere voice of it, and which he felt he was enjoined by Providence to communicate – his awareness of the historicity of his stand, of the fact that Europe, not just Florence or Italy, was his arena; his acute consciousness of the vastness and power of the opposition, and of the profundity and profusion of the rot which he felt he must eradicate – all this made him tremble, and purged him of much of the self-satisfaction and personal vindictiveness to which, wholly human that he was, he might otherwise have fallen a victim.

This urgency of purpose in Dante, and the directness of the means and manner of communication of it through his art in *The Divine Comedy*, enables today's readers, in the midst of a struggle of ideologies, to appreciate Dante as a writer more easily perhaps than the readers and critics of his works one hundred years ago; this is true despite the fact that a century ago Dante was held to be the very symbol of Italian independence in the struggles of a country which their national poet had seen disunited in his day and which only in the 1860s was to achieve the status of nationhood. For Dante's message (developed academically in his political treatise *De Monarchia*, yet achieving fullest expression in *The Divine Comedy*) was more than a call to unity to the mutually hostile cities and states of the Italian peninsula. Dante's dream, inspired by a prophetic vision of history of the sort current in the thirteenth century, was not national, but supranational; and if he wished to see Italy united, it was a fact only to be contemplated in the context of a Christendom similarly united and at peace within itself. Dante proposed a return to order, before the harm should become irreparable, under the enlightened leadership of a Christian emperor with unimpeded secular authority, and a pope who, tearing up both the pernicious document of Constantine's territorial donation and the bull *Unam Sanctam*, with its uncompromising claim of 'plenitude of power', would concern himself with purely spiritual leadership.

But *The Divine Comedy* is a poem, above all, of love. If religion and politics, civic life, literature and philosophy are important themes in the work, they are constantly developed and measured against the parameters of love. And the literal narrative of the work, the 'story' of *The Divine Comedy*, is the account of a man in love, Dante himself, who journeys beyond the grave to meet once more his lady snatched away by death some ten years before; and who finds the fullest satisfaction of that love in the vision of God. The love that is the measure of all human activity, for Dante, is that of God for his creation, "the love which moves the sun and the other stars" (*Paradiso* XXXIII.145). Its preeminent characteristics are justice and order. What does not accord with it constitutes injustice, disorder and irrationality in society, and imperfection and irrationality, or sin, in the heart of man. But Dante is a realist. The dialectics of *The Divine Comedy* predicate the authority of human reason in all man's activities: human rationality, that is, enlightened to a greater or lesser extent by wisdom. The source of that wisdom for mankind is firstly rational philosophy, which with the 'natural light' of the moral conscience illumines the paths to right living ('virtue'), and secondly theology, which arrives at the deepest truths by the revelation or 'divine light' of holy scripture. Philosophy and theology, represented in *The Divine Comedy* in Dante's guides, Virgil and Beatrice, are prescriptions for man's happiness both as a social animal and as an immortal soul.

As Dante the pilgrim and lover journeys through the Afterlife, therefore, he sees a reflection of *this* world in the three eternal realms. What he sees there is highly relevant to what he sees here as a citizen, because the fundamental parameters are the same. The difference is only one of perspective. In the Afterlife, God's love is free to structure the eternal realms according to his principles of justice and order; the souls there, having made their ultimate and immutable choice between accepting or rejecting his love, willingly dispose themselves into two different camps: the saved (in Paradise and Purgatory) and the damned (in Hell). In this life, the ultimate choices between justice and injustice, order and disorder, are still in the making, and the perfect pattern of love may be discerned to the extent that man in society lives and is encouraged to live according to justice and order. Dante's faith is that the patterns could come right in this life, for philosophy and theology reveal where the critical choices lie, and what the criteria of choice are.

The Divine Comedy is a work of literature that conforms closely in two important respects to the aesthetics and ethos of the medieval period, but which transcends 'medievalness' in one significant way, to suggest itself as first of the works of modern literature. Allegory and vision are perhaps its major medieval characteristics. Firstly *The Divine Comedy* has two major levels of meaning, the literal and the allegorical, whereas modern literature is generally content to develop only one level of sense, the literal. To use Dante's own definitions in his dedicatory letter to his patron Can Grande della Scala (*Letters* X), the work's literal subject is 'the state of souls after death', whilst its allegorical subject is 'man as deserving the reward or punishment of justice, according to his merits or demerits in the exercise of his free will'. This definition of the allegory thus has intimately to do with the didactic nature of the work; by observing the fate of souls in the Afterlife, the reader may deduce the standard of justice by which man's free choices and consequent actions *in this life* should be assessed. The allegory here is equivalent to the medieval understanding of the word, in harmony with the old dictum: *'littera gesta docet, quid credas, allegoria'* ('the literal sense teaches the facts; the allegory *what you should believe'*). Yet the allegory is richer even than Dante's statement suggests. The mind's eye, scanning beneath the surface of the literal sense, soon sees that subtending Dante's journey is not only the story of his conversion from sin to grace, but the progress too of the soul of Everyman; the other major figures of the story, Virgil and Beatrice, have secondary meanings, and these guides of Dante on his journey are operative on the allegorical plane not only in terms of Dante's own inner life, but also with universal significance.

The opening two cantos of *Inferno* place Dante in a forest with no precise topographical location; it is dark and confusing, and Dante has lost his path within it. The forest, then, represents error, Dante's own, but also that of Everyman. It may also represent Florence in 1300, or Christian Europe, in which the citizen wanders bereft of sound leadership and government. The hillside which Dante descries and towards which he makes in an attempt to escape from the forest is the notion of a more honourable and more satisfying life; the sun, which is wisdom, lights its flanks. But the way of escape for the traveller is barred by three wild animals, which are for Dante and Dante-Everyman the things within him that prevent him from realising his best aspirations: sensuality (the leopard), pride (the lion) and materialistic ambition, the frenetic pursuit of money and position (the she-wolf). If we see Dante as John-citizen of Florence, they may represent in political allegory the material promiscuity of Florence, the pride of the papacy (or France), and the political rapacity of France (or the papacy). How is Dante, in his manifold roles, to escape from these beasts, who push him back into the forest away from the sun and the open country? How may man free himself from the error into which his baser appetites thrust him, or from the corrupt society which alien forces have disfigured? It is now that Dante meets Virgil, who appears as a shadowy figure on the edge of the forest. Virgil offers Dante the chance of escape along an arduous path, for Virgil's voice is that of philosophical wisdom, or reason. To escape from error, one must

be able to identify it, perceive its causes and its agents. This is one of
the functions of philosophy, and Virgil undertakes to act as Dante's
guide and teacher as far as human wisdom can see ("what reason
may discern", *Purgatorio* XVIII.46). He will then hand over his
task to Beatrice, who as divine wisdom, the light of theology, can
show Dante the nature of the highest good. Philosophy and theo-
logy, human and divine wisdom, can bring man to a proper know-
ledge of himself, his propensity to evil, his capacity for good, of the
nature of the universe through which he moves, and of the cardinal
principle of its structure: the love of God as justice and order.

Virgil takes Dante through Hell (a subterranean world) and
Purgatory, as far as Earthly Paradise on the top of the mountain of
penance. Hell, literally the eternal realm of the damned, in the
allegorical scheme of *The Divine Comedy* is the city of man which
has become utterly corrupt, where justice and order, fair-dealing
and compassion have been totally subverted by loose-living,
violence, fraud and treachery. The 'sins' of the damned, as Kenelm
Foster has said, are largely crimes that would be condemned in any
rational society. Purgatory, where literally the souls of penitent
sinners are purged of their tendencies to sin, and the wounds in the
psyche caused by sin are healed, is allegorically a representation of
an imperfect but well-disposed society struggling upwards under
the discipline of secular and spiritual law towards the goal of a just
society. That ideal society is symbolised by Eden, on the summit of
the mountain, the domain from which the fallen Adam was driven
on the threshold of historical time. Dante, entering Eden, is both
himself and Everyman, with restored primal innocence, fitted to
repossess a perfect earthly society of justice and order where the
prescriptions of law are superfluous. It is in this Earthly Paradise,
appropriately, that Dante loses Virgil (the modulations of the
allegory here are exquisitely managed) and meets Beatrice once
more; and from here he rises with her into Paradise, to learn the
deeper truths that subtend man's relationship with the world and
with God. Paradise, literally the state of blessed souls in the eternal
presence of God, is an allegorical picture of the perfect life of
intellectual activity and contemplation, worship, prayer and specu-
lation in a renewed earthly society, and it is just possible that it
represents for Dante the new Age of the Spirit, according to the
eschatological vision of St Joachim of Flora.*

It is, indeed, the visionary element as much as the allegory of *The
Divine Comedy* that links it closely to its times. The visionary

* See *Paradiso* XII.140–1 and note to *Purgatorio* XXXIII.43.

characteristics of the work are, broadly speaking, the mystical and the historical. The progress of Dante through Purgatory and Paradise is punctuated by dreams and visions (Hell, the realm of the flesh, is notably and understandably bereft of such spiritual experiences), and the whole work, as literal narrative, culminates in Dante's direct sight of God, the so-called Beatific Vision, in the closing moments of the *Paradiso*. Dante arrives at, and records, the ultimate experience of the life of faith in a way that possibly reflects, in allegorical mode, the recognised steps of mystical contemplation: purification (Dante's experiences in Purgatory, culminating in the rites of purification in Earthly Paradise), illumination (Dante's intellectual enlightenment in *Paradiso* I–XXXI), and perfect union with God (beginning in the Empyrean, essential Paradise, XXXI–II, and ending in the Beatific Vision, XXXIII). The twelfth-century mystics proposed that perfect holiness and spiritual knowledge could ᵇ e achieved by contemplation rather than by good works or theological study. St Bernard's conviction that holiness rather than argument leads to divine knowledge was echoed by such as Hugh of St Victor, to the effect that 'the uncorrupted truth of things cannot be understood by reasoning',* and Richard of St Victor, his pupil, proposed the faculties of imagination and reason to be inferior to the faculty of mystical contemplation. It is significant, therefore, that just before Dante's sight of God, Beatrice, who is divine illumination ("who lights the intellect to truth", *Purgatorio* VI.45), resigns her role as Dante's guide to St Bernard, author of the fundamental medieval work on mystical contemplation *On Consideration*.† For Dante's "final satisfaction", as St Bernard puts it, vision not knowledge is given him, or rather, vision which is the spontaneous acquisition of knowledge; but certainly not knowledge derived from logic or dialectics. Dante's sight of God is a penetration of his light, a mystical union of the mind with God. So St Bernard commands Dante:

> 'And let us turn our eyes to the primal love
> So that, looking towards him, you may penetrate
> As far as possible through his refulgence.'‡

Dante's view of history, although remarkable for its range and grasp of significant movements and events, has little to do with

---

*St Bernard, *On Consideration*, translated by G. Lewis, Clarendon Press, 1908; p. 128.
†See *Paradiso* XXXI.59 f. and note.
‡*Paradiso* XXXII.142–4.

modern historiography. His 'reading' of history is, more exactly, visionary or prophetic. Certain significant historical patterns are predicated, and the activity of Providence is the force that moulds men and events. Dante's aim in writing *The Divine Comedy*, 'to lead men from a state of wretchedness into one of happiness' (*Letters* X, to Can Grande della Scala), was not merely evangelical. Happiness in this life, he believed, was one of mankind's two fundamental aims, and was contingent upon the maintenance of justice and order in a society ruled by one supreme monarch, the emperor of the Holy Roman Empire. In the course of the thirteenth century in Italy, the authority of that 'universal monarch' had been almost eradicated in the struggles between successive popes (from Gregory IX to Clement IV) and the imperial Hohenstaufen (Frederick II, Conrad IV, Manfred) over successional and territorial issues. It is arguable that Dante's own political fall and exile from Florence in 1302 may be attributed indirectly to papal ambitions to detach Tuscany from the Empire, as the price for the Church's recognition of Albert of Hapsburg's claim to the imperial crown. *The Divine Comedy*, begun very probably c. 1308, was undertaken with the aim not only of writing a work worthy of Beatrice, and vindicating Dante's own innocence of the corrupt practices of which he was accused in Florence, but also to vindicate the claim of the Holy Roman Empire as the supreme and independent secular authority of Christian Europe, against French imperialism, papal integrationalism, and their apologists. Dante's arguments, marshalled extensively in his treatise *De Monarchia*,* and most fully developed in *The Divine Comedy*, are of a historic-visionary nature. They propose the providential establishment of the Roman Empire as part of the necessary scenario for the atonement and the redemption of mankind. The *pax Romana* of Augustus' reign provided the necessary conditions of universal peace in which the Saviour of man was born in a corner of the Empire. The *lex Romana* of the Empire provided the universal legal authority required for Christ's crucifixion (Christ was handed over for execution to Pontius Pilate, the Roman governor). The Holy Roman Empire is for Dante the successor to the Roman *imperium*, and Roman law underpins the authority of each. The Roman people left Roman law as their legacy to the world, just as the Jewish people left the Gospels to mankind, both providential movements in history. The Holy

---

* The *De Monarchia* ('On Monarchy', lit. the government of a single ruler), was written either 1312–13, or c. 1318, at an interval during the composition of *The Divine Comedy*.

Roman Empire alone, Dante believed, as the legitimate heir of Rome, could provide the conditions of justice and order necessary for the pursuit of happiness in this world, and ensure the right conditions in which the Church might pursue its task of leading man to the achievement of his other legitimate goal, eternal happiness.

What *The Divine Comedy* adds, or appears to add, is a new chapter which is more properly eschatological in nature. The work contains, at significant junctures, veiled prophecies of a future champion who will rid the Church of its materialism, and the Empire of the political forces within it that disfigure and threaten to destroy it. Both the terms of reference and the manner of presentation of these predictions hint at the dawn of a new age of man, before the imminent winding-up of history. The prophecies of the Greyhound (*Inferno* I.101–11) and the apocalyptical 'DXV' (*Purgatorio* XXXIII.43), presage some future secular saviour, who, given Dante's reverence for the Holy Roman Empire, must surely be an emperor. Dante's world echoed with prophetic voices, and was rich in millenarian visions: Joachim of Flora, Alan of Lille, the so-called Tiburtine sibyl and the pseudo-Methodius.* In such prophecies the final age would be one of peace, preceding the brief appearance of Antichrist, who in turn would be overcome by Christ at his Second Coming on the Day of Judgement. The justification for these predictions rested in general on a belief in the cyclical nature of history, and particularly here in the replication of an older pattern embracing the advent of Augustus, the establishment of the 'Roman peace', Christ's incarnation (his first coming), and his victory over death at his Crucifixion. Dante's conception of the role of the Greyhound and 'DXV' is fully consistent with this sort of eschatological vision, as is his hint of the imminent end of time in the *Paradiso*. This is voiced by Beatrice as she surveys the court of heaven in the Empyrean, noting at the same time (the juxtaposition is significant) the throne prepared for Henry VII, the emperor who Dante had hoped would fulfil the role of saviour, before his untimely death in Italy, worn out by illness and papal, Angevin and Guelf opposition, in 1313:

> Look at our city, how far round it is;
> See how our places are so filled
> That not many people are wanted here now.

---

* See Bibliography, under Davis, C. T. and Reeves, M.

> And in that great seat you keep looking at
> Because of the crown you see placed above it,
> Before you sup at this marriage feast,
>
> Will sit the soul, Augustan upon earth,
> Of the great Henry, who will come to Italy
> To put her right before she is so disposed.*

Allegory and vision, then, link *The Divine Comedy* indissolubly to the medieval period. But the style of the work represents an advance in literature away from medieval norms towards more modern practice. In general, the medieval canons of literary style were conditioned by classical theory, or by what classical literary theory was believed to have been. Three levels of style were postulated in medieval rhetorical tradition: the high (or tragic), the middle (or comic) and the low (or elegiac). In his short poems, especially the *canzoni*, Dante aspires to the highest level of expression, the tragic or sublime, in which lofty thought is expressed in suitably elevated style; an 'aristocratic ideal of language and art' (C. Grayson) suited to the three 'noblest' subjects to which poetry can address itself: warfare, love, and virtue (see Dante's earlier work, *De Vulgari Eloquentia*). *The Divine Comedy*, however, cuts right across this rigid notion of art. Indeed, Dante felt constrained to call his work a 'comedy', not only because, contrary to tragedy, it begins badly (in Hell) and ends well (in Paradise) – for so does the *Aeneid*, which he nevertheless terms a 'tragedy'† – but because the range of subject matter and feeling determine a lexis and expressiveness that could only logically be equated with an 'average' style: the comic, which because of its inclusiveness appears 'unstudied and lowly', as belonging to the common people – 'in which even women-folk converse' (see Dante's *Letters* X).

What inspired Dante to break so completely away from the current normative stylistics of his period, and produce a major work which surely should have been, by prevailing canons, 'tragic' or exclusive in style (but which instead creates with its inclusiveness a new sublimity in western literature‡) is attributable to no known theoretical statement by Dante. Already by *c.* 1304 he had formulated a doctrine of *imitatio* of the classical poets in his *De Vulgari Eloquentia*: 'The more closely we copy the great poets, the more correct is the poetry we write.' It is not unlikely that by *c.* 1308,

---

* *Paradiso* XXX.130–8.
† *Inferno* XX.113.
‡ See Bibliography, E. Auerbach.

when beginning to write *The Divine Comedy*, Dante had already formulated an analogous theory with respect to the Bible. The proximity of *The Divine Comedy* to the Bible has been too often overlooked, and by the Bible I do not mean simply doctrine and imagery, with which *The Divine Comedy* is replete. We know from the pioneering work of E. H. Moore (see Bibliography) that the Bible, as a text, is used or referred to by Dante as many times as Aristotle and Virgil put together, but the deeper correspondences are only just becoming apparent as Dante scholarship progresses. Recent research has tried to establish organic and thematic links between the Italian text and the Bible in specific instances, and both E. Auerbach and C. S. Singleton have done work which would corroborate a theory of Bible-centred, as much as classically-orientated, stylistic praxis. From the start, it is clear that Dante intended that *The Divine Comedy* should carry, stylistically, a weight and authority commensurate with its message. The work was meant to convey a precise vision of the times in which Dante lived, which by its unimpugnable critique (this world is constantly measured by the eternal and immutable standards of the next) would carry a clear and ample warning to his generation of the dangers under which they lived, as well as a prophecy of the rewards of right-living. It is a vision that hints at the imminent collapse of the framework of Christian civilisation, as its leaders wilfully turned their backs on the divinely ordained institution and authority of the Holy Roman Empire, in favour of the schemes of ambitious city-states, domineering tyrants, petty monarchs and materialistic popes. The times might be gravid with a princely saviour, and a new age, but Christendom must be ready and rightly disposed to receive both. It was manifestly unprepared for either, and Dante arguably believed he was writing a gospel to convert his recalcitrant age. Close indeed are the aims of *The Divine Comedy* as formulated in the letter to Can Grande and the aims of divine law as postulated by St Thomas Aquinas in the *Summa Theologica*.* The poem's complement of invective and promise, of *exempla* of good and evil, of history and vision, of warning and prophecy, brings it often closer to the form and texture of the Bible than to either the *Aeneid* or the *Ethics*. *The Divine Comedy* has a gravity which is new to literature, and which it achieves by its inclusiveness,

---

*Dante: 'The object [of *The Divine Comedy*] is to remove those living in this life from their state of misery, and to lead them to a state of happiness.'
Aquinas: 'The object of Divine Law is to lead man to the goal of eternal happiness' (*Summa Theologica* II.I, q. 98, art. 1, resp.).

possessing the unprejudiced range of subject matter of the Bible
wedded to a sublime seriousness of purpose. It is biblical *imitatio*
which accounts to a significant extent for the large quotient of
realism that *The Divine Comedy* possesses.

Dante, it is clear, wrote *The Divine Comedy* as a work of
substantially 'theological' or 'scriptural' allegory. From *Inferno* III
onwards, as in accepted biblical exegesis, the literal sense of *The
Divine Comedy* is to be understood as factual or historical sense.
The forest, hill, and wild animals of *Inferno* I and II may be allegory
in the 'poetic' sense (such as is formulated in *Convivio* II.1.2–4),
where the literal level is merely a 'beautiful lie' conceived in order to
convey a hidden truth. But as C. S. Singleton observes, from the
moment Dante enters the gates of Hell, it is scriptural allegory that
is operative: Hell, and what lies beyond, is real, and Dante pre-
dicates a real journey through the Afterlife, with historical co-
ordinates. The characters of Hell, Purgatory and Heaven are there-
fore preponderantly of verifiable historicity: from Virgil to
Brunetto Latini, Lucretia to Beatrice, Constantine the Great to
Emperor Frederick II, they stand as concrete *exempla* of vices and
virtues, not mere ethical personifications such as are found without
exception in works of medieval literature before Dante. Profoundly
determining Dante's realism, however, is the figural interpretation
of history, of biblical inspiration, by which the lives of men, their
achievements and institutions are seen as figures, preceding an
eternal and therefore more real fulfilment in the Afterlife:
"shadowy prefaces of their reality", as Dante says in a different
context (*Paradiso* XXX.78). Augustan Rome prefigures medieval
Rome of the Holy Roman Empire, but both are figures of a more
significant fulfilment, in Heaven, of the City of God. Similarly,
human character is only fulfilled and brought to its highest level of
realisation in the Afterlife, in accordance with the choices for good
or ill made whilst on earth. Dante's characters in the Afterlife, as E.
Auerbach has shown, are significantly alive with a preternatural
intensity, as the mysterious sum of all their decisive acts and
decisions made on earth. In the accounts of their lives, the history of
families, cities and nations in the ancient and medieval world unfold
before the reader's eye, with an immediacy and realism it required
some five hundred years of evolving literary taste, from Humanism
to the nineteenth century, to fully recognise and acclaim.

In conclusion, does Dante's *Divine Comedy* need exegesis and
explanation at all, can it not exist as poetry without the apparatus of
learned comment? Both T. S. Eliot and Charles Sisson found in
their early acquaintance with Dante that, like all great poetry, his

work may communicate even before it is fully understood. The language of Dante, for Eliot, was written in the dawn of modern civilisation while words still possessed a primeval poetic lucidity, before their inspissation through the evolution of national literatures. Lucidity, if it is the property of Dante's words, is also the characteristic of his thought and imagery. Rarely is Dante purposely ambivalent in his poetry; he revered clarity, order and relevance. He accepted, moreover, the Dominican position of his master Aquinas, that knowledge is a prerequisite of love, and aimed primarily at the enlightenment of his readership in order to provoke their love of justice, order and truth. Since the life of a poem resides in its imagery perhaps as much as in its rhythms, then it follows that Dante's imagery must be allowed its intended *quantum* of intellectual translucency. Much of Dante's imagery is transparent because it is universal; from the everyday experiences of countryside, city street, hearth and home, trade, travel, warfare and civic life, to the cosmological: sun, moon, stars, planets, winds and seas. But a proportion of his imagery remains opaque, because of the intellectual and, nowadays, often esoteric allusions it carries. Dante exploits for his poetic needs Christian liturgy, classical myth, scholastic philosophy, biblical, ancient and contemporary history, theology, art, astronomy and science, and it is here surely that the scholar may legitimately remove any residual patina of age for the benefit of the reader, just as it is legitimate to remove the discoloured varnish from any Old Master, ignoring the complaints of those who find the charm of old things in their obfuscation. Dante, one feels, would not have required less.

Similarly, the historical allusions, taken for granted by Dante amongst his contemporary readership, must, where research has permitted it, be clarified; the history especially of Florence and Tuscany, of imperial and papal animosities, of Guelfism and Ghibellinism, need a hint, if nothing more, as to what they signified for Dante himself and his public. Dante's delphic utterances, and there are few of these, do not need any comment beyond the obvious reference to the background of the visionary and eschatological literature of his time; it would be wrong to be incisive where Dante was expressly vague. Opaque imagery, then, needs what clarification scholarship can provide, otherwise it remains poetically inert, and neither the poem nor the poet is faithfully served. The justification for publishing Dante's poem, now some six hundred years old, for a readership beyond the confines of college walls must rest ultimately on the theory that the reading of literature of any age is itself a sort of *imitatio*, a private and sensitive re-creation of the work itself, in as clear a light as it is possible to see it.

> Here may be seen how being blessed
> Has its foundations in the act of sight,
> And not in love, which comes afterwards.
> (*Paradiso* XXVIII.109–11)

David H. Higgins, University of Bristol

The Hereford 'Mappa mundi' *c.* 1290

An outline of the Hereford Map with some names in modern form, published by the Royal Geographical Society, London, 1948 (ed. G. R. Crone). This represents the inhabited world (the Northern Hemisphere of Land) much as Dante envisaged it, with Jerusalem at the centre. Earthly Paradise lies to the far East, however, whereas Dante places it on 'Mount Purgatory' in the Southern Hemisphere of Oceans, diametrically opposite to Jerusalem.

Political Panorama of
thirteenth and early fourteenth century in terms of Guelf and Ghibelline alignments

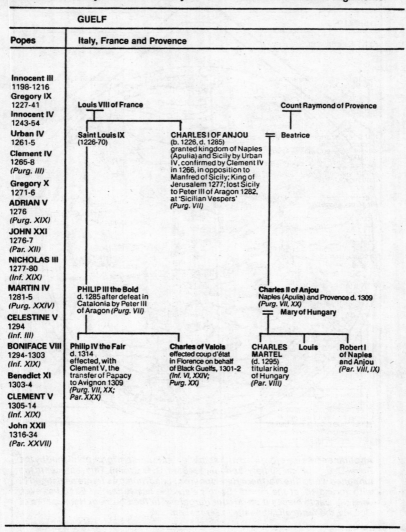

GUELF

Popes	Italy, France and Provence

Innocent III
1198-1216
Gregory IX
1227-41
Innocent IV
1243-54
Urban IV
1261-5
Clement IV
1265-8
(Purg. III)

Gregory X
1271-6
ADRIAN V
1276
(Purg. XIX)
JOHN XXI
1276-7
(Par. XII)
NICHOLAS III
1277-80
(Inf. XIX)

MARTIN IV
1281-5
(Purg. XXIV)
CELESTINE V
1294
(Inf. III)
BONIFACE VIII
1294-1303
(Inf. XIX)
Benedict XI
1303-4
CLEMENT V
1305-14
(Inf. XIX)
John XXII
1316-34
(Par. XXVII)

Louis VIII of France

Count Raymond of Provence

Saint Louis IX
(1226-70)

CHARLES I OF ANJOU
(b. 1226, d. 1285)
granted kingdom of Naples
(Apulia) and Sicily by Urban
IV, confirmed by Clement IV
in 1266, in opposition to
Manfred of Sicily; King of
Jerusalem 1277; lost Sicily
to Peter III of Aragon 1282,
at 'Sicilian Vespers'
(Purg. VII)

Beatrice

PHILIP III the Bold
d. 1285 after defeat in
Catalonia by Peter III
of Aragon *(Purg. VII)*

Charles II of Anjou
Naples (Apulia) and Provence d. 1309
(Purg. VII, XX)
Mary of Hungary

Philip IV the Fair
d. 1314
effected, with
Clement V, the
transfer of Papacy
to Avignon 1309
*(Purg. VII, XX;
Par. XXX)*

Charles of Valois
effected coup d'état
in Florence on behalf
of Black Guelfs, 1301-2
*(Inf. VI, XXIV;
Purg. XX)*

CHARLES
MARTEL
(d. 1295)
titular king
of Hungary
(Par. VIII)

Louis

Robert I
of Naples
and Anjou
(Par. VIII, IX)

Italy, Aragon and Germany	Emperors

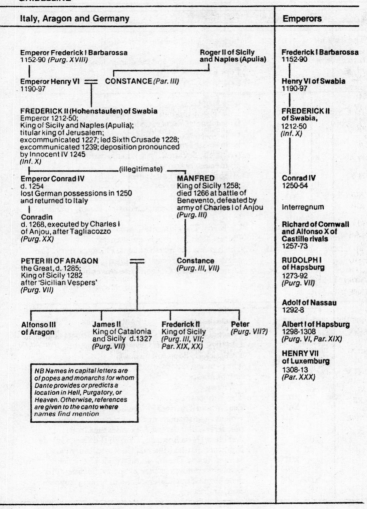

Emperor Frederick I Barbarossa
1152-90 *(Purg. XVIII)*

Roger II of Sicily and Naples (Apulia)

Emperor Henry VI ══ **CONSTANCE** *(Par. III)*
1190-97

FREDERICK II (Hohenstaufen) of Swabia
Emperor 1212-50;
King of Sicily and Naples (Apulia);
titular king of Jerusalem;
excommunicated 1227; led Sixth Crusade 1228;
excommunicated 1239; deposition pronounced
by Innocent IV 1245
(Inf. X)

────────────── (illegitimate) ──────────────

Emperor Conrad IV
d. 1254
lost German possessions in 1250
and returned to Italy

MANFRED
King of Sicily 1258;
died 1266 at battle of
Benevento, defeated by
army of Charles I of Anjou
(Purg. III)

Conradin
d. 1268, executed by Charles I
of Anjou, after Tagliacozzo
(Purg. XX)

PETER III OF ARAGON
the Great, d. 1285;
King of Sicily 1282
after 'Sicilian Vespers'
(Purg. VII)

Constance
(Purg. III, VII)

Alfonso III
of Aragon

James II
King of Catalonia
and Sicily d.1327
(Purg. VII)

Frederick II
King of Sicily
*(Purg. III, VII;
Par. XIX, XX)*

Peter
(Purg. VII?)

> *NB Names in capital letters are
> of popes and monarchs for whom
> Dante provides or predicts a
> location in Hell, Purgatory, or
> Heaven. Otherwise, references
> are given to the canto where
> names find mention*

Emperors:

Frederick I Barbarossa
1152-90

Henry VI of Swabia
1190-97

FREDERICK II
of Swabia,
1212-50
(Inf. X)

Conrad IV
1250-54

Interregnum

**Richard of Cornwall
and Alfonso X of
Castille rivals**
1257-73

RUDOLPH I
of Hapsburg
1273-92
(Purg. VII)

Adolf of Nassau
1292-8

Albert I of Hapsburg
1298-1308
(Purg. VI, Par. XIX)

HENRY VII
of Luxemburg
1308-13
(Par. XXX)

PLAN OF THE DIVINE COMEDY

LOCATION	CANTO	INFERNO
The dark forest	I, II	Leopard, lion, and she-wolf. Virgil
Gate of Hell	III	
Vestibule of Hell	III	The uncommitted and pusillanimous. Pope Celestine V
The Acheron	III	Charon's ferry

LOCATION	CANTO	UPPER HELL
1st Circle (Limbo)	IV	Unbaptised children, good pagans. The castle of the famed: poets (Homer, Ovid, Horace, Lucan, Virgil), rulers (Caesar, Saladin), leaders (Aeneas, heroes and heroines of Troy, Latium and Rome); philosophers (Aristotle, Socrates, Plato), mathematicians, physicians, historians, etc.
	V	Minos, judge of the damned *Sins of the Appetites*
2nd Circle	V	The sexually promiscuous: Francesca da Polenta and Paolo Malatesta; Dido, Cleopatra, Helen, Achilles, Paris, Tristram
3rd Circle	VI	Cerberus. The gluttons: Ciacco of Florence
4th Circle	VII	Plutus. Moneygrubbers and wasters
5th Circle	VII, VIII	The lagoons and marsh of Styx. Phlegyas' ferry. The angry: Filippo Argenti; the sullen
Gate of Lower Hell (City of Dis)	VIII, IX	Demons, Furies, Gorgon. The heavenly messenger

LOCATION	CANTO	LOWER HELL *Speculative Sin*
6th Circle	IX–X	Heretics and sceptics ('Epicureans'): Farinata degli Uberti, Cavalcante dei Cavalcanti; Emperor Frederick II, Pope Anastasius II
	XI	The plan and rationale of Hell (Virgil) *Sins of Malice* 1 *Violence*
7th Circle	XII	The Minotaur
	XII	*First Round* The river Phlegethon. Centaurs. The violent against others or their property. Tyrants, murderers, plunderers: Alexander the Great; Azzolino III da Romano, Obizzo II d'Este, Guy de Montfort; Attila; Rinier da Corneto, Rinier Pazzo
	XIII	*Second Round* The unnatural wood. The violent against themselves or their property. Suicides: Pier delle Vigne. Squanderers: Lano of Siena, Jacopo da Sant'Andrea

LOCATION	CANTO	INFERNO
	XIV–XVII	*Third Round* The burning sands. The violent against God (blasphemous): Capaneus. The violent against nature (sexual perverts): Brunetto Latini, Jacopo Rusticucci, Guido Guerra, Tegghiaio Aldobrandi. The violent against art (extortionate bankers): members of the Ubbriachi, Gianfigliazzi and Scrovegni families
The abyss	XVII	Geryon
		2 *Fraud*
		Malebolge
8th Circle	XVIII	1st chasm. Procurers and seducers: Venedico Caccianemico, Jason
	XVIII	2nd chasm. Flatterers: Alessio Interminei, Thais
	XIX	3rd chasm. Simoniacs: Pope Nicholas III (Boniface VIII, Clement V)
	XX	4th chasm. Futurologists: Tiresias, Manto, Michael Scott, Guido Bonatti
	XXI, XXII	5th chasm. Malacoda and the Malebranche. Grafters and swindlers: Ciampolo of Navarre; brother Gomita, Michael Zanche
	XXIII	6th chasm. Hypocrites: Catalano dei Malavolti and Loderingo of Bologna. Caiaphas, Annas
	XXIV, XXV	7th chasm. Thieves: Vanni Fucci; Cacus; five Florentines including members of the Donati, Cavalcanti, and Brunelleschi
	XXVI, XXVII	8th chasm. Corrupt advisers: Ulysses and Diomed, Guido da Montefeltro
	XXVIII, XXIX	9th chasm. Instigators of scandal and schism: Mahomet, Mosca dei Lamberti, Bertram de Born, Geri del Bello
	XXIX, XXX	10th chasm. Falsifiers (impersonators, liars, forgers, alchemists): Gianni Schicchi, Sinon, Adam of Brescia
The pit of Cocytus	XXXI	The giants: Nimrod, Antaeus, etc.
9th Circle (Cocytus)	XXXII–XXXIII	3 *Treachery*
		1st zone, *Caina*. Treacherous to family and relatives: Alessandro and Napoleone degli Alberti, Mordred, Camicione dei Pazzi
		2nd zone, *Antenora*. Traitors to country and cause: Bocca degli Abati, Gianni dei Soldanieri, Ganelon; Count Ugolino and Archbishop Ruggieri
		3rd zone, *Ptolomaea*. Treacherous to guests: brother Alberigo of Faenza, Branca d'Oria of Genoa
	XXXIV	4th zone, *Judecca*. Treacherous to legitimate superiors (lords and masters) and benefactors: Judas, Brutus, Cassius
Centre-point of the earth	XXXIV	Lucifer. Dante and Virgil leave Hell

	LOCATION	CANTO	PURGATORIO	
DAY 1 (Threshold of Purgatory)	Shore of Purgatory	I, II	Cato. The boat of souls	
			Casella	Dante's *canzone* 'Love that discourses with me in my mind'
	Excommunicated	III	Manfred of Sicily	The battle of Benevento (1266)
	Late-repentant: 1 Apathetic	IV	Belacqua (Virgil)	The sun's course in the Southern Hemisphere
	Late-repentant: 2 Unabsolved (violent death)	V, VI	Jacopo del Cassero	The ambush at Oriago (1298)
			Buonconte da Montefeltro	The battle of Campaldino (1288)
			Pia dei Tolomei	Domestic crime in the Maremma
	Late-repentant: 3 Negligent	VI–VIII	Sordello Valley of Christian rulers: Charles I of Anjou	
			Emperor Rudolph I, Ottocar II of Bohemia, Philip III of France	Dante's invective against negligent Emperors, Italy and Florence
DAY 2		IX	Dante's Dream of Eagle	
	Gate of Purgatory	IX	Three Steps of Confession, Contrition, Satisfaction (Seven *P*s)	
	1st Cornice: Proud	X–XII	Omberto Aldobrandeschi	Dynastic arrogance
			Oderisi da Gubbio	Artistic arrogance
			Provenzan Salvani	
	2nd Cornice: Envious	XIII–XIV	Sapia of Siena Guido del Duca Rinier da Calboli	Political and social degeneracy of Tuscany and Romagna
	3rd Cornice: Angry	XV–XVII	Marco Lombardo	Free will. The Church's appropriation of secular authority, and the consequent disorder of Christendom

	LOCATION	CANTO	PURGATORIO	
DAY 2 cont.	4th Cornice: Slothful	XVII–XIX	(Virgil)	The moral structure of Purgatory The nature of love
			The Abbot of San Zeno	
DAY 3		XIX	Dante's Dream of Siren	
	5th Cornice: Avaricious (including Ambitious) and Wasters	XIX–XXII	Pope Adrian V Hugh Capet	The crimes of the Royal House of France
	6th Cornice: Gluttonous	XXII–XXV	Statius Forese Donati	Statius' debt to Virgil Moral laxity in Florence .
			Bonagiunta da Lucca	Sicilian, Tusco-Sicilian poetry and the new poetry of Dante
			(Statius)	The generation of the body and the nature of the soul
	7th Cornice: Sexually Promiscuous	XXVI	Guido Guinizelli	Origins of the 'sweet new style' of Italian poetry. Provençal poetic technique
		XXVII	Arnaut Daniel Passage through Fire	
DAY 4		XXVII	Dante's Dream of Leah	
		XXVII	(Virgil)	Virgil's last speech to Dante: the acquisition of freedom
	Earthly Paradise	XXVIII	Matilda	Topology and climatology of Earthly Paradise
		XXIX	Procession of Revelation	
		XXX	BEATRICE	Virgil's departure. The rebuke of Dante
		XXXI		Dante's remorse. Lethe
		XXXII	The allegorical spectacle	Visionary history of Church/State relations
		XXXIII		The 'DXV' prophecy. Eunoë

HEAVENS (ANGELIC ORDERS)	CANTO	VIRTUES	ORDER OF SOULS	PARADISO	
1 Moon (Angels)	I			(Beatrice)	The order, material and spiritual, of the universe; the soul's return to God as fulfilment of that order
	II–V	Faith (blemished by inconstancy)		(Beatrice)	Natural phenomena and Angelic operation. The moon's dark areas
				Piccarda Donati Empress Constance (Beatrice)	The freedom, relative and absolute, of the will
2 Mercury (Archangels)	V–VII	Hope (marred by ambition)		Emperor Justinian (Beatrice) Romieu de Villeneuve	The Roman and Holy Roman Empires Guelf and Ghibelline factionalism Original sin, redemption; the logic of divine vengeance for the Crucifixion. Immortality of the soul, resurrection
3 Venus (Principalities)	VIII–IX	Love (spoiled by lust)		Charles Martel Cunizza da Romano Folquet of Marseilles Rahab	Social structure; paradoxes of heredity Guelf-Ghibelline strife in NE Italy Florence condemned as papal financiers
4 Sun (Powers)	X–XIV	Prudence	The wise: theologians, scholars and teachers	*1st Ring* St Thomas Aquinas (a Dominican) *2nd Ring* St Bonaventure (a Franciscan) Solomon	Life and work of St Francis. Decadence of Dominican Order Life and work of St Dominic. Decadence of Franciscan Order The resurrected body; radiance
5 Mars (Virtues)	XIV–XVIII	Courage	Hebrew and Christian soldiers	*The Cross of Souls* Cacciaguida (Joshua, Charlemagne, Roland, Robert Guiscard, Godfrey of Boulogne)	The civilisation of 12th-century Florence The corruption of 13th-century Florence Guelfism and Ghibellinism in the city Dante's future and fortune. The writing of the *Comedy*

6 Jupiter (Dominations)	XVIII–XX	Justice	Just rulers	*The Eagle of Souls* King David, Trajan, Hezekiah, Constantine, William II of Sicily, Ripheus	Castigation of Christian monarchs: Emperor Albert I, Philip IV of France, Edward I, Wallace, Ferdinand, Wenceslaus, Charles II of Naples; Sicily, Aragon, Portugal, Norway. Mystery of divine justice and providence
7 Saturn (Thrones)	XXI–XXII	Moderation	Contemplatives	St Peter Damian (a Benedictine) St Benedict *The Golden Ladder*	Mystery of predestination. Worldliness of monastic and ascetic orders. The decline of the Benedictine Order
8 Constellations (Cherubim)	XXIII–XXVII	Faith Hope Love	(The Church Triumphant)	(Dante) St Peter St James St John Adam St Peter	Vision of Church in Triumph. Dante's examination on Faith. Dante's examination on Hope. Dante's examination on Love. The fall of man. Origin of languages. Denunciation of materialism of the Church
9 Crystalline or Primum Mobile (Seraphim)	XXVII–XXIX		(Angels)	(Beatrice) (Dante) (Beatrice)	Anarchy in society. Vision of God and his angels. The Creation. The Angelic Hierarchies. Scriptural authority; errors of preachers
10 Empyrean	XXX–XXXIII	All virtues	True Paradise of the Redeemed	(Beatrice) St Bernard Blessed Virgin Mary Dante's Beatific Vision	Emperor Henry VII. Rebuke of Pope Clement V. Problem of elective Grace. St Bernard's prayer to the Virgin. The Divine Essence

ACKNOWLEDGEMENTS

For this translation I have used mainly the excellent three-volume edition of the *Commedia* by Barbi and Casini (Sansoni, Florence), a compendium of learning brought to bear exactly at the points where it is needed.

It was Michael Schmidt who suggested that I should undertake this work. He has, these six years and more, been so much more an instigator and abettor of my work, than a mere publisher, that it is only proper that the version should be laid at his door.

Finally, I must thank David Wright, though it is superfluous, for he has so long put an accusing finger on my verse, at the sensitive points, that I can hardly conceive of working without him. That does not – need I say? – give him any responsibility for my errors.

Benefiting in particular from the comments of David Higgins, I have made a number of minor changes from the text of the first (Carcanet) edition.

C. H. Sisson

Dante exegesis and scholarship have an ancient, extensive and impressive history, stemming from Giovanni Boccaccio, the acknowledged father of Dante studies, who in 1373 delivered the first official *lectura Dantis* in Florence. My debt, in composing the critical apparatus for this verse translation of *The Divine Comedy*, extends to Dante commentators and scholars from Boccaccio himself to the most recent of modern scholars of several nationalities, and especially to the editors and contributors of the *Enciclopedia dantesca* (5 volumes, Rome, 1970–6), Paget Toynbee, *A Dictionary of Names and Notable Matters in the Works of Dante* (revised by C. S. Singleton, Oxford University Press, 1968), G. Siebzehner-Vivanti, *Dizionario della Divina Commedia* (ed. M. Messina, Milan, 1965), and to the authors of three signal editions, with commentary, of *The Divine Comedy*: Natalino Sapegno (*La Divina Commedia*, Milan, 1957), J. D. Sinclair (Bodley Head, 1948), C. S. Singleton (Princeton, 1970–75). Other works which I have consulted with profit are listed in the Selected Bibliography. My thanks are also due to the translator of the present work, Charles Sisson, with whom I discussed several difficult points of interpretation; to Henry Gifford, Emeritus Professor of English in the University of Bristol; and to the Editor of *Words*, University of Wellington, New Zealand, for permission to use in the Introduction part of the transcript of my lecture delivered in Wellington to mark the Septcentenary of Dante's birth.

David H. Higgins

ON TRANSLATING DANTE

I

The encounter of a translator with a poet he is going to translate is a matter of some delicacy. As with other friendships, there is the chance that throws the two parties together, and the less fortuitous elements which make the acquaintance more or less agreeable, and more or less close. It may seem monstrous to talk in this way of so great a master as Dante, and one so remote from us in so many respects. But all literary encounters have a certain unceremonious- ness about them. We surround ourselves with books so that we can call up Montaigne, or Eckermann, or Virgil, or Andrew Marvell, as the mood takes us or the drift of our interests at the time suggests. There are scores or hundreds of merely casual encounters, and some of more intimate significance. The latter have their times, and their place in one's development as a reader or a writer. For a man who writes or will write verse, the question of the poets who will influence him has a special importance. He may – he must – think highly of many who have no evincible influence on his work; there are likely to be some – in the early part of his career – who influence him too patently. There may be a small number who remain as a point of reference, working more or less obscurely, as indicating a *ne plus ultra* along certain lines which he would like to follow, but somehow never succeeds in doing. In this class are the technical masters – for generations, since the Renaissance, the Roman classics; more recently and specifically in the twentieth century, Dante.

It would be absurd for me to claim any *special* relationship with the author of *La Divina Commedia*. He was first thrust under my nose by Eliot's essay of 1929, which came to me three or four years later when I was eighteen or nineteen – a prestigious recommenda- tion, at that time. Some of the lines quoted by Eliot have been part of the furniture of my mind ever since. It was to the Temple Classics edition – still the best introduction to the English reader who is finding his own way – that Eliot drew attention, and it was to that edition that I went. The volume containing the *Inferno* was one of the three little books I took with me when I went overseas in the army, and although my Heine seemed more accessible at that time the luminosity of a few lines of Dante, pecked at here and there,

settled invincibly in my mind at this restless period. You see, I am
slow. When I first saw the Mediterranean, sailing back through it
on a troopship, it was a Dantean light which played on it. The
references thus established have never left me, and through the
years that followed, with their miscellaneous preoccupations,
Dante has occasionally surfaced, like one of his own damned
emerging momentarily from the boiling pitch, though never more
visibly than *In Insula Avalonia* (1972), with its three-line stanzas
and its

> Look, for you must, upon the fine appearance,
> The creature had it and is formless dead.
> Now come no nearer than to straws in glass.

The last line is a direct theft. It may have been this poem which
induced my publisher, a few years later, to suggest that I should
translate *The Divine Comedy*: to which my profound sense of
incapacity before the text replied with a brutal negative. It was
certainly the recollection of *In Insula* which made it possible for
me, after a decent interval, to try my hand at the opening canto of
the *Inferno*.

These preliminaries may seem elaborate and perhaps egotistical,
but the point I wish to make is a general one. It is often assumed, by
people who have not wrestled with such tasks, that a decision to
translate this or that poet can be entirely wilful. It can be, in the
sense that anyone who can count up to ten on his fingers can
respond affirmatively to any publisher's request for a version of this
or that, but the man who has written verse of his own – and who else
should attempt to put any poem from another language into English
verse? – will generally find himself inhibited. At any particular
point in time, the range of possibilities is narrow, and it may in
practice be narrowed to one. That a translator has to take what
interests him, in matter and in technique, goes without saying.
What is sometimes less understood is that he has to take something
to which his own current work bears a special relationship. This
does not mean that the translator has to write like Dante before he
begins, any more than Dryden wrote like Virgil. If that were the
condition, a lot of labour would have been spared. But it means that
the translator has to be able to find both a metric and a tone in which
he can give the matter of his author so that a readable English work
is made out of it. It is *not* the case that someone who has written a
dictionary of a language is thereby qualified to translate out of it,
nor that the scholarship of an Edward Moore guarantees the tact to
set out inoffensively what the author has said. This is not to say that

linguistic or other scholarship is to be ignored by the translator. Far from it, but the *sine qua non* for the employment of any of these advantages in the making of a new version is the ability to write in the language into which the translation is to be made and, in the case of a verse translation, the ability to write verse in that language. Without these qualifications, the problem of finding the right tone, and the right metric, have no practical significance.

II

For one who has come to Dante through Eliot and who was set on course by the technical programme in Pound's *How to Read*, from the moment of setting eyes on that work in the early thirties, it is the luminous clarity of Dante's line which has been the great attraction. It is the great pressure of his matter which makes the clarity possible, as one comes later to see; but the first sight of Dante, for one who catches a glimpse from afar, is of a tailor narrowing his eyes to thread a needle, or a gaggle of cranes stretched across the sky. That does not give you a style to imitate; it gives you a perception of the maximum which can be done, in a few words, to evoke a physical presence. The lesson from this is, silence: there is certainly no encouragement to produce a few more pages of verse for the next reading, or the next poetry prize. Dante is, with Catullus, the best possible master for the writer of verse in our century, with its welter of words, spoken and written, its sheer lack of *silence* in which anything can be *heard*. Catullus is less formidable because the incipient verse-maker can soon work his way through a few small poems and feel the full effect of such directness. Looking now at the *Catullus* which was my first major exercise in translation, I find I did at least make an English book of it. It is not in translators' language and it can be read. This may seem a small merit, though to me it is an essential one – and rare enough, as one can see by flicking through any half-dozen volumes chosen at random from any shelf of nineteenth- and twentieth-century versions. Dante himself has suffered, and in some of the most widely circulated translations. To take lines at random from Laurence Binyon's version, which is certainly not without merit, and enjoys a certain repute through having been recommended – with whatever qualifications – by Ezra Pound, here is the opening of the *Purgatorio*:

> Now hoisteth sail the pinnace of my wit
> For better waters, and more smoothly flies
> Since of a sea so cruel she is quit,

> And of that second realm, which purifies
> Man's spirit of its soilure, will I sing,
> Where it becometh worthy of Paradise.
> Here let dead Poesy from her grave up-spring . . .

Let her indeed: it is enough to make her. Binyon's version of the *Comedy* was first published from 1934 onwards, when I was not only alive but already adult, and I can testify that this was not the language of the period. Nor is this, from Dorothy Sayers, that of the forties or fifties: I quote from where I opened the book, *Purgatorio* VII, lines 61–3:

> 'Nay', said my lord, as it were marvelling,
> 'Lead on then; bring us where thy speech conveys
> Such pleasant promise of fair harbouring.'

It is not any language, though nearest, no doubt, to the *quotha* and *forsooth* of Victorian knightly romanticism. There is an immense difficulty. Both Binyon and Sayers might have said that the language of their own time did not have the resources for the weight and dignity of Dante's speech. Maybe; but can one find in such fustian any trace of the acerb Florentine? Did he puff up his lines to impress the post-Victorian market, or to look dignified, like a lord mayor, while he utters nullities? Or does the weight of his lines come from the stringency with which he omits everything which does not reinforce his meaning, which therefore stands so barely before us? The first lesson of Dante is that one should write to *convey*, not to impress. It is admittedly difficult to see why anyone should be impresssed, at this time of day, by the model Binyon and Sayers have followed as an alternative to Dante, but it is the way of the world to attach the word 'beautiful' to the second-hand.

Once one has taken a decision to translate into the language of one's own day, or rather, once one has *not* taken a decision to write in Wardour Street or other dialect, but intends to write merely as one does write, there is still the real problem, which in all translations from another age, is that of *tone*. The problem presents itself to the translator – if he is any good – in an entirely concrete form. He is not looking for a critical adjective which will describe how he views the matter or how he will perform; he will be fumbling for a few lines which convince him that he can go on, and in some sort say what his poet says. That may sound a modest requirement; the rigour of it depends on the degree of rigour the translator is accustomed to exercise in relation to his own writing. In my experience, there is an identifiable moment when the translator can first say: I can translate a particular poet. Until that moment, all is uncertain. It is the point at which the first verses come to him convincingly in his own language; for the question of tone of course includes the question of the kind of verse one is going to use. What might be called the subjective authorisation to translate Lucretius came to me on the bus between Avignon and Tarascon; that for Virgil's *Eclogues* arrived one night in Sevenoaks. The phenomenon is as definite as that of writing a poem: more consciously prepared, perhaps, but finally as spontaneous. After that, the course of the labour before one is clear. Through whatever morass of linguistic and other scholarship you may pass before it is finished you know that, as the meaning clarifies itself line by line and page by page, it will take on itself that newly discovered form to which no further reflection can be given.

III

In the case of the translation of *The Divine Comedy*, there had been one preliminary decision which will certainly meet with some disagreement here and there. This was, not to follow Dante's rhyme-scheme. There were several reasons for this. The first was, that I should not dream of writing a poem of my own – certainly not a poem of any length – in *terza rima*. That may seem a poor reason, but it is in fact a good one, as anyone will understand who has understood that a translator must write as comes natural to him, in the language of his day and in the kind of verse which belongs to the current development of the language, and of his own technique. The real task is to give the matter of Dante, as one speaks most effectively. It will be obvious that the translations of Golding and Dryden follow this pattern, while those of Dorothy Sayers and Barbara Reynolds do not – if indeed these two could be said to write verse at all, in any but the most mechanical sense. The second reason is perhaps less a motive for the translator than a caveat for those who are tempted to think that the cultivation of such superficial resemblances between one poem and another is itself meritorious. It is that the differences between the English and Italian languages in general, and English and Italian rhymes in particular, are such as to make the imitation of *terza rima* (aba bcb cdc ded, etc.) rather like a clown following a ballet dancer. The lesser variety of sounds in Italian makes for a greater facility and elegance of rhyme. The result must be that any attempt to follow the Italian scheme through fourteen thousand lines or so, while following at the same time the matter and intent of another man, must lead to distortions which are intolerable to anyone who conceives that the first duty of a translator is to give his author's meaning as simply and directly as may be. This point can be abundantly demonstrated from *any* of the existing translations which follow Dante's scheme. Even Shelley, who managed the *terza rima* with great success in several of his own poems – that is, where he was following his own thoughts – was quickly led astray from the directness of his original when he translated the first fifty lines of Canto XXVIII of the *Purgatorio*. Moreover, neither he nor, I think, any other translator has carried imitation to the point to which it must be carried, if there is to be any real claim to follow the rhyme scheme – that is, to find feminine rhymes, as Byron has done in imitating an Italian scheme in *Don Juan*, with results which are excellent in that cynical medley but which would be ridiculous in a translation of *The Divine Comedy*. Finally, it is to be recalled that neither Cary, the first English translator of Dante, nor Longfellow – Professor of Modern Languages though he was – used rhyme in their versions, neither of which is without its merits, though neither offers a satisfactory approach to Dante for the reader of our own day.

Though I spoke of a 'preliminary decision' not to use rhyme, I mean no more than that, when the proposal to translate Dante was first put to me, it was clear to me at once that there would be no point in a further attempt at *terza rima*, as if Binyon had not done all that was needed in that kind, for the present century. When, after the initial revulsion from the whole project, the moment came when I thought I could after all try my hand at the first canto of the *Inferno*, the form of the verse to be used determined itself.

> Half way along the road we have to go,
> I found myself obscured in a great forest,
> Bewildered, and I knew I had lost the way.

One line of ten syllables, two of eleven; one of the latter with unstressed or feminine ending, one packing its extra syllable earlier in the line, with a little hiccup.

> It is hard to say what that forest is like,
> How wild and rough it is, how overpowering;
> Even to remember it makes me afraid.

All three lines here of eleven syllables. Then, as if gathering confidence, the line extended itself: 'So bitter it is, death itself is hardly more so.' Thirteen syllables, though without, I think, giving any sense of a break in the march of the verse. Clearly it was to be something other than the decasyllabic slide of the *Idylls of the King*. In the event, the length of the line varied between – generally speaking – thirteen syllables and nine, though incursions beyond those limits were admitted where the sense warrants it and the movement of the passage as a whole will bear it. So there are liberties with the length of line, as well as in the matter of rhyme, the translator's purpose being to convey Dante's meaning into English verse, not to comply with anyone's preconceptions as to how that should be done. Those who admire the smoothness of Binyon and Sayers should know that Binyon can count up to thirteen: 'I was of Siena, and here with the others I'; while Sayers's line, 'When some one faculty, by its apprehension', cannot be made out to be *less* than twelve. However, such wickedness, which with these two is no more than a rare aberration, is with me a settled course of life.

Without entering upon the question how far a translator should consider himself obliged to approximate to the length of Dante's line, which no one has followed exactly for the excellent reason of its complete unsuitability for English verse, it is worth looking at the way in which these famous hendecasyllabics are in fact arranged. Perhaps it is bold to say that they are not as regular as is usually supposed, but it is safe to say that they are far from any monotony. So, for example, line 128 of *Inferno* XXVIII is qualified in a footnote in Barbi and Casini's edition as '*lunghissimo verso*': '*levò 'l braccio alto con tutta la testa*'. Crescini is quoted as saying that 'the elision between *braccio* and *alto* matters little: it is there for metrical regularity but we are inclined not to notice it'. And elsewhere my editors: 'it is to be observed that in the old poetry the hendecasyllabic was much more varied in accent than it is with the moderns'. These observations do not undermine the formal regularity of the metre, but they are indications of how the verse should be read. More to the point for the contemporary English reader is this from Ezra Pound:

> I have never seen but one intelligent essay on Dante's 'metre' and that was in an out-of-print school-book found in a Sicilian hotel, the author cited an author who had examined Dante's actual practice and found that the 'eleven syllable' line was composed of various different syllable-groups, totalling roughly eleven syllables, and not running, so far as I can remember, to more than seventeen. Any pedant can verify the top limit, and it does not greatly matter as long as the student does not confuse the so-called 'syllabic' system with 'English pentameter', meaning a swat at syllables 2, 4, 6, 8, 10 in each line, mitigated by 'irregularities' and 'inverted feet'.

Peter Dale, introducing his honourable version of Villon, which

follows the rhyme-scheme of the original and approximates to the
metric scheme – if and so far as English verse could be said to
approximate to the unaccented French – says that an informal
version of a formal poem is as odd as 'to translate the *Cantos* into
heroic couplets'. The only objection to this plausible statement is
that it makes no sense. Pound's *Cantos* are already in English verse
of the twentieth century, and to turn it into an imitation of Dryden
would be an act of lunacy. The problem the translator faces – that of
producing, from the matter of the original, a readable work in the
language and verse of its day – simply does not exist. Dryden
himself, trying perhaps to fend off some such inchoate criticism,
gave reasons for not attempting any equivalent to Virgil's half-lines,
and for having occasionally used 'Pindarique lines' (of twelve
syllables), as well as 'Triplet Rhymes', breaking the regularity of his
verse. But he says all that needs to be said in his claim which,
terrifying as it is, must be that of every translator, that 'taking all the
Materials of this divine Author, I have endeavour'd to make Virgil
speak such *English*, as he wou'd himself have spoken, if he had been
born in England, and in this present Age'.

IV

It is not possible to take the reader into the workshop where for
hours and hours, on days and in weeks and months stretching into
years, the translator has lived with his author and tried to make
sense of him. 'Make sense of' not only in teasing out dictionary
meanings and weighing the alternatives offered by commentators in
the more obscure passages, but in advancing line by line and tercet
by tercet speaking in his own voice as modified by the presence of
that august original – for it must still be his own voice, even though
his success is to be measured by the degree to which it resembles
that imaginary English in which his author 'wou'd himself have
spoken'. His task, minute by minute and hour by hour, is not the
invention of a beautiful imitation – and did not Rémy de Gourmont
say that the imitation of a beautiful thing is always ugly? – but the
effacement of himself, so far as may be, before the text. For this
exhaustion the only preparation is a long experience of writing
poetry of one's own. This is because the poet has – however little
this discipline is understood by most of the versifiers who crowd
the platforms from which verse is emitted – to listen rather than to
dictate, to accept rather than to decide. In this intimate process the
best will sometimes be deceived, but they will be least deceived in
their best poems. With a translation, the internal situation is more
complicated. The translator's mind is an empty room in which the

verses float before him, surrounded as it were by what he has extracted, as possibly relevant, from the half-irrelevancies of dictionaries and the confusing propositions of commentators. The moment comes – sooner rather than later, later rather than sooner, according to the difficulty (for him) of the passage – when he sees through the original to the matter – the actual objects – of the original. It is at that moment that his own words form, and he has to take what he is given and to say what he sees. Of course, as with a poem of his own, he will have to return sometimes and admit that he has not seen clearly, or has not said what he has seen. Then he has to go through the process again or to make repairs as best he can. The result is an imperfect reading of the original, but it *is* a reading with something, however shadowy, of the coherence and stamp of the original. Such a translation is for those who have not read the whole of *The Divine Comedy* in the original, and very much for those whose interest in poetic technique is enough to have led them – amidst whatever other preoccupations – to dip here and there into the Italian, perhaps with the help of a crib, to establish for themselves who this Dante was, and something of what he did for the art of writing. 'I cannot imagine', says Pound, 'any serious writer being satisfied with his own work in this field, or indeed any serious writer being satisfied with his own product in this field or in any other.' And as Dryden with his great *corvée*, 'For my part I am lost in the admiration of it; I contemn the World, when I think on it, and myself when I Translate it.'

C.H.S.

DANTE'S ITALY c.1300

TRENTINO
FRIULI

L.COMO
Turin · MILAN
PIEDMONT LOMBARDY L.GARDA Verona Vicenza TREVISAN MARCH
Saluzzo Asti · Pavia · Cremona Padua · Este Venice · Treviso · Trieste
· Mantua
LIGURIA · Genoa Parma · Modena R.PO
EMILIA Ferrara
Pistoia BOLOGNA · Ravenna
Lucca Imola · Cesena
Prato Forli
Pisa ARNO FLORENCE ROMAGNA
TUSCANY Urbino
Volterra Arezzo Gubbio MARCHE
Siena Perugia · Ancona
CORSICA UMBRIA PAPAL STATE
Orvieto Spoleto Ascoli
Viterbo TIBER
LATIUM L'Aquila
SARDINIA ROME ABRUZZO
· Tagliacozzo
Anagni MOLISE
· Aquino
Gaeta Montecassino
CAMPANIA
Capua CAPITANATA
· Barletta
NAPLES · Bari
KINGDOM OF NAPLES & APULIA
APULIA · Brindisi
BASILICATA
Cosenza
CALABRIA
PALERMO
Messina · Reggio
KINGDOM OF
SICILY (TRINACRIA) Catania

INFERNO

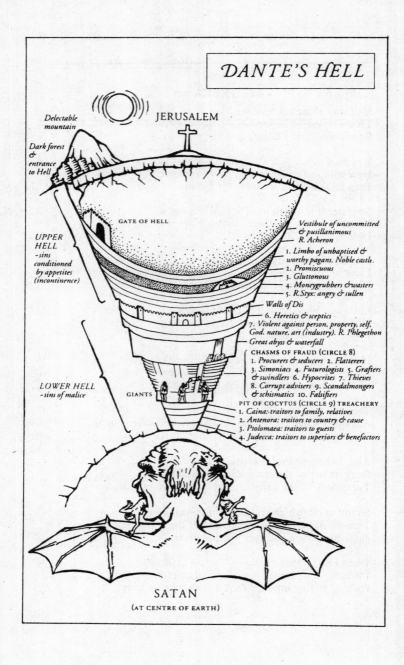

DANTE'S HELL

Delectable mountain

JERUSALEM

Dark forest & entrance to Hell

GATE OF HELL

UPPER HELL
– sins conditioned by appetites (incontinence)

Vestibule of uncommitted & pusillanimous
– R. Acheron

1. Limbo of unbaptised & worthy pagans. Noble castle.
2. Promiscuous
3. Gluttonous
4. Moneygrubbers & wasters
5. R. Styx: angry & sullen

Walls of Dis

6. Heretics & sceptics
7. Violent against person, property, self, God, nature, art (industry). R. Phlegethon

Great abyss & waterfall

CHASMS OF FRAUD (CIRCLE 8)
1. Procurers & seducers 2. Flatterers
3. Simoniacs 4. Futurologists 5. Grafters & swindlers 6. Hypocrites 7. Thieves
8. Corrupt advisers 9. Scandalmongers & schismatics 10. Falsifiers

LOWER HELL
– sins of malice

GIANTS

PIT OF COCYTUS (CIRCLE 9) TREACHERY
1. Caina: traitors to family, relatives
2. Antenora: traitors to country & cause
3. Ptolomaea: traitors to guests
4. Judecca: traitors to superiors & benefactors

SATAN
(AT CENTRE OF EARTH)

CANTO I

Half way along the road we have to go,
I found myself obscured in a great forest,
Bewildered, and I knew I had lost the way.

It is hard to say just what the forest was like,   4
How wild and rough it was, how overpowering;
Even to remember it makes me afraid.

So bitter it is, death itself is hardly more so;   7
Yet there was good there, and to make it clear
I will speak of other things that I perceived.

I cannot tell exactly how I got there,   10
I was so full of sleep at that point of my journey
When, somehow, I left the proper way.

But when I had arrived at the foot of a hill   13
Which formed the far end of that menacing valley
Where fear had already entered into my heart,

I looked up, and saw the edges of its outline   16
Already glowing with the rays of the planet
Which shows us the right way on any road.

Then my fear was a little put at rest,   19
Although it had lain in the pool of my heart throughout
The night which I had passed in that pitiful state.

And, as a man who, practically winded,   22
Staggers out of the sea and up the beach,
Turns back to the dangerous water, and looks at it,

So my mind, which still felt as if it was in flight,   25
Turned back to take another look at the defile
No living person had ever passed before.

When I had rested my weary body a little,   28
I took up my journey again on that stretch of desert,
Walking so that my firm foot was always the lower.

31   And, almost at the point where the slope began,
      I saw a leopard, extremely light and active,
      The skin of which was mottled.

34   And somehow it managed to stay in front of me
      In such a manner that it blocked my way so much
      That I was often forced to turn back the road I had come.

37   The time was the beginning of the morning;
      And the sun was climbing in company with those stars
      Which were with him when the divine love

40   First set those lovely things in motion; and this,
      With the hour it was, and the delightful season,
      Gave me reason to entertain good hope

43   Of that wild animal with the brilliant skin:
      But not so that I found myself without fear
      When a lion appeared before me, as it did.

46   When he came, he made his way towards me
      With head high, and seemed ravenously hungry,
      So that the air itself was frightened of him;

49   And a she-wolf, who seemed, in her thinness,
      To have nothing but excessive appetites,
      And she has already made many miserable.

52   She weighed down so heavily upon me
      With that fear, which issued from her image,
      That I lost hope of reaching the top of the hill.

55   And, like a man whose mind is on his winnings,
      When the time comes for him to lose,
      And all his thoughts turn into sorrow and tears:

58   So I was transformed by that restless animal
      Who came against me, and gradually drove me down,
      Back to the region where the sun is silent.

61   While I rushed headlong to the lower slopes,
      Before my eyes a man offered himself,
      One who, for long silence, seemed to be hoarse.

When I saw that fellow in the great desert,   64
I cried out to him: 'Have pity on me,
Whatever you are, shadow or definite man.'

And he replied: 'Not a man, though I was one,   67
And my parents were people of Lombardy,
Mantuans, both of them, they were born and bred there.

I was born *sub Julio*, although it was late   70
And I lived in Rome under the good Augustus
In the time of the gods who were false and told lies.

I was a poet, and I sang of the just   73
Son of Anchises, the man who came from Troy,
After the proud Ilion had been burnt down.

But you, why do you come back to such disturbance?   76
Why do you not climb the delightful mountain
Which is the beginning and reason of all joy?'

'Are you indeed that Virgil, are you the spring   79
Which spreads abroad that wide water of speech?'
When I had spoken, I bowed my head for shame.

'You are the honour and light of other poets;   82
My long study and great love give me strength
Now, as they made me pore over your book.

You are my master, and indeed my author;   85
It is from you alone that I have taken
The exact style for which I have been honoured.

Look at the animal which made me turn back;   88
Help me to handle her, you are famous for wisdom,
For she makes my veins and pulse shudder.'

'You will have to go another way than this,'   91
He answered, when he saw that I was weeping,
'If you want to get away from this wild place:

For that beast, which has made you so call out,   94
Does not allow others to pass her way,
But holds them up, and in the end destroys them;

97   And is by nature so wayward and perverted
That she never satisfies her wilful desires,
But, after a meal, is hungrier than before.

100   Many are the animals she makes herself a wife to,
And there will be more of them, until the Greyhound
Comes, who will make her die a painful death.

103   He will not feed on land nor yet on money,
But upon wisdom, love, and upon courage;
His nation will be between Feltro and Feltro.

106   What he will save is that unassuming Italy
For which the girl Camilla died, Euryalus,
Turnus and Nisus, all of whom died of wounds;

109   He will pursue that wolf in every city
And put her back in Hell where she belongs,
And from which envy first let her out.

112   The course I think would be the best for you,
Is to follow me, and I will act as your guide,
And show a way out of here, by a place in eternity,

115   Where you will hear the shrieks of men without hope,
And will see the ancient spirits in such pain
That every one of them calls out for a second death;

118   And then you will see those who, though in the fire,
Are happy because they hope that they will come,
Whenever it may be, to join the blessed;

121   Among whom you may climb, but if you do,
It will be with a spirit more worthy than I am;
With her I will leave you, when I depart:

124   Because the Emperor, who reigns up there,
Since I was one of the rebels against his law,
Does not wish me to enter into his city.

127   He commands everywhere, and there he rules,
There is his city, there he has his throne:
Happy are those he chooses for that place!'

I said to him: 'Poet, now by that God,   130
Who is unknown to you, I ask your assistance:
Help me to escape both this evil, and worse;

Lead me now, as you have promised to do,   133
So that I come to see St Peter's Gate
And those whom you represent as being so sad.'

Then he moved forward, and I kept behind him.   136

CANTO II

The day was going, and the brown evening
Was taking all the creatures of the earth
Away from toil: and I was the only one

Preparing himself to undergo the battle   4
Alike of the journey, and of that dutifulness,
Which the true memory will recollect.

O Muses! O profound inclination, help me!   7
O memory, which recorded what I saw,
Here will be shown what there is noble in you.

I began: 'Poet, you who are to be my guide,   10
Consider whether my strength is adequate
Before you trust me to make this terrible passage.

You tell me that the father of Sylvius,   13
While still in nature, went to eternity
And was there with the use of all his senses.

But, if the adversary of all evil   16
Was courteous to him—when one thinks of the great effects
Which followed from him, not only who, but what—

It does not seem unsuitable to a man of intellect: 19
Nor that he was chosen in empyreal heaven
To be the father of bountiful Rome and her empire;

22   The city and the power which, truth to tell,
     Were there established for the holy place
     Where the successor of great Peter sits.

25   By this journey, for which you praise him so,
     He came to understand what were the reasons
     Of his victory, and of the papal mantle.

28   And afterwards, the chosen vessel went there,
     To bring back reassurance for that faith
     Which is the beginning of the way to salvation.

31   But I, why should I go there? By whose permission?
     I am not Aeneas, neither am I Paul;
     Neither I nor others think that I deserve it.

34   Therefore, if I resign myself to going,
     I fear my journey may be a foolish one;
     You are wise, and understand more than I say.'

37   And just like somebody who shilly-shallies,
     And thinks again about what he has decided,
     So that he gives up everything he has started,

40   I found I was on that obscure hillside:
     By thinking about it I spoiled the undertaking
     I had been so quick to enter upon in the first place.

43   'If I have understood what you have said,'
     The reply came from that shadow of generosity,
     'Your spirit is touched by cowardice, which sometimes

46   Lies like a load on men, and makes them flag
     So that they turn back from the fittest task,
     Like an animal which mistakes what it looks at.

49   But, so that you may rid yourself from fears,
     I will tell you why I came, and what I heard
     At the point when first I became concerned for you.

52   I was among those who are in suspense;
     And a lady called me, so blessed and beautiful
     That I at once begged her to tell me what I should do.

The shining of her eyes was more than starlight;   55
And she began to speak, gently and quietly,
With the voice of an angel, but in her own language:

"O courteous spirit of that Mantuan   58
Whose fame endures still in the world, and will
Endure as long as the world itself shall last,

My friend, who is not also the friend of fortune,   61
On the desert hillside, is in such difficulty
Making his way, that he turns back for fear;

And I fear that already, he may be so far lost   64
That I have risen too late to be of help,
From all that I have heard of him in heaven.

Now leave this place, and with your apt speech,   67
And whatever may be necessary for his escape,
Help him, and so bring consolation to me.

I am Beatrice, and that is why I send you;   70
The place I come from I also wish to return to;
It is love which makes me speak to you as I do.

When I am back, standing before my master,   73
I shall often talk about you kindly to him."
So she was silent, and then I began:

"O lady of power, through whom, and through whom only,   76
The human race is better than all the rest
Under that heaven which bends closest to earth!

It pleases me so much to have your command   79
That if I had done it already, I should think myself slow;
There is no need to explain your wishes further.

But tell me why you do not hesitate   82
To come down here, into this central place,
From the ample heaven to which you burn to go back."

"Since you would like to be so far informed,   85
I will tell you briefly," so she replied to me,
"Why I am not afraid to come down here.

88   One has to fear only the things which have
     The power of hurting others; for the rest,
     They do not matter, they are not to be feared.

91   And I am made by God, I thank him, so
     That all your suffering has no effect on me,
     Nor am I touched by all these burning flames.

94   There is a gentle lady in heaven, who has pity
     On this difficulty I am sending you to,
     So that the sharp judgement of heaven is broken.

97   She called Lucy to her, and her request
     Was this: 'Your devoted follower needs help;
     I commend him to you, to do the best you can.'

100 Lucy, the enemy of all cruelty,
     Stood up and came to the place where I was
     And where I was sitting with the ancient Rachel.

103 She said: 'Beatrice, you who are a glory of God,
     Why do you not help him who loved you so greatly
     That for your sake he left the common crowd?

106· Do you not hear his pitiful complaint?
     Do you not see the death he is struggling with
     By that river over which the sea is powerless?'

109 Nobody on earth was ever more in haste
     To seek an advantage or to avoid an evil
     Than I, after such words as that had been spoken,

112 To come down here from my happy location,
     Trusting you on account of your noble language
     Which honours you and those who have listened to it."

115 When she had spoken to me in this manner,
     Her eyes shining with tears, she turned away:
     And that made me even more anxious to come.

118 And so I came to you, as she wished me to;
     Took you away from that wild animal
     Which stopped your short cut to the beautiful mountain.

What is it then? Why do you dawdle here?   121
Why do you let such cowardice sleep in your heart?
Why have you not more boldness and openness?

When three such ladies care for you in heaven,   124
Busying themselves about you in that court
And I report so promisingly to you?'

As little flowers, which in a frosty night   127
Droop and shut tight, when the sun shines on them
Stretch and look up, erect upon their stalks,

So I recovered from my failing strength,   130
My heart so filled with satisfying courage
That I began, like a man just released:

'How generous she was to give her assistance!   133
And how courteous you were, to obey her so quickly,
When she proffered her help and spoke the truth!

My heart is now so set in its desire   136
To come with you—and it is your words that have done this—
That I am back again with my first intention.

Now go, for a single will informs us both;   139
You are my guide, my master and my lord.'
So I spoke to him and, when he stirred from where he was,

I entered upon the deep and thorny way.   142

CANTO III

'Through me you go into the city of weeping;
Through me you go into eternal pain;
Through me you go among the lost people.

Justice is what moved my exalted Maker;   4
I was the invention of the power of God,
Of his wisdom, and of his primal love.

7   Before me there was nothing that was created
    Except eternal things; I am eternal:
    No room for hope, when you enter this place.'

10 These words, in an uncertain colour,
    Were written above a gate; and when I saw them,
    I said: 'Master, it is hard to follow the meaning.'

13 He answered as a man who understood:
    'Here you must leave all wariness behind;
    All trace of cowardice must be extinguished.

16 We have come now to the place where, I have told you,
    You will find the people for whom there is only grief:
    Those who have lost the benefit of the intellect.'

19 With that, he put his hand on top of mine,
    And looked glad, which made me feel more comfortable,
    And so he led me into that secret place.

22 Here, there were sighings and complaints and howlings,
    Resounding in an air under no stars;
    So that at first I found myself in tears.

25 A jumble of languages, deformities of speech,
    Words which were pain, with intonations of anger,
    Voices which were deep and hoarse, hands clapped together,

28 Made altogether a tumult, round and round,
    Unceasingly in that air in which all was colourless,
    Just as it might be in a perpetual sandstorm.

31 And I, who felt my head surrounded by horrors,
    Said: 'Master, what then is it that I am hearing?
    And what people are these, so crushed by pain?'

34 He answered: 'That is the manner of existence
    Endured by the sad souls of those who lived
    Without occasion for infamy or praise.

37 They are mixed with that abject squadron of angels
    Who did not think it worth their while to rebel
    Or to be faithful to God, but were for themselves.

Heaven chased them out, so as not to become less beautiful,   40
And the depths of hell also rejected them,
Lest the evil might find occasion to glory over them.'

I said: 'Master, what is it lies so heavily   43
Upon them, that they call out as they do?'
He answered: 'I will tell you very briefly.

They are without even the hope of death;   46
Their blind existence is of such abjection
That they are envious of every other fate.

The world does not remember them at all;   49
Mercy and justice treat them with contempt:
Let us not talk about them. Look and pass on.'

And as I looked at them, I saw a flag   52
Flapping wildly as it was carried forward,
As if it was not fit to rest a moment;

Behind it came a huge torrent of people;   55
So many that I never should have thought
Death had been able to undo so many.

When I had recognised a few of them,   58
I saw and knew the shadow of that man
Who out of cowardice made the great refusal.

I understood at once beyond all doubt   61
That this was the miserable and useless gang
Of those who please neither God nor his enemies.

That calamitous crowd, who never were alive,   64
Were naked, and their skins blown with the bites
Of swarms of wasps and hornets following them.

Their faces ran with blood from these attacks   67
And, mixed with tears, it streamed down to their feet,
Where filthy creeping creatures swallowed it.

And when I cast my eyes a little further,   70
I saw people on the bank of a great river;
And so I said: 'Master, if you are willing, tell me:

73   Who are those people, and what is it determines
     That they have such anxiety to cross,
     Or so it seems to me in this faint light?'

76   He answered: 'These are things you will be told
     When our steps come to a halt, as they will do,
     On that sad strip of land beside Acheron.'

79   Then, with my eyes cast downward out of shame,
     For fear that what I had said had given offence,
     Until we reached the river I said nothing.

82   And then, there came towards us in a boat
     An old man who was white with brittle hair,
     Calling out: 'Woe to you, perverse spirits!

85   You need not hope that you will ever see heaven;
     I have come to take you to the other side,
     Into eternal darkness, fire and ice.

88   And you who are there, and still a living soul,
     Keep well away from those there who are dead.'
     But, when he saw that I had made no movement,

91   He said: 'There are other crossings, other ways
     For you to reach the shore: do not pass here.
     And you should travel in a lighter craft.'

94   My guide said: 'Charon, do not torment yourself:
     It is willed there, where anything can be done
     If it is willed: no need for further questions.'

97   There was no more movement of the bearded cheeks
     Of that old pilot of the leaden marshes,
     Around whose eyes there burned red rings of flame.

100 But those spirits, who were worn out and naked,
     Changed colour and their teeth began to chatter;
     Such was the effect of hearing those harsh words.

103 Then they blasphemed God and cursed their parents,
     The human race, the place and time, the seed,
     The land that it was sown in, and their birth.

And then they gathered, all of them together,   106
Weeping aloud, upon the evil shore
Which awaits every man who does not fear God.

The devil Charon, with his eyes like coals,   109
Points at them, and collects them all together;
Whoever dawdles gets a blow from his oar.

As leaves in autumn, one after the other,   112
Are blown away until the branch has given
All of its spoil back to the earth again,

So was it with the evil seed of Adam;   115
They threw themselves from that shore one by one,
As they were beckoned, like birds obeying a call.

And so they went away on the dark water;   118
And even before they had been disembarked,
Another flock had collected on this side.

My courteous master spoke to me: 'My son,   121
Those who have died under the wrath of God
Assemble here from every land on earth;

And they are ready enough to cross the stream,   124
For the divine justice digs its spurs in
So that their fear is turned into desire.

There is no crossing here for any good spirit;   127
Therefore, if Charon says he will not have you,
You know what sense you may give to his words.'

When he had finished, the murky countryside   130
Trembled so much, that even to think of it
Still leaves me terrified and bathed in sweat.

The melancholy land belched out a wind   133
From which there came a flash of carmine light
That left me utterly insensible;

And I fell, as a man who falls asleep.   136

CANTO IV

There broke upon the deep sleep in my head
A solemn thunder, so that I started
Like someone who is wakened violently;

4   And so I cast my rested eyes around me,
And having stood up, I looked fixedly
To see what sort of place it was I was in.

7   The truth is, I was on the outer edge
Of the valley of the sorrowful abyss
Which echoes with infinite lamentations.

10   It was so dark, so deep, so filled with cloud,
That, when I fixed my eyes upon the bottom,
I could not there discern a single thing.

13   'Now let us go down into this blind world,'
Began the poet, and his face was pale:
'I will go first, you follow after me.'

16   And I, who had seen how his colour changed,
Said: 'How shall I come, if you are so afraid,
You who give comfort to me when I waver?'

19   He answered: 'It is the anguish of the people
Down there, which takes the colour from my face;
It is pity, although you take it for fear.

22   Let's go, it is a long way, we must not stop.'
So he moved forward, and made me follow him
Into that first circle round the abyss.

25   There, in so far as listening could tell me,
The only lamentations were the sighs,
Yet they made the eternal air tremble.

28   They came from the sadness, without any torment,
Felt by the crowds—there were many of them, and huge—
Of infants and of women and of men.

The master said: 'Are you not going to ask   31
What spirits these are which you see in this place?
I think you should know, before you go on;

They have committed no sin, and if they have merits,   34
That is not enough, because they are not baptised,
Which all must be, to enter the faith which is yours.

And, if they lived before the Christian era,   37
They did not adore God as he should be adored:
And I am one of those in that position.

For these deficiencies, and no other fault,   40
We are lost; there is no other penalty
Than to live here without hope, but with desire.'

It grieved my heart when I heard him say that,   43
Because I knew there were people of high value
Who were in that limbo, as it were suspended.

'But, sir,' I said, 'will you explain to me,'   46
I asked because I wanted to be certain
About the faith which overcomes all error:

'Did anyone, either through his own merit,   49
Or through another's, ever get out of here
And achieve blessedness?' He understood

What I implied, and said: 'When I was new here,   52
I saw a powerful spirit come this way,
Crowned with the insignia of victory.

He took away the shade of our first parent,   55
With that of Abel and his son, the shade of Noah
And of Moses, the obedient law-giver,

With the patriarch Abraham, and David the king,   58
Israel with his father and his children,
And with Rachel, for whom he did so much;

And many others, and he made them blessed;   61
I think that you should know, that before these,
There were no human spirits who were saved.'

64   We did not stop walking while he spoke,
     But went on through the forest none the less,
     That forest, I say, of spirits crowded together.

67   We had not gone very far on our way
     From the river of sleep, when I caught sight of a fire
     Which carved for itself a hemisphere in the darkness.

70   We were still some little distance from the spot,
     But not so far that I could not catch a glimpse
     Of the honourable people who stood there.

73   'O you who honour sciences and arts,
     Who then are these, who have so much honour, that
     In this manner they are separated from the others?'

76   He answered me: 'The honoured reputation,
     Which still re-echoes in your life up there,
     Wins grace in heaven, which gives them this advantage.'

79   Meanwhile, I heard a voice: 'Do honour,' it said,
     'To the magnificent poet, for his shade,
     Which had departed, is with us once again.'

82   And when the voice had stopped and all was quiet,
     I saw four immense shadows come towards us:
     They had no appearance either of grief or happiness.

85   The good master opened his mouth to speak:
     'Observe the one who, sword in hand, comes first,
     In front of the three others, as their chief.

88   That is Homer, there is no poet above him;
     The next who comes is Horace, the satirist;
     Ovid is third, then last of all comes Lucan.

91   Because they are all poets as I am,
     It was our common name the voice called out;
     They welcome me, and in that they do well.'

94   And so I saw together that excellent school
     Of those who are masters of exalted song
     Which, like an eagle, flies above the others.

When they had talked together a little while,   97
They turned towards me with signs of recognition;
And my master smiled to see them do so.

And then, they did me a still greater honour;   100
They took me as a member of their company,
So that I was a sixth among those great intellects.

So we went on in the direction of the light,   103
Talking of things of which it is well to say nothing,
Although it was well to talk of them at the time.

We came then to the foot of a great castle,   106
Encircled seven times by lofty walls,
And around which there flowed a pleasant stream;

We went over the stream as on dry land;   109
And I entered seven gates with those wise men:
We came into a meadow where the grass was cool.

And there were people whose eyes were slow and serious,   112
Of great authority in their appearance:
They were not talkative and their voices were gentle.

We moved away a little to one side,   115
To an open place, well-lit, upon high ground,
So that I could see the whole group easily.

There, straight in front of me, on a green background,   118
There were presented to me those great spirits,
Merely to have seen whom is an exaltation.

I saw Electra with many companions: 121
Amongst whom I knew Hector and Aeneas,
And the armed Caesar with the eyes of a hawk.

I saw Camilla there and Penthesilea   124
On the other side, and I saw the Latian king,
With his daughter Lavinia, sitting there.

I saw the Brutus who drove out the Tarquin,   127
Lucretia, Julia, Marcia and Cornelia;
And, standing by himself, I saw Saladin.

130 And, when I raised my eyes a little higher,
     I saw the master of knowledge, Aristotle,
     Sitting there with a company of philosophers.

133 All looked to him, and they all did him honour:
     I saw there Socrates, as well as Plato,
     The two who stood out and were nearest to him;

136 Democritus, who thought the world came by chance,
     Diogenes, Anaxagoras and Thales;
     Empedocles, Heraclitus and Zeno;

139 I saw the man who knew the virtue of herbs,
     I mean Dioscorides; and I saw, too, Orpheus,
     Cicero, Linus, and Seneca the moralist;

142 Euclid the geometrician, and Ptolemy;
     Hippocrates, Galen and Avicenna;
     Averrhoes, who wrote the great commentary.

145 I cannot give account of all of them,
     For my main theme is such it hurries me on,
     So that I often have to tell less than I saw.

148 The company of six was cut to two:
     My skilful guide led me another way,
     Out of the quiet, to where the air trembled:

151 And I came to a part where nothing is luminous.

CANTO V

     And so I went deeper down from the first circle
     Into the second, smaller in circumference,
     But greater in its cries, and stinging pain.

4   Minos was there, scowling and terrible,
     Examining the faults of new arrivals;
     He judges them, and sends each to his place.

I tell you, when the ill-born spirit comes   7
To him, there is nothing that is not confessed;
When he takes cognisance of any sin

He sees what place in hell is suited for it;   10
And whips his tail around himself as many
Times as the circles the sinner must go down.

A crowd of sinners always stands before him: 13
Each of them takes his turn to go to judgement;
They speak and listen; then they are swirled away.

'O you who come into this place of pain,'   16
Said Minos to me, when he saw me there,
And for a moment he paused from execution,

'Be careful how you enter and whom you trust: 19
Don't let yourself be tricked by the wide entrance.'
My guide said to him: 'Why do you call out?

Do not impede him, for his going is fated: 22
It is willed where everything is possible
If it is willed: and ask no further questions.'

And now the painful notes began to fall   25
Upon my ears; for now I am come indeed
To where a great lamentation strikes me.

I have come to a place where every light is silenced,   28
Which roars just as the sea roars in a storm,
When it is beaten by conflicting winds,

The infernal gale, which blows and never pauses,   31
Directs the spirits which it carries before it:
Harassing them with turning and buffeting.

When they arrive at the threshold of this ruin,   34
There, there are cries, complaints and lamentations;
And there, they blaspheme against the divine power.

I understood it is to this torment   37
That are condemned those who sin in the flesh,
And let their reason give way to their wishes.

40   And, as starlings are carried on their wings
     In the cold weather, in a vast wavering troop,
     So that breath carries the unfortunate spirits:

43   It drives them here and there, now down, now up;
     There is no hope ever to comfort them;
     They cannot stop, or ever suffer less pain.

46   And as the cranes go, chanting as they fly,
     Stretched out in a long ribbon in the air,
     I saw the approaching shadows, uttering cries

49   As they were carried by the trouble I have spoken of;
     And so I said: 'Master, who are those people,
     Who are so punished by the black air?'

52   'The first of those about whom you are asking,'
     He told me in reply, 'is that empress
     Who ruled over so many lands and languages.

55   She was so at the mercy of sensuality,
     That she made laws allowing what she liked
     So that her own conduct could not be blamed.

58   That is Semiramis, of whom we are told
     That she succeeded Ninus and was his wife;
     She held the land which the Soldan now rules.

61   The other is she who killed herself for love,
     And broke faith with the ashes of Sichaeus;
     And there you see the lustful Cleopatra.

64   See Helen, who brought about such evil times,
     Which lasted for so long; and great Achilles,
     Who in the end was in combat with love.

67   See Paris, Tristram,' and then more than a thousand
     Shadows he showed me, named and pointed out
     Those whom love had separated from life.

70   When I had heard my instructor in this way
     Naming the ladies and lovers of former times,
     I felt pity, and was as if bewildered.

I began: 'Poet, I should like, if it were possible,   73
To speak to those two who are coming side by side
And seem to be so light upon the wind.'

He said to me: 'You will see them when they come   76
A little closer to us: you have only to ask them,
Invoking the love that brings them, and they will come.'

As soon as the wind blew them to where we were standing,   79
I raised my voice: 'O you two panting spirits,
Come now and speak to us, if it is not forbidden.'

And just as doves called home to their desire,   82
With stretched and steady wings, back to the nest,
Come through the air because instinct carries them;

So, separating from the flock where Dido was,   85
They came towards us through the malignant air,
So strong was the affection of my cry.

'O kind and gracious living creature who   88
Go through the darkened air to visit us,
Although, when alive, we dyed the world with blood;

If only the king of the universe were our friend,   91
We would pray to him that you should have peace,
Because you pity our perversity.

Matters it pleases you to hear and speak of,   94
We will now hear and speak about to you,
While the wind is silent, as it is now.

The country I was born in lies along   97
The coast, just at the point the Po descends
To have some peace among its followers.

Love, which quickly fastens on gentle hearts,   100
Seized that wretch, and it was for the personal beauty
Which was taken from me; how it happened still offends me.

Love, which allows no one who is loved to escape,   103
Seized me so strongly with my pleasure in him,
That, as you see, it does not leave me now.

106   Love led us two to find a single death;
Caïna awaits him who brought us to this end.'
These were the words which came to us from them.

109   When I had heard those souls in their suffering,
I bowed my head, and kept it bowed so long
That at last the poet said: 'What are you thinking?'

112   When I replied, I started: 'Oh, alas,
That such sweet thoughts, desires that were so great,
Should lead them to the misery they are in.'

115   I turned to them again and spoke again,
Starting this time: 'Francesca, your great sufferings
Make me weep for you out of sadness and pity.

118   But tell me: in the time of those sweet sighs,
How and on what occasion did love allow
You to experience these uncertain desires?'

121   And she replied: 'There is no greater sorrow,
Than to think backwards to a happy time,
When one is miserable: your instructor knows this.

124   But if you have such a desire to know
The first root of our love, then I will tell you,
Although to do so, it will be as if I wept.

127   One day, when we were reading, for distraction,
How Lancelot was overcome by love—
We were alone, without any suspicion;

130   Several times, what we were reading forced
Our eyes to meet, and then we changed colour:
But one page only was more than we could bear.

133   When we read how that smile, so much desired,
Was kissed by such a lover, in the book,
He, who will never be divided from me,

136   Kissed my mouth, he was trembling as he did so;
The book, the writer played the part of Galahalt:
That day we got no further with our reading.'

While one of the spirits was speaking in this manner,   139
The other shed such tears that, out of pity,
I felt myself diminish, as if I were dying,

And fell down, as a dead body falls.   142

CANTO VI

When consciousness returned, after the darkening
Caused by my pity for the two kinsfolk
Which made me so sad that I was stunned,

I saw then, all around me, fresh torments   4
And tormented spirits I had not seen before,
As I moved on, turning this way and that, and looking.

I was in the third circle, where it rains   7
Eternally, icily and implacably;
Weight and direction are invariable.

Great hailstones, muddy water, mixed with snow,   10
Fall through the darkened air without respite;
They rot the ground they fall on, and it stinks.

Cerberus, a cruel and outlandish beast,   13
Barks like a dog, from his three throats, at those
Who, under that downpour, are there submerged.

His eyes are red, his beard greasy and black,   16
His belly huge, and his fingers are clawed,
He scratches the spirits, skins them, pulls them to bits.

They howl like dogs, the rain so batters them;   19
With nothing to shelter one flank, but the other,
The irreligious twist in their misery.

When Cerberus, the great dragon, saw us,   22
He opened his mouths wide and showed his fangs;
He shivered, and no part of him was still.

25   My guide then stooped, and opened his hands wide,
     Gathered up earth and then, his two fists full,
     He threw the lot down those rapacious throats.

28   Like a dog who barks when he wants food
     And quietens when he gets his teeth into it,
     Fighting and straining only in order to eat,

31   So was it with the filthy muzzles of Cerberus,
     The demon who so battered the ear-drums of those
     Spirits that they would like to have been deaf if they could.

34   We passed over the shadows which were beaten
     Under the heavy rain, we put the soles of our feet
     Down on the empty shapes which looked like bodies,

37   They lay upon the ground, strewn here and there,
     All except one of them, who sat up quickly
     When he saw us passing not far from him.

40   'O you who are conducted through this hell,'
     He said to me, 'acknowledge me if you know me:
     You were full-grown before I was unmade.'

43   I said to him: 'The anguish which you suffer,
     Is perhaps such, you are not recognisable;
     At least, it seems to me I never saw you.

46   But tell me who you are, put in this place
     Which is so dreary that, if perhaps other penalties
     Are more severe, none could be more displeasing.'

49   He answered: 'Your native city, which is full
     Of envy, till it is bursting at the seams,
     Was mine too, when I was in the open world.

52   You citizens called me by the name of Ciacco:
     For the pernicious fault of gluttony,
     As you see, now, the rain flattens me here.

55   And I, unhappy spirit, am not alone;
     All these suffer the self-same penalty
     For the same fault.' And then he said no more.

I answered him: 'Ciacco, your exhaustion and distress   58
Weigh on me heavily, and call up tears;
But tell me, if you know, what will become

Of those citizens of the divided city;   61
Will there be one just man? And tell me why
It has been troubled by so much dissension.'

He said to me: 'After an age of squabbles,   64
They will come to bloodshed, and the provincial party
Will drive the other out and do it viciously.

After which, that party is bound to fall   67
Within three summers, and the other come on top,
With the help of one who keeps an ambiguous course.

The other party will rule the roost for years,   70
Keeping its rival down with heavy exactions,
However great the tears and indignation.

There are two who are just, and no one listens to them;   73
Pride and envy and avarice are the sparks
Which set the hearts of that people alight.'

With that he ended his distressful utterance.   76
I said to him: 'I should like further instruction
If you will be so good as to tell me more.

Farinata and Tegghiaio, who were so excellent,   79
Jacopo Rusticucci, Arrigo and Mosca,
And the others who set their minds on doing well,

Tell me where they are now, that I may know them;   82
For I have the greatest desire to understand;
Does heaven delight them or does hell embitter them?'

He said: 'They are among the blackest souls: 85
For various faults have dragged them further down:
If you go lower, you will be able to see them.

But when you are once more in the sweet world,   88
Recall me to the memory of men:
I say no more: expect no further answer.'

91   His eyes, which had looked straight, were now askew:
       He looked at me a little, then bent his head
       And fell with it among the other blind men.

94   My guide said to me: 'He will not wake again
       Until he hears the sound of the angel's trumpet
       At the arrival of the enemy power:

97   Each one will see once more his bitter grave,
       Will put on once again his flesh and shape,
       Will hear what echoes through eternity.'

100   Thus we passed through the filthy mixture
       Of shadows and of rain, and with slow steps,
       Talking a little about the future life.

103   So I said to him: 'Master, will these torments
       Grow greater still after the great sentence,
       Will they be less, or burn as they burn now?'

106   His answer to me was: 'Go back to your science,
       Which teaches that the more perfect a thing is,
       The more it feels pleasure, and pain as well.

109   Although these people, because they are accursed,
       Will never reach the point of true perfection,
       They expect to approach it more nearly afterwards.'

112   We followed the road round a little further,
       Talking of more things than I will repeat;
       And so we came to the place where it goes down:

115   There we found Plutus, the great enemy.

CANTO VII

      'Papè Satan, papè Satan aleppé!'
      Plutus began, in his raucous voice;
      That wise and gentle man, who knew everything,

Replied, to comfort me, 'Do not let fear   4
Deflect you now; for, have what power he may,
He will not stop you climbing down the rock.'

Then he swung round towards the swollen face   7
And said: 'Be silent, you accursed wolf:
Consume yourself inwardly with your rage.

There is a reason for this downward journey: 10
For it is willed where the archangel Michael
Took revenge for that arrogant violation.'

As sails, when they are stretched out by the wind,   13
Wrap themselves in a heap when the mast breaks,
So that cruel animal fell to the ground.

So we went down the bank of the foul ditch,   16
Going a little further into the pit
Which is stuffed with all the evil of the universe.

Justice of God! Who except you could gather   19
As many pains and punishments as I saw?
And why is it our faults must so devour us?

Just as the water does above Charybdis,   22
Breaking upon the current that it meets,
So did these people in the circle of their dance.

Here the biggest crowd had come together   25
With great howls, from one side and the other,
And rolling heavy weights forward against their chests.

So they struck one another as they met;   28
And then turned round, and, rolling back again,
Some shouted 'Why hold on?' some 'Why let go?'

So they flowed back around the dark circle,   31
From each side of us, to meet on the other side,
Where once again they shouted their shameful chant:

When the two troops had met, they both turned round,   34
Went back through the semicircle, and met again.
And I, who felt as if my heart were punctured,

37   Said: 'My master, if you will, please indicate
      What people these are, and whether they were all clergymen,
      These tonsured ghosts on the left-hand side.'

40   He answered: 'The whole lot of them were cross-eyed,
      So to speak, in their minds, in their first life,
      And did not know how to spend moderately.

43   You may know their voices, they make outcry enough,
      When they arrive at the two points of the circle
      Where their contrary faults set them at odds.

46   Those were the clergy, who have nothing on top
      In the way of hair, and popes and cardinals;
      They are the ones in whom avarice does its best.'

49   I said: 'Master, among those who were like that,
      I certainly ought to recognise one or two
      Who were befouled with evils of that kind.'

52   He answered: 'You are wasting your time to think of it:
      They saw nothing in life, they wallowed in muck,
      And now they are so brown you cannot recognise them.

55   To all eternity they will run against each other:
      The one lot will arise out of their graves
      With fists clenched, the other with their hair cut off.

58   Ill giving and ill keeping have taken from them
      The lovely world, and put them in this scrum:
      What it is like, cannot be decently told.

61   Now you can see, my son, how short a life
      Have the gifts which are distributed by Fortune,
      And for which people get rough with one another:

64   So that all the gold there is beneath the moon
      And all there ever was, could never give
      A moment's rest to one of these tired souls.'

67   'Master,' I said to him, 'now tell me also:
      This Fortune, that you spoke about just now,
      What is she, that has the world's good in her clutches?'

He answered: 'How foolish people are!   70
How great is the ignorance which strikes them down!
Now listen to me and take in what I say.

He whose wise dispositions transcend everything,   73
Made the heavens, and gave intelligences to guide them,
So that each part shines on the other parts,

Distributing the light with equalness: 76
So is it with the splendours of the world;
He put in place an agent and director

Who at the proper time could change around   79
Vain possessions from one people to another,
Or between families, and no one could do a thing;

So that one race should rule, another languish,   82
According to the judgement of that female,
Who is as invisible as a snake in the grass.

Your science cannot take account of her: 85
She controls, takes decisions, executes them
In her kingdom, as other gods in theirs.

Her permutations go on without truce;   88
Necessity ensures that she is rapid;
So you no sooner have a thing than you lose it.

And this is she who is so crucified,   91
Even by those who ought to praise her most:
They blame her, but it is nothing but defamation:

But she is blessed and she does not hear;   94
With the other primal creatures, she is happy;
She rules her kingdom and enjoys her blessedness.

Now let us go down where there is more cause for pity;   97
Already the stars are sinking, which were rising
When I set out, and dawdling is forbidden.'

We crossed the circle to the other bank   100
Above a spring which boiled and flowed away
Through a concavity which it had made.

103   The water was more nearly black than blue;
       And we, in company with that dark stream,
       Went further down, following a difficult path.

106   It goes into the marsh which is called Styx,
       That sad brooklet, when it has tumbled down
       To the bottom of that long grey sloping hill.

109   And I, who stood there looking down intently,
       Saw people covered in mud, there in the swamp,
       All naked, and with anger in their faces.

112   They struck each other, and not only with their hands,
       But with their heads and chests and with their feet,
       Biting each other to pieces bit by bit.

115   The good master said: 'Son, now you see
       The spirits of those who were overpowered by anger;
       And I would also like you to understand

118   That underneath the water are people sighing;
       It is they who make the water bubble on top,
       As you can see, whichever way you turn.

121   Stuck in the slime, they say: "We chose to be sad
       In the sweet air enlivened by the sun,
       And our hearts smouldered with a sullen smoke:

124   Now we are sad instead in this black filth."
       That is the hymn they gurgle in their throats
       And cannot even get the words out properly.'

127   So we described a long arc round the bank
       Of that stinking pool, between the dry and the soft,
       With our eyes turned towards those who were swallowing
          the mud:

130   And so we came to the foot of a tower at last.

CANTO VIII

To go on with my story, long before
We actually reached the foot of the high tower,
Our eyes were drawn towards the top of it

By two little flames which suddenly appeared there,   4
And by another which answered from far away,
So far indeed that the eye could hardly see it.

I turned towards the ocean of intelligence,   7
And said: 'What does that say? And what reply
Comes from that other fire? And who are signalling?'

He answered me: 'Already on the filthy water   10
Can be seen what it is they are waiting for,
If the mist from the swamp does not conceal it from you.'

No bowstring ever sent an arrow off   13
To run through air with such precipitation
As the little boat which at that moment I saw

Advancing over the water in our direction,   16
Under the guidance of a crew of one
Who shouted: 'Now you are for it, wretched spirit!'

'Phlegyas, Phlegyas, your shouts are wasted,'   19
My master said, 'this time, for you will have us
Just as long as it takes to cross this marsh.'

As one who has heard about a great deception   22
That has been practised on him, and resents it,
So Phlegyas was, because his anger was checked.

My guide took a step down into the boat,   25
Then motioned me to board it after him,
And only when I was in did it seem loaded.

As soon as my guide and I were in the craft,   28
The ancient prow went on, and cut deeper
Into the water, than it did with other passengers.

31 While we scudded over the dead channel,
There arose before me one plastered in mud,
And said: 'Who are you, who come before your time?'

34 I answered: 'If I come, it is not to stay here:
But who are you, who have made yourself so filthy?'
He said: 'You see that I am one who weeps.'

37 I answered him: 'With weeping and with sorrow,
Accursed spirit, you stay where you are;
I recognise you, though you are dirty all over.'

40 Then he stretched out his two hands towards the boat;
The master, seeing this, pushed him away,
Saying: 'Away there with the other dogs.'

43 And then he put his arm around my neck
And kissed my face, and said: 'Disdainful soul,
Blessed is she who brought you into the world.

46 In his life he was full of arrogance:
And no good act embellishes his memory;
Therefore his shadow here is furious.

49 How many, up there, think themselves great kings
Who here will wallow in the mire like pigs,
Leaving behind them nothing but infamous horrors.'

52 And I: 'Master, I should very much like
To see that man pushed down into the soup
Before we get away from the lake, you and I.'

55 He answered me: 'Before the further shore
Comes into view, you shall see what you want:
Such a desire ought to be gratified.'

58 So, shortly afterwards, I saw such torture
Of that man, at the hands of those muddy people,
That I praise and thank God for it to this day.

61 They all cried: 'Down with Filippo Argenti!'
And that demented Florentine spirit turned
Upon himself and bit into his flesh.

Here we left him, so I will say no more of him;   64
But then fell on my ears a terrible wailing,
So that I looked ahead, straining my eyes.

Then the good master said: 'And now, my son,   67
We approach the city which takes its name from Dis,
With its grave citizens and huge armies.'

And I: 'Master, I already see its mosques,   70
Standing quite clearly there within the valley,
Pale red as if they came out of a fire.'

And he said to me: 'It is the eternal fire   73
Which lights them up inside and makes them glow,
As you see, in the deeper part of hell.'

We had now arrived inside the deep ditch   76
Which acted as a moat to that sad city;
The walls appeared as if they were made of iron.

Not without making first a huge circuit   79
Did we come to the place at which the boatman loudly
Called out: 'Ashore now, here is the way in.'

I saw above the gates more than a thousand   82
Spirits rained from heaven, and angrily
They said: 'Who is this creature who, without death,

Travels through the kingdom of the dead?'   85
And my wise master made a sign to indicate
He wished to have some secret talk with them.

Then they choked back their great disdain a little,   88
And said: '*You* come alone, let him go off;
He has been rash to enter into this kingdom.

He can take his fool's journey back alone,   91
If he knows how; for you are staying here
Because you brought him into this dark country.'

Imagine, reader, how I was discouraged   94
To hear them speaking this malediction,
Because I did not think I should get back.

97   'O my dear guide, who more than seven times
    Have brought me back to safety and rescued me
    From frightful dangers that stood in my way,

100   Do not leave me,' I said, 'so without help;
    But if we are forbidden to go further,
    Let us retrace our steps together, quickly.'

103   And that master who had brought me there
    Said to me: 'Have no fear; we will go our way;
    No one can stop us: such are our credentials.'

106   But wait for me here, your weary spirit
    Comforted and nourished with every hope,
    For I will not leave you in the low world.'

109   And so the gentle father went away
    And left me there, and I stayed with 'perhaps':
    And 'no' and 'yes' fought it out in my head.

112   I could not hear what it was he said to them;
    But he had hardly been with them a moment
    When, jostling each other, they ran in again.

115   And so our adversaries slammed the door
    In the face of my master, who stayed outside,
    And turned himself towards me with slow steps.

118   His eyes were downcast and his eyebrows showed
    No sign of cheerfulness, and he said, amidst sighs:
    'Who has denied me these houses of pain?'

121   And to me he said: 'Do not, because I am hurt,
    Lose heart, for I shall meet this trial successfully,
    Whatever the defence those inside put up.

124   That arrogance of theirs is nothing new;
    They showed the like once at a less secret gate,
    Which none the less is still without bolts and bars.

127   Above it you have seen the dead inscription:
    And already from the slope above us comes,
    Passing the circles without any escort,

130   One who is fit to open up the city.'

CANTO IX

That colour which my fear put on my cheek
When I saw that my guide turned back again
Made him quicker to repress his own pallor.

He stood still like a man who listens intently;   4
Because eyes could not take him very far
In the dark air and the closely drawn mists.

'There is no doubt we have to win this battle,'   7
He began, 'if not. . . But with the help that is offered us:
How long it seems before anybody comes!'

I observed the way in which he covered up   10
The first part of his speech with what came after,
Words of a different character from the first;

But none the less, what he said made me fearful,   13
Because I read into his broken phrase,
Perhaps, a worse meaning than it had.

'Does anyone ever come so far down   16
Into this sad pit, from the first step, in which
The only penalty is to lack hope?'

I put that question: he replied: 'Rarely   19
Does it happen that any one of us makes
The journey that I am making now.

It is true that I have been here once before,   22
Conjured by that intolerable Erichtho
Who used to call the shades back to their bodies.

My flesh had only just been stripped from me   25
When she made me enter within that wall
To take away a spirit from Judas's circle.

That is the lowest place, it is the darkest,   28
And the furthest from that heaven on which all turns:
I know the way well; you may be reassured.

31   That marsh, which sends out so much stinking breath,
     Surrounds on every side the weeping city
     Which we cannot now enter without wrath.'

34   The rest of what he said I have forgotten;
     Because at that moment my eye carried
     My attention to the high tower with the fiery top,

37   Where all at once there suddenly rose up
     Three infernal furies marked with blood;
     They had the shape and movement of women and

40   Around their middles were tied bright green hydras;
     They had small snakes and horned vipers for hair,
     And with that their fierce temples were bound.

43   And he, who knew the wretched creatures well
     As attendants of the queen of eternal weeping,
     Said to me: 'Look now at the fierce Erinnyes!

46   That is Megaera on the left-hand side;
     The one on the right hand, weeping, is Alecto;
     Tisiphone in the middle'; he stopped there.

49   All of them dug their nails into their breasts
     And clapped their hands together; and cried so loud
     That I drew close to the poet, in anxiety.

52   'Let Medusa come: then we can turn him to stone,'
     All of them said, looking down upon me;
     'It was a poor revenge we took on Theseus.'

55   'Now turn your back and cover up your face;
     If the Gorgon appears and you catch sight of her
     You will never go back to the world again.'

58   So my master said: and he himself turned me round;
     And, not relying on what my hands would do,
     He covered my face with his own hands also.

61   O you whose intellects are sane and well,
     Look at the teaching which is here concealed
     Under the unfamiliar veil of verses.

And now there came, over the troubled waves,   64
A crashing sound, which seemed to be full of terror,
And such that both the banks were shaken at once,

Not otherwise than as happens when a wind,   67
Rendered impetuous by the hostile blaze,
Tears through the forest without let or hindrance,

Shatters and beats down boughs, and carries them off;   70
Raising the dust as it goes proudly on,
Making wild beasts and shepherds flee before it.

He took his hands from my eyes and said: 'Now turn   73
The lash of vision on that ancient froth,
Just at the point where the smoke is most acrid.'

Like frogs scattering before a hostile snake,   76
And all at once disappearing in the water,
Not stopping until they reach the bottom,

I saw more than a thousand lost spirits   79
Making their escape before one who came
Over the Styx without wetting his feet.

He brushed the heavy air away from his face,   82
Passing his left hand over it repeatedly,
And that labour alone seemed to distress him.

I saw that he was the messenger from heaven,   85
And turned towards my master, who made a sign
That I should remain still and bow to the newcomer.

Ah, how full of disdain he seemed to me!   88
He came to the gate, and touching it with a baton,
He opened it, there was not the slightest difficulty.

'O you contemptible race, hunted from heaven,'   91
So he began, on that horrific threshold,
'Why does this insolence persist in you?

Why are you so recalcitrant to that will   94
Which cannot ever fail of its objective,
And which has more than once increased your pains?

97   What use, to run your head against the fates?
     Your Cerberus, if you have not forgotten,
     To this day has his throat and muzzle skinned.'

100   Then he turned back along the filthy road,
     And did not speak a word to us, appearing
     To be a man pressed and bitten by cares

103   Other than those that were before his nose;
     And we began to move towards the city,
     All being well after the sacred words.

106   We entered without any altercation;
     And I, who had a great desire to see
     The condition which that fortress shut within itself,

109   When I was inside, cast my eyes around;
     And I saw on every side a vast plain
     Filled with cries and with cruel torments.

112   Just as at Arles, where the Rhone is stagnant,
     Or as at Pola, near the gulf of Quarnaro
     Which shuts off Italy, washing its boundaries,

115   Tombs make the ground on every side uneven,
     So did they here, whichever way I looked,
     Except that the fashion of them here was bitterer;

118   Because among the tombs were scattered flames
     By which they were made completely incandescent,
     More so than iron need be, for any trade.

121   The lids of all of them were open and
     From the insides came a harsh lamentation
     Which seemed to be that of spirits wretched and vexed.

124   I said: 'Master, who are these people
     Who, buried inside these boxes, make themselves heard
     In these agonised sighs?'

127   And he replied: 'Here are the arch-heretics,
     With their followers, of every sect, and many more
     Than you imagine, are crammed into these tombs.

Those of the same kind are buried together,   130
Some monuments are hot and some are hotter.'
And then, when we had made a turn to the right,

We passed between these tortures and the battlements.   133

CANTO X

Now the way lies along a secret path
Between the city wall and the places of torture,
My master first, and I behind his shoulders.

'O supreme virtue, who through the pitiless circles   4
Take me round,' I began, 'just as it pleases you,
Speak to me now and satisfy my wishes.

The people that are lying inside the tombs,   7
Can they be seen? The lids are open already,
All of them, and there is no one on guard.'

He answered: 'All of them will be shut up   10
When they come back from the valley of Jehosophat
With the bodies they have left in the world above.

In this part we shall find the burial place   13
Of Epicurus and all his followers,
For whom the soul dies when the body dies.

Therefore the question that you put to me   16
Will be satisfied as soon as we are inside;
Also the desire of which you have said nothing.'

I said: 'Kind master, I do not keep my heart   19
Hidden from you, it is only that I wish to say little,
A habit to which you have more than once disposed me.'

'O Tuscan going through the city of fire   22
Alive, and talking in this sober manner,
Be good enough to stop in this place.

25   Your manner of speaking shows that you are from
That noble country of which you were a native,
And which, perhaps, I troubled too much.'

28   This sound came upon me unexpectedly
From one of the boxes; so that, being afraid,
I drew a little closer to my guide.

31   He said to me: 'Turn round: what are you doing?
Look now at Farinata who has straightened himself:
You will see all of him from the waist up.'

34   I had already turned and met his eyes;
And he rose upwards with his chest and forehead
As if he treated hell with great scorn:

37   And the confident, prompt hand of my guide
Impelled me among the tombs towards him,
Saying at the same time: 'Do not say very much.'

40   When I arrived at the place below the tomb,
He looked at me a little, then, as if disdainful,
He asked me: 'Who were your ancestors?'

43   I, who was desirous to obey,
Concealed nothing, but put the matter plainly;
So that he lifted his eyebrows a little.

46   Then said: 'They were fiercely in opposition
To me and my ancestors and my party,
So that on two occasions I scattered them.'

49   'If they were driven out, they came back
From wherever they were, both times,' I said;
'But yours have not well learned that trick.'

52   Then from the uncovered opening arose
A shadow which reached up to his chin:
I think that it had risen on to its knees.

55   It looked round about me, as if it wished
To see whether there was anyone with me;
And when that half hope was quite played out,

It said weeping: 'If through this blind prison   58
You go because of your exalted abilities,
Where is my son? Why is he not with you?'

I answered: 'I do not come here of myself: 61
The one who waits there, is leading me here;
And that person perhaps your Guido disdained.'

What he said, and the manner of his punishment,   64
Made his name clear as if it were spelt out;
For this reason my answer was so full.

Suddenly he called out: 'What did you say?   67
Disdained? Do you mean he is no longer alive?
Do his eyes no longer encounter the sweet light?'

When he perceived that I made some delay   70
Before I brought myself to answer him,
He fell down backwards and appeared no more.

But the other magnanimous spirit, at whose request   73
I had halted on my way, did not change his look;
He neither moved his neck nor inclined his body;

And going on with what he was saying before,   76
He said: 'If they have ill acquired that trick,
It tortures me more than the bed that I lie on.

But before fifty moons have lighted up   79
The face of that lady who reigns here,
You will yourself know what that trick is worth.

And if you would return to the sweet world,   82
Tell me: why is that people so relentless
Against my kindred in all the laws it makes?'

So I said to him: 'The tortures and the massacres   85
Which caused the Arbia to be coloured red,
Caused also these speeches in our temple.'

He sighed and shook his head, and then replied: 88
'In that I was not the only one; and certainly
I should not have moved with others, without reason.

91   But I was the only one, when it was agreed
     To carry out the plan of destroying Florence,
     To stand up openly in her defence.'

94   'As you would have your issue somewhen find peace,'
     I begged him, 'help me with the difficulty
     Which has obscured my reflections on this subject.

97   It seems, if I understand aright,
     You see beforehand what it is time brings,
     But with the present it is otherwise.'

100 'We see like people with imperfect sight,'
     He said, 'things which are a certain distance from us;
     The supreme ruler gives us that much light:

103 When they are closer or actual, our intellect
     Is useless; and, unless someone brings us news,
     We know nothing at all of your human state.

106 So you can understand that our knowledge
     Will be entirely dead, after the point
     At which the gate of the future will be shut.'

109 Then, as if my fault made me remorseful,
     I said: 'Now therefore you will say to that man who fell
     That his son is still among the living;

112 And if I was mute before, when he replied,
     Let him know that I was so because my thoughts
     Were in the confusion you have cleared up.'

115 My master was already calling me back;
     So I begged the spirit all the more pressingly
     To tell me what others were with him there.

118 He said to me: 'With more than a thousand others
     I lie here; within there is Frederick the Second,
     And the Cardinal; I say nothing of the others.'

121 Then he disappeared; and I retraced my steps
     Towards the ancient poet, thinking over
     What had been said which seemed hostile to me.

He stirred himself; and then, as he was going,   124
Said to me: 'Why do you look so bewildered?'
And I satisfied him as to the reason.

'But keep in mind the things that you have heard   127
Against yourself,' the wise poet directed,
'Attend to what I say'; he raised a finger:

'When you at last reach the sweet ray   130
Of her whose lovely eye sees everything,
From her you will know the course of your life.'

And then he turned his feet towards the left;   133
We left the wall and went towards the middle
By a pathway which struck into a valley

Which, even up there, was offensive by its stink.   136

CANTO XI

Coming to the topmost edge of a high bank
Made by great broken stones forming a circle,
We found ourselves above a crueller swarm;

And there, because of the horrible piling up   4
Of stenches thrown off by the deep abyss,
We made our way towards it under cover

Of a great tomb, on which I saw an inscription   7
Which said: 'I keep Pope Anastasius,
Whom Photinus seduced from the straight way.'

'We should delay our going down a little,   10
Till our sense grows accustomed to that breath;
And, after that, it need not trouble us.'

So said my master. 'Devise something,' I said,   13
'So that the time we spend here is not lost.'
And he replied: 'You see I am thinking of that.

16   My son, within the circle of stone,'
       He then began, 'there are three smaller circles
       Of graduated size, like those you are leaving.

19   All of them are filled with accurst spirits;
       But so that later you will have only to look at them,
       I will explain now how and why they are there.

22   The object of all malice, which earns heaven's hatred,
       Is injury; every object of that kind
       Causes distress to others by force or fraud.

25   And because fraud is an evil peculiar to men,
       It displeases God the more; and therefore the fraudulent
       Are placed beneath and greater pain assails them.

28   The first circle is given over to the violent;
       But as force may be against three persons,
       The circle is construed in three distinct rings.

31   Force may be used against God, one's self or one's neighbour,
       And against what belongs to each of them,
       As you will hear openly explained.

34   Violent death and wounds which cause pain
       May be given to a neighbour; while as to his belongings,
       There is wrecking, arson, and destructive extortion;

37   So homicide and those who use violence wrongly,
       Wreckers and robbers, are all of them tormented
       In the first ring, and in distinct troops.

40   A man can lay violent hands on himself,
       And on his goods; and therefore the second ring
       Is properly for the profitless repentance

43   Of those who deprive themselves of the world,
       Gamble away and waste their property
       And weep in circumstances which should make them happy.

46   Violence may be done to the deity,
       With the heart denying him and blaspheming against him,
       And treating beneficent nature with disdain;

And so the smallest ring seals with its mark 49
Not only Sodom but also Cahors,
And all who, despising God in their hearts, talk.

Fraud, by which every conscience is bitten, 52
A man may practise on a person who trusts him
Or upon one who has no confidence in him.

This latter mode cuts only the bond of love 55
Which nature of itself establishes;
And so there are, lodged in the second circle,

Hypocrisy, flatterers, and those who delude, 58
Falsity, thieving and simony,
Pimps, trouble-makers, and all such-like scum.

In the other mode, the love that is forgotten 61
Is not only what is natural, but what is added
By the creation of particular obligations;

So, in the smaller circle, at the centre 64
Of the universe, which is the seat of Dis,
Every traitor is for ever consumed.'

I said to him: 'Master, your exposition 67
Is extremely clear, and perfectly distinguishes
The abyss and the people which it contains.

But tell me: those in the sickening marsh, 70
Those who are driven by the wind and beaten by rain;
And those who rail at each other when they meet,

Why is it not within the glowing city 73
That they are punished, if God is angry with them?
And if he is not, why are they as they are?'

He replied: 'Why does your mind wander so 76
And so much more than it is accustomed to do?
Or are your thoughts perhaps on something else?

Have you no recollection of the words 79
With which your *Ethics* gives an account of
The three dispositions which heaven does not want,

82   Incontinence, malice and frantic bestiality?
     And how, of these, it is incontinence
     Which least offends God and incurs least blame?

85   If you consider this opinion well,
     And recall to mind who those spirits are
     Who, up there outside, undergo retribution,

88   You will see clearly why they are separated
     From these felons, and why the divine vengeance
     Uses less extreme torment to hammer them.'

91   'O sun who clear every obscure perception,
     You give such satisfaction when you enlighten me
     That, not less than knowledge, doubt is agreeable.

94   Now, go back to an earlier point in the argument,'
     I said, 'to where you said that usury offends
     Divine goodness, and unloosen that knot.'

97   'Philosophy,' he said, 'for those who understand it,
     Makes it clear, not only in one place,
     How nature takes her direction from

100 The divine intellect and from its arts;
     And if you pay attention to your *Physics*,
     You will find there, somewhere near the beginning,

103 That your art follows nature, as far as it can,
     Much in the way a student follows his master;
     So that your art is the grandchild of God.

106 From these two, if you recall to mind
     The beginning of Genesis, it is proper for man
     To win his bread and to advance his race:

109 And because the usurer takes another way,
     Treating nature and what follows from her
     Contemptuously, he puts his hopes elsewhere.

112 But follow me now, because I choose to go;
     For Pisces flickers over the horizon,
     And the whole Wain lies over Caurus,

115 And away over there we can go down the cliff.'

CANTO XII

The place to which, in order to descend the bank,
We came, was mountainous, and with what was there besides,
Such, that a look would make you shy away from it.

Like that landslide which, upon the bank   4
This side of Trent, struck at the Adige,
Either in an earthquake or because a support failed,

So that, from the top of the hill, from which it slid,   7
Down to the level, the rock is so broken up,
That anyone might pick a way down the cliff there;

Such was the track there down that ravine;   10
And at the top, where the ground had broken away,
The infamy of Crete spread out its limbs,

He who was conceived by the pretended cow;   13
When he caught sight of us, he bit himself,
Like one so angry he cannot help doing so.

My mentor called in his direction: 'Do you   16
Perhaps think that here again is the Prince of Athens
Who, in the upper world, put you to death?

Out of the way, beast! for this man does not come   19
Under your sister's guidance; he is going
Further to see the nature of your punishments.'

Like a bull who frees himself just at the moment   22
When he has received the fatal blow,
Who cannot escape, but leaps here and there,

I saw the Minotaur do the same thing;   25
My wary companion cried: 'Run to the gap;
While he is in a rage, you had better go down.'

So we took our way down on that discharge   28
Of stones, which frequently began to move
Under my feet because of the unusual burden.

31   I was thinking as I went, and he said: 'You are thinking,
      Perhaps, of this landslide which is guarded
      By that bestial anger which I extinguished.

34   You ought to know that, on the other occasion,
      When I came down here into deep hell,
      This rock had not yet cascaded.

37   And certainly, if I remember aright,
      A little before he came, who took
      The great booty from Dis, in the upper circle,

40   On all sides the deep foul valley trembled
      In such a manner that I thought the universe
      Felt love, by which, there are those who believe,

43   The world has more than once been turned to chaos;
      And at that moment all this ancient rock
      Here and elsewhere, was overturned like that.

46   But fix your eyes on that valley, we are approaching
      The river of blood in which everyone boils
      Who does harm to his neighbour by violence.'

49   O blind cupidity and senseless anger,
      Which so goads us in our short life here
      And, in the eternal life, drenches us miserably!

52   I saw a wide ditch bent like a bow,
      Like that which held the whole plain in its embrace,
      Just as my guide had indicated;

55   And between it and the foot of the bank, on a track,
      Ran centaurs one behind the other, armed with arrows,
      As they used, in the world, to go hunting.

58   Seeing us coming down, they all stood still,
      And from the company three of them broke away,
      With their bows, having first selected shafts;

61   And one cried from a distance: 'To what torture
      Are you coming, you who descend the slope?
      Tell me where you are from; or I draw my bow.'

My master said: 'We will make our reply   64
To Chiron who is standing near you there:
The worse for you, your will was always rash.'

Then he touched me and said: 'That one is Nessus,   67
Who died for the beautiful Dejanira
And took his own vengeance upon himself.

And the one in the middle, his head upon his breast,   70
Is the great Chiron, he who fostered Achilles;
The other is Pholus, who was so full of rage.

Around the ditch they go, thousand after thousand,   73
Loosing arrows at any spirit which rises
Further out of the blood than its guilt allows of.'

We approached these nimble beasts, and Chiron took   76
An arrow, and using the notch of it as a comb,
Put his beard back in place over his jaws.

When he had uncovered his great mouth,   79
He said to his companions: 'Have you noticed?
When the one behind touches things, they move.

The feet of the dead do not have that effect.'   82
And my good guide, who reached up to the chest,
Where the two natures are joined together,

Answered: 'He is alive, no doubt about it;   85
If I have to show him the dark valley alone,
It is because he must come, not for amusement.

One who broke off from singing Alleluiah   88
Committed this unusual office to me:
He is no thief, nor am I a suspicious character.

But, by that power by whose will I move   91
My steps along this road, which is so wild,
Let us have one of you, that, with us close to him,

He may show us the spot at which to ford the stream   94
And carry this man over on his crupper,
For he is not a spirit who goes through the air.'

97   Chiron then swung his right shoulder round,
     And said to Nessus: 'Turn, guide them as he says;
     If another troop gets in the way, make them skip.'

100 Then we moved on with our faithful escort,
     Along the edge of the boiling red liquid,
     From which came the shrill cries of the scalded.

103 I saw people who were in it to the eyebrows;
     And the great Centaur said: 'These are the tyrants
     Who gave themselves over to blood and rapine.

106 Here they weep for their pitiless offences;
     Here is Alexander, and fierce Dionysius,
     Who gave Sicily years of suffering.

109 And that forehead that has such black hair
     Is Azzolino; and that other, which is fair,
     Is Obizzo da Este, who—though some doubted it—

112 Was put out of the world by his bastard son.'
     Then I turned to the poet, and he said:
     'Let him be first now, I will be second.'

115 A little further on the Centaur stopped
     Above a group of shadows whose throats
     Were just emerging out of the boiling liquid.

118 He showed us one, who was set apart by himself,
     Saying: 'That one, in the bosom of God, pierced
     The heart which still bleeds beside the Thames.'

121 Then I saw those who kept out of the river
     Not only their heads but also the whole thorax;
     And I could recognise many of them.

124 So bit by bit the blood grew shallower,
     Until it was scalding nothing but the feet;
     And that was the point for us to cross the ditch.

127 'Just as, upon this side, you may see
     The boiling liquid growing less and less,'
     The Centaur said, 'So, I would have you know,

On the other side it presses down more deeply   130
Upon the river bed, until it reaches
The place in which tyranny must groan.

Here the divine justice stings Attila,   133
Who was a scourge when he was on earth,
And Pyrrhus and Sextus; and eternally milks

Tears, which it releases by boiling, from   136
Rinier da Corneto, and from Rinier Pazzo,
Who were so violent upon the roads.'

Then he turned back, and crossed the ford again.   139

CANTO XIII

Nessus had not yet reached the other side
When we set out to travel through a wood
Which had no path marked in it at all.

The foliage not green, but of dark colour;   4
The branches not wholesome, but knotted and twisted;
There were no apples but poisonous thorns.

The undergrowth is not so rough or dense,   7
Where the wild beasts, which hate all cultivation,
Live between Cecina and Corneto.

It is there that the filthy Harpies make their nests,   10
They who hunted the Trojans from the Strophades,
Announcing dismally their future loss.

They have broad wings, with human necks and faces,   13
Feet with claws, their great bellies covered with feathers;
They make lamentations on strange trees.

And the good master said: 'Before you enter,   16
Know that you are in the second ring.'
That is how he began, 'And you will be, until

19   You set your eyes on the horrible stretch of sand:
     Therefore look carefully; for you will see
     Things which you would not believe, if I reported them.'

22   I heard cries coming from every direction,
     And yet saw nobody who could be crying;
     I became so bewildered that I stopped.

25   I think he thought that I thought that those voices,
     And many there were, came from among the tree-stumps,
     From people who were hiding themselves from us.

28   Therefore the master said: 'If you break off
     A little twig from one of these plants,
     The thoughts you are thinking will be changed utterly.'

31   Then I stretched out my hand a little way,
     And picked a little branch from a great thorn;
     And the trunk of it called out: 'Why are you tearing me?'

34   It grew a little dark with blood and said,
     Once again: 'Why are you dismembering me?
     Have you no spirit of compassion?

37   Once we were men, now we are stumps and shoots:
     Surely your hand should have been more merciful,
     Even if we had been the souls of serpents.'

40   As a green stick, which is burning at one end,
     Sweats at the other end at the same time
     And hisses as the steam goes out of it;

43   So, from the broken shoot, came out at once
     Both words and blood; which made me let fall the top,
     And I stood there like a man afraid.

46   'If he had been able to believe at first,'
     Said my instructor, 'O you injured soul,
     What he had seen only in my verses,

49   He would not have stretched out his hand against you;
     But the thing was so incredible it made me
     Suggest an action which I myself regret.

But tell him who you were, so that, to make you   52
Some amends he may bring your name to life,
Once more, in the world, for he is allowed to return.'

The trunk said: 'You so tempt me, by speaking so gently,   55
That I cannot stay silent; do not take it ill,
If I allow myself to talk awhile.

I am the man who held the double keys   58
To Frederick's heart, and I it was who turned them,
Locking and unlocking, so delicately

That I kept almost everyone from his secrets;   61
I was so faithful in my glorious office
That, for its sake, I lost both sleep and strength.

The whore who never turned her lecherous eyes   64
From the palaces where Caesar entertained,
The common death of men, the vice of courts,

Inflamed the minds of everyone against me;   67
And those who were inflamed, inflamed Augustus,
Till all my happy honours were turned to sorrow.

My mind, with its taste for scorn and anger,   70
Thinking by death to escape the scorn of others,
Made me unjust against my just self.

By the new roots which shoot out from this tree,   73
I swear to you that I never broke faith
With my lord, who was so worthy of honour.

And if one of you is going back to the world,   76
Comfort my memory, which is still abject
Because of the reproaches made by envy.'

The poet waited a little, and then he said: 79
'Since he is silent, do not waste the time,
But speak, question him further, if you like.'

I said to him: 'Put to him some other point   82
On which you think I would have satisfaction;
For I could not, pity so stabs my heart.'

85 Then he began again: 'So that the man
Should freely do for you what you have asked him,
Incarcerated spirit, be pleased to tell him

88 How it is that the soul is so bound up
In this knotted wood; and tell him, if you can,
If any ever free themselves from such limbs.'

91 Then the trunk blew strongly, and, after a while,
The breath turned itself into a voice:
'The answer that you want can be put briefly.

94 When the fierce soul makes its way from the body,
From which it has managed to rip itself out,
Minos dismisses it to the seventh ravine.

97 It falls into the wood, there is no choice of place;
But wherever fortune happens to catapult it,
It germinates like a grain of barley.

100 It shoots up into branches and woody plants;
The Harpies, feeding then upon its leaves,
Inflict pain, and give pain a way out.

103 Like others, we shall look for our mortal bodies,
But none of us will ever put his on again;
It is not just for a man to have what he takes from himself.

106 We shall drag them here, and through the mournful wood
Our bodies will be hung, each one upon
The thorny tree of his tormented shade.'

109 We were still listening to the trunk,
Thinking that it had something else to say,
When suddenly we were astonished by an uproar

112 Like one who becomes aware of the approach
Of a boar and hunt coming close to where he stands,
When he hears the beasts, and the branches crashing,

115 And, look, two on the left-hand side,
Naked and scratched, and running away so fast
That they broke all the branches as they passed.

The one in front cried: 'Death, we need death!'   118
And the other, who seemed unable to catch up,
Called: 'Lano, you certainly didn't need legs like that

At the fighting around Toppo!' And, at that moment,   121
Perhaps because his wind was giving out,
He fell into a heap upon a bush.

Behind them, the forest was full of she-dogs,   124
Black creatures, hot on the scent, and running
Like greyhounds which had just got off the leash.

They fixed their teeth in the one who was hunched up,   127
And then tore him to pieces, shred by shred,
And carried off the limbs, which were still hurting.

And then my escort took me by the hand,   130
And led me to the bush, which was weeping tears
Through its bloody fractures, but in vain.

'O Giacomo da Sant'Andrea,' it cried,   133
'What have you gained by sheltering in me,
Am I to blame for your iniquitous life?'

When my master had stopped, he looked down on it and said: 136
'Who were you, who, through so many broken ends,
Sigh out your unhappy words with blood?'

He said to us: 'O you souls who have arrived   139
To see the shameless waste and laceration
Which has so taken my leaves away from me,

Gather them to the foot of this sad bush.   142
I was of the city which changed its first patron
For John the Baptist; for which reason the first

Will always try his tricks to make it grieve;   145
And if it were not that, at the crossing of the Arno,
Some slight trace of his image still remains,

Those citizens, who built the city again   148
Upon the ashes which Attila left,
Would have carried out all that work in vain.

I made a gallows for myself of my own house.'   151

CANTO XIV

Because the love I have for my own country
So seized me, I picked up the scattered leaves,
And gave them back to him, who had grown faint.

4   Then we came to the boundary which separates
The second circuit from the third, and where
There is to be seen a fearful device of justice.

7   To make clear what these novelties were,
I will tell you that we arrived at a sandy waste,
From the surface of which every living plant had been scoured.

10   The sorrowful wood stands like a garland about it,
As the sad ditch circles around the wood:
Here we stopped, standing just at the edge.

13   The ground was thickly covered with dry sand,
Not different in fashion from that which was
Trodden under the feet of Cato.

16   O vengeance of God, how much you ought
To be feared by everyone who reads
What was there manifested to my eyes.

19   I saw many droves of naked souls,
All of them weeping in great wretchedness,
But subject apparently to different laws.

22   Some of them lay supine on the ground;
While others were sitting there, all hunched up;
And others were continually wandering.

25   Those who were on the move were more numerous;
And those who lay down in the torment were fewer,
But had their tongues more loosened by cries of pain.

28   Upon them all the great sand, falling slowly,
Rained down dilated flakes of fire, just as
In the mountains snow falls without wind.

As Alexander in those hot regions   31
Of India, saw, falling upon his army,
Flames which fell to the ground without disintegrating;

So that he took care that his troops should tread   34
The ground, in such a manner that the burning
Was put out before more reinforced it.

So fell the eternal heat, and in this manner   37
The sand would catch alight, as if it were tinder
Under the steel, and so the pain was doubled.

There was no rest ever from the dance   40
Of wretched hands, which were now here now there,
Each one shaking from himself the fresh burning.

I began: 'Master, you who overcome   43
All things, with the exception of those hard devils
Who came out against us at the entrance gate,

Who is that great one who seems not to care   46
About the fire, and lies, scornful and twisted,
As if the rain would never ripen him?'

And he himself, when he perceived that I   49
Was questioning my escort about him,
Cried: 'As I was alive, so am I dead.

If Jove should weary out his smith, from whom   52
In fury he took the sharp thunderbolt
With which, on the last day, I was transfixed;

Or if he wearies the others, one after the other,   55
In Mongibello, at the black forge,
Crying: "Good Vulcan, help us, help us!"

As he did at the fight at Phlegra,   58
And send his bolts at me with all his strength;
Yet he should not find his revenge delightful.'

And then my escort spoke with a vehemence   61
Such as I had not heard from him before:
'Capaneus, if your pride is not lessened,

64   Your punishment will be that much the worse:
       No agony, except your rage itself,
       Would be a pain proportionate to your fury.'

67   And then he turned to me with gentler looks,
       Saying: 'That one was one of the seven kings
       Who besieged Thebes; he held and seems to hold

70   God in contempt, and treats him as not worth much;
       But, as I said to him, his own vexations
       Are exactly the right badges for him to wear.

73   Now come behind me, and watch that you do not put
       Your feet upon the burning sand;
       But always keep them close to the trees.'

76   Saying nothing, we came to where there spurts forth
       Out of the wood, a little rivulet,
       The redness of which still sends a shudder through me.

79   As from the Bulicame issues the stream
       Which prostitutes share among themselves,
       So that one went away across the sand.

82   The bottom of the stream, and both the shelving banks
       Were made of stone, and a strip on either side;
       So I saw that this would be the way for us.

85   'Among all the rest that I have shown you,
       Since we entered this place by that gate,
       The threshold of which is not denied to anyone,

88   Nothing which your eyes have perceived
       Is as remarkable as this river here,
       Which puts out all flames in the air above it.'

91   These were the words which my escort spoke:
       I begged him to give me food to satisfy
       The appetite which he had already given me.

94   'In the middle of the sea there lies a waste country,'
       He said then, 'and it is called Crete,
       Under whose king the world was once chaste.

A mountain is there which at one time was glad 97
With water and foliage, and it is called Ida:
Now it is deserted as a place condemned.

Rhea chose the place as a safe cradle 100
For her baby and, in order to hide him better
When he cried, she made it a place of cries.

Inside the mountain, upright, stands an old man, 103
Who keeps his back turned upon Damietta,
And looks at Rome as if it were his mirror.

His head is worked out of fine gold, 106
And his arms and chest are made of pure silver,
Then he is all brass down to the crutch;

From there downwards he is all of pure iron, 109
Except that his right foot is baked clay;
And he puts more weight on that than on the other.

Each part, except the golden, is broken 112
By a crack from which there drip tears,
Which collect and bore their way out through the stone.

Their course is downward over rock after rock: 115
They form Acheron, Styx and Phlegethon,
Then run away through this narrow gulley

Until they reach the lowest point of all: 118
They form Cocytus; and what that pool is like
You will see for yourself: so I will not tell you here.'

I said to him: 'If this rivulet here 121
Is drawn off in this manner from our world,
Why does it appear only at this side?'

And he replied: 'You know that the place is round; 124
And although you have come a long way,
Always to the left, descending to the bottom,

You have not yet done the complete circle; 127
So that if anything that is new appears,
It ought not to make you look astonished.'

130   I again: 'Master, will you tell me where
        Are Phlegethon and Lethe? About the one you are silent;
        Of the other, you say it is made of this rain.'

133   'In all your questions, certainly you please me,'
        He answered: 'but that boiling red water
        Ought of itself to answer one of your questions.

136   Lethe you will see, but not in this ditch;
        There, where the spirits go to wash themselves
        When they have repented and their sin is remitted.'

139   He added: 'Now it is the time to depart
        From this wood; see that you keep behind me:
        The side-tracks make a pathway, they are not burning,

142   And above them all fire is put out.'

CANTO XV

    Now one of these hard side-paths takes us further;
    And the stream's exhalation overshadows us,
    So that it keeps from the fire both water and banks.

4   Just as the Flemings between Wissant and Bruges,
      Fearing the tide which comes in violently,
      Build dykes so that the sea holds back;

7   And as the Paduans along the Brenta,
      For the defence of countryside and castles,
      Before the snows melt in the Chiarentana;

10   After the same pattern those banks were made,
      Though they were neither so high, nor so wide,
      Whoever might be the master who designed them.

13   Already we were so far from the wood
      That I should not have seen where it was
      If I had turned back to look,

When we encountered a troop of spirits   16
Who came along the bank, and each one of them
Looked at us, just as one might do at nightfall,

Looking at someone under a new moon;   19
And narrowed their eyes, which were turned in our direction,
As an old tailor does, threading a needle.

Eyed in this way by this company,   22
I was recognised by one of them, who seized me
By the edge of my cloak, and cried: 'How marvellous!'

And, when he had stretched out his arm to me,   25
I fixed my eyes upon his scorched appearance
So that his burnt face should not prevent

The recognition of him by my intellect;   28
And, bending my face towards his,
I answered him: 'Are you here, ser Brunetto?'

And he: 'O my dear son, be not displeased,   31
If Brunetto Latini comes back with you
A little way, and lets the file go on.'

I said to him: 'With all my heart, I beg you;   34
And if you want me to sit down with you,
I will, if he who goes with me is content.'

'O my dear son,' he said, 'if one of this troop   37
Stops for a moment, he lies for a hundred years
Without protection from the fire that strikes him.

So go on: and I will follow below you;   40
Then I will go back to my band,
Who go weeping for their eternal losses.'

I did not dare to go down from the road   43
To walk where he was walking; but, head bowed,
I went as one who goes with reverence.

He began: 'What fortune, or what destiny   46
Brings you down here before your last day has come?
And who is this, who is showing you the way?'

49   'Up there above, in the serene life,'
     I answered, 'I lost myself in a valley,
     Before the middle point of my life.

52   Only yesterday morning I turned my back on it:
     He appeared to me, as I was bent on resuming it,
     And he is leading me home by this path.'

55   He said: 'If you are following your star,
     You cannot fail to reach the glorious harbour,
     If I saw clearly in the agreeable life;

58   And if I had not prematurely died,
     Seeing heaven was so well-disposed towards you,
     I should have given you comfort in your work.

61   But that ungrateful and malignant people
     Which, anciently, came down from Fiesole,
     And still retains something of rocky hardness,

64   Will, for your doing well, be hostile to you:
     And, naturally, because the mountain ash
     Is no fit company for the sweet fig-tree.

67   They have long had a name on earth for being blind;
     A greedy race, envious besides and proud;
     With their ways you shall have nothing to do.

70   Your fortune reserves such honour for you,
     That both parties want to get at you;
     But the grass will be out of reach of the goat.

73   Let the Fiesolean beasts find their own fodder
     In their own kind, and leave the plant alone,
     If there appears one on their dung-heap

76   In which the holy seed comes to life again,
     Left by those Romans who remained there when
     That nest of so much malice was constructed.'

79   'If I had my way entirely,' so
     I answered him, 'you would not yet have been
     Put under ban from natural humanity;

For my mind is transfixed, and my heart stabbed,   82
By the dear, kind, paternal image of you,
When you were on earth, and time and again

Instructed me how man may be eternal: 85
And what pleasure I had in that, as long as I live,
It is appropriate that my tongue should show.

What you say about my course, I record,   88
And keep it to be glossed, with another text,
By a lady who will know, if I reach her.

This much I should like to make clear to you,   91
If only my conscience does not cry out,
That I am ready for what fortune wills.

There is nothing new to my ears in such promises: 94
And so, let fortune spin her wheel as she pleases,
And let the labourer hoe what row he will.'

My master then turned and I saw his cheek   97
Over his right shoulder, and he looked at me
And said: 'Those are the words of a good listener!'

In spite of that, I did not stop conversing   100
With ser Brunetto, and asking him who were
The best known and most eminent of his companions.

He told me: 'It is good to know some of them;   103
Of the rest, it is more creditable to be silent,
For time will be short for much talking.

Briefly, you should know that all of them were clerics   106
And learned men of distinction and reputation,
But, with the same fault on earth, befouled.

Priscian goes with that miserable crowd,   109
And Francesco d'Accorso; and you might have seen,
If you had any taste for such pestilence,

Him who, by the servant of the servants,   112
Was translated from the Arno to the Bacchiglione,
Where he at last left his ill-stretched nerves.

115 I could say more; but further walking and talking
There cannot be, because over there I see
Fresh smoke rising from the great sands.

118 People are coming with whom I may not be:
I recommend you to read my work, *The Treasure*,
In which I still live, and I ask no more.'

121 Then he turned back, and seemed to be one of those
Who, at Verona, run for the green cloth,
Through the open country; and he seemed to be the one

124 Who wins the race, and not the one who loses.

CANTO XVI

I was already where I could hear the roar
Of the water falling into the next circle,
Like the hum which bees make around a hive;

4 When three shadows together broke away,
Running, from a squadron which was passing
Under the rain of sharp torturings.

7 They came towards us, and all of them were crying:
'Stop! you who, from the way that you are dressed,
Seem to be someone from our deformed country!'

10 Alas, what wounds I saw on their limbs,
Fresh ones and old ones, burns made by the flames!
It still hurts me, recalling what I saw.

13 At their cry, my instructor listened;
He turned his face towards me, and said: 'Wait:
To these a certain courtesy is due.

16 And were it not for the fire which this place
Of its nature rains like arrows, I would say
That it would be better for you to hurry towards them.'

As we stopped, they began again to utter   19
Their ancient song; and when they had reached the point
Where we were standing, they all three formed a circle,

And then, as naked and oiled champions do,   22
Eyeing one another to see how best to grip
Before they come to blows and holds together;

And so, as they ran round, they kept their faces   25
Turned all the time towards me, so that their necks
Were all the time in movement, like their feet.

And, 'If the misery of this unstable ground   28
Makes you contemptuous of us and our wishes,'
One began, 'and our scorched, discoloured looks,

Our fame at least will perhaps induce your mind   31
To tell us who you are, who trail your feet,
While still living, over the floor of hell.

He, in whose footsteps you see me trample,   34
Although he goes naked and hairless now,
Was of a higher rank than you suppose.

He was the grandson of the good Gualdrada;   37
His name was Guido Guerra, and in life
He was active in council and in arms.

The other, who treads the sand after me,   40
Is Tegghiaio Aldobrandi, whose voice deserved
To have pleased more than it did, up in the world.

And I, who am put in torment with them here,   43
Was Jacopo Rusticucci; and certainly
My savage wife did me more harm than anything.'

If I had been protected from the fire,   46
I should have thrown myself among them down there,
And I believe my instructor would have approved;

But since I should have burnt and scorched myself,   49
Fear overcame the good will that I had,
Which made me want to run to their embraces.

52   Then I began: 'It was not with contempt,
      But with grief, that your condition pierced my heart,
      So deeply that it will be long before it is gone,

55   As soon as my master here addressed me
      In such words as made me begin to think
      That men such as you are might come this way.

58   I am of your country, and all my life,
      I have related, and heard of, with affection,
      Your achievements and your honoured names.

61   I leave the gall and go for the sweet apples
      Promised to me by the veracious guide;
      But first I must fall to the centre of the earth.'

64   'As you desire your soul long to accompany
      Your body,'—that was the manner of his reply—
      'And want your fame to shine after you,

67   Tell me if courtesy and courage still
      Live in our city as they used to do,
      Or whether all that has gone away;

70   For Guglielmo Borsiere, who has suffered with us
      Only a little time, and is here with the rest,
      Has much distressed us with his talk about it.'

73   'New families, who have made sudden gains,
      Have generated pride and immoderate ways,
      Florence, in you, you weep for it already.'

76   So I cried out as I threw back my head;
      And the three, who took that for a reply,
      Looked at one another, as if to say, Then it is true.

79   'If on other occasions it costs you so little,'
      They all replied, 'to satisfy other people,
      In this manner you are fortunate!

82   So, if you would get out of these dark places
      And go back to see the lovely stars,
      When you recall the time that you were here,

Do not omit to speak of us to people.'   85
And there they broke their circle, and fled away
As if their nimble legs had been wings.

In less time than it takes to say 'Amen'   88
All of them had completely disappeared:
So my master thought it time to go.

I followed him; and he had gone but a little way,   91
When the sound of water seemed so close to us
That, speaking, we should hardly have heard ourselves.

As that river, which follows its own course   94
At first, from Monte Veso towards the east,
Upon the left side of the Apennines,

And which up there is called Aquaqueta,   97
Before it flows down to its lower bed,
And at Forlì, goes by another name;

It roars down there over San Benedetto,   100
From the mountain, then falls in a cascade
At a point where a thousand could find refuge;

In such a manner, rushing down a steep bank,   103
We found the red water re-echoing
So that in a short time it would have stunned our ears.

I had a cord tied around my middle,   106
The one with which I had thought at one time
I would capture the leopard with the mottled skin;

When I had loosened it and taken it off,   109
As my escort commanded me to do,
I held it out to him, folded in a coil.

Then he turned himself towards his right side   112
And, standing back some distance from the edge,
He threw it down into the deep ravine.

'And surely something new must follow from that,'   115
I said within myself, 'a new sign,
Which my instructor watches so carefully.'

118   Ah, what extreme caution men should use
      With those who see, not only the outward act
      But have the judgement to see the very thoughts!

121   He said to me: 'Soon you will see up here
      What I expect and you are dreaming of:
      It must soon be discovered to your view.'

124   To that truth which has the look of falsehood
      A man should always close his lips, if he can,
      Because he incurs shame when there is no fault:

127   But I cannot be silent here; and swear,
      Reader, by the verses of this *Comedy*,
      As I wish they may long be acceptable,

130   That I saw, through that dark, heavy air,
      A figure coming, swimming up towards us,
      A marvel to any heart which stands firm,

133   As a man comes back when he has been below
      Some time, to loose an anchor which is caught
      On a rock, or something hidden in the sea,

136   Stretches himself upwards, and then draws up his feet.

CANTO XVII

      'This is the savage beast with the pointed tail,
      Who sails over mountains and breaks walls and weapons;
      There is the one who infects the whole world!'

 4   So my escort began to say to me;
      And made a sign that he should come to ground
      Just at the end of our marble path.

 7   And that foul representation of Fraud
      Came up, so that his head and chest arrived
      But the bank did not accommodate his tail.

His face was the face of a just man,   10
So mild, if you looked no deeper than the skin;
The rest of his body was a reptile's:

He had two tentacles, hairy to the arm-pits;   13
His back, his breast, and both his flanks were garish
With a variety of knots and whirls.

Tartars and Turks never made cloth with colours   16
Brighter than that, background and pattern together,
Nor did Arachne ever weave such webs.

As sometimes barges lie upon the shore,   19
Part of them in the water and part on land;
And as there among the gluttonous Germans

The beaver takes his position to make his ravages,   22
So that worst of wild beasts took his place
On the edge between the rock and the great sand.

His tail darted around still in the void,   25
Twisting upwards the envenomed fork
With which the point was armed, as in a scorpion.

My escort said: 'At this point we must take   28
A slightly circuitous path, until we reach
The evil beast who lies heaped over there.'

Then we descended, keeping on the right,   31
And took some ten paces towards the edge
To keep out of the way of sand and flames.

And when we reached the point where he was,   34
A little further on, I saw on the sand
People sitting near the empty space.

Here my master said: 'In order that you may have   37
A full acquaintance with what is in the circuit,
Go over there and see how those comport themselves.

Your conversation with them should be brief: 40
While I am waiting, I will speak with the beast,
And ask him to let us use his strong shoulders.'

43   So also on the extreme limit
       Of the seventh circle, all alone I went
       To where that dejected company was sitting.

46   Their grief was bursting forth out of their eyes;
       Their hands kept going here and there to shield them
       Now from the fire, now from the hot ground:

49   Just in the way that dogs will do in summer,
       Using their muzzles or paws, when they are bitten
       It may be by fleas, or flies or horse ticks.

52   When I had cast my eyes on several of them,
       On whom the agonising fire was falling,
       I knew none of them; but I perceived

55   That from the neck of each there hung a bag
       Which had a special colour and a crest,
       And each one had his eyes fixed on his own.

58   And as I went among them, looking at them,
       I saw upon a yellow purse an azure
       Which had the face and bearing of a lion.

61   Then my eyes wandering further over the group,
       I saw another purse as red as blood,
       And which displayed a goose whiter than butter.

64   And one who had an azure pregnant sow
       By way of crest on his white money-bag,
       Said to me: 'What are you doing in this ditch?

67   Now go away; and, as you are alive,
       You may like to know that my neighbour Vitaliano
       Is going to sit here on my left side.

70   With these Florentines am I, a Paduan;
       Repeatedly these deafen my ears, shouting,
       "You wait till we have that distinguished nobleman

73   Who will carry with him the pouch with the three goats!" '
       Here he twisted his mouth and stuck out his tongue
       As an ox does when he is licking his nose.

And I, afraid that to stay longer might anger   76
Him who had warned me not to stay long,
Turned my back on these exhausted spirits.

I found my escort, who had already mounted   79
Upon the crupper of that terrifying animal;
He said to me: 'Now be strong, and have courage.

Now that must serve us for a way down: 82
Get up in front, I want to be in the middle,
So that the tail cannot do any harm.'

Like one who feels malaria coming on,   85
And has already grown pale around the finger-nails,
And trembles when he merely looks at shade,

So I became when I heard Virgil speak;   88
But the menace in what he said made me ashamed,
As a servant is made brave by a good master.

I set myself upon those great shoulders: 91
I wanted to say, but the words did not come
As I thought they would: 'Mind you hold on to me!'

But he, who at other times had helped me out   94
In other troubles, as soon as I had mounted,
Seized me in his arms, and so supported me,

And said, 'Now Geryon, off with you; take care,   97
Make large circles, go down gradually;
Remember the unusual load you have.'

As a little boat pushed off from where it is grounded,   100
Stern first, and still stern first, so he made off;
And when he felt he was floating entirely free,

Turned his tail round to where his chest had been,   103
Extended it and then moved it like an eel,
And with his tentacles pressed back the air.

I do not think that there was greater fear   106
When Phaeton loosened his hold on the reins,
By which the sky, as still appears, was burnt;

109   Nor when the miserable Icarus
      Lost all his feathers as the wax was melted,
      His father crying to him: 'Where are you going?';

112   Than my fear was, when I saw that I was
      In air upon all sides, and saw extinguished
      Every seen thing except the beast itself.

115   It swam away, but it swam, oh, so slowly;
      Wheeled and went down, but I had a sense of nothing
      Except the wind in my face and from below.

118   I heard already, on my right, the gorge,
      Making a horrible thundering underneath us,
      And so, with my eyes down, I craned my neck.

121   Then I was in more fear of the dismounting,
      Because I saw fire, and heard lamenting;
      So, trembling, I crouched there hunched up.

124   I then saw, for I had not seen before,
      That we were descending and turning, for the great torments
      Seemed nearer, first on one side then the other.

127   As the falcon which has been much on the wing,
      And without seeing either bird or lure,
      Makes the falconer say: 'Ah yes, you are coming down,'

130   And comes back weary to the place it left so nimbly,
      Wheeling a hundred times, and lands far off
      From his master, angry and disdainful,

133   So at the bottom, Geryon set us down
      Right at the foot of that jagged rock
      And, lightened of the burden of us two,

136   Disappeared like an arrow from a bowstring.

CANTO XVIII

There is a place in hell called Malebolge,
Made all of stone which is the colour of iron,
As is the circle which delimits it.

Right in the middle of the malignant plain,   4
Opens a well, which is both broad and deep,
The plan of which I will speak of in its place.

The belt which this leaves therefore forms a circle   7
Between the well and the high, difficult bank,
And the bottom of it has ten distinct valleys.

As, when in order to guard the walls,   10
Ditch after ditch is dug around a castle,
The ground acquires a characteristic formation,

So was the appearance of the valleys here;   13
And as, from the doorways of such fortresses,
There are footbridges to the outside bank,

So from the base of the rock emerged projections   16
Which ran across the embankments and the ditches,
Down to the well where they ended and met.

In this place, shaken from the back   19
Of Geryon, we found ourselves; the poet
Kept to the left, and I followed him.

On the right hand I saw fresh cause for pity,   22
Fresh torments, and fresh devils, with whips;
With these all the first recess was filled.

Down at the bottom were the sinners, naked: 25
On one side of the track they came towards us,
On the other, marched with us, but with longer strides,

As the Romans, to deal with the great throngs,   28
In the year of the Jubilee, upon the bridge,
Ordered things so that streams of people could pass,

31 And so that on one side they would all face
    The castle, and go in the direction of St Peter's;
    And on the other go towards the hill.

34 On both sides, up on the dismal rock,
    I saw horned devils with great whips,
    Who lashed them cruelly from behind.

37 Ah, how they made them take to their heels
    At the first stroke! And there was nobody
    Who waited to have a second or a third.

40 While I went on, my eyes met somebody's;
    And I immediately said to myself:
    'I am sure that I have seen that man before.'

43 To look at him the better, I stopped in my tracks:
    And my kind master halted with me,
    And allowed me to go back a little way.

46 And that whipped spirit thought that he could hide
    By bowing his head; but it availed him little,
    And I said: 'O you with the downcast eyes,

49 If your manner and bearing are not deceptive,
    You are Venedico Caccianemico:
    But what brings you into this stinging mess?'

52 He said to me: 'I say it unwillingly;
    But I am forced to do so by your clear speech,
    Which makes me recollect my former world.

55 It was I who induced the beautiful
    Ghisola to do what the Marquis wanted,
    However discreditable the story may sound.

58 And I am not the only one from Bologna
    Who is weeping here; the place is so full of them
    That there are not so many tongues learning now

61 To say "sipa" between Savena and Reno;
    And if you want authority for that,
    Recall to mind how avaricious we are.'

While he was speaking one of the devils struck him   64
With his long whip, and said to him: 'Go on,
Pimp, you'll make no money from women here.'

I went back to where my escort was waiting;   67
Then, with a few steps, we reached a point
Where one of the rocks projected from the bank.

We climbed up on it easily enough;   70
And, turning to the right along the top,
We took our leave of those eternal circles.

When we were at the point where, underneath,   73
There was a gap to let the sinners pass,
My guide said to me: 'Stop and let the eyes

Of these other ill-born spirits meet yours;   76
You have not seen their faces hitherto
Because they were going the same way as ourselves.'

From the old bridge we looked down on the file   79
Which came towards us on the other side,
Driven on in the same fashion by the whip.

My helpful instructor, without my asking him,   82
Said to me: 'Look at that great spirit coming,
Who does not shed a tear because of pain.

How regal is his aspect even now!   85
That is Jason, who with his courage and cunning,
Went to Colchis and carried off the fleece.

He passed by way of the island of Lemnos,   88
After the furious, pitiless women there
Had put their menfolk one and all to death.

There, by his tokens and seductive words,   91
He tricked Hypsipyle, the young girl who
Had before that tricked all the other women.

He left her there, pregnant and on her own;   94
Such is the fault which brings him to the torment;
And there is vengeance here for Medea, too.

97   With him go all deceivers of this kind:
     And that is enough to know about this valley
     And about those who are bitten by its fangs.'

100 Already we were where the narrow path
     Reaches the second bank and forms a cross,
     And then goes on and forms a second arch.

103 There we heard people moaning
     In the other cleft; they snuffed around with their muzzles,
     And hit themselves with the palms of their hands.

106 The embankments were encrusted with a mould
     From the exhalation below, which thickened on them
     And violently attacked the eyes and nose.

109 The bottom was so deep, we could see nothing
     Without climbing on the back of the arch
     Until we were at the most commanding point.

112 We reached it; and then, down in the ditch,
     I saw people plunged in excrement
     Which seemed as if it had flowed out of a cesspit.

115 And, while I was searching down there with my eyes,
     I saw one with his head so covered with shit
     You couldn't see whether he was layman or cleric.

118 He shouted at me: 'Why are you so keen
     To look at me, rather than the other swine?'
     And I replied: 'Because, if I remember,

121 I have seen you before, when your hair was dry,
     And you are Alessio Interminei from Lucca:
     That's why I'm looking at you more than the others.'

124 And he then, smacking the top of his head:
     'So low I have been sunk by the flatteries
     Which my tongue was never tired of saying.'

127 Then my instructor said to me: 'Now, stretch
     Your face forward a little, so that your eye
     Can properly see the face

Of that filthy and dissolute bag 130
Who scratches herself with shit in her nails,
Now crouching, now standing on her feet.

That is Thais, the harlot who replied 133
To the customer who asked her: "Don't you think
That I deserve it?", "You do, you're marvellous."

And now I think we have seen enough of this.' 136

CANTO XIX

O Simon Magus, and his wretched followers,
Who turn the things of God—which ought to be
Married to goodness—in your rapacity

For gold and silver, into prostitutes; 4
Now is the time to sound the trumpet for you,
Because you are stationed in the third cleft.

We had already climbed to the next tomb 7
Upon that part of the projecting rock
Which hangs right over the middle of the ditch.

O highest wisdom, how great is the art 10
You show in heaven, on earth and in this evil place,
And how just are your dispensations!

I saw, on the sides and at the bottom, 13
The livid stone was full of perforations,
All of the same diameter, and all round.

The holes seemed to me to be neither smaller nor larger 16
Than those which, in my beautiful San Giovanni,
Serve for the priest to stand in during baptisms;

One of which, still not many years ago, 19
I broke, because someone was drowning in it:
And may this set the record right, where necessary.

22   From each of these mouths there stuck out in the air
        The feet, and the legs up to the calves, of a sinner,
        The rest remaining out of sight inside.

25   The soles of the feet of all of them were on fire;
        Which made the joints wriggle so violently
        That they would have broken plaited ropes or withies.

28   As a flame burning on a greasy surface
        Moves only over the object's outer skin,
        So it was there, from the heels to the tips of the toes.

31   'Who is that, master, who seems by his wriggling
        To suffer more than any of his companions,'
        I said, 'and whom a redder flame sucks dry?'

34   He said to me: 'If you care for me to carry you
        Down to that bank which lies below us there,
        You will learn from him about himself and his faults.'

37   And I: 'What pleases you is fine for me:
        You are my senior, and know I do not depart
        From your will, and you know what is left unsaid.'

40   Then we came to the fourth embankment;
        Turned and went down upon the left side
        To the narrow, perforated strip at the bottom.

43   The benign master did not set me down
        From his side, until we had reached the opening
        Of the one who waved his legs so much in torment.

46   'Whoever you may be, unhappy spirit,
        Who, upside-down, are stuck in like a stake,'
        I began, 'say something, if you can.'

49   I stood there like the friar who confesses
        The treacherous killer who, fixed in position,
        Calls him back so that death may be delayed.

52   And he cried: 'Are you standing there already?
        Boniface, are you already standing there?
        My information was out by several years.

Are you so soon sated with your wealth   55
For the sake of which you shamefully and deceitfully
Took the beautiful lady, and made havoc of her?'

I did as people do who are left standing,   58
Not taking in the answer they are given,
Ridiculous, not knowing what to say.

Then Virgil said to me: 'Now tell him quickly: 61
"I am not he, I am not the one you think." '
And I replied as he required me to.

At this the spirit twisted his feet to the limit;   64
Then, sighing with a voice that was in tears,
He said to me: 'Then what do you want with me?

If knowing is so important to you   67
That you have come all the way down the bank,
Know that I was clothed with the great mantle;

And true enough, I was the son of the bear   70
Who was so anxious to advance her cubs
That I filled a purse up there, and here I am in one.

Below my head others have been dragged down   73
Who were my predecessors in simony,
And they are flat between fissures in the rock.

I shall fall down there likewise, when I see   76
The one arrive that I mistook you for
When I put my sudden question to you.

But I have already been cooking my feet like this   79
And been in this place, upside-down, for longer
Than he will be planted here with red feet:

Because after him will come from towards the west,   82
From uglier malefactions, a lawless shepherd
Who will be fit to cover both of us.

The new Jason he will be, of whom we read   85
In Maccabees; and as to that one, his king
Was soft, so to this one will be the king of France.'

88   I do not know whether I was too rash here,
For I replied to him in this manner:
'Well then, tell me what was the amount of the treasure

91   Our Lord required of St Peter before
He handed over the keys to his keeping?
Surely he asked nothing but: "Follow me."

94   Neither St Peter nor the others took from Matthias
Gold and silver, when he was chosen to fill
The office which the guilty soul had lost.

97   Therefore stay there, for you are well punished;
And look after the ill-gotten money
Which made you so outrageous against Charles.

100   And if I were not still held back
By the reverence I have for the supreme keys
Which you held in a happier life,

103   I would have harder words for you than I have.
For your avarice brings much grief to the world,
Oppressing the good and helping on the wicked.

106   It was you and your like the Evangelist had in mind
When he saw her who sitteth on many waters
Committing fornication with the kings of the earth;

109   She that was born with the seven heads
And had her argument from the ten horns
As long as virtue was pleasing to her husband.

112   You have made a god of gold and silver:
And how do you differ from an idolater,
Except that he prays to one, and you to a hundred?

115   Ah, Constantine, how much ill you produced,
Not by your conversion, but by that endowment
Which the first rich father accepted from you.'

118   And, while I was singing that tune,
Either anger or conscience must have bitten him
For he kicked violently with both his feet.

I think indeed that my instructor was pleased,   121
He listened with such contentment on his lips
To the sound of the true words I uttered.

Therefore he took me in both his arms;   124
And after he had pulled me close to his chest
He climbed up by the path he had come down.

Nor did he tire of holding me in this manner   127
Until he had carried me to the top of the rock
Which crosses from the fourth to the fifth embankment.

Then he gently put down the burden,   130
Gentle throughout the rough, misshapen rock
Which would have been a difficult passage for a goat,

And so another valley was revealed to me.   133

CANTO XX

Now must my verses speak of new penalties,
To make matter for the twentieth canto
Of the first part, which is about the submerged.

I was already very much disposed   4
To look into the depths revealed to me,
Which were bathed with tears of anguish;

And I saw people coming through the round valley,   7
They were silent and weeping, advancing at the pace
Penitential processions use in the world.

As my gaze sank more deeply into them,   10
Each one of them seemed to be twisted round
Between the chin and the point where the thorax begins;

So that the head was turned, back to front,   13
And they were therefore obliged to walk backwards,
No longer being able to look the other way.

16   It may be that there are cases of palsy
        In which people are forced into such a twist,
        But I have never seen them, and do not credit it.

19   If you would have God let you profit by
        Your reading, reader, now consider for yourself
        How I was able to keep my face dry

22   When right before me I saw the human image
        So twisted, that tears coming from the eyes
        Rolled down into the crack of the buttocks.

25   I certainly wept, supported on one of the rocks
        Of the projecting stone, so that my escort
        Said to me: 'Are you too like the other fools?

28   Here pity is alive when it is dead:
        Who is more criminal than he who suffers
        Because he does not like the divine judgement?

31   Hold up your head now, hold it up and see
        The one for whom the Thebans saw the earth open;
        So that they all cried: "Where are you rushing headlong,

34   Amphiaräus? Why are you leaving the battle?"
        And he did not stop in his headlong course
        Till he reached Minos who catches them all.

37   Look how he has made a chest of his shoulders:
        Because he wanted to see too far ahead,
        He looks back and makes his way backwards.

40   See Tiresias, who transformed his appearance,
        When, from a man, he turned into a woman,
        Changing his physical structure entirely;

43   And afterwards, he had first to strike again
        The two copulating serpents with his rod
        Before he could resume his male plumage.

46   That is Aruns, with his back to the other's belly,
        Who, in the mountains of Luni, where you may see
        The people of Carrara hoeing below,

Had among the white marbles the cave   49
Where he lived; and from which his view of the stars
And the sea, was without interruption.

And she who covers up her breasts,   52
Which you do not see, with her flowing tresses,
And has all her hairy skin on that side,

Was Manto, who went seeking through many lands,   55
Before she settled there where I was born;
For which reason I should like you to listen to me.

After her father departed from life,   58
And when the city of Bacchus became enslaved,
She had a long period of wandering.

Up there in lovely Italy lies a lake,   61
At the foot of the Alps which lock in Germany
Above the Tyrol; it is called Benacus.

By a thousand springs and more, I think, the Apennine   64
Between Garda and Val Camonica is bathed,
With water which grows stagnant in that lake.

There is a place in the middle, where the Trentine shepherd,   67
And he of Brescia, and the Veronese,
Might give their blessing, if they went there.

Peschiera, which is a fine, strong castle   70
To hold the Brescians and the Bergamese,
Lies at the point at which the shore is lowest.

Thither must flow whatever cannot stay   73
Within the confines of Lake Benacus,
And make a river down through the green fields.

As soon as that water begins to run,   76
It is no longer called Benacus, but Mincio,
Down to Governo where it joins the Po.

After a little way, it finds a plain   79
In which it spreads and turns into a marsh,
And in summertime may be unwholesome.

82   The wild virgin, passing that way
      Saw land in the middle of the marsh,
      Without cultivation, bare of inhabitants.

85   There, to avoid all human intercourse,
      She halted with her slaves; practised her arts,
      And lived, and left her empty body there.

88   After, the men who were scattered round about,
      Collected in that place, because it was strong,
      Having the marshes on all sides of it.

91   They made a city upon those dead bones;
      And because of her who first chose the place,
      Without other auguries, they called it Mantua.

94   The population was much larger there
      Before the foolishness of Casalodi
      Fell to the stratagem of Pinamonte.

97   Therefore I warn you, if you ever hear
      Other accounts of the origin of my city,
      Do not let any lie obscure the truth.'

100   I said: 'Master, whatever you say
      Is to me so certain and commands my assent
      So that contrary talk would be nothing but ashes.

103   But tell me: among those who go by,
      Do you see anyone who is worthy of note;
      For it is to that alone my mind recurs.'

106   Then he said: 'That one with the beard
      Stretching from his cheeks down to his brown shoulders,
      Was, when Greece was so empty of males

109   That those in the cradle hardly stayed behind,
      An augur, and with Calchas signified
      In Aulis, the moment for cutting the first cable.

112   Eurypylus was his name, and he is celebrated
      Somewhere or other in my high tragedy;
      As you well know, since you know all of it.

That other, who is so thin about the flanks,   115
Was Michael Scott, who was certainly acquainted
With all the tricks of magical deception.

Look at Guido Bonatti; look at Asdente   118
Who now wishes he'd stuck to leather and thread,
But it is a bit late to repent now.

Look at the poor old women who left the needle,   121
The shuttle and the spindle, to become witches,
Working charms with herbs and images.

But come now; for already on the confines   124
Of both the hemispheres, stands under Seville,
And there touches the waves, Cain and the thorns,

And already yesterday night the moon was full: 127
You should remember that, for she did not hurt you
At any time in the depths of the forest.'

So he was speaking to me, as we went on.   130

CANTO XXI

And so from bridge to bridge, speaking of matters
Of which my comedy does not care to tell,
We came; and we were getting to the top

When we halted to see the next cleft   4
Of Malebolge, and a new set of vain tears;
I saw that it was preternaturally dark.

As in the arsenal of the Venetians   7
In winter, they boil up the sticky pitch
To caulk their vessels which are beginning to leak

Since they are unable to sail them; and, instead,   10
One builds his ship anew, and one stops up
The sides of a ship which has made many voyages;

13 Some rivet up the prow, and some the stern;
   Others make oars, or twist ropes for new rigging;
   While one repairs the mainsail or the jib;

16 So, not by fire, but by divine art,
   Now, down there boiled an inspissated pitch
   Which stuck on to the bank on both sides.

19 I saw it, but I could see nothing in it
   Except the bubbles which the boiling sent up,
   The rising of the whole, and its subsidence.

22 While I looked down upon it fixedly,
   My escort, calling, 'Look out there, look out!'
   Drew me to him from the place where I was standing.

25 Then I turned round, like a man who is anxious
   To see something which he should run away from,
   And who suddenly grows weak with fear,

28 So that after all he does not stop to look;
   I saw there was a black devil behind us,
   And he was running in our direction up the crag.

31 Ah, and how ferocious was his appearance!
   And in his bearing, how much cruelty,
   With his wings open, and his light-footedness!

34 His shoulders which were pointed and seemed proud,
   Were burdened with the two legs of a sinner,
   And in each hand he grasped the nerve of a foot.

37 From our bridge he called out: 'O Malebranche,
   Here is one of the Santa Zita council:
   Put him under, while I go back for more

40 To that city I have so well supplied:
   Every man there is a crook, except Bonturo;
   There they make Yeses and Noes, and do it for money.'

43 He threw him down, and over the hard rock
   Went back again; and never was a guard-dog loosed
   With such speed to follow up a thief.

The sinner plunged, and came up again, convulsed;   46
But the demons who were in cover under the bridge
Shouted: 'The Volto Santo has no place here!

Here it is not like swimming in the Serchio!   49
So, unless you want to feel our hooks,
Better not come up out of that pitch!'

Then they bit at him with a hundred prongs,   52
And said: 'You'd better dance there underneath;
If you can sneak a look out, you can have it!'

Exactly so a cook might make his underlings   55
Plunge meat into the middle of a cauldron
With long forks, so that it does not float.

My benign master said to me: 'Get down,   58
So that they cannot see that you are here;
A jagged rock will give you some shelter;

Whatever threats may be made against me,   61
Don't be afraid, I understand these things,
And once before was in trouble like this.'

Then he passed on beyond the top of the bridge;   64
And when he arrived upon the sixth bank
He needed to put on a bold front.

For with the fury and the impetus   67
That dogs come out upon a poor man
As soon as he stops outside a house to beg,

Came out those who were under the bridge, and raised   70
Against him all their mass of hooks;
But he called out: 'Calm yourselves, all of you!

Before you try to get me with your prongs,   73
Come forward, one of you, and listen to me,
And after that you can think about hooking me.'

They all cried out: 'Go on then, Malacoda!'   76
One of them moved, while all the others stood still.
And he came saying: 'What good will it do him?'

79 'Do you think, Malacoda, since you see
That I have come here,' so my escort said,
'And safely too, in spite of all your guards,

82 It is without God's will and a true destiny?
Let me go, for in heaven it is willed
That I should show another this wild track.'

85 At this, his pride fell suddenly, so far
That he let fall his pitchfork at his feet,
And said to the others: 'He must not be struck.'

88 And my guide said to me: 'Now, you who sit
Huddled up there behind that jagged rock,
You can come back to me in safety now.'

91 And so I moved, and went to him quickly;
And then the devils, all of them, came forward,
So that I doubted whether they would keep their word:

94 So I once saw the infantry afraid
When they came out, by treaty, from Caprona,
And saw themselves surrounded by enemies.

97 I approached closer with my whole person
To my escort, and did not tear my eyes
From their appearance, which was not encouraging.

100 They lowered their hooks, and said to one another:
'Shall I give him a touch of it on his behind?'
And answered: 'Yes, take a bit out of him!'

103 But that demon who was in conversation
With my escort, turned round suddenly
And said: 'Be quiet, quiet, Scarmiglione!'

106 Then to us he said: 'To go further along this ridge
Is not a thing you can do, because the sixth arch
Is lying in pieces down at the bottom;

109 And if you wish none the less to go on,
Keep up upon the ridge above the bank;
Nearby is another projection where there is a way.

Yesterday, five hours later than this hour,   112
One thousand two hundred and sixty six years
Had passed, exactly, since the path was destroyed.

I am sending some of my troop in that direction,   115
To make sure no one has come up for air:
Go with them, they will not be treacherous.'

'Forward then, Alichino and Calcabrina,'   118
He then began, 'and you too, Cagnazzo;
And let Barbariccia lead the platoon.

Let Libicocco come, and Draghinazzo,   121
Toothy Ciriatto, and Graffiacane,
And Farfarello and mad Rubicante.

Take a good look around the boiling pitch;   124
And see them safe as far as the other projection
Which goes the whole way over these dens.'

'Oh, master, what is it that I see?'   127
I said. 'No, let us go without an escort,
If you know how; I certainly want none.

If you observe them as your practice is,   130
Do you not see how they are grinding their teeth,
And how their brows threaten torture?'

He said to me: 'I would not have you afraid: 133
Let them grind their teeth as much as they like;
They are doing it for those who are stewing down there.'

On the left embankment they turned around,   136
But first each of them stuck out his tongue
Between his teeth, towards their chief, as a sign;

And he sounded a trumpet call from his arse-hole.   139

CANTO XXII

I have seen cavalry shifting their camp,
Beginning an assault, and on parade,
And, on occasion, seen them in retreat;

4   I have seen horsemen on reconnaissance,
Through your land, Aretines; and raiding parties,
Mock battles, and charging in the lists;

7   Sometimes with trumpets, and sometimes with bells,
With drums and with signals from castle walls,
With our devices, and those of foreigners;

10   But never with so strange an instrument,
Have I seen horsemen move, or foot-soldiers,
Not ships, by marks on land or by the stars.

13   We were advancing with the ten demons:
Oh! savage company! but, as they say,
In church with saints, and in the pub with rogues.

16   And yet it was the pitch that had my attention,
To see what this cleft was really like,
And the people who were there cauterised.

19   They were like dolphins, when they give a warning
To sailors, by the arching of their backs,
To look to their ship, if they want to save it;

22   So, now and then, to alleviate his pain,
One or other of the sinners would show his back
And disappear again, quicker than lightning.

25   And as, in a ditch, just at the edge of the water,
Frogs stand, with only their noses out of it,
So that their legs and the rest of them are hidden,

28   That is how the sinners were standing everywhere;
But as soon as Barbariccia came near them
They withdrew at once under the bubbles.

I saw, and the thought still makes me shudder,   31
One lag behind, as it will often happen
That one frog stays when another darts off;

And Graffiacane, who was nearest him,   34
Hooked him up by his pitch-covered hair
And pulled him out, he seemed to me like an otter.

I already knew the names of all those devils,   37
For I had noticed when they were selected,
And, when they called each other, I was listening.

'O Rubicante, see that you get your nails   40
Into his back, so that you take the skin off!'
The demons all shouted at him together.

And I: 'Master, see if you can contrive   43
To know the name of that unfortunate
Who has fallen into the hands of his adversaries.'

My escort then drew close to his side;   46
Asking him where he came from, and he replied:
'I was born in the kingdom of Navarre.

My mother placed me as a nobleman's servant;   49
She had been made pregnant by a scoundrel
Who destroyed himself and everything he had.

Then I was with the good king Theobald's family: 52
There I became an expert in corruption,
For which I settle accounts in this heat.'

And Ciriatto, from whose mouth protruded   55
On each side tusks which were like those of a hog,
Made him feel how one of them could rip him.

Among the greedy cats there had come a mouse;   58
But Barbariccia shut him in his arms
And said: 'Now stay there, while I get astride him.'

And to my master he turned his face and said: 61
'Ask him some more, if you have any desire
To learn more from him, before someone gets hold of him.'

64   My master then: 'Tell me, among the other
     Criminals, do you know of any Latins
     Under the pitch?' And he: 'I have just parted

67   From one who came from somewhere not far away:
     I wish I were still under cover with him,
     Where I should not be afraid of claws or prongs.'

70   And Libicocco said: 'We are too patient!'
     Then he took him by the arm with his hook,
     And tore off a piece of the muscle from it.

73   Draghinazzo also wanted to get hold of him,
     Down by his legs; upon which, the devil in charge
     Turned and turned again with threatening look.

76   And when they had become a little quieter,
     Addressing him who still gazed at his wound,
     My escort quickly put another question:

79   'Who was the one from whom you say you made
     An evil parting, when you came ashore?'
     And he replied: 'That was brother Gomita,

82   The one from Gallura, a bucketful of cheats,
     Who had his master's enemies in hand,
     And so disposed of them that they congratulated him.

85   He took their money and let them go quietly,
     As he says; and in other functions too,
     Corrupt on no small scale, a major operator.

88   With him keeps company Lord Michael Zanche
     Of Logodoro; and to talk of Sardinia
     Is something that their tongues are never tired of.

91   But now, look at the other one that's grinning;
     I would say more, but fear that he may be
     Turning his thoughts towards scratching my scabs.'

94   And the big boss turned towards Farfarello,
     Who opened his eyes wide, as if ready to strike,
     And said: 'Away with you, vicious bird.'

'If you would like to see or hear'—the terrified   97
Spirit at our side began again—
'Tuscans or Lombards, I will send them up;

But let the demons stand a little aside,   100
So that the spirits do not fear their vengeance,
And I, staying here on the same spot

For the one I am, will make seven of them come,   103
When I whistle, which is the way we do it
When any one of us gets out for a moment.'

Cagnazzo raised his muzzle at these words,   106
Shaking his head, and said: 'Listen to him,
He's cunning, if he thinks he can get down like that!'

Then he, who did not easily run out of tricks,   109
Replied: 'Cunning indeed, a bit too cunning,
When I put my friends in the way of greater torments.'

Alichino contained himself no longer,   112
Unlike the others, but said: 'If you go down,
I shall not come after you at a gallop,

But beat above the pitch with my wings: 115
With the top deserted and the bank as a shield,
Then see whether you can get the better of us.'

If you read on, you will hear of a new game: 118
They all turned their eyes to the other side;
And first of all, the one who was anxious not to.

The Navarrese acted at the right moment;   121
He put his feet on the ground, and in a flash
Leapt and freed himself from the chief devil.

Each of them felt remorse for this fault,   124
But most he who had been cause of the escape;
So he started and shouted: 'I will get you!'

It wasn't much use; for wings would not outstrip   127
The terror of the spirit who went under;
The devil, swooping, threw out his chest and rose:

130   It was just like a duck who with a smack,
      When the falcon is on top of him, plunges in,
      And the pursuer comes back, furious and disconsolate.

133   Calcabrina, angry at the trick,
      Kept flying after him; wanting the sinner
      To escape so that he could pick a quarrel.

136   And when that rascally spirit had disappeared,
      He turned his claws at once on his companion,
      And was grappled with him above the ditch.

139   But the other was a proper sparrowhawk;
      He gripped him tight, and both of them went down
      Into the middle of the boiling pond.

142   The heat loosed the clinch immediately;
      But then there was no rising out of it;
      They had got their wings so sticky in the pitch.

145   Barbariccia, disconcerted with the rest,
      Made four of them fly to the other side
      With all their hooks, and at great speed

148   They went down from every side to their posts:
      Reached out the hooks to the two caught in the bird-lime
      Who were already cooked inside the crust;

151   And we left them in that awkward situation.

CANTO XXIII

      Not speaking, on our own and without escort,
      We went on, one in front and the other behind,
      Like minor friars when they are on a journey.

  4   My thoughts, after the brawl that we had seen,
      Were turned upon that fable of Aesop
      Where he speaks about the frog and the mouse;

'Now' and 'immediately' are not more of a pair   7
Than those two situations, if you think hard
About the comparison between beginnings and ends.

And as one thought separates from another,   10
So from that thought another was born,
Which left my first fear redoubled.

What I thought was: 'These devils, through us,   13
Are put to scorn, hurt, and made the object
Of tricks, which must annoy them extremely.

If they get angry, on top of their malice,   16
They will come after us more cruelly
Than dogs who are snapping after a hare.'

Already I felt my hair standing on end   19
From fear, and stood still, looking over my shoulder,
As I said: 'Master, if you do not hide

Yourself and me quickly, I am terrified   22
Of the Malebranche: we already have them after us;
I imagine that I hear them coming already.'

And he: 'If I were a mirror,   25
I could not take the image of your appearance
More quickly than I do that of your thoughts.

They were entering among mine at this moment,   28
Behaving much the same and looking the same,
So that from both sets I drew one conclusion.

If there is a place where the right side slopes   31
So that we can go down to the next cleft,
We shall avoid the hunt that we imagine.'

He had hardly finished putting forward his plan   34
When I saw them coming with wings spread,
Not far away, and set on catching us.

My escort suddenly took me up,   37
Like a mother who is awakened by the noise
And sees flames leaping close to her;

40   She takes her son and flies, and does not stop,
     Being more concerned about him than herself,
     Even long enough to get into her shift;

43   And down from the ridges of the hard bank
     He slid full-length down the hanging rock
     Which blocks one of the sides of the next cleft.

46   Never did water run along a gulley
     So fast, to turn a millwheel upon land,
     When it is at the point nearest the paddles,

49   As my master went down that bank,
     Carrying me away, resting upon him,
     Like his son, and not as a companion.

52   Hardly had his feet reached the bed
     Of the depth below, when they were upon the ridge
     Just up above us; but there was nothing to fear;

55   For the high providence which had appointed
     That they should minister to the fifth ditch,
     Took from them all the power to go outside it.

58   Down there we came upon a painted people,
     Who went around with very slow steps,
     Weeping and looking weary and exhausted.

61   They had cloaks with the hoods drawn down
     Over their eyes, made in the same fashion
     As those which are made for the monks of Cluny.

64   Outside, they are gilded so that they are dazzling;
     But inside all lead, and so heavy
     That in comparison Frederick's were like straw.

67   What wearying gear for all eternity!
     We turned once more to the left-hand side, together
     With them, listening to their unhappy sobs;

70   But, with the weight, that weary people came
     So slowly that, with every step we took,
     We found ourselves beside fresh company.

So I said to my guide: 'See if you can find   73
Someone who is known for what he did, or his name,
And cast your eyes around you as we go.'

And one who understood the Tuscan speech,   76
Called to us from behind: 'Oh, hold back,
You who run so fast through the dark air.

Perhaps you will find in me what you are looking for.'   79
So my guide turned and said: 'Now wait for him,
And then go on, but at his own pace.'

I stood still, and saw two showing great haste,   82
In their minds—or their looks—to be with me;
But their burdens, and the narrow path, kept them back.

When they came up they eyed me sullenly,   85
Looking for a long time but saying nothing;
Then turned towards each other, and said to each other:

'It looks as if he's alive, the way his throat works,   88
And if they are dead, then what right have they
To go without wearing the heavy stole?'

Then to me he said: 'You, Tuscan, who have come   91
To the hypocrites' club, where they all wear sad faces,
Don't be above telling us who you are.'

I said to them: 'I was born, and grew up,   94
On the lovely river Arno, in the great city,
And am with the body that I have always had.

But tell me who you are, from whom pain wrings   97
Such drops as I see rolling from your cheeks;
And what is that glittering penalty which is yours?'

And one replied to me: 'The orange cloaks   100
Are of such thick lead that the weight of them,
As you might say, causes the scales to creak.

We were Wastrel Friars, and Bolognese: 103
I was called Catalano and he, Loderingo;
We were given a joint appointment by your city.

106   —Though, usually, a single man is chosen—.
       To keep the peace; and how we acted
       Is still to be seen, around the Gardingo.'

109   I began: 'O brothers, your evil . . .' but I spoke
       No further, for I caught sight of one
       Crucified on the ground with three stakes:

112   When he saw me, he twisted himself up,
       And blew the sighs he was making into his beard;
       And Brother Catalano, who saw this,

115   Said to me: 'The one you see nailed there
       Advised the Pharisees it was expedient
       That one man should be tortured for the people.

118   He lies across the path, naked, as you
       See him, and so he is obliged to feel
       The weight of everyone who has to pass.

121   And in this way his father-in-law also
       Suffers in this ditch, and the rest of the Council
       Which sowed so many evils for the Jews.'

124   Then I saw Virgil marvelling over
       The one who was there extended on a cross
       So ignominiously in eternal exile.

127   Afterwards he spoke to the friar with these words:
       'Be so kind, if it is not forbidden,
       To say whether, on the right, there is an outlet

130   Through which both of us can get away
       Without encouraging the black angels
       To come down to this place and get us out.'

133   He then replied: 'Nearer than you may hope,
       There is a rock which moves from the great circle
       And crosses over all the cruel valleys,

136   Except that in this one it is broken and doesn't cover it:
       You will be able to climb up on the ruins
       Which lie on the slope and are heaped at the bottom.'

My guide stood there a little, his head bowed,   139
Then said: 'He gave us false directions,
That one that hooks the sinners over there.'

The friar said: 'I heard once in Bologna   142
Of the Devil's many vices, among which
That he was a liar, and the father of lies.'

Then with long strides my guide went on his way,   145
Somewhat disturbed by anger, from his looks;
So I left those heavily burdened spirits,

Following the impressions of those dear feet.   148

CANTO XXIV

In that part of the early year when the sun
Tempers her hair under Aquarius
And the nights are already giving way to the noon,

When the frost copies upon the ground   4
The picture of her pale sister the snow,
But the coldness of her pen does not last long;

The farmer who has nothing left in store,   7
Gets up and looks, and sees the countryside
White everywhere, and hits himself with rage;

Goes back to the house, and grumbles round the place   10
Like a poor devil who doesn't know what to do;
Then out again, and suddenly takes hope,

Seeing that the face of the world has changed   13
In next to no time, and he seizes his stick
And chases his young sheep out to the pasture,

So the master filled me with dismay   16
When I saw him so cloud his face;
And so quickly after the trouble came the remedy;

19   For, as we arrived at the shattered bridge,
      My guide turned towards me with the gentle look
      Which I had first seen at the foot of the mountain.

22   He spread his arms out, having within himself
      Taken some decision, first of all inspecting
      The ruin, and then he took hold of me.

25   And, like a man who does his work with judgement,
      So that he always seems a step ahead,
      He, lifting me up towards the top

28   Of a great boulder, looked at another piece
      And said to me: 'Now climb on top of that;
      But first of all make sure that it will hold you.'

31   It was no way for those in the cloaks;
      For we could hardly climb—though he was light
      And I had help—up over the jutting rocks.

34   And had it not been that from that bank
      The slope was shorter than on the other side,
      I don't know about him, but I should have been beaten.

37   But since the whole of Malebolge goes down
      Towards the opening of the lowest well,
      The situation of every valley is such

40   That one side of it is higher than the other:
      We arrived somehow in the end at the point
      From which the last stone had fallen down.

43   The breath was so pressed out of my lungs
      When I got to the top, that I could do no more;
      I had to sit down as soon as I arrived.

46   'Now is the time for you to rouse yourself,'
      The master said; 'for sitting on a cushion
      Is not the way to fame, nor staying in bed;

49   And without fame, a man must spend his life
      Only to leave such traces upon earth
      As smoke leaves in the air, or foam in water.

Therefore get up: control your breathlessness   52
By force of mind, which wins in every battle,
If with its heavy body it does not sink.

You have much longer stairs to climb than these;   55
It is not enough to leave this lot behind:
If you have understood me, act accordingly.'

I then got up, showing I was provided   58
With more breath than I felt myself to be,
And said: 'Go, I am strong and have courage.'

Up on the jutting rock we took our way;   61
It was rough and narrow and more difficult
And steeper than the last section had been.

I talked as I went, not to appear feeble;   64
And then from the next cleft there came a voice
Which did not seem designed for forming words.

I don't know what it said, although I was   67
Already on the hump of the arch that crossed there;
But whoever spoke seemed to be moved by anger.

I bent over the cleft, but my living eyes   70
Could not pierce through the darkness to the bottom;
So I said: 'Master, will you contrive to get

To the next circle, and let us go down the wall;   73
Where I am I can hear but not understand,
And down there I can see but distinguish nothing.'

'I give you no other reply,' he said,   76
'Than to do as you say, because an honest request
Ought to be followed by action, not words.'

We went down from the bridge, having reached the end   79
Where it is joined on to the eighth bank;
And then the cleft was made clear to me:

And I saw inside it a terrifying heap   82
Of serpents, and of so strange a kind
That recollection of them makes my blood run cold.

85   Libya need boast no more, with its sand;
     Though it produces tortoises, darting snakes,
     Snakes that go upright, poisonous snakes and lizards,

88   Such pestilences, and such deadly creatures
     It could not show, neither could Ethiopia,
     Nor could that country by the Red Sea.

91   Among that cruel and miserable abundance
     Were running naked people, terrified,
     Without hope of a refuge or a cure;

94   They had their hands tied behind them with snakes
     The heads and tails of which pierced the small of the back
     While the rest of them was coiled together in front.

97   And suddenly, at one of the sinners at our side,
     A serpent leapt up, and transfixed him there
     At the point where the neck is fastened to the shoulders.

100 Never was 'o' or 'i' written so quickly
     As he caught fire and burnt, and turned to ashes
     Which fell together and showered to the ground;

103 And when he was in this manner destroyed,
     The dust collected itself without assistance
     And suddenly returned to the same shape.

106 So it is, according to the experts,
     That the phoenix dies and then is born again
     When it approaches its five hundredth year:

109 In life it eats neither grass nor corn,
     But tears of incense and grains of Paradise,
     And nard and myrrh are its winding sheet.

112 And as in one who falls, without knowing how,
     By a demonic force which drags him down,
     Or some other obstruction which brings a man to a stop,

115 When he gets on his feet and looks around,
     He is entirely bewildered by the anguish
     He has suffered, and as he looks he sighs;

Such was the sinner when he rose up again.   118
O power of God, with such severity,
Which out of vengeance will rain down such blows!

My guide asked the spirit who he was,   121
And he replied: 'I fell from Tuscany
Not long ago, and into this fierce throat.

Bestial life was what pleased me, and not human.   124
And I was like a mule; I am Vanni Fucci,
A beast, and Pistoia was the right hole for me.'

I said to my guide: 'Tell him not to sneak off,   127
And ask him what crime has brought him here;
For I knew him a man of blood and fury.'

The sinner, who understood, made no pretences,   130
But turned both mind and looks in my direction,
And gave the appearance of depressed shame;

Then said: 'I am more grieved that you have caught me   133
In this wretchedness in which you see me,
Than when I was taken from the other life.

I have no power to refuse what you ask: 136
I was put so far down here because I robbed
The sacristy of its fine furnishings

And falsely, it was put upon another.   139
But, so that you shall not enjoy this sight,
If ever you are out of these dark places,

Listen while I declare this prophecy: 142
Pistoia is first of all cleared of the Blacks
And then Florence renews her people and laws.

Mars brings exhalations from Valdimagra,   145
Which is encircled with dark clouds;
And with impetuous and bitter storm

There will be fighting on the Campo Picen;   148
So the mist will suddenly be dispersed
In such a manner that the Whites will suffer.

And I have said that because it should hurt you.'   151

CANTO XXV

When he had finished speaking the thief
Raised both his hands, making obscene gestures,
And called out: 'There you are God, so much for you!'

4   From that moment the serpents were my friends,
Because one of them wound about his neck
As if to say: 'I want you to say no more';

7   And another about his arms, and tied him again,
So fastening himself at his front
That he could not even give a shrug.

10   Oh, Pistoia, Pistoia, why not pass a law
To turn yourself to ashes, and have done with it,
Since you outdo your children in ill-doing?

13   Through all the darkened circles of hell
I saw no spirit so arrogant against God,
Not he who fell down from the walls of Thebes.

16   He fled without speaking another word;
And I saw a centaur full of rage
Come shouting: 'Where is he, where is that bitter one?'

19   I do not think Maremma has so many
Snakes as he had over his rump
To the point where his shape began to be human.

22   Over the shoulders, and at the back of the head,
With wings spread full out, there lay a dragon
Which set fire to everything in his way.

25   My master said: 'That creature is Cacus,
Who under the rock of the Aventine hill
Often spilt blood enough to make a lake.

28   He does not go the same way as his brothers
Because of the theft he fraudulently made
Of the great herd he had in his neighbourhood;

And that is why his ugly works ended   31
Under the club of Hercules, who perhaps
Gave him a hundred blows, and he felt less than ten.'

While he was talking, the centaur ran past,   34
And three spirits arrived somewhere below us,
Though neither I nor my guide saw them,

Until they cried out: 'And who are you?':   37
That put an end to our story-telling
And then we gave our minds only to them.

I did not know them: but it so happened   40
As it is likely to happen in such cases,
That one of them called another by his name,

Saying: 'Where has Cianfa gone?' So I,   43
In order that my guide should be attentive,
Laid a finger upwards from my chin to my nose.

If you now, reader, are slow to believe   46
What I shall tell you, it will be no wonder
For I who saw it can scarcely credit it!

As I kept my gaze fixed upon them,   49
I saw a serpent with six feet hurl himself up
In front of one of them, and hold him tight.

With the middle feet he wound about the belly,   52
And with the back ones, took hold of the arms;
Then fixed his teeth in one cheek, and the other;

The hind feet he spread out over the thighs,   55
And put his tail between the two of them,
And curled it up into the small of his back.

No ivy ever clung so closely   58
To any tree, as this horrible beast
Wound his limbs around those of the other.

Then they stuck together as if they had been   61
Hot wax, and their colours began to run;
Already neither appeared as it had been,

64   As, over a piece of burning paper,
Before the flame there runs a dark colour
So that it is not yet black, but the white is dying.

67   The other two looked at each other, and both
Cried out: 'Oh, Agnello, how you are changing!
See, already you are neither two nor one.'

70   Already the two heads had become one,
When there appeared to be two outlines mixed
In one face, in which both were lost.

73   The two arms were made of four limbs;
The haunches, legs, the belly and the chest
Became parts such as were never seen.

76   The whole of the first appearance was lost;
The perverse image seemed to be both and neither:
And like that it moved off at a slow pace.

79   As the lizard, under the great lash
Of the dog days, moving from wall to wall,
Looks like lightning if it crosses a path,

82   So appeared, coming towards the guts
Of the other two, a little fiery serpent,
Livid, and black like a peppercorn;

85   And that part through which we first take
Our nourishment, in one of them, he transfixed;
Then fell down, stretched out before him.

88   The one who was transfixed looked, and said nothing;
His feet did not move and he gaped
As if sleep or fever had assailed him.

91   He looked at the serpent, and the serpent looked at him;
And, one through his wound, the other through its mouth,
Billowed out smoke, and the two smokes met.

94   Let Lucan now be silent, when he tells
Of wretched Sabellus and Nasidius;
And let him listen to what is coming now.

Let Ovid be silent about Cadmus and Arethusa,   97
For if he makes one a snake and the other a fountain,
That is his art, which I do not envy;

For he never so changed two natures,   100
Front to front, that their essences
Were ready to alter their natural materials.

Together they responded to such principles   103
That the serpent's tail divided in a fork
And the wounded spirit's steps were locked together.

The legs and haunches so stuck to each other   106
That in a little while you could not see
Any trace of where the join was made.

The divided tail then took on the form   109
That was lost there, and the serpent's skin
Turned soft, while that of the man became hard.

I saw the arms entering the armpits,   112
And the two feet of the beast, which were short,
Growing longer as the arms grew shorter.

And then the hind feet, twisted together,   115
Became the member that a man hides,
And from his the man had two feet made.

While the smoke covered each of the two figures   118
With a new colour, and made the hair grow
On the one, while it depilated the other,

One rose up and the other fell down,   121
Still keeping their impious eyes fixed on each other,
By which light they saw their faces change.

The one who was upright drew his towards his temples   124
And out of the superfluity of skin
Ears issued on the unadorned cheeks:

That which was not pulled back, but still remained   127
Of the excess, turned into a nose for the face,
And the lips grew to the appropriate size.

130 The one who was lying down pushed out his muzzle,
And then drew his ears back into his head,
Just as a snail will draw back his horns;

133 And his tongue, which before was single, and designed
For speaking, split in two; and in the other
The forked tongue came together; the smoke's work is done.

136 The soul which had turned into a beast,
Hissing, fled down the valley, and the other
After him went talking, and spat.

139 Then he turned his new back upon him
And said to the other: 'I'm glad to see Buoso run
As I have done, crawling, along the road.'

142 And so I saw what filled the seventh pit
Change, and then change again: the novelty
May excuse any aberration of my pen.

145 And although my eyes were somewhat troubled,
And my mind, as well, somewhat bewildered,
They could not make their escape so secretly

148 That I did not perceive Puccio Sciancato;
He was the only one of the three friends
Who came first, who had not been changed:

151 The other was he whom you, Gaville, weep for.

CANTO XXVI

Rejoice, Florence, seeing you are so great
That over sea and land you flap your wings,
And your name is widely known in hell!

4 Among the thieves I found five of them,
Your citizens, enough to make me ashamed,
And you get no great honour by that.

But if near morning, all the dreams are true,   7
You will feel, in a little time from now,
What Prato, and others, think you have coming to you.

It would not be too soon, if it had happened already: 10
Would that it were so, since one day it must be!
It will seem worse to me, the older I grow.

We left the place, and up the stairs we went,   13
Which had served us before for our descent;
My escort climbed the steps, and took me with him;

And, following our isolated way   16
Among the jagged mass of jutting rock,
The feet could not get on without the hands.

Then I was grieved, and now I grieve again   19
When I direct my mind to what I saw,
And I restrain my ingenuity

Lest it should run where virtue cannot check it;   22
So that, if my good star or something better
Has given me benefits, I may not deny myself.

As the countryman, who is resting on a hill,   25
At the season when he who lights up the world
Hides his face from us for the shortest time,

When flies give way to gnats, sees in the valley   28
Thousands of glow-worms, perhaps in the very place
Where he has worked at harvest or at plough;

There were as many flames there glittering   31
In the eighth cleft, which I perceived
As soon as I arrived where I could see the bottom.

And as he who avenged himself with bears   34
Saw the departing chariot of Elijah
When the horses rose directly up to heaven

But could not follow what was happening with his eyes,   37
Further than to see only the flame,
Like a little cloud, that was going up and up;

40   So all those flames moved in the throat of the cleft,
     And none of them showed up what it had stolen,
     While every one of the flames concealed a sinner.

43   I stood upon the bridge, upright, to see,
     So that if I had not leaned upon a rock,
     I should have fallen, without being pushed.

46   My escort, when he saw me so attentive,
     Said: 'In each fire there is a spirit;
     Each one is wrapped in what is burning him.'

49   'My master,' I replied, 'now I have heard you,
     I am more certain; but I already thought
     It might be so, and wanted to ask you this:

52   Who is there in that fire which is so divided
     On top, that it appears to rise from the pyre
     That Eteocles was put on with his brother?'

55   He answered me: 'Inside there Ulysses
     And Diomed are tortured, and go together
     In retribution as they were in fury;

58   And so with their flame they now groan
     For that ruse of the horse which made the opening
     Through which came out the noble race of Romans.

61   They also weep inside for the cunning which makes
     Deidamia, dead, still mourn for Achilles,
     And there they pay for the Palladium too.'

64   'If they can, inside that glow, speak,'
     I said, 'master, I beg, and beg again
     That that asking may be worth a thousand askings;

67   Do not refuse my wish to wait until
     The flame with the two horns shall come this way:
     You see with what desire I bend towards it!'

70   And he to me: 'The request you make is certainly
     Praiseworthy; I will therefore do as you ask;
     Only make sure your tongue reins itself in.

Leave the talking to me, I have understood   73
What you are after; they perhaps would jib,
Since they were Greeks, at your way of speaking.'

After the flame had come to that point   76
Which to my guide seemed the right time and place,
I heard him speak to them in these terms:

'O you who are two inside one fire,   79
If I deserved of you, while I was alive,
If I deserved of you, little or much,

When in the world I wrote those high verses,   82
Then do not move; but let one of you tell
Where, having lost himself, he went to die.'

And then the bigger horn of the ancient flame   85
Began to shake itself and make a murmur,
Just like a flame that is buffeted by wind;

Then, pulling the top of it this way and that,   88
As if it were the tongue that was doing the talking,
Projected a voice outward, and said: 'When

I went away from Circe, who detained me   91
More than a year in the neighbourhood of Gaeta,
Before Aeneas had given it that name,

Neither affection for my son, nor duty   94
To my old father, nor the proper love
Which should have given Penelope happiness,

Could overcome, within me, the desire   97
I had to have experience of the world,
And of the vices and virtues of mankind;

I put out on the deep and open sea   100
With one boat only, and the company,
Small as it was, which had not deserted me.

I saw both shores of the sea as far as Spain,   103
As far as Morocco, and Sardinia
And the other islands bathed in that sea.

106   I and my friends had become old and slow
      When we arrived at the narrow opening
      Where Hercules had put his two marks

109   So that no man should go beyond that point:
      On the right hand I passed beyond Seville,
      And on the left had passed beyond Ceuta.

112   "Brothers," I said, "who through a hundred thousand
      Dangers at last have reached the occident;
      To this short vigil which is all there is

115   Remaining to our senses, do not deny
      Experience, following the course of the sun,
      Of that world which has no inhabitants.

118   Consider then the race from which you have sprung:
      You were not made to live like animals,
      But to pursue virtue and know the world."

121   I worked my friends to such a pitch of keenness
      With that little speech, for carrying on the journey,
      That afterwards I could hardly have held them back;

124   And, turning the stern towards the morning,
      We made the oars wings for that foolish flight,
      Always gaining a little on the port side.

127   All the stars of the other pole came up
      Already with the night, and ours went down,
      So that they were below the ocean floor.

130   Five times the light under the moon
      Had been lit up, and then again extinguished,
      Since we had set out on that dangerous passage,

133   When there appeared a mountain, which was dark
      Because of the distance, but to me it seemed
      Higher than any I had ever seen.

136   We all rejoiced, but soon it turned to grief;
      For from the unknown land a storm blew up
      And struck against the fore part of the ship.

Three times it turned her round, with all the waters;   139
At the fourth turn it raised the stern aloft,
And the head went down, as it pleased another it should,

Until the sea again closed over us.'   142

CANTO XXVII

The flame was now upright, and became still,
Saying no more, and now was going from us
With the permission of the gentle poet,

When another flame, which had followed behind,   4
Made our eyes turn towards its highest point,
From which there issued a confused sound.

Like the Sicilian bull which first bellowed   7
With the complaint of—as was only just—
The man who had first tuned it with his file,

And went on bellowing with the sufferer's voice,   10
So that, although it was all made of brass,
It seemed as if it was stabbed through with pain;

In the same way, because at first they had   13
No outlet from the fire, the miserable words
Were changed into the language of the fire.

But later, when they had made a way out   16
Up through the tip, and given that the flicker
Which the tongue had when it had formed the words,

We heard a voice: 'O you to whom I speak,   19
And who a moment ago were speaking Lombard,
Saying, "Now go, I ask no more of you,"

Although perhaps I am a little late,   22
Do not refuse to stay and talk with me;
You see I am willing to talk, and I am burning!

25   If you have only now, to this blind world,
    Fallen from that sweet Latin territory
    From which I bring my guilt in its entirety,

28   Tell me if the Romagnuols have peace or war;
    For I was from the mountains between Urbino
    And that shoulder from which the Tiber springs.'

31   I was still gazing down and leaning forward
    When my escort touched me on the arm
    And said: 'You speak to him: he is a Latin.'

34   And I who had my response on the tip of my tongue
    Began to speak without hesitation:
    'O soul, down there in your concealment,

37   Romagna is not, and it never was
    Without war in the heart of its oppressors;
    But it had no open war when I left there recently.

40   Ravenna fares as she has fared so long:
    The eagle of Polenta broods upon her,
    Stretching its wings also as far as Cervia.

43   The city, which already has experience of it,
    And of that sanguinary pile of Frenchmen,
    Finds itself once more under the green claws.

46   The old mastiff, and the young one, from Verrucchio,
    So good at maladministering Montagna,
    As usual there, tear people to pieces.

49   The cities of Lamone and Santerno
    Are ruled by the lion-cub on the white ground,
    Who changes sides between summer and winter;

52   And that city whose side the Savio waters:
    Just as she is between the plain and the mountains,
    So she lives half-way between oppression and freedom.

55   And now, I beg you, tell us who you are;
    Do not be harder than others have been on you,
    If you would keep your name up in the world.'

After the fire had roared a little while,   58
After its fashion, the sharp tip moved
To and fro, and then breathed out these words:

'If I thought that I was making my reply   61
To anyone who would ever go back to the world,
This flame would stay absolutely still;

But since no one ever came back alive   64
From this deep place, if what I hear is true,
I answer you without fear of infamy.

I was a soldier, then became a Franciscan,   67
Thinking to make amends by wearing the cord;
And certainly that thought would have come true

But for the high priest, the devil take him!   70
Who put me back among my early sins;
And how and why, I should like you to hear.

When I was still formed of the flesh and bone   73
My mother gave me, all that I achieved
Was done less by the lion than the fox.

The subtle ways of acting under cover,   76
I knew them all, and used all these devices
So well, that I was famous everywhere.

When I perceived that I had reached that point   79
Of my life on the earth, when everyone
Should lower his sails and pull the tackle in,

What had pleased me before, pleased me no longer;   82
Penitent and confessed, I became a monk;
Alas, alas, alas, it would have worked.

However, the Prince of the new Pharisees,   85
Having a war on near the Lateran,
And not a war with Saracens or Jews,

For every enemy of his was Christian,   88
And none of them had been to conquer Acre,
Nor been a merchant in the Soldan's country;

91   Forgot his supreme office, his holy orders,
And forgot also that I was wearing
That cord which used to make those who wore it, thinner.

94   As Constantine sought out Silvestro
On mount Soracte, to cure his leprosy,
So this man called me as his physician

97   To cure him of the fever of his pride:
He asked me my advice, and I was silent,
Because the words he spoke seemed drunken words,

100   And then he spoke again: "Do not be fearful,
I absolve you: now tell me what to do
To throw down Penestrino to the ground.

103   I can lock and unlock heaven, as you know,
Because in my possession are the two keys
Which my predecessor made so little of."

106   The powerful arguments then pressed upon me
Until I thought silence the worse course,
And said: "Father, since you wash me clean

109   Of that sin into which I now must fall,
A large promise followed by short payment
Will make you triumph on your lofty seat."

112   Francis afterwards, when I was dead,
Came for me, but one of the black cherubim
Said to him: "Do not take him: do not wrong me.

115   He must come down and be among my servants,
Because he gave the fraudulent advice,
Since when I have waited to seize him by his hair;

118   For absolution is for the repentant;
You cannot repent and will at the same time,
The contradiction is not allowable."

121   So much for me; oh, how I started back
When he came for me, saying to me: "Perhaps
You did not think that I was a logician!"

He carried me to Minos; and Minos twisted   124
His tail eight times around his fearful back;
And then, in great rage, he bit at it,

And said: "This one is for the thieving fire";   127
So I am lost in this place where you see me;
And, dressed in this way, I go in rancour.'

When he had finished what he had to say,   130
The flame went sorrowing away from us,
Twisting and turning the sharp horn.

We went further, I and my escort,   133
Up on the jutting rock to the next arch,
Which goes over the ditch in which the penalty

Is paid by those who are guilty of causing discord.   136

CANTO XXVIII

Who could, even in a prose description,
Give an account of all the blood and wounds
I saw then, even with several tellings?

No tongue, certainly, would be capable of it,   4
For our speech, and our intelligence,
Lack the capacity to comprehend so much.

If all the people were collected together   7
Who, up there in the fated land of Apulia,
Had to bewail the blood they had forced out

At the hand of the Trojans, and in that long war   10
In which there was so great a spoil of rings,
As Livy has recorded, who does not err,

And with those who felt the pain of wounds   13
Because they were opposed to Robert Guiscard;
And the rest of those whose bones are still picked up

16   At Ceperano, where the Apulians
     Were treacherous, and there at Tagliacozzo,
     Where old Alardo conquered without arms;

19   And if some showed where they had been run through,
     And some the limbs they had lost, it would be nothing
     To the ninth cleft, with its unspeakable ways.

22   Even a cask with the bottom knocked out
     Does not gape in the way that I saw one
     Ripped open from the chin to where he farts:

25   Between his legs, his guts were hanging out;
     His lights appeared, and that disgusting tube
     Which makes shit of what goes down our throats.

28   While I was all intent on looking at him,
     He looked at me, and his hand opened his chest;
     He said: 'Now see how I undo myself!

31   See how mangled Mahomet is:
     In front of me, Ali goes weeping,
     His face split open from his chin to his forelock.

34   And all the others you see in this place
     Were instigators of scandal and of schism,
     When they were alive, and so they are split here.

37   There is a devil behind here who hacks at us
     So cruelly, with cuts of his sword,
     And hacks again, everyone of our kind,

40   Every time we come round this road again;
     Because the wounds close themselves up each time
     Before anyone gets back to where he stands.

43   But who are you, who stand staring on that rock,
     Perhaps to put off going to that penalty
     Which was judged fitting for what you were accused of?'

46   'Death has not reached him yet, nor does guilt bring him,'
     Replied my master, 'to the torment here;
     But, to give him a full experience,

I, who am dead, have to act as his guide   49
Through hell, down here from one circle to another:
And that is sure as that I am speaking to you.'

More than a hundred of them, when they heard him,   52
Stopped in the ditch and then looked up at me
And, in astonishment, forgot their torture.

'Now say to Brother Dolcino, he should look to it,   55
You who perhaps will see the sun again soon,
Unless he wants to follow me here quickly,

That he has victuals, enough so that the snow   58
Does not bring victory to the Novarese,
Who otherwise would find it hard to get.'

Mahomet said these words to me while he   61
Had one foot lifted in the air, to go;
Then brought it to the ground, and he was off.

Another, who had a sword-wound through his throat,   64
And his nose cut off right up to the eyebrows,
And had been left with only one ear,

Stopping to look and wonder with the others,   67
Before the others he opened his windpipe,
Which was brilliant red on the outside;

And said: 'O you, whom guilt has not condemned,   70
And whom I have seen above on Latin ground,
Unless I am deceived by a resemblance,

Call to mind Pier da Medicina,   73
If ever you return to that sweet plain
Which stretches from Vercelli down to Marcabò.

And make it known to the two best men in Fano,   76
To Messer Guido and to Angiolello,
That, if what is foreseen here is not vanity,

They will be thrown overboard from their ship,   79
With a stone about their necks, near La Cattolica,
Through the treachery of a ferocious tyrant.

82   Between the islands of Cyprus and Majorca,
      So great a crime was never seen by Neptune,
      Not at the hands of pirates or the Greeks.

85   That traitor who sees only with one eye
      And holds the land which one who is with me here
      Would he had never set his eyes upon,

88   Will make them come to have discussion with him;
      And then will so act, that they will not need
      Vows or prayers for the Focara wind.'

91   And I to him: 'Show and declare to me,
      If you want me to carry back news of you,
      Who is he who views the scene so bitterly.'

94   He then put his hand upon the jaw
      Of one of his companions, and opened his mouth,
      Crying: 'This is the one, and he does not talk!

97   This exile overcame the doubts of Caesar,
      Affirming that, to a man who is ready to act,
      Hesitation can only bring disaster.'

100   O how demoralised he seemed to me,
      With his tongue cut off and his throat open,
      Curio, who was so daring when he spoke.

103   And one who had both his hands amputated,
      Holding the stumps up in the dark air,
      So that the blood poured over his face,

106   Cried: 'You will also remember Mosca,
      Who said, alas, "When it is done it is finished,"
      Which brought much trouble to the Tuscan people.'

109   And I added: 'And death to your family!'
      So he, seeing pain heaped upon pain,
      Went away miserable and demented.

112   But I stayed where I was to view the crowd,
      And saw something that I should be afraid,
      Without more proof, even to relate;

Were it not that I had the assurance   115
Of speaking the truth, which gives a man encouragement
When he is protected by a conscience.

I certainly saw, and I still seem to see,   118
A body without a head, and going along
Just as the rest of that sad troop was going;

It held the severed head by its hair,   121
Swinging in its hand like a lantern,
And the head looked at us, and said: 'Oh me!'

It made itself a lamp of itself,   124
And they were two in one and one in two:
How that may be, he knows who so disposes.

When it was right at the foot of the bridge,   127
It raised its arm up, and with that the head,
So that its words were brought nearer to us.

What it said was: 'Now you see the great penalty,   130
You who while still alive, visit the dead;
See whether any could be heavier.

And, so that you can take back news of me,   133
Know I am Bertram de Born, I am the man
Who gave the young king evil advice.

I made father and son rebel against each other: 136
Achitophel did no worse by Absalom
And David, with his incitements to harm.

Because I separated persons so close,   139
I carry my brain separated, alas,
From its beginning, which is in this trunk.

So in me is observed retaliation.'   142

CANTO XXIX

The number of people and the diversity
Of wounds had, so to speak, made my eyes drunk,
So that they wanted only to stay and weep;

4   But Virgil said to me: 'Why are you staring?
Why is your sight so fixed down there among
Those miserable, mutilated shadows?

7   You did not do that in the other chasms;
Think, if you hope to count how many there are,
The valley circles for twenty-two miles.

10   And already the moon is under our feet:
The time we are allowed is now short,
And there is more to see than you are looking at.'

13   'If you had,' I replied without interval,
'Seen what it was that made me look that way,
Perhaps you would have let me stand here still.'

16   Meanwhile my escort started off, and I
Followed him, and, replying as I went,
Added: 'You see within that cave,

19   Where I kept my eyes so firmly fixed,
I think a ghost from my family weeps
The fault which down there he must pay so dearly.'

22   And then my master said: 'Do not let your mind
Be agitated by thoughts of him in future:
Attend to other things; let him stay where he is;

25   For I saw him, down at the foot of the bridge,
Pointing you out, menacingly, with his finger,
And I heard some of them say: "Geri del Bello."

28   You were at that time so preoccupied
With one who at one time held Hautefort,
That you did not look that way; and he went off.'

'O my master,' I said, 'his violent death,   31
Which has not yet been avenged by any
Of us who are the consorts of his shame,

Made him contemptuous; that is why he went   34
Without a word to me, as I imagine:
And that has made me feel the more for him.'

And so we talked till we came to the beginning   37
Of the jutting rock from which we could have seen,
Had the light been better, the bottom of the next cleft.

When we were poised above the last cloister   40
Of Malebolge, so that its lay-brothers
Were able to appear before our eyes,

Terrible lamentations pierced me through   43
And pity tipped the arrows with her steel;
I could do nothing but cover my ears with my hands.

Such pain as there would be, if the diseases   46
Of summer in the hospitals of Valdichiana,
And those from the Maremma and Sardinia

Were all together in a single ditch;   49
So it was there, and such a stink came up
As you would get from limbs that had gone putrid.

We went down over the last embankment   52
Of the long rock, still moving to the left;
And after that I had a clearer view

Down to the bottom, where infallible justice,   55
As emissary of the high God,
Punishes the falsifiers here on record.

I do not think it can have been greater sorrow   58
To see, in Aegina, the people all struck down,
When the air was so full of sickness

That the animals down to the smallest worm   61
All dropped, and the ancient peoples afterwards,
According to what the poets give out for true,

64   Were brought back from the progeny of ants;
     Than it was to see, in that obscure valley,
     The spirits languishing in foul heaps.

67   One lay on another's stomach, another on the shoulders
     Of somebody else, and some of them went creeping
     As best they could along the dreary road.

70   Step by step we went, without speaking,
     Watching and listening to the sick there,
     Who could not raise their bodies from the floor.

73   I saw two sitting, leaning against each other,
     As dishes are propped up when they are put to warm;
     And they, from head to foot, were spotted with scabs;

76   And I have never seen a stable-boy
     Quicker to comb a horse, when his master wants him,
     Or when he is himself desperate for sleep,

79   Than these two scratching themselves with their nails
     Again and again, because of the insane itching
     Which has no other form of relief than that;

82   And their nails scraped down scabs, just as
     A knife scrapes down the scales of a bream
     Or other fish with larger scales than that.

85   'O you who take your mail off with your fingers,'
     Began my escort, speaking to one of them,
     'And who sometimes use them as pairs of pincers,

88   Tell us if there is any Latin among these
     Who are within here; and I hope your nails
     Will last eternally on the job they have.'

91   'We are both Latins, we whom you see here,
     Disfigured in this way,' replied one, weeping;
     'But who are you who put this question to us?'

94   My escort said: 'I am one who goes down
     With this man, who is living, from ridge to ridge,
     And my intention is to show him hell.'

The support they were giving each other collapsed,   97
And both of them turned trembling towards me,
As well as others nearby who happened to hear.

The good master pressed close to my side,   100
Saying: 'Now tell him what you want';
And I began, in accordance with his wishes:

'So that remembrance of you shall not grow weak   103
In the first world, and vanish from human minds,
But keep alive for many years to come,

Tell me who you are and of what people: 106
And do not let your disfiguring, filthy penalty
Make you afraid of such revelations.'

'I was an Arezzo man, and Albert of Siena,'   109
One of them answered, 'had me put to the fire;
But what I died for does not bring me here.

It is true I said to him—it was meant as a joke: 112
"I could fly through the air if I wanted to";
And he, who had curiosity but no brain,

Asked me to show him how; and only because   115
I would not make a Daedalus, he arranged
For me to be burnt by his father in God.

But to the last of the ten divisions here,   118
For the alchemy I practised in the world,
I was condemned by Minos, who makes no mistakes.'

And I said to the poet: 'Now was there ever   121
A people so frivolous as the Sienese?
Certainly not the French, by a long way!'

The other leper, who had heard what I said,   124
Replied: 'Of course you can make an exception for Stricca;
There was one who knew how to spend moderately!

And Niccolò who first discovered   127
Methods of cooking using plenty of cloves,
In a garden where such things easily took root;

130 And among the company in which Caccia
Of Asciano wasted his vine and forest,
And his crack-brained friend showed how clever he was.

133 But should you want to know who backs you up so
Against the Sienese, look hard at me,
So that my face provides the answer;

136 You will see that I am the shade of Capocchio,
Who falsified the metals, using alchemy;
You should remember, if I am seeing you right,

139 How good I was as one of nature's apes.'

CANTO XXX

At that time when Juno was furious,
Because of Semele, with all of Theban blood,
As she made clear on more than one occasion,

4 Athamas became so utterly mad
That, when he saw his wife with their two sons
—She was carrying the pair of them, one on each side—

7 He cried: 'Let's spread the nets, so that I catch
The lioness with her cubs, when they come this way';
And then spread out his pitiless claws,

10 Seizing the one who was called Learchus,
And swung him round and smashed him on a rock;
And she drowned herself with the other child.

13 And when the turn of fortune brought so low
The pride of the Trojans, who had courage for anything,
That both the king and the kingdom were erased,

16 Hecuba, mourning, bereft and prisoner,
When she had seen Polyxena sacrificed,
And her son Polydorus on the sea-shore

In her grief was presented to her sight,   19
She went out of her mind and barked like a dog;
So much had sorrow twisted her up.

But neither the Theban furies nor the Trojan   22
Were ever seen so cruel in anything,
Neither in wounding beasts or human limbs,

As I saw the two shadows, lifeless and naked,   25
Who ran along biting as if they had been
Pigs who had just been let out from their sty.

One went for Capocchio, the back of whose neck   28
He bit with his fangs, and in this way dragged him off
So that his belly scraped the solid ground.

And the Aretine, who stood there still, but trembling,   31
Said to me: 'That demon is Gianni Schicchi,
And, mad himself, he pitches into others.'

'Oh,' I said to him, 'that other—may it not fix   34
Its teeth in your back—be kind enough to tell me,
First of all, who it is, before it makes off.'

And he to me: 'That is the ancient spirit   37
Of the criminal Myrrha, who became
Her father's friend with a love that was out of true.

In this manner she came to sin with him,   40
With the pretence that she was someone else;
Just as that other one who is going off there,

In order to win the lady of the company   43
Disguised himself as Buoso Donati,
Making a will and giving it legal form.'

And when the demented pair, on whom   46
I had kept my eye, had gone on their way,
I turned to look at the other misborn spirits.

I saw one made in the shape of a lute,   49
Or who would have been, if he had had an amputation
And both legs had been cut off from the groin.

52   The heavy dropsy, which makes such disproportion
      Between the parts, with the fluid not assimilated,
      That the face does not match up with the belly,

55   Made him keep his lips always parted,
      As a feverish man does, who, because of thirst,
      Turns one lip down on his chin, and the other upwards.

58   'O you who are without any punishment,
      And I do not know why, in this poor place,'
      He said, 'look, and acquaint yourselves

61   With the deprivations suffered by Master Adam:
      When I was alive, I had all I wanted,
      And now, alas, I long for a drop of water.

64   The little streams which, from the green hills
      Of Casentino run down to the Arno,
      Making the channels they run in cool and wet,

67   Are always there before me, and not for nothing,
      For thinking of them dries me up far more
      Than the disease which wastes my face away.

70   The rigid justice which goads me now
      Finds reason in the place in which I sinned
      To make my sighs fly further than they would.

73   There is Romena, where I forged the coins
      With base metal, stamped with John the Baptist;
      It was for that I left my body burnt.

76   And if I could see the unhappy soul
      Of Guido, Alessandro, or their brother,
      I would not change the sight for Branda spring.

79   One is already in here, if the insane
      Shadows which circulate here tell the truth;
      What use is that to me? My limbs are tied.

82   If I were even only so much lighter
      That in a hundred years, I could go an inch,
      I should already have set out on my way,

Seeking him among the disfigured people,   85
Though the road winds round not less than eleven miles
And is not less than half a mile across.

It is through them that I am in such company: 88
It was they persuaded me to coin the florins
Which had a good three carats of alloy.'

And I to him: 'Who are these miserable two   91
Who steam the way that wet hands do in winter-time,
And who lie close to you on your right?'

'I found them here, and they have not budged since,'   94
He answered, 'I was thrown into this trough;
I do not think that they will ever budge.

One of them is the wife who falsely accused Joseph;   97
The other is the false Greek Sinon from Troy;
High fever makes them give off such a stench.'

And one of them, who took offence, perhaps   100
Because he had been given a bad name,
Struck with his fist at the unyielding belly.

It made a noise as if it had been a drum;   103
And Master Adam hit him in the face
With his arm, which seemed to be no less hard,

Saying to him: 'It is true that I have lost   106
The power of movement, with my heavy limbs,
But I have an arm free for a case like that.'

The other one replied: 'When you were going   109
To the fire, you didn't have it quite so ready:
But you moved it fast enough when you were coining.'

The dropsical spirit said: 'That's true enough;   112
But you were not so reliable a witness
When you were asked to tell the truth in Troy.'

'If I spoke false, you falsified the coins,'   115
Said Sinon; 'and I am here for one fault,
And you, for more than any other devil!'

118   'You perjurer, do not forget the horse,'
        Answered the one who had the blown-up stomach;
        'And may it hurt you that the whole world knows!'

121   The Greek said: 'May the thirst that cracks your tongue
        Be torture to you, likewise the festering water
        That makes your belly such a hedge around you!'

124   Then the coiner: 'So it is open wide,
        Your mouth, to speak ill as it used to do;
        If I am thirsty and am bursting with fluid,

127   You have that burning and that pain in the head;
        For you to lick the mirror of Narcissus,
        You would not need much of an invitation.'

130   In order to hear them I had stood stock still,
        When my master said to me: 'You are still looking!
        A little longer and I shall quarrel with you!'

133   When I heard him speaking to me in anger,
        I turned towards him and was so ashamed
        That I am so still when I think of it.

136   And as one who dreams of something harmful,
        Wishes in his dream that he was dreaming,
        And so desires what is, as if it were not,

139   So did I, for I was not able to speak;
        I wanted to excuse myself, and was doing so
        All the time, and did not think that I was.

142   'A lesser shame would erase a greater fault,'
        The master said, 'than you have been guilty of;
        Therefore let fall any unhappiness,

145   And take account of the fact that I am here,
        If it so happen that fortune should bring you
        Where there are people in the like disputes:

148   To want to hear them is an inferior wish.'

CANTO XXXI

The same tongue which had first so stung me
That it brought colour to one cheek and the other,
After that gave me the remedy:

So I have heard that the lance of Achilles,   4
And his father's, would first of all occasion
An evil gift but, after that, a boon.

We turned our backs on the unhappy valley,   7
And up the embankment which encircles it,
Crossing over without saying a word.

Here it was less than night and less than day,   10
So that I could see but a little ahead;
But I heard the sound of a deep horn

Such as would make any thunder seem faint;   13
My eyes followed the course of the sound in reverse,
And so were directed to a single place.

After the grievous defeat in which Charlemagne   16
Lost the sacred cause in which he had ventured,
There was no more terrible sound from the horn of Roland.

I had hardly turned my head in that direction   19
When I thought I saw a cluster of high towers;
So I said: 'Master, what city is that?'

And he to me: 'Because your sight must travel   22
Through the darkness from too great a distance,
It happens that your imagination plays you false.

You will see properly when you arrive,   25
How much the senses are deceived by distance;
So goad yourself on a little more.'

Then, kindly, he took me by the hand   28
And said: 'Before we go any further on,
In order that the fact may seem less strange,

31   You had better know that they are not towers, but giants,
     And they are in the well, around the banks,
     With all below the navel out of sight.'

34   As when a mist is fading, the perception
     Gradually gives a different shape to that
     Which was hidden by the vapour filling the atmosphere,

37   So, piercing there the dark and heavy air,
     And little by little coming nearer the brink,
     I mistook less and grew the more afraid;

40   For as upon its circular defences,
     Montereggione crowns itself with towers,
     So on the verges which surround the well

43   Towered to the height of half their bodies
     The horrible giants whom Jove still menaces
     From heaven when he hurtles down his thunder.

46   Already I could make out the face of one,
     The shoulders, chest, and a large part of the belly,
     And both the arms, which were hanging by his sides.

49   Certainly nature did well when she lost
     The art of making animals like these,
     Depriving Mars of such executioners.

52   And, if she has not given up elephants
     And whales, whoever thinks about it carefully
     Will find her just and more discreet for that;

55   For, where the argument of reason is
     Joined with an evil will and potency,
     There is no possible defence for man.

58   The face of this one seemed as long and broad
     As is the pine-cone at Saint Peter's in Rome,
     And all the other bones were in proportion;

61   So that the bank, which formed a sort of apron
     From the middle down, still left exposed above
     Certainly so much that it would have been a boast

For three Frieslanders to say they could reach his hair;   64
Because, from where a man buckles his mantle,
Downwards, I saw it was more than seven yards.

'Raphèl maỳ amèch zabí almí'   67
Was what that fierce mouth began to shout,
To which more gentle words were not appropriate.

And the guide, in his direction: 'Stupid soul,   70
Stick to your horn, and let it out that way,
When rage or other passion touches you!

Feel at your throat, and you will find the strap   73
Which holds it tied there, soul in disarray;
The horn itself is curved across your chest!'

Then he said to me: 'He stands self-accused;   76
That is Nimrod, through whose evil thought
There is more than one language in the world.

We'll leave him there and not waste talking on him;   79
For every language is the same to him,
As his own is to others, meaningless.'

We therefore set out on our way again,   82
With a turn to the left; a crossbow shot
Away we found the next giant, fiercer and bigger.

Who that master might be who tied him up,   85
I cannot say, but he had his left arm
Pinioned in front, and the right arm behind him,

Held by a chain which held him bound   88
From the neck down, and on the uncovered part
It went around him to a fifth loop.

'That proud spirit wanted to try his strength   91
Against high Jove,' my master said to me,
'And that is the reward he gets for that.

Ephialtes is his name; the great attempt   94
He made, when the giants frightened the gods;
The arms he used, he will never move again.'

97   And I to him: 'If it were possible,
    I should like my own eyes to have experience
    Of the unmeasurable Briareus.'

100   To which he answered: 'You will see Antaeus
    Near here, for he speaks and is unfettered
    And will take us to the lowest point of evil.

103   He whom you wish to see is much further off,
    And he is bound and looks as this one does,
    Except that he is fiercer in the face.'

106   Never was earthquake so violent,
    Nor ever shook a tower so powerfully,
    As Ephialtes when he shook himself.

109   Then I was more afraid of death than ever;
    The fear indeed would have been all that was needed
    If I had not seen that his arms were tied.

112   We went on our way further after that,
    And came to Antaeus, who, not counting the head,
    Stuck out of the pit some five ells.

115   'O you who, in that fortunate valley, which
    Made Scipio the heir of so much glory,
    When Hannibal and his followers showed their backs,

118   Took more than a thousand lions for your prey,
    And, if you had been in that ambitious war,
    With your brothers here, according to what some think,

121   The sons of earth would then have won the day;
    Take us down, and do not be unwilling,
    To where the cold imprisons Cocytus.

124   Do not make us go to Tityos or Typhon:
    This man can give what here is so desired:
    Therefore bend down, and do not twist your lips.

127   He can still give you back your fame on earth;
    For he still lives, and has long life to come,
    Unless before the time Grace calls him in.'

So said my master; and the giant in haste   130
Stretched out his hands, from which, in other times,
Hercules had felt stress; and took him up.

Virgil, when he felt the grasp upon him,   133
Said to me: 'Come here, so that I can take you';
Then made a bundle of himself and me.

As the tower of Garisenda seems to the eye   136
From the sloping side, when a cloud passes over it,
As if it were leaning in the opposite direction,

So Antaeus seemed to me, as I stood and gaped   139
To see him bend, and it was such a moment
That I should have wished to go some other way.

But lightly in that bottom which devours   142
Judas with Lucifer, he set us down;
And did not stay there bending over us,

But rose up as a mast does on a ship.   145

CANTO XXXII

If I could write in harsh and raucous verses,
As would be suitable to the sad pit
On which all the other rocks weigh down,

I could press out the juice of my conception   4
More fully, but because I have not that skill,
Not without fear I bring myself to speak;

For it is not a matter to take lightly,   7
Describing the lowest point of the universe,
Not something to be done in baby-talk:

And may those ladies help me with my verse   10
Who helped Amphion to put the wall round Thebes,
So that what I say may answer to the facts.

13   O you who are the lowest dregs of all,
       Put in this place which it is hard to speak of,
       Better if here you had been sheep or goats!

16   When we were right down in that dark well,
       Below the giant's feet, and much lower,
       And I was still staring at the high wall,

19   I heard someone say: 'Take care how you go by;
       Walk so as not to trample on the heads
       Of brothers who are wretched and exhausted.'

22   And so I turned round, and saw before me
       And below my feet, a lake, which was frozen
       Till it had more the look of glass than water.

25   The Danube, when she flows through Austria,
       Never in winter made so heavy a veil
       For herself, nor the Don under her cold sky,

28   As there was here; so that if Tambernic
       Had fallen on top of it, or Pietrapiana,
       It would not have creaked even at the edges.

31   And as the frog stations itself to croak
       With its muzzle out of the water, at the time
       When the peasant woman turns her thoughts to gleaning;

34   Discoloured, up to where disgrace appears,
       So were the shadows tortured in the ice,
       And, with their chattering teeth, sounded like storks.

37   All of them held their faces bowed down:
       The cold procured its testimony by the mouth,
       And their eyes showed the sadness of their hearts.

40   When I had looked around a little while,
       I glanced towards my feet, and saw two so close
       That the hair on their two heads was intermixed.

43   'Tell me, you who so press your fronts together,'
       I said, 'who are you?' And they bent their necks;
       And when they had lifted their faces towards me,

Their eyes, which before were moist only within,   46
Sent drops down to their lips, and the frost bound
Their tears between them and so joined them up.

Two beams were never bolted up so tightly: 49
And so it happened that, like two he-goats,
They butted one another in their fury.

And one shadow who had lost both his ears   52
Through the cold, with his face still looking down
Said: 'What is it makes you stare at us so hard?

If you would like to know who these two are,   55
The valley from which the Bisenzio falls
Was their father Albert's, and their own.

They came out of one body; and all Caina   58
You could search through, without finding a shade
Deserving more to be fixed in this icy place;

Not he whose breast was pierced to let the light through   61
By a single blow struck by the hand of Arthur;
Not Focaccia; not this one who obstructs me

So with his head, that I cannot see beyond him,   64
Sassol Mascheroni was his name:
If you are a Tuscan, you will know who he was.

And, so that you do not make me talk any more,   67
Know that I was Camicion de' Pazzi;
I wait for Carlino to make me look less black.'

Then I saw a thousand faces there,   70
Blue with the cold; it makes me shudder
And always will, when I think of those frozen shallows.

While we were going onwards towards the centre   73
At which all weights become a single weight,
And I was shivering in the eternal cold;

Whether it was will or fate or fortune,   76
I do not know; but, passing among those heads,
I struck one in the face hard, with my foot.

79   Weeping, he cried out: 'Why do you tread on me?
        If you have not come to increase the vengeance
        Of Montaperti, why do you molest me?'

82   And I: 'My master, now, wait for me here,
        So that, with this one's help, I may clear a doubt;
        After that, make me hurry as much as you please.'

85   My guide stood still, and I said to the one
        Who was still uttering frightful imprecations:
        'Who are you, who complain of other people?'

88   'And who are you, who go through Antenora,'
        He answered, 'striking other people's cheeks?
        If I were still alive I would not stand it.'

91   'I am alive, and it may matter to you,'
        Was my reply, 'if you want reputation,
        That I should put your name among my records.'

94   And he to me: 'I want the opposite;
        Get out of here and give me no more trouble,
        You do not understand how to flatter here.'

97   At that I took him by the scruff of the neck
        And said: 'You'd better tell me who you are,
        Or I will tear out every hair of your head.'

100   Then he to me: 'Even though you scalp me,
        I will not tell you who I am, nor show you,
        Though you stumble on my head a thousand times.'

103   I already had his hair coiled round my hand,
        And had pulled out more than one bunch of it,
        He yelping, and keeping his eyes lowered;

106   When another called: 'What is the matter, Bocca?
        Isn't it enough for your jaws to chatter,
        Without yelping? What devil is biting you?'

109   'Now,' I said, 'there is no need for you to speak,
        You filthy traitor; for now, and to your shame,
        I will take back a true report of you.'

'Go away,' he answered, 'tell them what you like;   112
And don't forget, if you get out of here,
The one who had his tongue so loose just now.

The thing he weeps for here is Frenchmen's money;   115
"I saw," you could say, "that man from Duera,
There where the sinners find it rather cool."

If you are asked who else was here, then say   118
You had beside you here the Beccheria
Who had his throat cut by the Florentines.

Gianni de Soldanier, I think, is further,   121
With Ganellone and that Tebaldello,
Who opened up Faenza while they slept.'

We had already gone away from him,   124
When I saw two so frozen in one hole
That the head of one made headgear for the other;

And, as in hunger people will gnaw bread,   127
So the one on top fixed his teeth in the lower one,
Just where the brain joins to the nape of the neck.

Not otherwise did Tydeus eat away   130
The temples of Menalippus in his fury,
Than this one did the skull and what comes next.

'O you who show by such a bestial mark   133
The hate you have for him whom you are eating,
Tell me why,' I said, 'on this condition:

If you have reason to complain of him,   136
I, knowing you and what his fault has been,
In the world above may make you recompense,

If my tongue does not wither as I speak.'   139

CANTO XXXIII

He raised his mouth from his ferocious meal,
That sinner, wiping it upon the hair
Of that head, the back of which he had spoiled.

4   Then he began: 'You are asking me to renew
A desperate grief, which presses on my heart,
Even to think of, and before I speak.

7   But if my words are to be a seed
Which may grow to infamy for the traitor I gnaw,
You shall see me speak and weep at the same time.

10   I do not know who you may be, nor how
You have come down here; but, when I listen,
It seems to me that you are a Florentine.

13   You should know that I was Count Ugolino,
And this is the Archbishop Ruggieri:
Now I will tell you why I am so close to him.

16   That, as a consequence of his ill thoughts,
Trusting myself to him, I was taken
And thereafter killed, no need to tell you;

19   But what you cannot have understood,
Is how cruel my death was; that you shall hear,
And you will know whether he offended me.

22   A narrow outlet in the close lock-up
Which, because of me, is called the Tower of Hunger,
And in which others must be shut up still,

25   Had shown me several moons through the slit,
When one evil night I had a dream
Which rent the veil of the future in two for me.

28   This man appeared as lord and master,
Hunting the wolf and the wolf-cubs on the mountain
Because of which the Pisans are unable to see Lucca.

With hounds that were hungry, eager, skilful,   31
He had put ahead of him, Gualandi,
With Sismondi and with Lanfranchi.

After a short run, so it seemed to me,   34
Father and sons were tired, and, with sharp teeth,
It seemed to me their sides were split open.

When I awoke, before the next day came,   37
I heard my little sons cry in their sleep,
Asking for bread, for they were with me there.

You must be cruel, if it does not hurt you   40
To think of the apprehension in my heart;
And if you do not weep, what do you weep for?

They were awake, and then the hour approached   43
When, ordinarily, food had been brought in,
And, on account of our dream, we were all anxious;

And I heard below the way out of the tower   46
Locked up; and then I looked into the faces
Of my sons without saying a word.

I did not weep, but turned to stone within: 49
They began weeping; and my Anselm said:
"Why do you stare so, father, what is the matter?"

But I neither wept nor could reply   52
All that day, nor the night that followed it,
Until the sun once more rose in the sky.

When a small ray of sunlight found its way   55
Into that grim prison, and I saw
On four faces the look that was in my own,

I bit into both my hands for grief;   58
And they, thinking I did it because I wanted
To eat, without any hesitation rose

And said: "Father, it would hurt us far less   61
If you ate us; it was you who made us put on
This miserable flesh, now you can strip it off."

64   I calmed myself, not to make them more unhappy;
That day and the next we all stayed silent:
Alas, hard earth, why did you not open?

67   When we had arrived at the fourth day,
Gaddo threw himself full length at my feet,
Saying: "My father, why do you not help us?"

70   Then he died: and, as you see me now,
I saw the three of them fall one by one,
Between the fifth day and the sixth; then I started,

73   Already blind, to grope over their bodies,
Calling them for two days, after they were dead:
And, after that, grief was less strong than hunger.'

76   When he had said that, with his eyes bulging,
He again seized the miserable skull with his teeth,
Which, on the bone, were as strong as a dog's.

79   Alas, Pisa, a shame to all the peoples
Of the fair country where the *Si* is heard,
Since your neighbours are slow to punish you,

82   Then let Caprara and Gorgona stir
And make a barrier of the Arno's mouth,
So that every man jack of you shall be drowned:

85   For if Count Ugolino is supposed
To have betrayed you so that you lost your castles,
You had no right to put his sons to torture.

88   Their tender age made them innocent,
You modern Thebes!—Uguiccione and Brigata,
And the other two whom I have named above.

91   We went further, to where the icy cold
Has harshly bound another group of people,
With their faces not turned down, but thrown back.

94   Their tears themselves do not allow them to weep,
And the grief which finds the ice blocking their eyes
Turns inwards to increase their anguish;

For the first tears form a coagulation,   97
And, in the manner of a crystal mask,
Fill all the cavity beneath the eyebrows.

Although, as if from a callosity,   100
Because of cold, there was no feeling left
Over the whole surface of the face,

I thought that I could feel a breath of wind,   103
So I said: 'My master, who causes this stir?
For is not all heat extinguished here?'

And he to me: 'Very soon you will be   106
Where your own eyes will answer that for you,
Seeing the reason why that blast beats down,'

And one of the wretches from the icy crust   109
Called out to us: 'O spirits so merciless
That you are assigned to the last station of all,

Remove the stony veils from my face,   112
So that the grief can issue from my heart
A little, before the tears freeze up again.'

I said to him: 'If you would have me help you,   115
Tell me who you are, and if I give no relief,
May I go down to the bottom of the ice.'

He then replied: 'I am Brother Alberigo;   118
I am he of the fruits of the evil garden,
Who get what I deserve for what I gave.'

'Oh,' I said to him, 'are you already dead?'   121
And he to me: 'How it stands with my body
In the world above, I have no knowledge here.

For Ptolomaea has this privilege,   124
That oftentimes a soul may sink down here
Before Atropos sends it on its way.

And so that you may the more willingly   127
Remove the glaze of tears from off my face,
Know, that as soon as any soul betrays,

130   As I did, then his body is taken from him
        By a demon, who afterwards governs it
        Until his time on earth comes to an end.

133   The soul crashes down into the pit;
        And it may be that the body of this shadow
        Who winters here behind me, is still on earth.

136   You should know that, if you have just come down:
        He is ser Branca d'Oria, and many years
        Have passed since he was shut up in this manner.'

139   'I think,' I said to him, 'that you deceive me;
        For Branca d'Oria has never died;
        He eats and drinks and sleeps and puts on clothes.'

142   'In the Malebranche's ditch above,' he said,
        'There where the sticky pitch is always boiling,
        Michael Zanche had not yet arrived

145   When this man left a devil in his place
        In his body, and in one of his kindred,
        Who did the treachery along with him.

148   But now stretch out your hand in my direction;
        Open my eyes.' I did not open them;
        It was a courtesy to treat him ill.

151   Ah, Genoese, men who are strangers to
        All usages, and full of rottenness,
        Why have you not been scattered from the world?

154   For, with the worst spirit of Romagna,
        I found one of you, such that for his works,
        His soul already bathes in Cocytus,

157   And, in his body, still seems alive on earth.

CANTO XXXIV

'*Vexilla regis prodeunt inferni*
Towards us now; so look ahead and see,'
My master said, 'whether you can discern him.'

As when a thick mist spreads itself around,   4
Or when night is falling, in our hemisphere,
And a turning windmill shows up in the distance,

I thought that I saw some such structure;   7
Then, for the wind, I shrunk behind my guide,
Because there was no other shelter there.

I was already, and with fear I put it   10
Into my poem, there where the shades were covered
Completely, and showed up like straws in glass.

Some lying flat, and some of them upright,   13
One on his head, another on his feet;
Another, like a bow, bent foot to face.

When we had made our way so far forward   16
That it pleased the master to point out
The creature which had once been so handsome,

He moved away from me and made me stop;   19
'That is Dis,' he said, 'and this is the place
Where you will need your courage to protect you.'

How frozen and how faint I then became,   22
Do not enquire, reader, description is useless,
For any speech would be inadequate.

I did not die, nor yet remain alive: 25
Think for yourself, if you have a trace
Of intellect, how I was, in that condition.

The emperor of the kingdom of pain   28
Had half his chest sticking out of the ice;
I am nearer to being as tall as the giants

31   Than the giants are to being as big as his arms:
      See now how great the whole of him must be,
      Proportionate to such parts as that.

34   If he was as beautiful as he now is ugly,
      And yet dared to rebel against his maker,
      Well may he be the source of all mourning.

37   Oh, what a wonder it appeared to me,
      When I saw three faces on his head!
      One, which was of fiery red, in front;

40   The other two, which were grafted on to that,
      Stood one above the middle of each shoulder,
      And came together where his crest was;

43   The right-hand one seemed between white and yellow;
      The one on the left had the look of those
      Who come from where the Nile has its source.

46   Under each face protruded two great wings,
      Each as would seem right for a bird of that size,
      Broader than any sea-sails I ever saw.

49   They had no feathers, but their make-up was
      More like a bat's; and he so fluttered them
      That three several winds went out from him.

52   It was by them all Cocytus was frozen;
      With six eyes he wept, and down three chins
      Dripped tears and dribble, mixed with blood.

55   In each mouth he was chewing with his teeth
      A sinner, as if pounding him with spikes,
      So that he kept the three of them in torment.

58   For the one who was in front, the biting was nothing
      Compared with the clawing, so that at times his spine
      Was left stripped of every scrap of skin.

61   'That soul there, which has the worst punishment,
      Is Judas Iscariot,' my master said,
      'With his head inside, and kicking his legs.'

Of the two other, who hang upside-down,   64
The one who hangs from the black face is Brutus;
See how he twists and says not a word;

And the other is Cassius, whose body looks so heavy.   67
But night is rising once more, now is the time
We should be off, for we have seen everything.'

As he wished, I put my arms round his neck;   70
And he chose his time and position with care;
And when he saw the wings were spread wide,

He caught hold of Dis's hairy sides: 73
And then went down from one knot to the next,
Between the thick hair and the frozen crust.

When we were at the point where the thigh hinges,   76
Just where the haunch begins to widen,
My guide, with laborious effort,

Turned his head to where his legs had been,   79
Catching hold of the hair as if to climb,
So that I thought we were going back to hell.

'Hold tight, for this is where we climb up,'   82
My master said, panting as if he were weary,
'We must do, to leave so much evil behind.'

Then he went out through a hole in the rock;   85
He made me sit on the edge of it,
And then warily climbed up to where I was.

I raised my eyes, and I expected to see   88
Lucifer just as I had left him;
I saw him with his legs uppermost;

And if I was perplexed at that moment,   91
Let stolid people judge, who do not see
What point it was that I had just passed.

'Get up,' the master said, 'get on your feet: 94
The way is long and the road difficult,
And the sun is already well up in the sky.'

97   It was not like a chamber in a palace,
     Where we were, but a natural dungeon rather,
     Ill-floored and with a want of light.

100 'Before I pull myself out of the abyss,
     My master,' I said when I was on my feet,
     'Tell me something, to rescue me from error.

103 Where is the ice? And how is he fixed like that,
     Upside-down? And how, in so little time,
     Has the sun moved from evening to morning?'

106 And he to me: 'You think that you are still
     The other side of the centre, where I took hold
     Of the hair of the beast who makes a hole in the world.

109 You *were* there, as long as I was going down;
     When I turned head-over-heels, you passed the point
     On which the weights bear down from every side.

112 And now you have arrived under the hemisphere
     Opposite to that which covers the dry
     Half of the world, under whose topmost point

115 There died the man who was born and lived without sin;
     You are standing above a little circular place
     Which corresponds to Judecca on the other side.

118 Here it is morning when it is evening there;
     And the beast down whose hair I climbed
     Is still fixed in the way he was before.

121 On this side he fell down from heaven;
     And the land which before rose on this side,
     Through fear of him, covered itself with sea

124 And came into our hemisphere; and so perhaps
     That which can still be seen here fled from him,
     Leaving an empty space and rushing upwards.'

127 There is a place down there, remote from Beelzebub,
     As far as that tomb-like passage runs,
     Which is known not from sight, but from the sound

Of a small stream which trickles down that way,   130
Through a hollow in a rock, which it has worn
In its course, which winds round, and slowly falls.

My guide and I started out on that road,   133
Through its obscurity to return to the bright world;
And not worrying about taking any rest,

We mounted up, he first and I second,   136
So that I saw some of the lovely things
That are in the heavens, through a round opening;

And then we emerged to see the stars again.   139

PURGATORIO

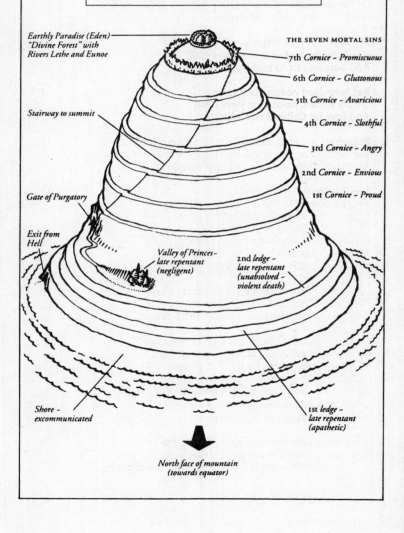

DANTE'S MOUNT PURGATORY
in the Southern Hemisphere of Oceans

Earthly Paradise (Eden)
"Divine Forest" with
Rivers Lethe and Eunoe

THE SEVEN MORTAL SINS

7th *Cornice* - *Promiscuous*

6th *Cornice* - *Gluttonous*

5th *Cornice* - *Avaricious*

Stairway to summit

4th *Cornice* - *Slothful*

3rd *Cornice* - *Angry*

2nd *Cornice* - *Envious*

1st *Cornice* - *Proud*

Gate of Purgatory

Exit from
Hell

Valley of Princes-
late repentant
(negligent)

2nd *ledge* -
late repentant
(unabsolved -
violent death)

Shore -
excommunicated

1st *ledge* -
late repentant
(apathetic)

North face of mountain
(towards equator)

CANTO I

To run on better water now, the boat
Of my invention hoists its sails and leaves
Away to stern that cruel stretch of sea;

And I will sing of this second kingdom
In which the human spirit cures itself
And becomes fit to leap up into heaven.

But here dead poetry rises again,   7
O holy Muses, since I am your own,
And here let Calliope rise a little,

Following my song with that sound from which   10
The pitiful Magpies felt so sharp a blow
That they despaired of ever being pardoned.

Sweet colour of oriental sapphire,   13
Which gathered in the clear face of the sky,
Right to the very edge of the first circle,

Restored to my eyes the touch of pleasure,   16
As soon as I issued from the dead air
Which had saddened my eyes and my heart.

The lovely planet which gives comfort in love   19
Was filling the whole eastern sky with laughter,
Hiding the Fish which followed in her train.

I turned towards the right, and fixed my mind   22
On the other pole, and there I saw four stars,
Never yet seen except by the first people.

The sky seemed to be glad in their sparkling: 25
O northern hemisphere, you are a widow
To be deprived of any sight of them!

When I had given up looking at those stars   28
And turned a little towards the other pole,
To where the Wain should have been, but it was gone;

31   I saw near me an old man, alone,
     With looks deserving as much reverence
     As ever any son owed to his father.

34   He wore his beard long and there were white strands
     In it, like his hair which tumbled down
     In two white bunches over his chest and shoulders;

37   The beams which came from those four holy lights
     So played upon his face and lit it up
     That I saw him as if he had been facing the sun.

40   'Who are you, who, going against the current
     Of the blind stream, have escaped the eternal prison?'
     He said, with a movement of his honoured plumage.

43   'Who was your guide? Whom did you have for lamp
     To bring you out of the profound night
     Which always darkens the infernal valley?

46   And are the laws of the abyss so broken?
     Or has there been a change of plan in heaven,
     So that, though damned, you come here to my rocks?'

49   My escort then took hold of me, and with
     Words and touch and other indications
     Made me bend knees and head in reverence.

52   Then he replied: 'It was not of myself
     I came: a lady from heaven asked me
     To help this man by bearing him company.

55   But since it is your will we should declare
     More fully what our true condition is,
     My will cannot be to say no to that.

58   This man has not yet seen his last evening;
     But, through his madness, was so close to it
     That there was hardly time to turn about.

61   As I have told you, I was sent to him
     To rescue him; and there was no other way
     Than this which I have set myself to follow.

I have shown him all the wicked people; now 64
I have in mind to show him all those spirits
Who cure themselves here under your care.

How I conducted him, would be a long story; 67
Virtue comes down from above and gives me help
In bringing him to see you and listen to you.

Now treat his coming as acceptable: 70
He looks for liberty, which is so loved,
As he knows who gives up his life for her.

You know this: that is why death was not bitter 73
To you in Utica, where you abandoned
That garment which will shine in the last day.

The eternal laws had no damage by us; 76
For this man is alive, I am not with Minos;
I am of the same circle as the chaste eyes

Of your Marcia, who is still to be seen praying, 79
O holy breast, that you will recognise her:
For her love, therefore, may you be inclined

To let us journey through your seven kingdoms: 82
I will convey your thanks to her, if you
Do not disdain to be mentioned in that place.'

'Marcia so pleased my eyes,' Cato replied, 85
'When I was still outside these present bounds,
That everything she asked of me, I did.

Now that she stays beyond the evil river, 88
She can move me no longer, by that law
Which was made when I issued from that place.

But if a lady from heaven moves and commands you, 91
As you assert, no need for flattery:
It is enough that you ask in her name.

Go therefore now, and put on him a girdle 94
Of simple rush, and wash his face, so that
Every trace of filth is removed from it;

97   For it would not do to go before
The first of the ministers of paradise
With the eyes dulled by any kind of mist.

100   All round about the base of this little island,
There where the waves are always beating on it,
Are rushes growing over the soft mud;

103   No other plant which puts out leaves and hardens
Itself, would ever live in such a place,
Because it would not give to the buffetings.

106   Afterwards do not come this way again;
The sun will show you, it is rising now,
A gentler way to take to climb the mountain.'

109   With that he disappeared; and I got up
Without a word, and went back to my escort
And turned my eyes entirely towards him.

112   He began: 'Follow my footsteps, let us turn
Back, for the plain slopes downwards here
Until it finishes at its lowest point.'

115   The dawn was conquering the morning hour
Which fled before it, so that far away
I recognised the trembling of the sea.

118   We went along over the lonely plain,
Like a man turning back to a road he has lost,
Who thinks he is wasting time until he finds it.

121   When we were at the point at which the dew
Resisted the sun, and, being on a stretch
Where there was shade, evaporated slowly,

124   My master gently stretched out both his hands
And touched the fine young grass; and when I saw
What his intention was, I proffered

127   My cheeks which were stained with tears, and there
He brought to light my natural complexion,
Which hell had hidden.

We came then to the deserted shore   130
Which never saw, sailing upon its waters,
Any who afterwards knew how to return.

Then he gave me the girdle another had willed for me;   133
And when he picked the plant of humility,
Miraculously it renewed itself at once,

Just in the very place from which he had taken it.   136

CANTO II

Already the sun had reached the horizon
Of which the meridian circle, at its highest
Point, passes directly through Jerusalem;

And the night, which circles on the opposite side,   4
Issued out from the Ganges with the Scales
Which fall from her hand when she is sovereign;

So that from where I was the white and red   7
Of the lovely Aurora seemed to be
Turning to orange as if she were old.

We were wandering along the shore still,   10
Like people who are thinking about their route,
Advancing in mind, but in their bodies, halting.

And there as, at the approach of morning,   13
Through the close-gathered mists Mars glows deep red,
Down in the west, above the level sea,

So appeared to me—may it not be the last time—   16
A light coming over the sea so swiftly
That its motion was faster than any flight;

So that when I had withdrawn my gaze   19
A little, to make enquiry of my escort,
I saw it again already brighter and bigger.

22   Then on each side of it appeared to me
        A little blob of white; and from underneath,
        Bit by bit, another blob appeared.

25   My master still stood there without a word,
        Until the first whiteness appeared as wings:
        Then he easily recognised the pilot.

28   He cried: 'Quickly, quickly, bend your knees:
        It is the angel of God: put your hands together:
        From now on you will see such officers.

31   See how he scorns all human implements,
        So that he does not wish to have other sail,
        Between such distant shores, than his own wings.

34   See how he has them straight against the sky,
        Striking the air with his eternal wings,
        Which are not ruffled as mortal hair would be.'

37   Then, as little by little the divine bird
        Advanced towards us, it appeared the brighter,
        Until my eyes could not bear it so near,

40   And I lowered them: and he then came ashore
        With a vessel so nimble and so light
        That it did not displace any water.

43   At the stern there stood the celestial helmsman,
        Whose blessedness was written all over him;
        And more than a hundred spirits sat on board.

46   'In exitu Israel de Aegypto'
        They sang together with a single voice,
        With all that follows those words in the psalter.

49   Then over them, he made the sign of the cross;
        And thereupon they threw themselves on the shore:
        And he departed, as he had come, swiftly.

52   The crowd left there seemed to be shy of the place
        And stared around them with the look of people
        Who are familiarising themselves with novelties.

On every side the sun was showering day,   55
Having already with its single arrows
Driven Capricorn from the middle of the sky,

When the newcomers raised their faces towards us,   58
And spoke to us: 'If you know where the way is,
Show us how we should go to the mountain.'

And Virgil answered: 'You perhaps may think   61
That we are people familiar with this place:
But we in fact are strangers, as you are;

We came just now, only a little before you,   64
By another way, which is so rough and hard
That climbing now will seem like sport to us.'

The spirits who, by their attention to me,   67
From my breathing, saw that I was alive,
Wondered at the fact, and became pale.

And as, to the messenger who bears the olive,   70
People are drawn in order to hear the news
And nobody seems to worry about being stepped on,

So on my face those spirits, who one and all   73
Were fortunate, fastened their gaze, almost
Forgetting to go and make themselves fair.

I saw one of them pull out of the crowd   76
To embrace me, with such a show of feeling
As moved me to make a similar gesture.

O shadows empty of all but appearances!   79
Three times at his back I clasped my hands,
And each time brought them back to my chest.

With wonder, I think, I must have changed colour,   82
Because the shadow smiled, and drew back,
And I followed him and moved forward.

Gently he told me that I should be still: 85
Then I knew who he was, and begged him
That he would stop a moment to talk to me.

88   He answered me: 'Just as I loved you in
      My mortal body, so I love you now I am free of it:
      Therefore I stop; but why are you going this way?'

91   'Dear Casella, in order to come back
      Where I now am, that's why I am making this journey,'
      I said; 'but how have you lost so much time?'

94   And he to me: 'No one has done me wrong,
      If he who takes when and whom he likes
      Has several times refused me passage here;

97   For it is of a just will that his is made:
      True enough that for three months he has taken
      Whoever wished to enter, in all peace.

100   So I, who then had turned to the sea-shore
      There where the water of the Tiber grows salt,
      Was with benignity received by him.

103   To that estuary he now directs
      His wings, because it is there that everyone
      Is received, who is not to sink to Acheron.'

106   And I: 'If a new law has not taken from you
      The memory or the use of that love-song
      Which used to quieten my every desire,

109   Will you be kind enough to console my spirit
      A little by that means, for it is very weary
      Since I have come here in my own body.'

112   'Love which discourses with me in my mind,'
      He began to sing, and so sweetly
      That the sweetness still sounds inside me now.

115   My master and I and those people
      Who were with him seemed to be so content
      That no other thing could touch their minds.

118   We were all fixed and listening to his notes
      When suddenly the good old man cried out:
      'What are you doing, all you idle spirits?

What negligence, what dawdling is there here?   121
Run to the mountain and strip the outer skin
Which stops God being manifest to you.'

As when, having found corn or greenstuff, pigeons   124
Are gathered in a flock at their feeding-ground,
Quietly and not showing their usual vanity,

If something appears which makes them afraid,   127
Suddenly they leave their feeding where it is
Because they are assailed by greater cares,

So I saw that band of newcomers   130
Abandon the song and go towards the hillside
Like people going without knowing where they will get to:

And our own departure was no less rapid.   133

CANTO III

Although they were being scattered over the plain
In sudden flight, turning towards the mountain
On which human beings are ransacked by reason,

I drew closer to my faithful companion: 4
And how should I have gone on without him?
Who would have brought me up the mountain?

He seemed to me bitten by his own reproaches: 7
O conscience so precious and so clear,
How small a fault is a sharp tooth to you!

When his feet had ceased from that haste   10
Which detracts from the honour of any action,
My mind which had before felt constrained,

Desirously let its purpose break out   13
And I set my face towards the eminence
That rises highest to heaven from the sea.

16   The sun, which was burning red behind us,
       Was interrupted in front by my shadow,
       For its rays were stopped as I stood there.

19   I turned to one side with the apprehension
       That I might have been abandoned, when I saw
       That it was only in front of me that the ground was darkened.

22   And my comfort said: 'Why are you afraid?'
       He began to speak, turning completely towards me:
       'Did you think I was not with you, guiding you?

25   It is already evening where there lies buried
       The body within which I made a shadow;
       Naples has it; it was taken from Brindisi.

28   Now, if there is no shadow before me,
       Do not be more amazed than at the heavens
       Which do not stand in the path of any ray.

31   Omnipotence disposes bodies like mine
       To suffer torments both from heat and cold,
       And how it does so, does not see fit to reveal.

34   Only a madman would expect our reason
       To follow all that infinite approach
       And understand one substance in three persons.

37   The human race should be content with the *quia*:
       For if it had been able to see everything,
       No need for Mary to have had a child.

40   And you have seen some whose desires would
       Have been satisfied, desiring fruitlessly,
       Which is their lot in their eternal grief:

43   I speak of Aristotle and of Plato
       And many more.' And here he bent his head,
       And said no more, and he continued troubled.

46   We arrived meanwhile at the foot of the mountain:
       And there we found the rock was so steep
       That though our legs were willing it was in vain.

Between Lerici and Turbia, the most deserted,   49
The most broken-down road, compared to this,
Is like an open and convenient stairway.

'Now who knows which side the slope comes down,'   52
My master said, and halted where he stood,
'So that we can get up there without wings?'

And while he, holding his head down,   55
Considered in his mind what way to go,
I was looking up around the rocks.

On the left hand appeared a crowd of spirits   58
Who, though they moved their feet towards us, appeared
Not to be coming, so slowly did they come.

'Master,' I said, 'if you raise your eyes   61
You will see those who will give us advice,
If from yourself there is none to be had.'

He looked, and with an appearance of relief   64
Replied: 'Let's go to them, since they come slowly;
And, my sweet son, may your hope be confirmed.'

The group was still at some distance from us,   67
I mean after we had gone a thousand paces,
About as far as a good slingsman can throw,

When they all pressed close to the hard rocks   70
Of the high bank and stood still, huddled together,
As a man stands to stare when he is uncertain.

'Spirits who finished well, already elect,'   73
Virgil began, 'by that peace which, I believe,
Is now awaited by each one of you,

Tell us where the mountain-side slopes so   76
That it is possible to go up higher;
For those who know most, dislike most to dawdle.'

As sheep do when they come out of a fold,   79
By ones and twos and threes, and the others stand
Timidly putting nose and eyes to earth;

82   And what the first one does, the others do,
     Crowding up to her if she happens to stop,
     Simple and quiet, without knowing why;

85   So I saw the heads of that happy flock,
     Moving as if to come forwards, their expression
     Modest and their deportment unpretentious.

88   As those in front saw that there was a break
     In the light on the grass to the right of me,
     So that the shadow went from me to the rock,

91   They stopped, and then they drew back a little,
     And all the others who were coming behind,
     Not knowing why they did so, did the same.

94   'Without you asking I will confess to you
     That this is a human body that you see;
     That is why the sunlight on the ground is broken.

97   No need to be astonished: but believe
     That it is not without virtue from heaven
     That he is seeking to surmount that wall.'

100 So spoke my master: and those honest people
     Said: 'Turn, you must then enter before us';
     And showed the backs of their hands, as they beckoned.

103 And one of them began: 'Whoever you may be,
     Going upon your way here, turn your face:
     Consider if you ever saw me anywhere.'

106 I then turned towards him and looked straight at him:
     He was fair and well-made and of gentle aspect,
     But one of his eyebrows split in two by a cut.

109 When I had modestly denied
     That I had ever seen him, he said: 'Now look!'
     And showed me a wound above his breast.

112 Then with a smile he said: 'I am Manfred,
     The grandson of the empress Constantia;
     And so I beg of you, when you go back,

Go to my lovely daughter, who is the mother   115
Of the two honoured in Sicily and Aragon,
And tell her the truth, if something else is told.

After I had had my body broken   118
By two mortal thrusts, I gave myself up,
Weeping, to him who pardons willingly.

My sins were horrible indeed: 121
But infinite goodness has so wide an embrace
That it takes everyone that turns to it.

If then the shepherd of Cosenza, set   124
On my tracks by Clement, to hunt me down,
Had but read carefully that page in God,

The bones of my body would still lie   127
At the head of the bridge by Benevento,
And still be guarded by those heavy stones.

Now the rain washes them and the wind moves them,   130
Outside the kingdom, and beside the Verde,
Where they were taken with extinguished lamps.

By their ill speaking men are not so lost   133
That they cannot turn to eternal love,
As long as hope has any touch of green.

True it is, he who dies in contumacy   136
Of Holy Church, although at last he repents,
Has then to stay here, below the slope,

For thirty times as long as he persisted   139
In his presumption, unless this decree
Is made shorter by efficacious prayers.

See if, hereafter, you can make me glad,   142
Revealing to my dear Constantia
How you have seen me, and this prohibition;

For here, advancement comes from those elsewhere.   145

CANTO IV

When as a result of pleasure or pain
Which any faculty of ours experiences
The soul withdraws itself into that faculty,

4   It seems to notice none of its other powers;
And this is contrary to that error which holds
That, in us, one soul lights up above another.

7   And so, when anything is heard or seen,
Which keeps the soul steadily directed towards it,
Time passes and the man is unaware;

10 Because the faculty which perceives time
Is different from the one which absorbs the soul:
The latter is bound while the former is free.

13 Of this I had actual experience,
While I was listening to that spirit and marvelling;
For the sun had risen full fifty degrees

16 Without my having observed what had happened,
When we arrived where those souls called out to us,
With one voice: 'This is what you were looking for.'

19 A bigger opening is often closed up by
A peasant with a forkful of thorns,
When he sees the grapes are ripening,

22 Than was the gap we climbed through
Alone, my guide first, and I after him,
As the company parted from us.

25 You can go through Sanleo and get down to Noli;
Or climb up to the top of Bismantova,
And keep on your feet; but here you have to fly;

28 I mean with the agile wings and feathers
Of strong desire, under the conduct of him
Who gave me hope and was a light to me.

We were climbing inside the split rock,   31
And had to squeeze between the two sides,
And the ground needed our hands as well as our feet.

After we had arrived at the top edge   34
Of the precipice and could see the open hillside,
I said: 'Master, which way shall we go?'

And he to me: 'Let no step of yours be wasted;   37
Only keep going up the mountain behind me
Until some experienced guide appears.'

The summit was so high that we could not see it,   40
And the slope was certainly steeper
Than forty-five degrees at this point.

I was exhausted when I began: 43
'O sweet father, turn round, and look,
I shall be left behind if you do not stop.'

'My son,' he said, 'drag yourself up there,'   46
And pointed to a terrace a little higher,
Which on that side circled the whole mountain.

His words spurred me so   49
That I forced myself to scramble after him,
Until at last the ledge was under my feet.

At that point both of us sat down,   52
Facing the east from which we had climbed
And which men usually look at with pleasure.

My first look was for the shore below;   55
Then I looked up at the sun, and marvelled
That its rays struck us from the left.

The poet clearly saw that I was astonished   58
To find that the vehicle of light
Was starting its course between us and the north.

So he said to me: 'If Castor and Pollux   61
Were in the company of that mirror
Which brings light up and down the world,

64   You would see the glowing part of the Zodiac
       Rotate even more closely to the Bears,
       If it was not to stray from its old path.

67   If you wish to consider how that may be,
       Reflect a little, and imagine Zion
       And this mountain and their position on earth,

70   With both of them having a single horizon,
       But different hemispheres; so that the route
       Which Phaeton did not know how to drive along,

73   Must, you will see, pass one of them on one side
       While it passes the other on the other,
       If you have that clearly in your mind.'

76   'Certainly, dear master,' I said, 'I have never
       Seen so clearly as I discern now
       Where my understanding was deficient;

79   The middle circle of the turning heavens,
       Which in one of the sciences is called the Equator
       And which is permanently between summer and winter,

82   Is, for the reason you give, as far away
       From us here, in a northerly direction
       As, for the Hebrews, it was towards the south.

85   But if it pleases you, I should like to know
       How far we have to go; for the hillside climbs
       Higher than my eyes can follow it.'

88   And he to me: 'This mountain is such
       That the first part of the ascent is always hard
       And the higher a man goes, the less hard it is.

91   Therefore, when it becomes so agreeable
       That the ascent becomes as easy to you
       As movement to a boat that is going with the current,

94   Then you will be near the end of this path;
       There you may hope to rest from your exertion.
       I can tell you no more, but that I know for certain.'

And when he had finished what he had to say,   97
A voice sounded near us: 'It may well be
That before then you will want to sit down!'

At that sound both of us turned round   100
And we saw on the left hand a great boulder
Which neither I nor he had noticed before.

We drew near; and there we saw people   103
Standing in the shade behind the rock
In the attitude of men in idleness.

And one of them, who seemed to me weary,   106
Was sitting, with his hands clasped round his knees,
And his head bowed down and touching them.

'O my sweet lord,' I said, 'look at that one   109
Who has the air of being more indifferent
Than if indolence herself was his sister.'

Then he turned towards us attentively,   112
Only moving his face without raising it,
And said: 'Then you go up, since you are so clever!'

I knew then who he was, and that weariness   115
Which still made it difficult for me to breathe
Did not prevent my going to him; and when

I had reached him, he hardly raised his head,   118
Saying: 'Have you really seen how the sun
Draws his vehicle over your left shoulder?'

His lazy actions and laconic speech   121
Moved my lips into a little smile;
Then I began: 'Belacqua, I am not worried

About you now; but tell me: why are you sitting   124
In this place now? Are you waiting for an escort,
Or are you simply going back to old habits?'

And he: 'Brother, what is the good of going up?'   127
The angel of God sits above the gate
And would not allow me to go to the torments.

130   Before that happens the heavens must revolve around me,
      With me outside here, as often as they did in my life,
      Because I postponed repentance to the end;

133   Unless before that some prayer which rises
      From some heart which lives in grace, should help me,
      For what use are the others, not heard in heaven?'

136   And already the poet was climbing before me,
      And he said: 'Come now: you see that the sun
      Touches meridian and, upon the shore

139   Night already sets foot on Morocco.'

CANTO V

     I had already parted from those shadows,
     And was following the footsteps of my guide,
     When one behind me pointing with his finger,

4   Cried: 'See, it does not look as if the light
     Shines on the left of the lower of those two,
     And surely he has the air of a live man!'

7   I turned my eyes at the sound of these words,
     And saw them staring with astonishment
     At me, and me again, and the broken light.

10   'Why is your mind so caught up in a tangle,'
     My master said, 'that you slacken your pace?
     And what does all this whispering matter to you?

13   Come on behind me, let those people talk:
     Stand like a solid tower which does not shake
     Its top whatever winds are blowing on it;

16   Because the man in whom thoughts bubble up
     One after the other, goes wide of the mark,
     Because one thought weakens the force of another.'

What could I say to that except: 'I'm coming'?   19
I said it, not without colouring a little
As men who deserve forgiveness sometimes do.

And meanwhile, there came across the hillside,   22
A little ahead of us, people who were singing
A *Miserere*, verse by verse in turn.

When they perceived my body did not yield   25
A passage to the rays of the sun, they changed
Their song into a hoarse, long-drawn out 'Oh!'

And two of them, as if they were messengers,   28
Ran over in our direction with the request:
'Will you inform us what state you are in?'

And my master replied: 'You can go back   31
And report to the others who sent you here
That this man's body is of real flesh.

If they stopped because they saw his shadow,   34
As I suppose, that is enough of an answer:
Tell them to honour him, he might be useful.'

I never saw meteors fall so fast   37
From the clear sky in a summer night,
Nor lightning from the August clouds at sunset,

So fast as they turned back and went uphill;   40
And, having reached the others, swept back with them
Like a troop of cavalry riding without rein.

'The people pressing round us is numerous,   43
And come to you asking,' the poet said:
'But go on, and listen as you go.'

'O soul going on the way to blessedness   46
With the same limbs you had when you were born,'
They came crying, 'will you not stop a moment?

See whether you have ever set eyes on any of us,   49
So that you can take news of us back there:
Oh, why do you go on? Why will you not stop?

52   We all are people who met a violent death,
     And were all sinners up to the last hour:
     But then the light of heaven made us wary,

55   So that, repenting and forgiving, we
     Came out of life having made our peace with God,
     Who stabs us with desire of seeing him.'

58   And I: 'However hard I look at your faces,
     I recognise none of you; but if anything
     I can do may please you, spirits happily born,

61   Tell me, and I will do it for that peace
     Which makes me seek it out from world to world,
     Following the footsteps of a guide like this.'

64   And one began: 'Each one of us will trust
     To your well-doing without your swearing to it,
     Unless not being able lames your will.

67   So I, who alone speak before the others,
     Beg you, if ever you see that country
     Which lies between Romagna and that of Charles,

70   That you should speak kindly for me in Fano,
     So that there may be good prayers said for me
     And I be able to purge my grave offences.

73   I was from there: but the profound wounds
     Whence flowed the blood in which my life resided
     Were dealt me in the midst of the Antenori,

76   There where I thought I should be most secure:
     The prince of Este had it done, he was angry
     With me beyond what could be held just.

79   But if I had made my escape towards La Mira,
     When I was set upon at Oriaco,
     I should still be there in the land of the living.

82   I ran to the marshes, and the rushes and the mud
     So caught my feet that I fell; and I saw there
     A pool from my veins form on the ground.'

Then another said: 'If you would satisfy   85
The desire which draws you up the high mountain,
Of your good charity help my desire.

I was from Montefeltro: I am Bonconte: 88
Giovanna and the others have no care for me;
Therefore I go among these with head bowed.'

And I to him: 'What violence or what chance   91
Led you so far astray from Campaldino,
That your place of burial was never known?'

'Oh,' he replied, 'at the foot of Casentino   94
Crosses a stream which is called the Archiano,
Which above the Eremo, rises in the Apennines.

There where there is no more use for its name,   97
I arrived, with a wound deep in my throat,
Fleeing on foot and leaving blood on the ground.

There I lost my sight and my speech;   100
I ended with the name of Mary, and there
My flesh fell and remained by itself.

I am telling the truth: you tell it again to the living: 103
The angel of God took me, and the angel of hell
Cried out: 'O you from heaven, why do you rob me?

You carry off the eternal part of him,   106
For one small tear he shed he is taken from me;
I will deal differently with what is left!'

You know that, in the air, damp vapour   109
Collects and turns to water again as soon
As it rises to where the cold condenses it.

He combined that evil will, which seeks ill only,   112
With intellect, and moved the mist and wind
By the power which his nature gave him.

Then, when the day was spent, he filled the valley,   115
From Pratomagno to the great yoke,
With mist; and he made the sky tense

118 So that the pregnant air changed into water:
The rain fell and into the channels ran
Whatever of it was not absorbed by the ground;

121 And as it came together in the great torrents
It rushed on towards the royal river
So swiftly, that nothing could hold it back.

124 The impetuous Archiano found my body
Frozen against its mouth; and pushed it on
To the Arno, and undid the cross on my breast

127 Which I had made when the pain overcame me:
It rolled me between the banks and along the river-bed,
And then covered and wound me in its spoil.'

130 'Pray when you go back to the world,
And are well rested after your long journey,'
The third spirit followed upon the second,

133 'Remember me then, who am La Pia:
Siena made me and Maremma undid me;
He knows it well, that man who, having declared

136 His formal intention, married me with his ring.'

CANTO VI

When people come away from a game of dice,
The loser stays on the spot, full of regrets,
Going over the throws, and is sadder and wiser:

4 Everybody else goes off with the winner;
One walks in front, another holds him back,
Another at his side says 'Don't forget me':

7 He does not stop, and listens to this one and that;
When he holds out his hand to someone, no more pressure;
And in this way he escapes from the crowd.

10 This is what I was like in that dense mob,
Facing first in one direction and then in another,
And by promises managed to get away.

There was the Aretine who met his death   13
At the fierce hands of Ghin di Tacco;
And the other who was drowned in the pursuit.

And there, imploring with outstretched hands,   16
Federigo Novello, and the Pisan
Who made the good Marzucco show how strong he was.

I saw Count Orso and the soul divided   19
From his body by envy and hatred,
As he said, and not for any wrong he did;

I mean Pierre de la Brosse; and while she still lives   22
The lady of Brabant had better look out
Or she will find herself in worse company.

When I had freed myself from all those shadows,   25
Whose prayer was only that other people should pray,
So that their own holiness would be accelerated,

I began: 'It seems to me that you deny,   28
O my light, expressly, in your book,
That prayer may deflect the will of heaven;

And that is all these people are praying for: 31
Must it not be then that their hope is vain,
Or is what you say not really clear to me?'

And he to me: 'My writing is quite plain;   34
And these people's hopes are not mistaken,
If the matter is considered with an open mind.

The supreme justice is not brought to nothing   37
Because the fire of love in an instant gives
Full satisfaction for the debt that is paid here.

And there, where I asserted this point,   40
A fault could not be put right by prayer,
Because the prayer was separated from God.

But certainly you should not make up your mind   43
On so profound a doubt unless you have it
From her who lights the intellect to truth:

46   I do not know whether you understand;
     I mean Beatrice: you will see her above,
     At the top of this mountain, smiling and happy.'

49   And I: 'Lord, let us go on faster,
     For already I am not so tired as I was before,
     And look, the hillside casts a shadow now.'

52   'We will go on as long as the day lasts,'
     He replied, 'as far as we may;
     But the fact of the matter is not as you suppose.

55   Before you reach the top, you will see the sun
     Rise again, already the hillside covers it,
     So that you do not interrupt the rays.

58   But see over there is a soul
     All on his own, and looking in our direction:
     He will tell us the quickest way to go.'

61   We came up to him: O you Lombard soul,
     How proud and full of disdain you were,
     And how courteously and slowly your eyes moved!

64   He did not utter a single word to us;
     But let us go on, only he kept us in view
     In the manner of a lion on the watch.

67   Only Virgil drew near him, asking him
     That he would show us which was the best way up;
     But he did not reply to that request,

70   But enquired about our country and condition;
     At which the gentle guide began: 'Mantua . . .'
     And the shadow, so withdrawn within himself,

73   Leapt towards him from the place where he had been,
     Saying: 'O Mantuan, I am Sordello,
     From your city.' And both of them embraced.

76   O enslaved Italy, a place of grief,
     A ship without a master in a great storm,
     Not mistress of provinces, but a brothel!

That noble mind was so ready,   79
Merely on hearing the sweet name of his city,
To give a welcome to his fellow-citizen;

And now your living children are always at war;   82
People thrown together within the same wall and ditch
Cannot live without biting one another.

Wretched country, look around your shores,   85
On every coast, and then into your heart
And see if any part enjoys peace.

What is the good of the Justinian code   88
To rein you in with, if the saddle is empty?
There would be less shame if you were without it.

And you people who are supposed to be devout   91
And to let Caesar sit well in his saddle,
If you understand properly what God prescribes,

Observe how this animal has grown vicious   94
For not having been corrected with spurs
Since you laid your hands upon the bridle.

O Albert the German, you who have abandoned   97
Her who has become untamed and wild,
When you should have been astride the saddle,

May a just judgement fall from the stars above   100
Upon your blood, strange and for all to see,
Such that it may be feared by your successor:

Because you and your father, preoccupied   103
By your greed there in Germany, have permitted
The garden of the empire to be turned into a desert.

Come and see, you who are negligent,   106
Montagues and Capulets, Monaldi and Filippeschi:
One lot already grieving, the other in fear.

Come, you are cruel, come and see the distress   109
Of your noble families, and cleanse their rottenness,
And you will see how dark Santafior is.

112 Come and see your Rome, which is in tears,
Widowed and alone, and calls day and night:
'My Caesar, why do you not bear me company?'

115 Come and see how the people love one another!
And if you are unmoved by pity for us,
Come and see what shame you have incurred.

118 And if it is allowed me, supreme Jove,
You who were crucified for us on earth,
Are your just eyes turned in another direction?

121 Or is it preparation in the depths
Of your counsel, for some future good
Which is quite hidden from our understanding?

124 For all the cities of Italy are full
Of tyrants, and any lout who chooses
To play with parties can become Marcellus.

127 My Florence, you may be well content
That this digression has nothing to do with you,
Thanks to your people who exert themselves so.

130 Many have justice in their hearts, and keep it there,
So that they don't let fly without reflection;
But your people have it on the tip of their tongues.

133 Many refuse to take public appointments;
But your people answer the call eagerly
Without being asked, and cry: 'I am ready to serve!'

136 Now rejoice, for you certainly have good reason:
You who are rich, at peace and so judicious:
If I speak truth, the facts are plain enough.

139 Athens and Sparta who were law-givers
In ancient times, and were so civilised,
Gave only a faint hint of how to do things,

142 Compared with you, who make so many clever
Arrangements that, by the middle of November,
You have used up all you earned in October.

How many times, in the years that you remember,   145
Have you changed laws and coinage, offices, customs,
And even brought in new inhabitants!

And if you see yourself in a clear light,   148
You will see that you resemble a sick woman
Who cannot stay quiet upon her bed

But twists and turns all the time to ease her pain.   151

CANTO VII

After the honourable and joyful greetings
Had been repeated three or four times,
Sordello drew back and asked: 'Who are you?'

'Before those souls worthy to climb to God   4
Had been turned in the direction of this mountain,
My bones were buried by Octavian.

I am Virgil; and for no other crime   7
Than not having had faith, I lost heaven':
That was the answer that my guide gave.

Like one who suddenly sees before him   10
Something by which he is filled with wonder,
Believing yet not, saying, 'It is . . . it isn't,'

So he seemed to be; and then he bent his head,   13
And in humility turned back towards Virgil
And embraced him with his arms about his knees.

'O glory of the Latins,' he said, 'through whom   16
Our language showed what it was able to do,
Eternal honour of my native place,

What merit or what grace show you to me?   19
If I am worthy to hear what you say,
Tell me if you come from hell, and from what corner?'

22   'Through all the circles of that painful kingdom,'
     He answered, 'I came here: it was a power
     From heaven moved me, and with that I come.

25   Not for what I have done but for what I have not done,
     I have lost the sight of the high sun you desire,
     And came to my knowledge too late.

28   There is a place down there where there is no torture,
     It is sad only from darkness, and the laments
     Have not the sound of woe, but they are sighs.

31   I am there with the innocent little children
     Bitten by the teeth of death before they were
     Exempted from the guilt of humankind;

34   I am there with those who did not put on
     The three holy virtues, and, without vice,
     Knew all the other virtues and followed them all.

37   But if you know, then tell us if you may,
     How we can most quickly reach the place
     At which Purgatory proper begins.'

40   He answered: 'No special place is given us;
     We are allowed to go up and around;
     So far as I may go, I will act as your guide.

43   But see how the day is declining,
     And there is no going up by night;
     We should, therefore, think where best to stay.

46   There are souls here, far away to the right:
     If you agree, I will conduct you to them,
     And knowing them will not be undelightful.'

49   'How is it?' was the reply. 'If anyone wanted
     To go up at night, would anyone hinder him,
     Or would he not go because he could not?'

52   And the good Sordello drew on the ground with his finger,
     Saying: 'You see, even that line
     You would not cross after the sun had gone;

Not that there would be any other impediment,   55
Except the nocturnal darkness, to stop you going:
But that would render your will impotent.

It is true that one might go down again   58
And wander round about the side of the mountain,
While the horizon keeps the day shut up.'

Then my lord, as if lost in wonderment,   61
Said: 'Lead us, therefore, where you say
We could rest and pass the time with delight.'

We had gone only a little distance forward   64
When I perceived there was a dip in the hillside,
Just as it might be with a valley here.

'There,' said the shadow, 'let us go in there,   67
Where the mountain makes a lap for us;
And there we will await the new day.'

Between steep and level was a crooked path   70
Which led us along the border of that hollow,
Where the edge more than half died away.

Gold and fine silver, cochineal and white lead,   73
Indigo, and brightly polished wood,
Fresh emerald at the moment it is split,

Would, all of them, be outshone by the colour   76
Of the grass and flowers growing in that hollow,
As the lesser is always outshone by the greater.

Not only had nature put colours there   79
But of the sweetness of a thousand odours
Made there a single vague and unknown scent.

I saw souls sitting there and they were singing   82
'*Salve Regina*' on the green and the flowers;
I had not seen them till we were in the valley.

'Do not desire that I should lead you there,'   85
Began the Mantuan who had guided us,
'Before what little sun there is takes its rest.

88   You will more easily be acquainted with
     All their faces and actions from this terrace
     Than if you were caught up with them in the dip.

91   The one with the highest seat, who has the look
     Of having neglected what he ought to have done,
     And does not move his lips when the others sing,

94   Was the Emperor Rudolph, who could have healed
     The wounds which have been mortal for Italy
     So that when another comes it will be too late.

97   That other, who appears to be comforting him,
     Ruled the land in which that water has its source
     Which the Moldau carries to the Elbe, and the Elbe to the sea;

100 Ottocar was his name, and he was better
     In infancy than Wenceslas his son,
     Lustful and idle, was when a full-grown man.

103 And that snub-nosed one who seems to be consulting
     The one who has so benign an aspect,
     Died retreating, and deflowering the lily.

106 Look at that one, how he is beating his breast!
     Then see the other who is resting his cheek
     In the palm of his hand, and as he does so, sighs.

109 They are the father and father-in-law of the blight of France:
     They know how tainted and depraved his life is,
     And for that reason they are transfixed with grief.

112 The one who looks so strong and sings together
     With that other one who has the aquiline nose,
     Wore his sword-belt with every mark of valour;

115 And if the young man who sits behind him
     Had remained king after he had died,
     The valour would have gone on from father to son,

118 Which cannot be said about the other heirs:
     Iacomo and Federigo have the kingdoms;
     But neither of them has the better inheritance.

Rarely does human worth rise through the branches;   121
That is the will of him whose gift it is,
So that it should be matter for petition.

My words apply to the one with the big nose,   124
As well as to Peter, with whom he is singing;
And that grieves Apulia and Provence.

So far was the seed degenerate,   127
That Constantia had more reason to boast
Of her husband, than Beatrice and Margherita of theirs.

Look at the king who led the simple life,   130
Sitting by himself, Henry of England:
But he had better fortune in his issue.

The one who stands lower than the others,   133
Gazing upward, is Guglielmo Marchese,
Through whom Alessandria and its war

Make Monferrate and Canavese weep.'   136

CANTO VIII

It was the hour when those who are at sea
Long to be back, and when their hearts grow tender,
The day they have said goodbye to their gentle friends:

The hour when the new pilgrim's heart is pierced   4
With love, if he hears the far-off bells
Which seem to weep for the dying day;

When I began to find my hearing empty   7
Of sound, and to fix my eyes on one of the souls
Who rose and with a gesture begged attention.

He put his hands together and raised them both,   10
With his eyes looking fixedly to the east,
As if saying to God: 'I care for nothing else.'

13   *'Te lucis ante'* came from his lips so devoutly,
      And with such sweet notes, that I was rapt
      Out of myself and every other thought:

16   And the others then sweetly and devoutly
      Accompanied him throughout the whole hymn,
      Fixing their eyes upon the spheres above.

19   Here, reader, look sharply to the truth,
      For the veil is now of such a fineness
      That it is easy to pass beyond it.

22   I saw that noble army turn its gaze
      Silently now, and still looking above,
      Pale and humble and as if expectant;

25   And saw come out of the sky and down to earth
      Two angels who carried flaming swords,
      Broken so that they were without points.

28   As green as little leaves just out of bud
      Were their robes, which fluttered as the green wings
      Beating behind them raised a little breeze.

31   The one took his stand a little above us,
      And the other came down on the opposite bank,
      So that the company was kept in the middle.

34   I could see their fair hair clearly enough;
      But looking at their faces, my eyes were dazzled,
      As any sense is, confounded by excess.

37   'Both of them come to us from Mary's bosom,'
      Sordello said, 'as sentinels for the valley,
      Because of the serpent which will appear any moment.'

40   So I, who did not know by what path,
      Turned round completely and drew closer,
      Suddenly frozen, to the reliable shoulders.

43   And Sordello said: 'Now at last let us go down
      Among the great shadows, and talk with them:
      To see you will be very welcome to them.'

I think I went down only three steps,   46
And was at the bottom, and I saw one gazing
Simply at me, as if he thought he knew me.

It was already the time when the air grows dark,   49
Yet not so much that, between his eyes and mine,
There were not revealed things which had been concealed.

He came towards me, and I advanced towards him: 52
'Noble judge Nino, what a pleasure it was
When I saw you were not among the offenders!'

We said all one can say by way of greeting;   55
Then he asked: 'How long is it since you came
To the foot of the mountain, over the distant waters?'

'From within the place of sorrow,' I said to him,   58
'I came this morning, and I am still alive,
Although, by my journey, I gain another life.'

And when my answer came to their ears,   61
Sordello and he made a movement backwards,
Like people who are suddenly bewildered.

One of them turned to Virgil, and the other   64
To one who was sitting there, and called: 'Up, Conrad,
Come and see what God, by his grace, has willed.'

Then he turned to me: 'By the singular love   67
You owe to him who hides his first reasons
So that there is no way to find them out,

When you are beyond the wide waters,   70
Tell my Giovanna she should pray for me,
There where there is an answer for the innocent.

I do not think her mother loves me now   73
That she has given up her white veils,
Which the poor woman will wish for again.

By her it may be easily understood   76
How little time a woman's love lasts
Without frequent rekindling by eye and touch.

79　The viper which the Milanese displays
　　Will not give so fine a burial
　　As she would have had from the Galluran cock.'

82　So he spoke, and his outward appearance
　　Was stamped with the marks of that just ardour
　　Which burns in the heart without excess.

85　My eager eyes looked only at the sky,
　　Only at the point at which the stars are slowest,
　　As a wheel is at the point nearest the axle.

88　And my escort: 'My son, what are you looking at?'
　　And I to him: 'I am looking at those three torches
　　With which the whole of the pole here is ablaze.'

91　Thereupon he to me: 'The four bright stars,
　　Which you saw this morning are low beyond there
　　And these have risen now to take their place.'

94　As he was speaking, Sordello drew our attention,
　　Saying: 'Look, there is our adversary';
　　And pointed with his finger where we should look.

97　On that side on which there was no bank
　　To the little valley, there appeared a snake,
　　Perhaps such as gave Eve the bitter food.

100　Among the grass and flowers, the evil serpent
　　Came, turning its head from time to time
　　And licking its back like an animal washing itself.

103　I did not see, and therefore cannot say,
　　In what manner the celestial hawks moved;
　　But I certainly saw both of them when they had moved.

106　Hearing the air split by the green wings,
　　The snake made off and the angels turned back,
　　Flying up to their stations unperturbed.

109　The shadow which had drawn close to the judge
　　When he called, throughout the whole attack
　　Had not taken his eyes off me for a moment.

'So may the light which is leading you above,   112
Find in your will as much wax as is needed
To bring you right to the enamelled summit,'

He began, 'if you have authentic news   115
Of Val di Magra and the neighbouring parts,
Tell me, for once I was important there.

I was called Conrad Malaspina; I am not   118
The elder of that name, but a descendant:
I bore my people the love which is here refined.'

'Oh,' I said to him, 'I have never visited   121
Your territories, but where in all Europe
Are there men by whom they are not talked of?

The fame which does honour to your house,   124
So cries up both the rulers and the country
That without having been there people know of them.

And I swear to you, as I would reach the summit,   127
That your race still is honoured, and has lost
Nothing in generosity or in valour.

Habit and nature have endowed it so   130
That, though the chief sinner twists the world,
Your race alone goes straight and scorns evil.'

And he: 'Now go: for the sun will not lie down   133
Seven times upon the bed the Ram bestrides
And covers with all its four feet, before

The courteous opinion you have uttered   136
Shall be nailed in the middle of your head
With bigger nails than the words of other men,

Unless execution of the judgement is stayed.'   139

CANTO IX

The concubine of ancient Tithonus
Was already growing pale at her eastern window,
As she issued from her lover's arms;

4 And her forehead was alight with jewels,
Set in the shape of that cold animal
Which lashes people with its tail;

7 And, in the place where we were, the night
Had made two of the steps by which she climbs
And the third already bending down its wings;

10 When I, who had with me something of Adam,
Defeated by sleep, lay down on the grass
Where all the five of us were already sitting.

13 At the hour at which the swallow begins
Her sad song at the approach of morning,
Perhaps in recollection of her first misfortunes;

16 And at which our minds are estranged
More from the flesh and less taken with thoughts,
And have visions which are almost divinations:

19 In a dream I thought I saw hanging
In the sky above, an eagle with golden feathers,
And wings open as if ready to drop;

22 And I thought that I was on that mountain
Where Ganymede abandoned his companions
When he was snatched up to the high consistory.

25 Within myself I thought: 'Perhaps it strikes
Only here ordinarily, and perhaps it disdains
To bear up in its claws prey from any other place.'

28 Then I thought that, when it had circled,
Terrible as lightning, it descended,
And carried me aloft into the fire.

There I thought that it and I burned,   31
And the imagined flames so stung me,
It could not be otherwise than that my dream was broken.

In such a manner was Achilles startled,   34
Casting his wakened eyes round about him
And not understanding where he might be,

When his mother took him away from Chiron   37
To Scyros, he being asleep in her arms,
To the place from which the Greeks later made him depart;

So I was startled, as from my face   40
Sleep fled, and I became pale,
As a man does when fear freezes him.

At my side there was only my comforter,   43
And the sun had been up more than two hours already,
And my face was turned towards the shore.

'Have no fear,' my master said to me;   46
'Be assured, we are in the right place:
Do not shrink, but put out all your strength.

You have now arrived at Purgatory: 49
See there the ridge which encloses it;
See the entrance where there is a gap.

Not long ago, in the first light before day,   52
When your soul was asleep inside you
Upon the flowers which adorn the place down there,

A lady came, and said: "I am Lucia: 55
Let me take that man who is asleep;
And so I will assist him on his way."

Sordello and the other noble essences   58
Remained: she took you, and as the day grew bright
Came up here; and I followed in her tracks.

She put you down here; and first her lovely eyes   61
Showed me where that open entrance was;
Then she and sleep both went away together.'

64   As a man whose misgivings are allayed,
     And whose fears are transformed into comfort,
     When once the truth has been revealed to him,

67   So I changed; and when my guide saw
     That I was calm, he moved up by the ridge,
     And I followed him towards the heights.

70   Reader, you see how my subject becomes
     More elevated; do not wonder if
     It is therefore presented with more art.

73   We were approaching, and were so placed
     That where at first had appeared to me a break,
     Or you might say, a sort of crack in the wall,

76   I saw a gate, which had three steps below it
     By way of approach, they were of different colours;
     And a porter who still did not say a word.

79   As my eyes were opened more widely,
     I saw him sitting on the top step,
     His face such that I could not look at him;

82   And in his hand he held a naked sword,
     Which so reflected the rays towards us
     That I tried often to look at it, but in vain.

85   'Stand there and answer: what is it you want?'
     He started by saying: 'Where is your escort?
     Look out, you may be worse for coming here.'

88   'A lady from heaven, who understands these things,'
     My master answered him, 'has just now told us:
     "You go that way: that is the gate there." '

91   'And may she assist your steps to blessedness,'
     The courteous gate-keeper began again:
     'Come forward therefore to these steps of ours.'

94   We came forward; and the first great tread
     Was white marble, so polished and smooth,
     That I saw myself in it as I appear.

And the second was coloured darker than purple,   97
Made of stone which was rough and charred,
And had cracks running through the length and breadth of it.

The third, which formed a heavy mass on top,   100
Appeared to me to be of porphyry as flaming
As blood which spurts out of a vein.

On this God's angel kept both his feet,   103
Sitting high up upon the threshold,
Which seemed to me to be of diamond stone.

My master took me up the three steps   106
In happy mood, and said to me: 'Ask
Humbly that the gate be opened up.'

Freely I threw myself at his holy feet;   109
I begged him to have pity and to open,
But first, I struck myself on the breast three times.

Seven P's he traced upon my forehead   112
With the point of his sword, and said: 'See that you wash
Those wounds, when you are in here.'

Ashes or earth which has been dug up dry   115
Would be the same colour as his garment was;
And from beneath it he drew out two keys.

One was of gold and the other was of silver: 118
First with the white one, after with the yellow,
He undid the gate, and I was content.

'Whenever one of these keys does not work,   121
So that it does not turn right in the lock,'
He said to me, 'then this road is not opened.

One is more precious; but the other needs   124
Skill and intelligence before it unlocks,
Because it is the one that unties the knot.

I have them from Peter; he has told me I should err   127
Rather on the side of opening than of closing,
If only people fall down at my feet.'

130 Then he pushed open the sacred gate,
Saying: 'Enter; but I give you warning
That anyone who looks back goes out again.'

133 And when the hinges of that sacred entrance
Turned on their pivots, because they are made
Of strong and ringing metal, there was not

136 A deeper groan, or one sounding more strident,
From the Tarpeia, when the good Metellus
Was taken from her, and she remained poor thereafter.

139 I turned attention to the first thunder
And seemed to hear a *Te Deum laudamus*
In a voice mingled with a delicious sound.

142 The impression made on me by what I heard
Was precisely that effect which is usual
When we hear people singing to an organ,

145 And only now and then understand the words.

CANTO X

When we were past the threshold of the gate
—Not used by souls which love perversity,
For that makes the crooked way look straight—

4 I knew it had been closed, by the clang;
And if I had turned my eyes towards it,
What excuse could have justified the fault?

7 We climbed through a division in the rock,
Which was moving on one side and the other
Like a wave which recedes and then approaches.

10 'Here we shall have to use a little skill,'
Began my escort, 'we must keep close in,
Now this way and now that, on the ebb side.'

This made our footsteps somewhat dilatory,   13
So that the diminished moon was gone
Back to lie down again in her bed,

Before we were out of the eye of the needle.   16
But when we were free of it, and in the open
Higher up, where the mountain towered above us,

I weary and both of us uncertain   19
Of our way, we stopped on a level place,
Lonelier than are roads through deserted lands.

From the edge which is the edge of emptiness   22
To the foot of the perpendicular high bank,
Would measure three times the length of a man;

And as far as my sight could wing its way,   25
First on the left side and then on the right,
The ridge appeared to be of the same pattern.

Before our feet had made any movement,   28
I noticed that the inner bank of the curve
(Which rose so sheer and had no way up it)

Was of white marble, and so decorated   31
With carvings that not only Polycletus
But nature herself would there be put to shame.

The angel who came to earth proclaiming   34
The peace which had been mourned for many years,
So opening heaven, long under interdict,

Appeared before us, so faithfully   37
Sculpted there, in a gentle attitude,
That he did not appear a dumb image.

You would have sworn that he was saying: 'Ave!'   40
For there also was the image of her
Who turned the keys to open the exalted love;

And her attitude was marked with those words: 43
Ecce ancilla Dei, as distinctly
As any figure stamped upon wax.

46 'Do not fix your mind on one place only,'
Said my gentle master, who was keeping me
On the side on which people have their hearts.

49 So I looked around me a little, and saw
Beyond Mary, and in the same direction
Where he was who was urging me on,

52 Another story carved upon the rock;
I therefore went past Virgil and approached it
So that it stood clearly before my eyes.

55 There, formed out of the marble itself,
The cart and the oxen, drawing the sacred ark,
To make us fear supererogation.

58 In front there appeared people; and they were all
Divided into seven choirs; of two of my senses,
One said: 'No'; the other, 'Yes, they are singing.'

61 Similarly, at the smoke from the incense,
As there portrayed, my sight and sense of smell
Found themselves in disagreement with each other.

64 There the humble psalmist went before
The blessed vessel, dancing with his skirts up,
And in that state seemed more and less than a king.

67 Opposite, at the window of a great palace,
The figure of Michal was shown, looking on
Like a woman who is scornful and sad.

70 I shifted my feet from the place where I stood,
To observe more closely another story,
Which beyond Michal shone white before me.

73 There was recorded the high glory
Of that ruler of Rome whose worth
Moved Gregory to his great victory;

76 I mean by this the Emperor Trajan;
And at his bridle a poor widow
Whose attitude bespoke tears and grief.

Around him was represented a great press   79
Of horsemen, and the banners with golden eagles
Could be seen moving above them in the wind.

The wretched woman, in the midst of all this,   82
Seemed to be saying: 'Lord, avenge my son,
Who is dead, so that my heart is broken.'

And he to be replying: 'Only wait   85
Till I come back.' And she: 'My lord, my lord!'
Like someone in whom grief is in a hurry,

'But if you don't come back?' And he: 'Whoever   88
Takes my place, will act.' She: 'What use to you
Are others' deeds, if you forget your own?'

So he said: 'Now be comforted, for I must   91
Carry out my duty before I go on:
Justice requires it and pity holds me back.'

He who never saw any new thing   94
Was the creator of this visible dialogue,
New to us because it is not found here.

While I was delighting myself with looking   97
At the images of such great humilities,
Which were dear to us for their maker's sake,

'See here—but they are not getting on very fast—,'   100
The poet murmured, 'are many people:
They will show us the way to the next stairs.'

My eyes, which were well content to look   103
To see something new, they were avid of such things,
Were not slow to turn in his direction.

I do not want, reader, to discourage you   106
From good resolutions, when you hear
How God wills that the debt should be paid.

Do not concern yourself with the form of pain: 109
Think what follows; and think that at the worst
It cannot go on beyond the last judgement.

112   I began: 'Master, what I can see
      Moving towards me, does not look like people;
      I don't know what, for looking tells me nothing.'

115   And he to me: 'The heavy condition
      Of their torment so bows them to the ground,
      That my eyes at first had conflicting impressions.

118   But look steadily there, and disentangle
      What is coming towards us beneath these rocks:
      Now you can see how each one beats his breast.'

121   O proud Christians, wretched and exhausted,
      Who, sick in mind, and not seeing aright,
      Go confidently in the wrong direction;

124   Do you not perceive that we are grubs,
      Born to turn into the angelic butterfly
      Which flies towards justice without defence?

127   Why does your mind float aloft
      Since you are no more than defective insects,
      Like the grub which has not reached its full development?

130   As, to hold up a ceiling or a roof,
      Sometimes you see, as a corbel, a figure
      Whose knees are pressed up against his chest;

133   Which, though not real, provokes a real discomfort
      In anyone who looks at it; that is how
      I saw these people were, when I looked hard.

136   True, they were either more or less contracted
      According as they had more or less on their backs;
      And the one who bore himself most patiently

139   Seemed, weeping, to say: 'I can stand no more.'

CANTO XI

'Our father, which art in heaven,
Not because circumscribed, but out of the greater love
You have for your first creation on high,

Praise be to your name and worthiness   4
From every creature, as it is appropriate
To render thanks to your sweet charity.

Thy kingdom come, and the peace of thy kingdom,   7
Because we cannot attain it of ourselves,
If it does not come, for all our ingenuity.

As of their own freewill your angels   10
Make sacrifice to you, singing Hosanna,
So may men also do of their freewill.

Give us this day our daily manna,   13
Without which, through the roughness of this desert,
He who tries hardest to advance, goes backward.

And as we forgive everyone the evil   16
That we have suffered, may you pardon us
Graciously, and have no regard to our merits.

Do not put our virtue to the test   19
With the old adversary, it is easily overcome,
But free us from him who spurs us on.

This last prayer, dear Lord, we no longer   22
Make for ourselves, having no need of it,
But for those who are left behind us.'

So those shadows, both for themselves and us,   25
Praying for a good journey, went, under their loads,
Like something that we dream from time to time,

Unequal in their anguish they went round   28
Wearily, upon the first cornice,
Purging themselves of the vapours of the world.

31   If there they always say good words for us,
      What can be said and done for them here
      By those who have a good root to their wills?

34   Surely we ought to help them wash away
      The marks they bear from here, so that, pure and light,
      They may go out into the starry heavens.

37   'So may justice and mercy soon relieve you
      Of your burdens, that you may move the wings
      Which will raise you in accordance with your desire,

40   Show us whether left or right is shortest way
      Towards the stairs; and if there is more than one opening,
      Instruct us as to which goes up less steeply,

43   For he who comes with me still has the burden
      Of Adam's flesh with which he is clothed,
      And, though against his will, can climb but slowly.'

46   There were words spoken in answer to these
      Which he whom I was following had uttered,
      But it was not clear from whom they came;

49   What was said was: 'Along the bank to the right,
      Come with us, and you will find the place
      Possible for a living person to climb.

52   And if I was not impeded by the rock
      Which so overmasters my proud neck
      That I am obliged to keep my face down,

55   I would look at that man who still lives
      And does not name himself, to see if I know him
      And to make him have pity on this load.

58   I was a Latin son of a great Tuscan:
      Guglielmo Aldobrandesco was my father;
      I do not know if you ever heard the name.

61   The ancient blood and all the pretty actions
      Of my ancestors made me so arrogant
      That, not thinking of our common mother,

I held every man in such scorn 64
That I died of it; how, the Sienese know,
And every child in Campagnatico.

I am Omberto; and not only me 67
Has pride damaged, it has dragged all my race
Down with it into calamity.

And here I must bear this weight among the dead, 70
Until I have given satisfaction to God,
Since I would not bear it among the living.'

Listening to him I bent down my head; 73
And one of them, but not the one who spoke,
Turned under the load that bore him down,

And saw me and knew me and called out, 76
Keeping his eyes fixed on me with difficulty,
As I, bent down, was going along with them.

'Oh!' I said to him, 'are you not Oderisi, 79
The pride of Gubbio, and the pride of that art
Which in Paris is called "illuminating"?'

'Brother,' he said, 'the sheets coloured by Franco 82
The Bolognese, are more brilliant than mine:
The honour is now all his, and mine is less.

Certainly I should not have been so polite 85
While I was alive, because of my great desire
To excel in this, my heart was engrossed in it.

The penalty of such pride is paid here; 88
And I should not be here yet, if it were not
That, while I could still sin, I turned to God.

O empty glory of human endeavour! 91
How little time the green remains on top,
Unless the age that follows is a dull one!

Cimabue thought he held the field 94
In painting, and now the cry is for Giotto,
So that the other's fame is now obscured.

97   So one Guido has taken from the other
       The glory of the language; and perhaps there is born
       One who may chase them both out of the nest.

100   Earthly fame is nothing but a breath of wind,
       Which first blows one way and then blows another,
       And brings a fresh name from each fresh direction.

103   What greater name will you have, if you are old
       When you put aside your flesh, than if you had died
       Before you had given up baby-talk and rattles,

106   Once a thousand years have passed? And that is a shorter
       Space to the eternal than the flash of an eyelid
       To the circle which turns in the heavens most slowly.

109   The one who moves painfully ahead of me
       Has a name which once rang through all Tuscany;
       There is hardly a whisper of him now in Siena,

112   Of which he was the lord, when they destroyed
       The rage of Florence, which was then as proud
       As at the present she is prostituted.

115   Your renown is like the colour of grass,
       Which comes and goes, and he discolours it
       Who causes it to spring fresh from the ground.'

118   And I to him: 'Your words are true and fill me
       With just humility, and cure my swelling:
       But where is he you were talking of just now?'

121   'That,' he replied, 'was Provenzan Salvani;
       And he is here because he was presumptuous
       To take the whole of Siena into his hands.

124   So he goes, and has gone since he died,
       Without rest: that is the coin which those
       Who dare too much, must pay in satisfaction.'

127   And I: 'If that spirit who waits
       Before he repents, right to the end of his days,
       Stays down below and does not ascend here,

Unless good prayers come to his assistance,   130
Until he has spent as much time as he lived,
How does it happen he was allowed to come?'

'When he was alive, in his greatest glory,'   133
He said, 'of his free will, in the centre of Siena,
He put aside all shame, and took his stand;

And there, to release a friend from the hardships   136
He was suffering at that time in Charles's prison,
He brought himself to quiver in every vein.

I say no more, and I know I speak darkly;   139
But little time will pass, before your neighbours
Will so behave themselves that you will understand it.

This action made him free of those confines.'   142

CANTO XII

Together, as oxen go in yoke,
I went in company with that burdened spirit
For as long as my gentle teacher allowed.

But when he said: 'Leave him and pass on;   4
For here it is good that, with sail and oars,
Each one should push his boat on as he can';

I drew myself up straight as one should for walking,   7
My body at least, because my thoughts remained
Bowed down, and their stature diminished.

I had moved forward, and was willingly following   10
My master's steps, and both of us already
Were demonstrating how light we were;

And he said to me: 'Turn your eyes downwards: 13
It will be good, and make the way more pleasing,
To see on what ground you put your feet.'

16   As, so that they may not be forgotten,
      The monuments on the ground above the buried
      Bear indications of what they once were,

19   So that they are wept over again many times,
      Because of the goading of remembrance,
      Of which only the compassionate feel the prick;

22   So I saw them, in better representations,
      Such was the skill of the artist, figures carved
      All over the ledge running around the mountain.

25   I saw him who was created nobler
      Than any other creature, falling from heaven,
      Down like a thunderbolt, on one side;

28   I saw Briareus, transfixed by the celestial
      Dart, lying on the other side,
      Heavy on the ground because of the chill of death.

31   I saw Thymbraeus; I saw Pallas and Mars,
      Still armed, gathered around their father,
      Staring at the scattered remains of the giants.

34   I saw Nimrod, at the foot of his great work,
      As if bewildered, and looking at the nations
      Who in Shinar, were proud with him.

37   O Niobe, with what sorrowing eyes I saw
      The image of you there upon the road,
      Between seven and seven of your lifeless children!

40   O Saul, how you appeared there,
      Fallen upon your own sword at Gilboa
      Which afterwards felt neither rain nor dew!

43   O crazed Arachne, so I saw you there,
      Already half a spider, grieving on the shreds
      Of the work which you did to your own harm.

46   O Rehoboam, your image no longer seems
      To threaten, in this place; but full of terror,
      Gets up to a chariot and flees away.

The hard pavement also showed 49
How Alcmaeon made his mother see
She had paid dearly for her unfortunate necklace.

It showed how the sons of Sennacherib 52
Threw themselves on him in the temple
And how, when he was dead, they left him there.

It showed the destruction and cruel havoc 55
Tomyris made when she said to Cyrus:
'You thirsted for blood, I will fill you with blood!'

It showed how the Assyrians were put to flight, 58
After the death of Holofernes,
And also the headless body left on the field.

I saw Troy cavernous and in ashes: 61
O Ilion, how base and vile you appeared
In the image which was drawn of you there!

What a master he was of painting and design, 64
Who drew the shadows and the features there,
Which would make any subtle mind gaze at them.

The dead looked dead, the living looked alive: 67
Those who had seen the real thing saw no better
Than I stepped on as I was walking bent down.

Now be proud, and on with arrogant looks, 70
You sons of Eve, and do not bend your heads,
In that way you will see your evil path!

Already we had gone round more of the mountain, 73
And more of the sun's course had been spent
Than had appeared to my preoccupied mind,

When he who was going ahead of me, 76
Always attentive, began: 'Hold up your head,
It is no longer time to walk so irresolutely.

See, there is an angel who is making ready 79
To come towards us; see the return
From the day's service, of the sixth handmaiden.

82   Put reverence in your looks and actions,
     So that he delights to send us further up;
     Reflect that this day will not dawn again.'

85   I was well accustomed to his admonitions
     Never to waste time, so that on that subject
     Nothing that he said could seem obscure to me.

88   The beautiful creature came up to us,
     Clothed in white, and in his face,
     Something of the trembling of a morning star.

91   He spread his arms, and then he spread his wings;
     He said: 'Come: the steps are close by here,
     And now you will find that they are easy to climb.'

94   For this invitation few are chosen:
     O human race, born to fly upwards,
     Why do you fall at such a little breeze?

97   He led us to where the rock was cut out:
     There he struck my forehead with his wings;
     Then he promised me a safe path for my journey.

100 As on the right hand, to climb the hill,
     Where stands the church which so dominates
     The well-run city, across the Rubaconte,

103 The precipitous rise of the hillside is broken by
     The stairs which were put there in an age
     When public record and weights and measures were safe;

106 So the gradient of the bank was reduced,
     Which falls steeply from the other circle,
     But on both sides the high rock grazes the climber.

109 While we were turning our bodies there
     Voices were singing: *Beati pauperes spiritu,*'
     And no words can tell how sweetly they sang.

112 Ah, how different these approaches are
     From those of hell! For here we have songs
     As we go in, and there ferocious laments.

Already we were climbing the holy steps,   115
And it seemed to me that I was very much lighter
Than I had seemed to be earlier on the flat.

So I said: 'Master, what heavy thing   118
Has been lifted from me, so that as I walk,
It seems that my progress is almost effortless?'

He replied: 'When the P's which have remained   121
Still on your face, although nearly invisible,
Are, like the first one, utterly erased,

Your feet will be so moved by goodwill   124
That not only will you have no sense of exertion,
But it will be a delight to be impelled upwards.'

Then I did what people do when they are walking   127
With something on their heads, but are not aware of it,
Until signs from others make them suspect it;

Then their hands help them to make certain,   130
And seek and find and carry out that function
Which cannot be provided for by sight;

And with the fingers of my right hand spread out,   133
I found only six of the letters which had been cut
Over my temples by the angel with the keys;

And, seeing that, my master gave a smile.   136

CANTO XIII

We were at the top of the flight of stairs
Where, for a second time, the mountain which
Purifies as one climbs it, is cut back:

There a cornice makes a belt round the hill   4
In the same manner as the first one did;
Except that the curve of it bends more sharply.

7   No shadows or figures were to be seen there;
Both the bank and the track appeared bare,
With the livid colour of the rock itself.

10   'If we wait here to make enquiries of people,'
The poet reflected, 'I am afraid, perhaps,
We shall find that we have chosen to wait too long.'

13   Then he set his eyes fixedly on the sun;
He made his right side a pivot and turned,
Swinging the left part of his body round.

16   'O sweet light, trusting in whom I enter
Upon the new way, conduct us in it,'
He said, 'as is necessary in this place.

19   You give warmth to the world, and shine upon it:
If no reason disposes us to the contrary,
We ought always to be led by your beams.'

22   We had already gone, from that spot,
About what you might reckon to be a mile,
In a short time, because we went with a will;

25   And, flying in our direction, we heard
But did not see, spirits who were uttering
Courteous invitations to the table of love.

28   The first voice which passed by us in flight
Said with great clearness: *'Vinum non habent,'*
And continued repeating those words behind us.

31   And, before it had died away completely
In the distance, another passed crying
'I am Orestes,' and that too did not stay.

34   'Oh,' I said, 'Father, what are those voices?'
And as I put my question, there was a third,
Saying: 'Love those who despitefully use you.'

37   And the good master said: 'This circle punishes
The sin of envy, and for that reason
The cords of the whip are made of love.

The bridle must be of a contrasting note;   40
I think you will hear it, that is my guess,
Before you arrive at the pass of pardon.

But look through the air as steadily as you can,   43
And you will see, in front of us, people sitting,
Each with a place along the side of the rock.'

Then I opened my eyes wider than before;   46
I looked ahead of me, and saw shadows with cloaks
Of the same colour as the rock itself.

And when we were a little further on,   49
I heard a cry: 'Mary, pray for us!';
A cry: 'Michael' and 'Peter' and 'All Saints'.

I do not think there is on earth today   52
A man so hardened that he would not be touched
By compassion at what I then saw;

For when I had approached closely enough   55
To make out clearly what state they were in,
Tears of deep grief spurted from my eyes.

The spirits seemed to be dressed in coarse sackcloth,   58
Supporting one another with their shoulders
And all of them supported against the bank.

Like blind people who are without means   61
And stand at a shrine, begging for what they need;
And one man's head fallen against another's

So that pity may be aroused in others,   64
Not merely by the sound of what they say,
But by their appearance, which also expresses longing.

And as the sun does not reach the blind,   67
So for the shadows of which I am now speaking,
The light of heaven does not wish to be vouchsafed.

For all had their eyelids threaded and sewn up   70
By an iron wire, as is done to wild hawks
Because they refuse to remain still as they should.

73 It seemed to me an outrage to go as I was going,
Seeing other people but not being seen by them:
And so I turned to my wise adviser.

76 He well knew what my silence meant,
And therefore did not wait for me to ask,
But said: 'Speak, but be short and to the point.'

79 Virgil was walking with me on that side
Of the cornice on which there was a risk of falling
Because there was no bank round the edge:

82 On the other side of me were the devoted
Shadows, through the horrible seams of whose lids
Burst tears which made their cheeks wet.

85 I turned to them, and began: 'O people assured
Of seeing the exalted light which alone
Is now the object of your desire,

88 So may grace dissolve the impurities
Of your consciences, that the river of memory
May run through them with perfect clarity,

91 Tell me, what to me would be gracious and pleasing,
Whether any soul among you is a Latin;
And perhaps it will be good for him if I recognise him.'

94 'O my brother, each one of us is a citizen
Of one true city; but you mean to say,
Someone who lived in Italy as a pilgrim.'

97 It seemed to me that this reply I heard
Came from a little ahead of where I was,
So I advanced, to make myself more audible.

100 Among the others I saw a shadow which looked
Expectantly; and if you ask how, I would say,
It pointed its chin upwards as the blind do.

103 'Spirit,' I said, 'in training for the climb,
If it was you who answered me just now,
Make yourself known to me either by place or name.'

'I was a Sienese,' she answered, 'and   106
With the others here, I cleanse my wicked life,
Weeping to him that he should bend to us.

I was not wise, although I was called Sapia,   109
And I was more delighted at others' losses
Than ever I was at good fortune of my own.

And lest you think I am deceiving you,   112
Hear whether I was as foolish as I say,
When already the curve of my life was downwards.

My fellow-citizens, quite near to Colle,   115
Were joined in battle with their adversaries,
And I prayed God for what he had willed.

They were broken and had turned with bitter steps   118
In a retreat; and when I saw the chase
I felt the greatest happiness I ever knew,

So I turned my impudent face upwards,   121
Calling to God: "Now I'm no longer afraid of you!"
As the blackbird does when he gets a little fine weather.

I wanted peace with God at the end   124
Of my life; and what I owed would still not
Have been reduced by penitence,

Had it not been that Peter from the comb-shop   127
Remembered me in his holy prayers,
For in his charity he was sorry for me.

But who are you, who come here with enquiries   130
About our condition, and have your eyes open,
As it seems to me, and are breathing when you speak?'

'My eyes,' I said, 'will yet be taken from me   133
In this place, though only for a little while,
For they have not offended greatly through envy.

My soul is in suspense much more with fear   136
Of the torments which are in the circle below,
For even now the load there weighs upon me.'

139   And she to me: 'Who then has brought you up
       Among us here, if you expect to go back?'
       And I: 'He who is with me, and says nothing.

142   And I am living; and therefore you may ask me,
       Elect spirit, if you will, back in the world,
       To go anywhere mortal feet may go.'

145   'Oh,' she replied, 'this is so new a thing
       To hear, it is a great sign that God loves you;
       Help me therefore sometimes with your prayers.

148   And I beg you, by all you most desire,
       If you ever set foot on Tuscan soil,
       You will tell my family all is well with me.

151   You will find among them people foolish enough
       To have hopes of Talamone, and to waste on it
       More enthusiasm than in finding the Diana;

154   But the contractors will lose more there.'

CANTO XIV

     'Who is that man who travels round our mountain
     Before death has given him the power to fly,
     And opens and shuts his eyes at will?'

4   'I do not know who he is, but he is not alone:
       You question him, for you are nearer to him,
       And greet him gently, so that he may speak.'

7   So two spirits, leaning against one another,
       Were talking about me, away there to the right;
       Then, to speak to me, they turned their faces up;

10   And one said: 'Soul, you who are still encased
       In your body as you go towards heaven,
       Of your charity be of consolation

To us and say whence you come and who you are;   13
For you make us marvel so at your grace,
As one must at a thing which never was.'

And I: 'Through the middle of Tuscany there spreads   16
A little river which rises in Falterona,
And a course of a hundred miles is not enough for it.

From a place on that river I bring this body: 19
To tell you who I am would serve no purpose,
For as yet my name is not greatly talked of.'

'If my mind manages to grasp the sense   22
Of what you say,' the one who had spoken first
Answered me, 'it is the Arno that you mean.'

And the other said to him: 'Why did he hide   25
The name of that river, as people do
When they speak of something which is horrible?'

And the shadow to whom the question was put   28
Explained himself: 'I do not know, but right
It certainly is, such a valley's name should perish;

Because from the beginning, where the mountain chain   31
Which cuts Pelorus off, is so pregnant
That few places are more remarkable,

To where it gives itself up and so restores   34
What the sky makes evaporate from the sea,
So providing the rivers with what goes with them,

Virtue is avoided as an enemy   37
By all, as if it were a snake, either because
The place is as it is, or because of bad habits:

With the result that there is such a change in the nature   40
Of the inhabitants of the wretched valley,
That they seem to have been put out to root by Circe.

Among filthy pigs, for whom acorns are fitter   43
Than any food intended for human use,
It first of all directs its trickling course.

46   Then it finds snapping curs, as it comes down,
      Snarling more than they have power to perform,
      And turns its snout from them in disdain.

49   It falls further; and the bigger it gets,
      The more it finds the dogs turn into wolves,
      This accursed and unfortunate ditch.

52   Then, having descended through deep rocky basins,
      It finds the foxes who are so full of tricks
      That they do not fear any mind getting the better of them.

55   I will not stop because another hears me;
      And it will be well for that man if he remembers
      What the true spirit disentangles for me.

58   I see your grandson who is now beginning
      To hunt those wolves upon the banks
      Of that fierce river, and terrifying them all.

61   He sells their flesh while they are still alive,
      And then slaughters them like old quarries:
      Depriving many of life and himself of honour.

64   Bloody he comes out of the sad forest;
      And leaves it such, that in a thousand years
      It will not grow back to its first condition.'

67   As when some great trouble is predicted
      A cloud may come upon the face of the listener,
      From whatever side the danger shows its teeth,

70   So I saw the other soul, who had turned
      And was listening, grow troubled and sad,
      When he had taken in what had been said.

73   What the one said and how the other looked
      Made me greatly desire to know their names,
      And I asked them, or half entreated them;

76   So that the spirit who first spoke to me
      Began again: 'You want me to bring myself
      To do for you what you will not do for me.

But since God wills that so much of his grace   79
Should shine through you, I will not treat you meanly;
Know therefore that I am Guido del Duca.

My blood was so set on fire by envy   82
That if I had seen a man with cause to be glad
You would have seen my face all discoloured.

As I sowed straw so I must reap it now: 85
O human race, why do you set your hearts
On benefits which cannot be shared with others?

This is Rinier; this is the glory and honour   88
Of the house of Calboli, where no one since
Has made himself the heir of his qualities.

And not only his family has been stripped   91
Between the Po and the mountains, the shore and the Reno,
Of the good required for truth and civic virtue;

For inside these boundaries is so full   94
Of poisonous shoots, that it would take great labour
To root them out or make the woods grow less.

Where is the good Lizio, and Arrigo Manardi?   97
Pier Traversaro and Guido di Carpigna?
Romagnols, you have become a crowd of bastards!

Where in Bologna will a Fabbro spring up?   100
Where in Faenza a Bernardin di Fosco,
A noble offshoot of a modest stock?

Do not wonder if I weep, you Tuscan,   103
When I remember, with Guido da Prata,
Ugolin d'Azzo who lived among us,

Federigo Tignoso and his circle,   106
The house of Traversaro, and the Anastagi
(Both families now without heirs),

The ladies and the knights, the exertions and recreations   109
Which love and courtesy made us so delight in,
There where the hearts have now turned to evil.

112   O Brettinoro, why do you not disappear,
      Now that your family has gone away,
      And many others, not to share the guilt?

115   Bagnacaval does well, to have no sons,
      And Castrocaro ill, and Conio worse
      For bothering to produce the counts it does.

118   The Pagani will do well when their demon
      Shall go away; though it cannot be that the record
      Will ever show them entirely in the clear.

121   O Ugolin de' Fantolin, your name
      Is safe, for now there is no reason to apprehend
      Degeneration could make it any worse.

124   But go your way, Tuscan, now; for now
      I would rather weep than talk, our conversation
      Has put my mind under such constraint.'

127   We knew that those dear souls heard us go;
      And therefore, because they said nothing, we knew
      That we could be confident of the way.

130   When we had gone a little way on our own,
      It was as if lightning split the air,
      And a voice hit us with the words:

133   'Every one that findeth me shall slay me';
      And it fled like thunder as it disperses
      If, suddenly, the cloud is ripped open.

136   As soon as our ears were safe from that voice,
      Another came upon us with a crash,
      Which seemed like thunder quickly following:

139   'I am Aglauros who became a stone';
      And then, to draw myself close to the poet,
      I took a step to the right, instead of forward.

142   And now the air was quiet on all sides;
      He said to me: 'That was the hard curb
      Which ought to keep man within his limits.

But you take the bait, so that the hook   145
Of the old adversary draws you to him;
And so check and recall do very little.

The heavens call you, and revolve around you,   148
Displaying to you their eternal beauties,
And yet your eye looks only on the ground;

It is for this you are punished by him who discerns all.'   151

CANTO XV

There appeared now to be left as much
Of the sun's course towards evening
As, between the third hour and the beginning of the day,

Appears of that sphere which for ever plays   4
In the manner of a child: for it was now
Vespers there, and midnight in Italy.

The rays struck straight in the middle of our faces,   7
Because we had so circled round the mountain
That we were now going straight towards the west,

When I felt weighing upon my forehead   10
A splendour much greater than before,
And I marvelled at I knew not what;

So that I raised my hand above my eyes   13
And made myself a shield from the sun's rays,
To file away the visible excess.

As when from water, or from a mirror,   16
A ray of light jumps in the opposite direction,
Rising at an angle which is identical

With the angle of descent, and in the same distance   19
Departs as far from the line of a falling stone;
As is demonstrated by experience and mathematics;

22   So I appeared to be struck by the light
      Which was refracted from the ground in front of me;
      And therefore my sight was quick to avoid it.

25   'What is that, gentle father, from which I cannot
      Shield my eyes in any effective way,'
      I said, 'and which seems to be moving towards us?'

28   'Do not be astonished, if the servants of heaven
      Still dazzle you'; so he replied to me;
      'It is a messenger who invites us to ascend.

31   Soon you will find that things of this kind
      Are no burden, but will give you delight
      As great as your nature allows you to feel.'

34   When we had approached the blessed angel,
      He said with a glad voice: 'Now come in here,
      By a stairway much less steep than the others.'

37   We climbed up, having already moved on,
      And *'Beati misericordes!'* was sung
      From behind us, and 'Rejoice in the victory!'

40   My master and I were going up together,
      We alone; and I thought, as we went,
      I would get some benefit from his talk;

43   And I turned towards him with the question:
      'What did that spirit from Romagna mean
      By talking about "benefits" and "sharing with others"?'

46   And he replied: 'He understands the harm
      Which comes of his greatest vice; so do not wonder
      If he reproves it, so that there is less to weep for.

49   For in so far as your desires are fixed
      On things which are diminished by being shared,
      Envy will pump sighs out of your lungs.

52   But if the love of the supreme heavens
      Turns your desires, so that they look upwards,
      You will not have that fear in your heart;

For the more there are who call the good "ours",   55
The more of it each one of us possesses,
And the more charity burns in that circle.'

'I am the more starved of satisfaction,'   58
I said, 'than if I had said nothing just now,
And more doubt collects in my mind.

How can it be that a good divided up   61
Among many, can make those who possess it richer
Than if it were possessed by only a few?'

And he to me: 'Because you are once more   64
Fixing your mind upon the things of earth,
You find obscurity in true light.

That ineffable and infinite good   67
Which is above, runs to love just as surely
As does a ray of light to a bright surface.

The gift is in proportion to the ardour   70
It finds; so that, the greater the charity,
The more the eternal good pours on the soul.

And the more people up there turn to each other,   73
The more there are to love, the more love there is,
Reflecting from one to another, as with mirrors.

And if my discourse does not satisfy you,   76
You will see Beatrice and she will fully
Take from you this and every other longing.

Try only to secure that the five wounds   79
Which are closed up by our contrition
Are taken from you as the two already.'

As I was going to say: 'You have contented me,'   82
I saw I had arrived on the next circle,
So that my eager eyes made me be silent.

There it seemed to me I was taken up   85
All at once, in an ecstatic vision,
And saw a number of people in a temple;

88   There was a woman who was about to enter,
      Saying with the gentle demeanour of a mother:
      'My son, why hast thou thus dealt with us?

91   Behold, thy father and I have sought thee sorrowing,'
      And as at that point she was silent,
      That which had first appeared then vanished away.

94   Then there appeared to me another woman,
      On her cheeks the water which grief distils
      When it arises in someone from great anger,

97   And she cried: 'If you are lord of this city,
      For whose name there was such strife among the gods,
      And which sparkles abroad with all knowledge,

100   Avenge yourself of those impudent arms
      Which have embraced our daughter, Pisistratus.'
      And the lord appeared to me, kindly and gently,

103   To answer her with a temperate expression:
      'What should we do to one who wishes us ill,
      If one who loves us is condemned by us?'

106   Then I saw people afire with anger,
      Killing a young man by stoning, and shouting
      To one another nothing but 'Kill him, kill him.'

109   And I saw him bowed down, since death
      Weighed upon him already, towards the ground,
      But of his eyes he always made gates for heaven,

112   Praying to the high Lord, amidst such war,
      That he would pardon those who persecuted him,
      With that look which brings out the onlooker's pity.

115   When my soul turned from these appearances
      To the things which are true independently of itself,
      I recognised my errors, which were not falsehoods.

118   My guide, who could see that I was acting
      Like a man who is loosing himself from sleep,
      Said: 'What is the matter, why aren't you keeping up,

But have come more than half a league 121
With eyes closed and legs staggering about,
Like someone overcome by wine or sleep?'

'O my gentle father, listen and I will tell you,' 124
I said, 'what it was appeared to me
When I so lost the use of my legs.'

And he: 'If you had a hundred masks 127
Upon your face, still your cogitations
Would not be closed to me, even the smallest.

What you saw was to stop you excusing yourself 130
From opening your heart to the waters of peace,
Which are poured out from the eternal fountain.

I did not ask "What's the matter?" as one might ask 133
A man who has only the eyes to see with
And they cannot see because the body is senseless,

But I asked in order to give your feet strength: 136
So must the lazy be shaken, if they are slow
To wake up for their watch when their turn comes round.'

We were going on through the evening, with our eyes 139
Straining to see as far ahead as possible
In the face of the bright evening sunlight.

And little by little a smoke came towards us, 142
It was dark as night, and yet there was no way
In which we could escape from that place:

It took from us our sight and the clear air. 145

CANTO XVI

Darkness of hell and of a night deprived
Of any planet, under a shrunk horizon,
Shadowed as much as may be by cloud,

4   Never made so thick a veil over my sight
As that smoke which covered us in that place,
Nor ever prickled so roughly to the touch;

7   So that my eyes could not bear to stay open:
For which reason my wise and faithful escort
Came close to me and offered me his shoulder.

10   Just as a blind man goes behind his guide,
Not to lose his way, and not to bump into anything
Which may do him injury or perhaps kill him;

13   I went through the bitter and filthy air,
Listening to my escort who kept saying:
'Take care that you don't get cut off from me.'

16   I heard voices, and all of them appeared
To be praying for peace and for mercy,
From the Lamb of God who takes away sins.

19   Always they began with an *Agnus Dei*;
The same words from them all, and the same mode,
So that there seemed complete accord among them.

22   'Are those spirits, master, that I hear?'
I said. And he to me: 'You are right,
And they are untying the knot of anger.'

25   'And who are you who cut through our smoke,
And who speak of us as if you still measured
Time by the divisions of the calendar?'

28   These words were spoken by one of the voices;
And my master said to me: 'Answer him,
And ask if this is the way to go up.'

31   And I: 'O creature, purifying yourself,
In order to go back beautiful to your maker,
You will hear a marvel, if you come with me.'

34   'I will follow you as far as is allowed me,'
He replied: 'and if the smoke prevents us seeing,
Hearing will keep us in touch instead.'

Then I began: 'With this bundle 37
Which death unties, I go on the upward journey,
And I came here through the anguish of hell.

And if God has so kept me in his grace 40
That he wills that I should see his court
In a manner strange to the custom of the day,

Do not hide from me who you were before death, 43
But tell me, and tell me if I am on the right road
For the opening; and your words be our escort.'

'I was a Lombard, and I was called Marco: 46
I knew about the world, and what I valued
Were the things that no one aims at any more.

To go higher you must go straight on.' 49
Thus he replied, and added: 'I beg you,
Pray for me when you are up there.'

And I to him: 'I bind myself, by my faith, 52
To do as you are asking; but I have a doubt
Which will burst inside me if I cannot get rid of it.

First it was simple, now it is redoubled 55
By your pronouncement, which confirms here
One made elsewhere with which I couple it.

The world indeed is, as your words convey, 58
Utterly empty now of every virtue,
And heavy and overlaid with malice;

But I beg you to indicate the reason, 61
So that I see it and point it out to others;
Some say it is in the stars, some, here below.'

He first gave a deep sigh, which my grief compressed 64
Into a sort of 'Whew!'; then he began:
'Brother, the world is blind, and you are of it.

You who are living attribute all causes 67
To the stars above, as if everything there is
Had of necessity to move with them.

70   If it were so, that would mean the destruction
     Of your free will, and it would not-be just,
     For good to be rewarded, and sinners punished.

73   The stars may initiate your movements;
     I do not say all of them, but suppose I should say so,
     There is a light to tell good from evil

76   And free will; which, if it makes an effort
     Throughout the first battles with the stars,
     Will be victorious, if it is well nourished.

79   Free as you are, you are subject to a greater law
     And a better nature; and that creates in you
     The mind the stars do not have in their charge.

82   So, if the present world is going off course,
     The reason is in you, and should be sought there;
     And I will tell you truly how the land lies.

85   Issues from the hand of him who contemplates it
     Before it is, in the manner of a child
     Who laughs and weeps and behaves childishly,

88   The simple little soul which knows nothing,
     Except that, moved by the gladness of its maker,
     It turns freely to what amuses it.

91   At first it relishes a trifling good;
     Is deceived by it, and runs after it,
     If guides and curbs do not deflect its love.

94   So there must be laws, to act as a curb;
     There must be a king, who might catch sight of
     At any rate the tower of the true city.

97   There are laws, but who puts his hand to them?
     No one, because the shepherd who goes ahead
     May chew the cud, but his hooves are not parted;

100   Because the people, when it sees its guide
     Go only for things that he is greedy for,
     Feed on that, and ask for nothing better.

You can see easily that bad government   103
Is the cause which has made the world wicked,
And not your nature, corrupted though it may be.

Rome, which was the maker of the good world,   106
Used to have two suns, by which could be seen
Both the road of the world and the road to God.

One has put out the other; and the sword is combined   109
With the pastoral crook, the two held together,
It must of necessity be that things go badly;

Because, combined, one does not fear the other: 112
If you doubt what I say, look at the ear of corn,
For every kind of plant is known by its seed.

Throughout the land by the Adige and the Po,   115
There used to be found courage and courtesy,
Before Frederick ran into trouble:

Now anyone can go through there safely enough,   118
If he has given up, because he is ashamed,
Having conversation or contact with good men.

It is true there are still three old men in · whom old times   121
Rebuke the new, and to them it seems long
Till God removes them to a better life:

Currado da Palazzo, the good Gherardo,   124
And Guido da Castel, who is better named
As the French call him, the straightforward Lombard.

You may now put it that the Church of Rome,   127
By confounding two powers within itself,
Falls in the muck and dirties itself and its load.'

'Marco,' I said, 'You set out the argument well;   130
And now I see why the sons of Levi
Were excluded from the inheritance.

But what Gherardo is that, who you say is left   133
As an example of the race that has gone,
And as a reproof to this barbarous age?'

136   'You are saying that either to trick or to tempt me,'
      He replied; 'for you are talking to me in Tuscan
      And yet seem not to have heard of the good Gherardo.

139   I do not know him by any other surname,
      Unless I take it from his daughter Gaia.
      Goodbye now, I am coming no further with you.

142   See the light, which streams through the smoke
      Already growing white, and I must go
      —The angel is here— before I appear to him.'

145   So he turned, and wished to hear me no more.

CANTO XVII

      Remember, reader, if ever in the mountains
      You were caught in a mist, through which you could see
      No better than a mole can through his skin,

4   How, when at last the thick and humid vapours
      Begin to clear away, the ball of the sun
      Comes in through them, though with great feebleness;

7   And your imagination will find it easy
      To arrive at understanding how I saw
      The sun again, just as it was ready to set.

10   So, keeping my steps with the trusted steps
      Of my master, I came out of that cloud
      When the sun was already dead on the low shore.

13   O faculty of imagination, which sometimes
      Takes us so far out of ourselves, that a man
      Does not notice though a thousand trumpets sound around him,

16   Who moves you, when the senses offer nothing?
      A light which takes its shape in heaven moves you,
      Of its own, or by a will which directs it down.

The pitilessness of her who changed her form   19
Into the bird that most delights to sing,
Appeared to me, traced in the imagination:

And here my mind was so sunk in itself   22
That nothing coming to it from outside
During that time, could be received by it.

Then fell into my heightened fancy   25
A crucified figure, full of scorn, and fierce
In his appearance, and dying in that state.

Around him were the great Ahasuerus,   28
Esther his wife, and the just Mordecai,
Who was complete in all he said and did.

And as those images broke of themselves   31
Much in the manner that a bubble will do
When there is not enough water to cover it,

There arose in my vision a young girl,   34
Bitterly weeping, and saying: 'O queen,
Why, through anger, did you do away with yourself?

You killed yourself so as not to lose Lavinia: 37
Now you have lost me: it is I who mourn,
Mother, for your ruin more than another's.'

As sleep is broken when suddenly   40
New light strikes on the closed eyes
And, broken, darts away before it dies;

So what I was imagining collapsed   43
As soon as my face was struck by a light
Greater than any we are accustomed to.

I turned round to see where I was,   46
When a voice said: 'It is here you come up,'
And took every other thought out of my mind;

And my desire became so extremely restless   49
To look at whoever it was who was speaking
That it would not rest until it was face to face.

52   But as at the sun which weighs upon our sight
        And hides its shape by an excess of brilliance,
        So my strength there was inadequate.

55   'That is a divine spirit who shows us
        The way up without waiting to be asked,
        And conceals itself within its own light.

58   It does with others as a man would do with himself;
        For he who waits to be asked, when he sees a need,
        Is already spitefully on the way to denial.

61   Now let our feet follow the invitation:
        Let us try to climb before it grows dark,
        For then it will not be possible, till day returns.'

64   So said my guide, and he and I together
        Directed our feet towards a stairway;
        And as soon as I was on the bottom step,

67   I felt near me as it were the movement of wings,
        And a wind in my face, and a voice said: ' Beati
        Pacifici, who are without evil anger.'

70   Already the last rays, which are followed by night,
        Had risen so far above us that the stars
        Made themselves seen in many directions.

73   'O my strength, why are you vanishing?'
        I said within myself, for I could feel
        The power of my legs ceasing to operate.

76   We were at the point at which the stairway
        Went no further, and we were stuck there,
        Just like a ship which has arrived at the shore.

79   And I listened, to see if I could hear
        Anything inside the new circle;
        Then I turned to my master, and said:

82   'My gentle father, tell me, what offence
        Is purged in the circle we are in now?
        If our feet stop, no need for you to stop speaking.'

And he to me: 'The love of the good, defective   85
Without its duty, is in this place made whole;
Here the idle rower dips his oar again.

But, so that you may understand more clearly,   88
Pay attention to me, and you will find
Our stay here will yield you some good fruit.'

'Neither creator nor creature was ever,'   91
He then began, 'my son, without love,.
Either natural or rational; you know that.

Natural love is always without error,   94
But the other kind may err, in the wrong object,
Or else through too much or too little vigour.

While it is directed to the primal good,   97
And keeps to its limits in relation to the secondary,
It cannot be the occasion of sinful pleasure;

But when it is twisted to evil, or seeks the good   100
With more or with less concern than it ought to have,
The creature is working against the creator.

So you can understand that love must be   103
The seed of every virtue that is in you
And of every action deserving of punishment.

Now, because love can never turn its face   106
From the well-being of the one who loves,
All creatures are free of hatred of themselves;

And since no being can be conceived as separate   109
And on its own, apart from the primal being,
Every creature is remote from hatred of him.

It follows, if my demonstration is correct,   112
That the evil which is loved is that of your neighbour;
And this love starts in three ways, in your dust.

There is the man who, through the suppression of his neighbour,   115
Hopes to excel, and for that reason only
Desires to see him cast down from his greatness:

118 There is the man who fears to lose power, favour,
Honour and glory because of another's success,
And so grieves for it that he loves the opposite:

121 And there is the man who takes umbrage at injury
So that he becomes greedy for revenge
And such a man must seek to harm another.

124 These three forms of love are repented of
Below us here: now I want you to understand
The other, which seeks good, but not as it ought to do.

127 Everyone has a confused notion of good,
On which he sets his mind, and which he desires;
And therefore everyone tries to attain it.

130 If the love which draws you to see or to reach it,
Is idle, then it will happen, here on this cornice,
That after proper repentance, you suffer for it.

133 There is another good which does not bring happiness;
It is not happiness, it is not the benign essence
Which is the root and fruit of every good.

136 The love which gives itself too much to this
Is wept for in the three circles above us;
But as to how the three modes are distinguished,

139 I say nothing, you can think it out for yourself.'

CANTO XVIII

When the exalted teacher had concluded
His exposition, and was looking in my face
To see whether I seemed satisfied;

4 I, who was once more pricked by a new thirst,
Was outwardly silent, and said inside myself:
'Perhaps I am asking him too many questions.'

But that true father, who observed   7
The timid desire which did not open up,
By speaking, gave me courage to speak.

So I: 'Master, my sight is so animated   10
By the light you give, that I discern clearly
All that your discourse imports or sets out.

Therefore I beg you, dear and gentle father,   13
Tell me the nature of love, to which you reduce
Every good operation and its contrary.'

'Direct towards me,' he said, 'the keen lights   16
Of your intellect, and you will see the mistake
Of the blind who have pretensions to lead the way.

The mind, which is created ready to love,   19
Is set in motion by anything that is pleasing,
As soon as pleasure wakes it up for action.

Your apprehension carries the impression   22
From a real object, and displays it inside you
So that it makes the mind turn towards it.

And if, when turned, the mind bends towards it,   25
That bending is love, and it is nature
Which through pleasure is bound in you afresh.

Then, as fire moves in an upward direction   28
By its constitution, which is such that it must rise
To where, being in its element, it endures longest,

So the captive mind enters upon desires,   31
Which is a spiritual motion, and does not rest
Until the thing that is loved makes it be glad.

Now it will be apparent to you how hidden   34
The truth is from people who declare
That every love is a laudable thing in itself,

Because perhaps the material of which it is made   37
Always seems good; but not every imprint is good,
Although there may be nothing wrong with the wax.'

40 'What you have said, and the attention I have paid,'
I answered, 'have made clear the nature of love,
But that has made me fuller of doubt than ever;

43 For if love is offered to us from outside
And if the soul is moved by nothing else,
It is not her fault whether or not she goes straight.'

46 And he to me: 'What reason may discern
In this matter, I can tell you; for the rest
Wait for Beatrice, for it is a point of faith.

49 Every substantial form, which is distinct
From matter and at the same time united with it,
Has within itself a specific virtue,

52 Which is not perceived except when in operation,
And is never manifest except by its effects,
As the life of a plant is by its green leaves.

55 So people do not know whence the understanding
Of the first apprehension may come,
Nor of the primary dispositions of appetite,

58 Which are in you as, in the bee, the instinct
To make honey; and this primary desire
Incurs no liability to praise or blame.

61 Now for accord between this wish and all the others,
There is the innate power which counsels you,
And which should stand on the threshold of assent.

64 That is the principle from which there comes
The notion of desert, depending on how
Good and evil loves are received and distinguished.

67 Those who went to the root of things with their reasoning,
Became aware of this innate freedom;
And so left a theory of morals to the world.

70 So, even supposing every love that is kindled
In you, arises out of necessity;
The power to entertain it is in you.

This noble virtue is what Beatrice
Understands by freewill; bear it in mind
In case she chooses to speak to you about it.' 73

The moon, which had waited till almost midnight, 76
Made the stars appear to us to be fewer;
It was shaped like a bucket which is on fire:

And its course from west to east was by those ways 79
The sun inflames when people in Rome
See him setting between Sardinia and Corsica.

And that noble shadow on whose account 82
Pietola is more famous than any Mantuan town,
Had taken from me the burden which oppressed me;

So I, who now had answers to my questions 85
Set out with plainness and clarity,
Was as it were lost in somnolence.

But that somnolence was taken from me 88
Suddenly by people who had run
Round the circle and appeared behind our backs.

A furious crowd such as in former times 91
Ismenus and Asopus saw by night,
Along their banks, when the Thebans called to Bacchus,

So, by what I saw of them, round this circle 94
Came those, with their feet moving like sickles,
While good will and just love rode on their backs.

They were soon upon us, because the whole company, 97
Great as it was, was moving at a run;
And the two in front were calling amidst weeping:

'Mary went into the hill country with haste; 100
And Caesar, intending to subdue Ilerda,
Struck at Marseilles and then raced into Spain.'

'Hurry! Hurry! and let no time be lost 103
Through lack of love,' the others cried as they followed,
'And zeal for good will make grace green again.'

106   'O people in whom this sharp fervour now
    Perhaps makes up for negligence and slackness
    You showed through tepidness in doing good,

109   This man who is alive—I do not lie—
    Wants to go up, as soon as the sun shines on us;
    Tell us therefore the shortest way to the opening.'

112   Those were the words that my master spoke;
    And one of the spirits said: 'Come behind us
    And you will find your way to the gap.

115   We are so full of desire to move on,
    We cannot stop; and therefore pardon us
    If you mistake our justice for ill manners.

118   I was abbot of San Zeno in Verona,
    Under the reign of the good Barbarossa,
    Of whom Milan still talks with bitter memories.

121   And one I know who has one foot in the grave
    Will soon weep because of that monastery,
    And will grieve that he had authority there;

124   Because he has put, in place of the true shepherd,
    His son, who is defective in his body,
    And worse in mind, and is besides a bastard.'

127   I do not know whether he said any more
    Or was silent, for he had gone so far beyond us;
    But this I heard and was glad to remember.

130   And he who helped me out whenever I needed it
    Said: 'Turn the other way: you will see two
    Spirits biting at idleness as they come.'

133   They were saying, as they followed the rest: 'The people for
      whom
    The Red Sea opened, were dead before the Jordan
    Saw their children come and sit down by it.

136   And those who could bear until the end
    The exertions they underwent with Anchises's son,
    Abandoned themselves to a life without glory.'

Then, when those shadows had gone so far from us,   139
That it was no longer possible to see them,
A new reflection was thrown up in my mind,

And after that, another and another;   142
And so I wandered from one to the next
Until, though rambling on, I closed my eyes

And then my drifting thoughts became a dream.   145

CANTO XIX

At the hour when the warmth of the daytime,
Cooled by the earth, and sometimes by Saturn,
Can no longer mitigate the cold of the moon;

When the geomancers see their Fortuna Major   4
Rise on the eastern horizon, before the dawn,
By a way which for a little time remains dark;

There came to me in a dream, a stuttering woman,   7
Crosseyed and lopsided on her feet,
With maimed hands, and all her colour washed out.

I stared at her; and as the sun brings comfort   10
To cold limbs which the night makes heavy,
So my look made her speech distinct

And afterwards, in a moment, made her straight,   13
And brought back colour to her washed-out face,
Until it was such as love would wish to see it.

When she had recovered the use of her tongue,   16
She began to sing, so that it would have been difficult
For me to give attention to anything else.

'I am,' she said, 'I am the sweet siren   19
Who leads sailors astray on the high seas;
So full of pleasure am I to those who hear me!

22   I turned Ulysses from the wandering path
With my songs; and he who gets used to me
Rarely escapes; so completely do I satisfy him.'

25   Before her mouth was shut up again,
There appeared a holy and spritely lady
Beside me, to put the other into confusion.

28   'O Virgil, O Virgil, who is this?'
She said haughtily; and he came forward
With his eyes fixed on the honourable one.

31   He seized the other, and opened her in front,
Dividing her clothes to show me her belly:
Which woke me up with the stink which came from it.

34   I moved my eyes, and my good master said:
'I have called you at least three times. Get up and come:
Let us find the opening through which you are to go in.'

37   I got up, and already all the circles
Of the holy mountain were full of broad daylight,
And we were walking with the new sun on our backs.

40   Following him, I bore my brow like one
Who has it weighed down by a load of thoughts,
So that it makes him look like the half arch of a bridge;

43   When I heard 'Come; this is the way through,'
Spoken in so kind and gentle a manner
As one does not hear in this world of ours.

46   With wide-spread wings which seemed those of a swan,
He who had thus addressed us directed us up
Between two walls of hard blue sandstone.

49   Then he moved his feathers and fanned us as
He affirmed *'Qui lugent'* to be blessed
Because their souls were to be comforted.

52   'Why do you keep your eyes fixed on the ground?'
My guide began to say to me, at the point
When we had both advanced a little above the angel.

And I said: 'I go in such doubt and fear   55
Because a vision I had just now so draws me
That I cannot stop myself thinking about it.'

'You saw,' he said, 'that ancient sorceress   58
On whose account alone there is weeping above us;
You saw how a man frees himself from her.

Let that suffice, beat down the earth with your heels: 61
Direct your eyes instead to that lure
The eternal king spins with the great spheres.'

Like a falcon, who first looks at his feet,
And then turns when he hears the falconer's call,   64
And stretches himself through desire for the food that draws
    him,

So I did; and the whole way the rock was split   67
To give passage to anyone going up,
I went, to where the track went round again.

As I issued upon the fifth circle,   70
I saw people upon it who were weeping,
Lying on the ground flat upon their faces.

'*Adhaesit pavimento anima mea*,'   73
I heard them saying with such deep sighs
That the words could scarcely be understood.

'O elect of God, O you whose sufferings   76
Justice and hope render the less hard,
Direct us towards the other ascents.'

'If you come without having to lie here,   79
And want to find the way as quickly as may be,
Keep the open side of the track on your right.'

That was what the poet asked, and that was the answer   82
Which came from a little ahead of us; so, during the talking,
I gave my attention to what else was hidden;

And turned my eyes towards my master's eyes: 85
So that he gladly showed his assent
To the desire which my look expressed.

88   When I was able to do what was in my mind,
I moved so that I was standing over that creature
Whose words had before made me pick him out,

91   Saying: 'Spirit, in whom weeping ripens
That without which there is no turning to God,
Interrupt for a moment your greater care.

94   Tell me who you were, and why you are lying
Face downwards; and whether you want me to obtain
Anything for you in the living world I came from.'

97   And he to me: 'Why heaven has put us with
Our backs towards itself, you will hear: but first of all,
Scias quod ego fui successor Petri.

100   Between Sestri and Chiaveri there descends
A lovely river, from the name of which
My family derives its chief title.

103   For a month, and a little more, I felt how heavy
The great mantle weighs to one who keeps it from the mud,
So that all other burdens seem as light as feathers.

106   My conversion was, alas, belated;
But when I was made the shepherd of Rome,
It was then I discovered how deceitful life is.

109   I saw that the heart was not at rest there,
Though there was no going higher in that life;
That is what set alight my love for this one.

112   Up to that point I was a wretched soul,
Divided from God, and greedy of everything:
And now, as you see, I am punished for it.

115   What avarice does, is here made manifest
In the purgation of the penitent souls;
And no punishment on the mountain is more bitter.

118   Just as our eyes before were not raised
To things above, but fixed on earthly things,
So here justice sinks them to the ground.

As avarice quenched our love for every good, 121
So that the faculty of doing good was lost,
So here, justice holds us constricted,

With our hands and feet bound and held; 124
And as long as it shall please the God of Justice,
So long shall we stay here, stretched motionless.'

I knelt down, and was about to say something; 127
But as I began and he became aware,
Merely by listening, of the respect I was showing,

He said: 'For what reason do you stoop?' 130
And I to him: 'Because of your dignity
My conscience bit me when it found me standing.'

'Straighten your legs, and get on your feet, brother!' 133
He answered. 'Make no mistake: with you and the others,
I am a fellow-servant to the one power.

If ever you understood the holy word 136
Of the gospel which utters the *"Neque nubent,"*
You will see well enough why I speak thus.

Now be off: I do not wish you to stay, 139
For your being there interferes with my weeping,
By which I bring to ripeness what you spoke of.

I have a niece back there, whose name is Alagia, 142
Good in herself, provided that our family
Does not make her evil by their example;

And back there she is all that is left to me.' 145

CANTO XX

The will puts up a poor show against a better will;
So against what I wanted, because of what he wanted,
I drew the sponge from the water without filling it.

4   I moved on; and my guide moved on where there were
Free spaces, which was only along the rock,
As one goes along a wall close to the battlements;

7   For the people who were melting, drop by drop,
Through their eyes, the ill that fills the whole world,
Were stretched too far towards the outside edge.

10   So curses be upon you, ancient she-wolf,
Who have more prey than all the other animals
Because your hunger is bottomless.

13   O heavens, through whose turning it seems to be thought
Conditions here below are changed about,
When will come the one who will drive her away?

16   We were going with slow steps, a few at a time,
And I watching the shadows, whom I heard
Pitifully weeping and complaining;

19   And by chance I heard 'Sweet Mary' called by one
Ahead of us; it sounded like the cry
That a woman makes when she is in labour;

22   It was followed by: 'You were in such poverty,
As may be seen by that poor stable where
You were delivered of your holy burden.'

25   And following that, I heard: 'O good Fabricius,
You desired virtue with poverty,
Rather than have great riches with vice.'

28   These words were so pleasing to me
That I drew on so that I could identify
That spirit from whom they seemed to come.

31   He went on to speak of the liberality
Nicholas showed towards the young girls
To bring their youth to honourable estate.

34   'O ghost who speak of so great a good,
Tell me who you were,' I said, 'and why you alone
Utter again these so deserved praises.

What you say will not go without recompense,   37
If I return to finish the short journey
Of that life which is flying to its end.'

And he: 'I will tell you, though not for any comfort   40
I expect from back there, but because so much
Grace shines in you before you are dead.

I was the root of that evil tree   43
Which darkens the whole territory of Christendom,
So that good fruit is rarely gathered from it.

But if Douai, Lille, Ghent and Bruges   46
Had it in their power, there would soon be vengeance;
And I beseech it of him who judges all.

Back there I was known as Hugh Capet: 49
From me are descended the Philippes and the Louis
By whom France has been ruled in these .te times.

I was the son of a butcher in Paris: 52
When the ancient kings had all disappeared,
Except one who was turned into a monk,

I found the reins of government of the kingdom   55
Firm in my hands, myself with so much power
From newly acquired lands, and so many friends,

That the widowed crown found its way to the head   58
Of my son, and that was the beginning
Of the whole line of consecrated bones.

As long as the great dowry of Provence   61
Had not taken all shame from my blood,
It was not worth much, but it did little harm.

Then it was that with force and falsehood   64
It became violent; and, to make amends,
Seized Ponthieu, Normandy and Gascony.

Charles came to Italy and, in his turn,   67
Made Conradin a victim, and afterwards
Pushed Thomas back to heaven, to make amends.

70   I see a time, not long after today,
     Which will bring another Charles out of France
     To make him and his race better known.

73   He comes without arms, and with only the lance
     That Judas tilted with, and sticks it in so hard
     That he makes the belly of Florence burst.

76   So he will win, not territory
     But sin and shame, so much the worse for him
     As he chose to regard such wrongs lightly.

79   The other, who was taken prisoner on his ship,
     I see selling his daughter, and haggling
     As pirates do about other slave-women.

82   O avarice, what more can you do to us,
     Since you have so attracted my family
     That it does not care about its own flesh and blood?

85   To make the future evil and the past look less,
     I see the fleur-de-lys enter Alagna
     And, in the person of his vicar, Christ made captive.

88   I see him mocked a second time in him;
     I see the vinegar and gall renewed,
     And him murdered between living thieves.

91   I see the new Pilate so cruel
     That that does not satisfy him, and without authority
     He bears his covetous sails against the Templars.

94   O my Lord, when shall I have the happiness
     Of seeing the vengeance which, though hidden from us,
     Makes your anger sweet in your secret counsel?

97   What I was saying about the only bride
     Of the Holy Spirit, and which made you turn
     To me for some sort of explanation,

100 That is the response to all our prayers
     As long as the day lasts; but when night comes,
     We take up a different music instead.

Then we tell again of Pygmalion,   103
Whose desire for gold was so ravenous
It made him traitor, thief and parricide,

And the misery of the avaricious Midas,   106
Because of his exorbitant request,
Which to this day makes us all laugh at him.

And all then remember the crazy Achan,   109
And how he stole the spoil, so that the anger
Of Joshua still seems to bite him here.

Then we accuse Sapphira and her husband;   112
We praise the kicks given to Heliodorus;
And round the mountain goes in infamy

Polymnestor who killed Polydorus: 115
And last of all the cry goes up here: "Crassus,
Tell us, you must know, what does gold taste like?"

Sometimes we talk, one loudly, another softly,   118
According as our feelings spur us to go
One at a faster, one at a slower pace:

So with the good which is our subject by day;   121
Before I was not alone; but close by here
No other person was raising his voice.'

We had already gone away from him,   124
And were battling to get the better of the road,
So far as that lay in our power;

When I felt, as if it were something falling,   127
The mountain tremble; and so a chill seized me,
Such as seizes someone going to his death.

Certainly Delos was not shaken so strongly   130
Before Latona made her nest in it,
To give birth to the two eyes of heaven.

Then there began on all sides a cry   133
Such that my master drew closer to me,
Saying: 'Have no fear, while I am your guide.'

136   *'Gloria in excelsis,'* all, *'Deo'*
     Were saying, from what I heard from those nearby,
     Whose cry could accordingly be understood.

139   We stood motionless, and in suspense,
     Like the shepherds who first heard that song,
     Until the trembling stopped and the song was ended.

142   Then we took up again our holy way,
     Looking at the shadows lying on the ground,
     Already back again at their usual complaint.

145   No ignorance ever assailed me
     With so extreme a desire to know,
     If my memory is not in error,

148   As I seemed then to have, reflecting;
     And because we were in a hurry I dared not ask,
     Nor could I see anything there myself:

151   So I went on, timid and thoughtful.

CANTO XXI

     The natural thirst which is never satisfied
     Except with that water which the woman of Samaria
     Asked to be given at Jacob's well,

4   Was tormenting me, and goading me to hurry
     Along the encumbered way behind my guide,
     And I was sorry at the just revenge.

7   And suddenly, just as Luke writes
     That Christ, already risen from the mouth of the sepulchre,
     Appeared to the two and went with them,

10   A shadow appeared to us, and came behind us
     While we were looking at the crowd which lay at our feet;
     Nor did we see him until he spoke,

Saying: 'My brothers, may God give you peace.'   13
We turned round quickly, and Virgil replied
With a salute which fitted the encounter.

Then he began: 'In the council of the blessed,   16
May you be put by that infallible court
Which relegates me to eternal exile.'

'How is it?' said the other as we pressed on,   19
'If you are shadows God thinks unfit for heaven,
Who has escorted you so far up this stairway?'

And my teacher: 'If you look at the marks   22
Which this man bears and which the angel drew,
You will see he should have freedom among the just.

But since she who spins day and night   25
Had not yet drawn the yarn which Clotho
Puts on the distaff and winds for each of us,

His soul, which is your sister and mine,   28
Coming up here, could not come up alone,
Because it does not see things as we do.

So I was taken out of the wide throat   31
Of hell to guide him, and I will guide him
As far as my teaching can be of service.

But tell me, if you know, why it was that just now   34
The mountain shook so, and why all with one voice
Seemed to shout, right down to the shore below.'

With this request he threaded so exactly   37
The needle of my desire, that mere hope
Made my thirst seem the less unsatisfied.

The spirit began: 'The rule which obtains here,   40
On the mountain, admits nothing without order,
And nothing outside the custom of the place.

It is free of any alteration: 43
What heaven receives from itself into itself
May be a cause here, nothing else may be.

46   For neither rain, nor hail, nor snow, nor dew,
Nor frost falls here above the three shallow steps
Which make the stairway at the entrance below:

49   Clouds are not seen here, either dense or scattered,
Nor flashes of lightning, nor Thaumas's daughter,
Who back there often changes her country:

52   Dry vapour does not rise higher than
The top of the three steps that I spoke of,
Where the vicar of Peter has his feet.

55   There are perhaps earthquakes, more or less, lower down;
But, I don't know why, there have never been any here
Caused by wind which is hidden in the earth.

58   There are quakes here when any soul feels purified,
So that it rises up or moves itself
In order to go up; and a great shout follows.

61   The proof of purification is the will,
Which, entirely free to change its company,
Surprises the soul, and gives it pleasure to will.

64   It wills before that, but its wish will not let it,
For divine justice makes it wish for torment,
As before it was turned towards sin.

67   And I, who have lain in this suffering
Five hundred years and more, have only just felt
My will free to come to a better threshold:

70   That is why you heard the tremors, and the pious
Spirits all over the mountain rendering praise
To that Lord I pray may send for them soon.'

73   This is what he said to us; and because the pleasure
Of drinking is proportionate to the thirst,
I could not say how much he delighted me.

76   And the judicious guide: 'Now I see the net
Which traps you here, and how you escape from it,
Why there are tremors here, and why such rejoicing.

Now may it please you to let me know who you were,   79
And why you have lain here so many centuries;
Let me understand all this from your lips.'

'In the time when the good Titus, with the help   82
Of the Supreme King, avenged the wounds
From which issued the blood that Judas sold,

Back there, I had the reputation which   85
Lasts longest and most honours a man,' he replied,
'I was very famous, but as yet without faith.

So sweet was the music of my words   88
That, from Toulouse, Rome took me to herself,
And there I merited a crown of myrtles.

Statius is what people still call me there: 91
I sang of Thebes, then of the great Achilles;
But fell by the wayside with the second load.

The seeds of my ardour were the sparks   94
Which emanated from the divine flame
By which more than a thousand have been set alight;

I speak of the Aeneid, which was at once   97
Mother and nurse to me in poetry;
Without which I should have been worth almost nothing.

And to have lived back there when Virgil was alive,   100
I would consent readily to an extra year
Of banishment before I am released.'

Virgil turned to me at these words,   103
With a look which, in silence, said 'Be silent':
But virtue cannot do everything that it will;

For laughter and tears follow so closely on   106
The passions from which they respectively proceed,
That they follow the will least in the most truthful.

I merely smiled as if to convey something;   109
At which the shadow said nothing, and looked at me,
Straight in the eyes, where the mind appears most clearly;

112   And he said: 'As you wish to complete your heavy task,
        Tell me why your face just now exhibited
        The flash of sudden laughter I caught sight of?'

115   Then I was in difficulties in both directions:
        One ordered silence, while the other conjured me
        To speak; so I sighed and was understood

118   By my master, who said: 'Don't be afraid
        Of speaking; but speak and let him know
        What he is asking so anxiously.'

121   So I: 'Perhaps you are wondering,
        Great spirit, at the laugh I gave just now;
        But I should like you to wonder more than that.

124   He who is guiding my eyes upwards
        Is the same Virgil who gave you the strength
        To sing as you did about men and gods.

127   If you supposed there was any other reason
        For my laughter, it is false, forget it;
        The reason is the words you spoke about him.'

130   Already he was stooping to embrace the feet
        Of my teacher, but the latter said: 'Do not,
        Brother, for you are a shadow and so am I.'

133   And he, rising: 'Now you can understand
        The quantity of love which warms me to you,
        When I put out of mind our vanity,

136   Treating shadows as if they were solid things.'

CANTO XXII

    Already the angel was left behind us,
    The angel who had shown us to the sixth circle,
    Having erased a scar on my face;

And declared those who hunger and thirst after righteousness   4
To be blessed, and he had accomplished that
With no other words than a *sitiunt*.

And I, lighter than when going through the other openings,   7
Went on, so that without any effort,
I was following the swift spirits as they went up;

When Virgil began: 'Love, set alight by virtue,   10
Has always set alight another love
If only its flame appeared outwardly.

So from the hour when Juvenal descended   13
Among us who are in the limbo of hell,
And made clear to me your affection for me,

My goodwill towards you had been such   16
As was never before felt for a person not seen,
So that now these stairs will seem short to me.

But tell me, and forgive me as a friend,   19
If, over-confidently, I slacken the rein;
And talk with me as you would with a friend:

How could avarice find any place   22
In your heart, where there was so much wisdom,
Which you gathered there so carefully?'

These words at first made Statius laugh   25
A little, and then he replied: 'Any word
From you I take as a precious mark of love.

It often happens indeed that appearances   28
Give mistaken occasion for suspicions
Because the true reasons are concealed.

Your question makes it clear that you think   31
That I was avaricious in the other life,
Perhaps because of the circle I was in.

Now you should know that avarice was too far   34
Removed from me, and that this lack of restraint
Was punished by thousands of months where you found me.

37 And were it not that I redirected my effort,
When I understood the place where you exclaim,
Distressed, as it were, by human nature:

40 "Why do you not control the appetite
Of mortals, O you accurst hunger for gold?"
—I should have felt the rolling weights below.

43 Then I perceived that our hands can spread their wings
Too far when they spend, and I repented
Of that as I had done of other sins.

46 How many will rise again with their hair cropped
Through ignorance which, with this sin,
Hinders repentance while living and at the last hour!

49 And know that the fault, which is such that it stands
In direct opposition to any sin,
Dries out its greenness here with the sin itself:

52 So, if I have been among those people
Who weep for avarice, to effect my cure,
It has happened to me on account of the contrary.'

55 'Now when you are singing of the cruel arms
Of the two who made Jocasta sorrowful,'
Replied the author of the bucolic poems,

58 'So far as appears from what Clio inspired,
It does not appear you had yet been made faithful
By the faith without which good deeds are not enough.

61 If that is so, what sun or what candles
So gave you light that you set your sails
To follow in the way of the fisherman?'

64 And he to him: 'It was you who first sent me
Towards Parnassus to drink in its caves,
And first lit me on the way to God.

67 You did as one who, walking by night,
Carries the light behind him, where it does him no good,
But is of advantage to those who come after him.

When you said: "The world begins anew;   70
Justice returns, and the first age of man,
And a new race descends from heaven."

Through you I was a poet, through you a Christian: 73
But so that you can see better what I am drawing
I will stretch my hand out to add colours.

The whole world was already pregnant   76
With the true faith, which had been sown abroad
By the messengers of the eternal kingdom;

And those words of yours to which I have alluded   79
So fitted in with what the new preachers taught,
That I got into the habit of visiting them.

Then they came to seem to me so holy   82
That when they were persecuted by Domitian
Their complaints were accompanied by my tears;

And while I was still living in that world,   85
I gave them assistance, and their honest ways
Made me despise every other sect.

And before, in my poem, I had conducted the Greeks   88
To the rivers of Thebes, I was myself baptised;
But, through fear, I was a secret Christian

For a long time, and outwardly a pagan;   91
Because of this lukewarmness I had to go round
The fourth circle more than four hundred years.

But you, who have lifted up the covering   94
Which hid from me the great good I mentioned,
While we are climbing to the top of the mountain,

Tell me where is our ancient Terence,   97
Caecilius, Plautus and Varro, if you know;
Tell me if they are damned, and in which section.'

'They, and Persius and I, and many others,'   100
My guide answered, 'are together with that Greek
To whom the Muses gave more milk than to any other,

103   In the first circle of the dark prison.
      We often talk together of the mountain
      Which still has our nurses on its slopes.

106   Euripides is there with us, and Antiphon,
      Simonides, Agathon and many other
      Greeks who once wore laurel on their brows.

109   Of the people you wrote about we see there
      Antigone, Deiphyle and Argia,
      And Ismene as sad as ever she was.

112   The girl who pointed out the spring of Langia
      Is there; the daughter of Tiresias; Thetis;
      And Deidamia is there with her sisters.'

115   Both the poets were already silent,
      Once more with their minds on what they saw around them,
      Free of the need to climb, as of the walls.

118   And already the four handmaidens of the day
      Were left behind, and the fifth was at the tiller,
      Still pointing the flaming tip upward,

121   When my guide: 'I think that we should turn
      Our right shoulders towards the outside edge,
      And go around the mountain in the usual direction.'

124   So custom indicated what we should do,
      And we followed the way with the less doubt
      Because of the ascent of that elect soul.

127   They went in front, and I was by myself
      Behind, and listened to their conversation
      Which gave me understanding in poetry.

130   But soon the pleasant talk was interrupted
      By finding a tree in the middle of the road,
      With apples which were sweet and good to smell;

133   And as a fir-tree grows smaller towards the top,
      From bough to bough, so this tree did towards the bottom;
      I think, so that no one could go up it.

On the side on which our path was barred   136
A clear liquid fell from the high rock
And spread itself over all the leaves.

The two poets drew near to the tree;   139
And a voice from within the foliage
Cried: 'You will go short of this food.'

And then said: 'Mary gave more thought to how   142
The wedding feast should be completed with honour
Than to her own mouth, which now answers for you.

And the women of ancient Rome, for their drink,   145
Were content with water; and Daniel
Despised food, and he acquired wisdom.

The first age had the quality of gold;   148
In it hunger made acorns tasty
And thirst turned every stream to nectar.

Honey and locusts were the provisions   151
Which nourished John the Baptist in the desert;
Therefore he is glorious, and as great

As is revealed to you in the Gospel.'   154

CANTO XXIII

While I was peering through the green leaves,
Like one of those sportsmen who are accustomed
To waste their lives going after birds,

My more than father said to me: 'My son,   4
Come now, for the time allotted to us
Should be bestowed more usefully than that.'

I turned my face, and my steps at the same time,   7
Towards those wise men, who were talking so
That it was no effort to walk with them.

10   And suddenly, weeping and singing were heard,
       '*Labia mea, Domine,*' so uttered
       That it produced at once pain and delight.

13   'O gentle father, what is that I hear?'
       I began. And he: 'Those are the shadows which go
       Perhaps, untying the knot of their obligations.'

16   As travellers do, when, deep in their own thoughts,
       They overtake people they do not know,
       Looking round at them, and not stopping,

19   So, behind us, moving more quickly,
       Catching up and passing by, a troop of souls,
       Silent and devoted, were staring at us.

22   They were all dark and hollow about the eyes,
       A pallor in their faces, and so wasted
       That their skins took the shape of their bones.

25   I do not think Erysichthon was so dried up
       To his final integument, by fasting,
       When he was in greatest fear from it.

28   Reflectively I said to myself: 'There
       Go the people who lost Jerusalem,
       When Mary ate a piece of her child!'

31   The sockets of their eyes were like rings without stones:
       Those who read 'omo' in the human face
       Would certainly have recognised the 'm' there.

34   Who would believe that the smell of an apple
       Had done all that, generating desire,
       For that and for water, if they did not know?

37   I was still wondering what had starved them so,
       Because it was still not clear to me
       What caused their thinness and wretched scurvy,

40   When from the depths of his head, a shadow
       Turned his eyes on me and stared hard;
       Then called out loud: 'What grace is accorded me?'

I should never have recognised him by his looks;   43
But by his voice, it was clear at once who he was,
Although his face was no longer recognisable.

This spark at once lit up again   46
All that I knew of that changed countenance,
And I saw once more the features of Forese.

'Oh pay no attention to the dry scales   49
Which discolour my skin,' he begged, 'nor
To the way my flesh is wasted away;

But tell me the truth about yourself, and say who   52
Those two spirits are who are your escort:
Don't stand there without speaking to me!'

'Your face, which I once wept over at your death,   55
Gives me no less pain to weep for now,'
I answered him, 'seeing it so distorted.

Tell me, for God's sake, what has made your leaves fall;   58
Don't ask me to talk while I am wondering,
For there is no talking when one wants something else.'

And he to me: 'From the eternal command   61
Virtue falls in the water and the tree
We left behind, and that makes me grow thin.

And these people here who sing as they weep   64
For having paid too much attention to their gullets,
In hunger and thirst work their way back to holiness.

Desire to drink and eat is begun in us   67
By the scent issuing from the apple and the spray
Which so spreads itself over the foliage.

And not once only, as we go round the ledge,   70
Is our punishment renewed: and though I say
Punishment, it would be better to say comfort,

For that desire which leads us to this tree   73
Is what led Christ to say "Eloi" in joy,
When he delivered us with his blood.'

76   And I to him: 'Forese, from that day
     In which you changed the world for a better life,
     Not five years have gone round till now.

79   If your power of sinning more came to an end
     Only when the hour of the good suffering
     Which reunites us with God, had supervened,

82   How is it that you are already up here?
     I thought I should find you down below
     Where time is made good for the time lost.'

85   And he replied: 'What has so soon brought me
     To drink the sweet wormwood of these torments,
     Is my Nella with her flood of tears.

88   With her devout prayers and her sighs,
     She has brought me from the hillside where they wait
     And set me free from the other circles.

91   The more dear and the more pleasing to God
     Is my little widow, whom I loved so much,
     Because she is so on her own in doing well;

94   For the Barbagia in Sardinia
     Is far more modest in its womenfolk
     Than the Barbagia where I left her.

97   O gentle brother, what do you want me to say?
     Already I can see a time ahead,
     Before the present hour is very old,

100 In which the impudent women of Florence
     Will be preached against from the pulpit because
     They go about showing their breasts to the nipples.

103 What women of Barbary, what Saracens
     Ever needed, to make them go covered,
     Either spiritual or other discipline?

106 But if the shameless creatures were assured
     Of what swift heaven is getting ready for them,
     They would have their mouths open already, to howl;

For if seeing the future does not deceive me,   109
They will be unhappy before there is down on the cheeks
Of baby boys now being soothed with lullabies.

Oh brother, make no attempt at concealment!   112
You see not only me, but all these people,
Keep their eyes on where you hide the sun.'

So I to him: 'If you bring back to mind   115
What you have been with me, and I with you,
The present memory will still be grievous.

From that life, he who goes ahead of me   118
Turned me, the other day, when, at full,
Was shown to you the sister of that one.'

(And I pointed to the sun): 'Through the deep night,   121
He has led me from those who are truly dead
With the real flesh with which I follow him.

'From there, with his help, I have been brought up,   124
Climbing up and circling round the mountain
Which makes you straight although the world has twisted you.

He says that he will be my companion until   127
I arrive at the place where Beatrice is;
There it must be that I am left without him.

Virgil is he who says these things to me'   130
(I pointed with my finger); 'the other is that shadow
For whom not long ago your kingdom shook

All its slopes; it now discharges him.'   133

CANTO XXIV

We hurried in spite of our talk, and talked in spite of our hurry;
And, still in conversation, we pushed on
Just like a ship blown by a favourable wind.

4   And the shadows, who appeared as things twice dead,
Looked at me through their sunken eyes, and wondered
When they perceived that I was still alive.

7   And, going on with what I had been talking about,
I said: 'He is perhaps mounting more slowly
Than he would do, because of his thought for another.

10   But tell me, if you know, where Piccarda is;
Tell me if there is any person of note
Among the people who are looking at me so.'

13   'My sister, as good as she was beautiful,
Or so it seemed to me, is now in triumph,
Delighting in her crown on high Olympus.'

16   First he said that; and then: 'It is not forbidden,
Here, to name anyone, for our appearance
Is so squeezed out to nothing by our diet.

19   He,' and he pointed, 'is Bonagiunta,
Bonagiunta from Lucca; and that face,
Beyond him, more puckered up than the rest,

22   Is that of a man who had the Church in his arms:
He was from Tours, and now fasts to purge himself
Of the Bolsena eels and the sweet wine.'

25   Many others he named to me, one at a time;
And all of them seemed well content to be named,
So that I did not get black looks from anybody.

28   I saw, hungrily using his teeth on nothing,
Ubaldino della Pila, and Boniface
Who shepherded many peoples with his staff.

31   I saw Messer Marchese, who at Forli
Drank as much as he liked, though less thirsty than now,
Yet somehow never felt he had had enough.

34   But as one who looks at a company and then chooses
One rather than the other, so I with this Luccan,
Who seemed to want my attention more than the rest.

He murmured; and I heard something like 'Gentucca'   37
From the place where he felt the sores
Of justice eating away at him.

'O soul,' I said, 'you who appear so anxious   40
To talk with me, speak so that I can hear you,
And so that I may be content with what you say.'

'There is a woman, born but not past her youth,'   43
He began, 'who will give you reason to like
My city, although everybody complains about it.

You will go from here with this piece of pre-vision: 46
And if my murmuring has left you in doubt,
Events will make the matter clear enough.

But tell me if you are he who invented   49
Those verses in the new manner, which begin
"Women who have intelligence of love." '

And I to him: 'I am one who, when love   52
Breathes on me, notices, and in the manner
That he dictates within, I utter words.'

'O brother, now I see,' he said, 'the knot   55
Which held back the Chief Clerk, Guittone and me,
From the sweet new style of writing that I hear of.

I see clearly enough how your pens   58
Follow closely what is dictated to you;
Something which certainly did not happen to ours;

And anyone who wants to look beyond that   61
Simply cannot tell one style from the other.'
So, as if satisfied, he said no more.

As the cranes who winter along the Nile   64
Sometimes make a great flock in the air,
And then fly faster and get into line;

So all the people who were with us there   67
Turned away, and then quickened their steps,
For they were light from thinness and desire.

70   And as a man who has grown tired of trotting
     Lets his companions go, and walks instead
     Until the panting frees itself from his chest,

73   Forese let the holy band go by,
     And then came on behind me, as he did so
     Saying: 'When will it be I shall see you again?'

76   'I do not know,' I answered, 'how long I shall live;
     But my return cannot be so soon
     That my wishes do not reach the shore first;

79   For the place where I was put to live
     Is more and more stripped of virtue every day,
     And seems set to become a sad ruin.'

82   'Now go,' he said; 'for the one who is most at fault,
     I see dragged at the tail of an animal
     Towards the valley where no one is justified.

85   The animal goes faster with every step,
     Accelerating until it makes an end of him
     And leaves his body miserably disfigured.

88   Those wheels'—he turned his eyes towards the heavens—
     'Have not to turn many times, before you will see
     What I cannot reveal more openly now.

91   Now stay behind, for time is precious here
     In this kingdom, and I am losing too much,
     Coming with you so far at your own pace.'

94   As sometimes, from a troop which is riding forward,
     A horseman breaks away and gallops on
     To have the honour of the first encounter,

97   So he parted from us with bigger strides;
     And I remained on the road with those two
     Who were such great marshals in the world.

100 And when he had gone so far ahead of us
     That my eyes followed him as far as they could,
     Just as my mind followed what he had said,

There appeared to me the green and laden branches 103
Of another apple-tree, and not far away,
Because I had only just come round the bend.

I saw people underneath it raising their hands, 106
And shouting I don't know what up at the leaves,
Like children who are clamouring for something,

Who beseech, and the one who is beseeched doesn't answer 109
But, to make them really keen to get it,
Holds up high what they want and doesn't hide it.

Then they went off as if they had changed their minds; 112
And we soon arrived at the tall tree
Which says no to so many requests and tears.

'Go past it without going near to it: 115
Higher up is the tree which Eve did eat of,
And this tree has been raised from that stock.'

So said I don't know who from among the branches; 118
Which made Virgil, Statius and me, close together,
Pass by on the rising side of the slope.

'Remember,' he said, 'those accurst creatures, 121
Formed in the clouds, who, having had more than enough,
Attacked Theseus, half horses and half human;

And the Hebrews who went on their knees to drink, 124
So that Gideon would not have them for his companions
When he came down the hill towards Midian.'

So, keeping against one of the two edges, 127
We passed, hearing about the faults of gluttony
Followed by the wretched rewards which came.

Then, spread out over the lonely road, 130
We took ourselves a thousand paces more,
All in contemplation, without a word.

'What are you thinking as you go, you three solitaries?' 133
A voice said suddenly; and I gave a jump,
As timid animals do when they are disturbed.

136   I raised my head to see who it might be:
        And never, even in a furnace, appeared
        Glass and metal so shining and so glowing

139   As I saw the one who said: 'If it should please you
        To go up, you had better turn here;
        This is the way to go, if you want peace.'

142   His appearance had taken my sight from me;
        So that I turned back to my instructors
        Like someone who has to listen to find his way.

145   And just as, when she announces the dawn,
        The May breeze stirs and brings her scent,
        All saturated by the grass and flowers;

148   So I felt a wind on my forehead,
        And was conscious of the movement of the wing
        Which made me feel a breath of ambrosia.

151   And I heard a voice: 'Blessed are those whom grace
        Has so enlightened that the appetite
        Does not inflame desire excessively

154   But lets them always hunger as much as is just.'

CANTO XXV

     It was the hour when climbing could not be put off;
     For the sun had left the circle of midday
     To Taurus, and the night to Scorpio:

4   So, as a man does not stop or delay,
        But goes upon his way whatever happens
        If he is spurred on by necessity,

7   So we went through the gap, one in front of the other,
        Going up the stairway which, for narrowness,
        Did not allow of going two at a time.

And as the baby stork which raises its wings   10
Because it wants to fly, and does not dare
To leave the nest, and lowers them again;

So was I, my desire to ask a question   13
Lit up and then put out, making the movement
Of one who is making an effort to speak.

Fast as we were going, that did not stop   16
My gentle father from saying: 'Let fly then,
Since you have drawn the bow to the arrowhead.'

With confidence then I opened my mouth   19
And began: 'How is it possible to grow thin
In a place where there is no need for nourishment?'

'If you call to mind how Meleager   22
Was consumed when a firebrand was consumed,
It will not be,' he said, 'so difficult for you;

And if you think how, every move you make,   25
Your image in the mirror moves in time with it,
What appears hard for you will appear easy.

But to put you at rest in your desire,   28
Here is Statius; I appeal to him and beg
That he will be the man who heals your wounds.'

'If I explain these eternal matters to him,'   31
Statius replied, 'while you are here at hand,
My excuse is that I cannot refuse you.'

Then he began: 'My son, if my words   34
Are heeded and received into your mind
They will light up how what you speak of happens.

Perfect blood, which is never drunk up   37
By the thirsty veins, and so is left unused
Like food which you clear up from the table,

In the heart takes on the power to inform   40
All parts of the human body, like that blood
Which runs through the veins to make it as it is.

43   A further transformation, and it descends
       To a place better not mentioned; from whence, afterwards,
       It is squirted on another's blood in the natural vessel.

46   There the two bloods welcome one another;
       The one disposed to suffer, the other to act
       Because of the perfect place from which it issues;

49   And, joined to the other, it begins to operate,
       First coagulating, and then giving life
       To what it has brought together as its material.

52   The active power having become a soul,
       Like that of a plant, but different in so far
       As the former is on the way, and the latter has arrived,

55   So operates that it moves and is sensitive,
       Like a sea fungus; and then it sets about
       Organising the potentialities it has the seeds of.

58   Now, my son, the power that comes from the heart
       Of the begetter, spreads and extends itself
       Where nature intends the various parts to be;

61   But how from animal, it becomes rational
       You do not yet see: and this is a point
       Which has made a wiser man than you go astray,

64   So that he taught that the intellectual faculty
       Existed in disjunction from the soul,
       Because he saw no organ assigned to it.

67   Open your breast to the truth which is coming;
       And know that, as soon as the foetus
       Has its brain completely articulated,

70   The prime mover turns to him in gladness
       At such a piece of nature's handiwork,
       And breathes a new spirit, filled with power,

73   Which draws the active element it finds there
       Into its own substance, and makes itself
       A single soul, living, sentient, and self-reflective.

And that you may wonder less at my words,   76
See how the sun's heat turns into wine
When it is joined with the juice that wells from the vine.

When Lachesis has run out of thread,   79
The soul gets away from the flesh and carries with her
Her human as well as her divine virtue:

The rest of the faculties, all of them, mute;   82
Only the memory, intelligence and will
Much sharper in action than they were before.

Without waiting, it falls of itself   85
Marvellously on to one of the two shores:
And there it first learns where it is going.

As soon as the place there circumscribes it,   88
The informing power radiates round about
In shape and size as in the living members;

And as the air, when the weather is showery,   91
Through the extraneous rays reflected in it,
Becomes brilliant with different colours;

So the neighbouring air there puts itself   94
Into the shape impressed upon it by
The virtue of the soul which comes to a stop there;

And then, in the same manner as a flame   97
Which follows the fire whatever shape it takes,
The new form follows the spirit exactly.

Because it is from this that it has its appearance,   100
It is called, thereafter, a shadow; and from this it has
All its sensitive organs, including that of sight.

It is by this we speak and by this we laugh,   103
By this we make the tears and sighs
Which you may have heard all over the mountain.

According as the desires and other feelings   106
Affect us here, the shadow takes its shape;
And that is the cause of what excites your wonder.'

109   Now we had come to the last circle,
      There we were, and we turned to the right hand,
      And we had other things to worry about.

112   In this place the bank throws out flames,
      And the cornice blows a breath upwards
      Which turns them back and keeps them away from the edge;

115   So we had to go on the open edge,
      One at a time; and on one side I feared the fire,
      And on the other, I was afraid of falling off.

118   My guide said: 'While you are in this place
      You have to keep a tight rein on your glances
      Because you could very easily make a mistake.'

121   Then somewhere in the heart of the great burning
      I heard 'Summae Deus clementiae' sung,
      Which made me want to turn nevertheless;

124   And I saw spirits moving through the flames;
      So I looked at them, and I looked at where I was going,
      Dividing my sight somehow between the two.

127   After that hymn had come to an end
      They shouted aloud: 'Virum non cognosco';
      Then they began the hymn again, softly.

130   When it was finished once more, they called out:
      'Diana kept to the wood and drove out Helice
      Because she had tasted the poison of Venus.'

133   Then they went back to their singing; then called out
      Examples of women and husbands who were chaste
      As virtue and marriage require of us.

136   And I think this goes on continuously
      All the time the fire is burning them:
      With such concerns and such entertainment

139   The wound must, in the end, be cured.

CANTO XXVI

While we were thus going along the edge,
One behind the other, my good master saying
At intervals: 'Look out, remember I warned you';

The sun was beating down on my right shoulder,   4
For with its rays, it was changing all the west
To a white appearance in place of the pale blue;

And with my shadow I made the flames seem   7
To glow more; and even at so slight a trace
I saw many shadows, as they passed, take note.

That was the reason which incited them   10
To speak to me; and they began to say
'That doesn't look like a ghostly body.'

So some of them made in my direction,   13
So far as they could, but always taking care
Not to come out where they would not be burnt.

'O you who go, not out of idleness,   16
But perhaps respect, after the other two,
Answer me who am burning in thirst and fire.

It is not only I who want an answer;   19
For all of these are thirsting more to know
Than Indians or Ethiopians for cold water.

Tell us how it is you keep the sun off,   22
Just as you would if you had not yet entered
Into the net of death.'

So one of them addressed me; and I should   25
Have made myself known, had not my attention
Been taken by something new which appeared then;

For along the middle of the burning track   28
Came people facing the opposite way from the others,
And they made me pause and look with wonder.

31   There I saw, on either hand, the shadows
      All hurrying, and one kissing another
      Without dawdling, content with a short greeting:

34   Just as within their dark companies
      Ants rub noses with one another,
      Perhaps to ask the way or how they are faring.

37   As soon as they break off the friendly greeting,
      Before they have taken another step
      They all call out as loudly as they can:

40   The new lot of people: 'Sodom and Gomorrah';
      And the others: 'Pasiphae entered the cow
      So that the young bull might run to her lust.'

43   Then, like cranes, some of whom may fly
      To the Rhiphaean mountains, some towards the deserts,
      The latter fearing the frost, the former the sun,

46   One lot of people went off, the other came on;
      And they turned, weeping, to their former songs,
      And to the cry which was most fitting for them.

49   And those who had before questioned me
      Drew near to me, as they had done before,
      Apparently intent on hearing what I would say.

52   I, who had twice seen what they wanted,
      Began: 'O you souls who are certain of achieving
      A state of peace, whenever it may be,

55   My limbs have not been left, either green or ripe,
      Back in the world, but they are here with me
      With their blood and all their joints and parts.

58   I am going up from here in order to be blind no longer:
      There is a lady above who obtains grace for me,
      Therefore I bring my mortal part through your world.

61   But—and so may your dearest wish be satisfied
      In a short time, and that heaven shelter you
      Which is full of love, and roomiest of all—

Tell me, that I may make some record of it,   64
Who you are, and what is that company
Which is now making off behind your backs?'

Not unlike a man down from the mountains,   67
Stupidly confused, as he looks round him speechless,
When, rough and wild, he finds his way into town,

Each of those shadows had that air about him;   70
But when they had thrown off their astonishment
—Which is quickly calmed in elevated minds—

'Blessed are you, who in order to die better,'   73
Began the one who had first questioned me,
'Load yourself with experience from our territories!

The people who do not come with us have offended   76
As once Caesar did, for which, in his triumph,
He heard the cry of 'Queen', meant for himself;

So when they leave, they all call out "Sodom,"   79
As a reproach to themselves, as you have heard,
And so they help the burning with their shame.

Our sin was hermaphrodite; but because   82
We ill observed the law of humanity,
Following our appetites as animals do,

We repeat, in order to disgrace ourselves,   85
When we leave them, the name of that girl
Who, to act the animal, disguised herself as one.

Now you know our acts and what we were guilty of: 88
If you would like to know who we are, by name,
There is no time to tell you, nor could I do so.

I will satisfy your desire, as regards myself;   91
I am Guido Guinizelli; and I am purging myself
Because I repented fully before the end.'

As, on the occasion of Lycurgus's sorrow,   94
The two sons did, when they saw their mother again,
So I did, but without rising so high;

97　When I heard that master of mine name himself
　　—My master and that of men better than I
　　Whose poems of love were always sweet and graceful.

100　And without hearing or speaking, I went thoughtfully
　　For a long time, gazing at him again
　　But, because of the fire, I did not go any closer.

103　When I had had my fill of looking at him,
　　I offered to do him any service I could,
　　Swearing as one does to make another believe.

106　And he to me: 'You leave such traces on me,
　　From what I hear, and they are so clear
　　That Lethe cannot remove or obscure them.

109　But if your words just now were truly sworn,
　　Tell me what is the reason why you show
　　In what you say, in your looks, that you hold me dear.'

112　And I to him: 'It is your sweet verses
　　Which, as long as the modern usage lasts,
　　Will make even the manuscripts beloved.'

115　'O brother,' he said, 'the man I am indicating
　　With my finger'—and he pointed to a spirit in front—
　　'Was a better workman in his mother tongue.

118　In love poems and in prose romances
　　He surprised everybody; never mind the fools
　　Who say that that man from Limoges is better.

121　Their minds are on reputation more than truth,
　　And so they settle their opinions
　　Before they listen to art or to reason.

124　So many in the old days did with Guittone,
　　Mouth after mouth giving him all the merit,
　　But in the end truth has won, with most people.

127　Now if you have so great a privilege
　　As to be allowed to go to that cloister
　　In which Christ is the abbot of the college,

Say a *Pater Noster* for me there   130
Or as much as we need to say in this world
Where sin is no longer in our power.'

Then, perhaps to give place to another   133
Who was close behind him, he disappeared in the fire,
As happens in water when a fish goes to the bottom.

I moved a little towards the one he had indicated   136
And said that my desire had ready for him
A place where there was gratitude for his name.

Then he began to speak freely to me: 139
'You please me so much with your courteous request
That I cannot conceal myself, nor would.

I am Arnaut, who weep and sing as I go;   142
Thoughtful now, I see my past folly,
And I see with joy the day I hope for ahead.

Now I beg you, in the name of that worth   145
Which guides you to the top of the stairway,
Be mindful in good time of my pain.'

Then he hid himself in the fire which refines them.   148

CANTO XXVII

As when the sun shakes out its first rays
In the place where its creator shed his blood,
While the Ebro falls beneath Libra at zenith,

And the waters of the Ganges are burnt up at nones,   4
So was its position now; for the day was going,
As the angel of God appeared to us in gladness.

He stood out of the flames, upon the bank,   7
And he was singing: '*Beati mundo corde!*'
In a voice which was far more alive than ours.

'There is no going further, without the fire biting you,   10
You holy souls: so enter into it,
And do not be deaf to the singing from beyond.'

13   He said this to us when we were near to him;
        So that, when I heard him, I became
        Like someone who is to be laid in his grave.

16   I stretched forward over my clasped hands,
        Looking at the fire and there were in my mind's eye
        Human bodies which I had seen burnt.

19   Both my kind escorts turned in my direction;
        And Virgil said to me: 'My dear son,
        There may be torture here, but not death.

22   Remember now, remember! And if I
        Managed to guide you safely upon Geryon,
        What shall I do now we are nearer to God?

25   Firmly believe that if you had to stand
        A thousand years in the belly of this blaze,
        It would not rob you of a single hair.

28   And if perhaps you think I am deceiving you,
        Get nearer, and so prove for yourself
        With your hands on the edges of your garments.

31   Put off all fear, now put away fear:
        Turn this way; come, and enter safely in!'
        And yet I stood there, though against my conscience.

34   When he saw me standing, fixed and stubborn,
        He said, a little troubled: 'Now see, my son:
        This wall is between you and Beatrice.'

37   As, at the name of Thisbe, Pyramus
        Opened his dying eyes and looked at her,
        When the mulberry tree became crimson;

40   So, my stubbornness having at last yielded,
        I turned to my wise master, hearing the name
        Which was for ever rising in my mind.

43   So he shook his head and said: 'What?
        Do you want to stay here?' And then he smiled
        As at a child persuaded by an apple.

Then he put himself into the fire in front of me,   46
Inviting Statius to come behind;
For a long time he had gone between us.

When I was inside, I could have thrown myself   49
Into boiling glass to make myself cooler,
So inconceivable was the heat in that place.

My gentle father, in order to comfort me,   52
Went on talking of nothing but Beatrice,
Saying: 'I seem to see her eyes already.'

A singing voice was guiding from beyond;   55
And we, with our attention wholly on that,
Came out at the point where the climb began.

'*Venite, benedicti Patris mei!*'   58
Sounded within a light that was there
So bright that it stunned me and I could not look at it.

'The sun is going,' it added, 'and evening comes;   61
Do not stop, but hurry on your way
While the western sky is not yet dark.'

The route went up directly through the rock,   64
And I was so facing that, in front of me,
I blocked the rays of the sun, which was low already.

And we had climbed only a few of the steps   67
When, by the disappearance of my shadow
My teachers and I saw that the sun had set.

And before the horizon in all its vast reaches   70
Became one in colour and appearance
And night had liberty to do as it pleased,

Each of us made his bed upon a step;   73
For the nature of the mountain took from us
The power of climbing, though not our pleasure in it.

As goats remain quiet while they are ruminating,   76
Although they have been restless and impudent
Up on the crags before they were fed,

79   Silent in the shade while the sun is blazing,
     Watched by the shepherd, leaning upon his staff,
     Who is of service to them while he is leaning;

82   And like a shepherd who lodges in the open,
     Reposing all night long beside his flock,
     Watching lest some wild animal should scatter them;

85   So we, all three of us, were at that time,
     I like a goat, the other two like shepherds,
     Bundled together by the rocks on both sides.

88   Little of the outside could be seen from there;
     But, in that little, I saw that the stars
     Were brighter and bigger than they usually are.

91   As I was ruminating, and wondering at them,
     Sleep took hold of me; the sleep which, often,
     Knows the news before the event occurs.

94   I think it was at that hour when, from the east,
     Cytheraea first shone upon the mountain,
     She who always seems burning with the fire of love,

97   That a young and beautiful woman appeared in my dream,
     And I saw her walking over an open plain,
     Gathering flowers as she went; and, singing, she said:

100 'If anyone should ask what my name is,
     Let him know, I am Leah, as I go,
     I move my beautiful hands to make a garland.

103 To please myself at the looking-glass, I adorn myself;
     But my sister Rachel never stirs
     From her mirror, and sits there all day long.

106 She is desirous of seeing her own lovely eyes,
     As I am of adorning myself with my hands;
     She takes pleasure in looking, and I in doing.'

109 And now, through the light before the dawn
     Which rises ever more welcome to the pilgrim
     On his way back, as he lodges less far from home,

The shadows were making off on all sides   112
And my sleep with them; so I then arose,
Seeing my great masters already up.

'That sweet apple which the care of mortals   115
Goes looking for upon so many branches
Will today bring peace to all your hungers.'

Such were the words that Virgil used to me;   118
And never at any time was there an announcement
Which gave me a pleasure equal to that.

Ever greater desire to be at the top   121
Came to me, and then, with every step I took,
I felt that I was growing wings to fly.

When the whole of the stairway had raced by   124
Under us, and we were on the highest step,
Virgil turned his eyes upon me fixedly

And said: 'You have seen the temporal fire, my son,   127
And the eternal; and you have come to a place
Where I, of myself, can see no further.

I have brought you here with intelligence and art;   130
Now you must take your pleasure for your guide;
You are out of the steep and narrow way.

You see the sun shining upon your forehead;   133
You see the grass, the flowers and little bushes
Which the ground here produces of itself.

While those beautiful eyes, happy and beautiful,   136
Which, in their tears, moved me to come to you,
Are coming, you may sit or wander here.

No longer wait for words or signs from me.   139
Your will is free, just, and as it should be,
And not to follow it would be a fault:

I leave you master of your body and soul.'   142

CANTO XXVIII

Eager now to explore in and around
The divine forest, which was dense and alive,
So that it tempered the new light to my eyes,

4   I left the slope, without waiting longer,
Making my way across the plain at leisure
Over the ground which was everywhere fragrant.

7   A soft air, without any trace
Of variation, struck me on the forehead,
But no harder than a gentle breeze;

10   It made the branches quiver without resistance,
As one and all they bent in the direction
In which the holy mountain cast its first shade;

13   Yet they were not so deflected from their stations
That the little birds who were perched on top of them
Interrupted the exercise of their art;

16   But, singing the first breezes in all gladness,
They welcomed them among the foliage
Which kept up an accompaniment to their songs,

19   Such as gathers from bough to bough
In the pine forest on the shore of Chiassi
When Aeolus lets loose the Sirocco.

22   Already my slow steps had carried me
Inside the ancient wood, so that I could not
Look back to the point at which I had entered it;

25   And there was a stream which stopped me going further;
It bent towards the left, with its little waves,
The grass which sprouted along its bank.

28   All the purest waters in our world
Seem to have some admixture of something else
In comparison with this, which hides nothing,

Although it flows so darkly, very darkly,
Perpetually in shade, which at no time
Admits either the sun or moon to shine there.

31

With my feet I came to a stop, but with my eyes
I crossed the little river, in order to gaze
At the variety of May-time flowers;

34

And there appeared to me, as there appears,
Suddenly, something which, for the wonder of it,
Sets every other thought one may have off course,

37

A girl by herself, who went along
Singing, and picking flower after flower,
Her entire path being coloured with them.

40

'Pray, lovely lady, who, if I am to believe
The looks which generally reveal the heart,
Are warming yourself in the sunshine of love,

43

May it please you to come forward a little,'
I said to her, 'towards the bank of the stream
So that I may hear what you are singing.

46

You bring to my mind where and what manner of person
Proserpine was in the time when her mother
Lost her and she herself lost her spring flowers.'

49

As a woman dancing turns herself
With her feet close to the ground and to each other,
And hardly advances one toe out of line,

52

She turned in my direction, looking over
The red and yellow flowers, exactly as
A virgin will modestly lower her eyes;

55

And then fully satisfied my request,
Moving so near to me that the sweet sound
Came to me so that it could be understood.

58

As soon as she was where the grass was bathed
Already by the waves of the lovely stream,
She graciously raised her eyes to meet mine.

61

64   I do not think that so much light shone
Under the brow of Venus, when she was pierced
By her son, who did not often strike carelessly.

67   She smiled straight at me from the other bank,
Further arranging in her hands those flowers
Which the high country bears though none is sown.

70   The river kept us three paces apart;
But Hellespont, at the point where Xerxes crossed
—And he should still be a caution to human pride—

73   Did not experience more hate from Leander
For high seas between Sestos and Abydos,
Than that stream did for opening no way for me.

76   'You are new, and perhaps because I am smiling,'
She began, 'in the place which was elected
To be the cradle of our human nature,

79   Doubt of some kind may keep you wondering;
But the psalm *Delectasti* gives light
Which can clear the mist from your understanding.

82   And you who are in front, and spoke to me,
Say if there is any more you would like to hear;
For I came so that I could answer any questions.'

85   'The water,' I said, 'as well as the sound of the forest,
Make me call in question something I recently
Came to believe, for I had heard something different.'

88   So she: 'I will tell you from what cause
Proceeds the thing that makes you marvel so,
And I will clear the mist that troubles you.

91   The supreme good, who pleases only himself,
Made man good and for good, and this place
Was given as an earnest of eternal peace.

94   Through man's default he did not stay here long;
Through his default he changed honest laughter
And sweet play for sorrow and for sweat.

So that the turbulence which is created 97
Down below, by exhalations of water and earth
Which follow as far as they can after heat,

Should not attack man in any way, 100
The mountain rose up towards heaven so high
That it would be clear of them above the gate.

Now, because in its circuit the whole air 103
Moves in a body with the Primum Mobile,
Unless the circle is broken at some point,

At this height, which is entirely clear, 106
In the living air, that motion can be felt
And makes the wood, because of its density, sound;

And the tree that is struck has the property 109
Of impregnating the air with its virtue,
Which the air, in its revolution, diffuses;

And the land, according to the merits 112
Of itself and its climate, conceives and produces
Different trees with different sorts of virtues.

To anyone who had heard this, it would not appear 115
To be a marvel on earth that some plants
Take root without any visible seed.

And you should know that this holy plateau 118
Where you are now, is full of all the seeds
And has fruits which are not to be gathered elsewhere.

The water that you see does not come from veins 121
Fed by an exhalation which cold condenses,
Like a river which breathes in and then out again;

But it issues from a steady and sure spring 124
Which replenishes, by the will of God,
As much as it pours out on either hand.

On this side it flows down with the virtue 127
Of taking from men the recollection of sin;
On the other side it brings all good deeds to mind.

130   It is called Lethe on this side; on the other
      It is called Eunoë; and it does not work
      Unless it is first tasted on both sides:

133   The flavour of it is above all others.
      And even though your thirst is fully quenched
      If I reveal to you no more than that,

136   I will give you a corollary as a grace;
      Nor do I think you will value my words less
      If they go beyond what I have promised.

139   Those who in ancient times wrote poems about
      The happy condition of the age of gold,
      Perhaps, on Parnassus, were dreaming of this place.

142   Here the root of the human race was innocent;
      Here it was always spring, every fruit is here;
      This is the nectar of which everyone talks.'

145   I turned right round in the direction of
      My poets, and I saw that they had heard
      The last portion of this discourse with smiles;

148   Then I turned my face again to the lovely woman.

CANTO XXIX

      Singing like a woman who is in love,
      She went on, at the end of her discourse:
      'Beati, quorum tecta sunt peccata.'

4   And, as nymphs who used to go alone
      Among the woodland shadows, some of them
      Desiring to see the sun, others to avoid it,

7   She then moved, going upon the bank,
      Against the stream; and I kept pace with her,
      Following her little steps with little steps.

The two of us had not taken a hundred paces   10
When the banks both made a turn at the same time
So that I was then facing the east.

And we had gone only a little way after that   13
When the woman turned around in my direction,
Saying: 'My brother, look now and listen.'

And as she did a sudden brightness transfused   16
The whole immense forest on every side,
So that I thought it might be lightning.

But since when lightning comes, it disappears,   19
Whereas this light lasted and shone more and more brightly,
I said inside myself: 'What can it be?'

And a sweet melody ran through the luminous   22
Atmosphere; so that a true fervour
Made me reproach the temerity of Eve

Who, there where heaven and earth were obedient,   25
The only woman, and only just created,
Would not put up with being under any veil;

Had she been dutiful, under that veil   28
I should have known these ineffable pleasures
Before this and for a much longer time.

While I was going among so many first-fruits   31
Of the eternal pleasure, in astonishment,
And desiring still greater felicities,

In front of me, under the green branches,   34
The air became like a fire alight;
And the sweet sound was audible as songs.

O sacrosanct Virgins, if I have ever   37
Felt cold for your sake or undergone long vigils,
I have reason now to ask for my reward.

Now Helicon should pour out through me   40
And Urania assist me with her choir
To put into verse things difficult to think.

43   Further on appeared seven golden trees
     —Or what looked like that at the great distance,
     Which stretched still between them and where we were—

46   But when I had approached them so closely
     That the common object which deceives the senses
     Lost none of its particularity through distance,

49   The faculty which prepares matter for reason
     Apprehended that they were candlesticks,
     And that the voices were singing 'Hosanna.'

52   Above, the splendid display sent out flames
     Much brighter than the moon in a clear sky
     At midnight in the middle of her month.

55   I turned round, full of admiration,
     To the good Virgil, and he responded to me
     With a look not less loaded with amazement.

58   Then I again looked towards the sublime objects
     Which moved in our direction so slowly
     That a bride coming out of church would have gone faster.

61   The lady called to me: 'Why are you so taken
     Only with the sight of these brilliant lights
     And do not look at what is coming behind them?'

64   Then I saw people dressed in white
     Coming behind, as if following their leaders;
     And such whiteness never was in this world.

67   The water shone to the left of me
     And gave back the reflection of my left side,
     When I looked into it, as a mirror would do.

70   When my position on my bank was such
     That only the river kept me at a distance,
     I halted my steps in order to see better,

73   And I saw the flames, as they advanced,
     Leaving the air behind them coloured,
     And they had the appearance of extended streamers;

So that there remained seven bands   76
Clearly marked, and all in those colours
From which the sun makes his bow, and Delia her girdle.

Those banners stretched further to the rear   79
Than I could see; and as far as I could judge
There were ten paces between the two outside ones.

Under the marvellous sky I have described   82
Came four and twenty elders, two by two,
And they were all crowned with *fleur-de-lys*.

All were singing: 'Blessed art thou   85
Among the daughters of Adam, and blessed also
Your loveliness to all eternity!'

When the flowers and all the young leaves and grasses   88
Opposite me upon the other bank
Were empty of those elect people,

As in the sky one star succeeds another,   91
After them there came four living creatures,
Each of them crowned with green branches.

Each of them was equipped with six wings;   94
The feathers were full of eyes: and the eyes of Argus,
If they were alive, would be like that.

I will waste no more verses on describing   97
How they looked, reader; I have other charges
To meet, and cannot waste any more on that;

But read Ezekiel who has depicted them   100
As he saw them coming from the cold north
In a whirlwind, with a great cloud and a fire;

And as you will find those creatures in his pages,   103
So they were there, except that as to the wings,
John the Divine is with me and differs from him.

The space between the four of them contained   106
A triumphal car upon two wheels,
Which came on with a griffin yoked to it.

109 He stretched his wings upwards so that the middle
Streamer was between them, with three on each side,
So that no harm was done to any of them.

112 They rose so high that they went out of sight;
The parts of them in which he resembled a bird
Were gold, the rest of him was white and carmine.

115 Neither Africanus, or even Augustus,
Delighted Rome with so splendid a chariot;
Even that of the sun would be poor beside it;

118 The sun's which, going off course, was burnt
At the devout entreaty of the earth,
When Jove performed his arcane act of justice.

121 Three ladies came dancing in a circle
By the right wheel; and one of them was so red
That she would hardly have been visible in a fire;

124 The next was as if her flesh and bones
Had been entirely made of emerald;
The third appeared to be of new-fallen snow;

127 And now they seemed to be guided by the white,
Now by the red; from the way that one sang
The others took the time, whether slow or quick.

130 By the left wheel, four disported themselves,
Dressed in purple, following the example
Of one of them who had three eyes in her head.

133 After the whole group I have described
I saw two old men, who were dressed differently
But had the same forthright and massive bearing.

136 One of them was attired like one of the familiars
Of the great Hippocrates, whom nature made
For the living creatures she holds most dear;

139 The other was dressed for the opposite profession,
With a sword, which was glittering and sharp
And which, even across the stream, made me afraid.

Then I saw four who were of modest appearance;   142
And behind them all an old man by himself,
Advancing, in a sleep, but keen-faced.

And these seven were dressed in the same manner   145
As the first group, but it was not lilies
That they had gathered around their heads

But rather roses and other red flowers: 148
From a short distance away one would have sworn
That above their eyes all of them were alight.

And when the chariot was opposite me,   151
There was a noise like thunder, and that great company
Seemed to have been forbidden to go further,

And stopped there with the standards which led them.   154

CANTO XXX

When the Seven Stars out of the first heaven
—Which never knew either setting or rising,
Nor any veil of mist, other than sin,

And which there put everyone on the alert   4
As to his duty, as the Seven Stars below do
For the man who turns the helm to come to port—

Had come to a halt, the truthful company,   7
Who had come between the griffin and them,
Turned towards the chariot as towards their peace;

And one of them, as if sent from heaven,   10
Shouted in a singing voice, three times, *Veni
Sponsa de Libano*, and the rest after him.

As the blessed, when the last trump sounds,   13
Will rise quickly, each one from his tomb,
Their flesh put on again, singing *hallelujahs*.

16   So there arose on the divine chariot,
      At the voice of that elder, a hundred
      Ministers and messengers of eternal life.

19   All were saying: *'Benedictus qui venis!'*
      And throwing flowers above and around,
      'Manibus o date lilia plenis!'

22   I have seen, at the beginning of day,
      The eastern part of the sky all roseate
      And the rest of it dressed in tranquillity;

25   And the face of the sun appear shadowy,
      And such that it was so tempered by mist
      That the eye could bear to look for a long time:

28   So, inside a great cloud of flowers
      Which leapt out of the angelic hands
      And fell inside the chariot and all around it,

31   Over a white veil, crowned with olive,
      A lady came to me, under her green cloak
      Clothed in the colour of flame.

34   And my spirit, which for so long a time
      Had not been in her presence,
      Trembled with wonder, crushed,

37   Without knowing her any more, with my eyes,
      But through the secret virtue which went out from her,
      Felt the great power of the ancient love.

40   The moment that, as I looked, I was struck
      By the high virtue which had already stabbed me
      Before I was out of my boyhood,

43   I turned round to my left, with that trust
      With which a child runs to his mother,
      When he is afraid or in trouble,

46   To say to Virgil: 'Less than a drop of blood
      Is left in me, that is not trembling:
      I know the signs of the ancient flame.'

But Virgil had taken himself away from us,   49
Virgil, my sweetest father, to whom
I had given myself up for my own well-being;

Nor was all that our ancient mother lost   52
Enough to keep my cheeks, although washed with dew,
From turning dark with tears, and I wept.

'Dante, weep no more for Virgil's going,   55
Weep no more yet, for you will have to weep
Presently because of another sword.'

Like an admiral who goes fore and aft   58
To see his people who man the other ships
And to encourage them to do well;

Upon the left side of the chariot,   61
When I turned round at the sound of my name,
—Which I mention only because I must,—

I saw the lady who first appeared to me,   64
Veiled under the angelic rain of flowers,
Direct her eyes towards me across the river.

Although the veil which fell around her head,   67
Encircled by Minerva's climbing branches,
Did not allow her to appear openly,

Regally, in her gesture still severe,   70
She went on, like a speaker who keeps back
The sharpest things he has to say till last:

'Look at me well! I am indeed Beatrice.   73
How were you able to climb the mountain?
Did you not know that men are happy here?'

My face fell and I looked at the clear water   76
But, seeing myself in it, switched to the grass,
So heavy was the shame on my brow.

As a mother may seem stern to her child,   79
So she appeared to me; because it is a bitter
Taste that is left by sharpness in pity.

82   She said nothing; and the angels sang
      Suddenly: '*In te, Domine, speravi*';
      But they did not get beyond '*pedes meos.*'

85   Just as the snow among the living beams
      Along the spine of Italy, is frozen
      When it is pinched and battered by the Slav winds,

88   Then, melted, trickles down through itself,
      Once there is a breath from the land without shade,
      Which seems like fire melting a candle;

91   So I was without a tear or a sigh
      Before the singing of those whose notes always
      Follow the notes of the eternal spheres;

94   But when I had heard in their sweet tones
      The compassion they had for me, more than if they had said:
      'Lady, why do you treat him so harshly?',

97   The ice which was packed round about my heart
      Turned into spirit and water, and with anguish
      Issued from my heart by the mouth and by the eyes.

100   She, still standing motionless on the side
      Of the chariot, as before, addressed herself
      To the merciful beings in these words:

103   'You keep watch in the eternal day,
      That neither night nor sleep may take from you
      One step the world takes along its ways;

106   Therefore my answer is made more carefully,
      That he who is weeping there may understand me,
      So that he may suffer as he has sinned.

109   Not only by the operation of the planets
      Which direct every seed to some end,
      According to their conjunction with the stars,

112   But by the abundance of divine graces
      Which rain on us from mists so far removed
      That they are utterly beyond our sight,

This man, in his youthful years, had such   115
Possibilities, that every propitious tendency
Would have produced some marvellous result in him.

But ground sown with bad seed and not cultivated   118
Becomes the more malignant and overgrown
The more wholesome vigour there is in the soil.

For some years I sustained him with my looks;   121
Showing my youthful eyes to him,
I led him with me in the right direction.

As soon as I was upon the threshold   124
Of my second age and changed my life, he took himself
From me, and gave himself to others.

When I had mounted from flesh to spirit,   127
And my beauty and virtue had grown greater,
To him I became less dear and less pleasing;

And he turned his steps along an untrue path,   130
Following false appearances of good
Which never kept any promise entirely.

It was no good my begging for inspiration,   133
With which in dreams, and in other ways
I called him back; little he cared about that!

So low he fell, that every remedy   136
Was short of what was needed for his salvation,
Except that of showing him the damned.

For this I visited the gate of the dead,   139
And to him who has conducted him up here
My prayers, with weeping, were carried.

God's high dispensation would be thwarted   142
If Lethe were passed, and such a feast
Tasted without any payment exacted

In the way of penitence where tears are shed.'   145

CANTO XXXI

'O you who are beyond the sacred river,'
She began, directing her speech towards me,
Point first, though it had seemed sharp enough sideways,

4 And then she went on without pausing,
'Say, say if this is true: an accusation like that
Needs your confession to go with it.'

7 My virtue was put in such confusion
That my voice stirred, but was extinguished
Before it could escape from throat and lips.

10 She waited a moment, then said: 'What do you think?
Answer me; for your unfortunate recollections
Have not yet been turned to nothing by the water.'

13 Confusion and fear mixed together
Forced such a 'Yes' out of my mouth
That to hear it it was necessary to see it.

16 As a crossbow breaks, when it goes off
After being pulled too tight, both bow and string,
And hits the mark with less impetus,

19 So I burst out under the heavy charge,
Pouring out tears and sighs, while my voice
Came to a halt somewhere in my throat.

22 So she said to me: 'In the midst of my wishes
Which were leading you to a love of the good
Beyond which there is nothing to aspire to,

25 What pitfalls or what barriers did you find
Across your path, that you had to give up hope
Of being able to go any further?

28 What attractions or what advantages
Showed themselves in the looks of the others
That you should walk up and down in front of them?'

After having heaved a bitter sigh   31
I hardly had a voice to answer with,
And my lips gave it shape with difficulty.

Weeping I said: 'The things that were at hand,   34
With their false pleasure, turned my steps aside
As soon as your face had gone from sight.'

And she: 'If you had kept silent or denied   37
What you confess, your fault would not be
Less known: there is a judge who knows!

But when the accusation bursts out   40
From the sinner's own cheeks, in our court,
The wheel turns back against the sharp edge.

Yet, in order that you may be ashamed   43
Of your errors, and so that another time,
When you hear the sirens, you may resist better,

Put aside the cause of your weeping   46
And listen to me: you will hear how my buried flesh
Should have moved you in the contrary direction.

Never did nature or art present you with   49
Such pleasure, as the beautiful limbs in which
I was enclosed, now scattered upon earth;

And if the highest pleasure thus failed you,   52
Through my death, what mortal thing soever
Ought afterwards to have drawn you to desire it?

Indeed you ought, at the first arrows from   55
Deceitful things, to have gone higher,
Following me, who was no longer of that kind.

You should not have let your wings be weighed down   58
To wait for further shots, by any girl
Or other vanity of such short use.

The young bird waits two or three times;   61
But before the eyes of the bird that is fully-fledged
Nets are spread and arrows shot in vain.'

64   As children, when they are ashamed, will stand
     Dumb, with their eyes to the ground, listening,
     Admitting they are wrong and sorry about it,

67   So I was standing; and she said: 'Since to hear
     Makes you sorry, you can raise your beard up
     And suffer a little more by looking at me.'

70   A great oak is uprooted more easily,
     Whether by a home wind or by a wind that blows
     Across the sea from the land of Iarbas,

73   Than I raised my chin at her command;
     And when she said my beard instead of my face
     I knew what venomous point she was making.

76   And when my face was raised in her direction,
     My eye grasped the fact that the primal creatures
     Had paused from their task of scattering flowers;

79   And my eyes, still not at all sure of themselves,
     Saw Beatrice turned towards the beast
     Which is a single person in two natures.

82   Under her veil on the other side of the river,
     She seemed to me to surpass her old self
     More than she had surpassed other women when she was with
          them:

85   The nettle of repentance so stung me
     That what had attracted me most to other things
     Became now most an object of hatred.

88   The consciousness of this so bit my heart
     That I fell down unconscious; what happened then
     She who was the cause of it best knows.

91   Then, when life had flowed back to my limbs,
     I saw above me the girl I had found alone,
     And she said: 'Hold on to me! Hold on to me!'

94   She had dragged me into the river up to my neck,
     And pulling me after her she was going along
     On top of the water, as lightly as a skiff.

When I was nearly at the blessed bank,   97
I heard 'Aspergas me' so sweetly
That I cannot remember, much less describe it.

The lovely woman opened her arms wide;   100
She put them round my head and ducked me under
So that I had to swallow some of the water.

She pulled me out, and conducted me, all wet,   103
Into the midst of the four lovely dancers;
And each one of them put her arm over me.

'We are nymphs here, and in heaven we are stars: 106
Before Beatrice came down into the world,
We were appointed to wait upon her.

We will lead you to her eyes; but the three there   109
Will sharpen yours to the happy light within them,
For they see more deeply than we do.'

Thus they began to sing; and after that   112
To lead me on towards the griffin's chest,
Where Beatrice stood, facing in our direction.

They said: 'Do not spare your eyes now: 115
We have stationed you before the emeralds
From which Love once drew his arms for you.'

A thousand desires hotter than flame   118
Held my eyes to those shining eyes
Which still remained fixed upon the griffin.

Like the sun in a mirror, that is how   121
The double animal shone in them,
Now one nature showing, now the other.

Consider, reader, whether I thought it wonderful   124
When I saw the object itself quite stationary
While the image of it was changing all the time.

While, full of astonishment and glad, my soul   127
Was tasting that food which of itself
Satisfies, but creates a longing for itself,

130 The other three, who by the way they moved
Showed themselves to be of the most exalted,
Came forward in angelic song and dance.

133 'Turn, Beatrice, now turn your holy eyes'
—This was their song—'to him who is faithful to you,
And who has come so many steps to see you!

136 For the grace of God be gracious to us, unveil
Your lips to him, so that he may discern
The second loveliness which you are hiding.'

139 O splendour of the live eternal light,
Who is there who has grown pale under the shade
Of Mount Parnassus, or has drunk from its basins,

142 Who would not find that his mind was encumbered,
Trying to render you as you appeared
When you showed yourself openly in the air

145 Where heaven in its harmony adumbrates you.

CANTO XXXII

My eyes were so fixed and attentive,
To quench the thirst I had had for ten years,
That the other senses were all extinguished.

4 And they were as if walled on either side
By unconcern—so much the holy smile
Drew me to itself with the old net!—;

7 When my gaze was forced to turn aside
Towards my left, by those goddesses,
Because I heard from them a 'Too intent!';

10 And my eyes were in that state that eyes are in
When they have just met the glare of the sun,
So that for a little while I could see nothing.

But when my sight had grown used to the lesser   13
(I say 'to the lesser' in relation to the greater
Object of sense from which I tore myself),

I saw that the splendid army had wheeled about   16
To its right flank, and was turning
With the sun and the seven flames at its head.

As in a retreat a troop of soldiers   19
Turn under their shields, and wheel with the standard
Before they can wholly change direction;

Those soldiers of the celestial kingdom   22
Which headed the column, had all passed us by
Before the first timbers of the car moved round.

Then the ladies went back beside the wheels,   25
And the griffin shifted the consecrated load
In such a way that no feather of him was ruffled.

The lovely woman who had pulled me across the ford,   28
And Statius and I, were following the wheel
Which, as it turned, described the smaller arc.

As we travelled through the deep forest, empty   31
Through the fault of her who listened to the serpent,
An angelic song set the time for our steps.

When we had advanced perhaps as far   34
As three bowshots from our starting-point,
Beatrice descended from the chariot.

I heard everybody murmur 'Adam';   37
Then they encircled a tree despoiled
In all its boughs, of foliage of any kind.

Its crown of branches, which spread out more widely,   40
The higher it went, would be taken for a wonder
Of altitude by Indians in their forests.

'Blessed are you, griffin, who with your beak   43
Take nothing from that tree, so sweet to the taste,
But giving pains in the belly afterwards.'

46   So, all around the sturdy tree,
      The others cried; and the animal with two natures:
      'Thus is the seed of righteousness preserved.'

49   And he turned to the shaft which he had drawn,
      And dragged it to the foot of the widowed bough,
      And left it bound to that from which it came.

52   As our trees, when the great light falls
      Downward on them, mixed with that which shines
      After the light of the celestial Pisces,

55   Swell in buds, and then renew themselves,
      Each one in its proper colour, before the sun
      Yokes his horses under a new constellation;

58   Displaying a colour which was less that of roses
      Than that of violets, the tree renewed itself,
      Although before the boughs had been so bare.

61   I did not understand it, it is not sung
      On earth, the hymn those people were singing there,
      Nor could I take in the notes entirely.

64   If I could depict how the pitiless eyes
      Went to sleep, hearing the tale of Syrinx,
      The eyes whose continuous watching cost so dear;

67   Just as a painter paints from a model,
      I would draw how I myself went to sleep;
      But let who will imagine the drowsiness,

70   I go on to the point when I awoke,
      And I tell you that a splendour ripped the veil
      Of sleep, and a call: 'Get up: what are you doing?'

73   As, to see some blossoms of the apple-tree
      Which makes the angels hungry for the fruit,
      And makes a perpetual marriage-feast in heaven,

76   Peter and John and James were led to the mountain,
      And fell upon their faces, and at the word
      By which deeper sleeps had been broken, came to themselves,

And saw the company diminished   79
By the departure of Moses and Elias,
And the raiment of the master changed;

So I came to myself, and saw standing over me   82
That compassionate woman who had gone with me
When I was walking beside the river earlier.

And all in doubt I said: 'Where is Beatrice?'   85
She answered: 'Under the new foliage,
Look, she is sitting on that root.

Look at the company she has around her: 88
The rest are going upwards after the griffin
With a sweeter and a more profound song.'

And whether she continued to speak after that,   91
I do not know, because before my eyes
Was she who shut out all my other thoughts.

She sat by herself upon the true ground,   94
Left there as sentry near the chariot
Which I had seen the two-natured beast make fast.

The seven nymphs had formed themselves into a circle   97
Round about her, in their hands those lights
Which are safe from the north wind and the south wind.

'For a little while you shall dwell in these woods;   100
And with me shall eternally be a citizen
Of that Rome of which Christ himself is a Roman.

Therefore, for the sake of the world which lives ill,   103
Keep your eyes on the chariot, and what you see,
Make sure that you write down, when you get back.'

So Beatrice; and I was all obedience,   106
Ready to kiss the feet of her commandments,
And directed my mind and my sight as she willed.

Never did fire descend with such swiftness   109
From thick cloud, when it falls from the remotest
Regions of the atmosphere,

112   As I saw the bird of Jove drop
      Down through that tree, ripping the bark,
      As well as the flowers and the new leaves;

115   And he struck against the car with all his strength;
      So that it reeled like a ship in a storm,
      Battered by the waves, first to port and then to starboard.

118   Then I saw the vixen rush into the cradle
      Of the triumphal car; she seemed to have been fasting
      From every kind of wholesome nourishment.

121   But, reproving her for her obscene faults,
      My lady put her to a flight as swift
      As those bones without flesh could manage.

124   Then, by the way by which it had first come,
      I saw the eagle descend into the inside
      Of the car, and leave it coated with his feathers:

127   And, as a voice comes from a grieving heart,
      There came a voice from heaven, with these words:
      'My little ship, how ill-laden you are!'

130   Then it seemed to me that the earth opened
      Between the wheels, and I saw a dragon come out;
      And it stuck its tail right up through the car;

133   And like a wasp which pulls back its sting,
      Drawing his malignant tail to himself,
      He pulled out a bit of the bottom and wandered off.

136   What remained covered itself again
      With the feathers—which perhaps had been offered
      In good faith and with the kindest intentions—

139   Like earth sprouting grass, and both wheels,
      And the shaft, were covered with them
      In less time than a sigh keeps the mouth open for.

142   The sacred construction, thus transformed,
      Put out heads from its different parts,
      Three over the prow and one on each side.

The first were horned like oxen, but the four   145
Had a single horn upon their foreheads;
Like monster there was never seen before.

Securely, like a city set on a hill,   148
Appeared to me a harlot, her clothes loose,
And casting her eyes around her all the time.

And as if to ensure that no one carried her off,   151
I saw a giant beside her, standing upright;
And from time to time they kissed one another.

But because she turned her lustful, wandering eye   154
On me, her fierce lover immediately
Whipped her from head to foot;

Then, full of suspicion and made cruel by rage,   157
He loosed the monster, and dragged it through the wood,
Which made that the only shield I had

From the harlot and the new monstrosity.   160

CANTO XXXIII

'*Deus, venerunt gentes*,' singing alternately,
Now three, now four, the ladies began
A sweet psalmody, and they were weeping;

And Beatrice, sighing and compassionate,   4
Listened to them, so changed in her looks
That Mary was hardly more so when she stood at the cross.

But after the other virgins had made room   7
For her to speak, she got up on her feet
And replied, coloured like fire:

'*Modicum, et non videbitis me;*   10
Et iterum, my beloved sisters,
Modicum, et vos videbitis me.'

13   Then she put all the seven in front of her,
        And indicated that behind her should follow
        I and the woman and the remaining poet.

16   So she moved off; and, I think, her tenth step
        Had not been put in position on the ground
        When with her eyes she subdued my eyes;

19   And in a tranquil manner she said to me:
        'Come more quickly, so that, if I speak to you,
        You will be better placed to hear what I say.'

22   As soon as I was, as my duty was, with her,
        She said to me: 'Brother, why don't you dare
        To question me, now you are coming with me?'

25   As those who, in the presence of their betters,
        Are too respectful in the way they talk,
        And do not bring their voices alive to their teeth,

28   It happened to me, who with half a voice,
        Began: 'My lady, you understand my need,
        And what is good for it.'

31   And she to me: 'I want you now to unwind
        From your entanglements of fear and shame,
        And not to go on talking as if you were dreaming.

34   Know that the vessel which the serpent broke
        Was and is not; let him who is to blame
        Know that God's vengeance will not be put off.

37   The eagle who left his feathers in the car
        Which then became a monster and a prey,
        He will not for ever be without an heir;

40   For I see certainly, and therefore tell it,
        Stars are already near which none may impede
        And none hinder, which will give us times

43   In which a five hundred, ten and five,
        A messenger of God, shall kill the whore
        Together with the giant who shares her sin.

And perhaps my prophecy, which is as obscure   46
As Themis and the Sphinx, persuades you less
Because in their manner it darkens the mind;

But soon the facts will show, the Naiads will   49
Solve the enigma, difficult though it is,
And leave both herds and crops meanwhile unharmed.

Take note: and as my words are carried from me,   52
Make sure that they are delivered to the living
Whose life is nothing but a race to death.

And bear in mind, when you are writing them,   55
Not to conceal how you have seen the tree
Which now has been twice robbed of its leaves here.

Whoever robs the tree or snaps off pieces,   58
Offends against God by a blasphemous act;
It was created holy for his use.

For biting it, the first soul hungered on   61
Five thousand years in torment and desire
For him who took the punishment on himself.

Your mind must be asleep, if you do not see   64
That it is for a special reason that this tree
Is so lofty and so wide at the top.

And if your idle thoughts had not encrusted   67
Your mind like the water of Elsa, and the pleasure of them
Been like Pyramus spattering the mulberry tree,

By so many circumstances you would have recognised,   70
On your own, the moral significance
Of the justice of God in his interdict on this tree.

But because I see you in your intellect   73
Made of stone, and turned to stone, coloured
So that the light of what I am saying dazzles you,

I want you to take back inside yourself,   76
At least an impression, if you do not write it,
As a pilgrim's staff is brought back wreathed with palm.'

79   And I: 'In the same way as wax under a seal,
So that figures stamped on it do not change,
My brain has now been marked by you.

82   But why do your words, I have so much longed for,
Fly so far beyond what I can see
That, try as I may, I lose most of them?'

85   'I do it so that you may know what school
You have followed,' she said, 'and may see how far its doctrine
Enables you to follow what I have said;

88   And that you may see that your way has been
As far from the divine way, as the earth
Is from the heaven which moves around the fastest.'

91   So I replied to her: 'I cannot remember
That I ever strayed away from you,
Nor does my conscience bite me on that account.'

94   'And if you cannot recall any of that,'
She answered smiling, 'now bring to your mind
How you have drunk the water of Lethe today;

97   And if, as they say, there is no smoke without fire,
That forgetfulness of yours demonstrates clearly
A fault in your will—your attention was elsewhere.

100   But truthfully, from now on my words
Will be naked, as far as it would be proper
To strip them before your boorish eyes.'

103   And, shining more brightly, and with slower steps,
The sun was holding the meridian circle,
Which is here or there, depending on where you are,

106   When there halted (as outriders will halt
When they are going ahead of the main party
And discover some strange thing or some new trace)

109   The seven ladies, at the edge of a slight shade
Such as may stretch over a cold mountain stream
Under green foliage and dark branches.

In front of them, it seemed to me I saw   112
Euphrates and Tigris issuing from a single spring
And, as friends might, being slow in parting.

'O light, O glory of the human race,   115
What water is this which spreads away
From one source, going further from itself?'

The answer to my enquiry was: 'Ask   118
Matilda to tell you.' And here the lady,
As if she were dissociating herself

From a fault: 'This matter as well as others   121
I have told him; and I am quite sure
That the water of Lethe has not hidden them from him.'

And Beatrice: 'Perhaps a greater care,   124
Which often takes a thing from memory,
Has made the eyes of his memory blind.

But look, that is Eunoë which flows there: 127
Lead him to it, and in your usual way,
Bring his fainting strength to life again.'

As a gentle soul who offers no excuse   130
But makes her own will of another's will
As soon as that other is disclosed to her;

So, when she had taken me with her,   133
The lovely girl set out; and to Statius,
Said in commanding manner: 'Come with him.'

If, reader, I had room to write more,   136
My poem could still not tell you everything
About the sweet drink of which I could never have had enough.

But since all the pages designed for this   139
Second part of the poem have been filled,
The rules of art stop me at this point.

I came back from that most sacred of streams,   142
Made afresh, as new trees are renewed
With their new foliage, and so I was

Clear and ready to go up to the stars.   145

PARADISO

CANTO I

The glory of him who moves everything
Penetrates the universe and shines
In one part more and, in another, less.

I have been in the heaven which takes most of his light,   4
And I have seen things which cannot be told,
Possibly, by anyone who comes down from up there;

Because, approaching the object of its desires,   7
Our intellect is so deeply absorbed
That memory cannot follow it all the way.

Nevertheless, what I was able to store up   10
Of that holy kingdom, in my mind,
Will now be the matter of my poem.

O good Apollo, for this final endeavour,   13
So make me the vessel of your virtue
As to be fit to receive your beloved laurel.

Up to this point one of the peaks of Parnassus   16
Has been enough for me: but now I need both
In order to enter upon the final contest.

Come into my heart, and so breathe   19
As you did when you extracted Marsyas
From the skin in which his limbs were enclosed.

O divine power, if you lend yourself to me   22
So that the ghost of the blessed kingdom
Traced in my brain, is made manifest,

You will see me come to your darling tree   25
And there crown myself with those leaves
Of which the matter and you will make me worthy.

So rarely, father, is any of it gathered   28
For the triumph of either emperor or poet,
Such is the aberration of human wishes,

31   That the Penean branch should bear gladness
     To the delighted delphic deity
     When it arouses longing in anyone.

34   A little spark brings a great flame after it:
     Perhaps after me better voices will pray
     In such a manner that Cirrha will respond.

37   It rises for mortals by different entrances,
     The lamp of the world; but when it comes from that
     Which joins together four circles with three crosses

40   It issues on a better course, and in conjunction
     With a better star, and so tempers and seals
     The wax of the world more to its own liking.

43   The east had already given us the morning there
     And, at home, evening, and the hemisphere
     Was all white there, as elsewhere it was dark,

46   When I noticed that Beatrice had turned round
     To her left hand, and was looking at the sun:
     An eagle never looked at it so steadily.

49   And as a reflected ray will always issue
     From the point at which the direct ray struck,
     Just like a pilgrim anxious to get home,

52   So from her action, received through my eyes
     Into my mind, my own action was made,
     And I gazed at the sun, in a way we don't.

55   Thanks to the place, much is permitted there
     To our faculties, which here is not
     —So suitable for mankind was it created.

58   I could not stand it long, yet not so little
     That I did not see sparks cast all around
     Like iron coming molten from the furnace;

61   And suddenly, it seemed that, to full daylight
     Full daylight had been added, as if he
     Who can had put another sun in the sky.

Beatrice was standing with her eyes firmly fixed   64
Upon the eternal heavens; and I kept mine
Fixed upon her, and so away from them.

Looking at her I became such within   67
As Glaucus was when he tasted the grass
Which made him, in the sea, one with the other gods.

What is involved in becoming more than human   70
Cannot be put into words; so may the example
Suffice for him for whom grace reserves the experience.

Whether I was only what of me was created   73
Latterly, O love which controls the heavens,
You know, who lifted me up with your light.

When the heavenly movements which you render eternal   76
By their desire for you, took my attention
With the harmony you regulate and distribute,

So much of heaven then seemed to me on fire   79
With the sun's flames, that rain and river never
Made a lake spread out as widely as that.

The newness of the sound and the great light   82
Lit in me such a desire to know the cause of them
That I have never felt anything so sharply.

So she, who now saw me as I did myself,   85
In order to quieten my agitated mind,
Before I could reply, opened her lips,

Beginning: 'You are making yourself stupid   88
By imagining what isn't, so that you do not
See what you would if you could shake that off.

You are not now on earth, as you think you are: 91
But lightning, flying from its proper place,
Never sped as you did who are coming back.'

If I was stripped of my first uncertainty   94
By these few words she uttered with a smile,
I was caught more completely in another,

97   And said: 'I am already satisfied and rest
     From one great wonder, but now my wonder is
     How I climb up through these light elements.'

100 So she, after giving a sigh of pity,
     Turned her eyes towards me with the look
     A mother casts upon a feverish child,

103 And began: 'Everything that is created
     Is part of a mutual order, and that is the shape
     Which makes the universe resemble God.

106 Here the superior beings see the traces
     Of the eternal power, which is the end
     For which the rule I have spoken of was made.

109 In this order all natures are arranged
     According to their conditions, more or less
     In the vicinity of their beginning;

112 So it is that they move to different harbours
     On the great sea of being, and each one of them
     By the instinct which is given it to bear it on.

115 One carries fire in the direction of the moon;
     Another is what moves all animal natures;
     A third pulls the earth together and makes it one:

118 It is not only the creatures which are outside
     Intelligence, for whom the bow is drawn,
     But also those which have intellect and love.

121 The providence which sets all this in order
     With its light gives quiet to the heaven
     In which there turns the fastest sphere of all;

124 And now thither, as to a pre-ordained place,
     We are carried by the power of that bowstring
     Which directs what it looses to a happy mark.

127 It is true that frequently the form
     Does not correspond to the intention of the art
     Because the material is deaf and does not answer;

So sometimes the creature which has the power to do so   130
Departs from this course, and although aimed,
Turns aside and goes in another direction

(In the same manner that fire may be seen to fall   133
Out of a cloud), if the original impetus
Is twisted towards the earth by false delight.

If I am right, then you should wonder no more   136
At the way you came up, than a river does
At the way it goes down a mountain to the bottom.

It would be a marvel if, without   139
Any impediment, you had settled below,
Just as it would if a live flame stayed on the ground.'

And then she turned her gaze back to the heavens.   142

CANTO II

O you who are in your little boat,
Anxious to listen, having followed so far
Behind my ship which puts to sea singing,

Turn back and revisit the shores you have left: 4
Avoid the high seas, in case, perhaps,
Losing me, you should find yourself bewildered.

The water I venture upon has never been sailed: 7
Minerva breathes, Apollo shows the way
And the nine Muses point to the Bears.

You other few, who have stretched up your necks   10
In time to the bread of angels, upon which
Life is lived here and no one has too much,

You may well put out on the salt deep   13
With your ships, following in my furrow
Before the water closes up again.

16   The heroes who made the voyage to Colchis
Did not marvel as much as you will do
When they saw Jason turned into a ploughman.

19   The thirst created with us, and for ever,
For the kingdom in God's image, carried us on
Almost as swiftly as the heaven you see.

22   Beatrice looked upwards and I looked at her;
And perhaps in as much time as it takes an arrow,
Set on a bowstring, to fly off and away,

25   I found myself arrived where a marvellous thing
Made me turn to look at it; and therefore she
To whom none of my concerns was hidden

28   Turned towards me, as glad as she was lovely,
And said: 'Direct your mind towards God in gratitude
Because he has brought you to the first star.'

31   It seemed to me we were covered by a cloud,
Shining and thick, as if solid and polished,
Like a diamond which has been caught by the sun.

34   The eternal pearl took us into itself
In the same manner that water receives
A ray of light through it, yet remains entire.

37   If I was body (and here we cannot conceive
How one dimension can contain another
As must happen if bodies interpenetrate)

40   The more should desire be inflamed
To see that essence in which it may be seen
How our nature combined itself with God.

43   There will be seen what we hold by faith;
It will not be demonstrated, but intuited
In the manner in which man believes the primal truth.

46   I replied: 'Lady, with all devoutness
That I am capable of, I thank him
Who has removed me from the mortal world.

But tell me: what are those dark markings   49
On this body, which down there upon earth
Make people invent talk about Cain?'

She smiled a little, and then she said: 'If mortal   52
Opinion is in error, in matters which
The key of the senses is unable to unlock,

The arrows of amazement should certainly   55
No longer pierce you for, following the senses, ·
You see that reason's wings are too short.

But tell me what you think about it yourself.'   58
And I: 'What appears different to us up here
I think is a matter of greater and lesser density.'

And she: 'Certainly you will find your view of the matter   61
Is profoundly wrong, if you will listen carefully
To the argument I shall deliver against it.

The eighth sphere exhibits many sources of light   64
Which, both as to quality and quantity,
May be observed to have different appearances.

If all that was produced by rarity and density,   67
There would be one single virtue in them all,
Distributed more or less equally.

Each different virtue must be the fruit   70
Of a formal principle, while, on your reasoning,
There could be no more than one in all the stars.

Again, if lack of density were the reason   73
For the dark patches you are asking about,
Either this planet would in places lack material

Or, the more or less dense would be divided   76
Like fat and lean in a body, as if in a book
A page of one were followed by a page of the other.

On the first hypothesis, it would be made clear   79
In eclipses of the sun by the light shining through
As it does when introduced into any non-dense medium.

82   That does not happen: therefore we have to consider
The second hypothesis; and if I destroy that,
Then clearly your whole case will fall to the ground.

85   If the rare matter does not go right through,
There must be a point at which its contrary,
The dense matter, allows it to go no further;

88   And from that point the sun's rays would be reflected
As colours turn back when they strike glass
Which has lead spread over it at the back.

91   Now you will say that the rays appear dark
Where the rays have to travel further than in other places,
Through being refracted from a greater distance.

94   This objection you can overcome,
If you care to try, by means of experiment,
Which is the only source of your rivers of science.

97   You will take three mirrors; and place two of them
At an equal distance from you; a third, further away
And so that you see it between the other two.

100   Turning towards them, arrange that behind your back
There is a light which shows in the three mirrors
And is reflected back to you from them all.

103   Although the size of the image will not be as great
In the most distant mirror, you will see
That it will shine just as brightly as the others.

106   Now, as when it is struck by warm rays
What is underneath is cleared of snow
And loses both the colour and the cold,

109   So I would clear your intellect
And animate you with light so alive
That it will tremble as you look at it.

112   Within the heaven of divine peace
Turns a body in the virtue of which
Lies the being of all that it contains.

The heaven after that, with so many visible bodies,   115
Distributes this being among different essences
Which are distinct from it and contained within it.

The other heavens dispose in various manners   118
The powers by which they differ from one another
So that they attain their ends and do their work.

These organs of the universe, as you see,   121
Are graduated one after another so that
They take from above and have their action below.

Now pay attention to the way I cross   124
This place to reach the truth that you desire,
So that you will know how to go over alone.

The movement and virtue of the several heavens   127
Must first be exhaled from the angelic movers
As the science of the hammer comes from the smith;

And from the profound mind which makes it rotate   130
The heaven rendered beautiful by so many stars
Takes its image and makes a seal of it.

And as the soul which is inside your dust   133
Acts through a variety of members
Which answer to a variety of powers,

So the intelligence spreads out its excellence   136
By multiplying itself among the stars
While still, itself, revolving as a unity.

Different virtues make different combinations   139
With the precious bodies which they bring to life,
And in which they are bound up as life is in you.

Because of the glad nature from which it flows   142
The embodied virtue shines through the material
As gladness does in the animated pupil.

That is how it happens that one light   145
Seems different from another; it is not density:
This is the formal principle which produces,

In accordance with its excellence, the troubled and the clear.'   148

CANTO III

That sun which first warmed my heart with love
Had shown me, by proof and refutation,
The sweet appearance of the naked truth;

4   And I, to admit that I was put right
And convinced, as the case indeed required,
Raised my head to address some words to her;

7   But an apparition appeared which held me
So closely to itself, to look at it,
That I did not remember my confession.

10   As through a glass which is transparent and polished,
Or through tranquil and translucent water
Which is not so deep that it is dark at the bottom,

13   The outlines of our faces are reflected
So faintly, that a pearl on a white forehead
Does not come less readily to our pupils;

16   So I saw many faces set to speak:
Which made me run into the opposite error
To that which made the man in love with the pool.

19   The moment that I caught sight of them,
Thinking that they were reflected images,
I turned my eyes to see whose they were;

22   And saw nothing, and looked back again
Straight at the light which came from my sweet guide
Which, as she smiled, blazed from her holy eyes.

25   'Do not be surprised if I smile,'
She said, 'at your childish way of thinking
Which does not rest its foot upon the truth

28   But, as usual, turns you round to walk on emptiness:
What you see here are true substances,
Relegated here for non-fulfilment of vows.

Speak with them therefore; listen and believe;   31
Because the true light which contents them
Does not allow their feet to turn away from it.'

And I directed myself to that shadow   34
Which seemed most desirous of conversation,
And began, like one confused by too much longing:

'O well created spirit, who in the rays   37
Of eternal life are conscious of the sweetness
Which, if not tasted, cannot be understood,

It would be pleasing to me if you would satisfy me   40
As to your name and your condition.'
So she, readily and with smiling eyes:

'Our charity does not lock the doors   43
On a just desire, any more than that charity
Which would have its whole court like itself.

In the world, I was a virgin sister,   46
And if your memory searches itself,
My being more beautiful will not hide me from you,

But you will recognise me as Piccarda   49
Who, placed here with these others who are blessed,
Am blessed in the slowest of the spheres.

Our affections, which are inflamed only   52
In what gives pleasure to the Holy Spirit,
Are glad to be placed as he disposes.

And this condition which seems so lowly a one   55
Is given to us because there was neglect
Of our vows, in some respect unfulfilled.'

So I to her: 'In your marvellous appearance   58
There shines I know not what of the divine
Which alters you from my first images of you:

That is why I did not at once call you to mind;   61
But now what you say helps me so that I can
Make out who you are in plain Latin.

64   But tell me: you who are happy here,
Do you desire a higher place than you have,
To see more, and be more friends with God?'

67   With the other shadows, she first smiled a little;
And then replied to me so happily
That she seemed to burn with love in its first fire.

70   'Brother, the virtue of charity brings quiet
To our will, so that we want only
What we have, and thirst for nothing beyond that.

73   If we desired to be higher up
Our wishes would not be in accordance
With the will of him who sets us here;

76   Which you will see could not be in these spheres,
If existing in charity is here necessity,
And if you properly understand what its nature is.

79   It is indeed the essence of this life
That we keep ourselves within the divine will,
So that our wills may be made one with his:

82   So that, how we are at various thresholds
Throughout this kingdom, pleases the whole kingdom
As it does the king who rouses us to his will;

85   And in his will we find our peace:
It is the sea to which everything moves
Which it creates and which nature makes.'

88   Then it was clear to me how everywhere
In heaven is paradise, although the grace
Of the highest good does not fall on all in one way.

91   But as it happens that, if we have had enough
Of one dish, but still fancy another,
We ask for one and say 'No, thanks,' to the other,

94   So I did, by gesture and by word,
To learn from her what piece of weaving it was
Through which she had not drawn the shuttle to the end.

'Perfected life and high merit,' she said,   97
'Place, higher in heaven, a lady by whose rule
Some clothe and veil themselves in your world

So that until death they wake and sleep   100
With that spouse who accepts every vow
Made by charity in accordance with his pleasure.

When a young girl, I fled from the world   103
To follow her, and hid under her habit,
And promised to go the way of her followers.

Then men more accustomed to ill than to good   106
Carried me off from that sweet cloister:
God knows what my life was after that.

And this other brilliance which shows   109
At my right hand, and lights itself up
With all the luminosity of our sphere

—What I say of myself applies to her: 112
She was a sister, and from her head, in the same way,
Was taken the shade of the sacred veil.

But when she was returned back to the world,   115
Against her will and contrary to good custom,
She never lost the veil about her heart.

This is the light of the great Constance   118
Who, from the second gale of Swabia,
Produced the third, which was also the last.'

Thus she spoke to me, and then she began   121
To sing *Ave Maria*, and, singing, vanished
As a heavy object does in deep water.

My sight, which followed her as far   124
As it could do, when it had lost her, turned
Towards the target of a greater longing,

And dwelt at last only on Beatrice;   127
But she flashed such lightning on my look
That at first my eyes could not bear it;

And that made me slower to question her.   130

CANTO IV

Between two dishes, equidistant from him
And equally attractive, a man would starve
Of his own free will, before he ate one of them;

4   So would a lamb stand still between the greeds
Of two fierce wolves, fearing both equally;
So would a dog stand still between two deer:

7   Therefore, if I was silent, I do not blame myself,
Equally impelled by my uncertainties;
It was necessity—nor do I commend myself.

10   I was silent, but the desire I felt
Was depicted on my face as well as my questioning,
Much more clearly than if I had spoken out.

13   Beatrice did exactly what Daniel did
When he relieved Nebuchadnezzar of his anger,
Which had made him unjustly cruel;

16   She said: 'I see how one desire and the other
Tug at you, so that your preoccupations
Are so fastened that they cannot breathe.

19   You reason: "If the will remains good,
How can the violence of another
Diminish the measure of my desert?"

22   You also find it matter for perplexity
That souls seem to find their way back to the stars
Which is in accordance with what Plato taught.

25   These are the questions which weigh equally
Upon your will; and so I am going to deal
First with the one which is the more bitter.

28   The seraphin who is nearest to God,
Moses, Samuel, and both the Johns,
Take which you will, and even Mary

Has its place in no other heaven   31
Than these have who appear to you now,
Nor is their being more or less eternal;

But all of them beautify the first circle   34
And in their different ways have sweet life
By feeling the eternal breath either less or more.

They show themselves here, not because this sphere   37
Is so assigned to them, but to indicate
What is the lowest of celestial states.

There must be such language for your mind   40
Because it learns only from what is sensible
Matter which, afterwards, it makes fit for the intellect.

For this reason Scripture condescends   43
To your capacities, and so attributes
Feet and hands to God, but means something else;

And Holy Church represents Gabriel   46
And Michael to you as having a human appearance,
As also the one who made Tobit well again.

What Timaeus argues concerning souls   49
Is not like that which can be seen here,
For he appears to be speaking literally.

He says that the soul returns to its star,   52
Believing that it has been carved out from there
When nature made use of it as a form;

Or perhaps his meaning is not what it seems   55
From the words he uses, and there may be some
Purport in them which is not to be derided.

If he means that praise and blame for their influence   58
Belongs to the revolution of the stars,
It may be he has hit upon some truth.

This principle, misunderstood, deflected   61
The whole world almost, so that it went too far
In calling on Jove and Mercury and Mars.

64 The other doubt which troubles you is less
Poisonous, because what there is wrong about it
Could not lead you from me in another direction.

67 Our justice appearing to be unjust
In the eyes of mortals, is a matter for faith:
There is nothing wicked or heretical in that.

70 But, because your intelligence is able
To penetrate this truth as you desire,
I will put your mind at rest.

73 If violence is to be understood
As meaning that the sufferer contributes nothing
To the force that moves him, these souls had not that excuse;

76 For the will does not weaken unless it wants to,
But operates as nature does in a flame
If it is violently twisted a thousand ways.

79 For if it bends itself either much or little,
It gives way to the force; and so did these,
For they could have gone back to the sacred place.

82 If their will had remained inviolate,
Like Lawrence's when he lay upon the grid
Or Mucius, who condemned his own right hand,

85 It would have put them back upon the road
From which they had been dragged, as soon as they were free;
But wills so positive are all too rare.

88 And by these words, if you have taken them
The way you should, the argument, which would
Often have troubled you, is rendered void.

91 But now there is another difficult stretch
Before your eyes, such that, left to yourself,
You would not get out till you were weary.

94 I have certainly made you understand
That a blessed soul will be unable to lie,
Because it is always close to the primal truth;

And since you might have heard Piccarda say   97
That Constance still kept her love for the veil,
So that in that she seems to contradict me.

Often before, brother, it has happened   100
That, to avoid danger, things were done
Reluctantly, which had better not been done;

As Alcmaeon, who because he was bid to do so   103
By his own father, took his mother's life,
And so for the sake of piety became pitiless.

At this point, I want you to consider   106
That force mingles with will, and so operates
That the offences may not be excused.

The absolute will does not consent to evil;   109
But consents in so far as it is afraid
That if it draws back, worse will befall it.

So, when Piccarda so expresses herself,   112
She has in mind the absolute will, and I
The other; so we are both speaking the truth.'

So was the rippling of that heavenly stream   115
Which issued from the spring from which all truth derives;
So both desires at once were set at peace.

'O love of the first lover, O divine lady,'   118
I said, at that, 'whose talk floods over me
And warms me so that I am more and more alive,

My love is not deep enough to render,   121
Sufficiently, grace for the grace that you give;
But he who sees and can may answer for me.

I see that our intellect can never   124
Have all it will, unless that truth enlighten it,
Beyond which there is no room for what is true.

It rests therein like a beast in its lair,   127
As soon as it has reached it; as it can do;
If not, every desire would be in vain.

130 Therefore there springs up, at the foot of truth,
  Doubt, like the shoots which spring at the foot of a tree,
  Which pushes us to the top, from tip to tip.

133 It is this invites me, this gives me assurance,
  Lady, to ask of you with reverence
  About another truth obscure to me.

136 I wish to know if a man can satisfy you
  For broken vows, by offering other good things,
  So that they are not too light in your balance.'

139 Beatrice looked at me and her eyes were full
  Of sparks of love of such divinity
  That, vanquished, my virtue ran away

142 And I was as if lost, my eyes lowered.

CANTO V

 'If I shine on you in the warmth of love,
 So beyond what is to be seen on earth
 That I am beyond the strength your eyes can bear,

4 Do not wonder: it comes from the perfection
  Of my sight which, as it apprehends,
  Advances in the apprehended good.

7 I see well how the eternal light
  Is already glowing in your intellect:
  The sight of it alone sets love burning:

10 And if any other thing seduces your love,
  It is nothing other than some trace of that,
  Ill-perceived, and shining through that thing.

13 You want to know whether, by some other service
  In place of broken vows, such reparation
  Can be made that the soul is safe from mischief.'

So Beatrice at the beginning of the canto;   16
And like one who proceeds without interruption
Continued in this manner the sacred discourse:

'The greatest gift which God in his open-handedness   19
Gave in creation, and the gift which most conformed
To his own excellence, and which he most values,

Was that of freedom of the will,   22
With which creatures created intelligent,
Each and all of them, were and are endowed.

Now there will appear to you, if you reason correctly,   25
The high value of vows, if they are such
That God consents to them when you consent;

Because, when the pact is made between God and man,   28
The treasure which I have shown the will to be
Is made a sacrifice by its own act.

What may be given then in compensation?   31
If you think that you make good use of what you have
      sacrificed
You want to do good works with ill-gotten gains.

You are now clear as to the greater point;   34
But because Holy Church gives dispensation,
Which seems to go against the truth I have shown you,

You must sit a little longer at the table   37
Because the hard food that you have taken
Calls for some further assistance to digest it.

Open your mind to what I am disclosing   40
And hold it in there; for there is no knowledge
If you merely understand, without remembering.

Two things together constitute the essence   43
Of the sacrifice: one is, the matter of it;
The other is the covenant itself.

The latter cannot be cancelled anyhow,   46
Except by carrying it out; it is on this point
That what is said above is so definite:

49   Therefore it was the law for the Hebrews
To offer sacrifice, but what they offered
Was subject to modification, as you should know.

52   What in my explanation I have called the matter
May be such that there is no deficiency
If it is changed against some other matter.

55   But let none shift the burden on his shoulder
By any judgment of his own, without
The turning of the white and yellow keys;

58   And you must think that any change is foolishness
If what is taken on, compared with what is shed,
Does not weigh at least half as much again.

61   Therefore anything which weighs so heavily,
Because of its worth, as to turn any scale,
Cannot be made good by any offering.

64   Let mortals never take the vow lightly:
Be faithful, but see what you are doing,
As Jephthah did not with his first gift;

67   He would have done better to say: "I did wrong"
Than to keep his vow and do worse; and no less foolish,
You may think, was the great king of the Greeks,

70   So that Iphigenia bewailed her beauty
And fools and wise men wept for her when they
Heard the tale of a vow so executed.

73   Christians, be more difficult to move
And do not be feathers in every wind;
And do not think that every water purifies.

76   You have the new testament and the old,
And the shepherd of the Church to be your guide;
This should be all you need for your salvation.

79   If evil covetousness shouts something else at you.
Behave like men and not like silly sheep
To make the Jew among you laugh at you.

Do not do as the lamb who leaves the milk   82
His mother gives him and, foolish and frivolous,
Amuses himself by fighting with himself.'

So Beatrice, as I have written it down;   85
And then she turned away, full of desire,
To that quarter of the sky which is most alive.

Her silence, and the change in her appearance,   88
Imposed silence on my covetous mind
Which already had fresh questions before it;

And as an arrow, which will strike the target   91
Before the string of the bow has come to rest,
So we sped onwards to the second kingdom.

There I saw my lady was so glad   94
As she entered the light of this heaven
That the planet itself shone more brightly for it;

And if the star so changed itself and laughed,   97
What did I do, whose nature is such that I
Am liable to change in every way!

As in a fishpond which is still and clear   100
The fish are drawn to anything dropped in
So that they think it might be something to eat,

So I saw far more than a thousand brilliances   103
Drawn towards us, and in each one I heard:
'There is someone who will increase our loves.'

And as each one of them came near to us,   106
The shadow appeared, full of happiness
In the clear radiance which issued from it.

Think, reader, if what is here begun   109
Did not go on, how you would suffer
Anguish from lack of knowing more about it;

And you will understand without my help   112
How I desired to hear about their condition
As soon as they were manifest to my eyes.

115 'O well-born, to whom grace permits
Sight of the thrones of the eternal triumph,
Before you have finished your soldiering on earth,

118 We are lit by the light which spreads itself
Throughout the heavens; and so if you desire
To light yourself by us, take what you will.'

121 Such were the words spoken to me by one
Of these charitable spirits; and Beatrice said: 'Speak, speak,
You may do so safely, and believe them as you would gods.'

124 'I see indeed how you are harboured in
Your own light, and that pours through your eyes,
Because they sparkle so when you smile;

127 But I do not know who you are, nor why you are,
Meritorious soul, classified in this sphere,
Which is veiled from mortals by another's rays.'

130 I said this in the direction of the light
Which had spoken to me before; and thereupon
It shone much more brightly than before.

133 Just as the sun which hides itself away
In too much light, when its heat has gnawed away
The softening of the thick mists around it,

136 So by increased happiness the sacred figure
Hid himself from me in his own rays;
And so entirely concealed, replied to me

139 In the manner which the next canto sings.

CANTO VI

'After Constantine had turned the eagle
Against the course of the heavens, which it had followed
Behind the ancient hero who took Lavinia,

Two hundred years and more the bird of God   4
Kept itself at the very edge of Europe,
Close to the mountains from which it first issued;

And under the shadow of the sacred wings   7
Governed the world there, changing in turn
From hand to hand until it came to mine.

I was the Caesar and am Justinian,   10
Who, by the will of the primal love I feel,
Removed from the laws what was superfluous or pointless;

And before I fixed my mind upon this work,   13
I believed that there was in Christ a single nature,
Not more, and with that faith I was content;

But the blessed Agapetus, who was   16
The chief shepherd, by his discourses,
Directed me to the unadulterated faith.

I believed him; and what was in his faith   19
I now see as clearly as you see
That every contradiction is false and true.

As soon as I was walking with the Church,   22
It pleased God by his grace to breathe upon
The great task to which I gave all I had:

And I entrusted the armies to Belisarius,   25
Who was so at one with the right hand of heaven
That it was a sign that I should give them up.

That is the end of what I have to say   28
To the first question; but the nature of my answer
Induces me to add something else,

So that you may see how much right   31
To move against the sacrosanct emblem have either
Those who make it their own, or those who oppose it.

For see what virtue entitles this emblem   34
To reverence.' And he began from the hour
When Pallas died so that it should prevail.

37   'You know that it remained fixed in Alba
     Three hundred years and more, until at last
     The three and three fought for it again.

40   And you know what it did from the rape of the Sabines
     Until Lucretia suffered, through the seven kings,
     Conquering all the peoples round about.

43   You know what it did, borne by the noble Romans
     Against Brennus, against Pyrrhus and against
     So many other princes and republics;

46   Whence Torquatus and Quinctius who was named
     From his neglected curls, the Decii and Fabii,
     All drew the fame which I am glad to honour.

49   It struck down the pride of the Arabs
     Who, following Hannibal, crossed the rocky alps
     From which you, Po, slide upon your way.

52   Beneath it Scipio and Pompey triumphed
     While they were still in their youth; and it seemed bitter
     To those hills beneath which you were born.

55   Then, near the time when all heaven willed
     To reduce the world to its serene way,
     Caesar, because Rome willed so, took it up.

58   And what it did, from the Var to the Rhine,
     The Isère saw, the Loire and the Seine,
     And every valley from which the Rhone is filled.

61   What it did when he went out from Ravenna
     And crossed the Rubicon, was with such speed
     That neither tongue nor pen could follow it.

64   It guided the army towards Spain, and then
     Towards Durazzo, and so struck Pharsalia
     That the blow was felt as far as the warm Nile.

67   Antandros and Simois, whence it came,
     It saw again, and the place where Hector lies;
     And then to the Ptolemy's loss roused itself again.

Thereafter it fell like lightning upon Juba;   70
And then it turned once more to your west,
Where it heard Pompey's trumpet.

For what it did with the next standard-bearer   73
Brutus and Cassius attest in hell,
And Modena and Perugia were sorry.

The unhappy Cleopatra wept because of it,   76
For as she fled away from it, she snatched
From the serpent her black and sudden death.

With Octavian it ran to the shores of the Red Sea;   79
With him established the world in such peace
That the temple of Janus was shut up.

But what that emblem which makes me speak   82
Had done and after was still to do
Through the mortal kingdom that was subject to it,

Looks like a small thing of no account,   85
If with a clear eye and pure affection
One sees what it did in the hand of the third Caesar;

For then the living justice which breathes through me   88
Granted it, in the hand of him I am speaking of,
The glory of retribution for God's anger.

And here wonder at the second point I make: 91
With Titus it then made retribution
For the retribution for the ancient sin.

And when the tooth of the Lombard bit into   94
The Holy Church, it was under the eagle's wings
That Charlemagne conquered, and so gave her assistance.

Now you may judge of such as those   97
Whom I accused just now, and of their faults,
Which are the reason for all the ills you suffer.

One party sets up against the public emblem   100
The yellow lilies; the other claims it for itself,
So that it is hard to say which is more at fault.

103 Let the Ghibellines pursue their devices
Under some other emblem; it is no way to follow
This one to separate justice from this.

106 And let that new Charles not beat it down
With his Guelfs; but let him fear the claws
Which have ripped the skin off bigger lions than he.

109 Many times before this children have wept
For their fathers' faults, and let him not imagine
That God will change his arms for those lilies!

112 This little star is studded with good spirits
Who exerted themselves in order to acquire
Honour and reputation:

115 And when the desires lean in that direction,
A little out of course, it must happen that
The rays of true love rise less full of life.

118 But in the appropriateness of our rewards
To our desert is part of our happiness,
Not to see them either more or less.

121 By this means the living justice so softens
Our affections that they may not be
Ever twisted by any iniquity.

124 Different voices make notes sound sweet;
And so different stations in our life
Make a sweet harmony among these spheres.

127 And within this present pearl there shines
The light of Romeo, the achievements of whom
Were great and excellent, but he got no thanks for them.

130 But the Provençals who so turned against him
Do not have the laugh; it is an ill course
They take who make trouble out of another's well-doing.

133 Raymond Berengar had four daughters, all
Were queens, it was Romeo who made them so,
And he himself was a humble man and a stranger.

And then ugly talk induced the count   136
To require this just man to account for his actions,
And he gave seven and five for every ten.

He went from there in poverty and old age: 139
And if the world knew the heart he had,
Begging his livelihood a crust at a time,

Much as it praises him, it would praise him more.   142

CANTO VII

'Osanna, sanctus Deus sabaoth,
superillustrans claritate tua
felices ignes horum malacoth!'

So, turning round in his own harmony,   4
That substance upon whom a double light
Played, was seen by me singing:

And that and the others moved into their dance   7
And rapidly, as if they had been sparks;
Suddenly they were veiled from me by distance.

I was in doubt, and said 'Speak to her, speak to her!'   10
Within myself; 'Speak to her,' I said—to my lady
Who quenches my thirst with drops of sweetness.

But that reverence which mastered me   13
Completely, just for *Be*—or for—*icè*,
Kept my head bowed like that of a man falling asleep.

Beatrice left me like that for a little while,   16
And began, shining upon me with a smile
Which would have made a man in flames happy:

'According to my thought, which is unerring,   19
How a just retribution can have been justly
Punished, is the thing that has set you wondering;

22   But I will clear your mind without delay;
      And if you listen, what I say will be
      Something gained on a great point of doctrine.

25   For not accepting a rein upon his will
      For his own good, that man who was not born,
      Condemning himself, condemned his whole issue;

28   So that the human race lay sick down there
      For many centuries in great error,
      Until it pleased the Word of God to descend.

31   Where he united to himself, in person,
      The nature which had distanced itself from its maker,
      And this he did only by his eternal love.

34   Now turn your eyes to this further discourse.
      This nature, united with its maker,
      As it was created, was pure and good;

37   But had been driven from paradise by itself,
      Because it had departed from the way
      Of truth and from its own proper life.

40   Therefore the penalty the cross exacted,
      If it is set against the nature assumed,
      Bit more justly than ever any did;

43   And likewise, never was any so unjust
      In relation to the person who suffered it
      And with whom that nature was conjoined.

46   So from a single act came different effects:
      That one death was pleasing both to God and the Jews;
      And through it earth trembled and the heavens opened.

49   Henceforward you should see no difficulty
      When it is said that a just retribution
      Found retribution itself in a just court.

52   But now I see your mind is tangled up
      From thought to thought into a knot, from which
      It awaits most anxiously to be released.

You say: "I understand what I hear;   55
But it is hidden from me why God willed
Only this means for our redemption."

This decree, brother, is buried from the eyes   58
Of everyone in whom the intellect
Has not grown fully in the flame of love.

None the less, because many look towards   61
The target, yet so few can make it out,
I will tell you why that manner was most fitting.

The divine goodness, rejecting all envy,   64
Burns in itself and is so radiant
That it displays its eternal beauties.

Whatever there is which drops directly from it   67
Is without end, because when it sets its seal
The imprint that it leaves cannot be changed.

Whatever rains from it without intermediary   70
Is entirely free, because it is not subject
To the influence of things newly created.

It is more like it and therefore pleases it more;   73
For the sacred blaze which shines in everything
Is most alive in what most resembles itself.

The human creature has the benefit   76
Of all these gifts; and if one should fail
He must fall from his nobility.

Sin alone takes his liberty from him,   79
And makes him not resemble the highest good
So that he benefits little from its light;

And he may never return to that dignity   82
Unless he fills the void left by his fault,
Just penalties in place of evil delights.

Your nature, when in its entirety,   85
It had sinned in its seed, was driven out
From these dignities as it was from paradise;

88 Nor might they be recovered, if you think
    Carefully about it, by any other way
    Than passing one or other of these fords:

91 Either that God alone, by his gentleness,
    Should have absolved man, or that man himself
    Should have made satisfaction for his fault.

94 Now fix your eyes deep inside the abyss
    Of the eternal counsel, and pay attention
    As closely as you can, to what I say.

97 Within his own limits man could never
    Give satisfaction, for he could not go as low
    In the obedience of humility

100 As he had aspired high in disobedience;
    And it is for this reason that man was
    Precluded from giving satisfaction himself.

103 Therefore it must be for God in his own ways
    To restore man to his complete life,
    Either in one way or both at once.

106 But since an operation gives more satisfaction
    To the doer, the more it shows the excellence
    Of the heart from which it comes,

109 The divine goodness which is stamped on the world
    Was pleased to make use of all his means
    To raise your condition up again.

112 Between the last night and the first day
    There never was and never will be so great an act
    Or so magnificent, by one or other means:

115 For it was more generous in God to give himself
    To make man able to raise himself again
    Than if he had merely remitted the sin;

118 And all the other methods would have been short
    Of justice if the Son of God had not
    Humbled himself in the incarnation.

Now, to satisfy your every desire,   121
I am going to explain one part
So that you may see things as I do myself.

You say: "I see water, and I see fire,   124
Air and earth and all combinations of them
Come to corruption, and last but a short time;

And yet these things were after all creatures;   127
So that, if what you have been told had been true,
They ought to be safe from all corruption."

The angels, brother, and the unaltering country   130
Where you are now, may be said to have been created
As they are now, in their complete being;

But the elements which you have named,   133
And the things which are compounded out of them,
Are all informed by a created virtue.

The matter contained in them was created;   136
Created also was the informing virtue
In these stars which circle round about them.

The soul of every animal and plant   139
Is drawn from its compounded potency
By the beam and movement of the sacred lights;

But your life breathes without intermediary   142
The highest goodness, and makes it in love
With him, so that it then always desires him.

And from that you may conclude too   145
For the resurrection, if you think again
How human flesh was made originally

When both the first parents were created.'   148

CANTO VIII

The world used to think, in its time of danger,
That the lovely Cyprian radiated the madness
Of love, as she turned in the third epicycle;

4   And therefore not only the ancient peoples
In the ancient error did her the honour
Of sacrifices and cried to her in prayer;

7   But they honoured also Dione and Cupid,
The one as her mother, the other as her son;
And told how the boy had sat in Dido's lap;

10   And from her with whom I begin my canto
They took the designation of the star
Which stares at the sun, now before it, now at its back.

13   I did not notice our rise into this element;
But of my being there I was assured
By the fact that I saw my lady become more beautiful.

16   And as, in a flame, it is possible to see a spark,
And as a voice may be heard through another voice,
When one is persistent and the other comes and goes;

19   I saw in that light there were other lamps
Moving in a circle at more or less speed,
Depending, I think, on their vision of the eternal.

22   Winds never came down from cold clouds,
Whether visible or not, so rapidly,
That they would not have appeared embarrassed and slow

25   To anyone who saw those divine lights
Coming towards us, leaving the circle formed
Earlier among the exalted seraphim

28   And among those who appeared first and foremost
'*Osanna*' sounded in such manner that I
Have since never been free from desire to hear it again.

Then one of them drew close to us   31
And, speaking by himself, began: 'We are all
Ready, at your pleasure, for you to rejoice at us.

We turn here with the celestial princes   34
In one circle, with one circling, in one thirst,
We to whom from the earth you once said:

"You who, understanding, move the third heaven";   37
And we are so full of love that, in order to please you,
A moment of stillness will not be less sweet.'

When my eyes had offered themselves in reverence   40
To my lady, and she had contented them
With the sight of herself, and had reassured them,

They turned back to the light which had so far   43
Engaged itself, and the words; 'Who are you?'
Came from me with tones of great affection.

And how much, and how, I saw it grow   46
By the new gladness which was superadded,
When I spoke, to the gladness that was its already!

Looking like this, he said: 'The world had me   49
For a short time down there; and had it been longer,
Much evil that will happen, would not have happened.

My happiness keeps me concealed from you,   52
For it radiates from me and hides me as if I were
A creature bundled up in its cocoon.

You loved me greatly, and you had good cause;   55
For if I had been below longer, I would have shown you
More than the mere foliage of love.

That left bank which is watered by   58
The Rhone, after the Sorgue has flowed into it,
Was expecting me as its lord in due time;

And that horn of Ausonia which is bounded   61
By Bari, Gaeta and then Catona,
From which the Tronto and Verde empty into the sea.

64   Already there shone on my forehead the crown
Of that country which the Danube waters
After it has abandoned its German banks.

67   And lovely Trinacria—which is darkened
Between Pachino and Peloro on the gulf
Which is battered most by the east wind,

70   —Not for Typhaeus but for the rising sulphur—
Would still have expected to have its kings
Who, through me, would have been descended from Charles
          and Rudolf,

73   If bad government, which always goes to the heart
Of subject peoples, had not moved
Palermo to cry out: "Death to them! Death!"

76   And if my brother had foreseen that,
He would already be avoiding the greedy poverty
Of Catalonia, in case it should work ill for him;

79   For true it is that something ought to be done
By him or by another, so that no more
Should be loaded on his overloaded ship.

82   His nature, which from liberality
Sank into meanness, had need of officers
Who were not only concerned to fill their coffers.'

85   'Because I think that the deep happiness
Which what you say pours upon me, my lord,
Where every good has its end and beginning,

88   Is seen by you as I see it myself,
It is the more pleasing; and this too I hold dear,
That you discern it as you look on God.

91   You have made me happy, now enlighten me,
For by what you have said you have made me wonder
How sweet seed can produce something so bitter.'

94   So I to him; and then he to me:
'If I can show you a truth, what you are asking
Will be before you, as now it is at your back.

The good which moves and pleases the whole kingdom   97
Through which you are climbing, makes its providence
A virtue in these immense bodies.

And not only are the natures provided for   100
In that mind which is itself perfection,
But provision is made also for their well-being:

So that whatever arrow leaves the bow   103
It falls ready for a foreseen object,
Like something that is directed to its mark.

If it were not so, this heaven where you are travelling   106
Would bring its effects about in such a manner
That they would be not constructions but ruins;

And that could not be, unless the intellects   109
Which move the stars were not themselves defective,
The primal intellect too, which had not perfected them.

Do you want further light on this truth?'   112
And I: 'No; I see it is impossible
That nature should tire, where there is need for her.'

And he again: 'Now say, would it not be worse   115
For a man on earth, if he were not a citizen?'
'Yes,' I replied; 'no need to explain that.'

'And is that possible, if life down there   118
Is not distributed in various functions?
No, if what your master writes is true.'

He reached this point by deductive argument;   121
And then concluded: 'It follows that the causes
Of your effects must be various too:

So that one is born Solon, another Xerxes,   124
Another Melchizedek, and another the man
Who, flying through the atmosphere, lost his son.

The influence of the stars, which is the seal   127
Upon the mortal wax, does its part well,
But does not distinguish one lodging from another.

130 So it comes about that Esau is different
From Jacob from his conception; and Quirinus comes
From a base father, yet is given to Mars.

133 Generated nature would always follow
The path that was trodden by the generator,
If divine providence were not in control,

136 Now what was behind you is in front of you:
But to let you see how I delight to serve you
I want to add a corollary to that.

139 Nature always, if she find a fortune hostile,
Just as she does with any other seed
Out of its region, makes a poor job of it.

142 And if the world down there would give its mind
To the foundation nature herself lays,
And was guided by that, it would have excellent people.

145 But you force into a religious order
Someone who would be better with a sword,
And make a king of someone who should be a preacher:

148 No wonder your journey takes you off the road.'

CANTO IX

As soon as your Charles, lovely Clemenza,
Had made these things clear, he told me the deceits
Which were to be practised upon his posterity;

4 But said: 'Keep quiet, let the years go by';
So that I can say nothing except that tears,
As is just, will follow the wrongs done to you.

7 And already the life of that holy light
Had turned back to the sun with which it was filled
As to the good which is so much to everything.

Alas, you deceived souls and impious creatures   10
Who twist your hearts away from the good so done,
Turning your faces towards vanity!

And then another one of these splendours   13
Moved towards me, and in order to signify
Its will to please, brightened visibly.

The eyes of Beatrice, which were steadily   16
Upon me, reassured me as before
Of her dear concurrence in my desire.

'Please satisfy my wish quickly,   19
Blessed spirit,' I said, 'and give me proof
That I can reflect in you what I am thinking.'

Then the light which was still new to me,   22
From its depths, in which it had been singing,
Continued as one who is happy to do good:

'In that part of the depraved land of Italy   25
Which is situated between Rialto
And the sources of the Brenta and the Piave,

Rises a hill, which is not very high,   28
From which once there came down a firebrand
Which made a great assault upon the country.

That brand and I came from a common root: 31
Cunizza was my name, and I shine here
Because I was conquered by the light of this star.

But I happily look with indulgence upon   34
The cause of my being here, and it does not grieve me;
Which may perhaps seem hard to ordinary people.

This luminous and beloved jewel   37
Of our heaven, which is nearest to me here,
Has great fame still; and, before that shall die,

Five centuries shall pass from this one's ending: 40
See whether a man should make himself excellent,
So that the first life leaves another behind it.

43   There is no thought of that in the present crowd
       Between the Tagliamento and the Adige,
       And though they are beaten they are not penitent.

46   But soon it will happen that Padua in the marshes
       Will change the waters which wash Vicenza,
       Because the people refuse to do as they should.

49   And where the Sile and Cagnano run together,
       A man lords it who goes with his head high
       Yet already the net is being woven to catch him.

52   Feltro will weep again for the default
       Of that pitiless man her shepherd, a crime so obscene
       That no one was thrown into Malta for the like.

55   It would certainly have to be an over-sized bucket
       That could hold all that Ferrarese blood,
       And it would tire anyone who had to weigh it ounce by ounce,

58   —All to be presented by that courteous priest
       To show he is on the right side; gifts such as these
       Will fit with the manners of the country.

61   There are mirrors above—you call them thrones—
       From which God in judgement shines upon us;
       So that we know that these words are true.'

64   Here she was silent; and she looked to me
       As if she was turning to other matters as
       She went back to her circle as before.

67   The other happiness, already made known to me
       As so valued, appeared in my sight
       As a fine ruby struck by the light of the sun.

70   To show happiness up there there is added brightness,
       As there are smiles here; but below the shadow
       Grows darker outside, as the mind is more sad.

73   'God sees all, and your sight is in him,
       Blessed spirit,' I said, 'so that no wish
       Can in any manner escape you.

So why does your voice—which entertains   76
Heaven for ever, with the song of those holy fires
Which make themselves a cowl with the six wings—

Not satisfy the longing that I have?   79
I would not wait until you questioned me,
If I knew your mind as you know mine.'

'The greatest valley in which water spreads'   82
—The words began to come from him at that moment—
'Out of that sea which flows around the earth,

Between the opposing shores is so far   85
From west to east, that the meridian
Of one part is the horizon of another.

I lived upon the shore of that valley,   88
Between the Ebro and the Macra which, in its short course,
Divides the Tuscans from the Genoese.

Almost the same sunset and the same sunrise   91
Have Bougiah and the city I came from,
The harbour of which was once warm with its own blood.

Folco is what I was called by those people   94
Who knew my name; and this heaven bears the mark
Of me, as I used to bear its mark;

So that Belus's daughter did not burn more fiercely,   97
Wronging at once Sichaeus and Creusa,
Than I, as long as I remained untonsured;

Nor that Rhodopeian girl who was deceived   100
By Demophoön, nor yet Alcides
When he had shut up Iole in his heart.

But here there is no repentance, there are smiles,   103
Not for the fault, which does not come to mind,
But for the power which ordered and foresaw.

Here there is admiration for the skill   106
Which renders the effect beautiful, and there is seen
The good which brings the lower world back to the upper.

109 But so that every wish which comes to you
   Here in this region, may be satisfied
   Before you go, I must tell you a little more.

112 You want to know who is in this light
   Which is sparkling in this manner close by me,
   As a ray of sun does in clear water.

115 Now know that the person inside it, who is tranquil,
   Is Rahab; and when she came to join our order,
   Her presence sealed it as of the highest kind;

118 By this heaven, in which the cone of shadow
   Which your world makes has its tip, she was taken up
   Before any other in the triumph of Christ.

121 It was indeed appropriate to leave her
   In some heaven as a palm of the great victory
   Which was achieved by one palm and the other,

124 Because she favoured the first glory
   Of Joshua in the Holy Land, which
   So little touches the papal memory.

127 Your city, which was planted by him
   Who first turned his back upon his maker
   And the envious ways of which are so grieved for,

130 Produces and diffuses that cursed flower
   Which has sent both sheep and lambs astray,
   Because it has turned the shepherd into a wolf.

133 In this manner the gospel and the great doctors
   Are abandoned, so that only the decretals
   Are studied, as may be seen by the margins.

136 It is on that that the pope and cardinals are intent:
   Their thought does not go as far as Nazareth,
   Where Gabriel opened his wings.

139 But the Vatican, and other choice parts
   Of Rome which have become the cemetery
   Of all the soldiery which followed Peter

142 Will soon be freed from the adultery.'

CANTO X

Looking upon his son with the love
Which both of them eternally breathe out,
The primal and ineffable power

Made whatever spins round in mind or place   4
In such order that he who contemplates it
Cannot but have some taste of God himself.

So, reader, raise your eyes with me   7
To the high spheres, and straight to the part
Where one motion strikes upon the other;

And there begin to brood upon the skill   10
Of that performer who, in his own mind,
So loves it that he never takes his eyes off it.

See how from that point there branches off   13
The oblique circle which carries the planets
To satisfy the world which calls on them.

And if their path had not been so deflected,   16
So much of the sky's virtue would have been vain
And almost every power upon earth dead;

And if the departure from the straight line   19
Had been more or less than it is, much would be lacking
In the order of the world, below and above.

Stay, reader, where you are seated now   22
And think over what is here adumbrated
If you want to find it pleasant and not wearisome.

I have put it before you, now help yourself;   25
For all my attention is taken by that
Matter which I have undertaken to write.

The greatest of the ministers of nature,   28
Which stamps the world with the virtue of heaven
And measures time for us with his light,

31   Having arrived at that point which is recalled
       Above, was circling in the spirals in which
       He arrives at an earlier hour every day;

34   And I was with him; but I had not noticed
       The ascent, except as a man notices
       His first thought before it comes to him.

37   It is Beatrice who leads so suddenly
       From good to better, that her action does not
       Extend itself through any instant of time.

40   How shining must a thing be of itself
       To be visible in the sun, which I had entered,
       Not by its colour but simply by its light.

43   Though I should call on talent, skill and practice,
       I could not say what would make you imagine it;
       Yet it may be believed; may the sight be longed for.

46   And if our fancies do not attain
       To such a height, there is no cause to wonder;
       For no eye sees a light beyond the sun's.

49   Such, in that place, was the fourth family
       Of the high father, who eternally contents them,
       Showing how he breathes forth and how he begets.

52   And Beatrice began: 'Give thanks, give thanks
       To the sun of the angels, who by his grace
       Has elevated you to the sensible sun.'

55   No mortal heart was ever so disposed
       To make submission, or so ready to give himself
       To God with such complete willingness,

58   As I was when I heard these words;
       And my love went out so utterly to him
       That Beatrice, eclipsed, was quite forgotten.

61   That did not displease her; but she smiled
       So that the splendour of her laughing eyes
       Divided my unified mind among several objects.

Then I saw several living and blinding brilliances;   64
We were in the middle and they made a ring,
More sweet in voice than shining in appearance:

So we may sometimes see Latona's daughter   67
Surrounded when the air is saturated
So that it holds the thread which makes her girdle.

In the court of heaven, from which I have come back,   70
Are many jewels so precious and beautiful
That they are inconceivable out of that realm;

And the song of these lights was one of those: 73
Whoever has no wings to fly up there
Must get what news he can of them from the dumb.

After these burning suns, singing as they went,   76
Had circled round about us three times
Like stars round about the fixed poles,

They seemed like ladies, not released   79
From their dance, but pausing silently,
Listening for the music to start again.

And I heard a voice within one of them: 82
'Since the ray of grace, from which the true love
Is set alight, and then grows more by loving,

So multiplied, shines so brightly in you   85
That it leads you upward by that stairway
Which none descends except to climb again;

Anyone who denied you wine from his flask   88
To quench your thirst, would no more be at liberty
Than water which does not find its way to the sea.

You want to know of what blossom this garland   91
Is woven, which circles and gazes on
The beautiful lady by whose virtue you are here.

I was one of the lambs of the holy flock   94
Which Dominic leads upon the way
Where there is good pasture for those who don't wander.

97   The one who is nearest to me on the right
       Was brother and master to me; and he is Albert,
       From Cologne, and I am Thomas Aquinas.

100   If you would like to know about all the others,
       Follow with your eyes above the holy wreath,
       Going round in a circle while I am speaking.

103   That next glowing issues from the smile
       Of Gratian, who was of such assistance
       To both systems of laws, as to please paradise.

106   The next after him who adorns our choir
       Was that Peter who with the poor woman
       Offered his treasures to the Holy Church.

109   The fifth light, the most beautiful among us,
       Breathes from such love, the whole world down there
       Desires vehemently to have news of it.

112   Inside there is the exalted mind to which
       Such deep wisdom was granted, that if truth is true
       No second ever arose who saw so much.

115   Next see the light of that great candle
       Which below, in the flesh, saw most deeply
       Into the angelic nature and its ministry.

118   In the little light beside it laughs
       That advocate for the Christian ages
       In whose work Augustine found assistance.

121   Now, if you are following with your mind's eye
       From light to light behind my praise of them,
       You are now thirsting to know about the eighth.

124   Therein rejoices, because he sees all good,
       The holy soul who shows anyone
       Who listens attentively, how deceitful the world is.

127   The body from which that soul was hunted
       Lies below in Cieldauro, while the soul
       Came from martyrdom and from exile to this peace.

See glowing next to that the ardent breath   130
Of Isidore, of Bede, and of that Richard
Who, in contemplation, was more than a man.

The one from whom your look turns to me   133
Is the light of a spirit in whose heavy thoughts
The approach of death seemed to him all too slow:

That one is the eternal light of Sigier   136
Who, teaching in the rue du Fouarre,
Syllogised truly and aroused envy.'

Then, just as the clock which summons us   139
At the hour when the spouse of God rises
To call her spouse with song, that he may love her,

With one part pushing and the other thrusting,   142
Sounding ding dong with such a sweet note
That the well-disposed spirit is tumescent;

So I saw the glorious circle before me   145
Move and answer voice to voice in harmony,
And with a sweetness which is not to be known

Except in that place where joy is eternal.   148

CANTO XI

O how insensate are the cares of men,
And how defective are the syllogisms
Which make them stretch their wings to fly downwards.

One was going after the law, one after medicine,   4
Another one chasing after the priesthood,
Another getting to power by force or sophisms,

One given to robbery, another to politics;   7
Another wearing himself out tied up
In the pleasure of the flesh, one was just idle;

10 While I was released from all these things
    And was received in so splendid a manner
    With Beatrice, there above in heaven.

13 When all these had gone back to their places
    In the circle where they had been before,
    They stood still, each like a candle in a candlestick.

16 And I perceived, from within that glow of light
    Which had first spoken to me, this beginning,
    With a smile as it made itself brighter:

19 'As I shine with a ray of eternal light,
    So, looking at that light, I understand
    The reason why you are thinking as you are doing.

22 You wonder, and want what I said
    Set out again in plain, discursive language
    Which will be easy for you to understand,

25 For just now I said: "Where there is good pasture,"
    And again I said: "No second ever arose";
    And here it is necessary to make a distinction.

28 The providence which governs the whole world
    With that design in which created sight
    Is always defeated before it gets to the bottom

31 —So that the spouse should go towards her beloved
    Who with a loud cry had espoused her
    With his blessed blood,

34 Secure in herself and more faithful to him,—
    Destined two princes for her benefit,
    Who were her guides on one side and the other.

37 The one was all seraphic in his ardour,
    The other in his wisdom was on earth
    A splendour of cherubic light.

40 I will speak of one of these, for he who speaks
    Of one is in fact praising both, whichever
    He takes, for both of them served the same end.

Between Tupino and the water which falls   43
From the hills chosen by the blessed Ubaldo,
Descends the rich slope of a high mountain,

From which Perugia feels the heat and cold   46
Through Porta Sole; and behind her weeps
Nocera, for her heavy yoke, and Gualdo.

From this slope, at the point where its steepness   49
Is most broken, was born into the world a sun
Such as sometimes rises from the Ganges.

Therefore let anyone who speaks of this place   52
Not say Assisi, which would not be enough;
Let him say, East, if he wants to get it right.

He was not far away from his dawn   55
When he began to make the world feel
Some comfort from the great power he had;

For while young he rushed out to battle   58
With his father, for the sake of a lady to whom,
As to death, no one willingly opens the door;

Before his spiritual court, and in the presence   61
Of his father, he was united with her;
After which he loved her more every day.

She, who had been deprived of her first husband   64
Eleven hundred years and more ago, was despised and obscure
Until he stood before her, without invitation;

It was of no effect that she was found safe   67
With Amyclas, within hearing of that voice
Which reduced all the world to fear;

It was of no effect to be constant and courageous   70
So that she, when Mary remained below,
Mounted with Christ upon the cross.

But, not to continue too obscurely,   73
Francis and Poverty are these two lovers
Of whom I have been talking all this while.

76   Their concord and the joy in their appearance
      Made love and wonder and looks of tenderness
      To be the occasions of holy thoughts;

79   So much so that the venerable Bernard
      Took off his shoes first, to run after peace
      And as he ran he thought that he was slow.

82   O unknown riches, O fruitful happiness!
      Egidius took off his shoes, Sylvester too,
      Following the spouse, the spouse pleased them so much.

85   Then he went away, this father and this master,
      With his lady and with the members of their household
      Already putting on the humble cord.

88   Nor did any sense of shame make him lower his eyes
      For being the son of Pietro Bernadone
      Yet dressed so pitifully as to astonish;

91   But he was regal when he told Innocent
      Openly of his hard purpose, and from him
      He had the first seal set on his order.

94   When the number of poor people grew,
      Following the lead of him whose marvellous life
      Were better sung in the glory of heaven,

97   The holy will of this archimandrite
      Was crowned with a second crown by Honorius
      At the inspiration of the eternal.

100   And when, in his thirst for martyrdom,
      He preached Christ and the followers of Christ
      In the proud presence of the Soldan,

103   And because he found the people too unready
      To be converted, not to stay in vain,
      He returned to gather Italian harvest,

106   When on the harsh rock between Tiber and Arno
      He received from Christ the final imprint
      Which was marked upon his limbs for two years.

When he, who chose him for such benefits,   109
Was pleased to draw him up to his mercy
Which he had earned by making himself negligible,

To his brothers, as to his proper heirs,   112
He recommended the lady who was most dear to him
And ordered them to love her faithfully;

And from her bosom the illustrious soul   115
Desired to go, turning to its own country,
And he wanted no other bier for his body.

Think now what he was who was a fit colleague   118
For such a one, in keeping Peter's ship
On the high seas, moving on the right bearing;

And such a man was our patriarch;   121
Whoever follows as he commands takes on,
As you must see, excellent merchandise.

But his flock has become so greedy   124
Of new fodder, that it cannot be
But that it wanders into some rough pastures;

And the further off from him his sheep go,   127
In their vagabond ways, the more empty they are
Of milk when they get back to their fold.

There are indeed those who fear loss   130
And keep close to their shepherd; but they are so few
That it does not take much cloth to make cowls for them.

Now, if my words have not been too feeble,   133
And if you have been listening as you should,
You have only to call to mind what I have said;

In part your will must now be satisfied   136
For you will see how the plant has been damaged
And you will see what correction is intended

By "There is good pasture, if they don't stray." '   139

CANTO XII

As soon as the blessed flame had taken
The last word up, to speak it, there began
A revolution of the sacred millstone;

4   And it had not turned once completely
Before another circle closed around it,
So joining movement with movement, song with song;

7   Song which surpassed our muses as much,
And our sirens, in those sweet trumpets,
As the first splendour does the mere reflection.

10 As two parallel rainbows with the same colours
Bend their way through the thin clouds
When Juno so orders her handmaiden,

13 The outside one born of the one inside
—Like the manner of speaking of that wandering girl
Whom love consumed as the sun consumes vapours—

16 And let everybody on earth know
By the covenant which God made with Noah,
That the world would never be flooded again;

19 So there circled around us those two garlands
Woven of sempiternal roses,
In such manner that the outer ring answered the innermost.

22 When the dance and the great festival
Alike of singing and of glowing lights,
One with another, in joy and gentleness,

25 Had reached, in a single will and moment, its end,
Like eyes which, in the pleasure which directs them,
Cannot help being raised and closed in unison;

28 Out of the heart of one of the new lights,
There stirred a voice which made me turn to it
—I seemed like a needle turning to the star;

It began: 'The love which makes me beautiful   31
Induces me to speak of the other guide
On whose account ours is so well spoken of.

It is fit, where one is, to introduce the other;   34
For, as their campaigns were to one end,
They should in glory now shine together.

The army of Christ, which it had cost so dear   37
To arm again, was moving behind its standard
Slowly and doubtfully, the troops few in number,

When that emperor who reigns eternally   40
Did something for the vacillating soldiers,
Of his grace only, not that they deserved it;

And, as has been said, gave help to his spouse   43
—Two champions, at whose doings and sayings
The erring rabble pulled themselves together.

In that part where the sweet Zephyr rises   46
To open up the early leaves with which
Europa sees herself covered anew,

Not far from the crashing of the waves   49
Behind which, after his lengthy course,
The sun at certain times hides from all men,

Lies Calaruega the fortunate   52
Under the protection of the great shield
On which the lion is subject and subduer.

Within it was born the passionate vassal   55
Of the Christian faith, the sacred athlete,
Kind to his followers and to his enemies, cruel.

As soon as it was created, his mind   58
Was so replete with living power
That, in his mother's womb, it made her prophesy.

When the marriage ceremony had taken place,   61
At the font, between him and the faith,
With its mutual endowment of benefits,

64   The lady who acted as his surety
      Saw in a dream the marvellous fruit
      Which was to issue from him and his heirs.

67   And so that he should be spoken of as he was,
      A spirit from up here moved her to call him
      By a name which showed in whose possession he was.

70   He was called Dominic; and I speak of him
      As a husbandman who was chosen of Christ
      To give him assistance in his garden.

73   He seemed indeed Christ's messenger and familiar;
      For the first love which was manifest in him
      Was for the first command that Christ gave.

76   Many times, silent and wide awake,
      He was found upon the ground by his nurse,
      As if he were saying: "It was for this I came."

79   O his father, truly called Felix!
      And his mother, who was Giovanna indeed,
      If that name has the meaning they say!

82   Not for the world, for which men labour now,
      Following the Ostian and Taddeo,
      But for the love of the authentic manna,

85   In a little while he became a great doctor;
      So that he set to work around the vineyard
      Which soon wilts if the dresser is no good.

88   And the demands he made to that seat
      Which was once kinder to the just poor
      —Degenerate, not in itself, but in its occupant—

91   Was, not to give away only a third or a half,
      Not to be given the first vacant preferment,
      Not for the tithes, which belong to God's poor;

94   But to be given permission to take up arms
      Against the erring world, for that seed
      From which grew the twenty-four plants around you.

With the doctrine and the will, and the authority   97
Of the apostolic office, he left the place,
Like a torrent which spurts out from a deep vein;

And his vehemence struck at the shoots of heresy   100
And struck most forcefully in those places
Where the resistances were most stubborn.

From him there flowed a variety of streams   103
With which the universal garden is so watered
That the young trees in it are fuller of life.

If such was the one wheel of the chariot   106
In which Holy Church defended herself
And overcame her civil strife in the field,

The excellence of the other, about which   109
Thomas was so polite before I came,
Should certainly be perfectly plain to you.

But the track left by what is now the highest part   112
Of the wheel of the chariot, has been abandoned,
And there is only mould where there was crust.

His household, which proceeded straight ahead   115
With their feet in his footprints, has turned round
So that the heel strikes where the toe once was.

And soon it will be seen what sort of harvest   118
Bad cultivation brings, when the tares complain
That they are not allowed into the granary.

I admit that if you turned our volume over,   121
Sheet by sheet, you would still find a page
On which you might read: "I am as I was."

But that will not be from Casale or Acquasparta;   124
From there only come the sort of people who
Either ignore the rule, or niggle about it.

I am the life of Bonaventure   127
From Bagnoregio, who in the great offices
Never let his left hand know what his right was doing.

130   Illuminato and Augustine are here,
       Who were of the first discalced brothers
       And in the cord made themselves friends of God.

133   Hugh of St Victor is here with them too,
       And Pietro Mangiadoro and Pietro Ispano
       Whose light shines below in twelve small books;

136   Nathan the prophet, and the metropolitan
       Chrysostom, with Anselm and that Donatus
       Who deigned to set his hand to the study of grammar.

139   Rabanus is here, and there shines at his side
       The abbot from Calabria, Joachim
       Who was endowed with a prophetic spirit.

142   To the celebration of this great paladin
       I was moved by the glowing courtesy
       Of brother Thomas and his honest discourse;

145   And all the company was moved with me.'

CANTO XIII

       Let anyone who really wants to know
       What I now saw, imagine (and let him hold
       The image, while I speak, firm as a rock)

4   Fifteen stars which in the various quarters
       Light up the sky with so much clarity
       That the air, however dense, is penetrated;

7   Let him imagine the Great Bear, for which
       Our latitudes are enough, by night and day,
       And which, as it turns, does not fade from our sight;

10   Let him imagine the mouth of that horn
       Which begins at the tip of the axis
       Around which the primal circle rotates,

Having made of themselves two constellations 13
Such as Minos's daughter made when she
Felt come upon her the chill of death;

And one of these with its rays inside the other, 16
And both of them rotating in such a manner
That one should take the lead and the other follow;

And he will have some notion of the actual 19
Constellation with its double dance,
Gyrating around the point where I was;

For it was as far from what we are used to 22
As the movement of the Chiana is from that
Of the heaven which goes faster than all the others.

There was no hymning of Bacchus or Apollo, 25
But of three persons in the divine nature,
The divine and human natures in one person.

The singing and the dancing were completed; 28
And those holy lights seemed to turn to us,
Happy to pass from one care to another.

Then that light which had narrated to me 31
The marvellous life of the poor man of God,
Broke the silence of those concordant powers,

And said: 'Since one lot of corn has been winnowed 34
And since the seed has been stored away,
Sweet love invites me to thresh the other.

You think that into that breast from which the rib 37
Was taken out to form the lovely cheek
Whose palate cost the whole world so dear,

And into that which, pierced by the lance, 40
Made such satisfaction for before and after
That it turns the scale against all our faults,

All the light that ever human nature 43
May have, was infused by that power
Which had created the one and the other;

46 And so you wonder at what I said before,
    When I reported there had never been a second
    To that good enclosed in the fifth light.

49 Now open your eyes to my answer,
    And you will see that what you believe and what I said
    Have truth for the centre of their circle.

52 What does not die, and that which can die,
    Is nothing but the reflection of that idea
    Which our father in his love generated;

55 For that living light which so issues from
    Its shining source, as to remain one with it
    And with the love which makes a third with them,

58 By its goodness gathers its rays together
    As if reflected in nine substances,
    Yet all eternally remaining one.

61 Thence it goes down to the remotest powers
    From act to act, until it becomes such
    As make no more than brief contingencies;

64 And by contingencies in this connection I mean
    The generated things which are produced,
    With or without seed, by the moving heavens.

67 Neither the wax nor what acts upon it
    Remains unchanged; so that live light more or less
    Shows through under the idea stamped on it.

70 So it happens that one and the same tree,
    According to its kind, fruits better or worse;
    And men are born with varying powers of mind.

73 If the wax had been brought to its perfection
    And heaven was acting in its supreme power,
    The whole brilliance of the seal would be apparent;

76 But nature always gives something imperfect,
    Working in the same manner as the artist
    Who has the skill, and yet his hand shakes.

But if the warm love, the limpid vision 79
Of the primal power disposes and sets the seal,
There a complete perfection is achieved.

In this way once the dust was made worthy 82
Of the completest animal perfection;
In this way too the Virgin was made to conceive:

So that I sanction your opinion 85
That human nature never was and never will be
As it was in those two persons.

Now if I did not carry my argument further, 88
Your first words would I suppose be:
"Well then, how was that one without an equal?"

But so that what is not plain may be so, 91
Consider who he was, what reason moved him
To ask what he did when he was told: "Choose."

I have not spoken so as to conceal from you 94
That he was a king and chose understanding
So that he might be a fully efficient king;

Not to know the number of intelligences 97
Up here, which move the world, or whether necessary
And contingent together can ever produce necessary;

Nor whether a *primus motus* must be assumed, 100
Or whether, in a semicircle, it is possible
To construct a triangle without a right angle.

So, if you observe what I say now and what I said earlier, 103
You will gather that the prudence of a king
Is what I was intending to indicate;

And if you look at the "arose" with clear eyes, 106
You will see that it relates only to kings,
Who are numerous, although good ones are scarce.

Take what I say with this distinction in mind; 109
And so it can stand with what you hold to be true
Of the first father and of our beloved.

112 And let this always make your feet like lead
So that you move like a man who is worn out
Towards a Yes or No you cannot actually see:

115 For a man is right down among the fools
In the case either of affirmation or denial,
If he proceeds without making distinctions;

118 Because it often happens that a quick opinion
Inclines in the wrong direction, and after that
The intellect is hampered by vanity.

121 It is worse than useless to put to sea
To fish for truth if you haven't got the skill,
Because you don't come back as you set out.

124 Parmenides, Bryson, Melissus and the rest
Are open proof of that to all the world,
For they went on without knowing where:

127 The same with Sabellius, Arius, and those fools
Who were like sword-blades to the scriptures;
The faces reflected in them were all awry.

130 Let people not be too sure of themselves
And their judgement, like someone who reckons
The field of corn before the ears are ripe:

133 For I have seen all the winter through
The thorn first show itself unyielding, wild,
And after all carry a rose on top;

136 And I have seen a ship sail straight and swiftly
Over the sea for the whole of its voyage
Yet perish at last at the harbour mouth.

139 Let not every Bertha and Martin think
Because they see one a thief, another respectable,
That they see how they are in the eyes of God;

142 For one may rise, and the other one may fall.'

CANTO XIV

Centre to circumference, circumference to centre,
Is how water moves in a circular vessel
Depending on whether you strike from without or within.

That was the thought which dropped suddenly   4
Into my mind, just as the glorious
Life of Thomas became silent again;

It was the likeness which occurred to me   7
With his speaking and that of Beatrice
Who, when he had finished, was pleased to begin thus:

'What he needs, although he does not tell you,   10
Either in words nor, yet, in his thoughts,
Is to get to the root of another truth.

Tell him whether the light with which   13
Your substance flowers now, will remain with you
Eternally in the manner it is with you now;

If it does remain, tell him how,   16
When you are made visible again,
It can happen without troubling your sight.'

As, drawn and impelled by an access of gladness,   19
People who are dancing in a circle
Sometimes raise their voices and move more briskly,

So, at this eager and freely offered prayer,   22
The holy company showed a fresh joy
In their circling and in their marvellous notes.

Anyone who laments that we must die   25
And go to live above, has not in view
The refreshment that is poured out on us here.

That one and two and three which lives for ever   28
And reigns for ever in three and two and one,
Uncircumscribed, and circumscribing all,

31   Was sung three times by each of these spirits
      With such melody as would itself be
      Appropriate reward for any merit.

34   And I heard in the divinest light
      Of the smaller circle a simple voice
      Perhaps like that of the angel who spoke to Mary,

37   Answer: 'As long as this festivity
      Of paradise shall last, so long our love
      Will shed around us such rays as clothe us.

40   Its brightness is proportionate to its warmth,
      The warmth to the vision, and that depends
      On how much grace it has beyond its worth.

43   When our flesh, then glorified and holy,
      Is put on us once more, our persons will be
      In greater perfection as being complete at last:

46   Because there will be an accession of that light
      Which is freely given us by the highest good,
      Light which enables us to see him;

49   In this way the vision must grow clearer,
      And the warmth produced by it must grow too,
      As well as the rays which shine out of it.

52   But, like charcoal which gives out a flame
      And yet glows more brightly than the flame itself
      So that it keeps its outline and appearance,

55   So the radiance which surrounds us now
      Will be outshone by the brilliance of the flesh
      Which now lies buried in the earth;

58   Nor will so much light weary us at all;
      For the organs of the body will be strong
      To everything able to give us pleasure.'

61   One and another chorus seemed to me
      So quick and eager to say 'Amen!'
      That it was clear they wanted their dead bodies;

Perhaps not just for themselves, but for their mothers,   64
For their fathers and others who were dear to them
Before they turned into eternal flames.

And then around us, shining with equal brightness,   67
Appeared a lustre beyond what was there already,
In the manner of an horizon growing clearer,

And as at the first rising of evening,   70
New objects begin to appear in the heavens
So that they seem to be there, then seem not to be,

I thought that I was beginning to see   73
Newcomers like the others, making a circle
Outside the other two circumferences.

Oh a true radiance of the Holy Spirit!   76
How suddenly it appeared and shone
Into my eyes, so that they could not bear it!

But Beatrice showed herself to me   79
So lovely and smiling that her appearance must be left
With those sights which the mind cannot retain.

From this sight my eyes recovered strength   82
To raise themselves; and I saw I had been translated
With my lady alone to a higher blessedness.

I saw clearly that I had risen higher   85
By the glancing smile of the star
Which seemed to me redder than ordinary.

With all my heart, and speaking with that tongue   88
Which is the same in all men, I made to God
Such holocaust as befitted this new grace.

And the ardour of the sacrifice within me   91
Was not spent, before I knew that indeed
My offering was accepted and propitious;

For a splendour appeared in two bands   94
With such radiance and with such red glow
That I said: 'O Helios, who so arrays them!'

97   As, with its lesser and its greater lights,
       The Galaxy spreads its white path between
       The poles of the world, and makes wise men reflect;

100   So those starry bands composed,
       In the depths of Mars, the venerable sign
       Which diameters crossing at right-angles make in a circle.

103   Here what I remember is too much for expression;
       For in that cross Christ himself shone
       So that I find no fit comparison:

106   But whoever takes his cross and follows Christ
       Will still forgive me for what I leave unsaid
       When he sees that that whiteness flashed out Christ.

109   Meeting together and passing one another,
       The lights sparkled brightly as they moved
       From side to side and up and down that cross:

112   It is thus that tiny specks may be seen,
       Straight and twisted, swift-moving and slow,
       Never staying the same, long and short,

115   Moving through the ribbons of light which sometimes
       Appear in the shadow which human skill
       And brains procure for our protection.

118   As rebec and harp with the strings well-tuned
       Make a sweet tintinnabulation
       To one who knows nothing of the notes,

121   So, from the lights which appeared to me there,
       Was gathered on the cross a melody
       Which carried me away, though the hymn was not clear.

124   Certainly I could hear it was a song of praise
       Because I could make out 'Arise' and 'Conquer',
       As one might, without understanding, hear.

127   I so fell in love at that point
       That there had been nothing hitherto
       Which had so bound me with sweet chains.

Perhaps what I am saying may seem too daring,   130
When I put second the pleasure from the lovely eyes,
Looking into which my desire reaches rest:

But anyone who considers how the living pledges   133
Of all beauty worked more the higher we were,
And that I did not turn to look at them,

Will be able to excuse what I accuse myself of   136
In order to excuse myself; and will see that I speak the truth;
For here the holy joy is not excluded

Because, as one rises, it becomes clearer.   139

CANTO XV

The gracious will, into which that love which is
Truly inspired, always resolves itself,
As does cupidity into ill-will,

Imposed silence upon that sweet instrument,   4
And caused the holy cords, which the right hand
Of heaven relaxed and tautened, to be still.

How could they be deaf to just requests,   7
Those beings who, to give me will enough
To make my prayer, agreed to be silent?

If, for the love of what does not endure,   10
A man gives up that love eternally,
He well deserves to suffer without end.

As through a clear and tranquil starlit sky   13
From time to time there runs a sudden fire,
Moving eyes which were gazing steadily,

And it seems as if a star is moving its station   16
Until one sees that, from the place where it lit up,
Nothing is lost, and that it does not last long;

19 So from the right-hand tip of that cross
    To its foot a star appeared to run,
    From the constellation which shone there.

22 Nor did the jewel come off its ribbon,
    But travelled along by way of the radial bands
    And seemed like a flame behind alabaster.

25 So did Anchises's shade present himself,
    If we are to believe our greatest muse,
    When, in Elysium, he perceived his son.

28 'O sanguis meus, o superinfusa
    gratia dei, sicut tibi, cui
    bis unquam coeli ianua reclusa?'

31 Thus spoke that light: so I paid attention;
    Then I turned to look at my lady,
    And in both directions I was stupefied;

34 For in her eyes there blazed such a smile
    That I thought my eyes had sounded the depths
    Of my grace and of my paradise.

37 Then—and both ears and eyes perceived his joy—
    The spirit added to what he had said at first,
    But I did not understand, so deep his meaning;

40 It was not by choice that he was obscure to me,
    But of necessity, for his conceptions
    Were placed above the limits of mortal men.

43 And when the bow of burning charity
    Was so let go, that what he said descended
    Towards the mark of our intellect,

46 The first thing that I understood
    Was 'Blessed be thou, O three and one,
    That you are so gracious to me in my seed!'

49 He went on: 'A long-felt, not unpleasing, hunger
    I had from reading in that great volume
    In which neither white nor black is ever changed,

You have satisfied, my son, within the light   52
In which I talk to you, thanks to that lady
Who gave you wings for so high a flight.

You think that your thought comes to me   55
From him who is the first, as out of unity,
Once known, may be derived five or six;

And so you do not ask who I may be   58
Or why I should appear to rejoice more in you
Than any other in this happy company.

You think right; for lesser and great here   61
In this life gaze into the mirror
In which you show your thought before you think it.

But so that sacred love in which I watch   64
In endless vision and which makes you thirsty
With a sweet desire, should be the better satisfied,

Let your voice, confident, fearless and glad,   67
Ring out your will, ring out with your desire,
To which my answer is already decreed!'

I turned to Beatrice, and she heard   70
Before I opened my mouth, and smiled assent
So that the wings of my desire grew.

Then I began like this: 'Love and intelligence   73
Became equally balanced in you
When the primal equality first appeared to you;

Because the sun which shines on you and burns   76
With heat and light, does so so equally
That all comparisons are inadequate.

But with mortals will and argument,   79
For reasons which are clear enough to you,
Have wings which carry very different feathers;

So I, who am mortal, feel myself   82
Unbalanced in this way, and can give thanks
For this paternal greeting only with my heart.

85   But I do indeed beg of you, living topaz,
     Who are the stone of this precious jewel,
     That you would satisfy me as to your name.'

88   'O my leaf, in whom I was well pleased
     As I awaited you, I was your root':
     That was the beginning of his answer.

91   And then he said: 'He who gave his name
     To your family, and who for a hundred years
     And more, has gone round the first cornice of the Mount,

94   Was my son and your great-grandfather:
     And it is proper that by your works
     You should shorten this long labour of his.

97   Florence within the ancient circle
     From which tierce and nones are still rung,
     Lived in peace, soberly, decently.

100 There were no golden chains or coronets,
     Embroidered gowns nor bands about the middle
     Which were more to look at than the person herself.

103 The daughter did not yet frighten her father
     Merely by being born; for then the age
     Of marriage and the dowry were both reasonable.

106 There were no houses empty of families;
     And Sardanapalus had not arrived
     To show what may be done in private rooms.

109 Montemalo had not yet been outdone
     By your Uccellatoio which, outdoing the rise,
     Shall just as certainly outdo the fall.

112 I have seen Bellincion Berti go dressed
     In leather and bone, and his wife come away
     From the mirror without having painted her face;

115 And I have seen the Nerli and Vecchietti
     Content to go about in skin jackets,
     And their wives at the spindle with flax.

O fortunate! every woman was sure   118
Of where she was to be buried, and none was yet
Abandoned in her bed because of France.

One would keep watch beside the cradle   121
And, rocking it, would use that way of speech
Which gives pleasure first to fathers and mothers;

Another, as she drew thread from the distaff,   124
Would tell her household all the old stories
About the Trojans, Fiesole and Rome.

Then a Cinghella, a Lapo Salterello   127
Would be as much a wonder as, in these days,
A Cincinnatus or Cornelia.

To so quiet and beautiful a life   130
Among the citizens, such loyal company,
To so delightful a place to live,

Mary—invoked with deep cries—gave me;   133
And in your ancient baptistry I was
At once made Christian and Cacciaguida.

Moronto and Eliseo were my brothers: 136
My wife came to me from the Po valley;
And from her your surname was derived.

Then I followed the emperor Conrad;   139
And he installed me as one of his knights,
So much did my manner of working please him.

In his train I marched against the iniquity   142
Of that law whose followers usurp,
Through the shepherd's fault, the justice you should exercise.

There by that obscene people I was   145
Unwound from the deceits of this world
The love of which corrupts so many souls;

And came from martyrdom to this peace.'   148

CANTO XVI

Nobility of blood, little as you are,
You make people glory in you although
Here below our affections are so weak;

4   That will now cause me no astonishment:
For there, where appetite is not awry,
I mean in heaven, I gloried in you myself.

7   You are a cloak which soon gets too small;
So that, if bits are not sewn on day by day,
Time will soon walk round with his scissors.

10   I found myself using that form of speech
Once more, which Rome had been the first to admit,
Although her people use it now less than any;

13   Then Beatrice, who stood a little aside,
Smiling, appeared like that lady who coughed
At the first fault recorded of Guinevere.

16   I began: 'You are my father, you give me
Entire confidence to speak to you;
You give me courage to be more than myself.

19   My mind is filled full of happiness
By so many streams, it rejoices in itself
Because it can bear it and not break up.

22   So tell me, my dear progenitor,
Who were your ancestors, and what were the years
Which were recorded in your childhood:

25   Tell me about the fold of St John the Baptist,
How big it then was, and who were the people
Fit for the highest seats of office in it.'

28   As charcoal livens into a flame
At the breath of the wind, so I saw that light
Burn more brightly at my gentle requests.

And as it made itself lovelier in my eyes,   31
So with a sweeter and softer voice,
But not in the manner in which we speak now,

He said: 'From the day when the first "Hail Mary" was uttered   34
To that birth in which my mother, now sainted,
Lightened herself of me whom she was carrying,

This fire came back five hundred times   37
And fifty, and thirty, to its Lion,
To rekindle itself under his feet.

My ancestors and I were born in the place   40
Where those who run in your annual games
First find themselves in the last of the wards.

That is enough to hear about my ancestors: 43
Who they were and whence they came there
It is more civil to keep quiet about.

At that time the whole number of those who were   46
Capable of bearing arms, between Mars and the Baptist,
Was only a fifth of the population now.

But the inhabitants, who are now a mixture   49
From Campi, Certaldo and from Fegghine,
Were pure-bred down to the last artisan.

Oh how much better to have the people I speak of   52
For your neighbours, and to keep your boundaries
Still at Trespiano and Galluzzo,

Than to have these inside and put up with the smell   55
Of louts from Aguglion and from Signa
Who still have a sharp eye for a swindle!

If the most degenerate crowd on earth   58
Had not been a stepmother to Caesar
But had been kind to her son as a true mother,

Some who have become Florentine bankers and merchants   61
Would have been sent back to Simifonte
Where their grandfathers went around as beggars;

64   Montemurlo would still belong to the Conti;
There would still be Cerchi in Acone district
And, perhaps, in Valdigrieve, Buondelmonti.

67   The confusion of people has always
Been the beginning of the city's trouble,
As, in the body, undigested food;

70   As a blind bull is quicker to fall over
Than a blind lamb; and a single sword
Often cuts better than five will do.

73   If you consider Luni and Urbisaglia,
How they have gone, and how, after them,
Chiusi and Sinigaglia are going:

76   To hear how families undo themselves
Will not seem strange or hard to understand,
Since even cities come to an end.

79   The things you make and do all have their deaths
As you have yours; though this is not evident
In things which last long, for your lives are short.

82   And, as the turning of the lunar heavens
Restlessly covers and uncovers the shores,
So does the tide of fortune in Florence:

85   Therefore it should not seem remarkable
When I tell you of distinguished Florentines
Whose fame is now hidden under time.

88   I saw the Ughi and the Catelleni,
Greci, Ormanni, Filippi, Alberichi,
Famous citizens, already in decline;

91   And I saw, when they were as great as they were ancient,
The families of Sannella and of the Arca,
The Soldanieri, Ardinghi and Bostichi.

94   Above the gate which at this hour is burdened
With new treason which lies so heavy upon it
That it will soon be the wreck of the ship,

Were the Ravignani, from whom are descended   97
The count Guido and those who have since
Taken the name of the great Bellincione.

Already the Della Pressa knew how to govern,   100
And Galigaio already had in his house
The gilded hilt and pommel of a knight's sword.

The stripe of grey fur was already great   103
And the Sacchetti, Guiochi, Fifanti and Barucci;
The Galli and those whose bushel was something to blush about.

The stock from which the Calfucci sprang   106
Was already great, and already the curule chairs
Were occupied by the Sizii and Arrigucci.

Oh what men I have seen who have been undone   109
By their pride! at that time the golden globes
Decked out Florence on all great occasions.

So did the fathers of those who,   112
Whenever there is a vacancy in your church,
Are to be found guzzling in consistory.

The outrageous family which is a dragon   115
To anyone who shrinks from it, but like a lamb
To anyone who shows his teeth, or his purse,

Was already coming up, but from small people;   118
So that Ubertin Donati was not pleased
To be related to them through his father-in-law.

Already the Caponsacco had come down   121
To the market place from Fiesole, and already Guida
And Infangato were good citizens.

I will tell you something incredible but true: 124
One used to go into the old city
By a gate which was named after the Pera crowd.

Everyone who bears any part of the arms   127
Of the great baron whose name and fortune
Are kept alive by the feast of St Thomas,

130   Derives his knighthood and privileges from him:
Even though he who surrounds it with a border
Nowadays joins forces with the people.

133   Already there were Gualterotti and Importuni;
And Borgo would still be a quiet spot
If they had managed to do without new neighbours.

136   The house from which your misfortune sprang
Because of the just scorn which brought you to death
And put an end to the pleasures of your life,

139   Was honoured, it and its associates:
O Buondelmonte, how ill-omened was your flight
From their wedding at the advice of another:

142   Many would be happy who are now sad
If God had delivered you to the river Ema
The first time you ever set foot in the city.

145   But it was fit that in her last hour of peace
Florence should give a victim to that battered
Statue which stands guard upon the city.

148   With these people and with others with them
I saw Florence enjoy such peace
That there was nothing for which she had to weep;

151   With these people I saw her inhabitants
In glory and justice, so that the lily
Was never turned upside-down on the flag-pole

154   Nor, through divisions, stained red with blood.'

CANTO XVII

As there once came to Clymene, to ascertain
The truth of what he had heard said against himself,
The young man who is still a caution to fathers;

So was I, and so was I felt to be   4
Both by Beatrice and by the sacred lamp
Which had already changed its position on my account.

And so my lady said: 'Show forth the heat   7
Of your desire, and let it so issue
That we may see of what temper it is;

Not that our knowledge is at all increased   10
By what you say, but you should be accustomed
To speak your thirst, enabling it to be quenched.'

'O my dear root, and yet so far above me   13
That, as an earthly mind can understand
A triangle cannot have two obtuse angles,

You see things which are contingent   16
Before they exist, looking upon that point
To which all times are present;

While I, in company with Virgil,   19
Was climbing up the mountain which cures souls
And going down into the dead world,

Grave words were spoken about the life ahead of me;   22
Although indeed I feel myself well set
To square up to any blows of fortune.

And therefore it is my wish to know   25
What fortune it is which comes my way;
For the arrow which is foreseen comes slowly.'

So I spoke to that same light   28
Which had spoken to me before; and, as Beatrice wished,
What I desired to know was confessed.

Without the circumlocutions in which people   31
Were swallowed up before the slaughter of
The lamb of God who takes away sins,

But in clear words and plain exact speech   34
That fatherly love replied to me,
Hidden, but appearing in his smile;

37   'Contingency, which does not stretch beyond
      The limits of your material world,
      Is all set out before the sight of God:

40   But does not on that account become necessity
      Any more than a ship which is drifting downstream
      Drifts as it does because a man sees it.

43   From God there comes into sight for me,
      As sweet organ music comes to the ear,
      The time which is in preparation for you.

46   As Hippolytus was driven out of Athens
      By his implacable and perfidious stepmother,
      So it will be with you, who must leave Florence.

49   This is willed and is already plotted,
      And soon will be brought about by him who devises it
      In the place where Christ is bought and sold every day.

52   It will as usual be the injured party
      Which gets the blame; but when vengeance comes
      It will bear witness to the truth which orders it.

55   You will leave everything you love most dearly;
      This is the arrow which is loosed first
      From the bow of exile.

58   You will learn how salt is the taste
      Of other people's bread, how hard the way
      Going up and down other people's stairs.

61   And what will weigh heaviest upon your shoulders
      Will be the evil and stupid company
      With which you will fall into the ravine;

64   For they will all turn against you,
      Ungrateful, mad, profane; but shortly afterwards
      They and not you will have to blush for it.

67   Their bestiality will be proved
      By their proceedings; and it will be well for you
      To have stood aside and on your own feet.

Your first refuge, and your first entertainment   70
Will be the courtesy of the great Lombard
Whose arms are a ladder bearing the sacred bird;

And his good will towards you will be such   73
That doing, which generally comes after asking,
As between you two, will be what comes first.

In him you will see one who at his birth   76
Was so marked by this powerful star
That his performance will be notable.

He is someone people have not yet noticed,   79
Because of his youth; for nine years only
Have these spheres circulated around him.

But before the Gascon has deceived the great Henry   82
Sparks of his virtue will begin to appear
Careless alike of money and exertion.

So well will his magnificence be known   85
That not even his enemies will be able
To keep their tongues from talking of his actions.

Look to him and the benefits he will bring;   88
Through him many people will be transformed,
Changing their condition, the rich and the beggars.

And you shall bear a record of him in your mind   91
But say nothing'; and then he told me things
Incredible to those who will live through them.

Then he added: 'These are the clarifications,   94
Son, of what was said to you; these are the snares
Which are concealed by only a few revolutions.

Yet I would not have you envious of your neighbours   97
Since your life will stretch far into the future
Beyond the punishment of their perfidies.'

When by his silence the blessed soul showed   100
That he had finished weaving that cloth
Which I had held out in readiness for him,

103   I began, like someone who, in his anxiety,
      Longs to take the advice of somebody
      Who sees clearly and is resolute and affectionate:

106   'I see clearly, father, how time rides
      Towards me, to give me such a blow
      As hurts most one who gives way to it;

109   And so it is well to arm myself with foresight
      So that, if the dearest place is taken from me,
      I do not lose the others by my poems.

112   Down in that world which is bitter without end
      And up the mountain from whose lovely summit
      The eyes of my lady raised me up,

115   And afterwards, through heaven from light to light,
      I have learned things which, if I repeat them,
      Will have a bitter taste for many people;

118   And if I am a timid friend to truth,
      I fear to lose the life I may have among those
      Who will call the present time, ancient times.'

121   The light in which the treasure I found there
      Was smiling, first began to sparkle brightly
      Like a ray of sun caught in a mirror of gold;

124   Then it replied: 'A conscience which is clouded
      By its own shame or by that of another,
      Will certainly feel that your words are sharp.

127   But none the less, all lying set aside,
      Make clear to everyone the whole vision;
      And let them scratch wherever they may itch.

130   For if your words are objectionable
      At the first taste, they will yield nourishment
      Afterwards, once they have been digested.

133   This cry of yours will do as the wind does,
      Strike hardest on the summits which are highest;
      And that is no small argument of honour.

Therefore we have shown you, in these spheres,   136
On the mountain and in the valley of pain
Only the souls of those who are known to fame;

For the listener's mind will not find its rest   139
Nor fix its faith unless it finds examples
Of which the root is known and not hidden,

And arguments which are as plain as day.'   142

CANTO XVIII

Already that blessed mirror was content
With his own thoughts, and I savoured mine,
Tempering the bitterness of them with sweetness.

And that lady who was leading me to God   4
Said: 'Have other thoughts; consider that I am
Close to him who has said, Vengeance is mine.'

I turned round towards the amorous voice   7
Of my comfort; and what love I discerned
In her holy eyes, I give up the attempt to tell;

Not only because I mistrust my own words   10
But because my mind is unable to turn back
So much above itself, with no one to guide it.

All I can tell of that moment is this: 13
That, as I gazed upon her, my emotion
Was free of any other desire whatever,

While the eternal pleasure, which radiated   16
Directly upon Beatrice, made me happy
With the appearance of it reflected in her looks.

Conquering me with the light of a smile,   19
She said to me: 'Turn round, and listen;
Paradise is not only in my eyes.'

22   As sometimes, here, what anyone is feeling
     May be seen in the way they look, if it is such
     That the soul is entirely taken up in it,

25   So in the blazing of that sacred brilliance
     To which I turned, I recognised the wish
     In him to talk with me a little longer.

28   He began: 'In this fifth stage of the tree
     Which lives from the top and always bears fruit,
     And at no time loses a single leaf,

31   Spirits are blessed who, below, before
     They came to heaven, were of immense fame,
     So that they would be spoil for any muse.

34   Look therefore at the arms of the cross:
     The one I name will carry out the movement
     The rapid fire within a cloud may do.'

37   I saw a light drawn along the cross
     And, as it happened, Joshua was named;
     The word and fact were perceived simultaneously.

40   And at the name of the great Maccabee
     I saw another move itself, spinning,
     And gladness was the whip for that top.

43   So for Charles the Great and for Orlando,
     My attentive look followed two more of them
     As the eye follows a falcon in flight.

46   Afterwards William and Renoardo
     And Godfrey of Boulogne and Robert Guiscard
     Carried my eye along the arms of the cross.

49   Then, moving and mixing with other lights,
     The soul which had spoken to me showed me
     What a singer he was among the choir of heaven.

52   I turned then upon my right side
     To see what Beatrice thought I should do,
     Whether she made it known by word or gesture;

I saw her two eyes were so clear,   55
So joyful, that her appearance surpassed
All she had seemed hitherto, even most lately.

And as, by feeling an increase of pleasure   58
In doing well, a man sees day by day
That his virtue is making some advance,

So I perceived that I was going round   61
Together with the heaven in a wider arc,
Seeing this miracle yet more beautiful.

And as the change which happens when a woman   64
Recovers her paleness, throwing off an embarrassment
Which has tinged her face with blushes,

So was the change then for my eyes, when I turned,   67
Because of the whiteness of the temperate star,
The sixth, which had received me into itself.

I saw in the sparkling light of Jupiter   70
The radiance of the love that was there
Signalling to my eyes in our language.

And as birds, rising from the river bank   73
As if congratulating on the food they have found,
Form themselves now in a round flock, now some other shape,

So within the lights the holy creatures   76
Sang in their flight, and formed themselves into
Different shapes, now D, now I, now L.

First, singing, they moved in time with their tune;   79
Then, turning into one of those letters,
They would stay like that a moment, in quietness.

O Pegasean goddess, giver of glory   82
To the inventive mind, and long life,
Which, with your help, it gives to cities and kingdoms,

Inspire me, so that I can set out boldly   85
Their figures, in the manner I have conceived them:
Let your power appear in these brief verses!

88   They showed themselves thirty-five times
      In vowels and consonants; and I noted
      The letters and syllables as they came out.

91   'DILIGITE IUSTITIAM' were the first
      Verb and noun to be so depicted;
      'QUI IUDICATIS TERRAM' were the last.

94   After the 'M' of the fifth word was formed
      They stayed in place; and then Jupiter
      Seemed silver there, inlaid with gold.

97   And I saw other lights descend where
      The top of the 'M' was, and there rest
      Singing, I think, the good that drew them to him.

100   Then, as when we strike burnt logs with something,
      There rise up innumerable sparks,
      Which foolish people tell their fortunes by;

103   There seemed to rise from there more than a thousand
      Lights, and climb, some far and some a short distance,
      Just as the sun which kindled them determined;

106   And each one resting in its place,
      I saw the head and neck of an eagle
      Represented by points of fire.

109   He who painted that has no need of a guide;
      He is himself the guide and it is from him
      The formative power recalls how to build a nest.

112   The rest of the blessed who appeared content
      At first to form a lily on the 'M',
      With a slight movement, followed the design.

115   O sweet star, how many and what gems
      Demonstrated to me that our justice
      Is made by the heaven in which you glitter!

118   Therefore I pray the mind in which begins
      Your movement and your power, that it will mark
      The source of that smoke which spoils your beams;

So that once more there may be anger against   121
The buying and selling inside the temple
Which is walled with miracles and martyrdoms.

O army of heaven which I contemplate,   124
Offer a prayer for those who upon earth
Are led out of course behind a bad example!

The custom once was to make war with swords;   127
But now it is made by taking from one or another
The bread the loving father keeps from none.

But you who write only to rub out,   130
Remember that Peter and Paul, who both died
For the vineyard you spoil, are still alive.

You may say: 'I have so set my heart   133
Upon the one who liked to live alone
And by a dance was brought to martyrdom,

That I do not know the Fisherman or Paul.'   136

CANTO XIX

There appeared before me with outstretched wings
The beautiful image made by those souls
Happy together in their sweet enjoyment.

Each one of them appeared a ruby in which   4
A ray of sunlight burned so brilliantly
That it was reflected in my eyes.

And what I have now to report   7
No voice has ever spoken, no ink written,
Nor any imagination comprehended:

I saw and also heard the bird talk,   10
In a voice which uttered both 'I' and 'mine',
When in conception it was 'we' and 'ours'.

13   It began: 'For being just and merciful
      I am exalted here to this glory
      Which is not to be achieved by wanting it;

16   And on earth I left a memory
      Such that even evildoers commend it
      Although they do not follow the example.'

19   As many coals give out a single heat,
      So from those many loves there issued out
      A single sound from the image before me.

22   Then I said: 'O you everlasting flowers
      Of eternal happiness, who so give out your scents
      That they seem to me to be a single scent,

25   Breathe on me so that I may break the fast
      Which has so long kept me in hunger,
      Not finding any food for it on earth.

28   I know certainly that if in heaven,
      Divine justice mirrors itself in other realms,
      Yours will not apprehend it through a veil.

31   You know how intently I prepare myself
      To listen; and you know what that question is
      Which has so long kept me in this fast.'

34   Like a falcon just out of the hood
      Who moves his head and claps with his wings,
      Looking eager and making himself fine,

37   Thus did I see that emblem, which was formed
      Only of praises of the divine grace,
      With songs known to those who rejoice there.

40   Then it began: 'He who drew with compasses
      The boundaries of the world, and within it
      Ordered so much both hidden and manifest,

43   His worth could not so mark itself upon
      The whole of the universe, that his word did not
      Remain in its infinite excess.

The truth of that you may see by the first of the proud, 46
Who was the noblest of all creation
But could not wait for the light, and fell unripe;

And so it appears that every lesser nature 49
Is too small a receptacle for that good
Which has no end, and is its own measure.

Therefore our understanding, which must be 52
No more than a glimmer from that mind
Of which everything in the universe is full,

Cannot of its nature be so powerful 55
That what it comes from does not see
Much beyond what is visible to it.

And so, in the sempiternal justice, 58
The understanding you have of the world
Loses itself as the eye does in the sea;

For, although near the shore it sees the bottom, 61
In the open sea it does not; none the less
The bottom is there although the depths hide it.

There is no light, except from that clear sky 64
Which never is troubled; otherwise, darkness,
The shadow of the flesh or its poison.

And now the hiding-place where the living justice 67
Lay concealed from you, is open enough
—That justice which you often called in question.

For you said: "A man is born upon the banks 70
Of the Indus, where there is none to tell of Christ
And no one to read or write about him;

And all his inclination and his actions, 73
As far as human reason sees, are good;
He is without sin in word or deed.

He dies unbaptised and without faith: 76
Where is the justice in condemning him?
Is it his fault, if he does not believe?"

79   Now who are you to set yourself up
       To judge of matters a thousand miles away
       With eyes that can hardly see nine inches?

82   Certainly for anyone who tries to be clever
       There is a marvellous subject for questioning,
       If scripture were not there to set you right.

85   O worldly creatures, O you gross minds!
       The primal will, which is good in itself,
       Is never less than itself, the supreme good.

88   Whatever is in accord with it, is just:
       No created good can attract the divine will
       Unless by its radiance the divine will so directs it.'

91   As a stork will circle above her nest
       When she has fed her young, and as the young bird
       Whom she has fed, fixes his eyes on her;

94   So did the blessed emblem, and so I
       Lifted my eyes, while he moved his wings
       At the instigation of so many counsels.

97   Wheeling he sang, and said: 'As what I sing
       Is to you, who do not understand it,
       So is the eternal justice to you mortals.'

100   When those shining fires of the Holy Spirit
       Came to a stop, still formed into that emblem
       Which made the Romans feared throughout the world,

103   He began again: 'No one has ever climbed
       To this kingdom without belief in Christ,
       Either before or after he was nailed to the cross.

106   But see: many there are who cry "Christ, Christ"
       Who at the judgement will be much less near
       To him than some who do not know Christ;

109   The Ethiopian will condemn such Christians
       When the two companies are separated,
       The one for ever rich, the other with nothing.

What will the Persian say to your kings   112
When they at last see the volume opened
In which their infamies are all set down?

There will be seen, among Albert's actions,   115
One which will shortly move the hand to write;
By it the kingdom of Prague will become a desert.

There will be seen the trouble on the Seine,   118
Induced by him who, falsifying the coinage,
Will die through being struck by a wild boar.

There will be seen the pride which makes men thirsty   121
And send the Scot and Englishman quite mad
So that they cannot stay within their frontiers.

Seen also the lechery and soft living   124
Of him of Spain and that other of Bohemia,
Who never knew valour or wanted to.

Seen also the lame man of Jerusalem   127
Whose good deeds you could count upon one finger
For every thousand ill deeds he performed.

Seen also the avarice and baseness   130
Of him who keeps the island of the fire
In which Anchises finished his long age.

And to make clear how little he is,   133
His record shall be written in clipped letters
So that a small space will contain them all.

His brother's and his uncle's filthy actions,   136
Which made bastards of what was a great family
And two crowns; all this will appear there.

And he of Portugal and he of Norway   139
Will be known there, as well as he of Rascia
Who saw the coin of Venice, with fatal consequences.

O happy Hungary, if she does not allow   142
Further mishandling! happy Navarre too,
If she can arm herself with her mountains!

145 It should be plain that it is an instalment
Of this that Nicosia and Famagosta
Already lament and shriek at their animal

148 Which keeps together with the other beasts.'

CANTO XX

When he who illumines the whole world
So descends out of our hemisphere
That the light in all directions is put out,

4 The sky, which before was only lit by him,
Suddenly makes itself visible again
By many lights, in which the one shines again:

7 And this act of the sky came to my mind
As the emblem of the world and of its masters
Became silent in its blessed beak;

10 Because all those living lights began,
Shining more brightly, to sing elusive
Songs which have escaped my memory.

13 O sweet love, dressing yourself in smiles,
How ardent did you appear in those flutes
Into which there breathe only holy thoughts!

16 When all the precious and shining stones
With which I saw the sixth light bejewelled
Had imposed silence on those angelic notes,

19 I thought I heard a river murmuring
As it descends clear from rock to rock,
Showing the abundance of the spring at the top.

22 And as the sound of the lute takes shape
At the neck of the instrument, and as the wind
Entering pipes does at the openings,

So, the interval of waiting over,   25
That murmur rose out of the eagle,
Up through his neck, as if it were empty;

There it became a voice and issued forth   28
From the beak in the shape of words
Such as the heart, on which I wrote them, expected.

'The part of me which sees, and in mortal eagles   31
Withstands the sun,' so it began to me,
'Should now be watched with attention,

Because of the fires of which I make my shape,   34
Those which make the eye sparkle in my head
Are the highest ranking among them all.

The one who shines in the middle as the pupil   37
Was the singer of the Holy Spirit
Who carried the ark around from city to city:

Now he knows the merit of his song,   40
In so far as it was the effect of his own counsel,
By the reward, which is proportionate.

Of the five who make the arch of my eyebrow,   43
The one who stands nearest to my beak
Consoled the widow for the loss of her son;

He now knows how dear it costs men   46
Not to follow Christ, by his experience
Of the sweet life and of its opposite.

The next one along the circumference   49
Of which I am speaking, on the upper arch,
Put off his death by true penitence:

He now knows that the eternal judgement   52
Is not altered, when a deserving prayer
Defers till tomorrow what was to have been today.

The next in line who, to give way to the shepherd,   55
With a good intention which produced bad fruit
Went with the laws and me to become a Greek:

58 He now knows that the evil derived
From his good deed is not hurtful to him,
Although thereby the world is destroyed.

61 And he whom you see where the arch bends down,
Was the William for whom that land laments
Which now weeps because Charles and Frederick are alive:

64 He now knows how heaven falls in love
With the just king and, by the appearance
Of his refulgence he still lets it be seen.

67 Who would believe, down in the wandering world,
That in this circle Ripheus the Trojan
Was the fifth among the holy lights?

70 He now knows much of the divine grace
Which the world below is not able to see,
Although his sight does not discern the bottom of it.'

73 As the lark who climbs into the air,
Singing at first, is then silent, content
With the final sweetness which satisfies her,

76 So seemed to me the image there imprinted
At the pleasure of the eternal, by whose desire
Everything comes to be the thing it is.

79 And although in relation to my question
I was as glass is to the colour behind it,
The question could not bear to wait in silence

82 But pushed out of my mouth with the strength
Of its own weight, the words 'What things are these?'
At this I saw a festive coruscation.

85 Then immediately, with eye brighter still,
The blessed emblem gave me its answer
So as not to keep me in suspense, wondering:

88 'I see that you believe these things
Because I tell you, though you do not see how;
So that, if they are believed, they are still hidden.

You do as one who learns the name of something   91
Perfectly well but not its quiddity
Unless someone will explain it to you.

The kingdom of heaven suffers violence   94
From warm love and from living hope
And the violent take it by force;

Not in the manner in which man overcomes man,   97
But conquering because they wish to be conquered
And, conquered, conquer with its own benignity.

The first spirit in the eyebrow, and the fifth,   100
Astonish you, because you see the region
The angels inhabit lit up by them.

They did not leave their bodies, as you think,   103
As Gentiles, but Christians with firm faith,
In the feet which were to suffer, or had suffered.

For the one came back to his bones, out of hell,   106
From which none ever returned to a right will;
And this was the recompense of living hope;

Of living hope, which put strength in the prayers   109
Which were made to God to raise him up again
So that he might have a will which could be moved.

The glorious soul of which I am speaking,   112
Returned to the flesh, though but for a short time,
Believed in him who had the power to help him;

And, believing, lit in himself so great a fire   115
Of the true love, that at his second death
He was worthy to come into this happiness.

The other, by that grace which mounts up   118
From so deep a spring, that no eye ever pierced
So far as to catch sight of the first wave,

Put all his love below upon justice;   121
So that, from grace to grace, God opened up
His eyes to our future redemption:

124   He so believed in it, that from that time
He could not bear the stink of paganism;
And reproved the perverse peoples for it.

127   The three ladies you saw by the right wheel
Did for him what had the effect of baptism,
A thousand years before baptising began.

130   Predestination, O how far away
Is your root from the sight of all those
Who do not see the primal cause entire:

133   And you, mortals, hold yourselves back
From giving judgement; for we, who see God,
Do not yet know who all the elect are;

136   And this deficiency is sweet to us
Because in this good our own good is refined
And we want whatever is God's will.'

139   So, to make my limited sight clear,
I was given by that divine image
This sweet medicine.

142   And as a good lutenist will make
The touch of the strings follow a good singer
So that the song becomes more delightful,

145   So, while he spoke, as I remember,
I saw the two blessed lights move,
Just as eyes blink at the same time,

148   So that their little flames kept time with the words.

CANTO XXI

Already my eyes were fixed again on the face
Of my lady and, with them, my mind was fixed
And so removed from any other purpose.

And she did not smile; but, 'If I smiled,'   4
She began, 'you would become as was
Semele when she was turned to ashes;

For if my beauty, which lights up the more,   7
(As you have seen) the higher we ascend
Upon the stairs of the eternal palace,

If it were not tempered, it would so shine   10
That at its brilliance your mortal power
Would be a branch split by thunder.

We have risen up to the seventh splendour   13
Which, under the breast of the blazing lion,
Now sends its beams down mixed with his virtue.

Fix your mind on what your eyes see   16
And make them mirrors to the figure which will
Make its appearance to you in this mirror.'

Anyone who knew with what delectation   19
My sight was feeding upon her blessed appearance
When I was directed to other concerns,

Would know how pleasing it was to me   22
To do as my celestial escort told me,
Weighing the pleasure of looking against that of obedience.

Within the crystal which, circling round the world,   25
Carries the name of its beloved leader
Under whom every malice lay dead,

The colour of gold, with refulgent rays   28
I saw a ladder which was erected aloft
So far, my sight could not follow it.

I saw too, coming down the steps,   31
So many splendours, I thought all the stars
Which shine in heaven were pouring down there.

And as, in accordance with their natural habits,   34
The daws stir at the beginning of the day,
All together, to warm their cold feathers;

37   Then some go off and do not reappear,
       While others return to where they started from,
       And others stay wheeling in the air;

40   That is how that sparkling seemed to me
       With those radiances which came all together
       As soon as they touched upon a certain rung.

43   And that one which came to halt nearest us,
       Became so bright, that I said to myself:
       'I see the love of which you give such signs.

46   But she, from whom I take the how and when
       Of speech and silence, is still; and therefore I,
       Against my wishes, do well not to ask.'

49   So she, who perceived my silence
       In the sight of him who sees everything,
       Said to me: 'Let your warm desire have its way.'

52   And I began: 'My merit is not enough
       To make me worthy of a reply from you
       But, for the sake of her who lets me ask,

55   You blessed life, who remain hidden within
       Your happiness, I beg you to inform me
       What it is that has brought you so close?

58   And tell me why in this circle the sweet
       Symphony of paradise is silent,
       Though below in the others it sounds so fervently.'

61   'You have mortal hearing, as you have mortal sight,'
       He answered me; 'so here is no singing
       For the same reason that Beatrice has not smiled.

64   I came so far down the rungs of the ladder
       Only in order to give you happiness
       With what I say and with the light which cloaks me;

67   Nor did a greater love make me more willing;
       For up there love as great as mine or greater
       Burns, as the flames by their brightness show.

But the deep charity which makes us prompt　　　　70
To serve the counsel which governs the world
Settles our places here as you observe.'

'I see well,' I said then, 'O sacred light,　　　　73
How in this court an unrestrained love
Is all that is needed for following eternal providence;

But this is what seems hard to understand:　　　　76
Why it was you, of all your companions here,
Who alone was predestined to perform this office?'

I did not come to the end of what I was saying　　　　79
Before the light, making its mid-point the axis,
Whirled round and round like a quick millstone.

And then the love that was within replied:　　　　82
'Divine light comes to a point upon me,
Penetrating what I am surrounded by,

The virtue of which, combined with my own sight,　　　　85
Raises me so far above myself
That I see the supreme essence from which it is drawn.

Thence comes the happiness I am alight with;　　　　88
For in proportion as my sight is clear,
So is the clarity of my flame.

But the most enlightened soul that is in heaven,　　　　91
That seraph whose eye is most fixed on God,
Would not satisfy this demand of yours;

Because the thing you ask is so deep　　　　94
Within the abyss of the eternal law
That it is cut off from all created sight.

And tell the mortal world, when you get back,　　　　97
What I have told you, so that it does not presume
To move its steps towards so remote a goal.

The mind, which is light here, on earth is smoke;　　　　100
Consider therefore how, below, it could achieve
What it could not do when heaven takes it up.'

103   His words set such limitations on me
That I gave up the question, and restricted
Myself to asking him humbly who he was.

106   'Between the two shores of Italy rise rocks
Not far distant from your own country,
So high, that thunder sounds much lower down,

109   And they make a hump which is called Catria,
Below which there was consecrated a retreat
Which used to be for prayer to God alone.'

112   So he began again the third discourse;
And then, continuing, said: 'In that place
I gave myself so solidly to God's service,

115   That with nothing but lenten foods I passed
Cheerfully through both hot and freezing weather,
Contented with contemplative thoughts.

118   That cloister yielded fruit to these heavens,
Richly indeed; and now it has become useless,
So much so that it must soon come to light.

121   In that place I was known as Peter Damian
And became Peter the Sinner in the house
Of Our Lady by the shore of the Adriatic.

124   Little mortal life remained to me
When I was put into one of those hats
Which seem always to have worse heads inside them.

127   Cephas came, and the great vessel of
The Holy Spirit, they were lean and barefoot,
Taking their food wherever they might get it.

130   Now the modern pastors have to be held up
On both sides, and to have someone to lead them,
They are so fat: and someone to push from behind.

133   They spread their cloaks over the backs of their horses
So that there are two beasts under one skin:
O patience, how great the load you have to bear!'

At these words I saw a number of little flames   136
Descend from rung to rung and spin round
And every turn made them look more lovely.

They surrounded the one that spoke, and came to a halt,   139
And uttered a cry which sounded so loud
That it resembled nothing upon earth:

Nor could I understand it; the roar flattened me.   142

CANTO XXII

Crushed and amazed, I turned to my guide,
Just like a little child who runs to find
The person in whom he has most trust;

And she, like a mother who at once   4
Reassures her pale and gasping boy
By her voice, which soon puts him right,

Said to me: 'Don't you know you are in heaven?   7
And don't you know that heaven is all holy
And that all that happens here is done out of charity?

What effect that song might have had upon you,   10
And my smiling, you may now comprehend,
Since the cry made so great a disturbance;

For, if you had understood their prayers,   13
You would already be aware of the vengeance
Which you will certainly see before you die

The sword which strikes from here will never strike   16
In haste or too late, though it appears so
To those who hanker after it, or fear it.

But turn to others now; and many and many   19
Illustrious spirits you will see before you
If you look in the direction I say.'

22   I turned my eyes as she wanted me to
     And I saw a hundred little spheres together,
     Beautiful in their own light and one another's.

25   I stood as one suppressing within himself
     The itch of his desire, and does not dare
     To ask, for fear·that he may ask too much.

28   And the greatest and most luminous
     Of those pearls came forward a little
     To satisfy my wishes regarding him.

31   Then I heard inside him: 'If you were to see
     As I do, the charity which burns in us,
     What you have in mind would come out.

34   But so that you, by waiting, are not kept
     From your high purpose, I will give an answer
     To the mere thought which you hesitate to utter.

37   That hill upon whose slopes Cassino lies
     Was formerly frequented, at the summit,
     By deceived and ill-disposed people;

40   And it was I who first carried up there
     The name of him who brought into the world
     The truth which so elevates humankind;

43   And upon me there shone so much grace
     That I converted all the country round
     From the impious cult by which the world was seduced.

46   Those other flames were all contemplatives
     Whose hearts were kindled with the heat
     Which brings to birth holy flowers and fruit.

49   Here is Macarius, here is Romoaldus,
     Here are my brothers who kept their feet
     Inside the cloister and were sound of heart.'

52   And I to him: 'The love which you show
     In speaking to me, and the benevolence
     I see and mark in all your burnings,

Has opened out my confidence as the sun   55
Opens the rose, until it has become
As full as ever it has power to be.

Therefore I pray you, father, to satisfy me   58
As to whether I am to obtain so much grace
As to see your likeness without concealment.'

He then said: 'Brother, your exalted desire   61
Will be accomplished in the final sphere
Where all, including mine, will be so.

There is perfection, ripeness, wholeness   64
For every wish: for there and there alone
Every part is where it always was,

Because it is not in space, nor has it poles;   67
And our ladder stretches into it
So that it disappears from your sight

The patriarch Jacob saw the upper part   70
Stretching away up there, when it appeared to him
With the angels ascending and descending on it.

But no one now lifts his feet from the ground   73
To climb it, and the rule of my order
Is left there simply as so much waste parchment.

The walls which enclosed a house of prayer   76
Now make a den of thieves, and the monks' hoods
Are now sacks full of rotten flour.

But the worst usury is not taken   79
Against God's will more surely than that fruit
Which makes the heart of the monks so mad;

For whatever the Church has, belongs,   82
All of it, to those who ask in God's name;
Not to relatives or something uglier.

The flesh of mortals is so susceptible   85
That down there a good beginning does not last
From the oak's first leaf to when it bears an acorn.

88   Peter began without gold and without silver,
And I with nothing but prayer and fasting,
And Francis humbly with his community.

91   And if you look at each of these beginnings
And then look again to see where they have got to,
You will see that the white has turned black.

94   But Jordan turning back to its source
Or the sea dividing, when God willed these things,
Were more marvellous than the relief needed now.'

97   He said that, and then at once rejoined
The company he came from, and they crowded closer;
Then, like a whirlwind, rose all together,

100   The gentle lady pushed me after them
With no more than a nod, up the ladder,
Her power so overcame my nature;

103   Never on earth, where movements up and down
Occur naturally, was ever movement so rapid
That it could be compared with my flight.

106   As I hope, reader, to return to that
Devout triumph on account of which I often
Weep for my sins and beat my breast,

109   You would not put your finger in a flame
And draw it out again, more speedily than I
Saw the sign after Taurus and found myself there.

112   O glorious stars, O light which is filled with
Immense power, from which I acknowledge
All my genius, whatever it may be,

115   Rising with you, and hiding myself with you,
Was he who is father of every mortal life,
When I first felt the air of Tuscany;

118   And then, when the grace was granted to me
To enter the high circle in which you turn,
It was in the quarter where you are.

My soul now sighs devotedly   121
To you that it may be given the power
For the hard passage which is now before it.

'You are so close to the ultimate salvation,'   124
Beatrice began, 'that your eyes should be
Able to see all clearly and sharply.

And so, before you go further in,   127
Look back below, and see how much of creation
I have already set under your feet;

So that your heart presents itself as joyfully   130
As ever it may, to the triumphant crowd
Which comes in gladness through this circle of ether.'

I turned my eyes back through every one   133
Of the seven spheres and saw the globe which looked
Such a miserable thing that I smiled;

And I recognise that the best opinion about it   136
Is that which makes least of it; and the man whose thoughts
Are elsewhere can truly be called just.

I saw the daughter of Latona burning   139
Without that shadow which was the reason why
I once thought some parts less dense than others.

I there found that I could look upon the face   142
Of your son, Hyperion; and saw the movement
About and near him, Maia and Dione.

Next there appeared to me the tempering Jove,   145
Between father and son; and it was clear to me
In what manner they changed their positions.

And all the seven were displayed to me,   148
How big they are, and how fast they move,
And what are the intermediate distances.

The little plot which makes us so fierce   151
Appeared to me, with all its hills and outlets,
As I swept round with the eternal Gemini.

Then I turned back my eyes to the lovely eyes.   154

CANTO XXIII

Like the bird which, within the beloved foliage,
Set on her nest with her sweet little ones,
At night, when things are hidden from us,

4   In order to see them looking up at her
And to find morsels she can feed them with,
A labour which she finds delightful to her,

7   Ahead of time, lights on an exposed twig,
Awaiting the sun in a blaze of love,
Fixedly gazing till the dawn appears;

10   So my lady stood erect and alert,
Turning to that quarter of the sky
Beneath which the sun shows least haste to move;

13   So that, seeing her full of expectancy,
I became as one who desires something
Other than what he has, and is content to hope.

16   It was but an instant between the moment when
I became attentive and the moment when I saw
The heavens growing brighter and brighter.

19   And Beatrice said: 'Look, there are the hosts
Of Christ's triumph, and there is all the harvest
Gathered from the circling of the spheres!'

22   Her whole face seemed to me to shine so,
And her eyes were so full of happiness
That I had better say nothing about it.

25   As in a cloudless sky at full moon,
Trivia smiles among the eternal nymphs
Who decorate all quarters of the heavens,

28   I saw, up above thousands of lamps,
A sun which lit up every one of them
As ours does what we see overhead;

And through the living light there shone through 31
The substance of light, which was so brilliant
To my eyes that they could not withstand it.

O Beatrice my sweet beloved guide! 34
She said to me: 'What overcomes you here
Is a power against which there is no defence.

Here is that wisdom and that power 37
Which opened the roads between heaven and earth,
For which there had been such longing so long.'

As fire bursts out of a cloud 40
Because it expands so that it will not hold
And, out of its element, rushes to the ground,

So my mind, among such feasts as these, 43
Grew greater and went out of itself,
And it cannot recall what happened to it.

'Open your eyes and see how I appear: 46
You have seen things which make it possible
Now, for you to sustain my smile.'

I was like one who still feels the effects 49
Of a forgotten vision, and tries in vain
To bring it back to his mind again,

When I heard this invitation, deserving 52
Of so much gratitude as never to be
Erased from the book which holds the past.

If now there were to sound all those tongues 55
Which Polyhymnia and her sisters made
Richest with the sweetest of their milk,

With these to aid me I should not arrive 58
At a thousandth part of the truth, as I sang
The holy smile and how clear the divine look made it.

And so, in presenting paradise, 61
The sacred poem has to make a jump
Like one who finds something in his way.

64   But anyone who thinks how weighty the theme is
     And that the shoulders it is loaded on are mortal
     Will not be disposed to blame them if they tremble.

67   It is no channel for a little boat,
     That which my daring prow cuts as it goes,
     Nor for a helmsman who is afraid of toil.

70   'Why does my face so fascinate you
     That you do not turn to the beautiful garden
     Which, under Christ's rays, bursts into flower?

73   Here is the rose in which the divine word
     Was made flesh; here also are the lilies
     The scent of which indicated the way.'

76   Thus Beatrice; and I, who readily followed
     What she suggested, gave myself up again
     To the battle my weak sight had undertaken.

79   As, by a brilliant sunbeam which poured down
     Through broken cloud, my eyes, though in the shade,
     Once saw a meadow full of flowers,

82   So I saw more than one crowd of brilliances
     Struck by blazing beams from above
     Without seeing where the blaze came from.

85   O benign power, setting your mark so on them:
     You had raised yourself in order to give place
     To eyes which were not able to behold you.

88   The name of the fair flower which I invoke
     Morning and evening, compelled my whole mind
     To fix my eyes upon the greatest flame.

91   And when both my eyes had painted for me
     The nature and brightness of the living star
     Which conquers up there as it did down here,

94   From within the heavens another light descended,
     Formed in a circle, in the manner of a crown;
     It settled around her and then moved about her.

The sweetest melody heard upon earth,   97
The most attractive to the listening soul,
Would be like a cloud split by thunder

In comparison with the sound of that lyre   100
With which the lovely sapphire was crowned,
Which filled the brightest heaven with sapphire.

'I am the angelic love which circles round   103
The exalted happiness whic. breathes from the womb
Which harboured once all we could wish;

And I will circle, lady of heaven, until   106
You follow your son, and make the supreme sphere
More divine because you enter it.'

So the melody which moved round and round   109
Came to a close, and all the other lights
Uttered aloud the name of Mary.

The royal mantle over all that enwraps   112
The universe, the mantle which burns brightest
And most lives in God's breath and his ways,

Had its inner border so far away   115
Above us that, from the place where I was,
How it looked did not yet appear:

Therefore my eyes did not have the strength   118
To follow as the flame with its crown
Lifted itself, as Mary rose to her son.

And as a child who holds out his arms   121
Towards his mother, when he has had his milk,
Having a mind which flames to what is beyond it;

So every one of these brilliances stretched up   124
With its flame, so that it was patent
How exalted was the love they bore to Mary.

Then they remained there in my sight,   127
Singing 'Regina coeli' so sweetly
That the delight of it has never left me.

130   O how great is the abundance which is contained,
      In those rich granaries, of those who were
      On earth the labourers of the good seed!

133   There they live and delight themselves with the wealth
      Which was acquired weeping in Babylonian
      Exile, when the gold was left untouched.

136   There, after his victory, there triumphs
      Under the exalted son of God and Mary,
      And with the company both old and new,

139   He who holds the keys of this glory.

CANTO XXIV

      'O fellowship called to the great supper
      Of the blessed lamb, who so feeds you
      That you always have all that you desire,

4   If, by the grace of God, this man has
      A foretaste of what falls from your table
      Before death prescribes the time for him,

7   Set your mind upon his immense affection;
      Refresh him with your dew: for you drink
      Always of the spring from which his thoughts flow.'

10   Thus Beatrice: and those joyful souls
      Became spheres moving on fixed poles,
      Flaming, as they circled, in the manner of comets.

13   And as the interdependent wheels in clocks
      Turn so that, while the first may be observed
      To be at rest, the last seems to fly;

16   So these groups of dancers, by the manner
      Of their dancing, whether swift or slow
      Enabled me to judge of their beatitude.

From the one I observed to be the most beautiful 19
I saw there emerged so exultant a flame
That none of the others there was more brilliant;

And it proceeded three times round Beatrice 22
With a song which was of such divinity
That my imagination cannot recall it.

So my pen takes a leap and I write nothing; 25
Because our speech, to say nothing of imagination
Is too bright to show up anything brighter.

'O my holy sister, who so religiously 28
Asks, because of your burning love
I free myself from this lovely circle.'

Then, when it had stopped, the blessed flame 31
Which had spoken as I have recorded
Directed his breath to my lady.

And she: 'Eternal light of the great man 34
To whom our Lord delivered over the keys
Of these marvellous joys, which he had brought down,

Examine him on easy or hard points, 37
As you please, regarding that faith
Which enabled you to walk upon the waters.

Whether he loves well, and hopes and believes 40
Is not hidden from you, because your sight
Is where everything is clearly seen;

But because this realm has admitted citizens 43
For the true faith, it is well for its glory
That he should have occasion to speak of it.'

As a student prepares himself and does not speak 46
Until the master has proposed the question,
To adduce the reason, not a definition,

So I prepared myself with all the reasons 49
While she was speaking, in order to be ready
For such an examiner and such a profession.

52   'Tell me, good Christian, make your position clear:
What is faith?' Then I raised my head
Into that light from which the words were breathed;

55   Then I turned to Beatrice, and she readily
Gave me an indication that I should pour out
The water which welled from my internal spring.

58   'The grace which permits me'—so I began—
'To make my confession to the old commander,
Enable me to make my ideas clear.'

61   I went on: 'Father, as was recorded
By the veracious pen of your dear brother
Who, with you, put Rome on the right track,

64   Faith is the substance of things hoped for
And the argument for what is not seen;
And that seems to me the quiddity of it.'

67   Then I heard: 'You have the matter right,
If you understand why he placed it
Among the substances and then among the arguments.'

70   And thereupon I: 'The profound matters
Which here vouchsafe their appearance to me
Are so hidden from the eyes there below,

73   That they exist there only in belief,
Upon which is founded the exalted hope,
And therefore they take on the nature of substance;

76   And from this belief we have to syllogise,
Without the intervention of sensible proof;
Therefore it partakes of the nature of argument.'

79   Then I heard: 'If all that is acquired below
As doctrine was understood in this manner
There would be no place for the inventions of sophists.'

82   This was what that burning love breathed forth;
Then added: 'You have examined well
The value and the weight of that coin,

But tell me if you have any in your purse.'   85
So I: 'I have, yes; so shining and so round
That there is no doubt about the mint.'

Then there issued from the deep light   88
Which was blazing there: 'And this dear jewel
On which every virtue is founded,

Where did you get it from?' And I: 'The downpouring   91
Of the Holy Spirit which is diffused over
The pages of the old and new testaments,

Is a syllogism in which the conclusion   94
Is so convincing that, beside it
Every demonstration appears feeble.'

I heard then: 'The old proposition   97
And the new, from which you so conclude
—Why do you take it for the word of God?'

And I: 'The proof which reveals the truth to me   100
Is in the works which followed, for which nature
Did not heat the iron or strike the anvil.'

The reply I was given was: 'Tell me, who assured you   103
That those works took place? The same scripture
That is to be proved, and no other, swears to it.'

'If the world turned to Christianity,'   106
I said, 'without miracles, it is itself so much
A miracle, that the others are nothing to it,

That you came, in poverty and hunger,   109
On to the field, to sow the good plant
Which was a vine and has become a thorn.'

That finished, the high court of heaven   112
Made 'We praise God' sound through the spheres
With the melody it is sung to up there.

And that great master whose examination   115
Had drawn me already from branch to branch
So that we were approaching the topmost leaves,

118 Began again: 'The grace which woos your mind
Has up to this point opened your mouth
In the manner in which it ought to open,

121 So that I approve what has come out:
But now you must say what you believe
And whence it is presented to your belief.'

124 'O holy father, you spirit who see
What you believe, as you went beyond
Younger feet into the sepulchre,'

127 I began: 'You desire me to make plain
The form of my ready belief, and ask
Me also what is the reason for it.'

130 And I replied: 'I believe in one God,
Sole and eternal, who moves all the heavens
With love and desire, and is himself unmoved.

133 And for this belief I have not only proofs,
Physical and metaphysical, but there is given me
Also the truth which is poured down on us

136 Through Moses, through the prophets, and the psalms,
Through the Evangelists and you who wrote
When the burning spirit had made you divine.

139 And I believe in three eternal persons, and these
I believe one essence, unity and trinity,
So that singular and plural are combined.

142 This mystery of the divine nature
I now speak of, is stamped in my mind
More than once by the doctrine of the gospel.

145 This is the beginning, this is the spark
Which spreads out into a living flame
And sparkles like a star in heaven.'

148 As a master who hears what pleases him
And so embraces his servant, to show his joy
At the news, the moment the man has finished;

So, giving me his blessing as he sang,   151
He circled me three times, when I was silent,
That apostolic light at whose command

I had spoken: so had what I said pleased him!   154

CANTO XXV

If it ever happens that the sacred poem
To which both heaven and earth have set their hands,
So that it has made me thin for many a year,

Should overcome the cruelty which shuts me out   4
From that lovely fold where I slept, a lamb,
The enemy of wolves who war against it;

With a different voice now, and with different fleece,   7
I shall come back poet; and at the font
Of my baptism I shall put on my wreath;

Because it was there I entered into the faith   10
Which reckons souls for God, and afterwards
For its sake Peter circles round my head.

Then a light moved towards me, from that sphere   13
Whence there had issued the original
Of all the vicars Christ has left on earth;

And my lady, full of happiness,   16
Said to me: 'Look now, look, there is the master
For whose sake there are pilgrims in Galicia.'

As when a dove takes his place beside   19
His companion, and they manifest
Their affection to one another, circling and murmuring,

So I saw the two great princes in glory   22
Received one by the other, both of them
Praising the food on which they feast up there.

But when the mutual greeting was completed,   25
They set themselves silently before me,
Alight so that I had to lower my eyes.

28   At that point, with a smile, Beatrice spoke:
       'Illustrious spirit, through whom the liberality
       Of our royal mansion was set on record,

31   Let the name of Hope resound through these heights:
       You know, for you gave it shape as often
       As Jesus showed more kindness to the three.'

34   'Raise your head and be more confident;
       For what comes up here from the mortal world
       Must be content to ripen in our rays.'

37   This comfort came to me from the second flame;
       So I lifted my eyes to the hills
       The weight of which had earlier bowed them down.

40   'Because through his grace our emperor
       Wills that before your death you should meet the nobles
       Face to face in his most sacred hall,

43   So that the verities seen in this court
       May strengthen in you and in others
       The hope which turns people to love below,

46   Say what it is, and how it is a garland
       For your mind, and say where it comes to you from.'
       That is how the second light continued.

49   And that compassionate lady who guided
       My feathered wings in that exalted flight,
       Gave the answer before I could do so myself:

52   'None of the sons of the church militant
       Has more hope than this man, as it is written
       In the sun which shines upon all our host:

55   Therefore it is permitted to him to come
       From Egypt, to our Jerusalem,
       Before the days of his soldiering are done.

58   The other two points—which are not put
       To find out what he thinks, but so that he
       May report how pleasing the virtue is to you—

I leave to him; for they will not be hard to him   61
Nor give occasion for boasting; let him reply
And may the grace of God allow him to.'

As a student who follows his teacher promptly   64
And willingly, when he knows the answer,
So that it may be seen how good he is,

I said: 'Hope is a certain expectation   67
Of future glory, and it is the product
Of divine grace and of precedent merits.

This light comes to me from many stars;   70
But he who first infused it in my heart
Was the supreme singer of the supreme head.

"They that know thy name," as he puts it   73
In his divine song, "will trust in thee":
And who does not know it, who has my faith?

Your dew lighted upon me, like his dew,   76
In your epistle; I am full of it
And overflow with your shower upon others.'

While I was speaking, there was a trembling flash   79
Inside the living heart of that fire;
It was sudden and repeated like lightning.

Then it breathed: 'The love with which I burn   82
Still towards the virtue which followed me
Right to the victory and my exit from the field,

Wills that I breathe on you who take delight   85
In it; and my pleasure is that you
Say what it is that hope promises you.'

And I: 'The new and old testaments   88
Set down the mark which points out to me
The souls of whom God has made his friends.

Isaiah says that every soul shall be   91
Dressed in a double garment, in his own land;
And "his own land" is this delightful life.

94   And your brother makes his revelation to us
      With more particularity, when he talks
      Of those who are "clothed with white robes." '

97   And then, as soon as these words were spoken,
      Sperent in te was heard up above us;
      To which all the dancing choirs replied.

100   Then from among them there flashed out a light
      Such that, if Cancer had so bright a star,
      Winter would have a month of complete daylight.

103   And as a happy girl gets on her feet
      And joins the dance, simply to honour the bride
      And not for any weakness of her own,

106   So I saw the splendour full of light
      Come to the two who were circling with such notes
      As were appropriate to their ardent love.

109   Then it joined their song and their circuit;
      And my lady kept her gaze upon them,
      Like a bride, silent and motionless.

112   'This is he who lay upon the breast
      Of our pelican in the wilderness, and he
      Who was chosen, from the cross, for the great office.'

115   So my lady; and her eyes did not stir
      From the fixed look they had,
      Either before or after speaking those words.

118   Like one who gazes and does all he can
      To see the sun when it is in part eclipse
      And, by looking, in the end ceases to see;

121   So did I with this last flame, until
      I heard a voice: 'Why do you blind yourself
      To see something which has no place here?

124   My body is earth in earth, and will be there
      With all the others, until the day when
      The number of the just shall be accomplished.

With two robes in this blessed cloister   127
There are only those two lights who rose:
And this you will report back in your world.'

At these words the flaming circle was still,   130
And with it the delightful intermingling
Which was made in the sound of the threefold voice,

As oars, which have been in and out of the water,   133
Suddenly, to rest or to avert danger,
All come to a stop at the sound of a whistle.

Ah what commotion there was in my mind   136
When I turned to see Beatrice
And did not see her, although I was near

To her, and in the world of the blessed.   139

CANTO XXVI

While I was perturbed with the loss of my sight,
From the brilliant flame which had caused that loss
Breathed a voice which held my attention;

It said: 'While you are recovering   4
The sight which you burned up in me, it is well
That you should make up for it by talking.

Begin therefore; and say to what end   7
Your soul is directed, and be assured that
Your sight has lost its way but is not dead;

For the lady who is conducting you here,   10
Through this divine territory, has in her looks
The power Ananias had in his hand.'

I said: 'As she pleases, sooner or later,   13
May there be a cure for these eyes which were the gates
Through which she entered with the fire I still burn with.

16   The good which is the satisfaction here
      Is Alpha and Omega of all the writings
      Love reads to me in low tones or aloud.'

19   The same voice which had taken away the fear
      I had felt at my sudden loss of sight,
      Gave me another occasion for conversation,

22   And said: 'Certainly, but you must undergo
      A further examination: for you must tell me
      What it was that directed you to the target?'

25   And I: 'By philosophic arguments
      And by authority which derives from here,
      This love must be imprinted upon me.

28   For the good, so far as it is apprehended,
      By its nature invites love, and does so the more
      The more goodness there is contained in it.

31   Therefore it is to the Essence so superabundant
      That every good which has an existence outside it
      Is nothing more than a light from its radiance,

34   Rather than to any other object of love,
      That must be moved the mind of everyone
      Who sees the truth on which this proof is founded.

37   This truth is made plain to my intellect
      By him who demonstrates to me the nature
      Of the primal love of all eternal beings.

40   It is made plain by the voice of that veracious
      Author, who said to Moses, speaking of himself:
      "I will make all my goodness pass before thee."

43   It is made plain by you also, at the beginning
      Of the great proclamation which cries on earth
      The secrets of the place above all other edicts.'

46   And I heard: 'By human reasoning
      And by authorities which accord with it,
      The chief of your loves looks to God.

But tell me if you are aware of anything else 49
Drawing you to him, so that you let me hear
How many teeth love has to bite you with.'

The holy intention of the eagle of Christ 52
Was not obscure to me, I saw indeed
In what direction he was leading my declaration.

So again I began: 'Every one of those bites 55
Which are able to make the heart turn to God
Work together with my charity;

For the creation of the world and my own existence, 58
The death which he sustained that I might live,
And what every believer hopes, as I do,

Together with the awareness I have spoken of, 61
Have dragged us out of the sea of perverted love
And put us on the shore of the love that is straight.

The leaves which make leafy the whole garden 64
Of the eternal gardener, I love according
As he has given them a share of good.'

When I stopped speaking a most sweet song 67
Resounded through the heavens, and my lady
Said with the others: 'Holy, holy, holy!'

And as a bright light which breaks on a sleeper 70
Because the power of sight runs through his membranes,
From one to another, to meet the brilliance,

And the waking man hates what he sees, 73
So undiscerning is the sudden awakening
Until reflection comes to his aid;

So from my eyes did Beatrice chase away 76
Every speck with the beams of her eyes
Which would shine from a thousand miles away!

So that I saw better than I had before; 79
And in a sort of stupefaction I asked
About a fourth light that I saw was with us.

82   And my lady: 'Within that radiance
The first soul that ever the first power
Created, gazes with longing upon his maker.'

85   As the top of a bough, which bends as the wind passes,
And then moves back into place once more
By its own energy which lifts it up,

88   So did I in the time that she was speaking,
Marvelling, and then I was reassured
By the desire to speak which flamed up in me.

91   And I began; 'Only apple that was ever produced
Ripe from the first, O you ancient father
For whom every bride is daughter and daughter-in-law,

94   Devoutly as I may I supplicate you:
Speak to me: you know what my wish is,
And to hear you the sooner I refrain from expressing it.'

97   Sometimes an animal under cover stirs
So that what he is after must appear
By the way the undergrowth follows his movements;

100   And so it was with the first of all souls;
He made it appear through the light that covered him,
How it delighted him to give me pleasure.

103   From it a breath: 'Although you do not utter it,
I can discern what you wish better
Than you can the things you see most clearly;

106   Because I see it in the true mirror
Which makes itself the image of other things
While nothing makes itself the image of him.

109   You want to hear how long it is since God put me
In that garden upon the mountain-top,
Where he prepared you for the long stairway.

112   And how long it delighted my eyes
And the exact reason for the great anger,
And the kind of language I used and indeed constructed.

Now my son, the tasting of the tree 115
Was not in itself the reason for our exile,
But only the fact of going beyond the bounds.

From that place whence your lady brought Virgil, 118
I longed for this assembly while the sun
Revolved four thousand three hundred and two years;

And I saw it return to all the stars 121
On its pathway, nine hundred and thirty times
While I remained upon the earth below.

The language I spoke had fallen into disuse 124
Before the work that could not be completed
Was ever attempted by Nimrod's people;

For because human wishes are always changing, 127
Following the stars, never was any product
Of human reason made to last for ever.

That man should speak is a natural phenomenon; 130
But whether this way or that, nature allows
You to work out, as seems best to you.

Before I went down to the infernal anguish, 133
YAH was, on earth, the name of the highest good
From whom there comes the happiness which surrounds me;

And then he was called *EL*; which is as it should be, 136
For mortal usage is like a leaf on a bough;
One goes away and another comes in its place.

On the mountain which rises highest above the waves, 139
I was, counting my pure life and the other,
From the first hour until the hour which follows

The sixth hour, when the sun passes meridian.' 142

CANTO XXVII

'To Father, Son and to the Holy Ghost,
Glory,' all paradise began to sing
So that I was drunk with the sweet song.

4   What I saw seemed to me to be
The universe smiling; so my intoxication
Came both from what I heard and what I saw.

7   Oh joy! and, ah, ineffable jubilation!
Oh life made up entirely of love and peace!
Assured wealth, with no longing for anything!

10   Before my eyes were standing the four torches,
Blazing, and the one which had come to me first
Began to make itself more alive,

13   And then, in its appearance, it became
As Jupiter would be if he and Mars
Were to become birds and then change feathers.

16   The providence which there assigns to all
Duties and offices, had imposed silence
Upon the blessed choir on every side,

19   When I heard: 'If you see me change colour,
Do not be astonished for, as I speak,
You will see all the others change colour too.

22   The man who now usurps my place on earth
—My place, my place, where there is now a vacancy,
At any rate in the sight of the Son of God—

25   Has made of my burial place a sewer
For blood and filth; so that the evil one
Who fell from here, is delighted to be down there.'

28   With that colour which paints morning and evening
The clouds which find themselves in the sun's way,
I saw then the whole of heaven covered.

And as a virtuous woman, who remains   31
Sure of herself, turns timid upon
Merely hearing of someone else's errors,

So Beatrice's looks underwent a change;   34
And so I believe the sun was darkened when
The supreme power suffered upon earth.

Then he went on with what he had been saying   37
In a voice so much changed from what it had been
That you could not say his appearance had altered more:

'The spouse of Christ was not brought up upon   40
My blood and that of Linus and of Cletus
So that she might be used for making money;

But, to point out the way here,   43
Sixtus and Pius, Calixtus and Urban,
Shed their blood after shedding many tears.

It was not our intention that one party should sit   46
Upon the right hand of our successor
While the rest of Christendom sat upon the other;

Nor that the keys which were entrusted to me   49
Should be turned into an emblem on a banner
Which was taken into battle against the baptised;

Nor that I should become a figure on a seal   52
For issuing corrupt and lying privileges:
For such things I redden and flash often.

In all the pastures there are seen from here   55
Ravening wolves dressed up in shepherds' clothing;
Up, Lord, why do you still lie there?

Men from Cahors and Gascony make ready   58
To drink our blood: as if a good beginning
Must sink until it reaches a vile end!

But the high providence which, with Scipio,   61
Preserved the glory of the world for Rome,
Will soon bring help, as I understand things.

64 And you, my son, who, heavy with mortality,
   Must go below again, open your mouth
   And do not hide what I have not hidden.'

67 As our atmosphere drifts down in flakes
   Of frozen mist, at the season when the horn
   Of the celestial goat touches the sun,

70 So I saw the adorned atmosphere
   Do, and send flakes of triumphant mist
   Upwards, of those who had been awhile with us.

73 My eyes followed their appearances,
   And followed till there was so much of the atmosphere
   Between them and their object, that they faded.

76 Whereupon my lady, who saw I had no need
   To gaze up longer, said to me: 'Lower your eyes
   And see what an arc you have described.'

79 From the hour when I had first looked down, I saw
   That I had moved through the ninety degrees
   Which the first zone makes from middle to end;

82 So that I saw beyond Cadiz the passage
   The demented Ulysses took, and on this side the shore,
   Almost, on which the gentle Europa was carried.

85 And more of the extent of this little ground
   Would have been shown me; but the sun had travelled
   Under my feet, a whole sign and more.

88 My enamoured mind was turned as always towards
   My lady to woo her, and now burned more than ever
   For my eyes to be brought to look at her again:

91 And if nature or art ever laid baits
   To catch the eyes, and so possess the mind,
   Whether with human flesh or pictures of it,

94 All of them together would seem to be nothing
   Compared with the divine pleasure which shone on me
   When I turned round to her smiling face.

And the power which that look poured on me   97
Swept me from the lovely nest of Leda
And carried me into the swiftest of the heavens.

The nearest and the most exalted parts   100
Are so uniform that I cannot say
Which Beatrice chose as a place for me.

But she, who saw what my desire was,   103
Began, smiling as she did so with such happiness
That God seemed to be rejoicing in her face:

'The nature of the universe, which is still   106
At the centre while all the rest moves round it,
Begins here as it were from its starting point.

And this heaven has no other location   109
Than the divine mind, in which is lit up
The love which turns it and the power it rains down.

Light and love contain it in one circle,   112
As it contains the others; and this surround
Is understood only by him who is round about it.

Its movement is not reckoned by any other;   115
But all the others are measured by this one,
As ten is by the multiples five and two.

And how time has its roots in this vessel   118
While all its foliage is in the others
Will now be made manifest to you.

Cupidity! which so pulls mortals down   121
Under its surface, that no one has strength
To get his eyes out clear above the waves.

Of course the will of men still comes to flower;   124
But the continual rain turns the real plums
Into a puffy mass covered with fungus.

Faith and innocence are now found only   127
In little children; and they both disappear
Before the young man has down on his cheeks.

130   Many a child who cannot speak properly
        Fasts, yet as soon as his tongue can wag freely
        Devours any food he can whatever the month is.

133   And many a child who, at that age, loves and takes notice of
        His mother, is no sooner talking properly
        Than he would like to see her in her grave.

136   So that white skin changes to black, as it does in the daughter
        Of him who brings the morning and abandons evening,
        As soon as she has put in an appearance.

139   That may seem to you quite extraordinary,
        But think: there is no one in the world who governs it;
        No wonder the human family is lost.

142   But before January ceases to be in winter
        Through the neglect on earth of the fractional days,
        From these high spheres will come such brilliance

145   That the destiny which has so long been awaited
        Will turn the ships around, the prows where the sterns were,
        So that the fleet will steer a true course

148   And true fruit will come after the flower.'

CANTO XXVIII

    When she who raised my mind to paradise,
    Denouncing the life which is at present led
    By wretched mortals, had revealed the truth;

4   As one behind whose back a torch is lit
        Will see the flame of it in a mirror
        Before he sees the thing itself, or thinks of it,

7   And turns around to see if that glass
        Tells him the truth, and sees that it fits
        As certainly as music fits to words;

So my memory remembers well   10
That I did too, looking into the lovely eyes
From which love had made a noose to catch me.

And as I turned and my eyes were touched   13
By what appears in that sphere as it circles
To any eye fixed in the right direction.

I saw a point which radiated a light   16
So intense that the sight it blazed upon
Had to close because of the brilliance:

And the smallest star which can be seen from here   19
Would seem a moon, set beside that point
As one star is placed beside another.

Perhaps as close as the halo seems to be   22
Around the light from which it takes its glow,
When the mist about it is at its thickest,

There was around the point a circle of fire   25
Which turned so rapidly that it would have beaten
The swiftest of the movements circling.

And this was surrounded by another,   28
And that by a third, and the third by a fourth,
The fourth by a fifth, and then the fifth by a sixth.

After that came a seventh, which was so wide   31
That Juno's rainbow, when it is complete,
Would be too narrow to contain it.

And so the eighth and the ninth; and each of them   34
Moved more slowly, according as it was
In order more distant from the first;

And that one burned with the clearest flame,   37
Which was least distant from the pure spark,
I think, because most in the truth of it.

My lady, who saw that I was anxious   40
And in suspense, said to me: 'From that point
Heaven and the whole of nature depend.

43   Look at the circle which is nearest to it,
And know that its movement is so fast
Because of the blazing love by which it is pierced.'

46   And I to her: 'If the whole universe
Were in the order I see in those circles,
I should be satisfied with what I am told:

49   But in the sensible universe we see
That there is more divinity in the circlings
The more remote they are from the centre.

52   So, if my desire is to have its end
In this marvellous and angelic temple
Which is bounded only by love and light,

55   I should hear also how it is that the model
And the image of it do not move similarly,
For by myself I cannot understand it.'

58   'If your fingers cannot manage this knot,
That is certainly nothing to wonder at;
It has become so hard because no one has tried!'

61   So said my lady and then: 'Listen
To what I tell you, if you want to be satisfied;
Then exercise your ingenuity on it.

64   The material circles are wider or narrower
According to the greater or less virtue
Which is distributed through all parts of them.

67   The greater the virtue the greater is the effect;
The greater effect involves more material
If the parts of it are all equally perfect.

70   Therefore the one which sweeps along with it
The rest of the universe, must correspond
To the circle which loves most and knows the most.

73   So, if you draw your measure, not around
The appearance of the substances which to you
Seem circular, but round the virtue instead,

You will see a marvellous correspondence   76
In every heaven, between what is greater and
The larger intelligence, and between smaller and lesser.'

Just as the hemisphere of heaven remains   79
Brilliant and serene when Boreas
Is blowing from the gentler of his cheeks,

So that the gloom which troubled it before   82
Is cleared away and melted, so that the sky
Laughs in its beauty throughout its length and breadth;

So did I, when my lady had provided me   85
With her answer, so clear that the truth
Was seen like a star in the heavens.

And when her words ceased, there was such sparkling   88
From the circles, as is seen in the sparks
Which are thrown off by iron when it boils.

Every spark followed the fire it belonged to;   94
There were so many that the number of them
Was greater than all the combinations at chess.

I heard Hosanna sound from choir to choir   97
To the fixed point which holds them to the *where*,
And will do always, in which they have always been.

And she who saw the uncertain thoughts   100
Within my mind, said to me: 'In the first circles
You have been shown the Seraphim and Cherubim.

So swiftly they follow as they are bound,   103
To be as like the point as they may be;
And they may so far as their vision is exalted.

Those other loves which encircle them   106
Are called Thrones of the divine gaze,
And with them the first group of three ends.

And you should know they all have the more pleasure
The more their vision penetrates deeply
Into the truth in which every intellect rests.

109   Here may be seen how being blessed
       Has its foundation in the act of sight,
       And not in love, which comes afterwards;

112   And merit is the measure of that sight
       For it is born of grace and of goodwill:
       And so it goes on from grade to grade.

115   The next group of three which, so to speak, sprouts
       In that everlasting spring, which Aries
       Does not come to despoil in the night,

118   Perpetually welcome spring with Hosanna
       In three melodies, which sound in those three
       Orders of happiness in which it is woven.

121   In that hierarchy are the other deities:
       First of all the Dominions and then the Powers;
       The third order is of the Majesties.

124   Then the two penultimate orders of happiness,
       The Principalities and Archangels move in circles;
       In the last all the angels are at play.

127   All these orders keep their gaze upwards,
       And downwards exert force, so that all are drawn
       Towards God and all draw others there.

130   And Dionysius with so much desire
       Set about contemplating all these orders
       That he named them distinctly, as I have done.

133   But Gregory departed a little from him;
       So that, as soon as his eyes were opened
       In this heaven, he smiled to himself.

136   And if so much secret truth was uttered
       By a mortal upon earth, it is no wonder;
       For he who saw it here above revealed it

139   With many another truth about these circles.'

CANTO XXIX

When both the children of Latona, covered
One by the Ram and the other by Libra,
Simultaneously have the horizon round their middles,

There is a moment when the zenith balances   4
The scales, till both of them let slip the girdle,
Unbalance themselves and change their hemispheres,

Just so long as that moment, Beatriçe,   7
A smile traced upon her face, was silent,
Looking hard at the point which had overwhelmed me.

Then she began: 'I do not ask, but tell you   10
What you would like to hear, because I have seen it
There where every *where* and *when* is gathered.

Not to obtain any more good himself,   13
Which is impossible, but so that his splendour
Might as it shone back, declare: "I am,"

In his eternity beyond time, and beyond   16
All other comprehension, as it pleased him,
The eternal love opened out in new loves.

Not that he lay idle before that;   19
For there was neither before nor after when God
Proceeded to move on the face of the waters.

Form and matter, joined together and simple,   22
Issued in being which was without fault,
Like three arrows from a bow with three strings;

And as in glass, in amber and in crystal,   25
A ray so shines, that from its arrival
To its being everywhere, is no time at all,

So the threefold working of its begetter   28
So shone into its being all at once
That there was no distinction of what came first.

31   Order was co-created and constructed
In substance; and these were the highest point
Of the universe; in them was pure act:

34   Pure potentiality was in the lowest place;
In the middle, potentiality and act
Were twisted together, never to be untwisted.

37   Jerome wrote about a long tract of centuries
In which the angels had already been created
Before the rest of the universe was made;

40   But the truth of the matter is written on many pages
By those who wrote what the Holy Spirit dictated;
And you will see for yourself, if you look carefully;

43   And even reason can see something here,
For it would not admit that motive powers
Could go on for so long and remain imperfect.

46   Now you know where and when those loves were created
And how they were created; so that already
Three of your burning questions are no more.

49   In less time than it takes to count twenty,
A party of the angels fell and troubled
The lowest of your four elements.

52   The rest of them remained, and so began
That manner of circling which you see here,
Which pleased them so much they never gave it up.

55   The reason for the fall was the accursed
Pride of the one you saw in constraint
Under the whole weight of the universe.

58   The ones you see here were modest enough
To acknowledge that they came from the goodness
Which made them apt to understand so much;

61   On this account their vision was exalted
By the enlightenment of grace and their merit,
So that their wills are firm and entire.

And do not doubt of it, but be assured 64
That to receive grace is meritorious
According as your love is open to it.

Now there is much for you to contemplate 67
Without further aid, in this consistory,
If my words have not been lost on you.

But since on earth it is taught in your schools 70
That the angelic nature is such
That it understands, remembers and wills,

I will go on, in order that you may see 73
The simple truth, which down there is confused
By the equivocation of your teaching.

These substances have never turned their sight 76
From the face of God, from which nothing is hidden,
Since first they found themselves glad in it:

So their sight is never interrupted 79
By a new object, and so it is not necessary
To recall it or to discourse upon it.

For upon earth they dream without sleeping, 82
Thinking they are telling the truth or knowing they do not;
There is more blame and shame in the latter.

Down there you do not follow a single path 85
When you philosophise; so carried away are you
By showing off and the ideas it gives you.

And even this incurs less anger here 88
Than when holy scripture is treated as secondary
Or when it is twisted from its meaning.

Men do not think how much blood it costs 91
To sow it in the world, nor how much he pleases
Who humbly keeps on close terms with it.

To show off, everyone tries to be subtle 94
And makes things up; this is the matter handled
By preachers, and the gospel is not heard.

97 One says that the moon went back on her traces
At the passion of Christ, and interposed herself
So that the sun's light could not reach the earth;

100 And lies, because the light hid itself
Of its own volition; which is why the eclipse was seen
At the same time by Spaniards and Indians and Jews.

103 Florence has not so many Lapos and Bindos
As there are stories of this sort every year
Cried from the pulpit on this side and that;

106 So that the lambs, who don't know anything,
Go back from their pasture fed with wind,
And it is no excuse that they don't see any harm in it.

109 Christ did not say to his first companions:
"Go and preach rubbish to the world";
But gave them truths that they could build upon.

112 And these sounded so loudly in their mouths
That in their fight to start the fire of faith
They used the gospel as both shield and lance.

115 Now they go out with idiotic jokes
To preach, and if people roar with laughter
The hood inflates with pride, and all are satisfied.

118 But the bird that nests in the point of the hood
Is such that, if the crowd saw it, they would see
What sort of pardon they were trusting to;

121 It has caused so much folly in the world
That, without asking for any sort of proof,
People would jump at any promises.

124 And that is how St Anthony's pig is fattened,
And many more who are more piggish still,
Paying with money which is worth nothing.

127 But we have wandered a long way; turn your eyes
Back again now to the direct path,
So that we shorten the journey and the time.

This nature is so far up the scale   130
Of number, that there was never mortal speech
Or indeed conception which could go as far:

If you see the revelation set out   133
By Daniel, you will see that in his thousands
All trace of determinate number is lost.

The primal light which covers everything   136
Is received by this company in as many ways
As there are splendours to reflect it back.

So, as love follows upon the act   139
Of the mind which conceives, the sweetness of loving
Is warm or warmer as the case may be.

Observe now how exalted and how capacious   142
Is the eternal power which has made for itself
So many mirrors on which to break itself

And yet remains one as before.'   145

CANTO XXX

Perhaps six thousand miles away from us
The noon is blazing, and this world extends
Its shadow almost to a level bed,

When what to us are the central depths of the sky   4
Begin to change so that, here and there
A star fails, and its light no longer reaches us;

And as the brightest handmaid of the sun   7
Comes further towards us, so that the sky closes up
One star after another until the loveliest has gone.

It was like that with the glory which for ever   10
Plays around the point which conquered me
And which seems embraced by what it itself embraces;

13   Little by little it put itself out of sight;
      So that seeing nothing, and my love, constrained me
      Once more to turn my eyes to Beatrice.

16   If all which has been said up to the present
      About her were to be packed into one encomium,
      It would not serve the turn on this occasion.

19   The beauty I saw went so far beyond
      Not only our capacity, but I believe
      That only her maker could enjoy it perfectly.

22   At this point I admit I am defeated,
      More than any comic or tragic writer
      Ever was by the crux of his subject;

25   For, as the sun does to the weakest eyes,
      So the remembrance of the sweet smile
      Did to my mind, as it were cut off from myself.

28   From the first day that I saw her face
      In this life, until that sight of her,
      Nothing ever kept my song from following her;

31   But now I must give up following
      Behind her beauty as I write my poem,
      Like any artist who has reached his limit.

34   I leave her to a greater proclamation
      Than that of my trumpet, which now at last
      Draws to a close with its hard subject-matter.

37   She went on, looking and speaking like a guide
      Who does not waste time: 'We have emerged now
      From the largest body to the heaven of simple light:

40   Intellectual light, full of love;
      Love of the true good, full of happiness;
      Happiness which transcends any sweetness.

43   Here you will see both the battalions
      Of paradise, and one with the appearances
      That you will see them wear on Judgement Day.'

Just as a flash of lightning which scatters   46
The powers of sight, and so deprives the eye
Of the power to apprehend even prominent objects,

So did living light shine about me;   49
And left me wrapt in such a veil of glory
That nothing was visible to me.

'The love which makes this heaven quiet   52
Welcomes newcomers with a salutation like this
To make the candle ready for the flame,'

These brief words had no sooner entered me   55
Than I became aware that my faculties
Had acquired more than their usual power;

And I was so strengthened with new sight   58
That there was no light, however clear,
Which my eyes could not have stood up against.

And I saw light in the form of a stream   61
Of resplendent brilliance, in between two banks
Painted with all the marvels of the spring.

From this river there issued live sparks   64
Which everywhere settled themselves in the flowers
Like rubies which have been set in gold.

Then, as if the scents had made them intoxicated,   67
They sank once more into the marvellous swirl;
And as one entered it, another flew out.

'The deep desire which now burns and urges you   70
To know what it is you are seeing,
Pleases me the more the more it wells up.

But you will have to drink of this water   73
Before this thirst of yours is satisfied.'
So spoke to me the sun of my eyes.

Then she added: 'The river and the topazes   76
Which enter and fly out, and the smiling grass
Are shadowy prefaces of their reality.

79   Not that they are themselves unripe things;
     The defect that there is is in yourself
     Whose sight is not yet equal to such things.'

82   No child ever makes so sudden a rush
     To where it sees the milk, if it wakes up
     A long time after its usual hour,

85   As I did, to make more perfect mirrors
     Of my eyes, bending down to the water
     Which flows that we may be the better for it.

88   And as the water splashed over the edge
     Of my eyelids, at once it seemed to me
     That that long river became circular.

91   Then, as people who have been masked
     Appear other than they were before
     If they take off the looks they disappeared into,

94   So were the flowers and sparks changed before me
     Into a greater ceremony, so that I saw
     Both of the courts of heaven made manifest.

97   O splendour of God, through which I saw
     The exalted triumph of the true kingdom,
     Give me ability to say how I saw it!

100 There is light up there which makes visible
     The creator himself, to his creature
     Who finds his own peace in seeing him.

103 And it stretches in the form of a circle
     So far, that the circumference of it
     Would be too large for a belt around the sun.

106 All its appearance is one radiance
     Reflected from the top of the Primum Mobile,
     Which takes from it its life and potency.

109 And as a hillside mirrors itself in
     The water at its foot, as if to admire itself
     When it is at its best with green and flowers,

So, standing above the light and all around,   112
I saw reflections from more than a thousand tiers
Of those of us who had got back there.

And if the lowest tier already embraced   115
So great a light, what was the amplitude
Of that rose at its extremist petals!

My sight did not lose itself in either   118
The width or the height, but took in everything,
The how much and the how of that jubilation.

There, near or far adds nothing, takes nothing away;   121
For where God governs without intermediary
The laws of nature have no relevance.

To the yellow of the sempiternal rose,   124
Dilating as it mounted, and giving off
An odour of praise to the sun which is always at spring,

Beatrice drew me, silent and wanting to speak,   127
And said to me: 'Now see how great it is,
The great congregation of white robes!

Look at our city, how far round it is;   130
See how our places are so filled
That not many people are wanted here now.

And in that great seat you keep looking at   133
Because of the crown you see placed above it,
Before you sup at this marriage feast,

Will sit the soul, Augustan upon earth,   136
Of the great Henry, who will come to Italy
To put her right before she is so disposed.

The blind cupidity which makes you silly   139
Has made you just like a little child
Who is dying of hunger but tells nurse to go away.

The man in charge of the divine market   142
Will then be one who does not deal in the same way
In the open and when he is under cover.

145   But after that God will not suffer him long
       In the sacred office; for he will be pushed down
       There where Simon Magus has his deserts

148   And that will push the Anagni man in further.'

CANTO XXXI

       In form then of a shining white rose,
       The holy army of those of whom, in his blood,
       Christ made his spouse, made its appearance to me;

4   But the other army which, as it flies, sees and sings
       The glory of him who fills them with his love
       And the goodness which made them as they are,

7   Like a swarm of bees, landing upon flowers
       At one moment and then at once returning
       To where its work is turned into sweetness,

10   Descended into that great flower, which is dressed
       In so many petals, and then rose up again
       To where their love lives eternally.

13   Their faces were all of living flame,
       Their wings of gold, the rest was all white
       To a degree which snow never reached.

16   When they went into the flower, from tier to tier
       They offered some of that peace and ardour
       They had acquired in their upward flight.

19   Nor did the interposing of so many
       In flight between the distant heights and the flower
       Interfere with my seeing or with the reflections;

22   For the divine light is such as to penetrate
       Wherever there is worthiness to receive it,
       So that nothing can stand in its way.

This tranquil and happy kingdom, so populous   25
With people of the old and new dispensations,
Had sight and love fixed on a single mark.

O threefold light which in a single star,   28
Sparkling upon their sight, so satisfies them!
Look down here upon us in our storm!

If the barbarians, coming from a quarter   31
Every day covered by Helice,
Circling with her son whom she adores,

Were stupefied upon seeing Rome   34
And her immense monuments, when the Lateran
Went beyond any other mortal construction;

I, who had come from human to divine,   37
From time to what is eternal,
From Florence to a people that is just and sane,

What stupefaction must I be filled with!   40
Between that and my joy I was more than willing
To hear nothing, and to stay silent myself.

And like a pilgrim who refreshes himself   43
In the temple he had vowed to go to and, looking round,
Already hopes to tell people what it looks like,

Travelling upwards through the living light   46
I ran my eyes over all the tiers,
Now high, now low, then going round again.

I saw faces full of charity,   49
Lit by another's light and their own smiles,
And gestures which bore all the marks of honour.

My glance had already taken in   52
How paradise in general was arranged
But had not yet rested anywhere;

And I turned with my eagerness alight   55
To ask my lady about those matters
Concerning which my mind was in suspense.

58   I intended one thing, but what happened was different:
I thought I should see Beatrice, and saw an old man
Dressed like one of the glorious company.

61   In his eyes and over his cheeks there was
An air of benign happiness, and his manner
Was what you might see in a tender father.

64   'And where is she?' I said suddenly.
He answered: 'It was for your final satisfaction
That Beatrice asked me to leave my place;

67   And if you look up in the third circle
Below the highest, you will see her again,
On the throne for which her merits destined her.'

70   Without answering, I lifted up my eyes
And saw her making a crown for herself
Reflecting as she did the eternal light.

73   From the highest region in which thunder begins,
No mortal eye is ever so far distant
Though it is plunged in the bottom of the sea,

76   As my sight was there, from Beatrice;
But it made no difference, for her image
Did not come down to me through any atmosphere.

79   'O lady in whom my hope always springs,
And who for my salvation have submitted
To leave the print of your feet in hell,

82   By all the many things that I have seen,
I recognise the grace and the capacity
There is in your power and your goodness.

85   You have brought me from servitude
To liberty, through all those ways and means
Which you had it in your power to use.

88   Continue your munificence to me
So that my soul, which you have made whole,
May please you when it is untied from my body.'

So I prayed; and she, so far away   91
As she appeared, smiled and regarded me;
Then turned away to the eternal fountain.

And the holy man said: 'So that you may   94
Perfectly finish the path on which you are set
—The end for which prayer and holy love sent me here—

Let your eyes wander over this garden;   97
For seeing it will make your sight more fit
To climb at last through the divine ray.

And the queen of heaven, for whom I am completely   100
Consumed with love, will grant the grace we need
Because I am her faithful Bernard.'

As one who comes perhaps from Croatia   103
In order to see our Veronica
And, from a long desire, cannot see enough,

But says to himself, as long as it is exhibited,   106
'My Lord Jesus, my Christ, my true God,
And was it like that that you appeared?'

So was I, gazing on the live charity   109
Of him who, by his contemplation,
Enjoyed this peace while still in the world.

'Child of grace,' he began, 'this manner of existence   112
In delight, will never be known to you
If you keep your eyes here at the bottom;

Look at the tiers up to the furthest of them   115
Until you see where the queen is sitting
To whom this kingdom is devoutly subject.'

I raised my eyes; and as, in the morning,   118
The eastern part of the horizon
Overwhelms that in which the sun goes down,

So, as if travelling from the valley to the mountain   121
With my eyes, I saw a point on the ridge
Which was brighter than all the rest beside it.

124 And as the point where we await the chariot
Which Phaeton drove so badly, is most ablaze
And on either side of it the light fades,

127 So that pacific red and gold oriflamme
Animated the centre, and on each side
The flames gradually lost their intensity.

130 And at that centre, with their wings outstretched,
I saw more than a thousand angels celebrating,
Each one different in brilliance and in manner.

133 I saw smiling on their games and songs
A beauty which was all happiness
In the eyes of all the other saints there.

136 And if I had as much wealth in words
As in imagining, I would not dare
To attempt even the least of her delightfulnesses.

139 As Bernard saw that my eyes
Were fixed attentively on the ardour of his ardour,
He turned his own to her with such love

142 As made mine burn the more to look again.

CANTO XXXII

Absorbed in his pleasure, that contemplative,
Unasked, took on the office of a teacher
And made a start with these holy words:

4 'The wound which Mary closed up and anointed
Was opened and made worse by her who sits
At Mary's feet, and is so beautiful.

7 Beneath her, in the third tier of places
In order from the top, there Rachel sits
With Beatrice beside her, as you see.

Sarah, Rebecca, Judith and the woman   10
Who was great-grandmother to that singer
Who for his fault said *"Miserere mei,"*

These you may see, descending tier by tier,   13
As I have named them to you, going down
Petal by petal through the great rose.

And from the seventh tier down, just as you see   16
Above it, is a line of Hebrew women
Set as a parting in the rose's hair;

Because, according as people looked to Christ   19
In faith, they are divided by the wall
These women make upon the sacred steps.

On one side, where the flower is in bloom   22
With all its petals, you will see seated
Those whose belief was that Christ would come:

On the other side, on which the semicircles   25
Are broken by empty places here and there,
Are those who looked towards the Christ who had come.

And as on this side there is the glorious seat   28
Of the lady of heaven and the other seats
Below her, which make the great division,

So, opposite there is that of the great John   31
Who, ever holy, endured the desert and martyrdom,
And after that was two years in hell:

And below him Francis, Benedict, Augustine   34
And others so on down from tier to tier,
Have the task of marking the separation.

Now marvel at divine providence;   37
For each of the two aspects of the faith
Will fill an equal part of this garden.

And know that downwards from this circle   40
Which cuts in two the two lines of separation,
Is the place of those here for no merits of their own,

43   But for those of others, under certain conditions;
        For all these are spirits which were released
        Before they had any real power of choice.

46   You can indeed see it by their faces
        And also by their having children's voices,
        If you look at them closely and listen carefully.

49   Now you are wondering and, wondering, say nothing;
        But I will loosen for you the hard bonds
        In which your subtle thoughts are tying you up.

52   Within the length and breadth of this kingdom
        There is no such thing as a place left to chance,
        Any more than there is sadness or thirst or hunger;

55   For whatever you see has been established
        By eternal law, so that everything fits
        As closely as the ring does to the finger.

58   And therefore these who came so early
        To true life are not without reason
        Divided into more and less excellent.

61   The king by whose power this kingdom stays
        In so much love and in such delight
        That no one dares to will anything beyond it,

64   Creating all minds in the happiness
        Of his own sight, endows them with grace
        Differently, as he pleases; and that is enough.

67   And this is set out clearly and expressly
        In the holy scripture about those twins
        Who quarrelled even in their mother's womb.

70   For the supreme light properly determines
        That how much grace each shall be crowned with
        Shall depend on the colour of his hair.

73   Because, without meritorious behaviour,
        They have been placed here in different tiers
        Only because of difference in endowment.

In the earliest centuries all that was needed   76
To gain salvation, for the innocent,
Was that the child's parents should have faith.

Then when the first ages were completed,   79
Male children had to be circumcised
If they were to find any strength in their innocent wings.

But then the time of the redemption came,   82
If they were without the perfect baptism of Christ
Such innocents were kept down below.

Look now upon the face which most resembles   85
That of Christ, because only its brightness
Can make you capable of seeing Christ.'

I saw rain down upon her so much happiness   88
Borne by those holy intelligences
Which were created to fly at such altitudes,

That all that I had seen before that   91
Did not keep me so suspended in wonder
Nor showed me so much of what God was like.

And that love which first came down to her   94
Singing '*Ave Maria, gratia plena,*'
Spread his wings out before her now.

There was answer to the divine versicle   97
From every side, in that court of the blessed,
So that every face was the more serene for it.

'O holy father who for my sake   100
Are willingly down here, leaving the sweet place
Where it is your eternal lot to sit,

Who is that angel who with such delight   103
Looks into the eyes of our queen
So in love that he seems to be all fire?'

So once again I went for my instruction   106
To him who took his beauty from Mary
As the morning star takes it from the sun.

109 And he to me: 'Resolution and gaiety,
As much as there can be in angel or human soul,
There is in him: and we all want it to be so,

112 Because he is the one who took the palm
Down to Mary, when the Son of God
Elected to take on the burden of flesh.

115 But now let your eyes follow me round
As I am speaking; observe the great patricians
Of this most just and charitable empire.

118 Those two who are sitting up there, most fortunate
In being placed closest to the Empress,
Are as it were the two roots of the rose.

121 He who is sitting next to her on the left
Is the father through whose audacious tasting
The human race tastes such bitterness.

124 On the right you see that ancient father
Of the Holy Church to whom Christ entrusted
The keys of this so beautiful flower.

127 And he who, before he died, saw
All the heavy days of that lovely spouse
Who was won by the spear and by the nails,

130 Sits beside him; and by the side of the other one
Is the leader under whom that ungrateful, changeable
Recalcitrant people once lived on manna.

133 Opposite Peter I saw Anna sitting,
So content to be gazing at her daughter
That she did not move her eyes to sing Hosanna.

136 And opposite the greatest paterfamilias
Sits Lucy, who sent your lady after you
When you, head down, were going to your ruin.

139 But because the time of your vision is fleeting,
Let us stop here, as a good tailor does
Who cuts his coat according to his cloth;

And let us turn our eyes to the primal love   142
So that, looking towards him, you may penetrate
As far as possible through his refulgence.

In truth, in case you should fall back   145
When you move your wings, thinking to go forwards,
It is proper that you should seek grace in prayer;

Grace from her who is able to assist you;   148
And you will follow me with your love
So that your heart does not stray from my words.'

And he began to pray this holy prayer.   151

CANTO XXXIII

'Virgin mother, daughter of your son,
Humble and exalted beyond any other creature,
The settled end of the eternal plan,

You are she who made human nature   4
So noble, that the maker of it himself
Did not scorn to have himself made by it.

In your womb was lit again that love   7
By whose warmth, in the eternal peace,
This flower has germinated as it is.

For us here you are a midday blaze   10
Of love; and down there, among mortals,
You are the ever-living spring of hope.

Lady, you are so great, and have such power,   13
That whoever seeks grace without recourse to you
Is like someone wanting to fly without wings.

You are so benign that you not only help   16
Whoever asks you but, very often,
Spontaneously give before the prayer is made.

19   In you there is mercy, in you there is pity,
In you magnificence, in you there is
Whatever goodness there ever was in creatures.

22   Now this man who from the lowest sink
Of the universe has seen one by one
How spirits live, from there to this point,

25   Implores you, of your grace, that he be given
Enough grace for him to lift his eyes
Higher towards the ultimate beatitude.

28   And I, who never burned more for my own vision
Than I do for his, I offer all my prayers,
And pray that they may not be insufficient;

31   That you may disencumber him of all
Clouds of mortality, with your own prayers,
So that the supreme pleasure may unfold.

34   Also I pray you, queen, who can do anything
You choose to do: after this great vision
Enable him to keep his affections sane.

37   May your protection extinguish human impulses:
See Beatrice, with how many of the blessed,
Putting her hands together for my prayer!'

40   The eyes beloved and venerated of God,
Fixed on the praying saint, made evident
How pleasing to her are devoted prayers;

43   Then they turned upwards to the eternal light
In which it is not to be thought that any
Creature's eye else would have found its way so clearly.

46   And I, who was drawing near the end
Of all desires, felt as I must do
The ardour of desire in me finished.

49   Bernard indicated I might look up,
And smiled at me; but I was already
Of my own motion as he would have me be;

For my sight, becoming clarified,   52
Entered deeper and deeper through the ray
Of that profound light which is true in itself.

From that moment what I saw was greater   55
Than our language, which fails at such a prospect,
As memory fails at something so out of its way.

As someone who sees something in his sleep   58
And after his dream has only an impression
Of what he felt, and can recall nothing else,

So am I, for my vision has almost gone,   61
And yet into my heart still, drop by drop,
Flows the sweetness which was born of it.

So the snow loses its shape in the sun;   64
So was it that the oracles of the Sibyl,
On the light leaves, were lost in the wind.

O supreme light who rise far above   67
Mortal notions, lend my memory
A little of what then appeared to me,

And give my tongue all the power it needs   70
So that a single spark of your glory
May be transmitted to people in the future;

For, if something of it comes back to my mind   73
And sounds a little in these verses of mine,
Your triumph will more easily be conceived.

I think I should have been quite bewildered   76
In the intensity of the living ray
If my eyes had been turned away from it.

And I remember that I was the bolder   79
To bear the rays, as long as my sight
Had intercourse with the infinite power.

O abundant grace, trusting whom I presumed   82
To fix my gaze through the eternal light
Until I had seen all that I could see!

85 I saw gathered there in the depths of it,
    Bound up by love into a single volume,
    All the leaves scattered through the universe;

88 Substance and accidents and their relations,
    But yet fused together in such a manner
    That what I am talking of is a simple light.

91 The universal form of this knot
    Is what I think I saw, because when I say that
    I feel that my gladness becomes more ample.

94 A single moment cost me more forgetfulness
    Than twenty-five centuries have the enterprise
    Which made Neptune marvel at the sight of Argo.

97 So my mind, held in complete suspense,
    Gazed fixedly, motionless and intent,
    And always as if on fire with the gazing.

100 In that light a man becomes such
    That it is impossible he should turn away
    Ever to look upon any other thing.

103 Because the good, which is the object of the will,
    Is there in its entirety; and outside it
    There is some defect in what there is perfect.

106 My language now will be more inadequate,
    Even for what I remember, than would that
    Of a child still bathing his tongue at the breast.

109 Not that there was more than a simple appearance
    In the living light which I gazed upon
    And which is always as it always has been;

112 It was my sight which was growing stronger
    As I was looking; so what looked like one
    Worked on me as I myself changed.

115 In the profundity of the clear substance
    Of the deep light, appeared to me three circles
    Of three colours and equal circumference;

And the first seemed to be reflected by the second,   118
As a rainbow by a rainbow, and the third
Seemed like a flame breathed equally from both.

O how my speech falls short, how faint it is   121
For my conception! And for what I saw
It is not enough to say that I say little.

O eternal light, existing in yourself alone,   124
Alone knowing yourself; and who, known to yourself
And knowing, love and smile upon yourself!

That circle which, conceived in this manner,   127
Appeared in you as a reflected light,
When my eyes examined it rather more,

Within itself, and in its own colour,   130
Seemed to be painted with our effigy;
And so absorbed my attention altogether.

Like a geometer who sets himself   133
To square the circle, and is unable to think
Of the formula he needs to solve the problem,

So was I faced with this new vision: 136
I wanted to see how the image could fit the circle
And how it could be that that was where it was;

But that was not a flight for my wings: 139
Except that my mind was struck by a flash
In which what it desired came to it.

At this point high imagination failed;   142
But already my desire and my will
Were being turned like a wheel, all at one speed,

By the love which moves the sun and the other stars.   145

Dante is lost in a forested valley. He makes towards a sunlit hillside, but finding his way barred by three wild animals, turns for help to Virgil.

1 Dante indicates here that his experiences recounted in *The Divine Comedy* begin in his thirty-fifth year, "half way along the road" of man's notional span of life of seventy years (see Psalms 90.10, and Dante, *Convivio* IV.XXIII 6–10). Born in 1265, Dante therefore places the events in the year 1300.

2 The first of the scenes of the poem is pointedly allegorical in the accepted style of the 'allegory of the poets' (see *Convivio* II.I.2 f.). In a general sense the "great forest" represents sin, and its darkness represents ignorance; its native creatures are savage animals representing specific sinful tendencies (see below note to l. 32). In another sense, for we should bear in mind that Dante's imagery may be intentionally polyvalent here, the forest could represent degenerate Christendom, or a corrupt Florence (cf. Florence, the "sad forest", in *Purgatorio* XIV.64) rife with private and social vices. See *Inferno* VI.74–5: "Pride and envy and avarice are the sparks/Which set the hearts of the people alight"; and cf. *Inferno* XV.67–9.

11 Dante's experience of the Afterlife in *The Divine Comedy* is represented as a supernatural journey rather than as a dream, which he begins in a state of spiritual degeneracy or 'sleep'. Dante draws specific and important parallels with his own *journey* here, and the experiences of Aeneas and St Paul, in *Inferno* II.13–36 (see notes).

12 "the proper way": cf. 'Jesus replied, "I am the way; I am the truth and I am life" ' (John 14.6).

13–18 The hill, bathed in sunlight, is described later by Virgil as "the delightful mountain/Which is the beginning and reason of all joy" (ll. 77–8). The hill represents the virtuous life to which Dante aspires. Cf. the 'holy hill of Zion' (AV Psalms 2.6), and see also Hebrews 12.22, Psalms 61.2, 121.1.

17–18 The sun, source and sustainer of terrestrial life, is a symbol of the illuminating grace and righteousness of the Creator. Cf. Dante, *Convivio* III.XII.6–8, and note to *Inferno* XX.127–9.

32 The leopard is the first of the three wild animals barring Dante's way. Leopard, lion and wolf belong to biblical tradition (see Jeremiah 5.6), but a precise allegorical identification of them in *The Divine Comedy* is not without its problems. Safest perhaps is to follow the interpretations of the early commentators of Dante, who represent the leopard as sexual promiscuity, the lion as pride, and the she-wolf as avarice (including, in modern terms, material and political ambition). These sinful tendencies may be seen as Dante's private weaknesses or, if Dante is seen as an Everyman figure, as the three most common vices of mankind (see 1 John 2.16, and Aquinas, *Summa Theologica* II.II, q. 77, art. 5). As political allegory the leopard may represent the material promiscuity of Florence, the lion the dangerous pride of the papacy (or France), and the she-wolf the political rapacity of France (or the papacy). In respect of the latter equation, see *Purgatorio* XX.10–12 and note.

37–40 The sun is rising in the Ram, the zodiacal configuration at the Creation, the beginning of spring and the period of the conception and crucifixion of Christ. From internal evidence (*Inferno* XXI.112–14), Dante's attempted escape from the forest begins on the morning of Good Friday 1300. The forest scene of Cantos I and II, constructed and elaborated with allegorical purpose, is given no geographically identifiable setting, unlike the location of Hell and Purgatory. Yet here, in the forest of sin, an intrusion of the real dimensions of space and time occurs, with a reference to a precise hour and season, as the ahistorical events of the opening cantos (I, II) give way to a historical journey through the Beyond, beginning at the Gates of Hell (Canto III onwards). The forest depicted here is a psychological or spiritual state, whereas Hell for Dante and his medieval public is a real location, under the earth.

63 f. Virgil, born 70BC in the era of Julius Caesar ("*sub Julio*", l. 70), died in 19BC. Virgil will be Dante's guide through Hell and Purgatory to the threshold of Earthly Paradise, where his role is assumed by Matilda and then by Beatrice. Virgil's initial appearance as "one who, for long silence, seemed to be hoarse" is conceived more in terms of his allegorical role as Reason than according to his literal role in the poem. In the allegorical sense Virgil represents the highest virtues of mankind before the enlightenment of Christianity; he variously epitomises reason, rational philosophy, poetry, classical civilisation and *imperium*. Virgil was above all the author of the epic poem *Aeneid*, which became an indispensable school-text of the art of high eloquence in the Middle Ages (see ll. 79–80). In this work Virgil sets out the origins and high destiny of Rome and its Empire, in incomparable verse and with profound human understanding. Believing that the Roman Empire had been divinely ordained as part of God's providential ordering of history (during the *pax romana* Christ was born and crucified), Dante took the *Aeneid* to be a historical work inspired by divine truth. Virgil also wrote *Eclogue* IV, which prophesied the birth of a Wonder-child and a new golden age of peace and prosperity under the emperor Augustus, and which later Christian commentators interpreted as prophetic of the coming of Christ and the Christian era (see *Purgatorio* XXII.70–2 and note). Dante's debt as a poet to Virgil was less obvious up to 1300 (the fictional date of the events of *The Divine Comedy*) than later when actually writing the great poem (probably *c.*1308 onwards), but a deep impression on Dante must have been made early on by the immense dignity, high religious tone and exalted aims of Virgil's epic, a masterpiece he would emulate in the post-classical, vernacular terms of *The Divine Comedy*, and surpass by the distance that separates Christian revelation from classical cerebration.

73–5 In the *Aeneid*, Virgil tells the story of Aeneas, "son of Anchises" (l. 74), who left Troy (Ilium) after its destruction by the Greeks, to journey to Italy and found the Roman race.

101–11 The Greyhound is one of two extended, cryptic references to a future champion or saviour of medieval Christendom (see also the 'DXV' of *Purgatory* XXXIII.43 f.). There are no certain solutions to the identity of the saviour in either obscure oracle, but it is worth noting that Dante may not have had any specific person in mind, and that had he provided a clear reference to a champion who would later fail, the credibility of the whole *Divine Comedy* would have suffered an irreversible blow. The terms of reference of the Greyhound, however, seem linked to an eschatological vision of the sort current from the twelfth to the fourteenth centuries. See note to *Purgatorio* XXXIII.43.

105 Several commentators have suggested the area lying between

Feltre (Veneto) and Montefeltro (Romagna), and thus the territories of Can Grande della Scala, Lord of Verona, one of Dante's patrons in his exile to whom the *Paradiso* would later be dedicated. However, there are chronological problems associated with this attribution, and historical problems with the proposition that between 'felt and felt' (*feltro*) refers to the rough cloth of the Franciscan habit possibly of some evangelical pope dedicated to returning the Papacy to its proper material poverty.

107–8 Heroes and a heroine of the battles for the territory of Latium fought between the invading Trojans under Aeneas and the native Volscians and Rutulians (see *Aeneid* VII, IX, XII).

111 See Wisdom of Solomon 2.24: 'it was the devil's spite [Vulgate 'envy'] that brought death into the world'.

117 Perhaps the fate of the damned after the Day of Judgement: 'But as for the cowardly, the faithless, and the vile, murderers, fornicators, sorcerers, idolaters, and liars of every kind, their lot will be the second death, in the lake that burns with sulphurous flames' (Revelation 21.8).

118–19 The redeemed souls in Purgatory, who voluntarily undergo the torments of their purgation.

120 The blessed in Heaven.

122 Beatrice (see note to *Inferno* II.53 f.), to whom, after Matilda, Virgil will finally relinquish his role as Dante's guide.

124 The "Emperor" is God, his "city" Heaven.

134 The Gate of Purgatory, in the authority of St Peter (*Purgatorio* IX.76, 127).

INFERNO II

Virgil's account of his commission as Dante's guide.

1–9 Following rhetorical tradition Dante opens with a formal exordium (ll. 1–3, a protasis of Virgilian inspiration, cf. *Aeneid* IX.224–5), including an invocation to the muses, perfunctory here, but more developed in *Purgatorio* I.7–12, and *Paradiso* I.13–36 where Apollo's aid is invoked.

13–15 Aeneas, father of Sylvius, visited the Underworld (Hades, Tartarus and Elysium) in Virgil's *Aeneid* VI.

16 God (Psalm 45.7: 'You have loved right and hated wrong').

18 "who" are the Roman offspring of Aeneas, the 'Gens Iulia', including Julius Caesar and, by adoption, the emperor Augustus; "what" is Rome and its Empire, divinely ordained

in "empyreal heaven" (see note to *Paradiso* I.4), and which prefigures Christian Rome (seat of the popes, successors to St Peter, l. 27) and her spiritual empire (cf. Dante, *De Monarchia* I and II).

25–7 In the course of his journey through the Underworld (*Aeneid* VI), Aeneas learned from the soul of his dead father, Anchises, of his future victories over the indigenous tribes of Italy, and of the foundation of Rome.

28–30 The account of the journey of St Paul (the "chosen vessel": Acts 9.15), who was 'caught up as far as the third heaven' (2 Corinthians 12.1–4).

35 The concept of the 'foolish journey' is developed in Dante's account of Ulysses, *Inferno* XXVI.

52 Virgil refers to himself as one of the "suspended" souls in Limbo, eternally existing "without hope, but with desire" (see *Inferno* IV.34–45, and note to *Inferno* IV.24).

53 f. Beatrice, whose presentation here recalls that in Dante's lyric poetry, was the object of Dante's love in his youth. Probably Beatrice Portinari, later a Florentine banker's wife, she died in 1290. Dante's *Vita Nuova* is the record in prose and verse of his love for her, written *c.*1292, a love that becomes increasingly spiritual as he discerns in her a profound, even supernatural, beauty and goodness. The final chapter of the *Vita Nuova* recalls Dante's intention to write a work in which he can 'treat of her more worthily', adumbrating a work of the sort that *The Divine Comedy* is. In *The Divine Comedy* Dante assigns her a central literal and allegorical function, as his guide through Paradise (she assumes Virgil's role) and as she "who lights the intellect to truth" ('*lume . . . tra 'l vero e l'intelletto*'; *Purgatorio* VI.45), revealed wisdom, divine doctrine, Theology.

58 Virgil was born in Andes, near Mantua, a city then in Cisalpine Gaul (North Italy).

71 The Celestial Rose of the Empyrean, the true Paradise, "Which is full of love, and roomiest of all" (*Purgatorio* XXVI.63). See also *Paradiso* XXXII.9.

76–8 Beatrice's allegorical role is referred to here (see note to l. 53 above).

78 "that heaven": i.e. the heaven of the moon.

83 Hell, in the centre of the earth.

84 "the ample heaven": see note to l. 71 above.

94–6 The Virgin Mary. See St Bernard's prayer to the Virgin on Dante's behalf in *Paradiso* XXXIII.16–18: "you not only help/

Whoever asks you but, very often,/Spontaneously give before the prayer is made".

97 f. St Lucy of Syracuse, martyred in the third century, the patron saint of sight. Dante records a failure of his eyesight in *Convivio* III.IX.13–16, and his son Jacopo attests Dante's special devotion to her. Her allegorical function may then be Illuminating Grace, but commentators have also seen her as Mercy (see l. 100, and Boccaccio's commentary), and even Justice. See also *Purgatorio* IX.55 f. (where St Lucy's eyes are particularly emphasised), *Paradiso* XXXII.137–8; *Convivio* III.V.10 f.

102 Rachel, Jacob's second wife (Genesis 29), symbolic of the contemplative life (see *Purgatorio* XXVII.104–8, and also *Paradiso* XXXII.8–9).

108 "that river over which the sea is powerless": death. The "river" is literally one of those associated with the Underworld in classical mythology, the Styx, Lethe or Acheron.

INFERNO III

Dante and Virgil pass through the Gate of Hell, into the vestibule of the uncommitted and the pusillanimous, to arrive at the river Acheron.

4 Justice is the quintessential mark of the righteous God, and characterises his ordering of the universe. Justice and order are therefore central themes of *The Divine Comedy*. See Introduction.

5–6 Power, wisdom and love are the specific attributes of the triune God as Father, Son and Holy Spirit.

7–8 Hell was created to receive Satan and the rebel angels, soon after (how soon, see *Paradiso* XXIX.49–51) the creation of the three "eternal things": angels (pure form or act), primal matter (or 'potential'), and the heavens (pure form combined with primal matter). Cf. *Paradiso* XXIX.22–4.

15 'Fear is nothing but an abandonment of the aid that comes from reason' (Wisdom of Solomon 17.12).

18 See Dante, *Convivio* II.XIII.6, echoing Aristotle: 'the truth is the good of the intellect'. God is "the truth in which every intellect rests" (*Paradiso* XXVIII.108). Cf. also *Convivio* IV.XXII.13: 'God the supreme object of the intellect.'

23 The stars symbolise God's presence. Cf. *Inferno* XXXIV. 139 and note.

34 f. For the condition of the pusillanimous, the uncommitted men and angels, see Revelation 3.15–16: 'You are neither hot nor cold. How I wish you were hot or cold! But because you are lukewarm, neither hot nor cold, I will spit you out of my mouth.' Such have no "hope of death": even the "second death" of final annihilation will apparently be denied them (see note to *Inferno* I.117). The whole conception of the fate of the pusillanimous reflects Dante's scorn for anything other than firm commitment in life, for 'life in man is exercising the reason. Therefore, if his life is the being of man, *renouncing the exercise of reason is renouncing his existence, and so it is being dead.* And does not he renounce the exercise of reason who gives himself no account of the goal of his life ... and who gives himself no account of the path he ought to take?' (*Convivio* IV.VII.12 f.) Dante's commitment to causes brought about his exile from Florence in 1302; but it also brought about his lasting achievements and glory. See Introduction.

52 f. Obliged to follow a banner such as they never followed when alive, the souls suffer an appropriate punishment based on the idea of *contrapasso*, retribution in kind (see *Inferno* XXVIII.142 and note).

59–60 Most probably Pope Celestine V, who was elected in 1294 in his eightieth year, but abdicated his office five months later at the insistence (it was widely reported) of his successor Boniface VIII. Dante, whose detestation of Boniface was boundless (his exile was largely due to Boniface's policies), had no compunction in subscribing to the rumour (see *Inferno* XIX.52–7 and note, *Inferno* VI.64–9 and notes).

71 The Acheron, first river of Hell (cf. Virgil, *Aeneid* VI.295 f.).

91–3 Charon refers to the boat of the angel who transports the redeemed souls from the mouth of the Tiber to the shores of Purgatory (see *Purgatorio* II.13–45). Dante hints here at his own certain salvation.

95–6 A ritual formula used again by Virgil in *Inferno* V.23–4 in order to proceed past Cerberus.

112–17 A natural simile of Virgilian inspiration (*Aeneid* VI. 309 f.).

133 Dante, in accordance with Aristotelian physics, ascribes earthquakes to the action of vapour or wind trapped within the earth (cf. *Purgatorio* XXI.55–7).

INFERNO IV

Dante and Virgil enter the First Circle of Hell, Limbo, containing souls of unbaptised children, virtuous pagans, and the great castle of the famed.

1–6 Dante had swooned on the far side of the Acheron, and recovers to find himself on the outer edge of the First Circle. The concept of 'circles' of sin is taken from St Augustine: "The wicked walk in a circle . . . because the path in which their false understanding runs is circuitous" (*City of God* XII.13).

24 Limbo is a concept of Dante's sanctioned amongst others by Aquinas (*Summa Theologica* part. III supp., q. 69, art. 1–6). Dante, however, elaborates his conception in some unorthodox ways with respect to his treatment of "people of high value" (l. 44), and with regard to the punishment, which is spiritual or intellectual rather than material, and occasions only sighs (l. 26). The souls exist "without hope, but with desire" (l. 42) of salvation, and all that that entails: not only joy, but for those with great minds, intellectual satisfaction, since they can never quench their intellectual thirst at the source of all wisdom, God. Cf. *Paradiso* XIX.69–90 and notes.

34 "They have committed no sin": except that they are tarnished as all humanity with Original Sin eradicable only by the grace of God through the self-sacrifice of Christ. Dante lends his Virgil (who died in 19BC) an understandly incomplete theology.

38 This line is based on Aquinas ('Nor were they wont to do all things well, because they did not pay due honour to God'), who considers the merits and demerits of virtuous infidels in his *Commentary on St John's Gospel* (Singleton), an essential gloss on this passage.

52 Virgil died nineteen years before Christ's birth, fifty-two years before the events of ll. 53–4.

53–4 Christ, whose name is never used in Hell, 'descended into Hell' (Nicene Creed) at his death, to rise again on the third day. See also 1 Peter 3.19.

55 "our first parent": Adam (Genesis 2–3).

59 "Israel" (the name given to Jacob); his father Isaac; his children the twelve sons, founders of the twelve tribes of Israel.

60 Jacob was obliged to work fourteen years for the hand of Laban's daughter Rachel (Genesis 29.9 f.).

68–9 The fire is the 'light of nature' (Romans 2.14), symbolising the intellect in its natural, pagan state, before the higher illumination offered by grace at the coming on earth of the Holy Spirit in New Testament times (Acts 2.1–4).

72 f. Aquinas held that if virtuous pagans did good things, they did them for the wrong reasons: not for love of virtue, but for love of 'empty renown'. Dante assesses their honourable contribution to history and civilisation in more rational and humane terms; as if some light were better than no light at all.

86–8 The texts of Homer's epics, the *Iliad* and *Odyssey*, were only known to Dante fragmentarily in quotation or glosses in Latin authors. Dante knew no Greek, and no MSS of the epics were known in the West early in the fourteenth century. Dante's esteem of Homer is based solely on his reputation as reported in later classical authors. Cf. *Purgatorio* XXII.101–2.

89 Horace, Roman poet, author of the *Satires* and *Ars poetica*.

90 Ovid, Roman poet of the *Metamorphoses*, used extensively by Dante as a source of mythology. Lucan, poet of the Latin epic *Pharsalia*, well known to Dante. All those poets were seen as inimitable masters of eloquence and learning (i.e. the 'illustrious style') by Dante and his age. Cf. Dante, *De Vulgari Eloquentia* II.VI.7.

106–11 The great castle contains the souls of those pagans who won honourable fame in their lives: intellectuals, including poets, moral and natural philosophers, mathematicians, physicians, rulers, leaders, warriors and other exemplary figures (cf. the Elysian Fields in Virgil, *Aeneid* VI.637 f.). The circles of seven walls with their gates may represent the seven 'liberal arts' of the Middle Ages (*trivium*: grammar, rhetoric, dialectics; *quadrivium*: arithmetic, geometry, music and astronomy), or the seven moral and intellectual virtues (prudence, justice, courage, moderation, understanding, knowledge and wisdom), or the seven parts of philosophy (physics, metaphysics, ethics, politics, economics, mathematics, dialectics), and the surrounding stream, eloquence (cf. the "wide water" of Virgil's works *Inferno* I.80, and similar metaphors applied to Beatrice's expositions, in *Paradiso* IV.115–20).

112–14 See note to *Purgatorio* III.10–11.

121 f. We must take it that the otherwise arid list of names would have been appreciated by Dante's public with something of the excitement and exaltation he himself professes.

121–2 Electra: earliest forebear of Aeneas (cf. *De Monarchia*

II.III.11) mother of Dardanus, the founder of Troy, the city from which Aeneas issued after its capture and pillage by the Greeks, to settle in Italy and found the Roman race (see note to *Inferno* I.63 f.). Hector, slain by Achilles in the siege of Troy, was the eldest son of King Priam of Troy.

123 Julius Caesar (d. 44BC), *imperator* of Rome and founder of the Empire, assassinated by republican conspirators, including Brutus and Cassius (see note to *Inferno* XXXIV.61–7).

124–5 The Volscian maiden Camilla, adversary of the Trojans in Italy, slain in ambush (*Aeneid* XI.759 f.). Penthesilea, queen of the Amazons, slain by Achilles in the Trojan war (*Aeneid* I.490–93).

125–6 Latinus, king of Latium, and his daughter Lavinia, second wife of Aeneas (*Aeneid* VI.764, VII.45 f.).

127 Lucius Junius Brutus, who in 510BC led the revolt against the last of the seven kings of Rome, Tarquin the Proud, and founded the Roman Republic (Livy, *History of Rome* I.57 f.).

128 Lucretia, wife of Collatinus, outraged by Sextus, son of King Tarquin, committed suicide. Julia, steadfast daughter of Julius Caesar, married at her father's insistence Pompey the Great, later her father's deadliest enemy in the civil war. Marcia, the wife of Cato of Utica (see note to *Purgatorio* I.79). Cornelia, wife of Scipio Africanus, mother of the Gracchi brothers, famed for her matronly virtues.

129 Saladin (d. 1193), Muslim sultan of Egypt (Babylon) and Syria, valorous opponent of Richard I Coeur de Lion in the Third Crusade. Renowned for his integrity as a ruler and generosity as a warrior, he was a password for magnanimity in the Middle Ages (cf. Boccaccio, *Decameron* I.3 and X.9).

131 Aristotle (d. 322BC), for Dante greatest of the philosophers, tutor to Alexander the Great, and leader of the 'Peripatetic School' of philosophy in Athens. Aristotle's impact on western thought from the twelfth century onwards was immense, influencing scholastic philosophy especially in the fields of natural history, metaphysics, ethics and politics. Of Aristotle's works, Dante knew best the *Nichomachean Ethics*, which he must have read in Latin translation (Dante knew no Greek), but his knowledge of Aristotle was augmented by reading the commentators, Albertus Magnus, Averrhoes, and St Thomas Aquinas. The latter's *Summa Theologica*, the most authoritative theological treatise of the Middle Ages, is a reconciliation of

Aristotelian thought and Christian doctrine. Quotations from
or references to Aristotle's works in *The Divine Comedy* come
only second in number to those from the Bible.

134 For Dante's appreciation of the place of Socrates and Plato in
the study of moral philosophy (which for Dante was brought
to perfection especially by Aristotle) see *Convivio* IV.VI.15.
Of Plato's works Dante had probably read only the *Timaeus*
(see *Paradiso* IV.49), but would have gleaned more from
references to his works in Latin authors and commentators.

136 Democritus (d. *c.*370BC) posited the creation of the world by
a chance concourse of atoms. Dante may have known
something of his works through Cicero or Albertus Magnus.

137 Diogenes the Cynic (fourth century BC) repudiated the
comforts of civilisation. Anaxagoras, the Greek philosopher
(fifth century BC), master of Pericles, was known to Dante
through Cicero's works. Thales of Miletus (seventh century
BC) was reputed founder of the first Greek school of
philosophy, one of the 'seven sages'; he left nothing written.

138 Empedocles of Sicily (fifth century BC), inventor of the art of
rhetoric and of the concept of the four elements, and
Heraclitus of Ephesus (fifth century BC), who posited fire as
the origin of all things, are both mentioned by Aristotle, and
the latter of the two by Cicero. Zeno of Cyprus (third century
BC) was the founder of the Stoic school, whom Dante eulogises
in *Convivio* IV.VI.9.

140–41 Dioscorides of Anazarba (first century AD), founder of
the science of pharmacy. Orpheus and Linus, mythical poets
mentioned by Ovid and Virgil respectively. Cicero (106–43BC),
Roman statesman, philosopher, author and orator, whose *De
Amicitia* and *De Officiis* Dante particularly esteemed. Seneca
(d. 65AD), Roman tragedian and moral philosopher of the Stoic
school.

142 Euclid, the Greek geometrician (fourth century BC). Ptolemy
(second century AD), astronomer and mathematician of
Alexandria, whose system posits that the sun, stars and planets
revolve around the earth, the basis of Dante's cosmography in
The Divine Comedy.

143 Hippocrates (fourth century BC), Greek physician, founder
of medical studies; Galen of Pergamum (second century AD),
physician and author; Avicenna (d. 1036), Arabic physician
and author.

144 Averrhoes (d. 1198), a Muslim physician and philosopher

born in Spain, best known in the Middle Ages as the influential commentator of Aristotle's works (see *Convivio* IV.XIII.8, and note to *Paradiso* X.133–8).

INFERNO V

The poets make their way past Minos. In the Circle of the Promiscuous, Dante encounters Francesca and Paolo, and at Francesca's account, falls senseless.

2–3 The disposition of the circles of Hell are as in an inverted cone, with the apex, containing Satan, at the centre of the earth. The punishments become more severe the deeper their location, corresponding to the fact that the graver sins are punished deeper down in Hell. Here, in Circles II–V of Upper Hell, sins of weakness or 'incontinence' are punished, i.e. where the sin, although of the will, is due to choice conditioned by the passions (lust, greed, avarice, anger), and where the object is not malice or 'injustice'. See notes to *Inferno* XI.22 f.

4 Minos is also judge of the dead in Virgil's Hades (*Aeneid* VI.432–3), but Dante's Minos is transformed from a Cretan king into a monstrous demon.

20 Cf. Virgil, 'black Pluto's door stands wide open' (*Aeneid* VI.127); 'The gate is wide that leads to perdition . . . but the gate that leads to life is small' (Matthew 7.13–14).

23–4 See note to *Inferno* III.95–6.

34 The ruin is most probably the fall of rock due to the earthquake which occurred at the death of Christ, and to which Virgil refers in *Inferno* XII.34–45, and Malacoda in *Inferno* XXI.112–14. See Matthew 27.51.

39 Reason is man's highest faculty, distinguishing him from the animal world. Lust is surrender to the lower animal nature in man, the mere sexual drive, irrespective of any rational order in the relationship of the sexes (love, fidelity to marriage vows, ideals of chastity) upon which society's stability ultimately rests. Cf. 'So when we say a man is living, it should be understood that the man has the use of his reason, which is special to him, and is the actualising of his noblest part. And so the man who cuts himself off from reason, and has recourse only to his animal senses, does not live as a man, but as an animal' (*Convivio* II.VII.3–4).

52–60 Semiramis: licentious ruler of the Assyrian empire, following the death of her husband Ninus, and founder of Babylon. She extended her territories with the same perfidy that she employed in increasing her train of luckless lovers. Cf. Paulus Orosius, *Adversus paganos historia* I.IV. Semiramis was finally assassinated by her son, for whom she had conceived an incestuous love.

60 The Sultan ("Soldan") of Egypt, in Dante's time, however, did not rule the Babylon of the old Assyrian empire, rather the Babylon (old Cairo) of Egypt. Dante repeats something of a widely held error in his times.

61 Dido of Carthage, who betrayed the memory of her dead husband Sychaeus through her infatuation for Aeneas, committed suicide when Aeneas left her to resume his journey to Italy (Virgil, *Aeneid* IV).

63 Cleopatra, queen of Egypt, mistress of Julius Caesar and later of Mark Anthony (whom she betrayed at Actium, afterwards deceitfully engineering his death), committed suicide when she failed to ensnare the victorious Octavian with her charms (see *Paradiso* VI.76–8).

64 Helen betrayed her husband, Menelaus of Sparta, by consenting to abscond with Paris to Troy, thus beginning the Trojan war. Post-homeric legend narrates her violent death at the hand of a friend, Polyxo, whose husband fell in the wars (Pausanias, *Descriptio Graeciae* III.19).

65 In the popular medieval accounts of Benoît de Sainte Maure and Guido delle Colonne (both known to Dante), Achilles agreed to betray the Greek cause in the Trojan war for the hand of Polyxena, daughter of Priam, but was ambushed and killed in Troy by Paris.

67 Paris, whose impious abduction of Helen caused the Trojan war, was (in the medieval account of Benoît) slain out of hand by Ajax. In yet another version, Paris was morally wounded by poisoned arrows, and died, the antidote having been witheld from him by Oenone, whom he had earlier betrayed. Tristram betrayed his lord, King Mark of Cornwall, in an adulterous relationship with Isolde the queen, and met his death from a poisoned spear wielded by the king.

74 f. Francesca and Paolo. See note to l.88 below.

82–4 "just as doves": cf. Virgil, Aeneid V.213–17 and VI.190–92. In his commentary on this canto, Boccaccio sees the doves more as creatures of instinct than of innocence. It would indeed be mistaken to see Francesca, and her love for Paolo, in the sentimental light of nineteenth-century romanticism. Her love is not the flame of pure passion, but is uncompromisingly represented by Dante as concupiscence. Francesca, however, seduced by the specious doctrines of courtly love, sees her passion wholly in the unreal but fashionable light of a powerful literary convention. See notes to ll. 88 and 100–106 below, and *Paradiso* XXV .19–24 and note.

88 The voice is that of Francesca da Rimini, who was killed, at some time between 1283 and 1286, together with Paolo Malatesta (her lover and brother-in-law), by Gianciotto Malatesta da Verrucchio of Rimini, her husband. The adulterous pair were not young, notwithstanding later embroidery by commentators. What is generally accepted is that Gianciotto (literally, 'John the Lame') was deformed whilst Paolo, the younger brother, was handsome and straight-limbed. Both brothers, however, to judge from history, were gifted and valorous, Paolo having been Captain of the People in Florence when Dante was eighteen (1282–3). The case of Francesca's and Paolo's joint death is not recorded before Dante, whose sources may have included Francesca's brother, Bernadino da Polenta, a colleague at Campaldino (1289). See note to *Purgatorio* V.88.

97–9 Francesca was born in Ravenna, daughter of its ruler Guido da Polenta. She was the aunt of Guido Novello of Ravenna, Dante's host in his exile from 1317 to 1321.

100–106 Francesca exculpates herself by blaming love, defined in ways familiar to Dante's contemporaries. We are dealing here with a concept of courtly love of Provençal origins, promulgated and developed in the thirteenth century by the poets of Sicily, Bologna and later Florence, including those of Dante's own 'school', the poets of the 'sweet new style' (*Dolcestilnovo*). *'Fino amore'* is characterised here in elegant, literary terms by Francesca, its true nature is represented as an ineluctable force before which the will is seemingly powerless. Dante is thus emphasising how attractive this fashionable concept of love is, and also how treacherously damning. For Christianity teaches that the human will is never bound, but remains at all times free in the choice between good and evil. See *Purgatorio* XXII.10–12 and note, and Bibliography, D. H. Higgins, op.cit., chapter 7.

107 Cain murdered his brother Abel (see Genesis 4.1–15), and therefore epitomises the whole breed of assassins of kinsmen.

He lends his name to a zone of lower Hell reserved for the treacherous of this sort (*Inferno* XXXII), to which Francesca clearly refers.

124–6 Cf. Virgil, *Aeneid* II.10–13.

128 The Arthurian stories, in several popular versions, were well known and loved in Italy in Dante's day. Chrétien de Troyes' highly literary versions, including his *Lancelot*, were perhaps best known amongst the French-speaking cultured classes in Italy. Lancelot fell in love with Queen Guinevere, King Arthur's wife, and pursued an illicit affair that cost him his quest to find the Grail.

137 Words uttered by Francesca in bitter reproach, in the same tone as l. 107. Galahalt arranged the clandestine meeting between Lancelot and Guinevere, betraying them in the way that Pandarus betrayed both Troilus and Cressida. It is significant that Francesca consistently transfers the blame for her predicament from herself to others—an important feature of Dante's characterisation of her as a less than immaculate woman.

140 "the other": Paolo, whose tears are a sorry continuum to the whole story. The passive role of the male here perhaps underscores how courtly love, and the passion attending it, are (for Dante) wholly unmanning. "Out of pity": the Old Italian word *pietade* used here means also 'distress' (see note to *Inferno* VI.2). Therefore Dante's emotions at this point may embrace not merely pity, but also anguish born of quite different feelings: even remorse or conscience, for he too had been, in his youth, a poet who had popularised what he now sees to be the treacherous doctrines of courtly love. It is perhaps significant that the only other time, following this, that Dante is shown as fainting occurs on the summit of Mount Purgatory when confronted by Beatrice's accusations of his having entertained a less than worthy love after her death (see *Purgatorio* XXXI.22–89 and notes).

INFERNO VI

Dante recovers from his swoon to find himself in the Third Circle of the Gluttonous, guarded by Cerberus, where he talks with Ciacco of Florence.

2 The Italian also allows: "Caused by the distress of the two kinsfolk".

7 The Circle of the Gluttonous.

13 Cerberus is adapted from Virgil's monstrous watchdog of Hades (*Aeneid* VI.417 f.), but Dante lends the beast grotesque human features, creating a demonic hybrid with the modified role of guarding only one of the regions of Hell.

38 f. Ciacco, a Florentine acquaintance of Dante, clearly of some social standing, but of whom no contemporary record exists. The name possibly derives from Giacomo, but equally was the popular name for pig (Buti). Boccaccio recalls Ciacco as 'the greatest glutton that ever was', but a highly cultured man (*Decameron* IX.8).

64 f. After ousting the pro-imperial Ghibelline party in 1266–7, the ruling Guelf party in Florence later split into two opposing factions, the Whites (led by the Cerchi, supported by Dante) and the Blacks (led by the Donati; see *Purgatorio* XXIV.82–7 and note). The Guelf party was as a whole the Church party, but the Whites were cautiously opposed to papal interference in the city's affairs (where the pope claimed territorial sovereignty), whilst the Blacks, for a mixture of financial and pious motives, wished to draw closer to the papacy.

64–6 Clashes between the factions led to serious bloodshed in May 1300. The dominant Whites, the "provincial party" (for the provincial origins of the Cerchi, see note to *Paradiso* XVI.65) instigated political persecution of the Blacks in June 1301, at the discovery of a conspiracy.

67–9 The Blacks finally turned for help to the tentative Pope Boniface VIII (l. 69), who ultimately sent Charles of Valois (brother of Philip IV of France) to restore the position in November 1301. The *coup d'état* of the Blacks, supported by French arms, occurred in 1302 ("within three summers", l. 68) bringing savage reprisals, the occasion of Dante's exile. See *Inferno* XXIV.142 f. and notes; *Purgatorio* XX.71–8 and notes.

73 The reference to the "two who are just" is obscure, perhaps intentionally so on Dante's part. What is clear is that 'two just men' are fewer than the three of the Bible who were unable to save Jerusalem (*Ezekiel* 14.12 f.). G. Villani, however, records two Florentines of exemplary character, alive in 1300: Barduccio, and Giovanni da Vespignano (*Cronica* X.129).

79 f. Dante indicates here the limitations of his own moral and political vision in 1300: all the political figures he optimistically inquires of are in Hell. The passage is also a damning comment on the qualities of political leadership in Florence in the previous half-century, whether Ghibelline or Guelf.

79–80 Farinata degli Uberti, a Ghibelline, is in the Circle of the Heretics and Sceptics (*Inferno* X); Tegghiaio Aldobrandi degli Adimari and Jacopo Rusticucci, both Guelfs, are amongst the homosexuals (*Inferno* XVI); Arrigo's identity is uncertain, but if Arrigo dei Fifanti, he was implicated in the murder of Buondelmonte, and party to the origins of the Guelf–Ghibelline quarrels in Florence in 1215; Mosca dei Lamberti, partisan of the Buondelmonti clan, and more seriously implicated, is amongst the schismatics (*Inferno* XXVIII.106–8).

95–6 The Last Trumpet will announce the Day of Judgement (the "great sentence", l. 104) at the Second Coming of Christ, "the enemy power" (see Matthew 24.27 f.).

97–9 The resurrection of the dead; see 1 Corinthians 15.51 f.

106 f. Developing the "science" of Aristotle, Aquinas posited that the soul achieves perfection only when united with the body, and its most complete perfection when united with the incorruptible, glorified body at its resurrection.

115 Plutus: see note to *Inferno* VII.1–2.

INFERNO VII

Dante and Virgil proceed past Plutus, into the Fourth Circle of the Moneygrubbing and Wasteful. Virgil expatiates on Fortune, and the two poets enter the Fifth Circle of the Wrathful and the Sullen, in the lagoons of the Styx.

1–2 Dante's Plutus, the demon guardian of the Fourth Circle of the Moneygrubbing and Wasteful, appears of mixed mythical origins: Plutus the god of wealth and Pluto the god of the Underworld. The gibberish he utters is understood by Virgil (l. 3) as an expression of outrage that a living man, Dante, should be seeking entrance to his Circle.

8 "Wolf" recalls the she-wolf of avarice in the dark forest of *Inferno* I.49 f.

11 A variation of Virgil's formula in *Inferno* III.95–6 and V.23–4.

11–12 The archangel Michael cast Satan (Lucifer) out of heaven (Revelation 12.7 f.).

22 In the straits of Messina, between Italy and Sicily, the currents of the Tyrrhenian and Ionian seas meet to form dangerous eddies and whirlpools above a deep cleft in the seabed (Charybdis). See Virgil, *Aeneid* III. 420 f.

39 The avaricious or moneygrubbing move round the circle on the left-hand side, the wasteful on the right.

56–7 The references are to the tightfisted and the wasteful. The latter's hair is symbolically cropped (see also *Purgatorio* XXII.46), as with lunatics, to indicate their diminished 'faculties' (Old Italian *facultade*: 'wealth' or faculty').

70 f. Virgil's definition of Fortune as a "primal creature" (l. 95), i.e. an angelic being, firmly places contingency within a providential ordering of events; inscrutable, but ultimately willed by God. It is an exalted Christian understanding of what others might call 'chance', and Dante must have borne in mind the text: 'And we know that all things work together for good to them that love God, to them who are called according to his purpose' (AV Romans 8.28).

87 The angels are referred to by Dante elsewhere as "deities" (*Paradiso* XXVIII.121), reflecting poetically the gentiles' misapprehension of them before the Christian era (see *Convivio* II.IV.6).

98 i.e. it is past midnight of Good Friday. Cf. *Inferno* II.1–3.

101–8 The spring of dark water supplies the lagoons of the river Styx in the Fifth Circle, to which the poets are now heading (see *Aeneid* VI.323).

INFERNO VIII

Dante and Virgil pass over the lagoons of the river Styx in Phlegyas' ferry, encountering Filippo Argenti amongst the angry and sullen. They arrive at the gates of Lower Hell, the City of Dis.

1–2 This protasis is unique in *The Divine Comedy*, for nowhere else does Dante look back to elaborate on events that he has omitted to mention in a preceding canto. The apparent fracture of the narrative may give support to earlier commentators who suggested that Dante had completed Cantos I–VII before his exile from Florence in 1302, to take up the poem again only some years later.

17 Phlegyas, demon ferryman of the Styx. In mythology he was credited with highly reputable origins (his father was Mars), but was sent by Apollo to Tartarus for the sacrilegious act of burning the god's temple at Delphi, enraged at Apollo's violation of his daughter. As such, a tragic figure, and no demon, he appears in Virgil, *Aeneid* VI.618–20.

32 Filippo Argenti (see l. 61), possibly of the de' Cavicciuoli, a branch of the Adimari family, whom Cacciaguida (Dante's revered ancestor) castigates for insolence in *Paradiso* XVI.115 f.

Stories of Filippo's ostentatious wealth, monstrous irascibility and overbearing arrogance multiply in the early commentators (even that Dante had been publicly humiliated by him in Florence). Boccaccio pictures him characteristically in *Decameron* IX.8: 'a tall, muscular, powerful man, who was more contemptuous, foul-tempered, and touchy than any other citizen of Florence'.

43–5 Virgil commends Dante for his righteous anger, quite different from the insensate rage displayed by the souls of the wrathful here (cf. Aquinas, *Summa Theologica* II.II,q. 158, art. 1–3).

68 The City of Dis: the territory of Lower Hell (see l. 75), where the souls of malicious sinners, whose natures were permanently disposed to violence, fraud or treachery, are punished. Dis is equated by Dante with Satan (*Inferno* XI.65). In Virgil, Hades is called the City of Dis (*Aeneid* VI.541), Dis being the Latin equivalent of Pluto, Greek god of the Underworld.

70 The mosques give Dis an oriental flavour, but stand as symbols of entrenched evil, inaccessible to the grace and reason of the Christian gospel.

78 As with the ramparts of Tartarus in Hades (*Aeneid* VI.630–31).

82–3 Cf. Revelation 12.9, which relates the fall of Satan and his angels.

115–16 The allegory of this passage is pointed: Reason (Virgil) is, of itself, inadequate to influence for good those who through volition and choice do evil.

125–6 The main gates of Hell (see *Inferno* III.1 f.) are permanently open, Christ having shattered them at his entrance into Hell (see note to *Inferno* IV.53–4). See also AV Matthew 16.18.

INFERNO IX

Dante and Virgil, prevented from entering the City of Dis by the hostile demons, have the gates opened for them by a heavenly messenger. They enter to find themselves in the Sixth Circle of Heretics and Sceptics.

8 The help offered by Beatrice: "whatever may be necessary for his escape" (*Inferno* II.68).

17–18 The First Circle, Limbo (see note to *Inferno* IV.24).

22–7 There is no known source for this experience of Virgil's, either in ancient or medieval literature. The Sibyl who guided Aeneas through the Underworld admitted previous experience

520 COMMENTARY AND NOTES

(*Aeneid* VI.562–5), and it is possible that Dante believed that his guide should be similarly qualified. Erichtho (l. 23) appears as a prophetess in Lucan's *Pharsalia* (well known to Dante) with the power to raise spirits to prophesy future events (VI.507 f.).

27 "Judas's circle": Judecca (*Inferno* XXXIV).

38 The three furies ("Erinnyes", l. 45) are drawn from sources in Virgil (*Aeneid* VI.555 f.), Ovid and Statius.

40 The hydra, considered the most venomous of snakes in Pliny's *Natural History*.

44 Hecate (Proserpine, Persephone), wife of Pluto, king of the Underworld.

52 Medusa, youngest of the Gorgon sisters (see l. 56).

54 Theseus, son of the king of Athens, escaped from Hell with the aid of Heracles (Hercules), having failed in his attempt to carry off Proserpine (Hecate).

61–3 An apostrophe to the reader, who is urged to look for the allegorical truth of the events beneath the literal sense (cf. *Purgatorio* VIII.19–21 and note). Reason is inadequate of itself to grapple with entrenched evil. Grace, the power of God (the heavenly messenger of l. 80 f.), alone can achieve this victory over evil which is both of the will and of choice.

67–72 The simile of the storm has its counterparts in classical literature (Virgil, *Aeneid* II.416 f.; Lucan and Lucretius), but Dante's version is a new creation of great vigour.

76–8 Cf. Ovid, *Metamorphoses* VI.370 f.

98 Cerberus: see note to *Inferno* VI.13. In the *Aeneid* (VI.391 f) Virgil recalls the legend of how Hercules dragged Cerberus from Hades with a chain.

112 At Arles, near the mouth of the Rhône, is the Roman cemetery of the Aliscamps, with the remains of several ancient sarcophagi.

113 Pola (Pulj), on the Istrian peninsula, near the Gulf of Quarnero (Velikì Kvarner), the site of a Roman cemetery.

132 Dante and Virgil now turn to the right, the first of only two such instances in Hell, where all their movements are normally to the left, clockwise. This symbolic departure from the poets' normal practice may indicate that human reason (Virgil), in order to reveal the perverted intellect behind heresy, must turn back upon itself in the unholy task and, uniquely at this point, where for once in Hell an intellectual sin is at issue. See also *Inferno* XVII.31 and note.

INFERNO X

In the Sixth Circle of the Heretics and Sceptics, Dante encounters Farinata degli Uberti and Cavalcante de' Cavalcanti, and learns that amongst the other shades is the emperor Frederick II of Swabia.

2 i.e. within the City of Dis, between the walls and the burning tombs of the heretics and sceptics.

11 The Last Judgement (Matthew 24.27 f. and 25.31 f.), according to long Jewish tradition, would take place in the valley of Jehosophat (the Kidron valley) outside Jerusalem (AV Joel 3.12). For the concept of the resurrection and the assumption of incorruptible bodies see 1 Corinthians 15.51 f., and notes to *Inferno* VI.95–6 and 106 f.

13–14 In spite of obvious anachronism, Dante uses Epicurus as an archetypal religious heretic. Positing the soul's mortality, Epicurus (d. 270BC) preached avoidance of pain as the highest good, and recommended a life of serenity, abstinence and moderation. But it was his disbelief in immortality that earned him notoriety in the Middle Ages, together with a later distortion of his teaching that proposed pleasure as the highest good. The name Epicurus thus became associated with heretical scepticism (free-thinking), materialism and hedonism. Such attitudes and ideas had found considerable, even militant, following in Florence a century before to judge from G. Villani's accounts (see *Cronica* IV.30, and Sapegno). Later, epicureanism and Ghibellinism became equated in Guelf propaganda, and must have determined Dante's choice of a great Florentine Ghibelline, Farinata, as his major figure in this canto.

22 Farinata degli Uberti's voice interrupts the earnest conversation of the poets. The Uberti were the leading Ghibelline (pro-imperial family of Florence in the middle of the thirteenth century, turbulent years that saw the expulsion of the anti-imperial Guelfs by the Ghibellines, and of the Ghibellines by the Guelfs, on more than one occasion. From 1258 to 1260 Farinata was in exile in Siena; from 1260 (after the battle of Montaperti) to 1264 in power in Florence, where he died a year before Dante's birth. He was condemned posthumously as a heretic in 1283 when Florence was once more Guelf, a symbolic political as well as religious act. Of impressive stature, bearing and speech, he was a cultured man with martial virtues, a born leader to whom even Guelf chroniclers paid tribute. Dante's tribute in this canto to Farinata's qualities (as well as implied criticism of his defects, notably his rigid party fanaticism) is no less sincere.

42 See *Paradiso* XVI.23 and note.

46–7 Dante was of a Guelf family, though not as notable a one as is implied here.

48 The Guelfs were expelled by the Ghibellines in 1248 (when imperial fortunes in Italy as a whole, led by Emperor Frederick II, were in the ascendant) and in 1260 (after a disastrous Guelf defeat at Montaperti).

49–50 The Guelfs returned to power in Florence in 1251 following the Ghibelline defeat at Figline, and in 1266–7 following the virtual collapse of the Ghibelline cause at Benevento, where Manfred was killed (see notes to *Purgatorio* III.103 f. and VII.113).

51 The Ghibellines, after their final expulsion by the Guelfs in 1267, the year following Benevento, were quite broken as a party, and never returned to power in Florence. In 1280 the most important of the Ghibelline families were specifically excluded from an amnesty, including the Uberti as the most powerful.

53 Cavalcante de' Cavalcanti, a Guelf, was reputed, according to Boccaccio and Benvenuto, an epicurean materialist. The families of the Cavalcanti and Uberti were linked in 1267 with the betrothal of Guido to Beatrice, Farinata's daughter.

58 f. Cavalcante's urgent questioning of Dante is reminiscent of a passage in Virgil, *Aeneid* VI.339.

60 Guido (d. August 1300), fervent supporter of the White Guelf faction, to which Dante himself belonged, Dante's 'first friend' to whom his *Vita Nuova* (1292) is dedicated, was a brilliant poet and intellect and an epicurean materialist like his father. The acute quality of his mind and his mordant wit are captured by Boccaccio in *Decameron* VI.9.

62–3 Guido's "disdain" of Virgil may reflect the divergency of thought that must have separated the two friends by 1300; Guido's sceptical attitudes could not have been further from the religiously inclined cast of Dante's mind at this time. Guido's favourite reading would not have been Virgil, an epic poet of deep religious sense such as is evidenced in the *Aeneid*.

73 Farinata, haughtily ignoring Cavalcante's interruption and predicament, continues his debate with Dante, which is shot through with animosity born of rigid political chauvinism. Dante's replies to Farinata have been hardly less hostile: very much in the frame of mind of the unregenerate Dante of the spring of 1300, a leading White Guelf shortly to accede to the influential Priorate in June.

79–81 In 1304 an attempted amnesty (initiated by the new pope, Benedict XI) between White and Black Guelfs failed, leaving the Whites (Dante amongst them) in continued exile. See notes of *Inferno* VI.64–9 and G. Villani, *Cronica* VIII.69.

80 Hecate (Proserpine), queen of the Underworld in classical myth.

82–4 The Uberti were specifically excluded from any amnesty after the return of the Guelfs in 1266–7.

85–6 The battle of Montaperti (see note to l. 48 above) was fought on the banks of the Arbia, into which the blood of the defeated Guelfs flowed in the ensuing rout. The Arbia flows some nine kilometres to the east of Siena. See note to Inferno XXXII.78.

87 Possibly a reference to the Baptistry of San Giovanni in Florence, where laws were ratified by the populace, although commentators do not concur over this (Santa Reparata and S. Piero Scheraggio were also used for public meetings).

91–3 After Montaperti, at a council in Empoli, the Ghibellines of Florence (with their Sienese allies, led by Provenzan Salvani, concurring) had in mind to destroy Florence itself. Villani records Farinata's stout and successful opposition to the measure (*Cronica* VI.81).

100–105 The condition which E. Auerbach calls 'hyperopia'. Farinata, for example, did not know of the Ghibellines' continuing exile from Florence in 1300 (the fictional date of Dante's journey), although he could foresee events of 1304. Cavalcante did not know of the whereabouts of his son, nor could foresee his death in the August of the same year. Ciacco's vision is less clouded (*Inferno* VI.64 f.), perhaps because his gluttony was the lesser sin.

119 Frederick II of Swabia, of the house of Hohenstaufen, was Emperor of the Holy Roman Empire from 1212 to 1250, king of Sicily and Naples (by succession from his mother), and titular king of Jerusalem (1227). His court in Palermo was the centre of a minor renaissance of learning, poetry and the arts, of which he was the inspiration. Here much of Arabic and oriental culture mingled with western traditions, and Frederick

was at home in both worlds. Of acute and unprejudiced intellect, he was reputed (not unreasonably) an epicurean materialist by his contemporaries. His excommunications resulted however from failure to prosecute his crusade (in 1227), and dynastic and territorial ambition which conflicted with papal interests (1239). The latter anathema was confirmed by Innocent IV, Frederick dying under the ban of the Church. During his lifetime Ghibellinism in Italy was at its most militant, promoted with a vigour and success that neither his son Conrad nor his natural son Manfred could hope to sustain (see note to ll. 49–50 above).

120 Ottaviano degli Ubaldini (d. 1273), created cardinal 1244, an ardent Ghibelline (as his nephew Archbishop Ruggieri, *Inferno* XXXIII.1 f., and brother Ubaldino della Pila, *Purgatorio* XXIV.29), was a churchman of strong personality and charm, but (for Dante) fatally weak on doctrinal principle; 'an epicurean in word and deed' (Benvenuto).

131 Beatrice; although Dante learns more from Cacciaguida in *Paradiso* XVII.37 f. See *Inferno* XV.55–78, 88–90.

INFERNO XI

While pausing before descending into the abyss of Lower Hell, Virgil teaches Dante the plan and rationale of Hell.

8 Anastasius II, pope 496–8, allegedly favoured the heretical doctrine of Acacius who proposed the exclusively human nature of Christ, whereas orthodoxy insists on his dual nature, true God and true man.

9 Plotinus, deacon of Thessalonica, an Acacian heretic and friend of Anastasius who may have unduly influenced him.

17 The Seventh Circle of the Violent, the Eighth of the Fraudulent, and the Ninth of the Treacherous.

22 f. Virgil begins by expounding the nature of the sins punished in Lower Hell; these are malicious sins committed by volition *and* by choice. The sins of Upper Hell, however, do not have malice as their aim, and although committed voluntarily are the result of 'incontinence' or weakness (a surrender to the passions) rather than of unconditioned choice.

23 "injury"; a term of scholastic philosophy, meaning 'injustice'.

24 Dante adopts here the distinctions of Cicero in *De Officiis* I.13. Cf. also AV Psalms 5.6(b): 'The Lord will abhor the bloody and deceitful man.'

25 Fraud is wanton misuse of the reason or intellect, the unique and differentiating faculty of man in the created orders (man, animal, plant, mineral).

28 i.e. the Seventh Circle in the total scheme of Hell.

31 Force (violence) is here classified into sins of diminishing gravity.

50 Sodom: destroyed by God for its unnatural vice of homosexuality and worse (Genesis 18.16 f. and 19.1 f.). Cahors: the southern French town, in the Middle Ages a centre of moneylending where excessive interest was charged on loans (usury).

51 Blasphemers.

52 "every conscience": i.e. the conscience of all those who practise fraud.

55–6 Natural love is 'the natural friendship of all men for one another by reason of their likeness in specific nature' (Aquinas, *Commentary on the Nichomachean Ethics of Aristotle* VIII.1).

57 The Eighth Circle of the Fraudulent, Malebolge, divided into ten concentric valleys.

65 "Dis": Satan (Lucifer). See note to *Inferno* VIII.68.

70–72 Dante here refers to the punishments in the four circles of the 'incontinent' in Upper Hell (although not in strict order): the wrathful and sullen, the promiscuous, the gluttonous, and the moneygrubbers and wasters.

73 The city of Dis, Lower Hell.

80 Aristotle, *Nichomachean Ethics* VII.I.

82 Dante would here seem to equate Aristotle's "frantic bestiality" with Cicero's "force", and the former's "malice" with the latter's "fraud" (cf. l. 24). "Incontinence": see note to l. 22 above.

94–6 See ll. 46–51. Usury was forbidden by Judaic law: 'He hath given forth upon usury, and hath taken increase [interest] . . . he shall surely die' (AV Ezekiel 18.13).

97 i.e. the philosophy of Aristotle.

98 e.g. in Aristotle's *Metaphysics* XII.7.

101–5 See Aristotle, *Physics* 11.2.

107–8 Genesis 3.19 f.: 'You shall gain your bread by the sweat of your brow.'

113–14 i.e. it is about 4 a.m. on Holy Saturday, shortly before sunrise (the sun rises after Pisces over the east horizon), when the Great Bear or Wain is on the north-west horizon. 'Caurus' is the north-west wind.

INFERNO XII

Dante and Virgil descend into the Seventh Circle of the Violent. Proceeding past the Minotaur, they enter the First Round, where in a river of boiling blood (the Phlegethon), and guarded by Centaurs, are the souls of those who committed violence against others or their property.

4–5 Probably the Slavini di Marco, twenty miles south of Trent, by the river Adige, in Northern Italy.

12 f. The Minotaur (l. 25), a hybrid beast, half human, half bull, sired on Pasiphae (wife of King Minos of Crete) by a white bull, by means of an ingenious contraption (l. 13). See Virgil, *Eclogues* VI. 45 f; Ovid, *Metamorphoses* VIII.131–7; and cf. *Purgatorio* XXVI.41–2, 86–7.

17 Theseus: son of the king of Athens (see note to *Inferno* IX.54).

18 The Minotaur, kept in a labyrinth on Crete, was killed by Theseus with the aid of Ariadne, Pasiphae's daughter by King Minos, who provided him with a sword to kill the beast and a thread with which to trace his path through the labyrinth.

34 See *Inferno* IX.22–7 and note.

38 "he": Christ, at the Harrowing of Hell (see notes to *Inferno* V.33–4 and VIII.125–6), who removed the patriarchs of the Israelites from Hell to Heaven.

39 "Dis": Satan. See note to *Inferno* VIII.68.

40 See Matthew 27.51 in reference to the earthquake at the crucifixion of Christ.

41–3 Empedocles (see note to *Inferno* IV.138) proposed that the world was subject to alternate periods of love and hate, causing respectively the destruction of things (a return to primitive chaos, when the four elements anarchically combine) and their reconstruction. This was a theory refuted by Aristotle.

47 The Phlegethon (see *Inferno* XIV.116).

56 Centaurs: mythical hybrids, with the body and legs of a horse, and the neck and head of a human, known for their fits of violence and destruction.

65 Chiron: the centaur charged with the education of Achilles (l. 71) and other famous men; see note to *Purgatorio* IX.34–9.

67–9 Nessus attempted the abduction of Dejanira, Hercules' wife, and was killed by the hero with a poisoned arrow. Before dying, Nessus gave Dejanira a piece of his clothing soaked in his blood purportedly as a love-charm, which Dejanira later gave to Hercules in order to win back his love from Iole, but which instead caused his death. See note to *Paradiso* IX.101–2.

72 Pholus dropped one of Hercules' poisoned arrows on his foot, and died.

88 Beatrice.

91–3 Cf. *Inferno* III.95–6 and note.

107 Probably Alexander the Great of Macedon, d. 323BC (Lucan, *Pharsalia* X.30 f); Dionysius the Elder, tyrant of Syracuse (d. 367BC).

110 Azzolino (Ezzolino) III da Romano (1194–1259), brother of Cunizza (see note to *Paradiso* IX.22), married the natural daughter of Emperor Frederick II (see note to *Inferno* X.119). Lord of the March of Treviso and leader of the Ghibellines in Northern Italy, he was remarkable for his energy and notorious for his savagery. Excommunicated in 1254. See G. Villani, *Cronica* VI.72.

111–12 Obizzo II d'Este (1247–93), Guelf lord of Ferrara, dedicated ally of Charles I of Anjou (see note to *Purgatorio* VII.113), aggressively appropriated much territory which he then quelled with ferocity. His "bastard son" (the illegitimacy may only be a calumny) Azzo VIII, only a slightly less successful tyrant than his father, was credited with having stifled his father to death (again a probable calumny). Cf. note to *Purgatorio* V.64.

116–17 Those guilty of homicide.

118–20 Guy de Montfort (d. 1298), son of Simon de Montfort and Eleanor, daughter of King John, Charles I of Anjou's vicar in Tuscany. In revenge for his father's death at the hands of Henry III's men at Evesham (1265), Guy stabbed to death Prince Henry of Cornwall, his cousin, in a church ("in the bosom of God", l. 119) in Viterbo in 1272, where King Philip III of France, Charles I of Anjou, and cardinals of the Church had assembled. G. Villani, in *Cronica* VII.39, states that Henry's heart was placed in a reliquary by London Bridge, although his body, it is known, was buried at Hailes Abbey, Gloucestershire.

133 Attila the Hun (d. 453), the "scourge" of God, invader and devastator of much of Europe.

135 Pyrrhus, either the king of Epirus (d. 272BC), ferocious enemy of the Romans, or the son of Achilles, whose slaughter of defeated Trojan nobles is recorded in Virgil, *Aeneid* II.526 f. Dante, however, speaks in admiration of the former in *De*

Monarchia II.IX.7. Sextus, son of Pompey the Great, was a pirate according to Lucan (*Pharsalia* VI.419 f.).

137 Rinier da Corneto, a bandit of the Maremma in Dante's time. Rinier Pazzo, a robber especially of Church grandees, possibly of the Pazzi family of Florence, was allegedly encouraged in his nefarious deeds by Emperor Frederick II; active in the first half of the thirteenth century.

INFERNO XIII

In the Second Round of the Violent, the wood of the suicides and squanderers, Dante hears Pier delle Vigne recount the story of his suicide, witnesses the punishment of the squanderers, and listens to the lament of an anonymous Florentine suicide.

1–9 These lines, heavy with negative particles ("not yet . . . no path . . . not green . . . not wholesome . . . no apples . . . not so rough or dense") reflect the use of anaphora in the Italian text, one rhetorical device amongst the several that distinguish the style of this canto.

9 Towns at the northern and southern edge of the Tuscan Maremma, which was formerly covered with dense forest.

10–15 See Virgil, *Aeneid* III.209 f. In the canto the Harpies may symbolise remorse, or the lack of self-charity of the suicide (see ll. 101–2).

19 i.e. of the Third Round of the Violent (Inferno XIV–XVII).

25 The rhetorical device of *traductio* ("I think he thought that I thought") employed with unobtrusive skill, to the end of complete narrative precision.

48 The episode of Aeneas and Polydorus (Virgil, *Aeneid* III.22 f.), upon which the incident of ll. 31–45 is partially based, although Dante's treatment has much that is entirely his own. See also Ovid, *Metamorphoses* II.352 f., the metamorphosis of Phaeton's sisters.

55 f. The voice is that of Pier delle Vigne, c.1190–1249, who rose from humble origins to become chancellor and intimate adviser of Emperor Frederick II (see note to *Inferno* X.119) at the courts of Naples and Palermo. Jurist, skilled administrator, master of eloquence (*ars dictandi*), and poet, Pier was responsible for the reform of the laws and administration of the Kingdom of Sicily (the *Regno*), and established an elaborate but effective style of Latin (*altus stilus*) in his reports, correspondence and edicts which was adopted by other administrations and by Dante himself in his Latin letters. At the height of his influence Pier was suddenly arrested and imprisoned by Frederick either on charges of embezzlement or treason. Blinded as a preliminary to execution, Pier anticipated matters by taking his own life.

55–78 Pier's speech is a small masterpiece of legal plea or defence, Ciceronian in structure and argument, in which he adduces calumny as the cause of his downfall (a *locus communis*), and revenge (*relatio criminis*) as the motive of his suicide (his aim to avoid the disgrace of public execution, and so deprive his enemies of the consummation of their triumph over him). At the same time he magnanimously exculpates Frederick II his master (*remotio criminis*) and with extreme scrupulousness (intended to sway the judgement of his listeners as to his innocence from treachery) blames himself for his predicament in a line (l. 72) that also pithily assesses the morality of suicide in the light of both divine and human (positive) law. The speech follows the rules of Ciceronian *inventio*: ll. 55–7 the *exordium* (a · dignified introduction), 58–61 the *narratio* (exposition of the facts), 62–3 the *partitio* (the main issue of the controversy: Pier's loyalty), 64–72 the *argumentatio* (the core of the forensic oration, in which the arguments are marshalled), 73–5 the *refutatio* (refutation of the case for the prosecution, which here is a simple charge of treason), and 76–8 the *peroratio* (aimed to arouse the indignation and pity of the judge for the plaintiff). Apart from the *refutatio* and the *peroratio*, the style of the whole speech is highly wrought, cunningly exploiting the devices of rhetoric (*ornatus*) without detriment to the intellectual content of the plea. See Bibliography, D. H. Higgins, op. cit. chapter 8.

58 "the double keys": the one to lock, the other to unlock.

64 "The whore": envy (*amplificatio* employing allegory).

65 "Caesar": Frederick II (*antonomasia*).

67–8 "inflamed . . . inflamed . . . inflamed": in rhetoric the trope of *traductio*.

68 "Augustus": Frederick II (see note to l. 65 above).

70 The line reflects Aristotelian and Thomistic thought on the nature of anger: any unwarranted slight provokes anger and with it the pleasure ("taste") of contemplating revenge (see Aquinas, *Summa Theologica* II.1, q. 48, art. 1).

72 Note the use of the rhetorical device of the antithesis, *ornatus* functionally employed.

96 Minos: see *Inferno* V.4 f. and note.

103 i.e. at the Last Judgement (see notes to *Inferno* VI.95–6, 97–9).

115 The souls of two squanderers.

118 "The one": possibly Ercolano (Lano) Maconi of Siena, member of the Spendthrifts Club, who dissipated nearly his entire fortune. He died in 1287 at the battle of Pieve del Toppo in an encounter with the Aretines.

119 "the other": Jacopo (Giacomo) da Sant'Andrea, a Paduan; insanely prodigal, he was reputedly executed by Azzolino III da Romano in 1239 (see note to *Inferno* XII.110).

143–4 Florence, in pagan times, was dedicated to the worship of Mars; in the Middle Ages its patron saint was John the Baptist, whose image appeared on the florin. See G. Villani, *Cronica* I.42,60.

145 "his tricks": the outbreak of conflict and dissension, the preliminaries of war of which Mars was god. As it happened, the crime that caused the beginnings of the disastrous Guelf–Ghibelline struggle in Florence was committed near the statue (see note to *Inferno* XXVIII.106–8).

147 The remains of an ancient statue of Mars stood in Dante's day by the Ponte Vecchio. Its preservation was believed to have guaranteed the city's revival after its reputed destruction by Attila (see note to *Inferno* XII.133) in the fifth century.

INFERNO XIV

The two poets enter the Third Round of the Seventh Circle, where on burning sands the violent against God, Nature, and her bounty are punished. Virgil indicates the soul of the blasphemer Capaneus, and discloses that the rivers of Hell can be traced to their source in the statue of an old man beneath a mountain in Crete.

1 i.e. Florence.

15 Marcus Porcius Cato, whose army crossed the Libyan desert in 46BC. See Lucan, *Pharsalia* IX.368 f., and note to *Purgatorio* I.31 f.

22–4 See *Inferno* XI.46–51 and notes.

22 The blasphemous, abusers of God. Cf. Revelation 16.9.

23 The usurers, who abused Nature and her benefits (crafts and skills). See *Inferno* XI.97–111 and notes.

24 The abusers of Nature's sexual law; sexual perverts.

29 "Rained down": cf. Genesis 19.24: 'and then the Lord rained down fire and brimstone from the skies on Sodom and Gomorrah'; and see note to *Inferno* XI.50.

31–6 Alexander the Great (see note to *Inferno* XII.107). The episode appears to have been taken by Dante from Albertus Magnus, *De meteoris* I.IV.8.

44–5 See *Inferno* VIII.82 f.

46 "that great one": Capaneus, one of the seven Greek kings at the siege of Thebes, who blasphemously challenged Jupiter and was struck dead by the god's thunderbolt. See Statius, *Thebaid* X–XI, and *Inferno* XXV.15.

51 An important feature of Dante's general presentation of the damned, whose characters are not diminished or distorted in Hell, but appear as intensified versions of their earthly personalities (E. Auerbach, *Mimesis*).

56 Mongibello: Mount Etna, in Sicily, the mythical location of Vulcan's forge.

58 Phlegra: see note to *Purgatorio* XII.28.

76–7 The outfall of the Phlegethon from the First Round of the Seventh Circle (*Inferno* XII).

79–80 Near Viterbo, a hot spring, reddish in colour, supplied the houses of prostitutes along the banks.

86 "that gate": the Gate of Hell, *Inferno* III.1 f.

96 Saturn, first of the mythical kings of Crete, whose reign coincided with the Golden Age of mankind.

100 Rhea, wife of Saturn, gave birth to Jupiter on Mount Ida. Obliged to keep the child's existence a secret (since Saturn would have devoured him) Rhea required her priests to maintain a constant clamour.

103 A gigantic statue, found inside a Cretan mountain, is mentioned by Pliny, *Natural History* VII.XVI.73 (Singleton).

104 Damietta in Egypt. See Anderson, pp. 290–4.

106 f. The statue represents the ages of mankind, as in Daniel 2.31 f., and Ovid, *Metamorphoses* I.89 f.

116 Acheron, Styx, Phlegethon: for their location see *Inferno* III.78, VII.106 and XII.47 respectively.

119 Cocytus, the fourth and final river of Hell; see *Inferno* XXXI.123.

136 Lethe rises on the summit of Mount Purgatory (*Purgatorio* XXVIII.25, 130).

INFERNO XV

In the Third Round of the Seventh Circle, Dante encounters his one-time teacher, Brunetto Latini, amongst the sinners guilty of sexual perversions.

9 "the Chiarentana": the old duchy of Carinthia, which contained the upper reaches of the Brenta in the Valsugana.

10 "those banks": i.e. those in the Third Round.

23 f. The soul of Brunetto Latini, *c.*1220–94, Florentine intellectual, rhetorician and public servant, by profession a notary. A Guelf, Brunetto was in exile during the period of Ghibelline hegemony in Florence, 1260–66 (see notes to *Inferno* X.22–51). During his exile in France, Brunetto wrote in French (*c.*1263) *Li livres dou Tresor* ("The Treasure", l. 119), an encyclopedic work of history, natural philosophy, ethics ('vices and virtues'), rhetoric and politics. On his return to Florence, where as a prominent Guelf he played an important part in the city's affairs (his name being mentioned in some thirty-five extant public documents), Latini brought out the *Tesoretto* (a didactic poem) and a fuller (but unfinished) commentary on Ciceronian rhetoric (the *Rettorica*), both written in exile. He may well have taught (formally or informally) rhetoric and other subjects in the city to such promising young students as Dante. See G. Villani, *Cronica* VIII.10.

41 "my band": the sexually perverted, probably pederasts and homosexuals.

50–51 See *Inferno*. I.1 f. The circumstances of the allegory (the road and the forest) here echo those in Latini's own *Tesoretto* ll. 186 f.

53 "He": Virgil.

54 i.e. heavenwards.

61–2 Fiesole is situated on a hill overlooking Florence. Its populace was believed to have settled in Florence after their own city had been destroyed during Cataline's rebellion (62BC). See G. Villani, *Cronica* I.37–8.

64 Brunetto refers to Dante's banishment from Florence by the Black Guelfs in 1302 (see notes to *Inferno* VI.64–9).

65 The mountain ash has a bitter berry (the rowan berry) containing sorbic acid.

68 Cf. Ciacco's analysis of Florentine degeneracy in *Inferno* VI.74–5, and see note to *Inferno* I.2.

71 i.e. the Black and White factions of the Guelf party. After
1304, Dante moved to a political position that was apart from,
and above, the narrow factionalism of either Guelf grouping,
and of the Ghibellines. See *Inferno* X, 79–81 and note and
Paradiso XVII.61–9.

77 According to an old legend, recounted by Latini and Villani,
Florence was founded by the nobler race of the Romans after
they had destroyed Fiesole. See note to ll. 61–2 above, and
Latini, *Tresor* I.37.1–2.

85 "how man may be eternal": the achievement of glory or
renown, Latini taught in his *Tresor* (II.120.1), guaranteed man
"a second life". This aspiration to immortality (the words
of Dante-character have a hollow ring, here in the eternity of
Hell) was nurtured particularly by contemporary rhetoricians,
who believed and taught that literary immortality was in their
gift (Wieruszowski). Latini's fate in *The Divine Comedy* may
perhaps be seen as part of Dante's criticism of contemporary
society in its cultural assumptions, just as the events of *Inferno*
X are part of his critique of contemporary political praxis.
Latini is in Hell primarily because of his sexual deviance, but
his tendency to subvert the order of nature in this respect
seems to be part of a general proclivity to deviation (Dante's
characters are invariably integrated in their psychological
profile: no sin of the damned is represented as out of
character). Man's object on earth is to glorify God, through his
works and words, whereas Latini the rhetorician is content to
promote and teach the glorification of man by offering an
illusory eternity of earthly renown. Dante, for all the gratitude
he expresses to Latini in this canto, is at the same time marking
the limitations of Latini's humanistic contribution to the
formation of his (Dante's) life and outlook. Dante as character,
tactfully, does not bring Virgil's name to Latini's attention
(Virgil is the reliable master, who leads to a true immortality of
the soul), and Dante as poet of the *Comedy* does not fail to
associate here the major (proto-humanistic) work of Latini,
The Treasure, with its author in his eternal destiny as an
outcast of heaven. See the expression of Dante's literary aim in
Paradiso XVII.118–20 and note. And cf. Romans 2.7–8, which
is most pertinent to Dante's theme here.

90 Beatrice; but cf. note to *Inferno* X.131.

109 Priscian, the great Latin grammarian of the sixth century AD.
His *Institutiones Grammaticae* were influential and

authoritative until modern times. There is no historical evidence of any sexual deviation. Dante seems to have heaped the alleged characteristic sin of the whole teaching profession on the luckless Mauritanian. Cf. *Paradiso* XII. 137 and note.

110 Francesco d'Accorso (d. 1293), son of the more famous lawyer and academic Accursius, was professor of civil law at Bologna and Oxford. No surviving record of any sexual crime attaches to his name.

111–14 Probably Andrea dei Mozzi, bishop of Florence 1287–95. Referred to by the early commentator Benvenuto as *magnus bestionis*, Andrea was removed ("translated") from Florence ("the Arno") to Vicenza ("the Bacchiglione") by Pope Boniface VIII ("the servant of the servants", l. 112; the irony is not to be missed).

119 *"The Treasure"*: see note to l. 23 f.

121–4 The annual cross-country race, known as the *palio*, was run outside the walls of Verona; the prize of a bolt of green cloth was given to the winner, and a cockerel to the loser. The runners were probably stripped down, if not actually naked as Boccaccio suggests. Dante's choice of the simile here, as his choice of the image of the naked runners (the sexually deviant) in this canto, may rest on his didactic intention to strip the dignity (cf. the slow-moving dignity of the noble pagans in *Inferno* IV.112–14, and note to *Purgatorio* III.10–11) from those unnatural sinners (pederasty and homosexuality being traditionally associated with intellectuals, as much as solemnity), and at the same time suggest that sexual malpractice is a private sin shamefully concealed by man in society but inevitably revealed for what it is by God in the Afterlife. Dante's clinching of the canto with the image of the cross-country runners of Verona may also point up his attack on presumptuous intellectuals (see note to l. 85 above) who perversely chase after the corruptible crown of worldly honours and an ephemeral immortality in this life (and preach so to others), whereas the Christian is a spiritual athlete who, seeking to glorify God, achieves the prize of eternal glory in the next life: 'You know (do you not?) that at the sports all the runners run the race, though only one wins the prize. Like them, run to win! But every athlete goes into strict training. They do it to win a fading wreath [AV 'a corruptible crown'], we, a wreath that never fades [AV 'an incorruptible crown'] . . . I bruise my own body and make it know its master, for fear that after preaching

to others, I should find myself rejected' (1 Corinthians 9.24–7).
Cf. *Convivio* IV.XXII.6 ('Many run for the prize [*palio*]'), and
Paradiso XII.56 (the "sacred athlete", St Dominic).

INFERNO XVI

On the burning sands of the Third Round of the Seventh Circle,
Dante encounters three more Florentines guilty of sexual per-
versions: Jacopo Rusticucci, Guido Guerra, and Tegghiaio Aldo-
brandi. Virgil then calls up the monster Geryon from the abyss of
Lower Hell.

20 "Their ancient song": their cries of pain as they suffer the
falling fire and the heat of the sands.

22 "as naked and oiled champions": Dante continues (with
Virgilian reminiscence in the detail of the image here, cf.
Aeneid III.280–82) his sad parody of the spiritual, Christian
athlete of Pauline inspiration (see 1 Corinthians 9.24–7, and
note to *Inferno* XV.121–4). The three Florentines, men of high
capabilities and standing (they were notable political figures of
late thirteenth-century Florence; see notes below), have been
fatally obsessed by the notion of human glory (see ll. 31, 36,
60, 66, 85), which Dante implies derives from a perversion of
spiritual impulses (the object of man's existence at all is to
glorify God), just as homosexuality derives from a perversion
of the natural impulses. Glory, honour and immortality in the
Christian life are only attainable by 'steady persistence in well-
doing', the reward of which is 'eternal life' (see Romans 2.7–8).
See also note to *Inferno* XV.85.

30 "One": Jacopo Rusticucci (see note to ll. 44–5 below).

34–9 Count Guido Guerra (*c.*1220–72), one of the leading Guelfs
of Florence, related to the powerful Conti Guidi family of the
Dovadola branch. Of exemplary vigour and prowess, Guido
suffered the critical reverses of the Florentine Guelfs at
Montaperti in 1260 as an opponent of Farinata degli Uberti (see
notes to *Inferno* X.22–50), but returned victoriously to
Florence after the battle of Benevento (1266), where he had
helped Charles I of Anjou in his defeat of Manfred and the
Ghibellines.

37 Gualdrada: daughter of the Florentine Bellincione Berti dei
Ravignani (see *Paradiso* XV.97–9 and note to XV.112),
virtuous daughter in a virtuous period of Florentine history.

41 Of the Adimari clan of Florence, and a Guelf, Tegghiaio was

podestà of Arezzo in 1256, but escaped the disaster of Montaperti in 1260 (see note to ll. 34–9 above). He did not live to see the Guelf revival of 1266. Although held in esteem by his contemporaries (if the early chroniclers are to be trusted), he is nevertheless described as being "among the blackest souls" by Ciacco in *Inferno* VI.79 f.

44–5 Jacopo Rusticucci, Florentine Guelf knight ("valorous and amiable" according to an early commentator), was of lesser family than Tegghiaio with whom he was closely associated in political events in the city. The name of his "savage wife" is unrecorded. See *Inferno* VI.80 and note to l. 41 above.

63 i.e. to witness the punishment of Satan in the deepest part of Hell.

70 Guglielmo Borsiere: described by Boccaccio in his commentary as a worthy citizen of the minor nobility (see also *Decameron* I.8), and by Benvenuto as a retired pursemaker with ready access to noble houses. Nothing is known of his sexual *mores*.

92 The Phlegethon.

94–102 "that river": the Acquacheta, which flows north-east from its source (Mt Veso) on the eastern slopes ("left side", l. 96) of the Apennines, past S. Benedetto dell'Alpe to Forlì, where it becomes the Montone (l. 99).

102 "where a thousand": i.e. where there would be room for very many cascades, instead of the one uninterrupted fall of some 200 feet to the river bed.

106 "a cord": possibly the cord of the Franciscan Order, of which Dante may have once been a novice (or even a Tertiary in the last years of his life). Using it as something of a hunter's lasso ("folded in a coil" l. 111), Virgil brings the beast Geryon up from the depths of the abyss (see next canto).

108 "the leopard": the symbolic wild animal of the forested valley, representing Dante's inclination to sexual promiscuity (see *Inferno* I.31–43 and notes).

128 "this *Comedy*": see note to *Paradiso* XXX.23.

INFERNO XVII

Geryon appears on the crags at the precipitous edge of the Seventh Circle. Dante talks with the soul of an extortionate banker of Padua before descending with Virgil, on Geryon's back, into the Eighth Circle.

1 f. Geryon: here a hybrid beast, part man, part animal, part reptile, explicitly representing Fraud (l. 7) the second and graver of the malicious sins (see notes to *Inferno* XI.24–5, 82). Dante's version of Geryon differs essentially from Virgil's (*Aeneid* VI.289) with its three bodies. It is closer to Brunetto Latini's *mantichora* (*Tresor* I.V.59) and to the 'locust' of Revelation 9.7–11, and in character to the serpent of Eden in its craftiness and cunning (Genesis 3.1; 2 Corinthians 11.3).

18 Arachne: see note to *Purgatorio* XII.43–5.

31 Dante and Virgil here turn to the right, the second of only two such instances in Hell, where movement is habitually to the left (clockwise). The significance may lie in the fact that Virgil (Reason) is moving, uncharacteristically, in the direction of fraud itself (Geryon, that "foul representation of Fraud", l. 7). See *Inferno* IX.132 and note.

36 "People": the extortionate bankers and moneylenders (userers). See *Inferno* XI.94–11) and notes.

59–60 The armorial device suggests a member of the Gianfigliazzi family of Florence, probably Catello, who died some time after 1283.

62–3 The device of the Ubbriachi of Florence.

64 Probably Rinaldo Scrovegni (d. *c*.1289) of Padua, whose son founded the Scrovegni Chapel, decorated by Giotto (see *Purgatorio* XI.94–6).

68 Vitaliano: according to early commentators, Vitaliano del Dente, *podestà* of Padua in 1307.

72–3 Gianni Buiamonte dei Becchi (*becco*: 'goat') died in 1310 in disrepute after a successful career as moneylender in Florence (he was created a knight before 1298), and as *Gonfaloniere della giustizia* in 1293 was responsible for carrying through the *Ordinamenti della giustizia* of *Giano della Bella* (see *Paradiso* XVI.131 and note).

107–8 Phaeton, son of Phoebus the sun god and Clymene, scorched the sky when he lost control of the chariot of the sun. Struck by a thunderbolt of Jupiter, Phaeton fell into the river Po, whilst the sky still bears marks of the escapade in the Milky Way (Ovid, *Metamorphoses* I.750–II.328 and see *Purgatorio* IV.71–2, *Paradiso* XVII.1–3, *Convivio* II.XIV.5.

109–11 Icarus, wearing the artificial wings made by his father, the inventor Daedalus, fell into the sea and drowned when, thrilled with the experience of flight, he flew too close to the sun (Ovid, *Metamorphoses* VIII.183 f.).

119 The noise is from the waterfall of the blood-red Phlegethon, as it falls into the abyss of Lower Hell.

INFERNO XVIII

The Eighth Circle of Fraud, Dante discloses, is called Malebolge, divided into ten valleys. In the first, amongst the procurers and seducers punished there, Dante talks to an old acquaintance, Venedico Caccianemico, and sees the soul of the Greek hero Jason. Passing across a natural bridge, they look into the second valley, where amongst the flatterers Dante recognises and speaks with Alessio Interminei of Lucca, and sees Thais.

1 "Malebolge": lit. 'evil bags'.

5 "a well": the lowest pit of Hell, the Ninth Circle of Treachery.

16 "projections": forming natural bridges of rock, the projections pass in a straight line over each of the ten valleys.

26–7 Looking on his right into the first valley (the poets are walking in a clockwise direction upon its outer edge), Dante sees two lines of sinners moving in opposite directions. Those closest to him, the go-betweens and pimps, are moving along the outer wall of the valley, in the opposite direction to the poets. Those moving along the inner wall, in the same direction (clockwise), are the seducers and are further from the poets at this point.

28–33 In 1300 Pope Boniface VIII proclaimed a jubilee year ('to honour Christ's birth'), and granted plenary indulgence to all citizens and pilgrims who visited certain shrines in Rome, including old St Peter's (see G. Villani, *Cronica* VIII.36).

29 "the bridge": the Sant'Angelo bridge, over the Tiber.

32 "The castle": the Castel Sant'Angelo.

33 "the hill": Monte Giordano.

35 The horns of the demons suggest those commonly ascribed to cuckolds, whilst their whips lash the procurers and seducers, providing a 'stimulus' in a cruel parody of that which they provided for their clients or roused in their victims. The punishment therefore follows the general principle of the law of retaliation (*contrapasso*) in Dante's Hell (see *Inferno* XXVIII.142 and note).

40 The "somebody": Venedico Caccianemico (l. 50) of Bologna, c.1228–1303 (Dante seemingly mistook the date of his death), an influential Guelf, who was *podestà* of several northern cities including Milan. He was reputed to have offered his sister

Ghisola (Ghisolabella) to his ally Obizzo II d'Este to gain money or advancement, presumably deceiving her by suggesting the possibility of marriage.

58–61 i.e. there are more Bolognese in this part of Hell than in Bologna.

61 "sipa": old Bolognese for 'yes'. Savena and Reno: the two rivers that delimit Bolognese territory.

72 "circles": i.e. the procession of the souls of the procurers around the outer wall of the valley.

74 "a gap": the archway of the natural bridge across the valley.

83 f. "that great spirit": Jason (l. 86), educated by the centaur Chiron (see note to *Inferno* XII.65), leader of the Argonauts in their quest for the Golden Fleece (l. 87), landed on Lemnos where the jealous women had revolted against their neglectful menfolk and were putting them to death. Here he seduced the princess Hypsipyle, who had craftily saved her father Thoas from the general slaughter of the males (l. 90). Subsequently landing at Colchis, having deserted the pregnant Hypsipyle, Jason procured the help of the passionate Medea (l. 96) in securing the Golden Fleece, by promising to marry her. He then abandoned Medea (and her two children by him) for Creusa, princess of Corinth. See Statius, *Thebaid* V.403 f.; Ovid, *Heroides* XII, *Metamorphoses* VII.1 f. See also *Paradiso* II.16–18 and note, XXXIII.96 and note.

104 "the other cleft": the second valley where the flatterers are punished.

116 Alessio Interminei of Lucca (l. 122), of whom little certain is known.

133 Thais, the courtesan in Terence's play *The Eunuch*. But Dante would probably have taken the relevant quotation (ll. 134–5) from Cicero, *De Amicitia* XXVI.98–9.

INFERNO XIX

In the third valley of Malebolge, where the clergy guilty of simony are punished, Dante speaks with Pope Nicholas III, who foretells the imminent arrival there of popes Boniface VIII and Clement V.

1 Simon Magus: Simon of Samaria, a magician (*magus*) baptised by Philip, offered the apostles money in exchange for the 'laying on of hands', the rite that transmitted the supernatural power of the Holy Spirit. He was castigated by Peter: 'Your money go with you to damnation, because you thought God's gift was for sale' (Acts 8.9 f.). 'Simony' is thus the name given to the offence of buying or selling positions in the Church, of providing spiritual offices, such as absolution or the imposition or lifting of bans of excommunication, for cash.

5 i.e. the trumpet of doom: see Matthew 24.31.

6 "the third cleft": the third of the ten valleys of Malebolge.

12 Dante is drawing attention here to the justice of the punishments in Hell. Their justice lies in their aptness, wherein also lies the allegorical heart of *The Divine Comedy*: 'if the work [*Divine Comedy*] be taken allegorically, the subject is man, as by good or ill deserts, in the exercise of the freedom of his choice, he becomes liable to the reward or punishment of Justice' (Dante, *Letters* X, to Can Grande della Scala).

14 "The livid stone": this possibly represents the 'rock' on which Christ built his earthly Church (Matthew 16.18–19), here represented as sadly perforated and spoiled by ecclesiastical corruption (the 'worm' of avarice is suggested).

17 San Giovanni: the Baptistry of Florence which in Dante's day served as the cathedral of the city.

19–21 Dante himself is the only reliable source of this fragment of autobiography.

25–30 The flame plays over the luckless sinners' feet, in a parody of the fire of the Holy Spirit which played over the heads of the apostles at Pentecost (Acts 2.1–4).

45 Nicholas III, pope 1277–80, was of the great Orsini clan of Rome; he unashamedly created cardinals and counts amongst members of his family, the "cubs" referred to in l. 71. The family name Orsini is derived from *orso* ('bear'). G. Villani, in *Cronica* VII.54, comments at length on the liberal nepotism practised by Nicholas.

52–7 Nicholas mistakes Dante's arrival for that of Boniface VIII, the pope in 1300. Created pope in 1294 in suspicious circumstances (see ll. 56–7 and note to *Inferno* III.59–60), Cardinal Benedetto Caetani lived to become the object of Dante's complete detestation. An expert in canon law and a skilful administrator, Boniface was also proud, quick-tempered and autocratic. His scheming led to the *coup* in Florence that resulted in Dante's exile (see notes to *Inferno* VI.64–9), but his peculation and nepotism are independently attested by G. Villani as being on a scale hardly less extensive than that practised by Nicholas III (*Cronica* VIII.6, 64). Boniface died in 1303. See also *Paradiso* XXVII.22 f. and note.

80-81 i.e. Boniface will in turn be pushed down into the hole in less time than twenty-three years after his arrival in Hell (the twenty-three years between Nicholas' arrival in the third valley of Malebolge in 1280, and Boniface's expected arrival in 1303). Boniface would have to wait only eleven years before Clement V's arrival there in 1314 (see note to l. 83 below).

83 "a lawless shepherd": Clement V, pope 1305–14. Of Gascon birth and thus pliable towards King Philip IV of France who had secured his election, Clement established the *Curia* in Avignon in 1309, removing the papacy from its historic seat in Rome (see Dante's condemnation of this in *Purgatorio* XXXII.148–60 and note). However, Clement's simony is attested independently by G. Villani, *Cronica* IX.59. See also *Purgatorio* XXXII.148 f. and note, *Paradiso* XXVII.58 and note, XXX.142–8 and notes.

85 "The new Jason": Jason "seized the high-priesthood" by offering a bribe to King Antiochus of Judaea in the second century BC (2 Maccabees 4.7 f.). Clement was alleged to have resorted to the bribery of Philip IV of France to secure his election as pope.

91–2 See Matthew 16.19.

93 See Matthew 4.18–19.

96 "the guilty soul": Judas Iscariot, the betrayer of Christ, whose place amongst the twelve disciples was filled by Matthias (see Acts 1.26).

99 Nicholas III, it was alleged (it cannot be shown historically), had received foreign money to oust Charles I of Anjou from his kingdom of Sicily. Nicholas's hostility towards Charles I of Anjou was not shared by his predecessors or successors, who looked upon Charles as the champion of the Church and Guelfism in their struggles against the Hohenstaufen and Ghibellines (see note to *Purgatorio* VII.113).

101 "the supreme keys": the Papacy, which in principle Dante totally supported, although openly hostile to certain of the popes, their materialism and their temporal ambitions.

106 "the Evangelist": John, author of the Book of Revelation. Dante takes the imagery of ll. 107–11 from Revelation 17.1 f.

107 "her": the Church, which compromises or 'fornicates' with kings, i.e. succumbs to material temptations, betraying her purity and essential poverty (cf. *Purgatorio* XXXII.148–60 and note).

109–10 "the seven heads": the seven gifts of the spirit; "the ten horns": the Ten Commandments.

111 "her husband": the Papacy.

115–17 Constantine, Emperor 306–37, transferred the seat of Empire from Rome to Byzantium, donating (it was alleged in a document accepted as authentic in the Middle Ages) the western part of the Roman Empire to the Church (under Pope Sylvester I, l. 117) into whose faith he had been baptised. See also *Purgatorio* XXXII.124–9 and note, and *Paradiso* XX.55–9. Dante always denied the legality of the Donation (e.g. *De Monarchia* III.X.4 f.), though did not doubt its authenticity (it was finally proved to be a forgery by Lorenzo Valla in the fifteenth century).

INFERNO XX

In the fourth valley of Malebolge, amongst the futurologists, Virgil points out Manto, and discusses with Dante the origin of Mantua.

11–12 The element of retaliation (*contrapasso*) in the punishment is, as usual, very apt. The futurologists attempted presumptuously to look into the future, and are therefore punished by looking for ever behind them.

28–30 Cf. "The primal will [God], which is good in itself,/Is never less than itself, the supreme good./Whatever is in accord with it, is just" (*Paradiso* XIX.86–8; and see note).

34 Amphiaräus: one of the seven Greek kings at the siege of Thebes. Gifted with prophecy, he foresaw his death there and hid, but his wife Eriphyle treacherously revealed his hiding-place (see *Purgatorio* XII.50–51 and note). Amphiaräus indeed died at Thebes, when he fell into a chasm that opened up in front of his chariot. See *Inferno* XIV.46 and note, and Statius, *Thebaid* VII–VIII.

36 Minos, Judge of Hell; see *Inferno* V.4–15 and note.

40 Tiresias of Thebes was granted the power of prediction by Jupiter, in compensation for his blinding by Juno. Tiresias had been consulted by the gods as to who derived more pleasure from sex, man or woman, since he had been changed into a woman for seven years (by foolishly striking at two intertwined snakes in a wood). Tiresias (truthfully but foolishly) confirmed Jupiter's opinion, against Juno's, that woman derived greater pleasure, and was struck blind by the goddess. See Ovid, *Metamorphoses* III.322 f.

46 Aruns of Luna (modern Luni) predicted that Caesar would win the civil war against Pompey, who would be killed (48BC). See Lucan, *Pharsalia* I.584 f.

52 Manto, fate-telling daughter of Tiresias (see note to l. 40).

58–99 With Virgil's lengthy story here of the founding of his native city Mantua, which elaborates the brief account in *Aeneid* X.198–200, Dante effectively destroys the link between Manto's witchcraft and the city named (later, Dante stresses) after her. Mantua is thus a 'clean' city, and Virgil its greatest son is by that much cleared of the stain of necromancy, an art which popular medieval legend ascribed to him.

59 Thebes, where according to legend Bacchus was born (see *Purgatorio* XVIII.91–2 and note), was governed by the Tyrant Creon after the siege.

63 Benacus (modern Benaco): Lake Garda, in Northern Italy.

65 The Val Comonica lies to the west of Lake Garda, and to the north of Lake Iseo.

67 "a place": probably the island of Lechi, in the middle of Lake Garda, where the dioceses of Trent, Brescia and Verona coincided.

72 Peschiera is at the southernmost point of Lake Garda, where the Mincio (old Mencio, l. 77) flows out southwards to Mantua, thence to join the Po at Governolo (old Governo, l. 78).

94–6 In 1272, Count Alberto da Casalodi lost the lordship of Mantua to Pinamonte dei Buonaccorsi by a ruse, having only just acquired it. The change of power involved the expulsion of many of Mantua's leading families.

106 Eurypylus: Dante mistakenly (and ironically, in view of ll. 113–14) attributed prophetic gifts to Eurypylus, by a misreading of the *Aeneid*. Calchas (l. 110) was the only augur in this incident.

108 The Greeks were largely absent, occupied with the siege of Troy.

111 Aulis: where the oracles of Apollo were uttered. "The moment for cutting the first cable": i.e. the propitious moment for the Greeks to set sail from Troy, after the siege and sack of the city.

113–14 In *Aeneid* II.114. For the use of the term "tragedy" here, see note to *Paradiso* XXX.23.

116 Michael Scott (d. c.1235) the Scottish scholar, translator and astrologer at the court of Emperor Frederick II (see note to

Inferno X.119), was reputed to have been a successful futurologist, but his scholarship and ability as a translator of several of Aristotle's works were probably more reliable.

118 Guido Bonatti of Forlì, author of a widely known treatise on astrology, served as court astrologer to Emperor Frederick II, Guido da Montefeltro, and other famous patrons in the thirteenth century. He may have accurately predicted the date of his own death, but it has not come down to us. Asdente: a shoemaker of Parma in the thirteenth century who turned futurologist, and achieved some notoriety (see Dante, *Convivio* IV.XVI.6).

124–6 The moon ("Cain and the thorns", l. 126; and see note to *Paradiso* II.49–51) is setting in the west ("under Seville", l. 125), seen from the position of an observer in Jerusalem. It is 6 a.m.

127–9 i.e. the moon, being full, was more of a help than a hindrance for Dante in finding his way through the forest. The moon, it was known in Dante's day, reflected the light of the sun, although imperfectly, and so we may perhaps see in these lines an allegorical sense: the wan light of the moon is that of an imperfect faith, whereas the sunlight ("the rays of the planet/Which shows us the right way on any road", *Inferno* I.17–18) is the perfect light of faith leading to salvation. See 1 John 1.5–7. Again, the moon may represent the wisdom of rational or classical philosophy, deprived of the fuller light of revealed or divine wisdom; but a guide nevertheless to life and truth, which if not perfect is better than none at all, and may lead onwards in the search for the source of all wisdom in God (as Virgil leads to Beatrice). The allegory here points up the differences between futurology, which uses the stars and planets for impious and fraudulent ends, and faith and knowledge which, however imperfect, are the only sure guides in resolving the problems of human destiny. Dante, moreover, had a clear idea of the uses as well as the abuses of astrology, which he did not altogether discount as a science. The limits of its truth and usefulness are treated in *Purgatorio* XVI.67–81 (see notes), where the issue of free will and astral determinism is debated. Cf. Psalm 121.6.

129 "the forest": the dark forest where Dante found himself at the beginning of the events of *The Divine Comedy* (*Inferno* 1.2).

INFERNO XXI

From the natural bridge across the fifth valley of Malebolge,
Dante sees the soul of a Lucchese guilty of corruption (barratry)
hurled by a devil into its depths. Virgil then parleys with a group of
demons led by Malacoda, who undertakes to see the poets safely to
an unbroken bridge across the next valley.

7 The Arsenal (military dockyard) of Venice would have been at
least two hundred years old when Dante visited it; it employed
many hundreds of craftsmen. The military and naval centre of
the Serenissima, its major activities were the building and
maintenance of the merchant and warships upon which the
fortunes of the city were founded. The docks may have just
been enlarged to include the New Arsenal when Dante was in
the city for the first time, presumably in the early years of
exile.

37 "Malebranche": lit. 'evil-claws'.

38 "of the Santa Zita council": i.e. of the council of Lucca. Santa
Zita (d. *c*.1272) is the patron saint of Lucca.

41 Bonturo: Bonturo Dati, a leader of the Popular Party in Lucca
in 1300, renowned, according to early commentators, for his
susceptibility to bribery and corruption. The irony of the line
is, of course, intentional. Dante's attack on Lucca for its
widespread corruption is part of a serious polemical intention;
likewise his equating Pisa with cruelty, Padua with extortion,
Pistoia with crime, Siena with gullibility, or Florence with
overwhelming pride (besides other defects). These summary
judgements seem to reflect current folklore in the fierce inter-
city rivalry of the period, where malice followed close on
mockery.

48 "The Volto Santo" (lit. 'holy face') is a crucifix of probably
Byzantine origin, of great antiquity, still venerated in the
cathedral of St Martin in Lucca.

49 the Serchio: a river a few kilometres to the north of Lucca.

76 "Malacoda": lit. 'evil-tail'.

95 Caprona: a castle some eight kilometres east of Pisa, overlook-
ing the Arno from the north. Caprona, held by Pisan
Ghibellines, was taken by the combined Guelf forces of
Florence and Lucca in 1289. The capture was part of an
offensive against Pisa, following the death there of Count
Ugolino earlier in the year (see *Inferno* XXXIII.1 f. and note)

and the expulsion from the city of the Guelf partisans. It is very likely that Dante was present at the fall of Caprona, amongst the Florentine contingent.

112 "this hour": 7 a.m. on the second day (Holy Saturday) of Dante's journey.

114 "since the path was destroyed": the destruction of the natural bridges over the sixth valley occurred at the earthquake which accompanied Christ's death at the Crucifixion, at noon on Good Friday. See Matthew 27.51; *Inferno* V.34 and XII.37–45.

125–6 Malacoda here compounds the lie in l. 111. All the projections (natural bridges) across the sixth valley are broken and impassable.

INFERNO XXII

A damned soul is fished out of the boiling tar of the fifth valley of Malebolge by the demons. A corrupt Navarrese, he willingly tells Dante what souls are under the pitch with him; then, making his escape, he plunges back into the cleft. The winged demons, disappointed at the escape, squabble, and two fall into the tar.

5 "Aretines": Dante refers here explicitly to the campaigns undertaken by Florence in 1288–9 against the territories of Arezzo. The battle of Campaldino in June 1289 decided the outcome, when the Guelfs of Florence roundly defeated the Ghibelline forces of the region they had invaded. See note to *Purgatorio* V.88.

44 f. "the name of that unfortunate": the name, however, is not disclosed by the sinner, who is happy merely to refer to his birthplace Navarre (l. 48), and his service under "the good king Theobald's family" (l. 52), i.e. the family of Thibault II, king of Navarre 1253–70. Early commentators of Dante identify him as Ciampolo (John Paul), but there is no extant documentary evidence concerning him. He lives, however, in this episode of Dante's, which is rich with satirical, grotesque and farcical elements, conceived with the dramatic persuasiveness of the best of Dante's art.

81 "brother Gomita": a friar of Gallura, Sardinia, chief administrator to the Judge of the Judicature (i.e. governor of the district) of Gallura, Ugolino (Nino) Visconti (see *Purgatorio* VIII.47 and note). He was hanged by his patron when his crimes of malversation and graft came to light.

88–9 Lord Michael Zanche: probably Judge of the Judicature (i.e.

governor of the province) of Logudoro, Sardinia. In the last decade or so of the thirteenth century he was murdered at a banquet by his son-in-law Branca d'Oria of Genoa, who hoped to succeed to the title. The soul of Branca d'Oria is in Ptolomaea, one of the zones of the Ninth Circle of the Treacherous (see *Inferno* XXXIII.134 f. and note).

INFERNO XXIII

Pursued by the Malebranche, and unable to find a bridge intact across the next valley of Malebolge, Dante and Virgil escape their clutches by descending hastily to the floor of the sixth cleft. Here, amongst the hypocrites, Dante speaks with brother Catalano of Bologna, a member of the Order of Knights of St Mary (the Wastrel Friars), who points out Caiaphas and Annas in torment.

3 "minor friars": Franciscan monks, so-called because of their dedication to poverty.

4–9 The two demons (engaged in "the brawl", l. 4) were themselves thwarted, having tried to discomfit the Navarrese grafter, in the episode recounted in the previous canto. They thus ended up in the position of the frog in "that fable of Aesop" (l. 5) who aimed to make a meal of the mouse but himself finished in the role of victim.

32 "the next cleft": the sixth valley of Malebolge, where the hypocrites are punished.

63 Cluny: the Benedictine monastery in Burgundy, founded in 910, once a centre of monastic reform but in Dante's day given to soft living.

66 Frederick: Frederick II of Swabia, Emperor 1212–50 (see note to *Inferno* X.119), whose punishments of traitors to the *Regno* were legendary for their oriental savagery, and not merely excogitated as unfavourable propaganda by Guelf historians. If an early commentator is to be believed, Frederick swathed his victim in a cloak of lead which was then melted on him over a slow fire.

95 "the great city": Florence.

103 "Wastrel Friars": the so-called *Frati Gaudenti*, a religious and military order founded in 1261 in Bologna. The Knights of St Mary were known as much for their high living as for their pious activities.

104 Catalano dei Malavolti of Bologna (d. *c*.1285), a Guelf, was one of two *podestà* of Florence in 1266, at a time when the

Ghibellines in the city, their party having suffered a national defeat at Benevento (see note to *Purgatorio* III.103 f.), were looking for an accommodation with the Guelfs. Neither Catalano nor Loderingo his colleague (justifiably, to the minds of modern historians) earned the trust of the Florentines at this critical juncture. See G. Villani, *Cronica* VII.13.

108 The residence of the Ghibelline Uberti family was destroyed under the brief rule of Catalano and his colleague. It was in the area known as the Gardingo, probably near to where the Palazzo della Signoria now stands.

115–17 "The one": Caiaphas, hypocritical high priest of the Temple of Jerusalem who, arguing expediency, proposed the death of Christ. See John 11.49.

121 "his father-in-law": Annas; see John 18.13.

129 "on the right": i.e. towards the next valley, the seventh of Malebolge.

136 Catalano here reveals the lie told and compounded by Malacoda in *Inferno* XXI (see notes to ll. 114, 125–6).

139–46 Virgil's head is bowed in shame as he realises he has been duped by Malacoda. The ingenuousness he has displayed is an indication of the limits of reason unenlightened by grace, that illumination of the mind which reveals evil (not merely good) for what it is. Catalano's definition of the Devil as a "liar, and the father of lies" (l. 44) employs Christ's own words in John 8.44, a piece of divine understanding which did Catalano little good but which might have saved Virgil, disposed to good, from embarrassment, had he but known the Gospels. The allegory of this passage is tactfully and masterfully conveyed in convincing dramatic terms.

INFERNO XXIV

After climbing laboriously out of the sixth valley of Malebolge, Dante and Virgil proceed to a vantage point from where they can observe the inhabitants of the seventh cleft. Here, amongst the thieves, Vanni Fucci talks to Dante.

1–2 "In that part": i.e. from 21 January to 21 February, when the sun is in conjunction with Aquarius. "Tempers her hair": i.e. when its rays become warmer.

3 i.e. towards the spring equinox.

19 "the shattered bridge": the broken bridge formerly spanning the sixth valley (see *Inferno* XXIII.136 and note).

46–57 The verses here exemplify, as few others, the rational, positive and active character of Dante's Virgil.

48 "the way to fame": see notes to *Inferno* XV.85 and XVI.22.

49–51 See Wisdom of Solomon 2.1–5 and 5.14; *Aeneid* 5.740.

55 i.e. both the steep way from the centre of the earth to the surface (to the shore of Purgatory in the Southern Hemisphere), and the climb up the mountain of Purgatory itself.

61 "the jutting rock": the slope of the natural bridge over the seventh cleft.

85–7 Libya: i.e. North Africa. Dante derived his list of snakes from Lucan's *Pharsalia* IX.708 f.

90 "that country": Arabia.

92 "naked people": the thieves and robbers. With their hands tied behind them by snakes, they suffer grotesque, protean transformations in their bodies, punishments reflecting the law of retaliation (*contrapasso*) that governs Hell; their light fingers are now immobilised, and their own most sacred property, their bodies, is subjected to a form of robbery.

107–11 See Ovid, *Metamorphoses* XV.392 f.

112–17 Dante probably refers to the epileptic, whose convulsions were thought to be of either a spiritual or physiological nature.

125 Vanni Fucci, who died in March 1300 (see ll. 122–3), was the illegitimate son ("mule") of a noble family of Pistoia, but given to violence, theft and brigandage. His looting of church treasures from the sacristy of the cathedral of San Zeno, Pistoia, probably occurred in 1293. His thoroughly vicious and depraved character, attested by early chroniclers and commentators, or well brought out by Dante, who because of Vanni's known adherence to the Black Guelf faction (Dante was a White Guelf) attributes to him political prophecy of malicious intent (ll. 142–51).

143 The White Guelfs of Pistoia, aided by the same faction from Florence, expelled the Blacks in May 1301 (G. Villani, *Cronica* VIII.45).

144 Florence's White Guelfs, having expelled or imprisoned their own Black faction in June 1301, were themselves expelled by the Blacks, with the aid of Charles of Valois, in 1302. See Ciacco's prophecy in *Inferno* VI.64 f. and notes, *Purgatorio* XX.71–8 and note. Dante was amongst the exiled Whites.

145–50 The periphrasis, developed with imagery of medieval climatology, most probably refers to the campaigns waged by the Black Guelf Moroello Malaspina, marquis of Giovagallo in the Lunigiana (Val di Magra), leader of the Guelf Alliance and of the Lucchesi (and later a patron of Dante). These, with their allies the Black Guelfs of Pistoia and Florence, waged war in 1302 against Pistoia, which had been held since May 1301 by the Whites of the city (see note to l. 144 above). The war ended with the capture of Pistoia in 1306. See Dante *Letters (Epistolae)* III, and note to *Purgatorio* XIX.142.

145 Mars: the god of war.

148 Campo Picen [Piceno]; it is not clear what precisely Dante meant by this name (a calque of Sallust's *Ager Picenus*), but probably the reference is to Pistoiese territory in general.

INFERNO XXV

Dante and Virgil observe the hideous transformations of five of the souls of the thieves, all Florentines, in the seventh valley of Malebolge.

1–3 "the thief": Vanni Fucci, the sacrilegious thief (see previous canto). Dante completes the portrait of this vicious Pistoiese with graphic detail.

10 "Oh, Pistoia": see note to *Inferno* XXI.41.

10–12 Dante may have had in mind not only the ancient tradition that Pistoia was founded *c*.62BC by the surviving members of the insurgent Cataline's ill-famed and ill-fated band, but also the fact that the destinies of Pistoia and Florence seemed harmfully and inextricably entwined (see notes to *Inferno* XXIV.143–50).

15 Capaneus, the blasphemer, in the Third Round of the Seventh Circle of Hell (see *Inferno* XIV.46 f. and note).

15–18 "a centaur": the centaurs are mainly employed by Dante as guardians of the perpetrators of violence, in the First Round of the Seventh Circle. Dante's use of one here, to persecute Vanni Fucci, emphasises the violent, aggressive nature of the thief from Pistoia, and also that his defiance of God, seen in ll. 1–3 of this canto, is to the order of violence of the blasphemous in the Third Round.

19 The Tuscan Maremma was then a wild, uncultivated region; see *Inferno* XIII.7–9 and note.

25 Cacus: Dante transforms this Virgilian monster (*Aeneid* VIII.193 f.) into a centaur. Having stolen some cattle belonging to Hercules, the hybrid beast was summarily choked (Virgil) or beaten to death (Dante, following Livy) by the hero.

26 The Aventine hill: one of the seven hills of ancient Rome.

43 Cianfa: a Florentine, contemporary of Dante, probably of the Donati clan, and according to an early commentator a thief of catholic accomplishments.

68 Agnello: probably Agnello dei Brunelleschi, of a Florentine patrician family, whose career of theft is recorded by one early commentator.

94–5 Lucan, in *Pharsalia* IX.763 f., recounts the horrifying death by snake-bite, in the Libyan desert, of Sabellus, whose body at once dissolved in putrefaction, and of Nasidius, who swelled enormously to burst his breastplate. Dante develops the matter of this canto with great imaginative verve and technical virtuosity in conscious emulation of the classical masters of the metamorphosis, particularly Ovid.

97–8 Ovid, in *Metamorphoses* IV.563 f., relates how Cadmus, the king of Thebes, was changed in old age into a snake as a punishment for killing a serpent sacred to Mars. The nymph Arethusa was transformed into a fountain by Dictynna (Diana) to save her from the embraces of Alpheus the river god (Ovid, op. cit. V.572 f.).

138 Human spittle was popularly believed to be poisonous to snakes.

140 Buoso: a Florentine, either Buoso degli Abati or, more likely, Buoso Donati, uncle of Forese (see note to *Purgatorio* XXIII.40).

148 Puccio Sciancato: Puccio Galigai of Florence, known as '*Sciancato*' ('lame').

151 Francesco dei Cavalcanti, '*il Guercio*' ('cross-eyed'), member of the Florentine patrician clan of that name (see *Inferno* X.53 f. and note), was killed by the oppressed and abused villagers of Gaville in the Val d'Arno, who were decimated by the Cavalcanti in revenge.

INFERNO XXVI

In the eighth cleft of Malebolge, amongst the advisers of deceit and strategems (souls guilty of the fraudulent use of intellect and eloquence), Dante hears Ulysses recount the story of his last, fatal voyage.

7 For the understanding in the Middle Ages of the reliability of the so-called dawn-dream, see note to *Purgatorio* IX.16–18. Dante experiences three such prophetic dreams in the course of his climb up Mount Purgatory (*Purgatorio* IX, XIX, XXVII).

9 Prato: the prophecy is obscure, and commentators from earliest times have proposed different solutions. The reference is either to the rebellion of Prato against its powerful and doubtless predatory neighbour, Florence, in 1309, or to the interdict that Cardinal Niccolò da Prato pronounced on Florence for its wilful failure, in 1304, to arrive at an accommodation with its White Guelf citizens in exile (amongst whom Dante; see *Inferno* X.79–81 and note).

19–24 Before embarking upon his description of the events in the eighth valley, where the corrupt advisers are punished for their misuse of intellect and eloquence, Dante, amply endowed with both faculties (cf. *Inferno* II.7 and X.59, *Purgatorio* XXX.109–17, *Paradiso* XXII.111–17), admonishes himself lest he too fall into the same error. See ll. 43–5, where this proclivity is confessed allegorically, and Virgil's admonition in l. 72.

23 "my good star": see *Inferno* XV.55–6, *Purgatorio* XXX.109 f., *Paradiso* XXII.111–17 and note.

26–7 i.e. during the summer, when the days are longer than the nights.

34–6 It was the fate of the children of Bethel, in punishment for their mockery of the prophet Elisha, to be devoured by a bear (2 Kings 2.23–4). Elisha had just witnessed Elijah's ascent into heaven in a chariot of fire, drawn by fiery horses (ib. v. 11).

47–8 The corrupt advisers, guilty of misapplying their intellectual powers, are similarly guilty of the abuse of eloquence. In Hell they are completely enveloped in flames, like burning torches, the flickering tips of which suggest moving tongues (see l. 89, and XXVII.13 f.) and seem to function as such. The imagery may have been in part suggested to Dante by St James' letter in the New Testament; 'And the tongue is in effect a fire . . . it pollutes our whole being . . . and its flames are fed by hell' (James 3.6; and see J. D. Sinclair's commentary). The tongue is seen in the Bible as the instrument of evil ('For the words that the mouth utters come from the overflowing of the heart', Matthew 12.34), and its wagging may produce much harm; Dante's reference here to the children of Bethel's gratuitous mockery of Elisha (l. 34) is pertinent, as are also the terms of Virgil's warning to Dante (l. 72). The didactic aim of this canto of *Inferno* may in many ways be summed up in terms of the same letter of St James: 'Who among you is wise and clever? Let his right conduct give practical proof of it, with the

modesty that comes of wisdom' (James 3.13); and Dante may
have exploited the same chapter of James for significant
imagery, other than that of the fiery tongue alone. The whole
conception of the sea voyage in this canto, and Ulysses'
exploitation of his comrades' loyalty, may have found its
genesis in: 'Or think of ships: large they may be, yet even
when driven by strong gales they can be directed by a tiny
rudder on whatever course the helmsman chooses. So with the
tongue. It is a small member but it can make huge claims'
(ib. 3.4). Dante's use of selected portions of the Bible at
important moments in *The Divine Comedy* as a source of
imagery as well as doctrine may be seen also in *Inferno* V and
XIII (see Bibliography, D. H. Higgins). See also Introduc-
tion.

52–4 Eteocles and his twin brother Polynices, sons of Oedipus,
were joint kings of Thebes, agreeing to reign in alternate years.
In dispute over the agreement, the twins killed each other in
combat during the war waged against Thebes by the seven
kings. Even the flame that rose from their joint funeral pyre
was divided. See Statius, *Thebaid* XII.429 f., and *Purgatorio*
XXII.55–6 and note.

55 f. Ulysses (Odysseus) one of the major Greek heroes at the
siege of Troy (see Homer's *Iliad*), was the son of the aged
Laertes (l. 95) and king of Ithaca. Rejected by Helen, he
married Penelope (l. 96) instead, by whom his son Telemachus
(l. 94) was born. His adventurous journey of return to Ithaca,
after the fall of Troy in which he played a principal part, is
recounted in Homer's *Odyssey*, a work which, with the *Iliad*,
Dante did not know at first hand for historical reasons (see
Inferno IV.86–8 and note). Together with Diomed, king of
Argos (l. 56), Ulysses enticed Achilles away from Deidamia
(l. 62; and see note to *Purgatorio* XXII.110–14) to join the
expedition against Troy (even though he knew of a prophecy
that predicted Achilles' death there), stole from Troy the
sacred statue of Pallas Athene ("the Palladium", l. 63) upon
which the security of the city depended, and was credited by
Laocoon (although he makes no mention of Diomed) with the
stratagem of the wooden horse. This contained Greek soldiers
and was brought unsuspectingly into the city by the Trojans,
who foolishly listened to the arguments of Sinon, the supposed
Greek renegade (see *Inferno* XXX.98 and note). The ensuing
fall of Troy, attacked treacherously from within is recounted in

Virgil, *Aeneid* II.13 f. The picture of Ulysses here in Dante, ruthless (l. 57), scheming and dishonest, an unprincipled but talented aristocrat who coldly applied his intellect and his considerable gifts of eloquence to sacrilegious ends, is part of the darker tradition of representation of the hero, alive in the post-homeric legend of classical times and the Middle Ages (see Bibliography, W. B. Stanford).

82 "those high verses": the *Aeneid*.

90 f. Ulysses' account of his death, given here by Dante, is not consonant with classical or medieval tradition. Dante probably did not know Homer's prediction of a peaceful end for Ulysses (although one early commentator points out that Dante would have known of the hero's return to Ithaca). Nor did Dante appear to know the post-homeric account by Dictys Cretensis, current in the Middle Ages, of his death at the hands of his natural son by Circe. Dante's version of Ulysses' end is original, compelling and certainly more consistent with the hero, as we know him, than the sordid parricide in Dictys.

91 Circe, the semi-divine enchantress of the island of Aeaea, requested Ulysses to remain with her for a year, as repayment for her transforming his comrades from pigs to men again. Dante took the detail of this stage of Ulysses' story (but not the account of the voyage, which is his own) from Ovid, *Metamorphoses* XIV (see Bibliography, B. Reynolds).

93 See Virgil, *Aeneid* VII.1–4.

97–9 Ulysses' inquiring mind and restless intellect are well conveyed here, characteristics of the hero that Dante would have found emphasised in Horace, Cicero and Ovid, certainly more than in Virgil. Dante's condemnation of Ulysses is not on the grounds of intellectual curiosity as such. Dante's reverence for knowledge is indicated by his epigrams, such as 'Knowledge is the distinguishing perfection of our soul' (*Convivio* I.I.1), and 'life in man is exercising the reason' (ib. IV.VII.12). Ulysses is in Dante's Hell because he was guilty of what in the Middle Ages was regarded as intellectual promiscuity (*'prostitutio nostrae virtutis rationalis'*, R. Montano): not only the use of ruses and cunning (see ll. 58–63), and the misuse of high eloquence to persuade men to commit foolishness or worse (see Ulysses' persuasive but specious arguments to his men in ll. 112–20), but also the intellectual folly of reaching out to explore areas of knowledge considered beyond the right, or good, of man to know, presumption which is swiftly recompensed (ll. 136–42). A certain sort of wisdom, as St James puts it, does not 'come from above; it is earth-bound, sensual, demonic' (James 3.15). See also *Purgatorio* III.37 and note.

107–9 The so-called Pillars of Hercules (Mount Abyla in North Africa, and Gibraltar), were considered to be the westernmost limit of man's knowable world, and hence endowed with primitive religious significance. See the Hereford 'Mappa mundi' (*c*.1290), on p. 25. In another context Dante quotes, from Proverbs, what is apposite here: 'Pass not the ancient boundaries which thy fathers set up' (*Convivio* IV.VII.9). See also Dante's description of Adam's sin, in *Paradiso* XXVI.117.

110–11 Seville: the straits of Gibraltar were also known as the straits of Seville. Ceuta: in Morocco.

112–20 Ulysses' words of encouragement to his men to effect a "foolish flight" (l. 125) reflect something of Aeneas's words in *Aeneid* I.198 f., rallying his men to fulfil a pious voyage (its divine purpose, to find Italy and establish the Roman race). Dante presents Ulysses here very much as the dark to Aeneas's light.

119–20 See Dante, *Convivio* II.VII.3–4, quoted in note to *Inferno* V.39.

125 "foolish flight": see *Paradiso* XXVII.82–3, and Bibliography, J. A. Scott.

126 Ulysses' ship bends its course southwards, into what was then regarded by most authorities as the Southern ('austral') Hemisphere of the globe, covered entirely by ocean. Here, however, Dante places his Mount Purgatory on an island, where the souls of repentant Christians are purged before ascending to heaven (see note to *Purgatorio* I.4–6). It is this holy mountain that the presumptuous Ulysses sights, l. 133.

130–31 i.e. five months had passed.

141 "another": God. Cf. Job 36.13–14: 'Dissemblers and crafty men prove the wrath of God . . . their soul shall die in a storm' (Vulgate), and Seneca's *Letters*, 88.7: "we daily encounter storms of the spirit and our depravity drives us into all the woes of Ulysses."

INFERNO XXVII

In the eighth cleft of Malebolge, Dante encounters Guido da Montefeltro, damned in Hell as an adviser of stratagems.

7–12 "the Sicilian bull": an instrument of torture in the shape of a bull constructed in brass by Perillus (l. 9) for his master Phalaris, tyrant of Agrigentum, Sicily. The cries for mercy of the victim, who was enclosed in the contraption, were turned to bellows as the device was heated. Perillus was its first victim. The story is recounted by several authors, including Ovid, Pliny, and Paulus Orosius.

19 f. According to the early commentators, the voice is that of Guido da Montefeltro, *c*.1220–98, captain-general of the Ghibellines in the Romagna, where he inflicted notable defeats on Guelf and papal forces. In 1283 the Romagna reverted to papal authority, and Guido was exiled. Appointed *podestà* of Pisa in 1289, shortly after the resignation of Archbishop Ruggieri from that office (see note to *Inferno* XXXIII.13–14), Guido led the city in its struggles with Guelf Florence (see note to *Inferno* XXI.95) until 1293 when a peace, disastrous to Pisa's interests, was concluded, and Guido's services were dispensed with. He retired to Urbino, where in spite of earlier excommunications he was reconciled to the Church, and in 1296 became a Franciscan monk (ll. 79–83). Guido was a noble of acknowledged courage and sagacity and long experience (he was known as "the fox", l. 75), but before his death, if Dante's account here is reliable, he advised Pope Boniface VIII on the most expedient way to defeat his enemies the Colonna, and in terms that earned him his damnation. See *Convivio* IV.XXVIII.8; G. Villani, *Cronica* VIII.23.

29–30 i.e. Montefeltro, which lies in the region of the Romagna and its Marches, between Urbino and Mount Coronaro in the Apennines.

37–9 In the course of the thirteenth century the cities of the Romagna were constantly in the turmoils of war, sedition, rebellion and repression, as the struggle between Guelf communes and Ghibelline 'tyrants' and overlords intensified. A general peace was initiated, however, in 1299 by Pope Boniface VIII.

40–42 Ravenna, together with Cervia and its salterns, had reverted to the authority of the Polenta family (whose arms bore a silver eagle) in the late thirteenth century. See note to *Inferno* V.97–9.

43–5 "The city": Forlì had been successfully defended by Guido da Montefeltro during 1281–3 against Italian troops and French mercenaries in the army of Pope Martin IV. In 1282 the French suffered heavy losses there (l. 44) at Guido's hands.

Later Forlì came under the Guelf rule of the Ordelaffi family, whose device was a green lion on a gold field.

46–8 "The old mastiff": Malatesta da Verrucchio (father-in-law of Francesca; *Inferno* V.88) and his eldest son Malatestino ("the young one"), were successively Guelf Lords of Rimini from 1295, after the Ghibellines had been ousted. The Ghibelline leader, Montagna dei Parcitati, was ruthlessly done to death, probably by Malatestino.

49–51 Faenza (on the river Lamone), and Imola (on the Santerno) were ruled in 1300 by Maghinardo Pagani da Susinana (d. 1302), whose arms were a blue lion on a white field. He was called 'the Demon' because of his craftiness (see *Purgatorio* XIV, 118 and note). His family was Ghibelline in his native Romagna, but Maghinardo was a fervent supporter of Guelf Florence on the field of battle, to which city he owed loyalty through his education there, and because of his Florentine wife. See G. Villani, *Cronica* VII.149.

52–4 "that city": Cesena, on the river Savio, was in 1300 a commune, Guelf in spirit, governed by one of the Ghibelline Montefeltro clan. Its freedom as an independent and virtually self-governing city was thus impaired by someone of Ghibelline sympathies who occupied, nevertheless, the influential position of Captain of the People and *podestà*.

70 "the high priest": Pope Boniface VIII.

85 f. Pope Boniface VIII ("the Prince of the new Pharisees") had been at loggerheads with the aristocratic Colonna family of Rome since his election as pope in 1294, following the abdication of Celestine V ("my predecessor", l. 105; see *Inferno* III.59–60 and note). The Colonna refused to recognise the validity of his election, and in 1297 Boniface retaliated by dismissing two cardinals in the family from office. The clan retreated to its strongholds, including their castle at Palestrina (old "Penestrino", l. 102) near Rome, in defiance. Boniface's troops took the castles the following year. See note to *Inferno* XIX.52–7.

86 "the Lateran": the Lateran palace, the main Roman residence of the medieval popes before the Vatican palace was built.

89 Acre, the major port of disembarkation in the Holy Land in the era of the crusades, was in Christian hands until 1291. When it was conquered by the Saracens, Pope Nicholas IV insisted that all Christian trade with Egypt ("the Soldan's country", l. 90) should cease.

93 The Franciscan Order was traditionally wed to poverty, but by 1300 had declined from its original purity. An ascetic movement (the Franciscan Spirituals) was alive in the Order in Dante's day, dedicated to reform. See *Paradiso* XII.112 f.

94–6 The Emperor Constantine (see *Inferno* XIX.115–17 and note) was reputed to have been stricken with leprosy in punishment for his persecution of the early Christians in Rome, and to have been cured by Pope Sylvester I who had taken refuge on Mount Soracte, north of the city. There followed Constantine's conversion to Christianity, and the recognition of Christianity as the official religion of the Roman world. The essential divergences between the circumstances of Constantine's cure and that effected on Boniface (in a purported simile) illuminate the sin of Guido himself; the gloss of eloquence is hardly adequate to disguise the perverted intellect that develops such a defective and fraudulent figure of speech.

104 "the two keys": the symbolic keys of the papacy; see note to *Purgatorio* IX.117–27.

112 Francis: St Francis of Assisi (d. 1226), founder of the monastic Order of the Franciscans. The dispute over the soul of Guido between St Francis and a black cherub will find a parallel in Dante's account of the fate of Guido's son Buonconte da Montefeltro who, although unabsolved, repented at the moment of his death and found salvation (see *Purgatorio* V.85 f. and note).

118–23 The intellectual dishonesty of Boniface VIII makes a dupe of Guido by promising an absurdity: absolution 'on account', in advance of a premeditated sin (ll. 108–9 and 118–19). Guido's perverted mind contrives the cunning and dishonest advice that brings down the Pope's enemies, but at the same time, caught in its own subtlety, fails to discern the intellectual fraud perpetrated on him by Boniface. The black cherub (a fallen angel of the order of Cherubim, dedicated to Knowledge) ironically uses truth to expose both the fraud of Boniface and the error of Guido. Guido is thus twice duped; and duped once more by Dante, who does not disclose to him that he is indeed alive and will return to the world to shame Guido's memory (see ll. 61–6). An appropriate commentary on this episode, of the sort which Dante may well have had in mind, is provided in the rich spiritual matter of Psalms: 'The wicked man's ways are always devious, but thy judgements are beyond his grasp . . .

His mouth is full of lies and violence; mischief and trouble lurk under his tongue' (ib. 10.5–7); 'He has made a pit and dug it deep, and he himself shall fall into the hole that he has made. His mischief shall recoil upon himself' (ib. 7.15–16).

124 Minos: see *Inferno* V.4 f. and note.

INFERNO XXVIII

Dante looks down into the ninth valley of Malebolge, where the instigators of scandal and schism are punished. Mahomet, Pier da Medicina, Mosca dei Lamberti and Bertram de Born are amongst the afflicted souls.

8 Apulia: i.e. the whole of Southern Italy, comprising in Dante's day the Kingdom of Naples, the arena throughout history of much political struggle and bloodshed.

10 "the Trojans": Dante probably refers, by antonomasia, to the Romans as descendants of the Trojans, and hence to the hard-fought wars of Rome's early period of expansion; "that long war": the Second Punic War when, following their victory at Cannae (216BC), the Carthaginians robbed the many Roman dead of their gold rings. See Livy, *History of Rome* XXIII.12.

14 Robert Guiscard: see note to *Paradiso* XVIII.47.

16–17 Ceperano: modern Ceprano, in Lazio. There was, in fact, no battle fought at Ceprano to account for the slaughter implied in l. 15. Dante most probably refers to the retreat from Ceprano, prior to the battle of Benevento in 1266. In this battle there was much cowardice on the part of the southern barons in King Manfred's army, and much blood spilt by the contending army of Charles I of Anjou. See G. Villani, *Cronica* VII.6–9, and note to *Purgatorio* III.103 f.

17–18 At the battle of Tagliacozzo in 1268 when Conradin, the last of the imperial Hohenstaufen, was defeated Villani records that the victorious Charles I of Anjou followed the tactical advice of a French knight Érard (Alardo) de Valéry, Constable of Champagne. See G. Villani, *Cronica* VII.26 f., and note to *Purgatorio* VII.113.

23 "one": Mahomet (see l. 31), otherwise Mohammed (d. 632), was believed to have been a Christian before founding the religion of Islam. See *Purgatorio* XXXII.130–35 and note.

32 Ali: Ali ibn-abi-Talib (d. 661) married Mohammed's daughter Fatima. His succession to the Caliphate brought about the split in Islam between the Shiites and the Sunnites.

55–60 Brother (Fra) Dolcino Tornielli, leader of the reforming sect of the Apostolic Brotherhood, took refuge with his followers in the hills near Novara following a papal decree to suppress them in 1305. After a severe winter of starvation, the sectarians fell victim to the troops of the Bishop of Novara, who massacred or burned many. Brother Dolcino was captured and burned to death in 1307. The Church's accusation of schism was clearly accepted by Dante, although the Brotherhood's original aims to bring the Church back to its primitive poverty were not inconsistent with Dante's own.

64 "Another": Pier da Medicina (see l. 73), probably related to the lords of Medicina, a resident of Bologna about whom nothing certain is known other than that he was an acquaintance of Dante. The early commentators, however, elaborate upon his unusual ability to create and exploit dissension amongst the lords and tyrants of the Romagna for his own material gain.

74 Vercelli in Piedmont, and Marcabo (formerly a fortress on the Po, near Ravenna) delimit the region of the Po valley.

76–90 Malatestino of Rimini (the "ferocious tyrant", l. 81; "That traitor" l. 85), known as the 'Young Mastiff' (see *Inferno* XXVII.46–8 and note), probably engineered the death in 1312 of two leading citizens of Fano, Guido del Cassero and Angiolello di Carignano, in order to secure the mastery of the city for himself.

86 "the land": Rimini.

86–7 "one . . . he": Curio (see note to l. 95 below).

90 "the Focara wind": the cape of Focara, near La Cattolica, was feared for its violent squalls, and it was customary amongst navigators to pray or offer vows when in its vicinity.

95 "one of his companions": Gaius Curio (d. 49BC), tribune of the people, abandoned Pompey to join Julius Caesar's faction. Dante follows Lucan (*Pharsalia* I.261 f.) by attributing to Curio the advice that Caesar should cross the river Rubicon (just north of Rimini) into republican Italy and begin thereby the civil war.

106–8 In 1215 Mosca dei Lamberti of Florence proffered the fatal advice to the Ghibelline Amidei clan that they should assassinate Buondelmonte dei Buondelmonti, a Guelf, for his jilting one of their daughters, thus beginning the disastrous feud between Guelfs and Ghibellines in the city. See note to *Paradiso* XVI.140.

119 The decapitated body is that of Bertram de Born (see l. 134), c.1140–1202, lord of Hautefort (Dordogne), a warrior-poet, the friend and confidant of Prince Henry the "young king" (l. 135), son of Henry II of England. Prince Henry's rebellion against his father continued intermittently between 1172 and 1183 when he died, and was believed to have been engineered by Bertram. Dante's earlier opinion of Bertram, as a man of generous character (*Convivio* IV.XI.14) and an accomplished troubadour poet (*De Vulgari Eloquentia* II.II.9), appears to ignore this darker side of his career, noted in one of the *razos* to his poems.

137–8 Absalom, the son of King David, was incited to rebel against his father by Ahithophel, David's trusted counsellor and friend. See 2 Samuel 15–19.

142 "retaliation" (Italian *contrapasso*) is the principle rigorously followed by Dante in his conception of the punishments of Hell. Its origins lie in the biblical injunctions of Exodus: 'Wherever hurt is done, you shall give life for life, eye for eye, tooth for tooth, hand for hand, foot for foot, burn for burn, bruise for bruise, wound for wound' (ib. 21.23–5). The word *contrapasso*, however, derives from the medieval Latin translation of a term in Aristotle's *Nichomachean Ethics*. Cf. also Wisdom 11.17: 'By what things a man sinneth, by the same he is tormented'.

INFERNO XXIX

In the tenth and final valley of Malebolge, where falsifiers are punished, Dante talks with two alchemists, Griffolino d'Arezzo and Capocchio.

1 f. "The number of people": in the preamble of this canto, Dante is still rapt in observation of the mutilated souls of the instigators of dissension in the ninth chasm of Malebolge.

9 An exact estimate of the size of a portion of Hell is given also in the next canto (*Inferno* XXX.86), where the circumference of the tenth valley is given as eleven miles. The distance across the ninth *bolgia* is thus seven miles (Dante had π in mind) narrowing rapidly to three and a half miles across the tenth.

10 It is about 1 p.m. on Holy Saturday with the moon over the meridian line of Purgatory in the Southern Hemisphere, diametrically opposite the sun, which would now stand over Jerusalem. The journey through Hell is now about eighteen hours old and is destined to last for twenty-four hours. For

other time references see *Inferno* XI.113–14 (4 a.m.) and XX.124–6 (6 a.m.).

20 "a ghost from my family": Geri del Bello degli Alighieri (l. 27), to whom Dante was cousin once removed, was reputed a trouble-maker. He was finally assassinated, most likely by one of the Sacchetti family, some time after 1276. Both law and custom in Florence sanctioned vendetta, but the Alighieri as late as 1300 had not yet avenged his death. Nor were they destined to do so, for the blood-feud between the two families was settled by a formal reconciliation in 1342, twenty-one years after Dante's death.

29 Bertram de Born, Lord of Hautefort. See *Inferno* XXVIII.119 f. and note.

46–8 The Valdichiana in Tuscany, the Tuscan Maremma, and Sardinia, were all notorious pockets of malaria in Dante's day.

58–64 Jealous and enraged by her consort Jupiter's love for the nymph Aegina, Juno struck the island named after her with a deadly plague. The king Aeacus, Aegina's and Jupiter's son, prayed to his father in desperation, who repopulated the island with men (Myrmidons) transformed from the ants which lived in an oak sacred to him. See Ovid, *Metamorphoses* VII.523 f.; and *Convivio* IV.XXVII.17.

109 "an Arezzo man": early commentators identify him as Griffolino d'Arezzo, an alchemist. The gullible Albert of Siena is the subject of some stories in Sacchetti's *Novelle*.

116 Daedalus constructed wings for himself and his son Icarus in order to escape from Crete where he had constructed the labyrinth of King Minos. See note to *Inferno* XVII.109–11.

117 "his father in God": the bishop of Siena, according to one of Dante's early commentators, who also suggests that Albert was the bishop's illegitimate son.

119 "alchemy": the early and entirely legal science of extracting metals from their ores. The knowledge and skills involved were put to illicit use in research for the 'philosophers' stone', which was supposed to produce gold and silver from base metals.

120 Minos: see *Inferno* V.4 and note.

121–3 See note to *Inferno* XXI.41.

124 "The other leper": Capocchio (l. 136), according to one early commentator, had been a Florentine student and acquaintance of Dante, gifted in mimicry. He was executed as an alchemist in Siena, by burning, in 1293.

125–32 The identities of Stricca and Niccolò are not known with certainty, but both (taking Dante's irony into account) would have been extremely frivolous men, probably spendthrift.

129 "a garden": Siena.

130 "the company": the Spendthrifts Club (*Brigata Spendereccia*), a group of young men of Siena in the second half of the thirteenth century, dedicated to dissipation. See also *Inferno* XIII.118 and note.

130–31 Caccia of Asciano (d. after 1293) swiftly dissipated his patrimony of vineyards and lands. He was related to the wealthy Scialenghi clan.

132 "his crack-brained friend": Bartolommeo dei Folcacchieri of Siena (d. 1300), who held important Guelf offices in Tuscany. The escapade referred to is not known.

INFERNO XXX

Amongst the falsifiers, Dante sees the souls of two impersonators, Gianni Schicchi dei Cavalcanti and Myrrha, and witnesses a sordid squabble between Master Adam, a counterfeiter, and the Greek perjurer Sinon.

1–12 Athamas, made insane by Juno as part of her revenge against the Thebans, in his madness took his wife Ino and their two children for a lioness with her cubs, with the horrifying results recorded in this lengthy simile (see Ovid, *Metamorphoses* IV.464 f.). For the story of Semele princess of Thebes and Juno see note to *Paradiso* XXI.6.

13–21 As prisoner of the Greeks after their capture of Troy, Queen Hecuba witnessed the sacrifice of her daughter Polyxena on the tomb of the Greek hero Achilles, and then found the mutilated body of her son Polydorus washed up on the shore. Polydorus and a sizeable treasure had been entrusted to Polymnestor, king of Thrace, for safekeeping during the Trojan war. Polymnestor, who had murdered Polydorus to gain the treasure, was in turn savagely mutilated by Hecuba, whose defiant cries were heard as the barking of a mad dog. See Ovid, *Metamorphoses* XIII.402 f.

31 "the Aretine": Griffolino d'Arezzo (see previous canto).

32 Gianni Schicchi dei Cavalcanti (d. *c.*1280), of Florence, a noted mimic, impersonated the recently dead father (Buoso di Vinciguerra) of his friend Simone Donati, in order to ensure for Simone a major share of his father's estate. Gianni, disguised as the dying Buoso, also nominated himself (to the chagrin of Simone) the beneficiary of some of the estate, including a valuable mare ("the lady of the company", l. 43).

38 Myrrha, daughter of the king of Cyprus, used disguise to gratify her incestuous passion for her father. She fled when her father discovered the deception, and was turned into a myrrh tree. See Ovid, *Metamorphoses* X.298 f.

49 f. "one": Master Adam (l. 61), most probably an Englishman in the employ of one of the branches of the Conti Guidi clan, the counts of Romena in the Casentino. The territories of the family of brothers (two named in l. 77) lay some kilometres to the east of Florence. In conflict with the burgesses of Florence, the brothers issued false and debased florins (ll. 89–90) coined by Adam; it was Adam who was caught, tried and burned at the stake for the crime, in Florence, in 1281.

78 "Branda spring": either a spring of that name near the castle of Romena, or that of Siena.

97 "the wife who falsely accused Joseph": Potiphar's wife, disappointed at Joseph's refusal to make love to her, brought about his immediate imprisonment on a charge of attempted violation. See Genesis 39.6 f.

98 The Greek Sinon, representing himself as a renegade, so gained access to Troy and persuaded the Trojans to admit the wooden horse, a subterfuge which led directly to the city's capture. See note to *Inferno* XXVI.55 f.; Virgil, *Aeneid* II.57 f.

128 "the mirror of Narcissus": water. See note to *Paradiso* III.17–18.

145 "I am here": the words reproaching Dante's unseemly curiosity draw attention to the allegorical role of Virgil as reason, which, counselling temperateness, preserves the proper dignity of the soul committed to virtue.

INFERNO XXXI

Leaving Malebolge, Dante and Virgil encounter the giants who guard the Ninth Circle. At Virgil's command Antaeus lowers them down into the icy well, Cocytus, where the souls guilty of treachery are punished.

4–6 The lance of Achilles, handed on to him by his father Peleus, had the property of healing the wounds that were inflicted by it. See Ovid, *Metamorphoses* XIII.171–2.

16–18 In his campaign of 778 against the Moors in Spain, Charlemagne suffered a severe reverse at Saragossa. In his retreat through the Pyrenees, the rear-guard of his army commanded by his nephew Roland was wiped out at Roncesvalles through the treachery of the legendary Ganelon of Mayence. Roland delayed blowing on his horn to summon help until it was too late. The slaughter of Roncesvalles is the climax of the ancient *Song of Roland*, well known to Dante as to the whole medieval world. See also *Paradiso* XVIII.43 and note; *Inferno* XXXII.122.

41 Montereggione (modern Montereggioni), a thirteenth-century castle in the Val d'Elsa near Siena, still stands with its fourteen encircling towers, which are now somewhat lower than in Dante's day.

44–5 Jove (Jupiter), hurling thunderbolts, and with the help of Hercules, defeated the Titans (the giant Sons of Earth) who rebelled against the gods and attempted to storm Olympus. The battle took place on the field of Phlegra.

51 Mars: the god of war.

55–7 This is the conclusion drawn by Aristotle in *Politics* I.1. It was the stupidity of the giants in Baruch 3.26–8 that brought about their fortunate extinction.

59 The stone pine-cone, some twelve feet high, now stands in the Vatican gardens. Of Roman origin, it stood originally near the Field of Mars in the city, and was transferred in the sixth century to old St Peter's, where Dante would have seen it.

64 Frieslanders were clearly noted for their stature in Dante's day, although no other corroboration of this popular belief has been found.

77 Nimrod, 'mighty hunter before the Lord', was commonly credited with the building of the Tower of Babel, when the confusion of languages occurred (see Genesis 10.8–10, 11.1–9; Brunetto Latini, *Tresor* I.24). He was represented as a giant by St Augustine and Paulus Orosius. See also *Purgatorio* XII.34 and note.

94 Ephialtes, with his brother Otus, giant sons of Aloeus, by piling Mt Pelion on Mt Ossa assaulted Olympus in an attempt to tear it down and unseat Jupiter (Virgil, *Aeneid* VI.580–84; Horace, *Odes* III.IV.42–52).

99 Briareus: or Aegaeon, one of the rebellious Titans (Virgil, *Aeneid* X.565–8).

100 Antaeus, a giant of Libya, was invincible provided his feet stayed in contact with his mother, Earth. Hercules defeated him by lifting him from the ground and crushing him to death, an event which took place near Zama, where Scipio Africanus the Elder defeated Hannibal (see ll. 115–17; Lucan, *Pharsalia* IV.585 f.).

119 "that ambitious war": see note to ll. 44–5 above.

123 Cocytus: the Ninth Circle of Hell, where the treacherous are punished.

124 Tityos was slain by Apollo and Diana for his attempt to violate their mother Latona (Virgil's *Aeneid* VI.595 f.). Typhon: or Typhaeus, a hundred-handed giant, was killed in the attempt to storm Olympus, and buried under Mt Etna (Ovid, *Metamorphoses* III.303 and V.354 f.).

136 The leaning tower of Garisenda, in Bologna, still stands and is of an impressive height, although several feet lower now than in Dante's day.

143 Judas, the betrayer of Christ, is eternally devoured in one of the mouths of Satan in Cocytus, the lowest depth of Hell (see *Inferno* XXXIV.61–3).

INFERNO XXXII

In Cocytus, the Ninth Circle of Hell, where the treacherous are punished, Dante and Virgil pass through the zone of Caina, where those guilty of treachery to family and relatives are gathered; here Dante talks to Camicione dei Pazzi. Then proceeding through the second zone, Antenora, where the traitors to their country and cause are located, Dante encounters, amongst others, Bocca degli Abati.

1–15 As always, Dante's concern is to choose the level of style and vocabulary fitting to the matter he is treating, a technical and poetic flexibility that is amply demonstrated in his poem which ranges from the torments of Hell to the bliss of Paradise, and across a human spectrum of infinite variety, from Adam to St Bernard, Ulysses to Brunetto Latini, Francesca da Rimini to Beatrice, and from the Emperor Justinian to the Emperor Rudolph of Hapsburg. In this extended exordium (ll. 1–15) Dante takes stock of what severe stylistic tasks lie ahead, as he prepares to describe the treacherous, the dregs of the moral life, in the frightful predicament of their punishment.

2 "the sad pit": the Ninth, and lowest, Circle of Hell, Cocytus, at the centre of the earth and of gravity. It is also the centre of the whole material cosmos in the Ptolemaic system adapted by Dante (l. 8).

10 "those ladies": the nine Muses of literature and the arts, who helped Amphion to build the walls of Thebes, the stones moving into place by themselves at the sound of his lyre. See Statius, *Thebaid* X.873 f.

15 "here": on earth. Sheep and goats are frequently used in biblical parables, designating mankind (cf. Matthew 25.31 f., although Matthew 26.24 is a better gloss for the sense of this verse: 'It would be better for that man [Judas] if he had never been born').

23 "a lake": formed by the river Cocytus, one of the rivers of Hell (see *Inferno* XIV.119).

28–9 Tambernic and Pietrapiana (modern Tambura and Pania della Croce) are mountains in the Apuan Alps, north-west Tuscany.

55 "these two": Alessandro and Napoleone degli Alberti (sons of Count Albert of Mangona), who died at each other's hands in a quarrel over their patrimony *c.*1282. The Conti Alberti possessed castles in the Val di Bisenzio (l. 56), west of Florence. See note to *Purgatorio* VI.19–21.

58 Caina: the first zone of the frozen lake of Cocytus, where the treacherous to family and relatives are punished; named after Cain who killed his brother Abel (Genesis 4.1 f.).

61–2 Mordred, who betrayed his uncle King Arthur and was killed by him in battle.

63 Focaccia: Vanni dei Cancellieri of Pistoia, according to an old chronicle of the city, who murdered his cousin Detto in a tailor's shop.

65 Sassolo Mascheroni, probably of the Toschi family of Florence, murdered a kinsman for his estate and was publicly executed in so gruesome a way that the whole event became legendary in the city, even in that brutal age. See the commentary by the *Anonimo fiorentino.*

68 [Alberto] Camicione dei Pazzi, of the Val d'Arno, killed his kinsman Ubertino, probably in order to take his property.

69 Carlino dei Pazzi: in 1302 Carlino betrayed his party, the exiled White Guelfs of Florence, by handing over the castle of Piantravigne (Val d'Arno) to the Blacks. See D. Compagni, *Cronica* II.28, and notes to *Inferno* VI.64–9. Carlino will make Camicione look "less black" because he will be destined for a lower zone of Cocytus, Antenora, where traitors are punished.

73 Dante and Virgil now proceed to the second zone of Cocytus, Antenora, where traitors are gathered.

78 "one": Bocca degli Abati (l. 106), a Florentine, fighting in the crucial battle of Montaperti, in 1260, against the forces of the Ghibellines of King Manfred of Sicily, cut the Florentine standard from the hand of its bearer, a prelude to the annihilation of the Guelfs and the triumphant return of the Ghibellines into power in Florence. See notes to *Inferno* X.22 and 85–6; and G. Villani, *Cronica* VI.77–8.

88 Antenora: the zone of Cocytus set aside for traitors, named after Antenor, who was reputed in most post-homeric accounts (including medieval material) to have betrayed Troy to the Greeks (see Benoît de Sainte-Maure, *Roman de Troie*; Guido delle Colonne, *Historia destructionis Troiae*, both very probably known to Dante).

106 "another": Buoso da Dovera (Duera, l. 116), one of the Ghibelline leaders of Cremona, treacherously allowed the army of the French Charles I of Anjou unmolested passage through his territory, despite the orders of King Manfred of Sicily to oppose him. The arrival in Italy of Charles's army in 1265 brought to a new pitch the struggle between Ghibellines and Guelfs for hegemony in Italy, and ensured the defeat and death, the following year, of Manfred himself at Benevento (see note to *Purgatorio* III.103 f.).

119 Tesauro dei Beccheria, abbot of Vallombrosa and papal legate of Tuscany, was accused of treachery towards the victorious Guelf cause in 1258, and was beheaded, following the expulsion of the Ghibellines from Florence in the same year.

121 Gianni dei Soldanieri, a Ghibelline of Florence, changed sides after the defeat of the Ghibellines at Benevento in 1266, and headed a popular movement in Florence which ousted his own party and put the Guelfs in power (see also note to l. 106 above).

122–3 Ganellone: (Ganelon) see note to *Inferno* XXXI.16–18. Tebaldello dei Zambrasi, a Ghibelline of Faenza, took private revenge on the Lambertazzi of Bologna, refugees in Faenza, by opening the city gates to their Guelf enemies the Geremei of Bologna in 1280.

125 "two so frozen": Count Ugolino della Gherardesca and Bishop Ruggieri of Pisa (see next canto).

130–31 Tydeus, one of the seven kings in the siege of Thebes, mortally wounded by Menalippus whom he nevertheless managed to kill, attacked the severed head of the dead Theban

with his teeth in a fury of joy and anger. See Statius, *Thebaid*
VIII.739 f.

INFERNO XXXIII

*In the second zone of Cocytus, Antenora, Dante hears the story of
the treachery of Archbishop Ruggieri of Pisa and the ensuing death
of Count Ugolino della Gherardesca, from the Count's own lips.
With Virgil, Dante then passes to the third zone, Ptolomaea, where
the treacherous to guests are punished. Here he encounters the
souls of Fra Alberigo of Faenza and Branca d'Oria of Genoa.*

13–14 Ugolino della Gherardesca, Count of Donoratico
(*c*.1220–89), was of a wealthy Ghibelline family, extensive
landowners in the Pisan Maremma and Sardinia. He joined
forces with his Guelf kinsman, Giovanni Visconti (a betrayal
which earns him his place here in Antenora), and after an initial
reverse, gained considerable power in Pisa in 1276, a normally
Ghibelline city. It was after Pisa's disastrous naval defeat by
Genoa (Meloria, 1284), leaving the city weakened and sur-
rounded by her enemies, that Ugolino was made *podestà*. He
ceded certain castles to the Guelf powers of Florence and Lucca
probably in order to buy time to consolidate the city's
position. When the city's disgruntled Ghibellines, under
Archbishop Ruggieri degli Ubaldini, began to regroup and
present a threat to Ugolino, the *podestà* agreed to join them,
disclaiming his Guelfism. The Archbishop first accepted
Ugolino's recantation, but then in 1288 treacherously im-
prisoned him with four of his family (two sons and two
grandsons—not, *pace* Dante, four "little sons", l. 38), causing
them to be starved to death, as Dante relates. In 1289, with the
city firmly Ghibelline, and following the Archbishop's
resignation as *podestà*, Guido da Montefeltro was appointed to
the office (see note to *Inferno* XXVII.19 f.).

23 "the Tower of Hunger": originally the Gualandi Tower, in
what is now the Piazza dei Cavalieri in Pisa.

29 "the mountain": Monte San Giuliano, north-east of Pisa.

32–3 The Gualandi, Sismondi and Lanfranchi were powerful
Ghibelline families in Pisa.

47 "Locked up": the Italian also allows the sense of 'nailed up'.

79 "Alas, Pisa": Ugolino's horrifying story, and bestial attack on
the Archbishop's skull, result not in the compassion he expects
from Dante (see ll. 40–42), but in Dante's invective instead, in

whom any warm human emotion is frozen out leaving room only for cold disgust. The emotions thus produced by the episode harmonise totally with the moral and physical setting of Cocytus.

81 "your neighbours": the Guelf cities of Florence and Lucca.

82 Caprara (mod. Capraia) and Gorgona: two islands then belonging to Pisa, lying between the mouth of the Arno and Corsica.

85–6 The Ghibellines under Archbishop Ruggieri used as a pretext for their imprisonment of Ugolino his surrender of Pisan castles to the Guelfs of Florence and Lucca in 1285 (see note to ll. 13–14 above).

89 "modern Thebes": as related by Statius in the *Thebaid*, Thebes was the scene of much tragedy and bloodshed, resulting from Juno's persecution of the house of Cadmus: the deaths of Semele (*Paradiso* XXI.6), of Ino and her children at the hands of her husband Athamas (*Inferno* XXX.1–12), of Laius at the hands of his son Oedipus (who married his mother, Laius's wife Jocasta; *Purgatorio* XXII.55–6), of Eteocles and Polynices (*Inferno* XXVI.52–4), and of many others in the war of the seven kings against the city (see *Inferno* XIV.46, XX.34 and XXXII.130–31).

92 "another group": the souls of the treacherous to guests, in the third zone of Cocytus, Ptolomaea (see l. 124 and note below).

103 "a breath of wind": the wind driven by Satan's wings, in the lowest zone, Judecca.

109 "one of the wretches": Brother (Fra) Alberigo dei Manfredi of Faenza, one of the 'Wastrel Friars' (see note to *Inferno* XXIII. 103). In 1285 Alberigo, in revenge for an insult, had a close relation, Manfred, struck down at a banquet he held for the purpose. According to one early commentator, the assassins were summoned by the words 'Bring on the fruit' (see ll. 118–20).

124 Ptolomaea: the name derives from Ptolemaeus, who assassinated Simon Maccabaeus and his two sons at a banquet in Dok (see 1 Maccabees 16.11 f.).

126 Atropos: the third of the three Fates, who cut the threads of life spun by Clotho and Lachesis.

129–33 Dante probably derived this notion from Psalms 55.15 and 23: 'may they [the treacherous] go down alive to Sheol . . . Cast them, O God, into the pit of destruction; bloodthirsty and treacherous, they shall not live out half their days.'

134 "this shadow": ser Branca d'Oria (l. 137) of Genoa, who died
c.1325, with the help of a relative assassinated his father-in-law
Michael Zanche (l. 144) at a feast. The latter is punished for
malversation and graft in the fifth valley of Malebolge (see
Inferno XXII.88–9 and note) in the care of the demons
Malebranche (l. 142).

150 Dante's own treachery here, and seeming lack of charity, is
consistent both with popularly accepted ethics of the time that
it is no treachery to deceive the treacherous (the sentiment
expressed is a literary commonplace), and with Virgil's remark
on Dante's misplaced compassion earlier: "Here pity is alive
when it is dead" (*Inferno* XX.28).

INFERNO XXXIV

*Leaving Ptolomaea, Dante and Virgil enter Judecca, the lowest
zone of Cocytus, where the souls who betrayed their legitimate
superiors and benefactors are totally immersed in the frozen waste.
At the central and lowest point lies Satan, who devours Judas,
Brutus and Cassius in his three mouths. Climbing down the Fallen
Angel's side, Virgil carries Dante to the safety of a tunnel, along
which they make their escape to the earth's surface in the Southern
Hemisphere.*

1 'The banners of the King of Hell advance': an adaptation of the
first line of a Latin hymn of the Cross, 'The banners of the
King [of heaven] advance', sung in Holy Week (the week
before Easter). Virgil appears not only to know Christian
hymnology, but well enough to offer an ironic variation; for
Satan, as will be seen, is immobilised in the lowest depth of
Hell.

11 "the shades": these are the betrayers of their legitimate
superiors and benefactors, to whom loyalty, love and gratitude
were due. The worst betrayal is that of one's proper superiors.
Fealty was the sacred bond which in principle cemented the
medieval world together, in both Church and Empire, institu-
tional pillars in a society of strictly hierarchical ordering. It was
this sort of world in the Middle Ages that Dante saw in peril of
imminent collapse, and for which his *Divine Comedy* was
written as a warning and inspiration.

28 Dante's Satan ("Dis", l. 20), the angelic betrayer of Jehovah, is
a grotesque mechanical monster in the popular iconographical
tradition of Doom mosaics and frescos (see the mosaics in the

cupola of the Baptistry in Florence, which Dante would have known from his earliest years). Satan may seem a disappointing creation of Dante's, after the profound characterisations of his major figures in Hell, but the evil *spirit* of Satan—as opposed to his 'literal' representation—has already been unfolded for us in all its attractiveness and ugliness by the poet throughout all the previous cantos. For the fall of Satan, see Isaiah 14.12–15, Luke 10.18, Revelation 12.7–9.

30 "the giants": see *Inferno* XXXI.

38–45 With three faces, Satan is a foul parody of the Holy Trinity. The three colours red, pale yellow and black represent Hate, Impotence and Ignorance (the opposite of the Love, Power, Wisdom of the Holy Trinity). Satan's tears are of rage and disappointment.

61–7 Satan's victims are archetypal sinners against the spiritual and temporal orders, Church and State, the twin institutional pillars of medieval society: Judas Iscariot the betrayer of Christ, founder or 'cornerstone' of the Church; Brutus and Cassius the treacherous assassins of Julius Caesar, the founder of the Roman Empire, the pattern of all subsequent secular authority.

68 "night is rising": the time is approximately 6 p.m. on the evening of Holy Saturday. The journey through Hell, begun at dusk on Good Friday, has taken twenty-four hours. See note to *Inferno* XXIX.10.

93 "what point": the central point of the earth. The pull of gravity towards "the point on which the weights bear down from every side" (ll. 110–11) is used by Dante as an analogy of the pull of sin towards Satan who sits at the midpoint of the material world.

96 "the sun": Virgil begins to reckon time in terms of the sunrise and sunset in the Southern Hemisphere, where they are now bound. It is about 7.30 a.m. (the Italian text refers to 'middle tierce') on Holy Saturday morning by this reckoning (see note to l. 68 above).

112 Dante conceived of the world as spherical (the 'flat-earth' theory was not widely maintained in the Middle Ages). But in common with other philosophers of his time before extensive voyaging began, Dante lacked precise knowledge of the Southern Hemisphere, and assumed that the Northern Hemisphere contained all the land, and the Southern all the ocean (see Dante's treatise *Quaestio de Aqua et Terra* of 1320).

When Satan fell from heaven, Dante proposes that he struck the Southern Hemisphere (whose land all fled to the Northern), penetrating to the centre of the earth. The displaced material accumulated on the surface of the Southern Hemisphere to form the island and mountain of Purgatory, where the two poets are now bound. They travel upwards to the surface along the shaft made by Satan's passage through the crust of the earth.

114–15 Jerusalem, where Christ was crucified, is represented on medieval *mappae mundi* as the midpoint of the Hemisphere of Land (the Northern Hemisphere). See the Hereford 'Mappa mundi', p. 25.

127 Beelzebub: Satan.

139 The stars are referred to also at the close of *Purgatorio* and *Paradiso*. As objects of God's handiwork in the perfect order of creation, they are here signposts for the travellers, pointing upwards towards the eternal Heaven of his dwelling. Cf. Psalms 19.1 (A.V.): 'The heavens declare the glory of God; and the firmament sheweth his handiwork'.

PURGATORIO I

On the morning of Easter Sunday, Dante and Virgil emerge from the abyss of Hell on to the shore of Mount Purgatory. Cato. The ritual of purification.

3 "that cruel stretch of sea": the metaphor refers to Hell.

4–6 The "second kingdom" is Purgatory, which in Dante's unique conception is a mountain set upon a solitary island in the Southern Hemisphere of Oceans, diametrically opposite Jerusalem in the Northern Hemisphere (see note to *Inferno* XXXIV.112). Here the souls of the repentant, their sins forgiven, voluntarily undergo the purgation of their sinful tendencies in order to fit themselves for Paradise. See note to *Purgatorio* IX.112.

7–12 The conventional invocation of a poet, seeking inspiration from some supernatural source (see *Inferno* II.7–9, *Paradiso* I.13–36). Here Dante calls upon Calliope, the Muse of epic poetry (see Virgil, *Aeneid* IX.525), first of the nine Muses.

11 The nine daughters of Pierus, king of Emathia in Macedonia, challenged the nine Muses to a singing contest and were changed into magpies for their presumptuous rivalry (see Ovid, *Metamorphoses* V.294 f.).

15 Either the horizon, or (in Dante's Ptolemaic cosmography) the first planetary circle of the moon.

19 The "lovely planet" is the morning star Venus, whose influence on earth, originating in the Holy Spirit, causes all things to love 'according to their several dispositions' (*Convivio* II.V.13 f.). Love is the currency of relationships in Purgatory, whereas in Hell it had been hate.

21 The constellation of the Fish, rising just before the Ram (see note to *Inferno* I.37–40), accompanies Venus at sunrise in spring. It is about five a.m. on Easter Sunday.

23 The "four stars" lie in the southern horizon, possibly the Southern Cross, although there is no certain evidence that voyagers by the early fourteenth century had crossed the equatorial line. Indeed, Dante insists (l. 24) that they had only been seen previously by Adam and Eve, "the first people".

31 f. Marcus Porcius Cato (94–46BC), whom Dante represents as guardian of the shores of Purgatory. Defeated on the field of battle at Utica, near Carthage in North Africa, Cato committed suicide rather than submit to his adversary Julius Caesar. Champion of the republican cause, then in collapse under the onslaught of the Triumvirate, Cato was revered in antiquity (Cicero, Livy, Lucan) and the Middle Ages for his stern character, complete integrity and dedication to the cause of liberty (cf. ll. 71–5; *De Monarchia* II.V.17, *Convivio* IV.XXVIII.15). With Cato, the political theme of the *Purgatorio* begins, for the liberty which Dante seeks, although liberty of the soul from the tyranny of sin, is consonant with the liberty of the citizen from the restraints of the law: 'if man had remained in the state of innocence in which God made him, he would not have needed the directives of law, since they are remedies for the weakness of sin' (*De Monarchia* III.IV.14).

37–9 The four stars now offer an allegorical interpretation. They represent the four cardinal virtues of the ancient world: prudence, courage, moderation and justice, which Cato signally exemplified in the course of a life free of the taint of vice or corruption. So much so that Dante overlooks the pagan stoicism and suicide of Cato, and daringly elevates him to a condition of quasi redemption, superior to that of even Virgil.

53 "a lady from heaven": Beatrice (see note to *Inferno* II.53 f.).

77 Minos, judge of the dead in classical myth, is placed by Dante as guardian and judge of Hell from the limits of the Second Circle downwards (see *Inferno* V.4 f. and note).

78 Limbo, Virgil's location, is in the First Circle of Hell (*Inferno* IV).

79 Marcia, Cato's wife, similarly in Limbo amongst the virtuous pagans, was given in marriage by Cato to his friend Quintus Hortensius. Upon the death of Quintus, Marcia was taken back by Cato as his wife, following her strenuous remonstrances (see *Convivio* IV.XXVIII.13 f.).

88 Acheron, the first river of Hell (*Inferno* III.71 f.).

95 The rush signifies humility, the Christian virtue that is the basic requirement of repentance, just as pride is the root cause of sin. A reed was placed in Christ's hand after his trial instead of a sceptre (AV Matthew 27.29). The washing of the face (a perfunctory rite in *Aeneid* VI.635 f., as Aeneas prepares to enter Elysium) is here done with dew, symbol of the grace of God (Old Testament *passim*; Dante's *Letters* V.5).

107 "The sun": symbol of God's illuminating grace.

130–32 A veiled reference to the disaster of Ulysses' presumptuous voyage (see *Inferno* XXVI.133–42).

135–6 Similarly the golden bough, which allowed Aeneas' entrance to the Underworld, when broken off was immediately replaced by a new growth (*Aeneid* VI.143–4).

PURGATORIO II

From the boat bringing redeemed souls to begin their penance in Purgatory a soul disembarks whom Dante recognises as Casella, a fellow Florentine. Casella's song is interrupted by a reproachful Cato.

1–9 Night is beginning to fall over Jerusalem in the Northern Hemisphere, as the sun rises over Purgatory in the Southern.

5 The mouth of the Ganges marked the eastern limit of the known landmass in the Northern Hemisphere, and there it is midnight. At the spring equinox the constellation of the Scales is diametrically opposite the Ram in the zodiacal circle, when the latter constellation is in conjunction with the sun (see note to *Inferno* I.37–40).

6 The Scales "fall from her [the night's] hand" after the autumn equinox, when night becomes longer than day.

17 The "light" emanates from an angel who guides and powers the boat bearing the souls of the redeemed to the shores of Purgatory from the mouth of the Tiber (see l. 101).

41 This then is the "lighter craft" to which Charon refers in *Inferno* III.93.

46 The first verse of Psalms 113 Vulgate (114 NEB), 'When Israel came out of Egypt', is particularly appropriate here as the souls of the redeemed are released from the bondage of the flesh into eternal life. The anagogical sense of the verse is explained by Dante in *Convivio* II.I.7: 'when the soul goes forth out of sin, it is made holy and free in its power'.

57 The constellation of Capricorn, which at dawn had stood directly over Purgatory, now is descending as the sun rises with the Ram (the constellations of Capricorn and Ram lie at ninety degrees to one another in the zodiac).

70 It was a common contemporary practice in Italy for a messenger bringing good news to a city to wear an olive garland on his head (cf. G. Villani, *Cronica* VI.78).

76 f. It is the soul of Casella, a musician of Florence (possibly of Pistoiese origins) who, it is clear from the text here, had set some of Dante's *canzoni* to music. A composition by Casella survives in the Vatican Library, and early commentators have no difficulty in identifying him (Buti, Benvenuto, *Anonimo fiorentino*), although no important historical document or chronicle refers to his career.

80–81 Reminiscent of Aeneas' vain embrace of Anchises his father, in *Aeneid* VI.700 f.

95–6 A delay possibly due to late repentance on Casella's part, although there is no textual evidence of this.

98–9 From Christmas 1299 Boniface VIII declared a year of plenary indulgence (the waiving of penance) to all attending the Jubilee in Rome, provided certain churches and shrines were visited.

107–8 Dante's keen appreciation of music is reflected in *Convivio* II.XIII.23 f.

112 f. The first verse of Dante's *canzone* in *Convivio* III. Although Dante expatiates on the allegorical sense in his treatise (as a poem praising Lady Philosophy), the poem's literal sense speaks of love's overpowering mastery of Dante's mind before a woman of more than normal beauty and grace. It is a song in harmony therefore with the spirit and mood of love in Purgatory, although Dante and Casella's rapt audience are guilty of too indulgent an appreciation at this early stage of their penitential pilgrimage; hence Cato's sudden outraged interruption in l. 119 f.

PURGATORIO III

Virgil remarks on his lack of a shadow, whilst a crowd of souls (of the excommunicate) remark on the shadow that Dante casts. Dante speaks with Manfred of Sicily, who died in battle in 1266.

3 "reason": may be here understood as wisdom, i.e. the law or justice of God.

10–11 Deriving from Aristotle, it was a commonplace notion that the dignity of the great is best indicated through gravity of movement, voice and discourse (*Nichomachean Ethics* IV.3).

16 Having emerged from Hell to face east on the shores of Purgatory, Dante and Virgil now turn westwards towards the mountain.

25 In Italy, which Dante puts three hours behind the time in Jerusalem, it is evening, i.e. between 3 and 6 p.m. See note to *Purgatorio* II.1–9.

26–7 The emperor Augustus (Octavian) transferred the remains of Virgil from Brindisi, where he died in 19BC, to Naples.

29–30 Dante, in harmony with Ptolemaic astronomy, regarded the spheres of the concentric heavens as 'diaphanous' (*Convivio* II.VI.9).

31–3 Statius, however, in *Purgatorio* XXV.37–107, attempts an explanation of the origins and nature of the visible appearance of the souls in the Afterlife, and goes some way to answer Dante's unspoken question here. Virgil might have done the same, but his mortification at Cato's rebuke seems to have got the better, for the moment, of his serene pedagogical spirit.

36 i.e. the nature of God as Father, Son and Holy Spirit.

37 i.e. man should be content to understand things only *as they exist*, as effects, and their causes (*propter quid*) only in so far as they can be ascertained from them, not the wherefore of their existence which is locked in the inscrutable mind of God (see *Purgatorio* VIII.67–9). The term *quia* was used in scholastic philosophy in *a posteriori* argumentation. Virgil here takes the same sort of stand against presumptuous speculation as Dante himself will later in his *Quaestio de Aqua et Terra* (1320), para. 22, quoting scriptural support. Cf. Aquinas, *Summa Theologica* II.II.174.3.

38–9 Had man been vouchsafed knowledge of the quiddity of all things, including God, then the incarnation of Christ, who reveals the nature of God to the point that is needful for man's salvation, would have been superfluous.

40–44 Dante places Aristotle and Plato, pagan philosophers, in Limbo, representing them as "without hope [of satisfying their intellectual thirst in God's presence], but with desire [so to do]" (*Inferno* IV.42).

49 The coastline between Lerici (near La Spezia) and Turbia (La Turbie, near Monaco) is largely precipitous, served by few roads in Dante's day.

52–4 Indications of Virgil's ignorance of the topography of Purgatory now begin to be apparent. Although he will later explain to Dante the moral scheme of this realm of the Afterlife (*Purgatorio* XVII), Virgil has no practical knowledge of the way. The allegory is clear: human reason alone is not sufficient to arrive at an understanding of the way of faith to salvation. Dante, as a Christian, is now in a position to advise Virgil in this exclusively Christian realm (see ll. 61–3).

58 f. Souls of the contumacious, those who died under the ban of the Church as excommunicates.

79–84 Appropriately the souls of the saved are likened to a flock of sheep, an image widely used in Scripture, but developed by Dante with realistic precision, emphasising here their submissiveness, gregariousness and natural timidity. Cf. Luke 12.32: 'have no fear, little flock; for your Father has chosen to give you the kingdom.'

103 f. Manfred, illegitimate son of Emperor Frederick II (see *Inferno* X.119 and note), was regent of the Kingdom of Sicily following the death of Frederick in 1250, assuming the role of leader of the Ghibelline cause in its struggle with the Papacy. Having taken the crown amidst popular acclaim in 1258, he was excommunicated by Pope Alexander IV. In 1266, near Benevento, Manfred was defeated and killed in battle by Charles I of Anjou (brother of the king of France, Louis IX) the papacy's candidate for the crown of the *Regno*. See G. Villani, *Cronica* VII.7–9, and note to *Inferno* XXVIII.16–17.

113 Constance of Sicily (d. 1198) wife of Emperor Henry VI, the mother of Emperor Frederick II (see *Paradiso* III.109 f.).

115–16 Manfred's daughter Constance (d. 1302) by his wife Beatrice of Savoy. Constance married Peter III of Aragon, who through her laid claim to the crown of Sicily. He assumed it in 1282 following the 'Sicilian Vespers' (see note to *Paradiso* VIII.72–5). Constance was the mother of Alfonso (king of

Aragon from 1285 till his death in 1291), Jacomo (king of Sicily 1285, and of Aragon 1291), and Federigo, who displaced Jacomo as king of Sicily in 1296. Dante later mentions Jacomo and Federigo-(but in somewhat disparaging terms) in *Purgatorio* VII.119, two of the "honoured" still alive and in power in 1300 (see note).

121 Although attested by chroniclers as 'handsome, generous, courteous and debonair' (Villani), and an effective ruler, his sceptical outlook and dissolute living are also the subject of comment.

121–3 'The man who comes to me I will never turn away': John 6.37.

124 The Archbishop of Cosenza (Calabria), whose identity remains uncertain.

125 Pope Clement IV confirmed his predecessor's choice of Charles of Anjou as rightful claimant to the crown of Sicily and Naples, in opposition to Manfred.

127 f. After the battle of Benevento (1266), Charles of Anjou refused Manfred burial in consecrated ground. The body was later disinterred from the cairn of "those heavy stones", and cast out of the territory of the kingdom upon the banks of the river Verde (now the Liri and Garigliano), most probably on the orders of Clement IV.

132 The ritual of excommunication included the symbolic extinguishing of candles.

138 i.e. outside the gate of Purgatory, awaiting entrance to begin the process of penance.

139 The penalty for contumacy is Dante's own invention, but perhaps based ultimately on *Aeneid* VI.325 f. If it is draconian, it shows that Dante took the interdict of the Church very seriously indeed.

140–41 Manfred refers to intercessory prayer by the faithful in this life (cf. James 5.16; 'Therefore confess your sins to one another, and pray for one another, and then you will be healed. A good man's prayer is powerful and effective'; and Aquinas, *Summa Theologica* III. supp., q. 71, art. 6, resp.).

PURGATORIO IV

Dante and Virgil begin their ascent towards the gate of Purgatory. Virgil resolves Dante's perplexity as to the position of the sun. They encounter Belacqua amongst the souls of those who through lethargy repented late.

2 "any faculty": i.e. any of the five senses of touch, sight, hearing, taste, smell.

4 "powers": i.e. the three bodily functions—life, sensation (see note to l. 2 above), and reason.

5–6 Aristotle, with Aquinas and Dante following him, accepted the notion of the one indivisible soul in man (having three "powers") in opposition to the Platonic concept of the plurality of souls (each associated with one "power"). See *Convivio* III.II.11.

14 The spirit of Manfred. See preceding canto.

15 It is now about 9.20 a.m. (the sun travels in its arc fifteen degrees in one hour).

19–21 The narrowness of the gap is emphasised: 'Enter by the narrow gate. The gate is wide that leads to perdition . . . but the gate that leads to life is small' (Matthew 7.13–14). See note to *Inferno* V.20.

25 San Leo (in the former Duchy of Urbino), situated on the top of a precipitous hill; Noli (on the Gulf of Genoa), approached in Dante's day only by sea or down a precipitous track; Bismontova, once a fortress surmounting a sheer, isolated crag in the Emilia, near Canossa.

61–6 i.e. 'If the constellation of the Twins [Castor and Pollux] were in proximity with the sun ["that mirror"], then you would see the sun glowing even further north [nearer the constellation of the Bears] than you do now.' Dante, in the Southern Hemisphere, has remarked on the strangeness of the presence of the sun in the northern horizon (instead of the southern horizon, as it appears to an observer in the Northern Hemisphere). Virgil confirms Dante's impression by this hypothetical statement, and then proceeds to the explanation.

64 The "glowing part of the Zodiac" is that part of the sky in which the sun is.

68–74 Jerusalem (Mount Zion) and Purgatory are diametrically opposite each other, respectively in the Northern and Southern hemispheres. They thus share a common horizon lying between the two of them.

71–2 i.e. the route followed by the sun. Phaeton, the child of the sun god, Phoebus, lost control of the chariot of the sun, almost setting the earth on fire (see *Inferno* XVII.107–8 and note).

81 Summer shares the same side of the equator as the sun, whilst in winter the sun is always on the further side, therefore the equator is permanently "between summer and winter".

88–90 The physical implication is that the slope of Mount Purgatory is convex in shape (cf. ll. 40–42). The spiritual implication of the lines is that as the redeemed sinner progresses in the process of penance, the weight or drag of his imperfections becomes less burdensome.

98 f. The voice is that of Belacqua, clearly a friend of Dante, whom the early commentators identify as a Florentine craftsman of musical instruments, noted for his slothfulness.

103–5 Presumably a category of souls, those who like Balacqua "postponed repentance to the end" (l. 132).

120 Dante and Virgil were sitting facing east (ll. 52–3), with the sun, in the northern horizon, on their left.

133–4 See note to *Purgatorio* III.140–41.

137–8 It is now noon, with the sun at the meridian point.

138–9 In Morocco, at the far western point of the known land-mass in the Northern Hemisphere, night is falling, six hours ahead of Purgatory.

PURGATORIO V

Still in Ante-Purgatory amongst the late-repentant, Dante meets and converses with three souls who met a violent end, unabsolved but repentant at the last minute: Jacopo del Cassero, Buonconte da Montefeltro, and Pia dei Tolomei.

1 The souls who repented late through spiritual apathy.

4–5 Dante's shadow again occasions comment from the dis-embodied spirits. It falls on his left, indicating that the two poets are proceeding westwards along the northern face of the mountain, i.e. in the correct anticlockwise direction.

23 The souls of those who died violently, unabsolved, yet repentant at the point of death.

24 From Psalms 50 (Vulgate), one of the so-called seven penitential psalms (NEB Psalms 51.1: 'Be gracious to me, O God, in thy true love').

64 Jacopo di Uguccione del Cassero of Fano (l. 70), an ally of the Florentine Guelfs in the war against Arezzo (1288–9), was *podestà* of Bologna eight years later, foiling the plans of the Ferrarese Azzo VIII d'Este (l. 77; and see *Inferno* XII.112) to annex the city. On his way to Milan in 1298, via Oriago (formerly Oriaco, l. 80), La Mira (l. 79) and presumably Padua, Azzo's men ambushed and assassinated him at Oriago in the marshes of the lagoons.

68–9 The March of Ancona lies between the Romagna (to the north) and the territory of the Kingdom of Naples (to the south), then ruled by Charles II of Anjou.

75 i.e. in Paduan territory. Antenor was the reputed founder of Padua, considered in some post-homeric accounts to be the traitor of Troy. Dante names a zone in deepest Hell Antenora (*Inferno* XXXII–III), the location of those who betrayed their country or cause. Clearly Jacopo is here inferring the treachery of the Paduans in the circumstances of his death.

88 Buonconte da Montefeltro, the son of Guido (*Inferno* XXVII.19 f.), a leading Ghibelline, who in 1289 led the army of Arezzo against the Guelfs of Florence at the battle of Campaldino (l. 92) and was roundly defeated, he himself falling in the struggle. His body could not be found on the field of battle. Dante himself was present in the Florentine ranks.

89 Giovanna, Buonconte's wife; "the others": his daughter and his brother.

94 The Casentino, a district in Tuscany in the higher reaches of the Arno east of Florence, where Campaldino is situated.

96 The Eremo ('Hermitage') is the monastery of Camaldoli, overlooking much of the Casentino.

97 i.e. where the Archiano flows into the Arno.

103–8 The debate between the angels of hell and heaven is paralleled in the story of his father Guido da Montefeltro (*Inferno* XXVII.112 f.), whose soul was the object of contention between St Francis and a devil, with a very different outcome. The struggle between the forces of good and evil for the soul at the point of death was a commonplace belief. St Bonaventure elaborates on this in his writings (Singleton).

115–16 The valley of the Casentino, containing the plain of Campaldino, stretches from Mount Pratomagno in the south-west to the main ridge ("the great yoke") of the Apennines above the monastery of Camaldoli.

122 "the royal river": the Arno.

133 Pia of Siena, whom early commentators identify as Pia dei Tolomei (possibly by a first marriage), wife thereafter (1295?) of Nello dei Pannocchieschi, one of the lords of the Sienese Maremma. Her violent death was contrived reputedly by Nello ("that man", l. 135) who, if it was not for reasons of jealousy, presumably regretted his hasty *ad hoc* marriage by the mere giving of a ring, and sought a more advantageous match.

PURGATORIO VI

Dante questions Virgil on the efficacy of intercessionary prayer. Their encounter with Sordello occasions an invective from Dante on the disunity of Italy, the turmoil in Florence, and the Emperor's neglect of his duty.

10 Dante is surrounded by the souls of the violently slain, clamouring for prayers to shorten their term of waiting in Ante-Purgatory.

13–14 Ghino di Tacco, a notorious bandit of noble blood, assassinated the Arentine judge (probably Benincasa da Laterina) who had sentenced one of his relatives to death *c.*1297.

15 The reference here cannot be elucidated with any certainty, although one early commentator suggests Guccio dei Tarlati, an Aretine Ghibelline, who was drowned whilst hunting down some exiled Guelf rivals, the Bostoli.

17–18 Federigo Novello, son of Guido Novello of the Conti Guidi of the Casentino, was killed (*c.*1290) by one of the Bostoli whilst aiding the Tarlati in their suppression of them; "the Pisan" is the son of Marzucco degli Scornigiani of Pisa, whose murderer was forgiven by his father. Marzucco, it is assumed, had by that time entered a religious order.

19–21 Count Orso degli Alberti was murdered by his ambitious cousin in 1286, part of a family feud that would continue in subsequent years. The fratricidal fathers of the pair are in the lowest parts of Hell (*Inferno* XXXII.41 f.). The "soul divided" is Pierre de la Brosse, executed for high treason in 1278 as a result (Dante opines) of the machinations of Marie de Brabant, second wife of Philip III of France, whom Pierre had accused of complicity in the death of Philip's son (the Dauphin) by his first wife.

28–30 In *Aeneid* VI.373 f., the Sibyl accompanying Aeneas in the Underworld rebukes the shade of the unburied Palinurus for presuming that 'divine decrees can be changed by prayers'.

37–9 i.e. God's justice is not annulled, even though loving prayers of intercession by the faithful may mitigate (even remit "in an instant", l. 38) the penalty.

42 Before Christ's 'full, perfect and sufficient sacrifice' at the Crucifixion, grace for the remitting of the penalties of sin was not normally available to those outside the Covenant between God and the Hebrews.

45 Beatrice is referred to here in her symbolic role as the light of revealed truth, which illuminates the human intellect with understanding of, and love for, the things of God. See note to *Purgatorio* XVIII.46–8.

48 "At the top of this mountain": in Earthly Paradise (see *Purgatorio* XXX.32 f.).

58 f. The soul in solitude is Sordello of Goito (near Mantua), courtier, poet and troubadour (*c*.1200 to *c*.1270), the northern Italian poet who wrote, in Provençal, love lyrics, didactic poems on the chivalrous virtues and fearless polemical verses. The latter include a *planh* (lament) on the death of Ser Blacatz, a Provençal noble, whom Sordello held up as a model of a ruler, whilst berating the contemporary Emperor (Frederick II), and the sovereigns of Christendom for their pusillanimity and neglect. It is poetry of this sort that earns Sordello his place in *The Divine Comedy*, at a point where the political theme becomes prominent. Cf. Proverbs 22.13.

71 Virgil was born near Mantua (see note to *Inferno* I.63 f.).

88 The Roman Emperor Justinian (d. 565) had drawn up the great *Corpus iuris civilis*, a complete reference work of Roman law. Dante assumes Justinian's conversion to Christian orthodoxy and places him in the Heaven of Mercury (*Paradiso* VI).

89 "the saddle": i.e. the imperial throne of the Holy Roman Empire, which Dante conceived as morally if not actually vacant in 1300, when Albert of Hapsburg was emperor. In *Convivio* IV.IX.10 Dante speaks of the Emperor as 'rider of the human will'.

91 "you people" are the rulers of the Church, who fiercely opposed imperial ambitions and authority in the thirteenth century.

93 'Then pay Caesar what is due to Caesar, and pay God what is due to God', Matthew 22.21.

97 f. Albert of Hapsburg, Emperor 1298–1308, son of Rudolph I (see ll. 103 and *Purgatorio* VII.91 f.), neither of whom came to Italy to be crowned, as tradition prescribed, with Charlemagne's iron crown in Monza, and with a golden crown in Rome. This omission was for Dante symbolic of their general neglect of Italy and her problems, and of their dereliction of duty to the Empire.

100–102 Dante appears to refer to the assassination of Albert's eldest son Rudolph in 1307, and Albert's own murder by his nephew John of Swabia in June 1308.

107–8 The family of the Montecchi ("Montagues") lent their name to the Ghibelline party of Verona, later led by Ezzelino III da Romano (d. 1259) in the wider political context of the struggle for control of Lombardy. The Cappeletti ("Capulets") were a Cremonese family whose name was assumed by the Guelf or anti-imperial faction in Lombardy, which by 1300 was in decline. In other words, by 1300 both "Montagues" and "Capulets" as parties were dead forces, destroyed or worn out by their endless warfare (Shakespeare's story in *Romeo and Juliet* of two feuding families in Verona is thus misconstrued history). The Monaldi and Filippeschi families of Orvieto, Guelf and Ghibelline respectively, were continually feuding by 1300, each living in fear that they might be destroyed by the other.

109–11 The aristocratic orders of Italy, who held their titles and lands ultimately from the Emperor (and ensured the ordered fabric of medieval society), were in decline, either through their own feuds or through the plundering advances of the *borghesia* into their patrimonies, as in the case of the Aldobrandeschi of Santafiora whose domains had been significantly eroded through war or treaties with the burgesses of Siena. See *Purgatorio* XI.49 and note.

126 The name of M. Claudius Marcellus, consul 51BC and eloquent opponent of Julius Caesar, stands here for 'demagogue'.

127 f. The invective against Florence is full of heavy irony.

PURGATORIO VII

Sordello greets Virgil, and with night falling guides the two poets to a beautiful valley occupied by a third group of late-repentant, the negligent among the rulers of Christendom.

6 See note to *Purgatorio* III.26–7.

22–36 See notes to *Inferno* II.52, IV.24, *Purgatorio* III.40–44.

35 The Christian virtues of faith, hope and charity.

36 The cardinal or pagan virtues: prudence, courage, justice and moderation.

42 Thus Sordello complements Virgil's role as Dante's guide in Purgatory, as later will Statius (*Purgatorio* XXI f.).

53–7 The sun's light is symbolic of God's illuminating grace (cf. *Inferno* I.17–18), which when absent impedes the soul's will to ascend on the path of sanctification. See John 12.35–6: 'The light is among you still, but not for long. Go on your way while you have the light . . . He who journeys in the dark does not know where he is going.'

83 *"Salve Regina"* ('Hail thou Queen'), the opening words of the anthem to the Virgin Mary sung at the close of vespers, the evening service, before compline.

84 f. The valley is set apart for the nightly vigil of the rulers of Christendom, who through spiritual neglect not only permitted the worldly cares of their office to delay their repentance, but also failed to rule in the manner required of Christian princes—that is, to govern with due deference to the Empire (the divinely ordained, supreme secular authority) and the Church (its spiritual authority and teachings), so that more often than not professed Christian rulers of Europe were at serious variance with one another. In the architecture of *The Divine Comedy* the valley here finds a parallel in the noble castle of the famed in Limbo (*Inferno* IV).

91–6 Rudolph I of Hapsburg, Emperor 1273–92, was full of energy and enterprise, yet he neglected his coronation in Rome, and his imperial responsibilities in a strife-ridden Italy, intent only upon the consolidation and expansion of his territories in and around Germany.

96 Some commentators see this verse as referring to Henry VII of Luxemburg (Emperor 1308–13), but if this is accepted in the context of the line ("too late") then it would be impossible to identify the mysterious 'DXV' as the same person. See the discussion in note to *Purgatorio* XXXIII.43 f.

97–102 Ottocar II of Bohemia, who is comforting Rudolph, was in life Rudolph's most dangerous rival for the imperial throne. Unable to accept Rudolph's authority as Emperor, Ottocar was finally defeated and killed by him in 1278. Ottocar's son, Wenceslaus II (who in spite of Sordello's strictures here was known as 'the Good'), married Rudolph's daughter.

103 Philip III the Bold, King of France 1270–85, whose fleet was defeated in the Gulf of Rosas by that of Peter III of Aragon, died not long afterwards. By waging war on Peter, Philip had entertained hopes of retrieving Sicily for the Angevins after it had fallen, in 1282 at the 'Sicilian Vespers' (see note to *Paradiso* VIII.73–5), into the hands of the Aragonese.

104 Henry I the Fat, king of Navarre 1270–74.

106–7 "that one": Philip III; "the other": Henry I of Navarre.

109 The "blight of France" is Philip IV the Fair, king of France 1285–1314, reigning in 1300 therefore, the year of *The Divine*

Comedy's fictional events. He was son of Philip III, son-in-law of Henry I of Navarre and brother of Charles of Valois (the 'peacemaker' whose support of the Black Guelfs in Florence earned Dante his exile in 1302). Philip IV had, in Dante's estimation, much to answer for. Dante never mentions him by name, always by a periphrasis, as if the name itself were unclean (*Inferno* XIX.87, *Purgatorio* XX.91). The crimes of Philip to which Dante refers include the attack on the person of the Pope, Boniface VIII, his suppression of the Order of the Knights Templar, and his undue influence on the papacy, resulting in the illegal and humiliating removal of the papal seat from Rome to Avignon in 1309 under Clement V. See also notes to *Purgatorio* XX.46, 66, 85–90, 92–3; *Paradiso* XIX. 118–20 and note.

112 Peter III, king of Aragon 1276–85 (see note to l. 103 above), laid claim to the crown of Sicily through his marriage with Constance the daughter of King Manfred of Sicily (see notes to *Purgatorio* III.103 f. and 115–16). He became virtual leader of the Ghibelline cause in Italy some years after Manfred's death.

113 Charles I of Anjou and Provence (1226–85), king of Sicily (1266–82) and of Naples (1266–85), brother of St Louis (IX) of France, was figurehead of the Guelf movement in Italy, and right arm of the papacy. Towards the end of his life he became the bitter enemy of Peter III of Aragon (note to l. 112 above), from whom he tried to wrest the kingdom of Sicily once his. Charles extinguished the last of the males of the imperial Hohenstaufen family, Conradin, in 1268, two years after his forces had slain Manfred at Benevento (see notes to *Purgatorio* III.103 f. and *Inferno* XXVIII.17–18).

115–17 Alfonso III the Magnificent, of Aragon, eldest son of Peter III of Aragon, who died in 1291 after a reign of six years.

119 Jacomo II (James, second son of Peter III of Aragon), king of Catalonia and Sicily from 1285, and of Aragon from 1291. Federigo II (third son of Peter III), displaced Jacomo as king of Sicily in 1296. See note to *Purgatorio* III.115–16, *Paradiso* XIX.131, XX.63, *Convivio* IV.VI.20.

121–3 Dante had already developed this basic tenet of his philosophy in *Convivio* IV.XX.5 f.

124 Charles I of Anjou (l. 113).

125 Peter III of Aragon (l. 112).

126 Charles II of Anjou inherited the Kingdom of Naples (Apulia) and the county of Provence from his father, the

nobler Charles I, in 1285. Dante's low opinion of Charles II is also expressed in *Purgatorio* XX.79 f. and *Paradiso* XIX.127–9.

127–9 The "seed" is Charles II, see note to l. 126 above; Constance, wife of Peter III of Aragon (see note to l. 112); Beatrice of Provence and Margaret of Burgundy, first and second wives of Charles I of Anjou (see note to l. 113). The sense is that Charles I's son is as inferior to him as Charles I was inferior to Peter III of Aragon.

130–32 Henry III, king of England 1216–72, whose presentation here is akin to that in G. Villani (*Cronica* V.4). His issue is Edward I, reigning in 1300, an energetic and enterprising monarch; but see *Paradiso* XIX.121–3 and note.

134 Guglielmo (William) VII, Longsword, marquis of Monferrat (1254–92). As imperial Vicar he waged war on the Guelf cities but, captured by the Alessandrians during a rebellion, was left to die in a cage exhibited to the public. His son Giovanni, together with the Visconti of Milan, invaded Monferrat and the Canavese, seeking vengeance.

PURGATORIO VIII

In the valley of the negligent rulers Dante speaks with Nino Visconti and Conrad Malaspina, remarks on a constellation of three stars, and witnesses the guardian angels drive away a snake which threatens the valley's security.

5 The bells of compline, the service, following vespers, which concludes the day's worship.

13 "*Te lucis ante* [*terminum*]" ('Before the ending of the light'), the hymn of compline.

19–21 An apostrophe to the reader to warn him to consider the allegorical truth that subtends the literal at this point of the narrative (cf. *Inferno* IX.61–3).

25 f. Still outside Purgatory proper, the souls, as those still on earth, are subject to temptation and fear (symbolised by the snake who will later appear, and the falling night) and need, and are freely afforded, grace to win through: a spirit of fortitude and hope, which the green-clad angels here symbolise. Cf. Psalms 34.7.

27 The broken swords would perhaps indicate their use more for defence than attack, otherwise their incandescence suggests that of the swords of the angelic guardians of Eden after the Fall (Genesis 3.24).

47 Ugolino (Nino) Visconti, son of Giovanni Visconti of Pisa, and grandson of the ill-fated but treacherous Count Ugolino (see note to *Inferno* XXXIII.13–14), was appointed Judge of the Judicature (i.e. governor of the district) of Gallura, Sardinia (then under Pisan authority), where he died in 1296. A notable Guelf (he headed the Guelf League, the *Taglia guelfa* in 1293), he promoted attacks on Pisa, which had reverted to Ghibellinism under Archbishop Ruggieri, and was known to have been in Florence on several occasions between 1288 and 1293, when Dante might well have met him.

64 "One of them": Sordello; "the other": Nino.

65 Conrad (Currado) Malaspina, see note to l. 109.

67–9 "to him": to God. See note to *Purgatorio* III.37.

71 "my Giovanna": daughter of Nino Visconti and Beatrice d'Este. Orphaned in 1296 on the death of her father, she was sent to Volterra, and later married the lord of Treviso, Rizzardo da Camino (subject of Dante's reproaches, because of his militant Ghibellinism, in *Paradiso* IX.49–51).

73–4 Beatrice gave up her "white veils" of widowhood to marry, in 1299 or 1300, Galeazzo Visconti of Milan. Galeazzo was expelled from Milan in 1302, to live in abject dependency on allies. This will be a cause of regret on Beatrice's part, Nino suggests, who stresses her inconstancy in ll. 76–8.

79 The device on the coat of arms of the Visconti of Milan.

81 The device of the Visconti of Pisa (Nino's branch).

86 i.e. towards the southern horizon.

89–93 The cluster of three stars (l. 89) probably represents the three Christian virtues (faith, hope and charity), whereas those of the morning symbolised the four cardinal virtues (see note to *Purgatory* I.37–9) of the ancient world.

99 "the bitter food": see note to *Paradiso* VII.26.

109 "The shadow" is Conrad (Currado) II Malaspina (l. 118), Ghibelline marquis of Villafranca in the Lunigiana (grandson of Conrad I, "The elder", l. 119), who died in 1294. Dante's paean of praise for the Malaspina here is due in large measure to the courteous reception and employment which the family gave him in 1306, at Villafranca in the Val di Magra (l. 116). See note to *Purgatorio* XIX.142.

114 The splendid territory of Eden (Earthly Paradise) on the summit of the mountain.

131 "the chief sinner": possibly Pope Boniface VIII.

133–5 i.e. not seven years shall pass before Dante will have striking and concrete confirmation (see ll. 136–9) of the generosity of the Malaspina.

134 "the Ram": at the time of the beginning of Dante's journey through the Afterlife, the sun was rising in the Ram (see note to *Inferno* I.37–40).

PURGATORIO IX

At first dawn of Dante's first night on the mountain, he dreams he is snatched up by an eagle, whilst in reality he is being carried up, asleep, to the gates of Purgatory by St Lucy. Here the angelic guardian of the gates, having ritually prepared Dante for his ascent of the mountain, opens the gates with St Peter's keys.

1–9 The opening lines (1–6) here most probably represent the first 'white' dawn as seen in the Northern Hemisphere, where Dante (in Italy) is writing his poem. There then follows (ll. 7–9) a reference to the equivalent time as it was in Ante-Purgatory: the night being some two and a half hours old "in the place where we were". Dante has adopted a similar procedure in *Purgatorio* II.1–9, representing the time in Purgatory initially in terms of the equivalent time in the Northern Hemisphere.

1–3 Aurora (goddess of the dawn) fell in love with Tithonus (brother of Priam of Troy). She secured immortality for him, but not, through inadvertency, dispensation from ageing. Cf. Virgil, *Georgics* I.446–7.

4–6 The constellation of Scorpio, high over the western horizon at sunrise in the Northern Hemisphere, is contiguous with the whitening eastern horizon at daybreak.

7–9 "the steps" are the hours of night. With night over two hours old, and the third 'folding its wings', it is betwen 8.30 and 9 p.m.

10 Dante is still in the old body of the flesh ("Adam"), subject to sleep.

12 Dante, Virgil, Sordello, Nino and Conrad.

15 Philomela was turned into a swallow, and her sister Procne into a nightingale, by the gods to prevent their violent death at the hands of Procne's husband Tereus, seeking vengeance for Procne's murder of their son. Procne had so acted on receipt of the news that Tereus had raped and mutilated her sister Philomel (Ovid, *Metamorphoses* VI.412 f.).

16–18 So-called 'dawn-dreams' were commonly reckoned

prophetic (cf. *Inferno* XXVI.7). The capacity to see into the future during sleep was proposed among others by Cicero and accepted by medieval theologians such as Albertus Magnus and Aquinas. Cf. *Convivio* II.VIII.13.

20 f. Cf. 'I have carried you on eagle's wings and brought you here to me' (Exodus 19.4). The significance of the eagle of Dante's dream, as with other elements of his imagery, cannot be precisely delimited. It is possible that Dante intended the eagle here to be symbolic not only of grace, but also of empire (cf. the symbolic Eagle of *Paradiso* VI), or more exactly, of an *ideal* of universal government which, inspiring the mind of man, raises him towards attempting the achievement of a society of perfect justice. If that perfected society is prefigured by Terrestrial Paradise on the summit of the mountain, towards which the pilgrim poet will shortly begin his ascent, then the way to the realisation of this social and political ideal must be through obedience to the Church's spiritual laws of penitence and prayer (required on the mountain), as well as by obedience to secular law symbolised perhaps by the philosophical rationale of the mountain (transposed into the particular shape and disposition the mountain takes, the nature of which the poet must take account of, if he is to ascend at all). It is significant that the symbolic eagle is the dream (though a 'true' dream, see note to ll. 16–18 above), whilst St Lucia (l. 55 f.) is the reality. With perfect spiritual vision, it is she who carries Dante up to the gates of Purgatory so that he might begin the actual achievement of the conquest of the mountain's summit, and all it signifies.

23 Ganymede was carried off by an eagle to become cupbearer to Zeus.

34–9 The mother of Achilles, Thetis, took him away whilst he slept from Chiron his teacher, to the court of Lycomedes at Scyros. From here he was inveigled by Ulysses to join the Greek armies on their way to Troy (see note to *Inferno* XXVI.55 f.). Cf. Statius, *Achilleid* I.104 f.

55 St Lucia (Lucy): see note to *Inferno* II.97 f., and note to l. 20 above.

58 "essences": souls, as forming the essential nature of men.

75 "a sort of crack": see notes to *Inferno* V.20, and *Purgatorio* IV.19–21.

82 Cf. the flashing sword of the Cherubim set to guard Terrestrial Paradise (Eden) after the Fall (Genesis 3.24).

94–102 The first step is symbolic of recognition and confession of sin, the second contrition, the third satisfaction through works (penances): the three stages leading to the forgiveness of sins.

104 "the threshold" probably represents the 'rock' on which the Church was founded, the authority of Christ delegated to St Peter and his successors (Matthew 16.18–19).

105 "diamond": possibly denoting the unimpugnable principle and justice of the process of forgiveness of sins.

111 The ritual gesture, expressing penitence for sin by 'thought, word and deed', accompanied by the words '*mea culpa, mea culpa, mea maxima culpa*'.

112 The "seven P's" stand for the soul's "wounds" (l. 114; Ital. *piaghe*, Lat. *plagae*) which remain after the seven mortal sins (Lat. *peccata*) have been forgiven. The "wounds" are what is left blemishing the soul, leaving it with 'resistance to good and tendency to evil' (St Bonaventure). Acts of penance are prescribed precisely to incline the will once more to the good and away from evil, and such are the aims of the torments on Mount Purgatory (Singleton).

117–26 "two keys": the silver and gold keys of ecclesiastical authority (see Matthew 16.19), the silver representing spiritual discernment, the golden the power 'to bind or loose' the sin (see also *Paradiso* V.57).

124 "One": the golden.

126 "the knot": the complexity of the sin, as to motive, circumstances and effect.

131–2 'No one who sets his hand to the plough and then keeps looking back is fit for the Kingdom of God' (Luke 9.62); cf. also Genesis 19.15–26, and the myth of Orpheus and Eurydice (Ovid, *Metamorphoses* X.1 f.).

137–8 The Roman treasury was in the temple of Saturn on the Tarpeian hill; it was plundered by Julius Caesar in 49BC in spite of the attempts of Metellus to defend it (see Lucan, *Pharsalia* III.153 f.).

140 The hymn 'We praise thee, O God', in use in church services since the fourth century.

PURGATORIO X

Dante and Virgil, on the First Cornice of Purgatory, find its wall sculptured with scenes exemplifying humility, and encounter the souls of the proud.

2 For love as the motive of all good and evil actions, see *Purgatorio* XVII.91 f.

3 Cf. 'all the paths they [the wicked] follow are crooked', Isaiah 59.8.

4–6 See note to *Purgatorio* IX.131–2.

14 The setting moon is now on the wane, after appearing full when Virgil and Dante were in the dark forest at the beginning of the journey (see *Inferno* XX.127).

16 Cf. Matthew 19.24, and notes to *Inferno* V.20 and *Purgatorio* IV.19–21.

32 Polycletus (*c.*452–412BC) the famous Greek sculptor, mentioned in Aristotle and Roman authors.

33 For Dante, Nature is God's child, and Art his grandchild. Art follows Nature as "a student follows his master" (see *Inferno* XI.101–5 and note).

34 f. The sculptured scenes are *exempla* of the virtue of humility, the opposite of pride, the sin purged on the first cornice.

34 The archangel Gabriel, who announced the Incarnation to Mary. See Luke l. 28 f.

35 Cf. Luke 2.13–14.

36 Cf. note to *Paradiso* VII.48.

44 'Behold the handmaid of the Lord [be it unto me according to thy word]', Luke 1.38.

55 f. The biblical episode engraved is from 2 Samuel 6.2 f.: King David's bringing the Ark (chest) of the covenant into Jerusalem, Uzzah's sin in presuming to touch it as it swayed (v. 57), David's dance of worship, and his wife Michal's contempt for her husband's lack of dignity. See *Paradiso* 37–9 and note.

73 f. The emperor Trajan (d. 117AD), according to legend, after some altercation postponed his departure for battle in order to redress the wrong done to a widow whose son had recently been murdered. See *Paradiso* XX.44–8 and note.

75 Pope Gregory the Great (d. 604) was held to have swayed the justice of God by prayer ("his great victory"), releasing Trajan's soul from Hell, who, resuscitated, was converted to Christianity. Dante accepted this, as Aquinas before him, and places Trajan in Paradise (*Paradiso* XX.44–8).

94 i.e. God.

100 The souls of the proud, bowed under the weight of boulders.

111 See note to *Inferno* X.11.

On the Cornice of the Proud, Dante hears the souls intoning the Lord's Prayer, and converses with Omberto Aldobrandeschi and Oderisi da Gubbio. The latter points out to Dante also the soul of Provenzan Salvani.

1–21 Dante paraphrases the Lord's Prayer (Matthew 6.9–13).

3 "your first creation": the angels and the heavens.

7–9 See note to *Paradiso* III.85.

13 "manna": the food with which God fed the Israelites during their forty years in the wilderness (see Exodus 16.35).

20 "the old adversary": Satan.

22 The souls in Purgatory are beyond earthly temptations, therefore do not need to say ll. 19–21 for themselves.

26 "loads": the boulders each of the proud bear on their backs (*Purgatorio* X.119).

32 "here": on earth, as Dante writes the *Purgatorio*.

44 Cf. *Purgatorio* IX.10 and note.

49 The speaker is Omberto Aldobrandeschi, second son of Guglielmo Aldobrandesco (l. 59), lord of Compagnatico (l. 66), slain by the Sienese in 1259. See *Purgatorio* VI. 109–11 and note.

58 "Latin": i.e. Italian.

61 The Aldobrandeschi were Ghibelline counts of Santafiora in the Sienese Maremma.

67–9 See note to *Purgatorio* VI.109–11.

74 f. Oderisi da Gubbio (c.1240–99), a friend of Giotto and Dante, an illustrator of manuscripts, according to Vasari was employed in the Vatican Library by Boniface VIII. Oderisi, to whom no work can be certainly ascribed, was of the Bolognese school of miniaturists, a colleague of Franco of Bologna (ll. 82–3), and former pupil of Cimabue.

94–6 Cimabue (c.1240 to c.1302), the Florentine artist and mosaicist, introduced a more naturalistic style into painting of the Duecento which was dominated by Byzantine traditions. His pupil was the great Giotto di Bondone (c.1266–1337), now regarded as the founder of modern painting, who took the potentially original style of his master into totally new fields of plasticity and expression.

97–9 "one Guido": probably Guido Cavalcanti (see note to *Inferno* X.60); "the other": probably Guido Guinizelli of Bologna (see note to *Purgatorio* XXVI.92 f.).

108 The (eighth) heaven of the fixed stars, which moves in its precession from west to east (as opposed to its diurnal movement east to west), one degree per century.

109 Provenzan Salvani (l. 121), c.1220–69, the leading Ghibelline of Siena (ll. 122–3) and ally of the Florentine Farinata degli Uberti at the battle of Montaperti (see notes to *Inferno* X.22, 91–3), where the Florentine Guelfs were utterly defeated (ll. 112–13). Provenzan was beheaded when captured by the Florentine Guelfs in 1269, after the battle of Colle. His houses and property in Siena were then obliterated by the returning Guelf partisans (l. 111). See *Purgatorio* XIII. 106 f. and note.

115 Cf. Isaiah 40.6–8, James 1.11.

116 "he": the sun.

133–8 One of the early commentators relates the story that Provenzan begged for money in the centre of Siena, to pay a huge ransom for a friend imprisoned by Charles I of Anjou after the battle of Tagliacozzo in 1268.

140 "your neighbours": Dante's fellow-citizens in Florence, who were to exile him in 1302.

141 i.e. Dante in his exile will come to know the courage it takes to put aside pride and beg from others (cf. *Convivio* I.III.4).

PURGATORIO XII

Still on the Cornice of the Proud, Dante firstly pauses to examine the scenes sculptured in bas-relief on the path which depict the downfall of the arrogant, then submits himself to the guardian angel of the cornice.

2 Oderisi da Gubbio (see previous canto).

25–60 In the Italian text an acrostic is formed from the initial letters of the *terzine* to read *VOM* (i.e. *uomo*, man), a device to emphasise that pride is the gravest sin of man, from which all others stem. See note also to ll. 61–3 below.

25 Lucifer (Satan) the highest of created Intelligences, whose rejection from heaven was due to his pride and rebellion. See Revelation 12.7–9, Luke 10.18.

28 Briareus, one of the Titans (giants) who rebelled against Jupiter on Olympus and were defeated at the battle of Phlegra (see note to *Inferno* XXXI.99).

31 "Thymbraeus": Apollo; "Pallas": Athena (Minerva).

32 "their father": Jupiter.

34 Nimrod: the supposed architect of the Tower of Babel

(Babylon) in Shinar, "his great work" (see Genesis 10.8–10, 11.1–9). The completion of the tower was prevented by God by confusing the language of its presumptuous builders; hence Nimrod's bewilderment (l. 35). See also *Inferno* XXXI.77–8, and *De Vulgari Eloquentia* I.VII.4–5.

37–9 Niobe, queen of Thebes, inordinately proud of her fourteen children and her divine origins, required the Thebans to worship her instead of Latona. The latter's children, Apollo and Diana, at their mother's request, killed all the presumptuous queen's children (see Ovid, *Metamorphoses* VI.182 f.).

40–41 Saul, the first king of Israel, arrogantly disobeyed God (1 Samuel 15). Defeated by the Philistines on Mount Gilboa, Saul committed suicide (1 Samuel 31.1–6).

42 See 2 Samuel 1.21, David's curse on Gilboa.

43–5 Arachne challenged Athena (Minerva) to a contest in weaving tapestries. The perfection of Arachne's work, her choice of subject (the love affairs of the gods), together with her hubris, earned the destruction of her work by the enraged goddess. To avoid the goddess's anger Arachne hanged herself, but was transformed in the nick of time by Athena into a spider (Ovid, *Metamorphoses* VI.5 f.).

46–8 Rehoboam, king of Israel, arrogantly refused to alleviate the heavy taxation imposed on the people by his father Solomon. When his general Adoram was stoned by the rebellious Israelites, Rehoboam mounted his chariot and fled to Jerusalem (1 Kings 12.1–19).

50–51 Alcmaeon's mother Eriphyle was bribed with a necklace (formerly belonging to Venus's daughter) to reveal the hiding place of her husband Amphiaräus, who was unwilling to join the Theban wars. Her presumption in yearning to possess something belonging to the gods, as well as her treachery, was punished by her death at the hands of her son Alcmaeon. See note to *Paradiso* IV.103–5, and *Inferno* XX.32–6 and note.

52–4 Sennacherib, blasphemous king of Assyria, was killed by his sons after his decisive defeat by divine intervention, following his expedition against King Hezekiah of Israel (2 Kings 18.13–37, 19.1–37).

55–7 Tomyris, queen of Scythia, avenged the death of her son by decapitating his defeated killer Cyrus, the arrogant Persian king, and throwing his head into a basin of blood with the words in l. 57 (Orosius, *Adversus Paganos Historia* II.VII.6).

58–60 The blasphemous Assyrian Holofernes, Nebuchadnezzar's general, was decapitated in his tent by Judith, during the siege of Bethulia; his army fled (Judith 8–14).

61–3 The Trojan war ended with the capture and pillage of 'proud Troy' by the Greeks. Cf. *Inferno* I.75, Virgil, *Aeneid* III.2–3. In the Italian text the initial letters of the *terzina* form the word *VOM* (*uomo*, man), as if this legendary episode were really a monument to man's overweening pride and foolish vainglory.

81 i.e. it is just past noon on Easter Monday. In classical literature the hours were frequently represented as divine attendants upon the sun.

94 Cf. Matthew 22.14: 'For though many are invited, few are chosen.'

100–105 Just outside the earlier walls of Florence (ironically referred to as "The well-run city", l. 102) on the south-eastern side, the church of San Miniato al Monte, which still stands, was reached in Dante's day by steps; access from Florence was over the Rubaconte bridge (now the Ponte alle Grazie).

105 See note to *Paradiso* XVI.105.

110 'Blessed are the poor in spirit' (AV Matthew 5.3), the first of the beatitudes in Christ's sermon on the mount; 'the poor in spirit' is rendered in the New English Bible as 'those who know their need of God', i.e. an attitude diametrically opposite to that of pride.

118 Pride is the heaviest of all the sins, 'the beginning of all sins' (Aquinas).

121 See note to *Purgatorio* IX.112.

135 The guardian angel of the gates of Purgatory (*Purgatorio* IX.78 f.).

PURGATORIO XIII

On the Second Cornice, where the sin of envy is purged, the poets hear disembodied voices recalling exempla *of charity, and encounter Sapia among the penitents.*

13–15 The sun is almost due north, since it is shortly after midday. Virgil now turns to the right, to move round the cornice anticlockwise.

29 "*Vinum non habent*" ['They have no wine']: the words of concern of Mary, to her son Jesus, at the feast of Cana-in-Galilee, where Jesus turned water into wine. See John 2.1–11.

33 Having avenged his father's death, Orestes, son of

Agamemnon, was duly apprehended. His friend Pylades, in order to save him, declared that he (Pylades) was Orestes. See Cicero, *De amicitia* VII.24, and John 15.13.

36 Based on the words of Christ, in Matthew 5.44.

39–40 The pattern of the corrective punishments in Purgatory as a whole is here established: "the whip", examples of the virtue to be imitated; the "bridle", examples of the sin to be avoided. The implied image is of the horse, representing the unruly appetites (as in *Convivio* IV.XXVI.5 f.).

50–51 Part of the Litany of the Saints.

70–72 The training of hawks, caught in the wild, required the expedient of sewing the eyelids together, to exact quiet and obedience.

95 "one true city": the City of God (cf. Hebrews 11.16).

96 "pilgrim": cf. Hebrews 11.13–14.

106 f. Sapia (Sapía), d. before 1289, wife of Ghinaldo Saracini, lord of Castiglioncello (Montereggioni), aunt of Provenzan Salvani (see note to *Purgatorio* XI.109). A Guelf sympathiser, she joyfully witnessed the defeat of the Ghibellines of Siena (amongst whom was Provenzano, her nephew) by the Florentines at the battle of Colle, in the Val d'Elsa, Tuscany, in 1269. See *Purgatorio* XI.109 and note.

109 Sapia plays here on etymologies, and the belief in the mysterious equivalence of names and things (see note to *Paradiso* XII.69): 'Sapia' has the same root as 'sapient' (wise).

127 According to early commentators, a Franciscan hermit of great piety who died in 1289.

152 Talamone: a small silted port on the coast of Tuscany (purchased by Siena in 1303) which the Sienese vainly hoped to develop, in order to capture some maritime trade from Pisa.

153 "the Diana": a supposed underground stream of Siena, which, it was vainly hoped, would provide the city with a constant supply of fresh water.

PURGATORIO XIV

On the Cornice of the Envious, Guido del Duca reproves the degenerate cities and families of the Val d'Arno, and laments the moral decline of the dynasties of the Romagna whilst commending their more virtuous forebears. Exempla of envy are then heard as disembodied voices.

10 "And one said": Guido del Duca (see l. 81) degli Onesti of

Ravenna (c.1170 to c.1250), renowned for the nobility and integrity of his character. He was *podestà* of Rimini (1199) and possibly of other towns of the Romagna. No record is extant attesting his sin of envy.

14 "your grace": i.e. the grace of God that allows Dante to make his journey.

17 The Arno rises just south of Monte Falterona in the Apennines.

25 "the other": Rinier (see ll. 88–9) de Paolucci da Calboli (c.1225–96), a Guelf leader of the Romagna, was *podestà* of Parma and other towns of the region, and much involved in the conflicts there between Guelfs and Ghibellines. He died in the defence of Forlì against a Ghibelline attack.

31–2 "the mountain chain": the Apennines, thought to have been formerly connected in the far south to "Pelorus" (Cape Faro, North East Sicily).

34 i.e. at its mouth, not far from Pisa.

42 Circe, daughter of the Sun, transformed Ulysses' men into hogs. See Ovid, *Metamorphoses* XIV.248 f., Virgil, *Aeneid* VII.10 f.

43 Perhaps the Conti Guidi of Porciano (see *Inferno* XXX.64 f.) or the inhabitants of the Casentino in general.

46 The Aretines.

50 The Florentines. Cf. *Paradiso* XXV.6.

53 The Pisans.

58 Fulcieri dei Paolucci da Calboli, Black Guelf *podestà* of Florence in 1303, a cruel persecutor of the White Guelfs including Dante. See G. Villani, *Cronica* VIII.59.

64 "sad forest": Florence. Cf. *Inferno* I.2 and note.

87 Possessions, high office and honours belong to individuals, and provoke envy since they cannot be shared, whereas love is in the ownership of no individual, provokes more love and increases as it is shared.

92 i.e. the Romagna, "the shore" being that of the Adriatic.

97–8 Romagnole nobles of the middle thirteenth century, of honour and reputation, though of no great fame, whom Dante cites as belonging to the 'good old days' of an earlier generation (see ll. 109–11).

100 Fabbro dei Lambertazzi of Bologna (d. 1259), Ghibelline leader in the Romagna, in the heyday of Bologna's power.

101 Bernadin di Fosco, leading Guelf of Faenza, gallantly defended the city against the forces of Frederick II in 1240.

104 Guido da Prata: possibly a local grandee of Ravenna, in the early thirteenth century.

105 Ugolino d'Azzo, probably degli Ubaldini (d. 1293), of Tuscan origins, related to cardinal Ottaviano (*Inferno* X.120), and Archbishop Ruggieri (*Inferno* XXXIII.14). He had settled in the Romagna and acquired estates there.

106 A nobleman of Rimini, probably of the early thirteenth century, given to hospitality.

107 The Traversari: an influential Ghibelline family of Ravenna. Cf. l. 98: Piero had been one of its most distinguished members. The Anastagi: a once powerful Ghibelline family of the same city.

112 Brettinoro: Bertinoro, near Forlì, with a castle held by the Manardi family, who were extinct by 1300 (cf. l. 97).

115–17 i.e. the Malvicini family, Ghibellines, counts of Bagnacavallo, were near extinction by 1300, whereas the counts of Castrocaro and Conio (Cunio) were obstinately producing degenerate sprigs.

118 A Ghibelline family of Faenza, whose surviving head in 1300, Maghinardo, was known as 'the demon' (see *Inferno* XXVII.50).

121 Ugolino dei Fantolini of Faenza (d. 1278), according to early commentators, was a nobleman of outstanding integrity, whose two sons were both dead by 1300.

133 The voice of Cain, who out of envy had just murdered his brother Abel (Genesis 4.14).

139 The daughter of a king of Athens, whose envy of her sister Herse earned her the punishment as described, at the hands of Mercury. See Ovid, *Metamorphoses* II.708 f.

146 "the old adversary": the Devil.

147 Equivalent to the "bridle" and "whip" of *Purgatorio* XIII.39–40 (see note).

PURGATORIO XV

The guardian angel of the Cornice of the Envious absolves Dante, who with Virgil ascends to the Third Cornice. Virgil, during the ascent, talks of the doctrine of charity. On reaching the next cornice, containing the souls guilty of anger, Dante is subject to an ecstatic vision of examples of meekness.

1–6 It is 3 p.m. (three hours before sunset), in Purgatory the beginning of "Vespers" (l. 6), and midnight in Italy.

4–5 "that sphere": the sun, restlessly moving across the sky, in the course of the year follows different paths, depending on time and season.

20 i.e. as far from the vertical.

21 "experience": i.e. experiment. See *Paradiso* II.95 f. and note, where the science of optics is again exploited.

38 'How blest are those who show mercy [mercy shall be shown to them]', from the Sermon on the Mount, Matthew 5.7. Mercy is glossed by Aquinas as the virtue opposite to the vice of envy, *Summa Theologica* II.II. q. 36, art. 3.

44 Guido del Duca; see preceding canto.

45 See *Purgatorio* XIV.86–7.

47 "his greatest vice": envy.

49 f. The root idea of Virgil's disquisition is found in St Augustine (*De Civitate Dei* XV.5), and later theologians.

73 "up there": in the Empyrean, true Paradise.

75 Again Dante's predilection should be noted for imagery from the science of optics. See note to l. 21 above.

76 Virgil is constantly aware of his intellectual limitations in Purgatory. His metaphysical explanations have resort to analogies in philosophy or the sciences, and he humbly looks to Beatrice (divine wisdom) for a fuller mastery of the transcendental. See *Purgatorio* XVIII.46 f., where, on the matter of the doctrine of free will, he again defers to Beatrice.

79 i.e. the remaining five P's inscribed on Dante's forehead. See note to *Purgatorio* IX.112.

83 "the next circle": the Third Cornice of the Wrathful.

85 f. A vision of *exempla* of meekness (the virtue opposite to the vice of wrath) now occupies Dante's whole mind and attention.

87–92 With the meekness but firmness of a mother, Mary remonstrates with Jesus who, still a child, had taken himself off to the Temple in Jerusalem to listen to, and debate with, the teachers (Luke 2.41–8).

94–105 When a suitor of a daughter of Pisistratus, tyrant of Athens, kissed the girl in public, the enraged mother urged that a savage punishment should be imposed on the youth. Pisistratus, unmoved, answered temperately in terms of ll. 104–5 (Valerius Maximus, *Memorabilium Libri*, Book V.I).

98 The naming of the city of Athens was at first subject to a dispute between Minerva and Neptune. See Ovid, *Metamorphoses* VI.70 f.

106–14 The death of St Stephen, first Christian martyr (Acts 7.54 f.).

132 "the eternal fountain": God (as in John 4.14).

PURGATORIO XVI

Enveloped by smoke on the Cornice of the Angry, Dante and Virgil hear the Agnus Dei recited. Dante then converses with Marco Lombardo, who refutes astral determinism and asserts that the will of man is free. He then inveighs against the bad government of Christendom due to the popes' acquisition of temporal authority, and proposes the independence of the Empire as to its origins and secular role.

5 "that smoke": the blinding cloud of smoke, covering the cornice, which effects the purging of anger. In the smoke the souls learn reliance on their spiritual resources in order to conquer their easy subjection to its power (see Virgil's words, in his role as reason, l. 15).

18 See John 1.29.

19 "*Agnus Dei*": 'Lamb of God [who takest away the sins of the world have mercy upon us . . . have mercy upon us . . . grant us thy peace]', a prayer of the Holy Communion or Mass.

46 Marco Lombardo: of no certain identification, the early commentators agree that he was of the petty nobility of North Italy, living in the middle of the thirteenth century. Legends about him attest his generosity of spirit and integrity of character. The use that Dante makes of Marco here is typical in one respect of the polemical semantics of the *Comedy*: of no great social or intellectual renown, Marco is yet employed to castigate popes for their rapacity and assert the sacred doctrine of man's free will. Similar is the role of Sordello (*Purgatorio* VI–VIII), Guido del Duca (*Purgatorio* XIV), Cacciaguida (*Paradiso* XV–XVIII). 'Few of you are men of wisdom, by any human standard, few are powerful or highly born. Yet, to shame the wise, God has chosen what the world counts folly, and to shame what is strong, God has chosen what the world counts weakness. He has chosen things low, and contemptible, mere nothings, to overthrow the existing order' (1 Corinthians 1.26–8).

57 "elsewhere": by Guido del Duca, *Purgatorio* XIV, 37–9.

63 "here below": i.e. due to merely human causes.

67–9 The false doctrine of astral determinism.

73 A philosophical stance accepted by Aquinas, who restricted the influence of heavenly bodies to man's sensitive appetites alone, whilst his intellectual functions of will and reason remain essentially unaffected: e.g. *Summa Theologica* II.II, q. 95, art. 5.

75 "light": the power of ethical discrimination. See Ecclesiasticus 17.7.

76 "free will": this doctrine, central to the question of man's relationship to God, is discussed by Dante in *De Monarchia* I.XII.2–4 following Aquinas. The subject is developed in the *Comedy* by Virgil in *Purgatorio* XVIII.61–75, and Beatrice in *Paradiso* V.19–24. See Ecclesiasticus 17.6: 'He gave men . . . the power of choice and a mind for thinking.'

78 "well nourished": not least on the Christian doctrine that asserts the inviolable principle of the freedom of the will.

79–80 "a greater law . . . a better nature": God. Marco states the seeming paradox of Christian doctrine, that man is most free when his will and reason most conform to those of God (whereas man's bondage lies in his apparent freedom: the indulgence of his appetites or the pursuit of injustice).

91–3 For clarification see Dante's earlier statement in prose in *Convivio* IV.XII.14–18.

95–6 Dante's ideal state of universal justice, under a single monarch (the emperor of the Holy Roman Empire), is discussed in *De Monarchia*, written either *c.*1312, or *c.*1318.

97 "laws": Roman law as codified by Justinian. See note to *Paradiso* VI.10. A revival and study of Roman law had taken place in Bologna in the twelfth and thirteenth centuries.

98 "No one": since the death of Emperor Frederick II in 1250 (see note to *Inferno* X.119) Dante had held the throne of the Empire to be morally vacant. See notes to *Purgatorio* VI.97 f., VII.91–6.

98–9 The pope ("shepherd") meditates ("may chew the cud"), but has no discernment ("his hooves are not parted"), confusing spiritual and temporal matters (the latter the responsibility of the Emperor). Dante almost certainly has in mind the papal bull of 1302, *Unam Sanctam*, issued by Boniface VIII in which papal *plenitudo potestatis* is claimed, a notion Dante strenuously opposed. The moral implication of the integral hoof is that the contemporary popes are 'unclean' animals (see Leviticus 11.1–7). The political implications are developed in ll. 106 f.

106 Ancient Rome prepared the time of universal peace (*pax romana*), for the birth of the Saviour. See Dante, *Convivio* IV.V.3 f., *De Monarchia* I.XVI.1–2.

107–8 Christian Rome was the seat (in theory) of the Holy Roman Emperor, and traditionally the seat of the pope (the "two suns"), each responsible, in Dante's view, for guiding man to his twofold end: temporal happiness and eternal happiness respectively (*De Monarchia* III.XVI). The image of the "two suns" was Dante's answer to the wide employment in contemporary polemics, by supporters of papal supremacy, of the traditional sun–moon metaphor. Here the moon was asserted to represent the Empire, its authority a mere reflection of the Church's divine authority (the sun). See *De Monarchia* III.IV.12–22. Dante ever maintained the divine, autonomous origins of both Church and Empire, as well as the independence of their institutional roles in Christian Europe.

109–10 The images of the crook (the shepherd's, i.e. the pope's) and the sword (of the Emperor) here refute by implication the notion of the Church's two swords, spiritual *and* temporal, developed by Boniface VIII in the bull *Unam Sanctam* (see note to ll. 98–9 above).

115 Rivers delimiting the territory of old Lombardy, Marco's homelands.

117 Frederick II (see note to l. 98 above) had been checked in his territorial ambitions by the combined military power of the papacy and the rebellious league of northern Italian cities.

124 Currado da Palazzo: of Brescia, vicar of Charles I of Anjou in Florence in 1276, and *podestà* of Piacenza in 1288, a Guelf leader of reputedly exemplary character. Gherardo da Camino (d. 1306) of Treviso: 'he was noble, and so will his memory be for ever' (Dante, *Convivio* IV.XIV.12).

125 Guido da Castello: of Reggio Emilia who, according to one early commentator, entertained any French guests with openhanded generosity (cf. *Convivio* IV.XVI.6).

131–2 "the sons of Levi": the priesthood, i.e. the Church; "the inheritance": worldly possessions, wealth (see Numbers 18.20–24).

140 Gaia: early commentators are divided on her character; she appears to have been either a paragon of virtue, or a wanton. Sapegno, Singleton and others prefer to see her as the latter, but the gratuitous lowering of the moral and poetic tone of the passage through such an interpretation is hard to accept in *Purgatorio*.

PURGATORIO XVII

On the Third Cornice; Dante is subject to visions of exempla *of anger. Submitting to the guardian angel of the cornice, Dante, with Virgil, mounts to the next terrace, where night falls. Virgil in the meantime explains to Dante the moral structure of Purgatory.*

3 It was believed in antiquity and the Middle Ages that the mole's eyes were covered by a membrane. See Brunetto Latini, *Tresor* I.197.

11 "that cloud": the cloud of smoke (see note to *Purgatorio* XVI.5).

16–18 Following Aristotle, it was thought that the faculty of the imagination (*fantasia*) stored and retained the 'material phantasms' received from the senses alone (Aquinas, *Summa Theologica* I, q. 78, art. 4, resp.; Dante, *Convivio* III.IV.9 f.). Dante proposes (following, according to Bruno Nardi, certain neo-Platonist interpretations) that the imagination can in fact be stimulated directly by God (the "will" of l. 18) in visions. See note to *Paradiso* XXXIII.85 f.

19–20 Procne was transformed into a nightingale, having, in her rage, killed her son Itys and served him to her unfaithful husband Tereus. For Tereus's infidelity, see note to *Purgatorio* IX.13–15.

26–30 Haman, the chief officer of Ahasuerus, the king of Persia, was hanged (Dante has "crucified") at the insistence of Queen Esther as punishment for his attempted suppression of the Jews. Mordecai, the Jew who had innocently provoked the anger of the arrogant Haman, was promoted to Haman's office (Esther 3–7, 10).

34–9 Lavinia ("a young girl", l. 34), princess of Latium, was promised by her father to Aeneas, in preference to Turnus. Amata, the mother of Lavinia, incensed by her husband's decision and distraught at the false news of Turnus's death, committed suicide (Virgil, *Aeneid* XII.595 f.).

44 "a light": the guardian angel of the Third Cornice.

63 See note to *Purgatorio* VII.53–7.

68–9 Another P is wiped from Dante's forehead by the angel, who pronounces the appropriate beatitude 'Blessed are the peacemakers [for they shall be called the children of God]', AV

Matthew 5.9. Aquinas discusses the difference between just and unjust anger in *Summa Theologica* II.II, q. 158, art. 1–3; and cf. Christ's anger in Matthew 21.12–13.

80 "the new circle": the Fourth Cornice of the Slothful.

85–6 Virgil refers to the sin of sloth, and especially spiritual sloth (Chaucer: 'accedie', *The Parson's Tale* l. 388).

87 "the idle rower": cf. the metaphor of the 'boat' of the soul in its journey over the 'sea' of life in *Convivio* IV.XXVIII.2.

91–3 This proposition is developed more fully by Dante in *Convivio* III.III.2 f., following Aquinas.

94 "natural love": the instinctive love of all created things for their 'proper place', or their perfect fulfilment, e.g. fire moves upwards, it was believed, towards the Sphere of Fire; plants seek their sustenance in specific terrain, animals love their own kind, and man's soul as intellective and 'angelic' (his 'essence' as man) seeks to return to God whence it came. This love is instinctive, and thus not subject to praise or blame. See Dante, *Convivio* IV.XII.14 f.; *De Vulgari Eloquentia* II.II.48 f.; Aquinas, *Summa Theologica* I, q. 60, art. 1, f.

95 "the other kind": rational or elective love, where free will or choice is exercised (the prerogative only of man and angels), and where praise or blame may properly attach. This is the conscious attraction to a particular object in experience (K. Foster), to an 'apprehended' good or 'apparent good'. See *Summa Theologica* I.II, q. 27, art. 1, ad. 1.

95–6 It is elective love, so classified, that is purged in Purgatory on the seven cornices. Elective love may err if it is:

> (i) directed to the "wrong object" (the harm of one's neighbour) through pride (1st Cornice), envy (2nd Cornice), anger (3rd Cornice); (ii) directed to the good, but with "too little vigour": sloth (4th Cornice); (iii) directed to the good, but with "too much . . . vigour": avarice (5th Cornice), gluttony (6th Cornice), sexual promiscuity (7th Cornice).

The order of the Seven Mortal Sins adopted by Dante is that of St Augustine and St Bonaventure.

97 "it": elective love: "the primal good": God.

98 "the secondary": the good as apprehended by man that answers (or seems to answer) directly or indirectly to his 'animal' and 'vegetable' appetites for sex and sustenance respectively.

103–5 See Aquinas, *Summa Theologica* I.II, q. 27, art. 4, resp., and elsewhere.

106–8 Thus suicide may be seen as the consequence of choosing death as an 'apparent good'; for example, to escape the evils of dishonour or pain. Dante shows that the suicide of Pier delle Vigne was not due to self-hate, but was motivated by the 'apparent good' of revenge, an aim accomplished by avoiding the total dishonour of a public execution. See note to *Inferno* XIII.55–78.

110 "the primal being": God. God may only be hated in his effects, not in his essence: see Aquinas, *Summa Theologica* II.II, q. 34, art. 1, resp., and Romans 8.7.

115–17 The sin of pride (cf. Aquinas, *Summa Theologica* II.II, q. 162, art. 3).

118–20 The sin of envy (cf. Aquinas, ib., q. 36, art. 1 f.).

121–3 The sin of anger (cf. Aquinas, ib., q. 158, art. 2, ad. 3).

127 "a confused notion of good": God, as *the* good of man, is implied here. Cf. Aquinas: 'To know that God exists in a general and confused way is in our nature, in so far as God is the beatitude of man' (*Summa Theologica* I, q. 2, art. 1, ad.1).

133 "another good": the "secondary" goods of l. 98 (see note).

134–5 "happiness": this lies in the contemplation of God, the "benign essence".

137 "the three circles": the cornices where avarice, gluttony and promiscuity are purged respectively (see note to ll. 95–6 above).

PURGATORIO XVIII

Prompted by Dante, Virgil explains to him the nature of love and, as far as he is able to discern, its relation to the concept of free will. A crowd of souls of the formerly slack and apathetic rush past the poets on the Fourth Cornice, relating exempla *of keenness and commitment. The abbot of San Zeno indicates the way up to the next cornice, and two souls recite examples of sloth and pusillanimity. Dante falls asleep in the middle of his reflections.*

14–15 Virgil had ascribed all our actions to motivation by love, in the preceding canto, *Purgatorio* XVII.91–139.

17–18 See Matthew 15.14: 'they are blind guides, and if one blind man guides another they will both fall into the ditch'.

19–21 "The mind": i.e. the intellective soul as appetitive, which in its naïve state, "ready to love", has been described by Marco Lombardo in *Purgatorio* XVI.85–93.

22 "Impression": not merely a visual impression, but also its notion. The term is from the scholastic philosophy of the time, with its origins in Aristotle.

26–7 "it is nature": Virgil is speaking here, therefore, of 'natural' (instinctive) love (see *Purgatorio* XVII.93–4) as opposed to 'rational' (conscious, elective) love (ib. 95–102).

28–30 See *Paradiso* I.115 and note to ib. 109 f.

30 i.e. in the Sphere of Fire, believed to lie between the earth and the heaven of the moon. See note to *Paradiso* I.79–80.

31 "the captive mind": i.e. the soul 'captured' by desire for the object it is moved to love.

31–3 The three stages of love (following perception, or "apprehension", l. 22) identified by scholastic philosophy are here described: inclination towards the thing perceived (love, properly speaking, l. 26), desire (a spiritual movement of the appetite towards the thing loved, l. 31), joy (the tranquillity, "rest", l. 32, of possession). See Aquinas, *Summa Theologica* I.II, q. 26, art. 2, resp.

37 "the material of which it is made": i.e. the essential disposition to love implanted in human nature.

38 "imprint": i.e. "the impression/From a real object" (l. 22–3); in effect, here, the object itself.

39 "the wax": i.e. the essential disposition to love (the "material" of l. 37; see note).

45 The implication of this line would be that the notion of free will (central, with the notion of Original Sin, to the Christian doctrine of man) is erroneous. Virgil now expends time and effort, at this most important juncture, in relating the philosophy of the soul as a loving entity to that of the soul's essential freedom and responsibility; ll. 46–75.

46–8 These important lines serve not only to indicate the medieval view of Virgil as a philosopher (see *Inferno* I.89), but also his allegorical role as natural reason, and in this respect, his relation to Beatrice who is divine Wisdom (reason illuminated by divine grace). Beatrice's elucidation of the doctrine of free will and its relation to faith occurs in *Paradiso* V.19 f.

49–51 "substantial form": the essential character or constitution of a thing that possesses independent existence. Here, in the context of man, it is the soul, which exists "distinct/From matter" (and is thus eternal), but is temporarily "united" with matter (the body) in its earthly existence.

51 "a specific virtue": the soul's dual faculties of intellect and will.

56 "the first apprehension": the primary notions or conceptions of things for which the intellect (a faculty of the soul, see note to l. 51 above) needs no explanation, e.g. the notions of being and not being, completeness and incompleteness and so on. There is also, most importantly, the primary notion of the goodness of right and truth, by which the soul instinctively knows God, even before it knows that it knows Him.

57 "the primary dispositions of appetite": the natural, instinctive movement of desire in the soul (i.e. will; see note to l. 51 above) towards fulfilment of its needs (the soul's end or purpose) which are: God and his attributes such as goodness, truth, beauty (the fulfilment of man's intellectual or 'angelic' nature), pleasure of the senses, including sex (the fulfilment of his 'animal' nature), sustenance, i.e. food and warmth (the fulfilment of his 'vegetable' nature). See note to *Purgatorio* XVII.94.

61 "this wish": i.e. the "primary desire" of l. 59; "all the others": i.e. those wishes (desires) that arise from the soul's attraction towards *particular* objects (or concepts) in experience, i.e. desires for things as *means* to the soul's fulfilment (regarding fulfilment as the 'end' of the soul's natural inclinations, see note to l. 57 above); "this wish" is instinctive and naturally good; "all the others" will "accord" with it if they too are good.

62–3 "the innate power which counsels you", etc.: i.e. the exercise of reason or judgement, as to the rightness or wrongness of a thing or of a course of action. Such judgement should precede the retention or release of the will towards its fulfilment in the desired object.

69 "a theory of morals": i.e. ethics.

71 "out of necessity": because, as has been stated, the soul is "created ready to love" (l. 19, and cf. *Purgatorio* XVI. 85 f.).

79–81 The moon's position appears to be in Sagittarius, where the sun is when it sets south-west of Rome ("between Sardinia and Corsica"), near the winter solstice.

79 The monthly easterly 'backing' of the moon across the sky.

82 "that noble shadow": Virgil, born in Andes (modern Pietole), near Mantua.

89 "by people": souls of the slothful, whose lack of keenness is purged on this cornice.

92 "Ismenus and Asopus": rivers of the city of Thebes, in Boeotia, where Bacchus was born. He was worshipped in orgiastic rites, hence the "furious crowd" of l. 91.

100 Mary's visit to her cousin Elisabeth, following Gabriel's news of the latter's pregnancy at the Annunciation, was made in haste (see Luke 1. 39–40).

101–2 Events of 49BC in the civil wars between Ceasar and Pompey. The latter's stronghold in Ilerda (modern Lérida, Catalonia) was conquered by Caesar in a swift and brilliant manoeuvre. See Caesar, *De Bello Civile*, I.32 f., Lucan, *Pharsalia* III.453 f.

117 "justice": i.e. the just penalty for their slackness, to run without pausing.

118–20 Gherardo, d. 1187, abbot of the monastery of San Zeno, Verona, in the era of Frederick I ("Barbarossa", l. 119), emperor 1152–90. Frederick destroyed Milan in 1162, one of the rebellious communes of Northern Italy.

121–6 The reference is to Alberto della Scalla, lord of Verona, who died in 1301, the year following the events of *The Divine Comedy*. Although Alberto legitimately sired the great Can Grande (Dante's revered patron in his exile; see note to *Paradiso* XVII.71) he had the audacity to place his illegitimate, ill-favoured and immoral son Giuseppe as abbot of San Zeno in 1292.

133–8 The two spirits cite examples of spiritual tepidity: the Israelites, whose lack of faith and love for God was tantamount to betrayal, so that he vowed that they should not live to see the Promised Land (Numbers 14.1 f.); and those Trojans who remained in Sicily rather than pursue their destined journey to Italy under Aeneas (Virgil, *Aeneid* V.604 f.).

PURGATORIO XIX

In the early hours of the morning of the third day in Purgatory, on the Fourth Cornice, Dante dreams he is confronted by a Siren. On awakening, he submits to the guardian angel of the cornice, and with Virgil climbs up to the Fifth Cornice where the souls of the avaricious and wasters are purged of their sin. Amongst them Dante talks with Pope Adrian V, who refers to his niece Alagia.

1 "At the hour": before sunrise, at about 3.30 a.m.

2–3 Saturn was believed to shed cold on earth when it stood above the horizon. See Virgil, *Georgics* I.336. Similarly, the moon's light was thought to be literally cold.

4 "their Fortuna Major": geomancers, in 'casting figures', termed *fortuna major* the fortuitous configuration of shapes (obtained by the casual tapping of a stick on sand) resembling six of the stars in the constellations of Aquarius and the Fish (Pisces). The Fish rises just before the Ram, the constellation in which the sun rises on the eastern horizon at the spring equinox (see *Inferno* I.37–40 and note, *Inferno* XI.113–14 and note).

7 "in a dream": this, the second of Dante's dreams in Purgatory, also occurs before dawn, the time of the true dreams. See note to *Purgatorio* IX.16–18.

19 "the sweet siren": "that ancient sorceress" (l. 58) is symbolic of sins of the flesh (avarice, gluttony and lust) purged on the remaining cornices. Dante employs the same imagery in *Letters* V to the rulers of Italy: 'And do not allow greed with her illusions, siren-like ['*more sirenum*'], to seduce you, stifling the vigil of reason by her seductions' (para. 4). There may also be in Dante's Siren something of the adulteress of Proverbs 2.16–19, with her 'seductive words': 'No one who resorts to her finds his way back or regains the path to life.' See also *Purgatorio* XXXI.34–45.

22 Ignorant of the detail of Homer's *Odyssey* (Dante knew no Greek, and both MSS and translations of the complete work were lacking until the fifteenth century), Dante may have assumed the seduction of Ulysses by the Sirens from Cicero's translation, in *De Finibus* V, of a passage in *Odyssey* XII (E. Moore).

26 "a holy and spritely lady": the lady, like the Siren, is of Dante's dream; she should not be equated with any of the real figures of his journey (Beatrice, St Lucy, St Mary). Her symbolic function, to warn Reason (Virgil) of the danger against the seductive but illusory qualities of temptations of the flesh (the Siren), suggests that she is the "light upon good and evil" (see *Purgatorio* XVI.75 and note), ethical discrimination: 'The Lord gave men the power of choice and a mind for thinking. He filled them with discernment and showed them good and evil' (Ecclesiasticus 17.6–7).

43 The invitation of the guardian angel of the Cornice of the Slothful.

49 "and fanned us": with this movement, the angel erases the fourth P from Dante's forehead.

50–51 "Qui lugent": '[Blessed are] they that mourn [for they shall be comforted]', in AV Matthew 5.4, the second beatitude pronounced by Christ in the Sermon on the Mount. This is appropriate for those who, spiritually keen, may mourn in the flesh for the life of physical ease they have renounced.

62–3 Cf. *Purgatorio* XIV.148–50.

70 The Fifth Cornice of the Avaricious (including those who grasp at power and privilege, as well as material wealth) and the Wasters.

73 'My soul cleaveth unto the dust', AV Psalms 119.25.

81 i.e. they should move anticlockwise around the mountain, in the usual direction.

91–2 i.e. repentance leading to purification. See *Purgatorio* XXXIII.145.

97 Adrian V, pope 1276. With Martin IV on the Sixth Cornice of the Gluttonous, they are the only popes in Purgatory. In Paradise, Dante places only John XXI (Peter the Spaniard, *Paradiso* XII.134), apart from the martyred popes of the primitive Church. Four contemporary popes on the other hand are in Hell, or destined for Hell (see *Inferno* III, XIX and notes).

99 'Know that I was the successor of Peter'; St Peter was the first Bishop of Rome.

101 The river Lavagna in Liguria; Adrian's family were the Fieschi of Genoa, counts of Lavagna.

137 "*Neque nubent*": 'They neither marry' (AV Matthew 22.30); i.e. in the Afterlife, earthly rank, title and condition have no meaning.

142 Alagia; virtuous wife of Moroello Malaspina of the Lunigiana, a friend of Dante in his exile. Other women of the Fieschi were notoriously immoral. See note to *Inferno* XXIV.145–50.

PURGATORIO XX

On the Fifth Cornice, Dante hears the souls of the avaricious and the wasters recite examples of true liberality, then converses with Hugh Capet who reproaches his descendants amongst the royalty of France for their political rapacity. An earthquake shakes the mountain, and strains of the 'Gloria' are heard.

8 "the ill that fills the whole world": avarice in its various guises:

greed for material possessions or power; rapacity and miserliness.

10 "ancient she-wolf": the she-wolf is one of the three animals of the dark forest of *Inferno* I. Dante's explicit equating of the she-wolf with avarice on this cornice, where a pope (Adrian V, see previous canto) and a French monarch play a major role, lends support for a political as much as moral interpretation of the forest and its animals; see *Inferno* I.32 f. and notes.

15 The Greyhound (*Inferno* I.105) or the 'DXV' (*Purgatorio* XXXIII.43), the future champion and saviour of Christendom, is implied here. See notes.

19–24 Mary, mother of Jesus, the supreme example of the renunciation of material possessions. Although the mother of God incarnate, she humbly accepted to give birth to him in a stable: See Luke 2.6–7.

25–7 Fabricius Luscinus, Roman commander of the third century BC, famed in antiquity for his integrity and frugality. He rejected attempts of the invader Pyrrhus, king of Epirus, to corrupt him, and although occupying important official posts in Rome, died owning little but his farm. Cf. Dante, *De Monarchia* II.V.11.

31–3 St Nicholas, fourth-century bishop of Myra (Lycia), of whom a popular legend relates that he saved three daughters of an impoverished nobleman from prostitution by secretly providing them with dowries.

40 f. The speaker is Hugh (Hugues) Capet (l. 49), father of the founder of the Capetian dynasty (987) which was still ruling France in Dante's day. The historical inexactitude of some of Dante's statements on the early Capetians may be ascribed to error common amongst historians in his day.

46 Principal towns of Flanders, which the Capetian monarch Philip IV the Fair of France invaded, not without treachery, between 1297 and 1304. See note to *Purgatorio* VII.109, and *Paradiso* XIX.118–20; "vengeance" (l. 47) came in 1302, when the French were disastrously defeated by the Flemish at Courtrai, in the Battle of the Spurs.

52 "son of a butcher": this was part of the distorted legend, current in the Middle Ages.

53 "the ancient kings": the Carolingians.

54 Charles of Lorraine (who, as a son of Louis IV, should have succeeded his childless nephew Louis V in 987, but was supplanted by Hugh) was not in fact a monk.

58–9 Hugh Capet the Younger, King of France 987–996.

61–3 Provence fell into the sphere of influence of the French monarchy in 1246, when Charles I of Anjou, brother of Louis IX, married (not without political chicanery; hence l. 62) Beatrice of Provence.

63 "It": Hugh's line, the Capetian dynasty.

65 "to make amends": words, repeated as a refrain in succeeding verses, heavy with irony.

66 Philip IV annexed the county of Ponthieu and Gascony in 1294, seizing them from the King of England, Edward I. Normandy, ceded by King John of England, had first passed into French hands in 1206.

67–9 Charles I of Anjou, made king of Naples and Sicily in 1266, was employed by the popes and the Guelfs as their champion against remaining imperial Hohenstaufen in Italy, Manfred and Conradin. See note to *Purgatorio* VII.113.

69 Thomas Aquinas (1226–74) was believed to have been poisoned by agents of Charles I of Anjou. G. Villani, in *Cronica* IX.218, repeats the story, which is probably untrue. See note to *Paradiso* X.82 f.

71–8 "another Charles": Charles of Valois, brother of Philip IV of France, was invited by Pope Boniface VIII into Italy to support his campaigns against the Aragonese Frederick II of Sicily (see note to *Paradiso* XIX.131 and 136), and was employed also to settle the quarrel between the Black and White Guelfs in Florence. The latter he accomplished in 1301–2. Following Boniface's strategy, Charles effected a *coup* on behalf of the pro-papal Blacks against the Whites, an event that resulted in Dante's exile (see notes to *Inferno* VI.64–9, XXIV.144).

78–81 "The other": Charles II of Anjou (see notes to *Purgatorio* VII.126, and *Paradiso* XIX.127), before his accession to the title, was given command of the fleet by his father Charles I, in a campaign to recover the Kingdom of Sicily which had been lost in 1282 at the 'Sicilian Vespers' (see note to *Paradiso* VIII.72–5). The Angevin fleet (like that of their French allies; see note to *Purgatorio* VII.103) was soundly defeated in battle in 1284 by the fleet of Peter III of Aragon under Ruggiero di Loria, and the young Charles was taken prisoner. In 1305, Charles II gave his daughter Beatrice in marriage to Azzo VIII d'Este, following allegedly profitable bargaining.

85–90 The quarrels between Philip IV of France and Pope

Boniface VIII reached their culmination in September 1303 when Guillaume de Nogaret, Philip's emissary ("the fleur-de-lys", l. 86), together with Sciarra Colonna, in order to prevent a papal act of excommunication against Philip, seized the Pope at his residence in Anagni (old "Alagna", l. 86). The occasion of the disputes had been the refusal of the Pope, in 1295, to allow the French clergy to make contributions to the French exchequer. Philip's sharp response was met by the issue of papal bulls, claiming the full sovereignty (*plenitudo potestatis*) of the papacy over the secular state and its rulers; the most extreme of these was the bull '*Unam sanctam*' of 1302. The shock at Philip's temerity was widespread in Europe, many seeing in it the symbolic defeat of the theory of pontifical supremacy. The removal of the seat of the papacy from Rome to Avignon by Pope Clement V, in 1309, was felt to be a tragic but logical outcome.

88–90 The events of Christ's capture, trial and crucifixion are found in the gospel of Matthew 26.47–75, 27.1–56.

92–3 In 1307 Philip IV accused the Crusader order of the Knights Templar of heresy and sacrilege. Their vast wealth finally fell into his hands when the Order was suppressed by Pope Clement V at the Council of Vienne in 1312.

97 "the only bride": St Mary, l. 19 above.

103–5 Pygmalion, king of Tyre, treacherously murdered his uncle Sychaeus (hence "parricide", l. 105, in the broader sense of the Latin), the husband of his sister Dido, for his wealth. See Virgil, *Aeneid* I.340 f.; and *Inferno* V.61 and note.

106–8 Midas, king of Phrygia, was given by Bacchus the power to turn anything he touched into gold, so that even his food and drink were transformed. See Ovid, *Metamorphoses* XI.85 f.

109–11 Achan stole part of the forbidden spoils of Jericho, and with his family was stoned to death on Joshua's orders (Joshua 7.1 f.).

112 Sapphira and her husband Ananias deceitfully witheld from the apostles part of the money they had received from selling their worldly goods and, reproached by Peter, fell dead (Acts 5.1 f.).

113 Heliodorus was ordered by the king of Syria to despoil the Temple of Jerusalem, but was struck down by a mysterious horse and rider (2 Maccabees 3.1 f.).

115 Polymnester, king of Thrace, treacherously killed and robbed Polydorus the son of Priam of Troy, the latter having entrusted

his son to the Thracian's care before the fall of the city. See Virgil, *Aeneid* III.19 f., Ovid, *Metaphorphoses* XIII.429 f., *Inferno* XXX.13–21 and note.

116–17 Crassus, one of the Triumvirs with Caesar and Pompey in 60BC, was excessively wealthy. He was killed in 53BC by the Parthians, whose king, according to legend, filled the mouth of the severed head with molten gold.

130–32 Delos, a floating island, was at the mercy of wind and storm, until it was anchored by Jupiter to provide a safe refuge for Latona's confinement. Here she gave birth to Apollo and Diana "the two eyes of heaven" (i.e. as sun and moon respectively). See Ovid, *Metamorphoses* VI. 189 f.

136 "*Gloria in excelsis . . . Deo*": 'Glory to God in the highest', the words of the angels to the shepherds announcing the birth of Christ (Luke 2.14).

PURGATORIO XXI

Virgil and Dante encounter the poet Statius on the Fifth Cornice, who has just completed his purgation.

1 "The natural thirst": the innate appetite of the intellective or 'angelic' soul of man for truth, and for God as truth and the source of truth, "that truth . . . beyond which there is no room for what is true" (*Paradiso* IV.125–6). See also Dante, *Convivio* I.I.1 and 10 for the basis in Aristotelian thought of the concept, and note to *Purgatorio* XVII.94 on the subject of the "natural love" of the soul.

2–3 "that water": i.e. the illuminating grace of the revealed truth of God. For the episode of the encounter of Jesus with the Samaritan woman at Jacob's well in Sychar, see John 4.4–15.

7–9 For Jesus's encounter with the two disciples on the road to Emmaus after his resurrection, see Luke 24.13–32.

10 "A shadow": Statius; see note to l. 67 f. below.

25 "she who spins": Lachesis, one of the three Fates, who together with Clotho was believed to spin the yarn of a man's mortal life. Atropos, the third sister, was supposed to measure and cut off the yarn at the appointed time.

31–3 For Virgil's role as Dante's guide, see *Inferno* I.63 f. and note, *Purgatorio* XVIII.46–8 and note.

43–57 The part of the mountain of Purgatory above the gates is not subject to the variations of earthly climate, but to the laws of the 'unalterable heavens' alone.

50–51 "Thaumas's daughter": Iris, the rainbow (Ovid, *Metaphorphoses* XIV.845), whose location varies with the angle and position of the sun.

52 "Dry vapour": i.e. wind, believed to derive from an exhalation of dry, thin vapour from the earth.

53–4 The gate of Purgatory (see *Purgatorio* IX.90 f.).

55–7 See note to *Inferno* III.133.

62 "change its company": i.e. move upwards from Purgatory to Heaven.

63 "gives it pleasure to will": i.e. allows the soul fulfilment of its natural desire (will) to rise to heaven.

64–6 Freed from the flesh, the soul wills (with its 'natural' or instinctive desire) to rise at once to heaven, but its wish (its conscious desire, governed by an act of free choice) is to purge itself in the "torment" (l. 65) of Purgatory, whereas before it had inclined to indulgence in wrong (l. 66). The soul's wish is here, in its penitential state, conditioned by the grace of God, which inclines it to conform freely to the norms of "divine justice" (l. 65; and see notes to *Purgatorio* XVIII.57–63). Because the principle of *contrapasso* (retaliation) is operative in the torments of Purgatory (as in Hell; see note to *Inferno* XXVIII.142), the *particular* sinful disposition of these souls now becomes their penance.

67 f. "And I": Statius, Roman poet of the so-called Silver Age of Latin literature, was born in Naples (not Toulouse, l. 89) and died *c.*96AD. Author of the epic poems the *Thebaid* and the *Achilleid* (the latter unfinished, see l. 93), he also wrote the *Silvae* which would however have been unknown to Dante and his century. The *Achilleid* begins the account of the life of Achilles and his part in the Trojan war, and thus would have complemented the *Aeneid* of Virgil, the indispensable epic poem amongst the antecedents of *The Divine Comedy*. Clearly Dante attributes to Statius attitudes to the *Aeneid* of Virgil that he himself had entertained. Dante also shows Statius as having been converted secretly to Christianity through his reading of Virgil, an unlikely ascription from an historical point of view. C. S. Lewis, however, saw in the *Thebaid* a work whose pantheon and 'theology' are closer than any other classical work to Judaeo–Christian traditions (see Bibliography). Such traces, if detected by Dante himself (as is possible), would lend

credence to his theory of Statius's conversion to Christianity, and justify the linking here in the *Comedy* of Dante and Statius as poets who, at very different times in history, perceived something of divine light and truth in Virgil's work.

82–4 "the good Titus": see *Paradiso* VI.91–3 and note.

PURGATORIO XXII

Reaching the Sixth Cornice of the Gluttonous, Statius tells Virgil the circumstances of his conversion to Christianity, and inquires as to the fate of Terence and other poets. A voice issuing from a tree enjoins moderation, and provides examples of the virtue.

3 "a scar": the fifth of the P's with which Dante's forehead is branded. See note to *Purgatorio* IX.112.

4–5 The reference is to the beatitude of Christ's sermon on the mount: 'Blessed are they which do hunger and thirst [Vulgate: "*sitiunt*", l. 6] after righteousness', AV Matthew 5.6. This is the beatitude appropriate to the Fifth Cornice where avarice, an insatiable "thirst" for worldly wealth and power, is purged.

10–12 "Love, set alight by virtue": for Dante, the highest love of which man is capable is that engaging his highest nature, the rational or angelic: 'And by the fifth and last nature, by which I mean the truly human, or angelic, that is the rational, man entertains love for truth and virtue; and from this love true and perfect friendship is born', *Convivio* III.III.11. It is the love of virtue, Dante states here, that is the only truly compelling love; and so the passage here may be taken as a gloss on *Inferno* V.103 and 106, where Francesca erroneously, and fatally, assumes that it is sensual love that is ineluctable: "Love, which allows no one who is loved to escape ... led us two to find a single death."

13 Juvenal the satirist, *c*.65 to *c*.140AD, attacked the vices and extravagances of Roman life in verses heavy with irony and indignation; but where the victims of this social injustice came under his purview, his compassion is unmistakable. He was a younger contemporary of Statius (see *Satires* VII.82 f.).

14 "the limbo of hell": see *Inferno* IV.24 f. and note.

40–41 The quotation is from Virgil's *Aeneid* III.56–7, although Statius here appears to adapt the verses slightly to allow for his own case (i.e. prodigality, rather than avarice).

42 "below": in Hell, the Fourth Circle of the Moneygrubbers and Wasteful (*Inferno* VII).

46 See note to *Inferno* VII.57.

55–6 The lines refer to the subject of Statius's *Thebaid*. Jocasta, consort of the king of Thebes, was the mother of Oedipus and later became, in her ignorance, his wife. She bore Oedipus twin sons, Eteocles and Polynices, who became sworn enemies and killed each other in the war against Thebes waged by the seven kings. See Statius, *Thebaid* XII; *Inferno* XXVI.52–4 and note.

57 Virgil was the poet of the *Bucolic Poems* or *Eclogues*; see ll. 70–72 below and note.

58 Clio: the Muse of history.

60 "the faith": i.e. the Christian faith; 'For by grace are ye saved through faith . . . not of works, lest any man should boast', AV Ephesians 2.8–9.

62 Cf. 'God . . . who has called you out of darkness into his marvellous light', 1 Peter 2.9.

63 "the fisherman": St Peter (Simon), see Mark 1.16–17.

65 Parnassus: the mountain in Greece sacred to Apollo and the Muses of poetry.

70–72 Lines from Virgil's *Eclogues* IV.5–7, slightly adapted by Dante in harmony with his gloss in *De Monarchia* I.XI.1. These prophetic lines, written *c.*40BC, were interpreted from early Christian times as a prediction of the birth of Christ and the coming of the Christian era. See note to *Inferno* I.63 f. More than a small hint of Dante's own debt to Virgil can be gleaned from this exposition of Statius's indebtedness to him.

83 Domitian, Emperor of Rome 81–96AD, instigated a cruel persecution of the early Church, the most signal crime of the many perpetrated in his reign.

88–9 i.e. before Statius began writing the *Thebaid*; see note to *Purgatorio* XXI.67 f.

97 Terence, d. 159BC, Roman writer of comedies. Not known to Dante at first-hand, he nevertheless uses lines from *The Eunuch* as quoted by Cicero, in *Inferno* XVIII.133–5 (see note).

98 Caecilius: d. 166BC, comic dramatist, whose name was known to Dante through Horace and St Augustine. Plautus: d. 184BC, Roman comic dramatist known to Dante only by name. Varro (or Varius): a minor Roman poet, and friend of Horace and Virgil through whose works Dante became acquainted with his name.

100 Persius: d. 62AD, a Roman satirical poet, known to Dante only by name and reputation in other authors.

101–2 "that Greek": Homer; see *Inferno* IV.86–8 and note.

104 "the mountain": Parnassus (see note to l. 65 above).

105 "our nurses": the Muses of poetry.

106–7 Euripides, Antiphon, Simonides, Agathon: Greek playwrights and poets, whose names alone were known to Dante.

110–14 Characters in Statius' epic poems whom Dante treats as historical personages. Antigone: daughter of Oedipus and Jocasta (see ll. 55–6 above), interred alive by Creon; Deiphyle: wife of Tydeus (*Inferno* XXXII.130–31 and note), condemned to death by Creon; Argia, wife of Polynices of Thebes, sister of Deiphyle; "The girl who pointed out the spring of Langia": Hypsipyle, daughter of the king of Lemnos (*Inferno* XVIII.83 f. and note); "the daughter of Tiresias": Manto (whom Dante places, nevertheless, not in Limbo, but in the valley of the futurologists, in the Eighth Circle of Hell, *Inferno* XX.52 f.); Thetis: mother of Achilles (*Purgatorio* IX.37); Deidamia: one of the princesses of Scyros, deserted by Achilles at the insistence of Ulysses (see Statius, *Achilleid* I.536 f.; *Inferno* XXVI.62).

111 Ismene: sister of Antigone (l. 110), daughter of Jocasta and Oedipus (see note to ll. 55–6 above), witnessed the violent deaths of all in her family, including her lover Cyrrheus.

118–20 The "handmaidens" are the hours (see *Purgatorio* XII.80–81 and note). With the "fifth [handmaiden]" . . . at the "tiller" (the pole of Apollo's sun-chariot) the time is approaching 11 a.m.

141 These words are addressed to any fasting soul on the cornice who approaches the tree.

142–4 The virtue of restraint, opposite to the vice of gluttony, is exemplified by Mary's intervention at the wedding reception at Cana (see *Purgatorio* XIII.29 and note).

145–6 The reputation for temperance enjoyed by the women of ancient Rome is reported by, amongst others, Valerius Maximus and Aquinas.

146–7 See Daniel 1.3 f.

148–50 See Ovid, *Metamorphoses* I.102 f.

151–4 See Matthew 3.4, 11.11.

PURGATORIO XXIII

On the Sixth Cornice a crowd of souls, lean with hunger, pass by Dante, Virgil and Statius; one of these is Forese Donati, Dante's

Florentine friend. Forese castigates the women of Florence for their immodest dress.

4   "My more than father": Virgil.

11   *"Labia mea, Domine"*: 'Open my lips, O Lord [that my mouth may proclaim thy praise]', Psalms 51.15. The biblical verse is apt for the souls of the penitent gluttons of this cornice, whose mouths had been opened, in life, to less spiritual nourishment.

25   Erysichthon, prince of Thessalia, sacrilegiously felled a sacred oak in Ceres' grove which contained a nymph dear to the goddess. Ceres afflicted the prince with an insatiable hunger, so that he finally fed his body by consuming it. See Ovid, *Metamorphoses* VIII.738 f.

30   In the siege of Jerusalem by Titus in 70AD (see note to *Paradiso* VI.91–3), a Jewess by the name of Mary was forced by hunger to eat her own child. See Paulus Orosius, *Adversus paganos historia* VII.9.

32   "omo": the Italian (or low Latin) for 'man' (cf. Lat. *homo*; modern Ital. *uomo*), which can be easily read into the emaciated features (eyes, eye-sockets and nose) of the penitents. The concept is a commonplace in medieval sermons and theological tracts.

40   "a shadow": Forese (l. 48) Donati, brother of Piccarda (*Paradiso* III.34 f. and note) and Corso (see *Purgatorio* XXIV.82 f.). Known familiarly as Bicci (Dante, *Lyric Poetry* 72.2), Forese was a friend of Dante and a poet, who died in 1296. After Beatrice's death, Dante exchanged a series of sonnets in a *tenzone* with Forese (1293–6) where (unless the poems are to be taken antiphrastically) friendly banter is less in evidence than wounding malice. Dante attacked Forese for his gluttony (*Lyric Poetry* 73, 74), and made malicious fun of Forese's wife, Nella (*Lyric Poetry* 72). In this canto Dante as poet may be making amends to both victims of his verses, not least to Nella (see ll. 87–93). Dante was married to Gemma, Forese's cousin.

73   "that desire": i.e. the desire to submit to God's will.

74–5   See Matthew 27.46, 50.

83   "down below": in Ante-Purgatory. See *Purgatorio* IV.130–34.

94   "the Barbagia": a remote mountainous region in central Sardinia (Arborea) whose inhabitants were reputed uncivilised in the Middle Ages.

106–11 On such prophecies by Dante, see note to *Paradiso* XXII.14–15. Some commentators have linked this passage with Dante's *Letters* VI to the 'most infamous Florentines' of March 1311, where there is phrasing similar to l. 109. Here the promised punishment might be part of the avenging justice of Emperor Henry VII, from whom Dante expected so much, but see notes to *Purgatorio* VII.96, XXXIII.43.

118 Virgil, in the dark forest (*Inferno* I).

120 "the sister": the moon (Diana), sister to the sun (Apollo), both children of Zeus and Latona.

131 "the other": Statius.

PURGATORIO XXIV

The poet Bonagiunta da Lucca amongst the gluttonous on the Sixth Cornice compliments Dante on his poetry in the new manner, and indicates the deficiencies of his own and of others. Forese Donati foretells the violent death of his brother Corso Donati. Passing by a second tree on the cornice, Dante submits to the Angel of Temperance.

8 "He": Statius.

9 "another": Virgil.

10 Piccarda Donati, the sister of Forese, whom Dante encounters in the Sphere of the Moon. See *Paradiso* III.34 f. and note.

15 Piccarda's crown is the metaphorical 'crown of righteousness' of the justified and redeemed souls (AV 2 Timothy 4.8, 1 Corinthians 9.25); "high Olympus": lit. the home of the gods, Mt Olympus. By this Forese means the heaven of the true God. Dante as poet constantly indulges in this elegant mannerism.

19–20 Bonagiunta Orbicciani degli Overardi, *c.*1220 to *c.*1300, judge, notary of Lucca, and poet of the 'Central School' (the Tosco-Siciliani). Perhaps an underestimated follower of Guittone d'Arezzo (see l. 56 and note, and *Purgatorio* XXVI.124–6 and note), Bonagiunta may nevertheless be considered an important transitional poet between the earlier courtly lyric of the Sicilian school (early thirteenth century; see note to *Inferno* X.119) and the *Dolcestilnovo* of Dante and the Florentine *fedeli d'amore*. Dante, who may have known Bonagiunta personally, seems to write him down deliberately, here and in *De Vulgari Eloquentia* I.XIII.1.

21–4 Martin IV, pope 1281–5, a Frenchman, formerly treasurer of the cathedral of Tours. Notorious for his gluttony, he was yet sufficiently active on behalf of French interests in Italy, particularly those of Charles I of Anjou and Provence, king of Naples and Sicily (see *Purgatorio* VII.113 and note). Dante's election here of Martin IV for eventual beatitude, despite his condemnation in *Purgatorio* XX.67 f. of all the activities in Italy and elsewhere of the imperialistic Capetian monarchy, its kin and its henchmen, may perhaps only be explained in terms of the lofty and objective political stance of the mature poet.

24 Bolsena: a lake near Viterbo, "the sweet wine": Vernaccia.

29 Ubaldino della Pila, d. 1291, brother of Cardinal Ottaviano degli Ubaldini (see *Inferno* X.120 and note) and of Ugolino d'Azzo (recalled in *Purgatorio* XIV.105), was father of the notorious Archbishop Ruggieri degli Ubaldini of Pisa (see *Inferno* XXXIII.1 f. and notes). Ubaldino della Pila was lord of a castle in the Mugello, near Florence, noted for his magnanimity and gluttony. Boniface: probably of the Genovese Fieschi family, and Archbishop of Ravenna 1274–95.

31–3 Messer Marchese degli Argogliosi of Forlí (related to the da Polenta family of Ravenna, later Dante's patrons) was *podestà* of Faenza in 1296. He was possessed, according to an early commentator, of a widely renowned thirst, about which anecdotes circulated.

37 Gentucca: commentators have long been divided on the exact meaning of this word, but it is perhaps safest to see it as the proper name of some lady of Lucca who gave Dante hospitality during his exile (see also ll. 43–5).

51 The first line of the first *canzone* in Dante's *Vita Nuova* (XIX). The poem represented for Dante himself, as he tells us in the commentary, a new approach to lyric writing, the *stilo de la loda* (lit. 'laudatory style') in which the object of his love, Beatrice, would be the constant inspiration and focus of his themes, rather than himself with his sense of inadequacy, frustration and failure. As a consciously made, new and original beginning to his poetic output, the poem became something of a model for the school of poets who were associated with Dante (see l. 58, "your pens"), the *Dolcestilnovisti* (lit. 'poets in the sweet new style'; see l. 57, and note to *Purgatorio* XXVI.92 f.). The poem marks a departure from the earlier lyric poetry of Italy, which was based closely on Provençal antecedents. Such was the poetry of the so-called 'Central School' (the 'Tosco-Siciliani': including Guittone d'Arezzo,

l. 56, and Bonagiunta himself, amongst others), and of the still earlier Sicilian school of Jacopo da Lentini (the "Chief Clerk", l. 56), to which belonged Stefano Protonotaro, Pier delle Vigne (see *Inferno* XIII.55 f. and note), Jacopo Mostacci, Giacomino Pugliese, Frederick II, and Prince Enzo. The *canzone* in question may also mark a break, in an important way, with the poetry and thought of Guido Cavalcanti, Dante's friend and fellow-poet, so influential in Dante's early period (see *Inferno* X.60–63 and note). But the essential point of difference between Dante's lyric poetry and his predecessors' lies, as Dante himself points out (ll. 52–4), in his fidelity to inspiration rather than a reliance on the reworking of traditional forms and concepts. It is an inspiration which derives in part from a better understanding of the nature of love in its philosophical and theological dimensions (for which Dante was indebted initially to Guido Guinizelli, see *Purgatorio* XXVI.92 f. and note). The new poetry of Dante was also marked by a sharper, more discriminating sense of style.

54 The word 'dictate', here and in l. 59, belongs properly to the vocabulary of chancelleries and places of learning in the Middle Ages. A *dictator* was a highly placed functionary, highly educated, a master of eloquence, who often controlled the administration of a court, *curia* or chancellery, and was responsible for the drawing up (by 'dictation' to scribes and copyists) of all the important documents (treaties, declarations, agreements, petitions and the like) vital to commerce, litigation and diplomacy. *Ars dictandi* was the name given to the matter of the normative style-books of the chancelleries. Pier delle Vigne (*Inferno* XIII) and Brunetto Latini (*Inferno* XV) were celebrated *dictatores* of the imperial *Curia* and of the Guelf commune of Florence respectively. Of relevance also to the use of the term 'dictate' here is the notion of Alcuin of York that God is the 'dictator' under whom holy men write (*Poetae* I.285).

56 "the Chief Clerk": the imperial notary Jacopo da Lentini, *c.* 1200 to *c.*1250, the most prolific and accomplished of the Sicilian school of poets (see note to l. 51 above), considered the inventor of the sonnet form. Highly regarded both by Guittone and Dante (*De Vulgari Eloquentia* I.XII.8), Jacopo da Lentini has left some thirty pieces of reliable attribution showing exceptional metrical skill and a lively, graceful treatment of the themes and style of Provençal troubadour

verse. Guittone: Guittone d'Arezzo, c.1230–94, a Guelf partisan like Bonagiunta, master of *ars dictandi* and poet, he entered in 1265 the Order of the Knights of St Mary (the 'Frati Gaudenti', see note to *Inferno* XXIII.103), changing both the mode of his life and of his poetry, in which he adopted henceforth a highly moral and religious tone. The poetry of his earlier period is often heavy with rhetorical *ornatus*, difficult in expression, and sometimes conforms to the style of the *trobar clus*. His virtuosity often overreached his expressive powers, so that while Dante may have appreciated his technical achievement, he thought him lacking (as this canto indicates) in significant inspiration in the composition of love poetry.

79 "the place": Florence, where in April 1300 (the fictional date of *The Divine Comedy*) Dante was highly placed in the government of the city.

82–90 "the one who is most at fault": Forese refers to his brother, Corso Donati, who led the Black Guelf faction in Florence (see notes to *Inferno* VI.64–9), and was probably instrumental in persuading Pope Boniface VIII to send Charles of Valois to settle the issue in favour of the Blacks. Corso, ambitious for supreme power in Florence, met a violent death in October 1308, when the citizens of Florence turned against him, charging him with conspiracy and treason. See G. Villani, *Cronica* VIII.43, 49, 96.

84 "the valley": Hell.

98 "those two": Virgil and Statius.

104 "another apple-tree": the first one is mentioned in *Purgatorio* XXII.130 f.

116 "the tree": the tree of the knowledge of good and evil in the Garden of Eden, whose fruit Eve ate, ultimately bringing about the fall of man. See Genesis 2.15–17, 3.1–24. This tree is on the summit of Dante's Mount Purgatory (*Purgatorio* XXXII.37 f.).

121–3 The voice from the tree recites examples of gluttony, the intemperate or untimely desire for food and drink. The "accurst creatures/Formed in the clouds" are centaurs (born of the shapely Nephele, herself cloud-born), who in their drunkenness attempted the rape of the women at the wedding of Pirithous and Hippodamia, and were successfully checked by Theseus and the Lapiths in a lengthy fight. See Ovid, *Metamorphoses* XII.210 f.

124–6 In the campaign against the Midianites, Gideon refused to allow the more self-indulgent of his soldiers, who had fallen to their knees in order to drink from a pool, to participate in the battle and subsequent victory. See Judges 7.1 f.

133 The voice of the guardian angel of the cornice of gluttony breaks into the events of the canto in a way which bespeaks a new realism and conception of scene in western literature. Dante has used this device before, in the scene with Farinata, in *Inferno* X.22 f. See E. Auerbach, *Mimesis*, 'Farinata' (cf. Bibliography).

151–4 The angel's pronouncement is based on the fourth beatitude of Christ's Sermon on the Mount (as is also that of the angel of the previous cornice). See Matthew 5.6.

PURGATORIO XXV

During the climb to the Seventh Cornice, Statius expounds the genesis of the human body, its acquisition of a soul, and the form and appearance of the disembodied soul in the Afterlife. On arriving upon the next cornice the three poets hear the souls of the sexually promiscuous, purged in fire, recite examples of chastity.

1 The factor of time is especially important in the context of Purgatory, where the soul is anxious to be away to Paradise yet must stay (although it happily consents so to do) its appointed time in torment. It is a time of spiritual correction, but also of learning, and Dante is always happy to dawdle, to satisfy his intellectual thirst. Dante calls attention to the need for dispatch here (following Virgil's admonition in *Purgatorio* XXIII.4–6), and Forese terminates his talk with Dante observing that "time is precious here/In this kingdom, and I am losing too much" (*Purgatorio* XXIV.91–2).

2–3 Dante indicates the time as approximately 2 p.m. in Purgatory (2 a.m. in Jerusalem). Taurus now occupies the meridian, the sun having left it two hours previously to sink westwards, whilst in the Northern Hemisphere, where it is night, Scorpio (diametrically opposite Taurus in the zodiac) now touches the great meridian circle.

8 See *Purgatorio* IV.19–21 and note.

22 Meleager, the son of Althaea and prince of Calydon, as a babe was granted by the Fates the same span of years as a log burning in the hearth. Althaea snatched the log away and extinguished it, but years later burned it deliberately to avenge the deaths of her brothers whom Meleager had killed for having insulted Atalanta. See Ovid *Metamorphoses* VIII. 260 f.

22–7 Virgil's point seems to be as follows: Meleager's vital spirit was, and was not, his own (his life was connected, in a mysterious but critical way, to that of the log); likewise, the image in a mirror is, and is not, the person reflected in it; and similarly, the visible 'shadow' of the disembodied soul (which is 'act' not material) in the Afterlife is, and is not, the soul itself. Thankfully, Virgil has recourse to the Christian Statius for a properly theologically based and 'scientific' explanation of the phenomenon, which discloses the significant link between the soul and its visible manifestation.

37–108 Statius's explanation of the apparent emaciation of the souls on the cornice "In a place where there is no need for nourishment" (l. 21), begins from first principles (the genesis of the body and soul), in the same way that Beatrice's explanation of the moon's dark patches will entail an exposition of the whole ordered system of the visible universe (see *Paradiso* II.61 f. and note). The didactic programme of *The Divine Comedy*, thus typically extended beyond the contingent issue, is significantly enhanced—part, no doubt, of Dante's intention. Statius's exposition is in three parts: (i) the generation of the physical body (ll. 37–60); (ii) the divine origin of the soul, as a direct creation of God (ll. 68–75); (iii) the soul's nature after the death of the body, and its visible manifestation in the Afterlife (ll. 79–107). The intervening verses convey refutation of mistaken conceptions, and analogies. Dante's academic sources, as a basis for Statius' largely orthodox explanation, include Aquinas, Aristotle, Avicenna, St Augustine, Albertus Magnus, and finally Averrhoes (whom he refutes).

37 "Perfect blood": i.e. blood which has had "power to inform" (l. 40) conferred on it in the heart. The 'formative power' mends old tissue, develops new, and in the semen develops parts of a new organism.

38 "veins": blood vessels in general, the distinction between veins and arteries was not yet formulated in Dante's day.

43 "A further transformation": here any "Perfect blood" (l. 37) which is superfluous to the body's immediate need for nourishment becomes semen, when its "power to inform" becomes generative also.

45–7 "another's blood": i.e. the menstrual blood in the matrix, which provides the passive matter in the process of generation.

This "Perfect blood" of the female has not passed through the final stage of 'activation' of the male process, which takes place in the seminal vessels.

48 "the perfect place": the heart; see note to l. 37 above.

51 "To what it has brought together": i.e. the menstrual blood which it has "brought together" in a sort of coagulation, in the matrix.

52–5 The human soul (cf. *Convivio* III.II.11–16) develops according to medieval scholastic philosophy, through the 'vegetative' (vital) and 'sensitive' stages (i.e. appropriate to plant and animal life respectively) before the 'intellective' or properly human stage is attained. The vegetable and animal stages are subsumed in the complete human soul, not separated or suppressed.

52 "The active power": that in the sperm.

55 Motion and sensitivity (the animal faculties) are at this stage amorphously combined as in a sponge ("sea fungus", l. 56).

57 i.e. the five senses (touch, hearing, sight, taste, smell).

58–60 The material body now develops organs appropriate to the vital (or 'vegetative') and 'sensitive' (or 'animal') needs of the soul.

63 "a wiser man": Averrhoes (see note to *Inferno* IV.144).

64–6 Averrhoes' position, as he understood Aristotle, was that the intellect was not an individuating attribute of the soul, but a universal faculty actually independent of man in which he merely shared. Seeing the soul as merely 'sensitive' and therefore corruptible, he thus appeared to deny its immortality. It was orthodox Christian belief that the intellective soul (affording man his reason) was individual and immortal, and actually conferred immortality on the merely 'sensitive' or 'animal' aspect of it. But see note to l. 82 below.

70 "The prime mover": God.

72 Cf. 'Then the Lord God formed a man from the dust of the ground, and breathed into his nostrils the breath of life' (Genesis 2.7); 'It was [God] that inspired him with an active soul and breathed into him the breath of life' (Wisdom 15.11). The "new spirit, filled with power" is the so-called 'possible intellect', the faculty of the intellective soul which affords man will and understanding. As a direct creation of God (with the angels and primal matter), it is individual and immortal.

73–5 Dante insists here, with proper orthodoxy, on the unity of the soul. See note to *Purgatorio* IV.5–6.

73 "the active element": the combined powers of the sentient and vital (or vegetative) soul.

76–8 An apt analogy, here an immaterial power (the sun's heat) acts upon a material object (the grape juice) to produce a third and different thing, wine.

79 i.e. at death. For Lachesis, see note to *Purgatorio* XXI.25.

81 "virtue": i.e. potential, or latent power.

82 At death the vital (or vegetative) and animal (or sensitive) faculties of the soul become inactive ("mute"), and revert to latency.

83 "memory, intelligence and will": the faculties of the immortal nature of man, of his intellective soul or 'form'.

86 "the two shores": i.e. Hell and Purgatory.

88 "the place there": i.e. definable space in the two locations of l. 86.

89 "the informing power": see notes to ll. 37 and 52 above.

93 i.e. as in the rainbow.

96–102 "The virtue of the soul": i.e. the latent power or potential of the soul, in its intellective, sensitive and vegetative aspects, to organise and shape to its purposes the matter with which it is united (on earth, the body, but here it is the "neighbouring air", l. 94).

97–8 Flame is the visible manifestation of combustion or fire.

102 "sensitive organs": i.e. organs of the senses.

106–8 The apparent emaciation of the souls on this cornice is the expression of the desire, or will, to suffer as if desperately hungry.

109 "the last circle": the Seventh Cornice of the Sexually Promiscuous.

119 An allegorical sense is intended: it was a commonplace of the medieval casuistry of love, and repeated endlessly in the lyrical poetry, that passion or carnal love was a power ("the poison of Venus"; l. 132) that struck at the heart of the victim through the eyes.

122 "*Summae Deus clementiae*": 'God of supreme clemency', a matins hymn in the old Roman breviary, which contains, besides a prayer for power to overcome the lusts of the flesh, also a reference to 'refining flames'.

128 '*Virum non cognosco*': 'I know not a man', the words of Mary to the archangel Gabriel at the Annunciation, protesting her virginity (AV Luke 1.34). This is the first of the two *exempla* of

chastity proposed by the souls, who when alive were given to sexual laxity.

131–2 Helice (Callisto), one of Diana's nymphs, seduced by Jupiter, was driven away by the chaste goddess lest she should contaminate the others. Juno spitefully transformed her into a bear; and then Jupiter, to save her from her own son Arcas' hunting spear, set both of them as stars in the sky as the constellations of the Great Bear (or Wain) and Little Bear. See Ovid, *Metamorphoses* II.401 f.

132 "the poison of Venus": carnal love.

139 "The wound": the disfigurement made in the soul by frequent concessions to the temptation to sexual promiscuousness. The "wounds" of the seven mortal sins have been symbolically engraved as P's (Ital. *piaga*) on Dante's forehead. See *Purgatorio* IX.112 and note.

PURGATORIO XXVI

On the Seventh Cornice, the highest, of Purgatory, Dante talks with the Bolognese poet Guido Guinizelli amongst the souls of the sexually promiscuous, and with the Provençal poet Arnaut Daniel.

4–6 It is now late afternoon, and the sun is sinking in the sky. The climb to the Seventh Cornice had begun at 2 p.m. (see *Purgatorio* XXV.2–3 and note).

15 The souls of the sexually promiscuous are purged in flames, a fitting torment in view of the ancient and enduring poetic metaphor sanctioned even by St Paul: 'Better be married than burn', 1 Corinthians 7.9.

16–17 The courteous and elegant mode of address (a *captatio benevolentiae*) is part of an ancient rhetorical tradition surviving from antiquity. Cf. Francesca to Dante (*Inferno* V.88–93), Pier delle Vigne to Dante (*Inferno* XIII.55–7), Virgil to Ulysses (*Inferno* XXVI.79–82), Dante to Hugh Capet (*Purgatorio* XX.34), Cacciaguida to Dante (*Paradiso* XV.28–30).

29 "people facing the opposite way": the souls of sexual perverts, whose circling of the cornice is against the normal direction, to remind them constantly of the specific nature of their promiscuity.

32 The speed and chasteness of the kiss here is part of the conscious purging of the soul's lasciviousness. Cf. 'Greet one another with the kiss of peace', Romans 16.16.

40 "Sodom and Gomorrah": the cities destroyed by God for their gross sexual immorality. See Genesis 18.16 f., 19.1 f.; *Inferno* XI.50, and the cantos of *Inferno* (XV, XVI) dedicated to the punishment of this vice.

41 Pasiphae: see note to *Inferno* XII.12 f. Since it is the heterosexuals who call her to mind, Pasiphae's sin must be viewed not as bestiality, but as excessive lasciviousness. See ll. 82–4 and note below.

43 "like cranes": cf. *Inferno* V.46–7.

44 "the Rhiphaean mountains": according to ancient authorities, these mountains, unknown to modern geography, lay to the north-west of the Carpathians, and were considered the source of the river Don.

58 Dante is undertaking the journey through Purgatory to acquire salvation, which is seen in this canticle in terms of spiritual freedom and intellectual enlightenment, release from the bonds of sin and from the blindness of ignorance; the virtue and wisdom, in short, of prelapsarian man.

59 "a lady": Beatrice.

62–3 "that heaven": the Empyrean, true Paradise.

78 "Queen": Julius Caesar's homosexuality is attested by Suetonius, and became a commonplace of medieval historiography.

82–4 "hermaphrodite": i.e. heterosexual. These souls had indulged excessively and uncontrollably in sex, thereby infringing the sacred "law of humanity" (i.e. reason; see note to *Inferno* V. 39). For the legend of Salmacis and Hermaphroditus, see Ovid, *Metamorphoses* IV.285 f.

86 "that girl": Pasiphae (see l. 41 above and note).

92 f. Guido Guinizelli (*c.*1230 to *c.*1276) judge, lawyer and poet of Bologna. First of all a poet in the style of Guittone d'Arezzo, Guinizelli later superseded all his models, and with the great *canzone* '*Al cor gentil rempaira sempre amore*' ['Love ever finds shelter in the noble heart'] furnished new directions for the love lyric in Italy. Both in expression (a controlled, somewhat scholarly lyricism) and in idea (love is presented in new terms, as an exclusive, cultural pursuit, a source of moral elevation) the poem set a new standard, so that with this and his other lyrical poems Guinizelli became a model and "master" (ll. 97–8) for the poets of Dante's own 'school' the *Dolcestilnovisti* (see notes to *Purgatorio* XXIV.51, 56; and Dante, *Vita Nuova* XX, *Convivio* IV.XX.7, *De Vulgari*

Eloquentia I.XV.6). The placing of Guinizelli here in Purgatory, on the cornice of the promiscuous, must reflect something of Dante's sense of having superseded Guinizelli himself both in the range of his poetry and the concept of love that inspires it. In Dante's concept, free of all the deterministic and therefore earthly elements still detectable in Guinizelli, the highest love is intellectual, entirely transcending the flesh. Such will be seen from the *Paradiso*, where the mind and spirit of Beatrice, and Dante's feelings for her in these terms, is one of the major focal points of his poetry. See note to *Purgatorio* XXVII.36.

94–5 Lycurgus, king of Nemea, in grief and anger ordered the death of Hypsipyle for having brought about, through neglect, the death of his infant son. He was forestalled, however, by Hypsipyle's two other sons, who arrived in time to save her. See Statius, *Thebaid*, V.499 f.

108 Lethe: the river of forgetfulness, which Dante situates on the summit of Mount Purgatory. See *Purgatorio* XXVIII.130 and note.

115 "the man": Arnaut Daniel (*c.*1180 to *c.*1210), one of the greatest and most influential of the Provençal troubadours, both in expression and technique. Revered by Dante (here, and in *De Vulgari Eloquentia* II.II.9, etc.), and imitated by him in some of his lyrical compositions, he was held also in high regard by Petrarch. But the implied criticism of Guinizelli, referred to in note to l. 92 f. above, must also apply to Arnaut.

120 "that man from Limoges": Giraut de Bornelh (*c.*1150–1220), a Provençal troubadour whom many considered the greatest of his era. Dante quotes him, oddly, as one of the 'distinguished vernacular poets of rectitude' (i.e. intellectual or moral poetry), and Arnaut as a signal love poet, in *De Vulgari Eloquentia* II.II.9. Guinizelli's asperity in regard both to Giraut and Guittone d'Arezzo may not be entirely Dante's own, but the order of merit indicated almost certainly is.

124 For Guittone d'Arezzo, see *Purgatorio* XXIV.56 and notes to ib. ll. 51–6.

128 "that cloister": the Empyrean (true Paradise).

130 "*Pater Noster*": the Lord's Prayer.

140–47 Arnaut Daniel's speech here, in the original text, is in Provençal, a striking demonstration (as was intended) of Dante's linguistic virtuosity as well as a tribute to Arnaut and the whole corpus and ethos of Provençal lyric poetry.

PURGATORIO XXVII

Dante submits to the guardian angel of the Seventh Cornice of the Promiscuous, and with Virgil and Statius passes through its flames. Night falls, and in his sleep Dante dreams of Leah. On the threshold of Earthly Paradise, on the summit of the mountain, Virgil pronounces his final speech and offers his last advice to Dante.

1–5 Dante, in what purports to be a simile, indicates that it is sunset in Purgatory, whilst it is sunrise in Jerusalem (the place of Christ's crucifixion, ll. 1–2), midnight in Spain (l. 3), and midday in India (l. 4).

6 "the angel of God": the guardian angel of the Seventh Cornice.

8 *"Beati mundo corde!"*: 'Blessed are the pure in heart [for they shall see God]', the sixth Beatitude. See AV Matthew 5.8.

23 Geryon: see Inferno XVII.1 and note, and 79 f.

27 The verse recalls the events of Daniel, where Shadrack, Meshach and Abednego stood unharmed in the furnace of Nebuchadnezzar: 'the hair of their heads had not been singed' (Daniel 3.27). The fire of Purgatory is the final corrective torment for all the redeemed sinners, before they enter, purified, into Earthly Paradise, and rise from there to Heaven. The flames are cleansing, not destructive (l. 21): 'Then . . . I will refine them as silver is refined, and assay them as gold is assayed' (Zechariah 13.9).

36 Beatrice: it is finally human love, not intellectual argument, that inspires Dante with the courage to face and pass through the daunting flames. The allegory here resolves itself into the proposition that the higher love is unaffected by the fire of earthly passion, whilst the latter is transcended, not suppressed by the higher love. Through Beatrice, Dante was able to love God, and even love him better. Dante did not (because he did not need to) reject her in his search for Him, whereas Petrarch's love for Laura proved an impediment to his love for the Creator, and Laura is renounced at the last, in the final poem of the *Canzoniere*. Dante's love for Beatrice is movingly expressed in *Paradiso* XXVII.88–96.

37–9 After a series of unhappy accidents, Pyramus stabbed himself in despair in the mistaken belief that his love Thisbe had been killed by a lioness. The berries of the mulberry tree, near which he was standing, were stained with his blood and remain crimson in sympathy for his fate. Thisbe's last words were heard by the dying Pyramus, before she too took her own life. See Ovid, *Metamorphoses* IV.55 f.

58 'Come ye blessed of my Father [inherit the Kingdom prepared for you from the foundation of the world]', AV Matthew 25.34.

59 "within a light": the light radiates from the angel who is the guardian of Earthly Paradise (the Garden of Eden; Genesis 2.8 f.) near where the poets have now arrived, on the summit of the mountain of Purgatory.

61–3 "The sun is going": see note to *Purgatorio* VII.53–7.

91 f. Dante falls asleep once more on this, the third night of his time in Purgatory. Again he experiences a dream towards dawn, the time of true or prophetic dreams (cf. *Purgatorio* IX.13 f., XIX.1 f. and notes).

95 Cytheria: Venus, who rose from the sea near Cythera in the Peloponnese.

97 f. "a young and beautiful woman": Leah, Jacob's first, more prolific wife, for whom he toiled seven years. His second wife, for whom he toiled a further seven, was Rachel, for long barren of children (l. 104). See Genesis 29.1 f. From the early Middle Ages, Leah was understood as a symbol of the active life and Rachel of the contemplative life. See Richard of St Victor, *Benjamin Minor* chap. 1.

109–11 Cf. the pilgrim figure in *Purgatorio* VIII.4–6.

115 "That sweet apple": fulfilment, or satisfaction of desire.

127 "the temporal fire": the fire of Purgatory (but referring, through synecdoche, to all the torments of Purgatory) will be extinguished as the last redeemed sinner completes his penance on the Last Day.

128 "the eternal": the fires of Hell, which will never go out. See Matthew 25.46.

128–30 Virgil, who has had merely the natural light of the intellect and its "art" (or skills) to guide him so far, and who has been granted that modicum of grace to see into Earthly Paradise, if not to enjoy it (see note to *Inferno* I.63 f.; *Purgatorio* XVIII.46–8 and note; and cf. Romans 2.14), has now come to the end of his task as Dante's guide. Dante is henceforth his own master, since his "pleasure" (l. 131) is now, after the corrective torments of Purgatory, naturally inclined to seek its proper fulfilment in the knowledge and love of God, and in those activities which are appropriate to such an aim.

Likewise, Dante's judgement (his 'free will', as it is translated in l. 140), no longer distorted or distracted by ignoble aims or by the lower appetites, is able to discern what is right for his soul's ultimate good, in the choices it will face in its journey back to God. Virgil's last words (l. 142), in the original Italian, also include the concepts of 'crown' and 'mitre' (lit. 'I crown and mitre you over yourself') as if to imply that Dante, as Everyman, has achieved a condition of perfect citizenhood, where rules and laws, of either Church or State, are superfluous (see *De Monarchia* III.IV.14); he is now the perfect citizen for the perfect society which is symbolised, appropriately, by Earthly Paradise, the home of man before the Fall; cf. 'the blessedness of this life [the second of man's two aims, the other being the blessedness of eternal life] consists in the exercise of man's proper power, and is figured by the Earthly Paradise' (*De Monarchia* III.XVI.7).

136-8 Virgil refers to Beatrice, and to his promise in *Inferno* I.121-3.

PURGATORIO XXVIII

Deep in the forest of Earthly Paradise (Eden), Dante comes across a stream, Lethe, on the further bank of which he sees Matilda. She resolves Dante's perplexity over the presence there of water and breezes, in an explanation of the special climate of the place.

2 "The divine forest": this "ancient wood" (l. 23) is the chief natural feature of Earthly Paradise (Eden; see Genesis 2.8), "cradle of our human nature" (l. 78) and the home of man before the Fall. The forest is suggested by Genesis 2.9: 'The Lord God made trees spring from the ground, all trees pleasant to look at and good for food', and thus the wild and inhospitable forest of *Inferno* I is probably a debased and corrupted version of this biblical one. Its iconographical features are not, however, purely biblical; there attaches also a redolence of the Golden Age, a classical element explicitly suggested by the corollary of Matilda's discourse (ll. 139-44), and implicit in some of the imagery deriving from Ovid's description in *Metamorphoses* I.89 f. For the geographical siting of Earthly Paradise in the Middle Ages ('away to the East', Genesis 2.8), see the thirteenth-century Hereford 'Mappa mundi' on page 25. Here 'Paradise' occupies the most easterly position, but it is separated from the main land-mass by a stretch of water. Dante's modified world-map places Eden squarely in the Southern Hemisphere of Ocean, but its separation from the main land-mass appears to have been at least sanctioned by medieval cartography.

20 Chiassi: the Roman town of Classis, near Ravenna, now disappeared except for the basilica of S. Apollinare. The pine forest still survives, extending some thirty-three kilometres along the shore.

21 Aeolus: god of winds; "the Sirocco": the sultry south wind which blows across from the African shore.

25 "a stream": Lethe; see l. 130. The Genesis version of Eden (ib. 2.10) indeed sanctions a river, but Dante does not hesitate to apply a classical name and function.

40 "A girl": her name will be given later as Matilda (see *Purgatorio* XXXIII.119). Matilda's significance and identity have long been the subject of debate amongst Dantists. Earthly Paradise is her domain, and most probably Dante intended her to be a living symbol of 'the blessedness of this life' which is 'figured by Earthly Paradise' (see *De Monarchia* III.XVI.7). She is therefore the realisation of Leah of Dante's dream in *Purgatorio* XXVII.97, symbolic of the moral and intellectual virtues of the perfected active life, attained through the teachings of philosophy (see *De Monarchia loc. cit.*). Active in moral virtue, she will later bathe Dante in this stream of Lethe and then Eunoe; with intellectual mastery she will explain to Dante the climatology of Earthly Paradise. But Matilda is a symbolically complex creature. In so far as she symbolises the perfection of this life, she represents Philosophy through whose teachings, according to Dante, that fulness is attained by acting in accordance with the moral virtues (the 'practical exercise of the mind'; see *Convivio* IV.XXII.10–11, 18). In so far as she fulfils here a Christian role, she is 'infused' Philosophy which operates to the ends of Christian love (*caritas*). Matilda is thus the Christian fulfilment of Virgil, whom she replaces as Dante's guide. It is this perfection that brings her joy, a loving delight deriving from the perfect liberty that obedience to the moral or cardinal virtues (prudence, courage, justice and moderation) can procure, and from intellectual fulfilment, which consists precisely in 'considering *the works of God and of nature*' (*Convivio loc. cit.*). Whence indeed derives the relevance to her meaning of the "psalm *Delectasti*" (l. 80): 'For thou Lord hast made me glad

through thy work: I will triumph *in the works of thy hand.*' She
is thus the new Eve in a Christian Earthly paradise. Matilda, as
will be seen later, is at the command of Beatrice, which is to be
expected, because Reason's natural light is subordinate to the
'divine light' of Christian wisdom which transcends it, and
proposes to it the higher goal of eternal blessedness along the
paths of faith, hope and charity (see *De Monarchia loc. cit.*).
Beatrice will be the fulfilment of Rachel in Dante's dream,
symbol of the contemplative life. In her symbolic role in *The
Divine Comedy*, Beatrice is precisely that 'divine light': she
"who lights the intellect to truth" (*Purgatorio* VI.45), Wisdom
as 'the flawless mirror of the active power of God' (Wisdom of
Solomon 7.26). Matilda's appearance in Earthly Paradise, when
Dante, no less than the reader, was expecting to find Beatrice,
may be elucidated perhaps from the mystical literature of the
twelfth century:

> Rachel is the teaching of truth, Leah the discipline of virtue.
> Rachel is the search for wisdom, Leah the desire for
> righteousness ... It often happens that a soul not yet
> wholly cleansed from a low way of life, and not yet fit for
> contemplation of heavenly things, hastening to the marriage
> bed of Rachel and preparing itself for her embrace, at the
> moment when it thinks to hold her, finds suddenly and
> unexpectedly, that it is being embraced by Leah.
> Richard of St Victor (d. 1173), *Benjamin Minor* chapters 1,
> 4.

The problem of Matilda's historical identity has never been
happily resolved. That she has historicity (is not merely a
symbolic creature, such as the seven virtues of the Procession
in *Purgatorio* XXIX) is suggested by structural considerations
if none other: Dante's guides and teachers are all historical
personages (Virgil, Statius, Beatrice, St Bernard, Sordello,
Marco Lombardo), and it is unreasonable to think of Matilda
as otherwise. The Countess of Tuscany, Matilda of Canossa (d.
1115), champion and benefactor of the Church, renowned for
her active and inspired role as a ruler, has been most frequently
proposed since the fourteenth century. The nuns Matilde of
Hackenborn and Matilde of Magdeburg, authoresses of mystical
works, both of whom died shortly before 1300, have also been
suggested in recent years, but as *exempla* of the secular (moral)
virtues hardly qualify. Other commentators have proposed

that Matilda (because of Dante's description of her, redolent of the women of the Florentine poetry of his era) is the anonymous 'gentle Lady' of the *Vita Nuova* (chap. 36 f.), whom Dante later elevated to the role of Lady Philosophy in the *Convivio*. But see note to *Purgatorio* XXX.130.

50–51 Proserpine: at play and gathering flowers with her friends, Proserpine, daughter of Jupiter and Ceres, was carried off by Pluto, king of the Underworld, to be his consort. See Ovid, *Metamorphoses* V.385 f.

65–6 Venus was accidentally pierced by an arrow of her son Cupid as she embraced him, and at once fell in love with Adonis. See Ovid, *Metamorphoses* X.525 f.

71 Xerxes crossed the Hellespont (Dardanelles) to attack Greece in 480BC, but was defeated at Salamis, and forced to retreat in confusion and humiliation across the narrows.

73–4 Leander swam nightly across the Hellespont to visit his love Hero, priestess of the temple of Venus Aphrodite at Sestos. Undeterred by rough water, Leander was finally drowned in a tempest.

80 "the psalm *Delectasti*": AV Psalms 92.4: 'For thou Lord hast made me glad through thy work: I will triumph in the works of thy hands.'

85–7 Dante's perplexity arises from what he has just now seen in Earthly Paradise: a running stream and a breeze through the trees, all of which appears to be in conflict with Statius' remarks (see *Purgatorio* XXI.43 f. and note) that earthly climate extends only up to the gate of Purgatory.

91 "The supreme good": God, whose own perfect goodness is the only worthy object of his perfect love.

94–6 Adam will inform Dante (*Paradiso* XXVI.139 f.) that his stay in Eden was just over six hours. In the biblical account, Adam's sin was disobedience, motivated by presumption (his eating the forbidden fruit of the tree of the knowledge of good and evil), and his punishment was expulsion from Eden, and the necessity to earn his bread by the sweat of his brow. See Genesis 2.15–17, 3.1–24.

98 "exhalations of water and earth": i.e. the so-called moist vapours that are drawn upwards by the sun's heat, and then are transformed into rain in the colder zone of the 'middle atmosphere'. Earthly Paradise is situated in the third zone of the 'higher air', beyond meteorological variation.

103–4 The Primum Mobile or Crystalline Heaven, is the ninth, outer, transparent heaven of the Ptolemaic astronomical system. It imparts its swift motion, from east to west, to all the heavens within and below it, and also to the sphere of air surrounding the earth.

112 "the land": i.e. the land in the Northern Hemisphere (the Southern Hemisphere was held to be entirely ocean).

121–2 i.e. 'fed by rain' (see note to l. 98 above).

123 i.e. 'Like a river whose level rises and falls'.

130 Lethe: the name of the river of oblivion of the classical Underworld. See *Inferno* XIV.136–8, and Virgil, *Aeneid* VI.748 f. The waters of Dante's Lethe remove the painful memory of past sins.

131 Eunoë: a name invented by Dante, based on Greek elements (lit. 'pleasant' and 'mind/memory'), to suggest the function of its waters, which is to freshen the memory of good deeds, just as Lethe removes the memory of evil deeds.

140 "the age of gold": see note to l. 2 above.

141 Parnassus: the mountain near Delphi sacred to Apollo and the Muses; "on Parnassus" is to be understood metaphorically.

PURGATORIO XXIX

Following Matilda, who sets off along the opposite bank of the stream Lethe, Dante is met by an allegorical procession which represents the Revelation of Divine Truth.

3 Matilda's song is based on Psalm 32.1: 'Happy the man whose disobedience is forgiven, whose sin is put away' [AV 'whose sin is covered']. Dante, like all Christian believers, is 'happy' because he is justified in God's eyes by faith, and thus his sins are covered or 'put away'. This faith is based precisely on what the Scriptures reveal of God's truth, and therefore it is apt that the allegorical procession which Dante is about to witness has as its subject the revelation of Divine Truth in the Scriptures, and through the Church. At the centre of the procession are symbolic representations of Christ, 'on whom faith depends from start to finish' (Hebrews 12.2), and of his earthly Church, the repository, vehicle and proponent of scriptural truth.

24 "the temerity of Eve": Eve's motive for eating the fruit of the tree of the knowledge of good and evil, in spite of God's ban, was to attain to his likeness, a sin of presumptuous pride or temerity. See Genesis 3.1–6. That Dante inserts this reference to Eve within the context of his guidance by, and dependence

on, Matilda, emphasises one aspect of the identity of Matilda as a 'new Eve' (see note to *Purgatorio* XXVIII.40). Dante the wayfarer, indeed, is here a new Adam, reborn to innocence, and his reliance on *this* Eve will not lead to betrayal ('Eve also gave her husband some of the fruit and he ate it', Genesis 3.6), but to a revelation of divine truth.

27 "any veil": the veil of ignorance: 'The serpent said . . . as soon as you eat [the fruit], your eyes will be opened and you will be like gods, knowing both good and evil' (Genesis 3.4).

37 "sacrosanct Virgins": the Muses of poetry and the arts.

40 Helicon, a mountain in Boeotia, was sacred to Apollo and the Muses ("sacrosanct Virgins", l. 37). From it ran two streams, Hippocrene and Aganippe.

41 Urania: the Muse of astronomy and heavenly things.

47 "the common object": a term of scholastic philosophy, indicating an object perceptible to several or all of the five senses, not merely to one alone.

49 "The faculty": the *vis cogitativa*, or faculty of perception, which supplies to the reason notions about the thing perceived.

50 "candlesticks": these represent the sevenfold spirit of God, and the seven gifts of the Holy Spirit. See Revelation 1.12–13, 4.5; Isaiah 11.2.

51 "Hosanna": the cry of welcome from the crowds as Jesus entered Jerusalem before the Passover and his crucifixion (Matthew 21.9).

68 "my left side": symbolic of Dante's worst side, his unworthiness.

78 "Delia her girdle": the halo around the moon (Delia is Diana, the moon goddess).

81 "ten paces": a probable reference to the Decalogue (Ten Commandments).

83 The twenty-four elders represent the twenty-four books of the Old Testament, on the reckoning of St Jerome (who had in mind the twenty-four elders of Revelation 4.4).

84 *"fleur-de-lys"*: the lily, whose whiteness symbolises the purity of faith.

85–7 The words are an adaptation of those of Gabriel to Mary at the Annunciation (ll. 85–6; see Luke 1.28), to which is added (ll. 86–7) something of the words of the Bridegroom to his Bride (Christ to his Church) in Song of Songs 4.7. The verses are therefore prophetic, and may apply equally to the advent of Beatrice (*Purgatorio* XXX.32) as to Christ and his Church at the centre of the procession (see notes to ll. 107, 108–14 below).

92 "four living creatures": symbols of the Evangelists (and hence the Gospels) common in medieval iconography; Matthew (the man), Mark (the lion), Luke (the ox) and John (the eagle). Cf. Ezekiel 10.4 f., and Revelation 4.6–7.

93 The green signifies the hope of eternal life, which is the message of the Gospels.

95 Argus: the creature of a hundred eyes, guardian of Io. See Ovid, *Metamorphoses* I.622 f.

100–102 See Ezekiel 1.4 f.

105 "John the Divine": St John, the author of Revelation. See ib. 4.8.

107 "A triumphal car": the car, or chariot, represents the Church on earth (the Church Militant); its two wheels probably signify the monastic Orders of the Dominicans (dedicated to the pursuit and propagation of divine knowledge) and the Franciscans (dedicated to the practice of *caritas*, or Christian love). For the imagery of the wheels of the Church's car, elaborated in those terms, see *Paradiso* XII.106–11 and notes. The car in this procession is typical of the two-wheeled war chariots employed in triumphal processions in ancient Rome (see ll. 115–16 below).

108–14 The griffin, half eagle and half lion, represents Christ in his dual nature as God and man. See Daniel 7.4, and Isidore of Seville, *Etymologiae* XII.2.17. The gold, an incorruptible metal, represents his divinity; the white and carmine symbolise respectively the purity of his manhood and the blood of his sacrifice on the Cross.

115 Africanus: either Scipio Africanus the Younger, the destroyer of Carthage in 146BC, who was held by Cicero to be greatest of the Romans, or Scipio Africanus the Elder, the conqueror of Hannibal at Zama in 202BC. Augustus: the first Emperor of Rome (d. 14AD).

118–20 The myth of Phaeton is referred to. See note to *Inferno* XVII.107–8.

121–9 "Three ladies": the theological virtues, love, hope and faith (see 1 Corinthians 13.13) with their traditional symbolic colours red, green and white. The three theological virtues are essential to the attainment of eternal life, and therefore these three ladies dance by the right wheel of the Church, on the favoured side.

130–32 The four ladies, at the left wheel, represent the four moral, cardinal or active virtues of prudence, courage, justice and moderation of which prudence is the principal (her three eyes represent vision towards the past, present and future; see *Convivio* IV.XXVII.5). Their purple (i.e. deep red) dress signifies both the Christian love that infuses them (for they are the former 'pagan virtues' now transformed in their service of the true God), and hints at their special relevance to the secular state (the royal purple of Empire). For their origins as 'fruits of Wisdom's labour', sanctioned by the Bible, see Wisdom of Solomon 8.7.

134–41 "two old men": Luke (representing, as author, the Acts of the Apostles) and St Paul (representing the major Epistles). Luke, the doctor (Colossians 4.14), is suitably dressed as a follower of Hippocrates (see note to *Inferno* IV.143), whilst Paul carries the Sword of the Spirit, 'the words that come from God' (Ephesians 6.17).

142 "four": the four modest men represent the minor or General Epistles of Peter, Jude, James and John.

143–4 "an old man by himself": he represents the last book of the Bible, Revelation (Apocalypse), written, it was believed, by St John the Evangelist following a profound visionary experience.

148 The red signifies the fire of Christian love (*caritas*).

PURGATORIO XXX

Beatrice appears miraculously on the chariot of the Church in the middle of the Procession of Divine Revelation. Dante, turning to find that Virgil has already gone, becomes the object of Beatrice's detailed reproaches for his disloyalty to her memory.

1 "the Seven Stars": the seven candlesticks leading the procession (see *Purgatorio* XXIX.50 and note); "the first heaven": the Empyrean, essential Paradise, where the sevenfold spirit of God, and the seven gifts of the Holy Spirit, belong.

4 "there": the movement of the procession is controlled by the seven candlesticks at its head.

5 "the Seven Stars below": the stars of the Great Bear or Wain, which indicate the position of the North Star for navigators.

7 "the truthful company": the twenty-four elders representing the books of the Old Testament (see *Purgatorio* XXIX.83 and note).

11–12 "*Veni/Sponsa de Libano*": 'Come from Lebanon, my

bride' (Song of Songs 4.8). The Vulgate adds 'and you shall be crowned'. The words of the Bridegroom to his Bride (in scriptural allegory, Christ to his Church) in the Song of Songs are turned to the welcoming of Beatrice as the 'divine spirit' of Christian doctrine, the Wisdom of God in the new dispensation.

13–15 For the Last Judgement and the general resurrection of the dead, see notes to *Inferno* VI.95–9.

18 i.e. angels.

19 'Blessed thou that cometh': the words, slightly adapted, are those of the crowds that welcomed Jesus into Jerusalem before his crucifixion (AV Matthew 21.9), and used by the Church in the service of Mass.

21 'Give lilies from full hands': words used here in welcome to Beatrice (the lilies suggest the purity of her faith), but which are taken from Virgil's *Aeneid* VI.883, where Anchises prophesies and mourns the premature death of his descendant Marcellus, nephew of Augustus. In this sense they are fitting as welcome to Beatrice, whose early death in 1290 cut short a life of exemplary virtue.

31–3 The colours of Beatrice's clothing symbolise the three theological virtues faith (white), hope (green) and love (red). She is the 'divine light' of Christian wisdom that illuminates these virtues, and inspires spiritual teachings, by which man may attain the 'blessedness of eternal life' (see *De Monarchia* III.XVI.7, and note to *Purgatorio* XXVIII.40). The olive crown she wears signifies wisdom; the olive is the tree sacred to Minerva, goddess of wisdom.

42 Dante tells how he fell in love with Beatrice when they were still children; both were in their ninth year. See *Vita Nuova* II.

48 These words are a translation of Virgil, *Aeneid* IV.23.

51 Dante's commitment to follow Virgil as his guide begins at *Inferno* I.130.

52 "all that our ancient mother lost": the joy of Earthly Paradise, the loss of which began with Eve's succumbing to the temptation of Satan. See note to *Purgatorio* XXIX.24.

58 Beatrice is 'admiral' on 'Peter's ship', the Church. See *Paradiso* XI.119 and note.

63 Dante adheres to the ancient rhetorical convention that discouraged the author's mention of his own name 'except on needful occasion' (*Convivio* I.II.3).

83–4 AV Psalms 31.1–8: 'In thee O Lord do I put my trust . . . thou hast set my feet in a large room.' The angels take Dante's

644 COMMENTARY AND NOTES

part, expressing through the psalm his belief in the mercy and protection of God, his justice, forgiveness and bounty.

89 "the land without shade": Africa; Dante probably alludes to the Libyan desert.

110 "every seed": the human seed. The stars, in conjunction with the planets, were held to determine the complexion of the soul as to its qualities. Dante was born beneath the sign of Gemini. See *Paradiso* XXII.111 f. and note.

112 "divine graces": the seven gifts of the Holy Spirit, wisdom, understanding, counsel, strength, knowledge, piety and fear of God. See *Convivio* IV.XXI.11.

121-3 These events, of 1274-90, are recorded in poetry and prose in Dante's *Vita Nuova*, where Beatrice's beneficent effects on Dante are noted and recalled in love and awe.

124-5 "the threshold/Of my second age": i.e. of youth, which was held to begin, after adolescence, at the age of twenty-five.

125 "changed my life": i.e. when Beatrice passed from her earthly to her heavenly life. Beatrice died in 1290.

126 "to others": the reference is to the episode of the anonymous 'gentle Lady', who offered Dante consolation and love after Beatrice's death. It was only a brief lapse, if the account in the *Vita Nuova* is to be trusted (see chapters 36-40). However, certain *canzoni* (odes) and several sonnets of Dante also, mostly written before his exile, are an expression of passionate love for some other girl or woman, who is neither Beatrice nor the 'gentle Lady'. These include four poems known, for their play upon the word *pietra*, as the 'stony verses' (Foster and Boyde, *Dante's Lyric Poetry*, nos. 77-80).

130 "an untrue path": this cannot be associated, as some commentators have suggested, with the period of the composition of the *Convivio* (1307-8), as if it were a time during which Dante indulged in purely rational philosophy and put revelation or the study of theology at a discount. A careful reading of the *Convivio* could not possibly suggest such a view. In spite of Dante's equating the 'gentle Lady' of the *Vita Nuova* (see note to l. 126 above) with his Lady Philosophy in *Convivio* II.II and XIII, the allegorising is artificial, and in the end, false. The "false appearances of good" (l. 131) followed by Dante, for which Beatrice rebukes him, are more probably the goals of private ambition and worldly fulfilment, associated with his life and political career in Florence up to 1300, a period which Dante symbolises in the dark forest of *Inferno* I (see notes to

Inferno I.32, VI.64 f., 79 f., X.73; and cf. *Purgatorio* XIX.7–24 and note to l. 19; XXXIII.85–90 and note).

133–5 Two such interventions by Beatrice are recorded in the *Vita Nuova*, chapters 40 and 43.

140 "him": Virgil. See *Inferno* II.52 f., where Virgil recalls Beatrice's charge to him to save Dante from certain death in the dark forest of sin.

PURGATORIO XXXI

Beatrice's reproaches arouse in Dante a profound remorse and exact a heartfelt confession. He faints; and on recovering finds himself in the waters of Lethe, in Matilda's charge. Having drunk from the waters, Dante is brought before Beatrice to gaze once more upon her undiminished beauty.

12 "the water": Lethe, the "sacred river" (l. 1), whose waters remove the memory of sin.

23–4 "the good/Beyond which there is nothing to aspire to": God, as the source of all good known to man, and the only perfect fulfilment of the soul's aspirations.

22 f. Beatrice persists in her examination of Dante in order to elicit from him not merely a monosyllabic affirmation of his sin of disloyalty and worldliness (l. 14), but a coherent confession indicating a new and conscious humility (ll. 34–6). The term 'contrition' implies not merely the breaking of the sinner's pride (as the root of all sin), but the total crushing of it. Beatrice's extended interrogation is therefore theologically justifiable.

29 "the others": the other, less worthy, objects of Dante's desires (see note to *Purgatorio* XXX.126).

45 "the sirens": Beatrice's specific mention of sirens in the context of "false pleasure" (l. 35) recalls the substance of Dante's dawn-dream on the Fourth Cornice. See *Purgatorio* XIX.7 f., 19 and note.

56 "Deceitful things": beauty of the flesh, which is transitory and therefore not worthy of the soul's devotion.

59 "any girl": (Ital. *pargoletta*). The female subject of some of Dante's *canzoni* and sonnets is so designated. See note to *Purgatorio* XXX.126.

72 Iarbas: king of the savage Gaetulian tribe from the area of Carthage in North Africa (Virgil, *Aeneid* IV.196).

74–5 Although "fully-fledged" (l. 62) in manhood, Dante had allowed himself to be distracted by "false pleasure" (l. 35) like any ingenuous child. Cf. *Purgatorio* XVI.85–93.

77 "the primal creatures": the angels surrounding Beatrice.

80–81 "the beast": the griffin, symbolising Christ in his dual nature, as perfect man and perfect God. See note to *Purgatorio* XXIX.108–14.

89 Dante's fainting here, caused by the extremities of his remorse, recalls his swooning upon the tragic conclusion of Francesca's story of love in *Inferno* V. There, although pity may have played a part, remorse and distress were arguably the emotions dominating Dante, who witnessed in Francesca's plight the damning effects of a love affair of the sort he, as poet in the courtly love tradition, had helped to promote, and who had, initially at least, considered Beatrice as merely a lady to whom to pay court, and even compromise, in the same traditional way (see *Inferno* V, and notes to l. 88 f.). Here the remorse is for lapses, as lover and poet, of the same shameful order.

92 "the girl": Matilda, here as active in virtue as she has been zealous in intellect. See note to *Purgatorio* XXVIII.40.

98 "*Asperges me*": 'Sprinkle me [that I may be clean]', Psalms 51.7; words at one time pronounced by the priest whilst sprinkling holy water on the confessed sinner.

104 "the four lovely dancers": the four 'infused' moral or cardinal virtues (Singleton). See note to *Purgatorio* XXIX.130–32.

106 "we are stars": see *Purgatorio* I.23–4, and notes to ib. ll. 23, 37–9.

109 "the three there": the three maidens of the procession, who represent the three theological virtues. See note to *Purgatorio* XXIX.121–9. As stars in the night sky of the Southern Hemisphere they are referred to in *Purgatorio* VIII.85–93.

111 The theological virtues are Christian virtues, of spiritual origin, and therefore 'see' more deeply than the moral and intellectual virtues into the truths and purposes of God.

121–3 Beatrice's eyes function now as those of Wisdom: as 'the flawless mirror of the active power of God' (Wisdom of Solomon 7.26). In these verses Dante discloses her allegorical role as Wisdom and, more precisely, Christian wisdom, which reveals divine truths (here, the dual nature of Christ as perfect man and perfect God).

122 "The double animal": the griffin (see note to ll. 80–81).

128 "the food": the food is true knowledge, as defined by Wisdom's own words in Ecclesiasticus 24.19–21.

133–8 Cf. Dante's own words as gloss: 'the eyes of Wisdom are her demonstrations, whereby the truth is seen most certainly, and her smile is her intimations, whereby the same light of Wisdom is revealed behind a certain veil; and in these two is felt that loftiest joy of blessedness which is the supreme good in Paradise' (*Convivio* III.XV.2–3).

141 Mount Parnassus: see note to *Purgatorio* XXII.65. The Castalian spring and pools are found on its lower slopes.

PURGATORIO XXXII

The Procession of Divine Revelation in Earthly Paradise moves on; the griffin attaches the pole of the chariot of the Church to a bare tree, which at once blossoms. The Procession mostly withdraws and Dante witnesses an allegorical spectacle, in which the chariot and the tree are central, representing crucial phases of the Church's history in its relations with the secular state.

2 As Dante records in the *Vita Nuova* XXX.1, Beatrice died on 8 June 1290, whilst the fictional date of *The Divine Comedy* is 1300.

8 "those goddesses": the three theological or Christian virtues (see note to *Purgatorio* XXIX.121–9), who have taken up their position on Beatrice's right.

11 Cf. Wisdom of Solomon 7.29: 'She [Wisdom] is more radiant than the sun.'

18 The Procession, led by the seven candlesticks (see note to *Purgatorio* XXIX.50) turns to face the east whence it has come and where the morning sun still lies.

22 "Those soldiers": the twenty-four elders (see note to ib. 83).

25 "the ladies": the seven Virtues (see notes to ib. 121–9, 130–32).

26 "the griffin": see note to ib. 108–14; "the consecrated load": the chariot of the Church (see note to ib. 107).

28 "The lovely woman": Matilda (see note to *Purgatorio* XXVIII.40).

32 Eve, the wife of Adam (see note to *Purgatorio* XXIX.24).

37–9 The tree is literally (i.e. historically) that of 'the knowledge of good and of evil', planted by God in the Garden of Eden, whose fruit, in spite of God's ban, Adam ate (see Genesis 2.15–17, 3.1–6). In its 'mystical senses (see Dante, *Letters* X.7) it is (i) allegorically, the spirit of the Law of God (right) infringed by Adam's disobedience (the tree is defoliated, l. 38–9), and (ii) 'morally' (see *Purgatorio* XXXIII.71–2) the Law of God in its application (justice), as it finds expression in the laws of the State, or Empire. In this latter, intellectual sense, as the justice of God apparent on earth, the tree represents the 'soul' of the Empire; but it is not, as some commentators have suggested, the 'body' of Empire as a political entity (this the eagle of the allegorical spectacle represents, which comes next). The murmuring of the name 'Adam' (l. 37) is in reproach of him both as an erring soul and as a less than perfect citizen.

42 "Indians": the inhabitants of India, which was celebrated for the height of its trees (see Virgil, *Georgics* II.122–4).

48 These words are an adaptation of Christ's: 'it becometh us to fulfil all righteousness' (AV Matthew 3.15). Christ was obedient to the will of God in both its manifestations; as divine providence (which required Christ's act of atonement for the sake of sinful man), and as law (to which he submitted as a man, born and crucified in a corner of the Roman Empire). In neither sense did the griffin (Christ) damage the tree (the 'righteousness' of God, as right and justice).

49–60 The shaft of the chariot of the Church is symbolic of the cross of Christ, and hence his sacrificial death. This the griffin attaches to the tree, so that it becomes a bond between the tree and the chariot. The blossoming of the tree which then ensues is the result of Christ's atonement (see 1 Corinthians 15.21–2; Romans 5.12, 19) for the sin of Adam both as soul and citizen. The infringement of God's righteousness (both as right and justice) has been made good. Again colour is significant (ll. 58–9). The deep red of the fruit suggests both the colour of Christ's blood, and the royal colour of Empire. We are left with a picture of the cross of Christ uniting what is essential in both Church and State: the Law of God, restored by Love in the new dispensation to mankind. This is the *raison d'être* of the one, and the inspiration of the other. This deep mystical union of the institutions is one which is not emphasised in the *De Monarchia*, Dante's prose treatise on the character, role and relations of Church and Empire, and may point to its antedating *Purgatorio*, if not the whole of *The Divine Comedy*. For the achieving in practice of the perfect society, through the harmonising of the functions of Church and State, see note to *Purgatorio* IX.20 f.

52–7 i.e. when (in spring) the sun is in conjunction with the constellation of the Ram (the constellation following Pisces,

l. 54), and before it moves one month later into conjunction with the constellation of Taurus (the "new constellation", l. 57).

64 "the pitiless eyes": the hundred eyes of Argos, who was set by Juno to guard Io, her rival for the affections of Jupiter. Mercury was sent by Jupiter to slay Argos, which he accomplished by first singing him to sleep with the story of Syrinx and Pan. See Ovid, *Metamorphoses* I.568 f.

73–81 The extended simile, incorporating metaphor (ll.73–5), employs the episode of the Transfiguration of Christ in Matthew 17.1–8. Here he appeared in supernatural splendour to Peter, James and John, on Mount Tabor, in the company of Moses and Elias. In the metaphor, the apple-tree is Christ, and the blossoms an earnest of his heavenly glory as the risen Saviour, the contemplative 'food' of the angels and the elect in Paradise (cf. AV Song of Solomon 2.3, Revelation 19.9).

78 "deeper sleeps": for example, the 'sleep' of the dead Lazarus (John 11.1 f.).

94 f. The griffin (Christ) has risen, with the company of the procession, leaving only Beatrice (divine Wisdom) behind as guardian, with the Virtues, of the chariot (the Church). The story of the historical Church is about to begin, told in the form of allegorical spectacle (l. 109 f.).

98 "those lights": the seven Virtues probably hold in their hands the seven candlesticks which led the procession, signifying here the seven gifts of the Holy Spirit (see note to *Purgatorio* XXX.112), the 'Comforter' of the earthly Church (see AV John 14.26).

102 "that Rome": Paradise, the eternal City of God.

109–17 The persecution of the early Church under the Emperor Nero and his successors, doing violence to the Law of God, is enacted here.

112 "the bird of Jove": the eagle, symbol of empire (see *Purgatorio* IX.20 f., *Paradiso* VI.1 f., XVIII–XX).

118–23 The vixen represents heresies, principally Gnosticism, which distressed the early Church. She is driven off by Beatrice (the divine light of Christian Wisdom). Cf. AV Ezekiel 13.4, where false teachers are likened to foxes.

124–9 The eagle's 'gift' of feathers is the so-called 'Donation of Constantine', the alleged gift made by the Emperor of Rome in the fourth century, to the Church, of the western half of the Roman Empire. See note to *Inferno* XIX.115–17. From this misplaced generosity, as Dante saw it, the Church's materialism and loss of spiritual authority derived.

130–35 The dragon is the religion of Islam, begun by Mohammed in the seventh century. The dragon's splitting and pulling away a fragment of the chariot reflects Dante's understanding of Mohammed as a Christian heretic, apostate, and finally schismatic (see *Inferno* XXVIII.23 f.).

136–41 The additional feathers represent the donations to the Church of territories and wealth by the Frankish kings Pepin and Charlemagne in the eighth century, compounding the Church's temporal cares, blunting its spirituality and sharpening its rapacity; so that the contemporary Church of Dante's age represents, for him, a monstrous parody of the primitive Church (ll. 142–7), born originally out of material poverty and spiritual wealth.

142–7 The metamorphosis of the chariot into a monstrous beast with seven heads and ten horns closely reflects the imagery of Revelation 13.1.

148–58 The harlot is the corrupted Bride of Christ, the perverted spiritual authority of the Church of Dante's era (see Revelation 17.1 f.). The giant represents the kings of France in the fourteenth century, with whom the papacy was initially on friendly terms (Urban IV and Clement IV were Frenchmen), but who, in the person of Philip IV, antagonised and finally dominated it. Under pressure from Philip IV, and with the compliance of the Gascon pope Clement V, the papacy was transferred (see ll. 157–8) to Avignon in 1309. See *Inferno* XIX.83 f. and note.

PURGATORIO XXXIII

Beatrice prophesies the advent of a champion sent from God to deliver Church and Empire. Dante drinks from the waters of Eunoë in the final ritual of his spiritual cleansing, in preparation for his ascent to Paradise.

1 The first line of Vulgate Psalms 78 (AV 79): 'O God, the heathen are come into thine inheritance', appropriate at this point in the narrative in view of the final episode in the allegorical Spectacle (see end of *Purgatorio* XXXII).

10–12 Words of Christ to his disciples recorded in the Gospel of John AV 16.16: 'A little while, and ye shall not see me: and again, a little while, and ye shall see me.' Beatrice prophesies the ebb and flow of the Church's history in terms of Christ's death and resurrection. She looks forward to a reformed and regenerated Church, following the advent of an unspecified champion to whom she obscurely alludes (l. 43; see note below). The nine paces that Beatrice takes (l. 16) may possibly hint at a timescale, but there are no sure grounds for this speculation.

23 "Brother" (*Frate*) is the standard form of address in the almost monastic atmosphere of Purgatory, and adopted here by Beatrice to put her love for Dante, her former earthly suitor, at once in the orthodox and disinterested perspective of Christian love (*caritas*).

34–9 In words reminiscent of Revelation 17.8, Beatrice hints at the lack of authority of the occupant of the papal throne, Boniface VIII (see *Paradiso* XXVII.22–7), in the same way that she sees (l. 37–9) the throne of Empire to lack genuine authority in 1300, due to the failure of Albert of Hapsburg to attend his coronation as Emperor in Rome, and his neglect of Italy, "the garden of the Empire" (see *Purgatorio* VI.97 f., *Convivio* IV.III.6).

43 Transposed into Roman numerals (DXV) the cryptogram has been variously interpreted. What is certain is that the numerology employed here is in the tradition of apocalyptic literature (see Revelation 13.18), and that the 'number' of the saviour of Christendom here (515) stands opposed to the 'number of the beast' (666), the Antichrist in the biblical text. Identification of the DXV remains uncertain, depending in part on the dating of *Purgatorio* itself. Briefly, if written before August 1313 (but see *Purgatorio* VII.96 and note), then the avenging 'messenger of God' would be Henry VII of Luxemburg, crowned in Rome in 1312, to whom Dante wrote an ecstatic letter of welcome (*Letters* VII), together with others to the Lords of Italy (V) and to the 'accursed Florentines' (VI) urging them to accept Henry's suzerainty. If it is considered to have been written after August 1313 (the date of Henry's death) then the DXV may signify either an unspecified future emperor or even Christ at his Second Coming (see Bibliography, R. E. Kaske). Recent scholarship, however, indicates that the former intepretation anticipating a future emperor is more probable. Dante lived in an era when prophecies of new ages and the imminent end of time were widespread, including those of Joachim of Flora (see *Paradiso* XII.140–41 and note), Alan of Lille, the

Tiburtine Sibyl and the pseudo Methodius. In prophecies such as these the final age would be characterised by the emergence of a supreme, victorious temporal ruler, who would suppress materialism in both the secular and ecclesiastical orders, convert the Jews and defeat the Saracens. This would initiate a reign of peace, which would precede the brief emergence of the Antichrist. He in turn would fall to Christ at his Second Coming on the Last Day. The events would, it was believed, repeat a pattern of earlier history embracing the *pax romana* of the invincible emperor Augustus, the first appearance of Christ at his incarnation under Augustus' reign, and Christ's victory over death at the Crucifixion. Dante's prophecies of the Greyhound (*Inferno* I.101–11) and the DXV here, as well as hints in *Paradiso* XXVII.61–3, 148, seems consistent with this sort of eschatological vision, as also his sense of the imminent end of historical time in *Paradiso* XXX.131–2. See Bibliography, C. T. Davis, M. Reeves.

47–51 Themis, mother of Prometheus and of the Seasons, enraged at Oedipus's solving of the Sphinx's riddle, and its consequent death, sent a wild fox to devastate the crops and herds of the Thebans. The reference to the Naiads here (l. 49) is due to Dante's misreading of Ovid's text, where *Laiades* (i.e. Oedipus) not *Naiades* was intended (Sapegno).

56 The Tree of the Knowledge of Good and Evil (see note to *Purgatorio* XXXII.37–9).

58–60 The warning is directed in the first instance to Philip IV of France, hinting in a prophetic way at the removal of the papal seat from Rome to Avignon in 1309 (see note to *Purgatorio* XXXII.148–58).

61–3 "the first soul": the reference is to Adam, who according to biblical chronology waited at least 5,000 years after the Fall, on earth and in Limbo, until his release by Christ at the Harrowing of Hell.

68 The Elsa is a tributary of the Arno, whose water was known for its furring qualities.

69 As Pyramus's blood stained the mulberry red so Dante's mind is dulled by unwonted delight in vain thoughts (see note to *Purgatorio* XXVII.37–9). Beatrice is using the allusive and difficult language of oracular utterance.

78 "a pilgrim's staff": the palm-wreathed stick was the palmer's proof of his visit to the Holy Land.

85–90 "what school": the 'school' of thought, materialistic in its nature, that determined Dante's moral, political and intellectual career "along an untrue path,/Following false appearances of good", until his reconversion to the faith in 1300. The circumstances of his conversion are hypostasised in the events of *The Divine Comedy* itself. See *Purgatorio* XXX.130–31 and note.

90 The Priumum Mobile, the most distant of the nine material heavens.

96 Lethe: see *Purgatorio* XXXI.91 f., and note to XXVIII.130.

104–5 It is noon on the Wednesday of Easter Week. The "meridian" differs according to the longitude of the observer.

109 "The seven ladies": the three Theological Virtues, and the four Cardinal Virtues (see notes to *Purgatorio* XXIX.121–32).

113 Rivers of Asia Minor, which flow out of the legendary site of the Garden of Eden (Genesis 2.10 f.). The two rivers of Dante's Earthly Paradise, Lethe and Eunoë, similarly have a common source.

127 f. As Lethe removes memories of evil deeds committed, so Eunoë revives memories of all the good the soul has performed on earth (see note to *Purgatorio* XXVIII.131). Purged of its tendency to sin, freed from the memory of sins, and quickened by memories of good, the soul is renewed as a new plant ready to rise to its true home in God's presence in Paradise. The will is now corrected to love only the good, and the soul's appetite is now only for what is good.

PARADISO I

Dante's invocation to Apollo. Dante and Beatrice rise from Earthly Paradise. Beatrice expounds the principle of order governing the universe.

1–36 An essential commentary on the Prologue (ll. 1–36) of *Paradiso* is provided by Dante himself in his letter to Can Grande della Scala, Lord of Verona, to whom the *Paradiso* is dedicated (see *Letters* X.17–32).

1 Appropriately, the last line of *Paradiso*, as the first, refers to God as the Unmoved Mover of all creation (cf. "the love which moves the sun and the other stars", *Paradiso* XXXIII.145), symbolically 'closing the circle' of the final canticle.

2 'The glory of the Lord fills his creation', Ecclesiasticus 42.16.

4 The Empyrean, true Paradise, beyond the bounds of time and space (*Paradiso* XXX–XXXIII), is "the heaven of simple light/

Intellectual light, full of love" (*Paradiso* XXX.39–40, and see *Letters* X.22 f.).

7–9 See *Letters* X.28–9 and the note to *Paradiso* XXXIII.85 f.

13 f. Apollo, the sun god, as well as providing oracles at Delphi (l. 32), appears in Virgil's *Eclogues* as the patron of poetry and music. The poet's crown in antiquity, like that of the military victor, was a laurel ("the Penean branch", l. 31) the tree beloved by Apollo (see the Daphne myth in Ovid, *Metamorphoses* I.452 f.). Sacred to Apollo was Cirrha (l. 36), one of the two peaks of Mount Parnassus, the other sacred to the Muses to whom Dante addresses his invocation in *Inferno* II.7 and *Purgatory* I.8.

20 After unsuccessfully challenging Apollo to a musical contest, the satyr Marsyas was skinned alive by the god for his artistic presumption (Ovid, *Metamorphoses* VI.382 f.).

37–48 For Dante and Beatrice, standing on the summit of Mount Purgatory, the sun ("The lamp of the world") now appears at its midday point, having risen at the "entrance" (l. 37) on the eastern horizon where three of the "four circles" (equator, ecliptic, colure) intersect the fourth (the horizon) to produce, notionally, "three crosses". It is the favourable period (l. 40) of the spring equinox still (see note to *Inferno* I.37–40), although some days after the exact equinoctial point which marks the beginning of springtime, traditionally the time of the Creation and Christ's Conception.

41 The sun rises in the Ram (the "better star") at the spring equinox.

43 "there": in Earthly Paradise, on the summit of Mount Purgatory in the Southern Hemisphere.

45 "elsewhere": i.e. the entire Northern Hemisphere.

46–7 Beatrice had been looking eastwards, then turns "left" (northwards) to face the sun at the midday point.

49–51 This striking simile, showing Dante's precise grasp of the concrete and scientific, is used also in *Purgatorio* XV.16 f.

68–9 Glaucus: the Boeotian fisherman who, noticing that his catch revived when laid on a certain sward of grass, tasted the herbage himself, and was transformed into a sea god (Ovid, *Metamorphoses* XIII.898 f.).

73–5 The soul is what of man is created last ("Latterly") after the procreation of the body (see *Purgatorio* XXV.61 f.). Dante, like St Paul, is uncertain whether his ascent into the heavens was made 'in the body or out of it' (2 Corinthians 12.2–4).

What Dante emphasises, however, is that his experiences in *The Divine Comedy* were actual, and not merely dreamed, a journey not a vision (see *Paradiso* XXVII.64, and note to *Paradiso* XXXII.139).

78 The music of the spheres, a Platonic concept, was refuted by Aristotelians, but possibly accepted by Dante because found in Cicero, Macrobius and some Church fathers.

79–80 Dante is seemingly passing through the Sphere of Fire (located between the earth and the moon), towards which flames rise as to their "proper place" (see l. 115), and from which lightning descends (l. 92). See *Convivio* III.III.2.

99 The elements of air and fire.

103 f. In this philosophical disquisition, framed in order to answer Dante's puzzlement over his ascent, and developed with the exquisite simplicity and ease of the highest poetry, Beatrice represents the whole of creation as a harmonious order of dynamic forces held in check, or released to act, as time and Nature ordain (and the ordaining is ultimately that of Providence). The whole is the *forma* (essential formative character or "shape", l. 104) "Which makes the universe resemble God". The presence of order in the material and spiritual world of creation, but its conspicuous lack in the affairs of men, is one of the central themes of the *Paradiso*.

109 f. All created things have implanted in them an 'instinct' or 'natural love' (*Purgatorio* XVII.91–4) which carries them to their "pre-ordained place" (l. 124, and see *Convivio* IV.XII.14 f., III.III.1–5): for example that in fire draws it towards the Sphere of Fire, and that in matter draws it downwards towards the central point of the earth. But man's 'instinct' as a rational soul is a natural love, or 'primal will' (see *Purgatorio* XVIII.49–60) that draws him back (*qua* intellective soul) to the "intellectual light, full of love" (*Paradiso* XXX.40) of the Creator in the Empyrean (l. 122).

111 Their beginning (*principio*) in God (see *Convivio* III.VII.2).

120 Mankind, made in God's image (Genesis 1.26–7), is endowed with the essential attributes of God: intellect and love.

122 The Empyrean, essential Paradise (see note to l. 4).

123 The "fastest sphere of all" is the Primum Mobile or Crystalline Heaven, which imparts its motion to all the eight material heavens below it, and is where time and Nature have their origins (see *Paradiso* XXVII.106–20). See note to *Paradiso* II.113 f.

133–5 Lightning. The "false delight" in man is treated in *Purgatorio* XVI.85–93, XVII.95–102.

PARADISO II

Dante and Beatrice rise to the Heaven of the Moon. Beatrice expounds the disposition and workings of the heavenly bodies, in the course of her explanation of the dark patches on the surface of the moon.

1–6 Dante's apostrophe to the reader, employing the metaphor of the ship (cf. also *Purgatorio* I.1–3) again points up the contrast between his divinely sanctioned voyage in faith and the 'foolish flight' of Ulysses' presumptuous voyage in *Inferno* XXVI.

8 Minerva, goddess of wisdom; Apollo the god of highest poetry (cf. *Paradiso* I.13 f.).

9 The Bears are the constellations of Ursa Major and Minor, the latter containing the North Star, principal 'lodestar' of navigators. The nine Muses are the daughters of Mnemosyne, goddesses of literature and the arts.

10–11 Those who have profoundly studied philosophy and theology to gain wisdom (see Psalms 78.25 where the reference is to manna, 'the bread of angels'; and cf. *Convivio* I.I.6–7).

11–12 See the words of Wisdom in Ecclesiasticus 24.21: 'Whoever feeds on me will be hungry for more, and whoever drinks from me will thirst for more.'

16–18 The Argonauts on their journey to Colchis to seek the Golden Fleece were astonished to see Jason, their leader, guiding a plough drawn by a team of fire-breathing oxen and sowing serpent teeth, which sprouted into armed men (Ovid, *Metamorphoses* VII.100 f.; and see *Inferno* XVIII.83 f. and note, *Paradiso* XXXIII.96 and note).

21 The Heaven of the Fixed Stars, rotating across the night sky.

30 The planet of the moon; Dante's Ptolemaic astronomy did not always distinguish between stars and planets.

31 f. Dante and Beatrice enter into the moon itself.

42 i.e. in the person of Christ, true man and true God.

43 "There": in Heaven.

45 Primal truths are axiomatic, requiring no proof; their apprehension being innate in man (cf. "the first apprehension", *Purgatorio* XVIII.56 and note).

49–51 In the popular imagination of the time, the moon's variegated surface was believed to be caused by Cain's presence, bearing a bundle of thorns on his back, banished thither as punishment for the murder of his brother Abel (Genesis 4.1 f.).

59–60 Dante the pilgrim repeats here his understanding of the solution as it stands in his earlier work *Convivio* (II.XIII.9), an Aristotelian hypothesis of Averrhoes (*De substantia orbis* II).

61 f. Beatrice refutes the materialistic solution of Averrhoes (based on the rarity and density of matter) and proposes a developed neo-platonic hypothesis accepted by Aquinas, namely that the range of luminosity in heavenly bodies is due to differences and modulations in their 'virtue' or specific nature. This explanation entails Beatrice's going back to first principles (l. 112 f.), incidentally but importantly explaining the whole ordered system by which the heavens operate, a spiritual or God-centred exposition of immense significance in the didactic 'programme' of the *Paradiso*.

64 The Sphere or Heaven of the Fixed Stars, the outermost visible canopy of the cosmos.

67–72 If merely rarity and density were adduced in explanation of the variety and quantity of the stars, then one could only conclude that there was but one "formal" (or formative) principle obtaining, "distributed more or less equally". Such a proposition, in terms of medieval philosophy, would be inadmissible, for it is clear that the qualitative variety (variety of "virtue[s]") in created phenomena on earth *must* predicate a similar variety in the heavens, since from the heavens alone come the formative influences that make the world what it is.

79 "The first hypothesis" is in l. 75.

83 "The second hypothesis" is in ll. 76–8.

89–90 The glass of a mirror is equivalent to the rarer matter; its lead backing represents the denser matter.

95 Arguments from experiment are sanctioned by Aristotle.

105 i.e. with the same integrity of light. The quality of reflected light is shown *not* to be determined by its distance from the observer, therefore the darker areas on the moon's surface cannot be due to the reflection of the sun's light from denser matter deeper within it.

112 The Empyrean (Tenth Heaven) outside time and space (see *Paradiso* XXX.39–42).

113 f. The Primum Mobile or Crystalline Heaven (the Ninth) is material but translucent, and takes its existence and power ("virtue") from the Empyrean, distributing it to the material world below and within it, from sphere to sphere. See *Convivio* II.III.7 f.

115–20 In the Eighth Heaven of the Fixed Stars (l. 115) the constellations sift out the "being" and undifferentiated power of the Primum Mobile, distributing it as differentiated "virtue[s]" through the seven planetary spheres below, finally to the earth at the centre of the system.

127–9 Each order of the angels controls one of the heavens and its influence, and thus the universe exists and operates with the intention of the Creator. The image of the smith comes ultimately from Aristotle.

133–5 The human bodily characteristics of limb, organ and senses are determined as such by the inherent powers of the soul, according to the soul's needs and requirements to express and actuate itself through the body.

136 The "intelligence" here means the angelic order in question, which produces the differentation and distribution of heavenly power and being as "virtue[s]" (see note to ll. 115–20 above).

140 The "precious bodies" are the incorruptible heavenly bodies of stars and planets.

142 f. The angelic "virtue", united with the incorruptible substance of primal matter, produces luminosity. The variety of "virtue[s]" accounts for the range of luminosity in the heavenly bodies, and for the modulation of luminosity within the individual planets such as the moon. We have thus arrived at a spiritual rather than material solution to Dante's original question.

PARADISO III

Within the moon's sphere, where the souls gather of those who failed to fulfil their holy vows, Dante converses with Piccarda Donati, who relates her story and that of the Empress Constance.

1 Beatrice, with whom Dante fell in love in his ninth year, in Florence (see *Vita Nuova* II).

3 The "truth" is that of Beatrice's long disquisition on the nature of the moon's dark patches in the preceding canto.

17–18 "the man in love with the pool" is Narcissus, who fell in love with his own reflection, as a penalty for rejecting the love of Echo (Ovid, *Metamorphoses* III.339 f.). Narcissus took for real what was only a reflection, whereas Dante takes for a reflection what is real.

21 Dante looks behind him for the real source of the supposed reflections.

29 A *substance*, in scholastic philosophy, is an entity possessing independent existence (see note to *Paradiso* XXXIII.88).

34 f. Piccarda Donati (see also *Purgatorio* XXIV.10 f.), cousin to Dante's wife Gemma, was the sister of Dante's friend Forese Donati (*Purgatorio* XXIII.40 f.), and also of Corso Donati (whose dire fate is predicted in *Purgatorio* XXIV.82 f.), a political enemy of Dante. It was Corso, according to some early commentators, who carried her away against her will from her convent, to marry her off to Rossellino della Tosa, a political crony.

51 The Sphere of the Moon, the lowest of the heavenly spheres. The speed of the first eight of the heavens which, invisible, carry round with them the planet or stars that belong to them, drops away in proportion to their distance from the outermost Crystalline Heaven or Primum Mobile.

56–7 The moon's changeable appearance, as it waxes and wanes, is thus an apposite symbol of inconstancy.

63 Latin was the supreme language of the medieval world; its clarity and conciseness remained unsurpassed for centuries by the less developed vernacular tongues. Dante, it should be noted, was the most conspicuous of the authors of the period who began the overthrow of Latin (whilst eulogising and employing it), by composing his greatest work in the vernacular. Here, "in plain Latin" is metaphor, meaning 'clearly'.

85 For one of the most famous of all the lines in *The Divine Comedy*, *'E'n la sua voluntade è nostra pace'*, Dante drew upon St Augustine, *Confessions* XIII.9: *'In bona voluntate tua pax nobis est.'* Cf. Ephesians 2.14.

86 Dante makes wide use of metaphors of the sea in *The Divine Comedy*, nowhere more effectively than when referring to God as the unlimited, measureless source and medium of all life (cf. *Paradiso* I.112–13, XIX.58–63).

87 The human soul is a direct act of creation by God. All purely earthly phenomena are indirect creations by Nature (the activation of 'potential complexes' by power or 'virtue' from the heavenly bodies). See *Purgatorio* VII.139–41 and note.

89–90 God did not create all men equal. Rather he treats them with equality, in the sense that by his grace he perfectly fulfils the desires of individual souls in proportion to their innate capacity for love and knowledge. More 'noble' souls have a larger capacity for love and knowledge than less 'noble' souls. (See *Convivio* III.XV.10).

98 St Clare of Assisi (1194–1253) founded, in collaboration with St Francis, an order of nuns, the Poor Clares, in 1212.

101 "that spouse" is Christ, whose Bride is the Church.

109 f. The Empress Constance (d. 1198), daughter and heir of the Norman king of Naples and Sicily, Roger II, was wife of Emperor Henry VI of Swabia, and mother of Emperor Frederick II (see also *Purgatorio* III.113). Dante accepts the contemporary account of her life, in which she was forcibly removed from a convent for the purposes of a marriage, of political and dynastic implications, with Henry Duke of Swabia, later emperor (see G. Villani. *Cronica* V.16).

119 The "gales" of Swabia, so-called because of their imperious characters and tumultuous lives, were three in number: Frederick I Barbarossa, Henry VI his son, and Frederick II his grandson.

PARADISO IV

Following Piccarda's statement in the previous canto, Dante's perplexities are resolved by Beatrice: firstly the problem of the inviolability or otherwise of the will, secondly the problem of the eternal location of the blessed souls.

1–12 Following Piccarda's explanation in the previous canto, Dante is beset by two doubts of equal seriousness, so that he is logically unable to decide which of the two he should put first to Beatrice. His condition is like that in the medieval paradox of 'Buridan's donkey' caught between two equally attractive bales of hay. This category of logical problem had been framed as early as Aristotle.

13 Daniel allayed Nebuchadnezzar's anger against the ineffectual wise men of his court by stating and interpreting the King's dreams for him (Daniel 2.1–45).

19–21 Piccarda and Constance (see previous canto) had been obliged by others to quit their convents and thus break their vows, even though their *will* to remain true to them was apparently unaffected by these circumstances. Dante's question is whether they can then be said to have fallen short of their vows, and thus to have merited something less than their full reward in heaven (their souls appear in the lowest sphere of heaven, that of the moon).

23–4 Plato in the *Timaeus* conceived that souls proceeded from the stars and were noble, more or less, according to the nobleness of the star, and then returned or 'reversed' to the star in a process of reincarnation. This was refuted by orthodox Christian theologians, who denied reincarnation and posited the creation of the soul by a direct intervention of God, at the moment after conception when the brain is articulated (see *Purgatorio* XXV.67–75). Dante is confused, having assumed that Piccarda's appearance in the Sphere of the Moon was due to the fact that her soul is eternally confined there, seemingly verifying Plato's hypothesis. See Dante, *Convivio* IV.XXI.2.

27 f. Beatrice deals first with the Platonic problem (see note to ll. 23–4 above) the more serious of the two, since it would allow excessive astral influence on the destiny of the soul, and deny the possibility of the return of the soul to the full, uninhibited presence of the Creator.

28 The Seraphim are the first order of angels, closest to God.

29 "both the Johns": John the Baptist, and John the Evangelist (author of the Gospel and, it was supposed, of Revelation).

31–2, 34 The Empyrean, true Paradise, beyond space and time. See note to *Paradiso* I.4.

35–6 See note to *Paradiso* III.89–90.

37 "They show themselves here": the idea that the souls of the blessed issue, as it were, from the Empyrean to welcome Dante home is adumbrated in Dante's earlier work, the *Convivio*, treating the ideal approach of an old man to the threshold of eternal life: 'And as to him who cometh from a long journey ere he enter the gate of his city, the citizens thereof come forth to meet him; so come, and so should come, to meet the noble soul those citizens of the eternal life' (ib. IV.XXVIII.5).

40–48 Dante held the Aristotelian and Thomist view of the mechanics of comprehension, viz. that cognition is based on sensory experience (e.g. 'all our knowledge originates from sense', *Summa Theologica* I, q. 1, ad. 9, resp.). Since Dante is still alive in the flesh, his acquisition of knowledge in the Beyond is limited to this pedestrian process (sensation > imagination > intellection), whereas angels and the disembodied souls achieve cognition directly, with no intermediary stages. Piccarda's appearance in the Sphere of the Moon is momentary, and merely in charitable condescension to Dante's limited means of cognition.

46–8 Gabriel, Michael and Raphael ("the one who made Tobit well again", Tobit 11.1–15) are archangels.

49 f. See note to ll. 23–4 above.

54 "a form": i.e. an essential formative principle. This is unacceptable to Christian doctrine, where the soul's 'form' is an eternal, rational entity created by God's direct 'inspiration'.

55–6 Dante (through Beatrice) appears to hint at the possibility of a reconciliation of Platonic and orthodox thought, suggesting that Plato might have been referring obliquely to astral influences as determining man's attributes and personality, an idea partially accepted by Dante but with important reservations (see *Purgatorio* XVI.67–81, and *Paradiso* XXII.111–17 and notes).

61–3 However, the doctrine of astral influences went too far in pagan antiquity, so that planets such as Jupiter, Mercury and Mars were worshipped as gods by man, who mistakenly believed his actions were *predetermined* by them, irrespective of the principle of free will.

64–9 "The other doubt": the problem of the inviolability of the will. A mistake on this point of doctrine would not be heretical and thereby damnable.

67 "Our justice": i.e. the justice of Heaven, as opposed to man's fallible justice. To question the justice of God is not heretical (a distortion of sound doctrine), merely faithlessness. However, the second hemistich of l. 68 might be construed: 'argues faith not heresy'; that is to say, only a man believing in God's infallible justice would question its infallibility in particular cases. Dante is thus no heretic, since a heretic might posit the fallibility of God's justice in principle.

70–72 Logic, not faith, is required to solve the problem of Piccarda's and Constance's occupation of "the lowest of celestial states" (l. 39).

73 f. Beatrice is proceeding on the assumption, of course, that Piccarda and Constance were guilty to some extent of faithlessness to their vows as nuns, not only because God's infallible justice has accorded them the "lowest of celestial states", but because it is known (ll. 81–6) that they did not return to their conventual life when the actual physical constraint that carried them off was removed. If human will is inviolable it is the "absolute will" (l. 109), which allowed both women honestly to retain their first love for convent life whilst consenting not to return. The consenting not to return belonged to the "other [will]" (l. 114), the conditioned or relative will (see Aquinas, *Summa Theologica* II.I, q. VI, art. 4 f.).

83–4 St Lawrence was a deacon of the early Church in Rome, grilled to death in 258. C. Mucius Scaevola, having failed to kill the Etruscan invader Lars Porsena, destroyed his own right hand in the fire Porsena had kindled to execute him. The act earned for him and Rome Porsena's reprieve (Livy, *History of Rome* II.12, *De Monarchia* II.V.14).

94–6 cf. *Paradiso* III.31–3.

103–5 The story of Alcmaeon (see also *Purgatorio* XII.49–51), who murdered his mother at the instigation of his father, mortally wounded in the Theban war (in which he had participated on the treacherous advice of his wife), is recounted in Ovid, *Metamorphoses* IX.407 f. and referred to in *Aeneid* VI.445–6. It is also found in Aquinas's commentary on Aristotle's *Nichomachean Ethics*, at the point where the discussion turns on actions committed in a context of conflicting principles (Singleton).

118 "the first lover" is God, primal Love.

125 "that truth": what is eternally true, the revealed truth of God as seen in His Word, Christ, and as found in Scripture and orthodox theology. This is the truth that Beatrice imparts, in her symbolic role as divine Wisdom.

129 For Dante, following Aristotelian thought, there is nothing in nature that is vain or futile ('*Natura nihil facit frustra*'). The intellectual problems that man poses for himself therefore must have answers, to be found, if not in rational philosophy alone, then (for Dante) in philosophy illuminated by revealed Christian truth and doctrine (for example, in a work of the scope of Aquinas's *Summa Theologica*).

PARADISO V

In the context of her disquisition on the nature of vows, Beatrice touches on the vital Christian doctrine of free will, then with Dante rises to the Heaven of Mercury.

1–9 The light of God, which is wisdom and love, illuminates Beatrice; his knowledge floods her intellect ("the perfection/ Of my sight", ll. 4–5), and his love shines from her eyes. From this light Dante himself is illuminated, for 'in thy light shall we see light' (AV Psalms 36.9).

10–13 Traces of the eternal light shine through all things, but man lacks judgement in assessing to what extent he should will to love all the things that please him: cf. Purgatorio XVI.85–96. It is love of 'apparent good' that is the cause of sin in Thomistic doctrine (Summa Theologica II.I, q. 73, art. 8, ad. 2).

22 See Purgatorio XVI.67–81, and XVIII.70–75 where Virgil promises Dante this fuller consideration of the doctrine of free will by Beatrice.

23 Angels and mankind.

31 By this question Beatrice implies that nothing can compensate for the willing sacrifice to God of God's greatest gift to mankind, the freedom of the will.

44–5 "the matter of it": i.e. what is vowed; "The other": i.e. the nature of the vow as a compact between man and God.

49–50 Jehovah's election of the Hebrews as His people in the old Covenant entailed a binding obligation on their part to make sacrifices and offering as a symbolic compensation for their unworthiness. The offerings might be in property and tithes, and could only be 'modified' (normally redeemed; "subject to modification") if suitable compensation were paid, as laid down in Leviticus 27. Thus the sacred compact was never in principle broken.

57 "keys": see note to Purgatorio IX.117–26.

61–3 Beatrice returns to the cases of Piccarda and Constance recounted in the previous canto. The vow as a compact with God cannot in principle be remitted, though it may be commuted. But it may be commuted only if something worthier can be put in its place. Since religious (monastic) vows involve the willing sacrifice of the free will to God (his gift than which nothing is more valuable) then it follows that the notion of the commutation of such vows (as those made by Piccarda and Constance) is absurd.

66–72 Jephthah (Judges 11.29 f.), following a vow of rash conditions made to Jehovah, was finally obliged to sacrifice his only daughter ("his first gift"). Agamemnon (l. 69), in order to appease the goddess Diana for an act of sacrilege, vowed to sacrifice to her the most beautiful child born in his kingdom in that year, and was obliged to offer up his own daughter Iphigenia; see Cicero, De Officiis III.25.95.

79–81 The reference is possibly to the cynicism of certain religious orders, who did financial business in the matter of encouraging, remitting and commuting vows.

87 The Empyrean, the true Paradise of the Creator and his redeemed souls.

93 "the second kingdom": the Heaven of Mercury.

97 Laughter, for Dante, is the 'gleam of the joyous soul' (see *Convivio* III.VIII.11).

117 Cf. AV 1 Timothy 6.12: 'Fight the good fight of faith, lay hold on eternal life, whereunto thou art also called.'

123 Cf. AV Psalms 82.6: 'I have said, Ye are gods; and all of you are children of the most High.'

128–9 Mercury, for Dante the smallest 'star' of heaven, circles closest to the sun and is hidden by its rays.

PARADISO VI

In the Sphere of Mercury, Justinian outlines the history of the spread of the Roman 'Eagle' through the ancient world, and into medieval times, then briefly recounts the story of Romieu de Villeneuve (Romeo).

1–3 The Emperor Constantine removed the seat of Roman authority ("the eagle") eastwards from Rome to Constantinople (formerly Byzantium) in 324AD, in the opposite direction to that taken by the founder of the Roman race, Aeneas (husband of Lavinia), in his westward voyage from Troy to Italy, recounted in the *Aeneid* of Virgil. See *Inferno* XIX.115–17 and note.

10 Justinian the Great ruled what then existed intact of the Roman Empire from Constantinople, from 527 to 565. His lasting monument is the great legal work ("The great task", l. 24) he supervised, the *Corpus iuris civilis*, the bible of Roman law for the late Empire and medieval world. See note to *Purgatorio* VI.88.

11 "primal love": i.e. the love of God (cf. *Inferno* III.6).

14–15 The Eutychian or monophysite heresy proposed only the divine nature in Christ whereas orthodoxy insists on his dual nature, true God and true man. That Justinian held this heretical view was a common but probably mistaken belief in Dante's time.

16 Agapetus I (pope 535–6). The known dates of Agapetus and those of Justinian's revision and codification of Roman law (528–33) hardly tally with Dante's version (cf. ll. 22–4). For J. H. Whitfield, 'the whole providential sequence [here] is Dante's invention, not historic fact'.

21 i.e. of any pair of contradictory statements, it is logical that one must be true and the other false; therefore Justinian is stating that his new, orthodox understanding of the dual nature of Christ is now as clear to him as logic.

25 Belisarius: Justinian's general, to whom he entrusted the reconquest of Italy from the Gothic invaders.

32–3 The imperial emblem of the Eagle was appropriated by the Ghibellines in Italy, and opposed by the pro-Church Guelf party, in the course of the thirteenth and early fourteenth centuries.

35 f. Justinian now embarks on the history of Roman imperial authority (the Eagle) from the earliest times to its reconfirmation as the Holy Roman Empire by Charlemagne, establishing its divine authority, its providential spread, and its unbroken historical tradition. His aim is to show how this transcendental concept of empire, with its roots deep in history, stands above and apart from the narrow political factionalism of the Ghibelline–Guelf struggles of Dante's politically fragmented era.

36 Pallas, son of the king of Latium, died helping Aeneas against Turnus and the Rutuli (*Aeneid* X.479 f.). When Aeneas married Lavinia, Pallas's sister, the kingdom of Latium (and the site of Rome) reverted to him by right.

37–9 The descendants of Aeneas established their rule (that of the Eagle) firstly in Alba Longa. After Rome's foundation by Romulus (a descendant also of Aeneas), three Roman champions, the Horatii, defeated three Alban champions, the Curiatii, to establish Roman supremacy in the struggle between Rome and Alba.

40–41 Romulus and his companions carried off the Sabine women as wives, whilst their husbands were watching the games he provided for them. Romulus was the first of Rome's seven kings. Sextus, the son of the last king, Tarquinius Superbus, cruelly violated Lucretia, of patrician blood, a scandal which brought about the end of the monarchical period in 510BC and the foundation of the Republic (Lucretia: see note to *Inferno* IV.128).

44 Brennus: a Gaulish chief (fourth century BC). Pyrrhus: king of Epirus (third century BC).

46–8 Roman heroes who distinguished themselves in repelling the invaders of early Rome and her possessions from the fifth to third century BC. Lucius Quinctius is better known as Cincinnatus, who was called from his farm to the dictatorship during one such crisis (see note to *Paradiso* XV.129).

49–51 The Arabs i.e. Carthaginians, under Hannibal, were defeated finally by Scipio Africanus the Elder (l. 52) in the second Punic War at Zama in 202BC.

52 Pompey the Great (106–48BC) waged successful campaigns in Sicily, Spain, Africa and the Mediterranean. Later, in the civil war, he was defeated by Caesar.

54 "those hills": i.e. where Fiesole stands, above Florence, destroyed according to G. Villani in the war against Cataline's conspirators *c*. 62BC (see *Cronica* I.31 f.).

57 Julius Caesar (102–44BC), the most brilliant and successful of the Romans, *imperator* and founder of the Roman Empire, although not its first emperor.

58–60 The rivers define Gaul, scene of Caesar's early campaigns (58–50BC).

61–2 Caesar began the Civil War by crossing the river Rubicon (between Ravenna and Rimini) in default of orders from the Senate (49BC). See *Inferno* XXVIII.95 and note.

65–6 Durazzo, formerly Dyrrachium in Illyria, where Caesar besieged Pompey the Great. At Pharsalia he defeated Pompey, who fled to Egypt for refuge.

67 Antandros (with its nearby river, the Simois) was the port from which Aeneas sailed (*Aeneid* III.5–6).

68 "the place where Hector lies": Hector's tomb, outside the walls of Troy.

69 Caesar took Egypt from the Ptolemies, and gave it to Cleopatra.

70 Juba: king of Numidia.

72 Pompey's sons, after his defeat, raised an army in opposition to Caesar.

73–75 After Caesar's assassination (44BC), Augustus (Octavian, l. 79) his nephew defeated two of the assassins, Brutus and Cassius (see *Inferno* XXXIV.64–7) at Philippi, Mark Antony at Modena, and the latter's brother at Perugia.

76–8 After Mark Antony's defeat at Actium (31BC), and his subsequent death, Cleopatra his mistress committed suicide, having failed to ensnare Augustus and fearing his vengeance (see note to *Inferno* V.63).

80 With Octavian (Augustus) master of the whole Roman Empire, the doors of the temple of Janus in Rome (which were always open during wars) were ceremoniously closed, marking the start of the long period of the *pax romana*.

87 "the third Caesar": Tiberius, emperor 14–37AD.

90 The crucifixion of Christ, God's retribution for the sin of man exacted by means of the sacrifice of his Son, occurred in 34AD. Christ, condemned by the Jews, suffered death under Roman jurisdiction.

91–3 Under Titus (i.e. Vespasian), emperor 70–79AD, his son Titus besieged and destroyed Jerusalem in 70AD, an act regarded as just retribution for the Jews' condemning the Son of God to death.

94 The occupation of much of Italy by the Germanic Longobards (Lombards), Arian invaders, was brought to an end by Charlemagne, to whom Pope Adrian I appealed in 773. Charlemagne was crowned emperor of the now Holy Roman Empire in 800.

100–103 The Guelfs, in league with the French ("The yellow lilies"), compounded their opposition to the Empire ("the public emblem"), whilst the Ghibelline party ("the other", l. 101) deceitfully appropriated the banner of the Empire as if they owned it. But the Eagle belongs to neither party (see note to l. 35 f. above).

104–5 i.e. the Ghibelline cause is unjust (since despite its protestations it seeks not the good of the Empire, but its own factional interest), and therefore can have no part in the essential affairs of Empire, which above all is the sacred fount and instrument of justice in temporal affairs.

106 The acknowledged leader of the Guelf cause in Italy in 1300 was Charles II of Anjou, Naples and Provence, who inherited his titles from his more august father Charles I of Anjou (see *Purgatorio* VII.113 f., 126 f. and notes) in 1285.

111 Charles must not deceive himself that the divine right of the Empire can pass into the ambitious hands of the French, so that the Lilies usurp the Eagle ("his arms").

112 f. Mercury is the smallest planet, with which are associated the souls of the faithful who yearned excessively for honour and reputation.

124–6 The music of the spheres referred to in *Paradiso* I.76–8. See note.

128 f. Romeo (Romieu de Villeneuve, 1170–1250), who rose from obscurity to become seneschal of Count Raymond Berengar IV of Provence (l. 133), justly and ably administered the

country, and arranged the marriage of Raymond's four daughters to kings. Accused unjustly of embezzlement, he was stripped of his rank and died in poverty. This canto, then, begins with the exalted theme of the transcendental justice of imperial authority, and ends with the example of a humble but just man unjustly accused, a wry comment on the way of the world, and a very personal comment if we may descry just beneath the figure of Romeo that of Dante himself, in his exile, whose own fortunes were not dissimilar (Whitfield). Cf. also Wisdom of Solomon 3.1–5.

PARADISO VII

In the Sphere of Mercury, Beatrice firstly answers Dante's unspoken question arising from Justinian's account of the role of the Empire in the aftermath of the Crucifixion, then answers two supplementary questions on the doctrine of the redemption of man, and the difference between primary and secondary creation.

1–3 'Hosanna, holy God of hosts, who doubly lightens with thy brightness the happy fires of these realms'.

5 Justinian (see previous canto).

12 cf. 'For food she [Wisdom] will give him the bread of understanding and for drink the water of knowledge', Ecclesiasticus 15.3.

14 *"Be"* (the letter B), and the syllables *"ice"*, first letter and last syllables of *Beatrice* give 'Bice', the shortened, affectionate form in Italian.

19–21 Dante's unspoken question arises from Justinian's words in *Paradiso* VI.91–3.

22 f. The solution to the problem is given by Beatrice in the wider (and more significant) context of the account of the origin of Original Sin in mankind.

26 "that man" is Adam, his sin that of presumption and disobedience. By eating of the fruit of the tree of the knowledge of good and evil (Genesis 2 and 3) Adam not only disobeyed God's direct injunction, but presumed to exalt himself towards the condition of God.

30 Christ. Cf. John 1.1.

31–3 The incarnation of the Word of God. Cf. John 1.14.

35–6 i.e. before the Fall, human nature in Adam was naturally disposed to the good. See note to *Paradiso* XXXII.4.

37 i.e. Eden, Earthly Paradise.

40–42 The crucifixion of Christ represented a full and just retribution in God's eyes, in so far as it exacted a perfect penalty for the original sin in human nature. The forfeit was that "nature assumed" by Christ, his perfect humanity.

43–5 The penalty of the Crucifixion, however, was unjust in human law, because of the sinlessness of "the person who suffered it", Christ the Son of God. The Jews, in their disbelief at Christ's divinity, crucified the divinity. This is the crime which also demanded retribution, and was exacted by the destruction of Jerusalem in 70AD by Titus, the instrument of imperial authority (the "just court", l. 51).

48 "earth trembled": see Matthew 27.51; "the heavens opened" to receive those henceforth redeemed by faith in Christ.

55–7 Beatrice formulates Dante's second unasked question, and proceeds to answer it.

58–63 Human intellect alone is inadequate to understand God's motives in selecting the death of His Son as the means to man's redemption. Only revealed wisdom, the truth of God, the wisdom that is love, can clarify this.

67 i.e. direct, 'unmediated' creation: angels, the soul of man, and primal matter.

72 i.e. the influence of things of indirect or secondary creation: purely natural phenomena.

73 Things directly created by God are more like him in their immortality and freedom, and therefore more pleasing to him than things of indirect or secondary creation.

74 the "sacred blaze" is God's love, of which all things bear traces.

86 "its seed": Adam. All mankind is contained potentially in Adam, the first man, as a plant is 'contained' in a seed.

100 See note to l. 26.

103 See AV Psalms 25.10: 'All the paths of the Lord are mercy and truth [justice].'

112 i.e. Between the Last Judgement and the day of the Creation. Dante's reversal of the normal (chronological) order (*hysteron proteron*, Singleton) reflects Beatrice's 'eternal' perspective of history, when the last events appear like the first because most recent.

115 "more generous": cf. 'Christ died for us while we were yet sinners, and that is God's own proof of his love towards us' (Romans 5.8). "God to give himself": cf. 'My Father and I are one' (Christ's words in John 10.30).

124–9 Dante's third unspoken question is answered by Beatrice as a corollary to her previous statements, specifically ll. 67–72, regarding the distinction between direct and indirect creation. Cf. *Paradiso* XIII.52–81 and notes.

124–5 The four elements of matter, identified by Empedocles (see note to *Inferno* IV.138).

127 "creatures": i.e. created things.

130 "the unaltering country": i.e. the heavenly places (see note to *Paradiso* II.140).

135 "created virtue": i.e. the influence of the heavens (the stars and planets) controlled by the several angelic intelligences. In this sense, the creation of the elements, and what is made from them, is due to secondary causes rather than to direct creation by God. See note to *Paradiso* II.115–20.

136–8 "The matter": i.e. primal, undifferentiated matter, with the *potentiality* to become anything, is a direct creation of God. Similarly the "informing virtue", which combines with primal matter to become something specific, is a direct creation of God. However, primal matter only becomes 'something' through the intermediacy of the heavens, which transmit the "informing virtue" of the Creator into it. Anything that is thus indirectly created is corruptible and bound (not free).

139–41 The informative influences or 'virtues' of the stars and planets act on 'potential complexes' (complexes of primal matter that have the potential to become what they do become) to produce the souls of animals and plants: the 'sensitive' souls of animals (which operate only through their senses) and the 'vegetative' souls of plants (which possess life but not sensation). These lower souls thus depend for their creation on a secondary cause (the heavens), and as such are mortal and bound.

142–4 The "highest goodness" is God, subject of the verb "breathes" in l. 142. The human soul is a direct creation of God, thus immortal, and its natural love is for God as supreme good (see *Purgatorio* XXV.67 f., XVI.85 f., *Paradiso* I.109 f. and note).

145 f. The bodies of Adam and Eve (the "first parents", l. 148) were direct creations of God, but the incorruptibility of human flesh was forfeited at the Fall. The recuperation of the incorruptible body will take place at the general resurrection of the dead on the Last Day. See 1 Corinthians 15.51 f., and notes to *Inferno* VI.95–6 and 97–9.

PARADISO VIII

Dante, with Beatrice, rises to the Sphere of Venus, where Charles Martel, amongst the souls of those whose love was tarnished by promiscuity, answers Dante's question on the apparent paradoxes of heredity.

1 i.e. before the redemption of mankind offered by grace in the Christian era.

2–3 Venus was born in the sea off Cyprus, where her cult probably originated (cf. Ovid, *Metamorphoses* X.270). As Aphrodite Pandemos she was worshipped as the goddess of physical love.

3 The epicycle of the Third Heaven (Venus). As well as revolving around the earth, the planets in ancient astronomy were believed (with the exception of the sun) to revolve also in a smaller orbit (the epicycle) around a point upon the larger orbit. This accounted for the varying distances from the earth that the planets were observed to maintain at different times in their cycles.

9 Cupid, disguised as Ascanius, Aeneas's son, thus deceitfully kindled the fatal passion of Dido for Aeneas (*Aeneid* I.657 f.).

12 Venus appears, according to season, as either the morning star (see note to *Purgatorio* I.19) or evening star, as Dante explains in *Convivio* II.II.1. It is located in turn in front of the sun and behind it.

13 i.e. into the planet of Venus.

15 The radiance of Beatrice's beauty increases as she draws nearer to the Empyrean, true Paradise, source of the Truth of which she is the mirror. See *Purgatorio* VI.45, and cf. Wisdom of Solomon 7.26: 'She [Wisdom] is the brightness that streams from everlasting light, the flawless mirror of the active power of God and the image of his goodness.'

23 Visible in the form of lightning as 'kindled vapours'.

26 "the circle": the Empyrean.

31 Charles Martel (see also *Paradiso* IX.1), 1271–95, eldest son of Mary of Hungary and Charles II of Anjou (see note to *Purgatorio* VII.126) who survived him, was husband to Clemenza, daughter of Emperor Rudolph I of Hapsburg (see note to *Purgatorio* VII.91–6). Heir to his father's throne of Naples (Apulia) and to Provence, he was created king of Hungary in 1292, though never resided there. In March 1294

he was in Florence (G. Villani, *Cronica* VIII.13) with a magnificent retinue of knights to meet his father Charles II bound for Naples. It was here that Charles made Dante's acquaintance, to judge from his generous words and his familiar greeting of Dante here as the poet of the *canzone*: "You who, understanding, move the third heaven" (l. 37; see *Convivio* II where the poem is treated).

34 The Principalities, the order of angels governing the Heaven of Venus.

49–51 Charles Martel died prematurely at the age of twenty-four. He predicts further misgovernment by his father Charles II, whom Dante held in low esteem, and by his brother Robert, who succeeded as his father's heir to the throne of Naples and the county of Provence.

58–60 The county of Provence.

61–3 "that horn of Ausonia": the southern portion of Italy, corresponding to the Kingdom of Naples, delimited by the three towns of l. 62, and the rivers of l. 63 (to the north of which lie the Papal States); see note to *Purgatorio* III.127 f.

65 "that country": Hungary.

67 f. Sicily, its eastern coast delimited here by references to Pachino to the south and Peloro (modern Cape Faro) to the north, appears darkened by the smoke of Mount Etna (smoke that is caused not, as legend has it, by the interred giant Typhaeus, but by the "rising sulphur", l. 70). Charles draws heavily and impressively on Ovid for much of this periphrasis.

72 Charles I of Anjou (see note to *Purgatorio* VII.113) and Rudolph I of Hapsburg (ib. 91–6); see note to l. 31 above.

73–5 The "subject peoples" of Sicily, in 1282, rose spontaneously against their Angevin rulers in Palermo, expelled them, and installed the Aragonese in their place. Known as the 'Sicilian Vespers', the revolution cost Charles I of Anjou the crown of Sicily, which passed to Peter III of Aragon (see notes to *Purgatorio* VII.103 and 112).

76–84 Robert was in Catalonia from 1288 to 1295 as hostage of the Aragonese in place of his father. When he succeeded to the crown of Naples in 1309 he appointed a number of Catalans as officials, their "greedy poverty" leading them easily to corruption (Sapegno). In this way and others Robert signally mismanaged the administration of his unwieldy government ("his overloaded ship", l. 81), so that parsimony (more than the generosity of his grandfather Charles I of Anjou) came to be the distinguishing mark of his rule (ll. 82–3).

87 i.e. in God.

93 The question follows from Charles' observations on his brother's parsimony in ll. 82–3. How is it that Robert did not inherit the generous nature of his forebears?

97–102 The "good" of the Creator, transmitted down through the spheres via the angelic intelligences (see notes to *Paradiso* II.112 to end), makes its "providence" (its preordaining of events, and of men's characters so to influence those events) an operating power ("virtue", l. 99). Such "provision" (l. 102) 'work[s] together for good to them that love God' (AV Romans 8.28).

109 "intellects": angels.

111 "The primal intellect": God.

113–14 i.e. 'it is impossible that universal Nature should fail in its preordained tasks', a cornerstone of Aristotelian thought (cf. Dante, *De Monarchia* I.X.1, and elsewhere in Dante's works).

115–16 Man as essentially a 'social animal' is another key concept in Aristotle, found in the *Politics*, and a commonplace in scholastic philosophy (cf. *Convivio* IV.IV.1).

118–20 Another commonplace of Aristotelian thought, from the *Politics* and elsewhere, and used by Dante in his minor works also.

122–3 "the causes": i.e. the character, and personality of men; "the effects": i.e. the different functions men perform.

124–6 Solon, a statesman; Xerxes, a warrior; Melchizedek, a priest; "the man", Daedalus, an inventor (his son Icarus: see note to *Inferno* XXIX.116).

129 i.e. has no regard as to whether its 'target' is a prince or a pauper; it pays no deference to mere rank or to any deterministic concept of heredity.

130–32 Esau and Jacob (Genesis 25.21 f.), twin brothers but quite different in disposition. Quirinus (Romulus, builder of Rome) had a royal mother, but, according to Dante, a "base father", yet his disposition earned him a divine paternity in legend.

133–5 Divine Providence thus prevents a deterministic law of genetic heredity from operating amongst humans.

139–41 It is a matter of observation that plants do not prosper away from the conditions that best suit their species. Similarly, if the human character, adapted by its nature to one sort of occupation, is forced to follow another, then it, likewise, will not prosper.

143 i.e. in the natural disposition of the individual.

145-6 It is not clear who this is, even granted that Dante had someone in mind (early commentators suggest Louis, younger brother of Charles and Robert of Anjou, who was in religious orders and later canonised).

147 Possibly Robert of Anjou, whose output of sermons alone was impressive.

PARADISO IX

In the sphere of Venus still, Cunizza da Romano and Folco (Folquet) of Marseilles talk with Dante, and the latter tells Dante of the redemption of Rahab the harlot.

1 Charles Martel (see previous canto). Clemenza: very probably Clemenza, widow of Charles (see note to *Paradiso* VIII.31), who died very shortly after her husband in 1295; less likely the attribution to Charles' daughter of the same name, future queen of Louis X of France.

3 "his posterity": i.e. his son Charles Robert, whose rightful claim to the throne of Naples in 1309, following the death of his grandfather Charles II of Anjou, was waived in favour of his uncle Robert, Charles Martel's younger brother (see note to *Paradiso* VIII.76–84). Pope Clement V confirmed Robert's succession to Naples, and Charles Robert's claim to the throne of Hungary, of which his father had been titular monarch.

8 "the sun": God.

22 Cunizza da Romano (*c*.1198 to *c*.1279), sister of the energetic but tyrannical Azzolino III (l. 29; and note to *Inferno* XII.110), whose life of liaisons (one with Sordello the poet and troubadour, see note to *Purgatorio* VI.58 f.), and four husbands, made her a living legend in Florence in Dante's day (cf. Benvenuto). Here she came finally to reside, and died at about the age of eighty.

25-7 The March of Treviso; Rialto is the largest island in the cluster forming Venice.

28 The hill of Romano, site of the castle of the Azzolini.

34-6 Cunizza humbly and joyfully accepts her predisposition to love, being so influenced by her 'star' Venus. Through the grace of God, her inclination turned from carnal lust to fervent love of God at the end of her long career. Cf. Folco's words, ll. 103–5 below.

37 Folco (Folquet) of Marseilles (see note to l. 82 f. below).

44 The March of Treviso, defined by the rivers on its eastern and western boundaries.

46–8 In 1314 Can Grande della Scala, Imperial Vicar of Vicenza, defeated the Paduan Guelfs who had taken control of the city some forty-nine years before.

47 The reference is to Paduan blood 'changing' (i.e. staining) the river that runs through Vicenza and forms marshes around the city.

48 The Paduans were Guelfs, and thus refuted any loyalty to Can Grande, a Ghibelline.

49 At Treviso.

50–51 Rizzardo da Camino, in 1300 heir to Gherardo da Camino, lord of Treviso (mentioned respectfully in *Purgatorio* XVI.124; see note), was later the husband of Giovanna Visconti daughter of Nino (see note to *Purgatorio* VIII.47 and 71). A militant and unpopular Ghibelline, Rizzardo was assassinated in 1312 in a Guelf plot.

52–60 The Guelf bishop ("shepherd") of Feltro (mod. Feltre), Alessandro Novello in 1314 betrayed certain refugee Ghibellines of Ferrara under his protection by handing them back to Ferrara, where they were executed together with many of their following on charges of treachery.

54 Possibly a papal prison for recalcitrant clerics.

59 "the right side": i.e. Guelf.

61 "thrones": the order of angels in control of the heaven of Saturn, who execute God's judgements.

66 See *Paradiso* VIII.20.

70–71 See note to *Paradiso* V.97.

77–8 The six-winged Seraphim, angels of divine love (cf. Isaiah 6.2).

82 f. The voice is that of Folco (Folquet) of Marseilles, Provençal poet and troubadour who died in 1231, having renounced the world to become a Cistercian monk in *c.*1195. His fame remains as a love poet (Dante respectfully cites one of his *cansos* in *De Vulgari Eloquentia* II.VI.5–6), but his career as a cleric was hardly less impressive, becoming bishop of Toulouse in 1205, notorious for his part in the persecution of the Albigensian heretics of Provence in the crusade of 1209.

82 The Mediterranean.

88–9 The river Ebro is in Spain. The Magra (old Macra) flows out near La Spezia, and divided Genoese territory from Tuscany. Thus the whole Mediterranean littoral is referred to ("the shore of that valley").

91–2 Bougiah, a port east of Algiers on the North African coast, shares the same meridian (longitude) as Marseilles.

93 The reference is to the slaughter of the citizens of Marseilles, supporters of Pompey, by the fleet of Julius Caesar led by Brutus in 49BC.

97–8 Dido, falling passionately in love with Aeneas, defiled both her dead husband's memory (Sychaeus), and that of Creusa, Aeneas' late wife (see note to *Inferno* V.61).

99 i.e. before becoming a monk (see note to l. 82 f. above).

100–101 Phyllis, daughter of the king of Thrace (whose palace was near Mount Rhodope), hanged herself, believing herself abandoned by Prince Demophoon (Ovid, *Heroides* II.147–8).

101–2 Hercules (Alcides), deceiving his wife Dejanira, fell madly in love with Iole. By her jealousy Dejanira unwittingly brought about his death (see note to *Inferno* XII.67–9; Ovid, *Heroides* IX.127 f.).

103–5 Cf. Cunizza's words, ll. 34–6 above.

106–7 "Here," etc.: here in heaven the souls admire God's skill in drawing divine love out of carnal love; "there", on earth, such a transformation in the lives of sinners is an example which will lead men's thoughts from earthly to divine things.

116 f. Rahab, a prostitute of Jericho, saved the lives of two spies from the besieging army of Israelites, as a result of which Jericho fell to Joshua, and Rahab's life was spared (Joshua 2.1 f., 6.15 f.). Rahab's betrayal was seen not merely as justified in the light of Jehovah's plan for Israel, but as an act of faith, earning her eternal salvation (see Hebrews 11.31, James 2.25).

118–19 The conical shadow of the earth, according to Ptolemy, reached as far as Venus, touching the first three heavens. Dante uses this fact for allegorical ends, since the souls associated with these heavens are shown with their perfection diminished by their earthly careers (moon: inconstancy; Mercury: greed for fame; Venus: carnal passion).

119–20 After his death on the cross, Christ entered Hell (1 Peter 3.19) and drew forth in his Triumph those of the ancients elected for salvation.

123 The two palms of Christ, nailed to his cross at the Crucifixion.

125–6 The zealous Folquet, one of the leaders of the Albigensian Crusade of 1209 (see note to l. 82 f. above), reproaches contemporary popes for their failure to mount crusades to the Holy Land; the last, the Eighth Crusade, had been proclaimed in 1270.

127 "Your city": Florence; "him": Satan. Cf. *Inferno* VI.49–50, 74–5, XV.67–8, XXVI.1–3; *Purgatorio* VI.27 f.

130 The florin, with a lily on the reverse.

132 "the shepherd": the popes, who were heavily dependent on Florentine bankers.

133 "doctors": the so-called Church fathers, whose exegeses and interpretations of the faith date from the earliest times of the Church (Gregory, Ambrose, Augustine, Bede, etc.).

134–5 "the decretals": the texts of canon (Church) law, deriving from papal edicts, much studied and glossed by (for Dante) a legalistic more than spiritually minded clergy.

137–8 Nazareth, where the angel Gabriel announced the incarnation of Christ to the Virgin Mary (Luke 1.26 f.).

139 The Vatican hill, where St Peter was crucified and buried, surmounted by old St Peter's in Dante's day.

141 The early Christian martyrs.

142 A veiled reference, perhaps, to the advent of the 'DXV' (*Purgatorio* XXXIII.43. See also *Paradiso* XXII.14–15 and note).

PARADISO X

Entering the Fourth Sphere, of the Sun, Dante learns from St Thomas Aquinas the identities of the ring of souls (the wise, including theologians, philosophers and scholars) who gather to meet him.

1 "his son": God the Son, Christ the Word of God; "the love": the Holy Spirit.

3–6 Cf. 'The heavens tell out the glory of God, the vault of heaven reveals his handiwork' (Psalms 19.1).

3 God the Father.

5 "such order": see notes to *Paradiso* I.103, II.112 f.; and cf. Wisdom of Solomon 7.17–22, Psalms 8.3.

9 i.e. where the sun lies at the spring equinox (the time of Dante's journey) in the constellation of the Ram. The two celestial "motion[s]" that coincide are the diurnal revolution of the

planets along the celestial equator, and the annual revolution of
the sun along the ecliptic.

13 "that point": the Ram, where the ecliptic crosses the celestial
equator (see note to l. 9).

14 "The oblique circle": the zodiac, an imaginary band eighteen
degrees wide around the stellar heaven, in which the solar
ecliptic traces its path.

15 All created phenomena on earth receive from the planets their
being and specific informing "virtue" that makes them become
what they are, with the right dispositions to perform as they
must in the ordered realm of creation.

16–18 If the zodiac were not deflected, or slanting, in relation to
the equator, then the planetary influences would be severely
limited in their scope (see note to l. 15).

18 "power": i.e. potential in complexes of primal matter to
become something, a potential that the heavenly influences
activate. See note to *Paradiso* III.87.

19–21 If the zodiac were deflected in a different way than it is,
then the pattern of seasons, hours of night and day, and
climates would be quite different from their present pattern
(which must be perfect, because so ordained by God) and thus
"lacking".

19 "the straight line": the equator.

21 "below": in the Southern Hemisphere; "above" in the
Northern.

28 "The greatest of the ministers of nature": the sun.

31 "at the point": in the constellation of the Ram.

32 "the spirals": the course of the sun round the earth in the year
may be plotted as a spiral, as it moves between the winter and
summer solstices.

33 In springtime, the sun's 'spiralling' results in an earlier sunrise
each morning.

40–42 Thus Wisdom: 'She is more radiant than the sun, and
surpasses every constellation; compared with the light of day,
she is found to excel' (Wisdom of Solomon 7.29).

49 The souls of those learned in sacred knowledge, in the Fourth
Heaven.

63 "unified": i.e. concentrated on God (see l. 53), who himself is
the unity behind the variety of his creation.

67 "Latona's daughter": Diana, the moon.

79–81 Probably as in the contemporary *ballata*, a poem set to
music and dance.

82 f. The voice of Thomas Aquinas (1226–74), Dominican monk (ll. 94–5), scholastic theologian and teacher (Cologne, Paris, Naples) and author of the *Summa Theologica* (profoundest and most influential of his theological works, in which he reconciles Aristotelian philosophy with Christian doctrine), the *Summa contra Gentiles*, the *Commentary on the Nichomachean Ethics of Aristotle* and many other works. Dante's own debt to Aquinas is inestimable, as is Aquinas' contribution to orthodox Catholic theology as a whole. Aquinas was canonised in 1323, after *The Divine Comedy* had been written. His untimely death is referred to in *Purgatorio* XX.69; see note.

98–9 Albertus Magnus (1193–1280), bishop of Regensburg (1260), theologian and teacher (Cologne, Paris), master of Aquinas; a prolific scholar, his work on Aristotle is an important antecedent to that of Aquinas.

104 Francesco Graziano of Chiusi, twelfth-century monk, scholar, and important theoretician of canon law, who attempted to reconcile ecclesiastical and secular traditions of law.

107–8 Peter Lombard (d. 1160), born near Novara, professor of theology in Paris, and Bishop of Paris, whose four books of *Sentences* were the official texts of dogmatics in the theological schools. In the course of this work he offers it to God as the widow (the "poor woman", l. 107) did her two small coins (cf. Luke 21.2).

109 f. King Solomon, son of King David of Israel, author of Wisdom of Solomon, The Song of Songs, Proverbs, Ecclesiastes. See 1 Kings 3.12: 'I give you a heart so wise and understanding that there has been none like you before your time, nor will be after you.'

115–17 Dionysius the Areopagite (Acts 17.34), first bishop of Athens, presumed author of *De coelesti hierarchia*, a work on the Orders of Angels (see *Paradiso* XXVIII.130–32 and note).

118–20 Most probably Paulus Orosius (fifth century), Spanish ancient historian whose major work was dedicated to St Augustine and used by Dante (*Historiarum adversus Paganos libri VII*). Other commentators think that Dante intended Marius Victorinus, whose translations of Plato were used by St Augustine.

124 f. Boethius, Saint Severinus (d. 526AD), author of the *Consolation of Philosophy*, a work of Christian inspiration widely known and respected in the Middle Ages, to which Dante pays

a personal tribute in *Convivio* II.XV.1 and which has affinities
with *The Divine Comedy*, particularly *Paradiso*.

128 St Peter in Ciel d'Oro, Pavia, where Boethius was buried
after his martyrdom at the hands of Theodoric, king of the
Ostrogoths.

131 Isidore, Bishop of Seville (d. 636), author of the *Etymologies*,
a compendium of scientific knowledge much used and imitated
in the medieval world. The Venerable Bede of Jarrow (d. 735),
author of the *Ecclesiastical History of the English* and other
pious works. Richard of St Victor (d. 1173), possibly of
Scottish origin, colleague of Peter Lombard and author of
biblical commentaries and contemplative works, particularly
the *Benjamin Minor* (see note to *Purgatorio* XXVIII.40).

133–8 Sigier of Brabant (d. *c.*1283), philosopher and theologian
in the University of Paris, around whom controversies raged
on matters of orthodoxy. A seeming proponent of Averrhoism
(Aristotelian thought interpreted in the light of the Muslim
Averrhoes' commentary, which was generally condemned as
heretical by the Church, especially by Aquinas), he was
arraigned on a charge of heresy, in spite of his protestations
that he "Syllogised truly" (l. 138), i.e. expounded Aristotle
honestly in the light of Averrhoes. Dante seems to include him
in Paradise as a man of intellectual integrity (even if his
Averrhoism remains), and it is significant that he should be
introduced to Dante by Aquinas, one of his fiercest opponents.

137 "rue du Fouarre": in Paris, now the Rue Dante.

140 "the hour": at matins. The "spouse of God": the Church. See
Ephesians 5.22 f.

142 The parts of a chiming clock's mechanism, an innovation in
Dante's time. Mechanical chiming clocks were first known in
the West towards the end of the thirteenth century. They are
known to have been employed in monasteries, where they
were of inestimable use in ordering the daily services. Dante's
reference here is amongst the first recorded in medieval
literature. See also *Paradiso* XXIV.13–15.

PARADISO XI

*Within the Sphere of the Sun, St Thomas Aquinas, in clarifying an
obscure statement in his previous discourse, enlarges on the story of
St Francis of Assisi and the decadence of his own Dominican
Order.*

16 "that glow of light": St Thomas Aquinas, who now resumes the dialogue. See note to *Paradiso* V.97.

18 Dante assumes that St Thomas smiles, because he notes the increased resplendence of the saint's soul (see note to *Paradiso* V.97).

25 See *Paradiso* X.96.

26 See *Paradiso* X.114.

28 f. Aquinas now proceeds to clarify the first problem, l. 25.

31 "the spouse": the Church; "her beloved": Christ.

32 'Jesus again gave a loud cry, and breathed his last' (Matthew 27.50). For Christ as mystical spouse of the Church, see Ephesians 5.22–32.

35 St Francis of Assisi and St Dominic.

37 The Seraphim, angels of love, the highest angelic order.

38 The Cherubim, angels of wisdom.

40 "one of these": St Francis of Assisi, whose story follows.

43–4 The location of Assisi, Umbria, indicated by the river Topino (formerly Tupino), and the Chiascio with its source near the hermitage of St Ubaldo, north-east of Gubbio.

45 The "high mountain": Monte Subasio, above Assisi.

46 Perugia, lying to the west of Assisi.

47–8 Nocera and Gualdo Tadino lie to the east of the range to which Monte Subasio belongs (thus "behind her", l. 47), on the cold side.

49 i.e. the western slope of Monte Subasio.

51 i.e. when the sun works its most favourable influence, at the spring equinox, as it rises in the Ram over the Ganges, the most easterly point of the inhabited land-mass in the Northern Hemisphere (see note to *Paradiso* I.37–48).

53–4 Dante is playing on the name 'Ascesi' (the old Italian form of Assisi) with its fortuitous meaning in Latin 'I have risen' (suggesting the sunrise). The "East" with its unmistakable religious connotations is, for Dante, more appropriate.

58–9 When about twenty-four years old, St Francis (1182–1226), the son of a rich wool-merchant, began his life of total dedication to God following a time devoted to pleasure and ambition that had ended in severe illness.

61–2 The bishop's court in Assisi, where St Francis openly avowed his dedication to a life of poverty in 1207. Here his father attempted to oblige him to renounce his hereditary rights to the family property, lest he should squander it on charity.

64 "her first husband": Christ.

68 Amyclas, a fisherman of the Adriatic coast, relied on his extreme poverty as protection against interference from the armies of Caesar and Pompey then in conflict; "that voice": of Julius Caesar, who called at Amyclas' door (Lucan, *Pharsalia* V.507 f.; Dante, *Convivio* IV.XIII.12).

72 Christ was stripped of his robe at the Crucifixion (Mark 15.24).

79 Bernardo da Quintavalle, a rich merchant of Assisi, the first disciple of St Francis. See St Francis' biography by Tommaso da Celano, the *Vita Secunda*, c.1247, and by St Bonaventure, *Legenda Maior*, c.1263.

83 Two of the earliest followers of St Francis.

87 The Franciscans were to adopt a belt of rope to signify their material poverty, hence their title 'Cordeliers'.

91 Pope Innocent III gave his verbal blessing to the Order of St Francis (the Friars Minor or Cordeliers) in 1210.

98 Pope Honorius III gave definitive recognition to the Order in 1223, although St Francis had drawn up the rules as early as 1209.

102 The Sultan of Babylon (Egypt), whom St Francis attempted to convert in 1219 during the fifth crusade.

106 i.e. in St Francis' retreat on the Monte della Verna, ten kilometres east of Bibbiena in the Apennines.

107 The stigmata.

113 "the lady who was most dear to him": poverty.

116 "its own country": heaven.

117 St Francis wished to die, as he had lived, in poverty. According to his last wishes he was laid to rest before his burial on the bare ground, his "bier". He was canonised in 1228 by Pope Gregory IX.

118 St Dominic (see note to l. 35 above).

119 "Peter's ship": the Church.

121 St Dominic was the founder ("patriarch") of the order of which Aquinas was a monk, the Dominicans, on whose present decline Aquinas now elaborates.

PARADISO XII

In the Sphere of the Sun, a second circle of souls forms around the first, from which St Bonaventure embarks on the story of St Dominic, and gives an account of the decadence of his own order, the Franciscans.

3 i.e. the first ring of souls of the wise (see previous canto). The millstone was a not infrequent image in medieval science, denoting the heavens' circling around the north pole (Sapegno).

12 "her handmaiden": Iris, the rainbow, messenger of the gods and especially of Juno (Ovid, *Metamorphoses* I.270–71).

14 Echo, the nymph, whose love for Narcissus was not returned, so that she pined away to a mere voice; cf. Ovid, *Metamorphoses* III.339 f., and note to *Paradiso* III.17–18.

17–18 See Genesis 9.8 f.

29 The voice of St Bonaventure (see note to l. 127 below).

38 "its standard": the Cross.

43 "his spouse": the Church. See Ephesians 5.22 f.

44 St Francis and St Dominic; see *Paradiso* XI.35–9.

46 Zephyr: the west wind of spring.

49 "the crashing of the waves": i.e. on the Atlantic shore of Spain.

50–51 At the summer solstice the sun sets due west of the coast of Spain, beyond which it was believed no land lay.

52 Calaruega: a town in old Castile, province of Burgos.

54 The arms of the kingdom of León and Castile displayed lions and castles in alternate quarters.

55 St Ðominic (*c.*1170–1221, canonised 1234), founded his order of preaching friars, the Dominicans, in 1215 (recognised by Pope Honorious III in 1216), and from 1219 directed its activities from Bologna.

60 A legend tells how Dominic's mother, before his birth, dreamed she would give birth to a black and white dog (the colours of the Dominican habit) with a burning brand in its mouth (the zeal of the Order, particularly dedicated to the identification of heresies; cf. l. 57). The word 'Dominican' was accorded the false etymology *domini canis*, the 'Lord's dog'. See note to l. 69 below.

62 St Dominic's spouse was Faith, while that of St Francis was Poverty.

64–6 Legend has it that Dominic's godmother dreamed the child bore a star on his forehead, signifying the role of the saint in enlightening the world with the doctrinal truth of the Christian gospel (l. 65: "the marvellous fruit.").

69 Dominic means 'the Lord's', the name therefore being 'the consequence of the thing named', in accordance with a doctrine of medieval etymology (cf. Dante, *Vita Nuova* XIII.4).

75 "the first command": the first beatitude of the Sermon on the

Mount, 'Blessed are the poor in spirit' (AV Matthew 5.3); see note to *Purgatorio* XII.110. See l. 77: "He was found upon the ground".

79 Felix literally means, in Latin, 'Happy'; "truly called" see note to l. 69 above.

80 Giovanna (Joanna) literally in Hebrew means 'God's grace'.

83 "the Ostian": a thirteenth-century commentary on the decretals used as a textbook in schools of canon law. "Taddeo": possibly Taddeo dei Pepoli, renowned Bolognese scholar of canon law of Dante's time.

84 "the authentic manna": see note to *Paradiso* II.10–11.

88 The papal throne, occupied by Innocent III when in 1205 Dominic was in Rome to request authority to preach against the Albigensian heresy in Provence.

90 Dante has in mind the contemporary pope (in 1300), Boniface VIII (see note to *Inferno* XIX.52–7).

95 "that seed": the true faith (cf. Luke 8.5 f.).

96 The souls composing the two concentric rings around Dante.

100–102 The reference is to Provence and the Languedoc as a whole, where the Manichaean or dualistic heresy of Catharism was widespread. A Crusade was proclaimed against the so-called Albigenses in 1209, in which St Dominic took part as propagandist of the true faith. See note to *Paradiso* IX.82 f.

106 Cf. the two-wheeled Chariot of the Church as it appears in *Purgatorio* XXIX.106 f. The one wheel is the Dominican Order, the other (l. 109) the Franciscan.

109 i.e. St Francis.

110 St Thomas Aquinas, in the previous canto.

112 f. St Bonaventure, a Franciscan, now proceeds to reproach his own order for their deviation from the true path of their founder.

114 An image from wine-making: bad wine leaves a mould in the barrel, whilst good wine leaves a crust.

119–20 "tares": cf. AV Matthew 13.30.

124–6 Ubertino da Casale (d. 1338) and Matteo d'Acquasparta (d. 1302), two Franciscans who represented opposing trends in the Franciscan Order; the former (leader of the Spirituals) advocated discipline, and was hostile to the relaxation in the Order's rules introduced by the latter (General of the Order from 1287).

127 St Bonaventura (Bonaventure), 1221–74 (canonised 1482), born in Bagnoregio, near Orvieto, was as a child miraculously healed by St Francis of Assisi (hence his name, lit. 'good

fortune'), and became General of the Franciscans in 1257, later cardinal. He was a prolific writer in the mystical tradition of St Bernard and St Augustine. Of his works, the *Itinerarium mentis in Deum* may have been most influential on Dante particularly for the anagogical structure of *Purgatorio* (see Bibliography, F. Fergusson).

129 i.e. he put spiritual priorities first, before the temporal.

131 i.e. of the Franciscans.

132 "cord": see note to *Paradiso* XI.87.

133 Hugh of St Victor: twelfth-century Flemish mystic, scholar and theologian, author of the *Didascalicon* and the *De sacramentis Christianae fidei*.

134–5 Pietro Mangiadoro (Petrus Comestor), d. 1179. Of huge scholarly appetite (hence his name), this Frenchman became Chancellor of the University of Paris, and wrote the *Historia Scholastica*, an authoritative commentary on Biblical history. Pietro Ispano (Petrus Hispanus, Peter the Spaniard), born 1226 in Lisbon, was elected pope as John XXI in 1276, eight months before his death; author of *Summulae logicales*, in "twelve small books" (l. 135).

136 Nathan: the bold prophet who admonished King David for his treachery in the circumstances of his marriage to Bathsheba (2 Samuel 12.1 f.).

137 St John Chrysostom: d. 407; Patriarch of Constantinople, fearless preacher against laxity in the Church and the court, left a large collection of homilies and sermons. Anselm: b. Aosta 1033, d. 1109 (canonised 1494), Archbishop of Canterbury from 1093 under William Rufus (with whom he clashed on questions of Church jurisdiction), and Henry I; author of theological treatises. Donatus: fourth-century scholar, reputed teacher of St Jerome (the translator of the Bible) and whose Latin grammar was a standard textbook up to the Middle Ages.

139 Rabanus Maurus: d. 856, a German, pupil of Alcuin; Abbot of Fulda and later Archbishop of Mainz. He was author of a commentary on the Bible, and of *De institutione clericorum*.

140–41 Joachim of Flora: *c.*1145 to *c.*1202, a Cistercian abbot of Corazzo, founded the monastery of S. Giovanni in Fiore. Author of a commentary on Revelation, he prophesied and preached the Reign of the Holy Spirit, a period of perfection in the affairs of men. Opposed by St Bonaventure (who now is reconciled to him, l. 141), he was influential amongst the Franciscan Spirituals, and did much to create the atmosphere of eschatological expectation that characterised Dante's century. He may have fed Dante's hopes of a heaven-sent champion to right the wrongs of Christendom (see note on the Greyhound, *Inferno* I.101–11, and the 'DXV', *Purgatorio* XXXIII.43). See also *Paradiso* XXVII.148 and note.

PARADISO XIII

Within the Sphere of the Sun, St Thomas Aquinas resumes his instruction of Dante by explaining the nature of perfect creation in Adam and Christ, and the circumstances of Solomon's gift of wisdom, concluding with a peroration on the foolishness of ill-considered judgements on transcendental matters.

4–24 The reader is asked to imagine twenty-four of the brightest stars of the sky in northern latitudes (the fifteen major stars of Ptolemy's system, the seven of the Great Bear, and the last two from the Little Bear) forming two concentric rings of twelve stars each.

10 "the mouth of that horn": the two stars of the Little Bear furthest from the North Star (l. 11).

12 "the primal circle": the circling heavens.

13–15 Deserted by Theseus on Naxos, Ariadne (daughter of Minos, king of Crete) was befriended by Bacchus who, to bring her fame, set her crown as a constellation in the sky (the Corona Borealis or the Crown). Dante's reference to Ariadne's death here (l. 15) may be due to his misreading of Ovid, *Metamorphoses* VIII.176 f.

23 The river Chiana in Tuscany, noted for its sluggish current.

24 The Primum Mobile. See note to *Paradiso* II.113 f.

25 One would not, in any case, have expected here such a hymn to pagan gods. Dante's intention may be to refute by implication the pagan explanation of the origin of the Corona Borealis as due to the intervention of Bacchus (see note to ll. 13–15 above).

31–2 St Thomas Aquinas had told Dante the story of St Francis in *Paradiso* XI.

34–5 St Thomas refers to the question implied in *Paradiso* XI.25, that he had then answered.

36 "the other" is the question implied in *Paradiso* XI.26 (but not hitherto answered) by the statement "No second ever arose". Dante's question, which St Thomas intuits, derives from the seeming exclusion of Christ and Adam, perfect in their natures as man, in the class-list of wisdom which Solomon, judging from this statement, would appear to lead. The saint proceeds to confirm Dante's understanding of the perfection of human creation (and therefore human wisdom) in Christ and Adam, but finally points out that Solomon chose, as God's gift, wisdom such as specifically befits a king not as befits one of perfect human nature, nor as befits a theologian, logician, mathematician and so forth.

37–8 "that breast": Adam's; from one of his ribs Eve was formed. See Genesis 2.21–3.

39 Eve first succumbed to temptation, leading to the Fall of Man. See Genesis 3.6–7.

40 The breast of Christ, pierced by a lance at the Crucifixion. See John 19.34.

43 "light": wisdom.

44 "that power": God.

48 i.e. King Solomon.

53 "that idea": the Word of God (Christ) second Person of the Holy Trinity, through whom 'all things came to be' (John 1.2).

57 The Holy Spirit, third Person of the Trinity.

59 The nine Orders of Angels. See note to *Paradiso* II.127–9.

61–2 "the remotest powers": i.e. the complexes of 'primal matter' of the world, with the potential ('power') to become something by the action ("act") of the creative power of the Word ("that living light", l. 55) as transmitted through the nine Angelic Orders (l. 59) and their associated Heavens ("from act to act", l. 62). See also notes to *Paradiso* VII.135, 136–41.

63 "brief contingencies": natural phenomena of necessarily finite duration.

66 "with seed": animals and plants; "without seed": minerals. In so far as from the heavens comes, transmitted, the power of creation, the "moving heavens" here represent Nature (see ll. 76–8).

67 "the wax": primal matter; "what acts": the 'informing virtue' (see note to *Paradiso* VII.136–8) of the creative power of the Word of God.

79–80 i.e. the Trinity itself, as Holy Spirit ("warm love"), Word or Wisdom ("the limpid vision"), and God the Father.

83 "the completest animal perfection": Adam.

84 The Virgin Mary gave birth to Christ, who shared Adam's perfect human nature, whilst retaining his own divinity.

90 "that one": King Solomon.

97–102 Items in theology, logic, physics and geometry, exemplifying branches of wisdom other than "the prudence of a king" (l. 104) that Solomon chose.

97 "intelligences": angels. See the discussion by Dante in *Convivio* II.V.

98 "necessary" (Lat. *necesse*): a necessary or absolute premise (a scholastic term).

99 "contingent": a conditional premise; "necessary": a necessary conclusion. The answer to this problem of logic was disputed between Plato and Aristotle.

100 The idea of 'prime motion' (*primus motus*) was proposed by Christian theologians in terms of God, the Unmoved Mover.

106 See note to l. 36 above.

111 Adam and Christ.

124 Minor philosophers or mathematicians of the early Greek world, whose teachings were reproved by Aristotle. Bryson attempted unsuccessfully to 'square the circle' (see note to *Paradiso* XXXIII.133–5).

127 Sabellius (d. *c.*265): an early Antitrinitarian heretic. Arius (d. 336): originator of the widely held heresy, named after him, that Christ was not (as the Nicene Creed has it) 'one substance with the Father'.

139 i.e. every Tom, Dick or Harry.

PARADISO XIV

The soul of Solomon, amongst the wise of the Heaven of the Sun, expounds to Dante the doctrine of the resurrected body. A third group of souls encircles the first two rings of the wise. Dante and Beatrice rise to the Fifth Heaven of Mars.

7–8 Dante and Beatrice are at the centre of the double ring of souls. St Thomas' words move from the circumference of the ring to the centre, whilst Beatrice's move from the centre to the souls on the circumference.

10 "he": Dante.

14 "substance": here, the soul itself. See note to *Paradiso* III.29.

18 The brightness of the souls, if it remained, would arguably be unbearable to the eyes of their restored bodies at the general resurrection.

28–9 The Holy Trinity is one in substance (God), two in nature (Christ unites the human and the divine), three in person (Father, Son, Holy Spirit).

35 The voice of King Solomon. See note to *Paradiso* X.109 f.

40 "its warmth": the intensity of love. Thus sight or vision precedes love, an important principle in Dante's thought. See *Paradiso* XXVIII.109–11 and note.

43–5 i.e. at the general resurrection. See 1 Corinthians 15.35 f., and especially ib. vv. 51–3. Cf. also *Paradiso* VII.145 f. and note.

47 "the highest good": God.

84 "a higher blessedness": the Heaven of Mars.

90 "holocaust": a sacrificial burnt offering; here, Dante's unspoken prayer of thanks.

96 Elios: a synthetic etymology, from *Helios* (Gk. 'sun') and *Eli* (Heb. 'God').

98–9 The Milky Way, whose origins are learnedly discussed by Albertus Magnus in *De meteoris* I.II.2–5, and referred to by Dante in *Convivio* II.XIV.5 f.

101–2 i.e. as in the Greek cross.

106 Cf. Matthew 16.24.

112–17 Called 'Brownian motion' in modern physics, the phenomenon had been recorded by Lucretius (*De rerum natura* II.114 f.), and Lactantius (*De ira Dei* X.9).

133 "the living pledges": Beatrice's eyes.

136 "what I accuse myself of": i.e. of apparently relegating the beauty of Beatrice's eyes (l. 131).

136–7 Note the use of the rhetorical device of *adnominatio*, "excuse ... accuse ... excuse". Dante's use of *ornatus* is always functional, as well as formally deft.

PARADISO XV

In the Sphere of Mars within the Fifth Heaven, Dante is addressed by the soul of his ancestor Cacciaguida, who extols the civic virtues of Florence in the twelfth century.

4 "the sweet instrument": the Greek cross of the warrior saints (cf. *Paradiso* XIV.118).

14 "a sudden fire": of a shooting-star or meteor.

25 Aeneas encountered the spirit of his father Anchises in the Elysian Fields of the Underworld; see Virgil ("our greatest muse", l. 26), *Aeneid* VI.684 f.

28–30 'O blood of my blood, O excessive grace of God; to whom, as to you, have the gates of Heaven ever been twice opened?'

30 "bis ... reclusa" ('twice opened'): the gates of Heaven are opened now for Dante in the flesh, and will open again for his disembodied soul after his death; the like not having occurred since the time of St Paul (cf. note to *Inferno* II.28–30).

31 "that light": Cacciaguida (l. 135), the great-great-grandfather of Dante (c.1090–1147) of whom nothing is known outside *The Divine Comedy* beyond casual references in contemporary documents. He was knighted by Emperor Conrad III and died during the second crusade in the Holy Land.

47 i.e. God as Holy Trinity.

50 i.e. the book of past and future events, divinely ordained. Cf. *Inferno* XIX.54.

53 "that lady": Beatrice.

56 "him who is the first": God.

56–7 The conception of numbers is derived from the conception of unity.

62 "the mirror": God. See *Paradiso* IX.20–21, 73–5; XXVI.106–8.

73–5 i.e. 'When God ["primal equality", l. 75] first appeared to you, love and understanding in you became one.' Beatrice, therefore, is able to grasp and formulate the deepest spiritual truths.

79 "argument": a scholastic term, meaning 'operation'; here, of course, the activity of speech. The will of mortals, imperfect creatures, often outruns their capacity for performance.

84 Dante implies here that his speech was inadequate to express the fulness of his gratitude.

91 Alighiero, Cacciaguida's son, took his name from that of his mother. Dante assumed him dead by 1200 (see ll. 92–3), but a document points to his being alive in 1201.

93 i.e. the Cornice of the Proud, in Purgatory.

95 "by your works": by intercessory prayer.

97 "the ancient circle": the earliest city walls of medieval Florence (ninth century).

98 i.e. the bells rung at 9 a.m. and 3 p.m., presumably from the Badia, the abbey which is adjacent to the quarter where the Alighieri lived.

107 Sardanapalus: king of Assyria, renowned for his dissolute living.

109 Montemalo (modern Montemario): a hill affording a view of Rome.

110 Uccellatoio: a hill overlooking Florence from the north.

112 Bellincion Berti dei Ravignani (c.1150 to c.1200), virtuous

ancestor of the great, but by 1300 degenerate, Conti Guidi family of the Val d'Arno (see *Purgatorio* XIV.43; and G. Villani, *Cronica* III.2).

115 Old noble families of Florence. See G. Villani, *Cronica* IV.12–13.

126 Proud legends of the city's origins. See notes to *Inferno* XV.61–2, 77.

127 Cinghella (or Cianghella): a Florentine lady of Dante's time, renowned for her vicious temper. Lapo Salterello: a prominent but utterly corrupt White Guelf and colleague of Dante.

129 Cincinnatus (Lucius Quinctius) was called from his farm in 458BC to defend Roman liberties as supreme commander. Having accomplished his mission, he retired at once to his farm. Cornelia: virtuous Roman matron (see note to *Inferno* IV.128).

133 Mary, mother of Jesus, invoked during childbirth.

134 The Baptistry of St John, of uncertain but ancient date. Its basic structure probably dates from the fourth century AD, whilst its exterior is Romanesque.

139 Conrad III of Swabia, Emperor 1138–52, led the second crusade (1147–9) with Louis VII of France.

143 "that law": Islam, the Mohammedan faith. The "followers" of Mohammed still ruled the Holy Land in Dante's time, usurping the government ("justice", l. 144), which by right belonged to the Christians but by default of the pope ("the shepherd") remained in the hands of infidels.

148 Those who died on a crusade were deemed martyrs who would go directly to Heaven.

PARADISO XVI

Cacciaguida, in the Sphere of Mars, discusses the extinction or decline of the great families of old Florence and speculates on the corresponding decline in the moral life and social harmony of the city.

1–6 Dante defines nobility in terms other than of blood-stock or wealth in the *canzone* and commentary in *Convivio* IV; yet faced with his illustrious ancestor Cacciaguida, the old theories lose something of their former authority.

10 "that form of speech": Dante addresses Cacciaguida with the honorific pronoun of second-person plural *voi*, which he has employed so far only with Farinata degli Uberti (*Inferno* X),

Brunetto Latini (*Inferno* XV), Pope Adrian V (*Purgatorio* XIX), Guido Guinizelli (*Purgatorio* XXVI), and Beatrice.

13–15 The Dame de Malehaut coughed discreetly at Guinivere's indiscreet questioning of Lancelot, following the confession of his love for her. Here Beatrice's meaningful smile perhaps dissuades Dante from making too free with his marks of respect for Cacciaguida (Cato rebukes Virgil for his well-meant flatteries, in *Purgatorio* I.91–3).

23 The question here recalls that of Farinata to Dante (*Inferno* X.42), thus hinting at a significant parallelism between Cacciaguida, the virtuous and truly patriotic Florentine, and Farinata the Florentine whose patriotism had declined into a socially and politically destructive partisanship.

25 Florence, whose patron saint is St John the Baptist.

33 See *De Vulgari Eloquentia* I.9.6 f., where Dante points out the tendency of vernacular languages to mutate in the course of time, a unique and original observation for the period, when linguistic theory was generally most primitive.

34 i.e. at the Annunciation to Mary of the immaculate conception of Christ (see Luke 1.26 f.).

37 "This fire": Mars.

38 "its Lion": the constellation Leo. Mars was thought to complete one revolution in approximately 1.8 solar years. Cacciaguida would seem to have been born therefore around 1090.

41–2 i.e. in the ward of Porta San Piero, near the modern Via de' Speziali. The "annual games", held on St John's Day, included a horse race which ended along the Corso.

45 "civil": i.e. modest.

47 The statue of Mars stood near the Ponte Vecchio on the south side of the earliest city walls (see note to *Inferno* XIII.147), and the Baptistry of St John just inside the north walls.

48 "a fifth": i.e. some 6,000 men. Cf. G. Villani, *Cronica* VIII.39.

50 Small towns in the district around Florence.

54 Trespiano: a village some four miles to the north of the old walls of Florence; Galluzzo: some three miles to the south.

56 The references are probably to Baldo da Aguglione and Fazio da Signa, eminent men in public office in Florence in the late thirteenth and early fourteenth centuries, both especially tarnished in Dante's eyes by their opposition to the Emperor Henry VII (d. 1313), on whom Dante had placed so much hope for the reestablishment of order and justice in Italy (see note to *Purgatorio* XXXIII.43, and *Letters* V, VI, VII). As a Prior of Florence, Baldo, for good measure, had also reconfirmed Dante's banishment in 1311, some nine years after the *coup* against the White Guelfs.

58 i.e. the papacy and clergy.

59 "to Caesar": to the emperors of the Holy Roman Empire.

61–3 The lines allude to the practice of the popes to borrow money especially from Florentine bankers to finance their anti-imperial measures. Dante alleges here that the Church's opposition to the emperors was not only unnaturally wrong, but that it helped to stoke up the economy of Florence as a centre of finance and trade, leading to its material growth, increase in population and moral decline.

61 "Some": probably the Velluti family, who originated in humble circumstances in Simifonte (Semifonte) in the Val d'Elsa, south-west of Florence.

64 With the economic expansion of Florence occurred also its political expansion. Since it was linked to the Church for financial reasons (see note to ll. 61–3 above), the city's espousal of Guelfism naturally followed. The growing city acquired the castle of Montemurlo, lying to the north-west, in 1254, forcing sale from the Ghibelline Conti Guidi and upsetting the balance of power in the district.

65 The Cerchi family, originating from Acone, became militant leaders of the White Guelf faction around 1300 (see note to *Inferno* VI.64–9) and were thus partially responsible for the political crisis which resulted in Dante's banishment in 1302.

66 The Buondelmonti family from Montebuoni in the Val di Greve (south of Florence) were Guelfs, and were credited with partial responsibility for the outbreak of the Guelf–Ghibelline quarrels in Florence in the early thirteenth century (see note to *Inferno* XXVIII.106–8, and note to l. 140 below).

67 "confusion": the entry of alien blood into Florence mixed with and contaminated the pure stock as the city expanded commercially and politically in the course of the late twelfth and thirteenth centuries.

73–5 Italian cities of ancient foundation and former power, by 1300 quite fallen from their greatness or in decline.

88–93 Old Florentine families either disappeared from public prominence or extinct.

94–6 The Gate of St Peter (Porta San Piero) of Florence, adjoining the property of the 'foreign' Cerchi family (see note to l. 65 above), who had recently acquired it from the Conti Guidi.

98 See note to *Inferno* XVI.34–9.

99 See note to *Paradiso* XV.112.

103 A stripe of grey fur (a pale of vair) characterised the coat of arms of the Pigli family.

105 The family of the Chiaramontesi were involved in 1283 in a scandal over the fraudulent weighing of salt (cf. *Purgatorio* XII.105).

109–10 Most commentators are agreed in seeing here an allusion to the Uberti family, whose dynastic ambitions led to strife in the city in the twelfth century and whose most famous member, Farinata, led the Florentine Ghibellines in their chequered fortunes in the thirteenth (see note to *Inferno* X.22).

110 "golden globes": the golden balls on the arms of the Lamberti family (see note to *Inferno* XXVIII.106–8).

112–14 The Visdomini and Tosinghi families controlled and allegedly exploited the revenues of the See of Florence during a vacancy of the bishop's seat.

115 The Adimari family (see notes to *Inferno* VIII.32, and XVI.41).

119–20 Ubertino of the noble Donati family married a daughter of Bellincione Berti. The latter married off another daughter to the thrusting Adimari family.

126 The Porta Peruzza.

128 "the great baron": Ugo of Brandenburg, Marquis of Tuscany, who died in 1001 on St Thomas' Day (21 December).

131 Giano della Bella, who in 1293 introduced the reforms of the *Ordinamenti della giustizia* to restrict the power of the *grandi* in Florence, in favour of the *popolani*. See note to *Inferno* XVII.72–3.

134 The ward of Borgo Santi Apostoli in Florence.

135 "new neighbours": the Buondelmonti (see note to l. 66 above).

136 "The house": that of the Amidei (see note to l. 140 below); "your misfortune": i.e. of Florence.

140 Buondelmonte dei Buondelmonti, a Guelf, in 1215 jilted a daughter of the Ghibelline Amidei family and married instead into the Guelf Donati. The offence was avenged by the Amidei's assassination of Buondelmonte near the ancient statue of Mars ("that battered/Statue", ll. 146–7), following the advice of Mosca dei Lamberti (see note to l. 110 above, and notes to *Inferno* VI.79–80, XXVIII.106–8). The murder of Buondelmonte initiated the strife between Guelfs and Ghibellines in Florence (see G. Villani, *Cronica* V.38; Dino Compagni, *Cronica* I.2), the end of the "peace" of l. 145.

143 The river Ema is crossed by the road from Montebuoni (where the Buondelmonti originated; see note to l. 66 above) to Florence.

147 "Statue": see notes to *Inferno* XIII.143–7.

152 "the lily": the white lily on the standard and coat of arms of Florence.

153 "turned upside-down": i.e. in defeat.

154 "stained red": after the Guelfs had banished the Ghibellines in 1251, they substituted a red lily for the white on the city's standard (see G. Villani, *Cronica* VI.43).

PARADISO XVII

In the Sphere of Mars, amongst the blessed Christian warriors, Cacciaguida prophesies Dante's future, and entrusts him with the task of writing the Comedy.

1–3 Phaeton, son of Phoebus the sun god, approached his mother Clymene to ascertain who his father was. Clymene sent Phaeton to Phoebus, who, to reassure him he was his father, rashly allowed him any favour. Phaeton chose to drive the chariot of the sun, with disastrous consequences to himself, the earth and heaven. See Ovid, *Metamorphoses* I.750–II.328, and *Inferno* XVII.107–8 and note.

5 "the sacred lamp": Cacciaguida.

17 "that point": God, in his eternal existence.

22 "Grave words": the prophecies bearing upon Dante's future spoken particularly by Brunetto Latini (*Inferno* XV.55–78), but also by Ciacco (*Inferno* VI.64–72), Farinata (*Inferno* X.79–81), Vanni Fucci (*Inferno* XXIV.140–51), Conrad Malaspina (*Purgatorio* VIII.133–9), and Oderisi (*Purgatorio* XI.139–41). See also *Inferno* X.131 and note.

23–4 Cf. Dante's words to Brunetto Latini, *Inferno* XV.91–6.

25–7 Fortitude is the specific virtue associated with the heaven of Mars and its warrior saints. In his discussion on courage, Aquinas makes the same point with something of the same imagery as Dante here (*Summa Theologica* II.II, q. 123, art. 9, resp.).

31–3 i.e. the obscure oracular utterances of pagan diviners and sibyls.

37–42 God's foreknowledge of events does not imply that their causes are 'necessary', they may still be contingent; i.e. foreknowledge and contingency are not incompatibles.

46–7 Hippolytus, son of Theseus, was falsely accused by his stepmother Phaedra (Pasiphae's daughter) of attempting to outrage her. Theseus sent his son away from Athens under a curse (see Ovid, *Metamorphoses* XV.497 f.).

50 "by him": Pope Boniface VIII. The plot in question was to send Charles of Valois to Florence and effect a *coup* in favour of the Black Guelfs; see notes *to Inferno* VI.64–9.

51 "the place": Rome. See *Inferno* XIX.52–7, and St Peter's denunciation in *Paradiso* XXVII.40 f.

57 Dante's exile from Florence began by decree on 27 January 1302 whilst he was (according to D Compagni, *Cronica* II.25) in Rome appealing to Boniface to desist from his political pretensions in the government of Florence. On 10 March, Dante was condemned to death in his absence.

62 The White Guelfs, banished from Florence simultaneously with Dante.

71 "the great Lombard": Can Grande della Scala (1291–1329), lord of Verona from 1312, Imperial Vicar in the province of Vicenza (1312), and Captain-General of the Ghibelline League (1318), to whom Dante dedicated the *Paradiso* (see Dante's *Letters* X, probably genuine), although Can Grande died excommunicate (see note to *Paradiso* XVIII.128–9). Dante may have been in Verona *c.*1303 and again in 1316. See notes to *Inferno* I.101, 105. An alternative reading of l. 76, accepted by some commentators, may suggest that "the great Lombard" (l. 71) is Can Grande's eldest brother, Bartolommeo (d. 1304), whilst the references to Can Grande begin only with l. 76.

82 i.e. before June 1312, when Pope Clement V, a Gascon, withdrew his support for Emperor Henry VII of Luxemburg during the latter's ill-fated expedition in Italy. See *Paradiso* XXX.133–48 and note.

99 A dark prophecy of the sort in *Inferno* I.101–11, *Purgatorio* XXXIII.43 f., *Paradiso* XXVII.61–3.

110 "the dearest place": Florence.

112 Hell.

113 Mount Purgatory, with Terrestrial Paradise (Eden) on its summit.

114 "my lady": Beatrice.

119 "those": Dante's readership in future generations. Dante's literary aim is to serve the truth, not self-glory. Cf. the episode of Brunetto Latini in *Inferno* XV (and note to l. 85), where Brunetto's literary aims are shown as perverted, serving primarily his fame and memory rather than the truth or God.

PARADISO XVIII

When Cacciaguida has pointed out significant representatives of warrior saints in the cross, Dante and Beatrice rise from Mars to the Sixth Heaven, where in the Sphere of Jupiter the souls of just monarchs and governors spell out messages, and delineate the symbolic profile of an eagle.

1 "that blessed mirror": Cacciaguida, who reflects the thoughts and prescience of God as a mirror (cf. Wisdom, 'the flawless mirror of the active power of God', Wisdom of Solomon 7.26).

6 'The Lord will give his people justice', Deuteronomy 32.36; 'Vengeance is mine; I will repay, saith the Lord', AV Romans 12.19.

11 "mind": i.e. memory. For Dante's insistence on the limitations of the memory in Paradise, see notes to *Paradiso* XXXIII.94–6.

25 "that sacred brilliance": Cacciaguida.

28 "this fifth stage": the Fifth Heaven of Mars.

38 Joshua succeeded Moses as leader of the Israelites, and led them into the Promised Land. See Deuteronomy 1.38, and note to *Paradiso* IX.116 f.

40 Judas Maccabaeus, in the second century BC, at first successfully defended Israel from the incursions of the Syrians, but was finally defeated and killed by them. See 1 Maccabees 2.66–9.22.

43 Charles the Great: Charlemagne, king of the Franks, and first Emperor of the Holy Roman Empire, was crowned in 800 on Christmas Day in Rome by Pope Leo III, and died in 814. His defence of Christendom from Longobards and Moors, chronicled in romances and ballads in the Middle Ages, earned him canonisation in 1165. Orlando: i.e. Roland, reputed nephew of Charlemagne, and one of his twelve Paladins. The medieval French *Chanson de Roland* (eleventh century) recounts his death at the hands of the Saracens in the pass of Roncesvalles whilst leading the French rearguard against overwhelming odds (778). See *Inferno* XXXI.18 and note.

46 William Duke of Orange, and Renoardo (Renoart), heroes of
medieval *chansons de geste* in the battles in Southern France
against the Saracens in the late eighth and early ninth centuries.
William was an historical figure, who died in 812, whilst
Renoart was most likely only fictional whom Dante nevertheless
takes as historical.

47 Godfrey of Boulogne (Bouillon), 1061–1100, leader of the
First Crusade in 1096, and later crowned King of Jerusalem.
Robert Guiscard (the Weasel), Duke of Apulia and Calabria
(1056), leader of the Normans who took Southern Italy from
the Byzantine Empire in campaigns from 1059 to 1084. See
Inferno XXVIII.14.

68 "the temperate star": the Sphere of Jupiter, in the Sixth
Heaven, between the 'heat' of Mars and the 'cold' of Saturn.
Dante's authority is Ptolemy.

82 "O Pegasean goddess": Pegasus, the winged horse, pro-
duced the spring Hippocrene on Mount Helicon, the home
of the Muses, by striking the ground with his hoof (see
Ovid, *Metamorphoses* V.250 f.). To which of the Muses
("goddess[es]") Dante refers is not certain; either Calliope
(Muse of epic poetry, as in *Purgatorio* I.9), or Polyhymnia
(Muse of sacred song, as in *Paradiso* XXIII.56).

91–3 "DILIGITE IUSTITIAM ... QUI IUDICATIS TERRAM":
'Love justice, you rulers of the earth [set your mind upon the
Lord as is your duty]', Wisdom of Solomon 1.1.

94 "M": the first letter of the word *monarchia* (lit. government by
one ruler), a reference to the supreme temporal authority,
divinely ordained, of the Emperor of the Holy Roman Empire,
defended by Dante in his political treatise *De Monarchia*
(written either *c.*1312 or *c.*1318). See *Purgatorio* XVI.107–8
and note.

97–8 The "M" (of Gothic style) is transformed into a lily (see
Paradiso VI.100), the emblem of France and the Guelfs in
Italy.

107 The lily, formed from the "M", now is transformed into the
outline of an eagle, the emblem of the Holy Roman Empire. In
view of Dante's strictures in *Paradiso* VI.103–5, the eagle
cannot be seen as that of the Ghibelline cause, which is
condemned there for its factionalism, and as unrepresentative
of the high cause of Empire. In the metamorphosis of the "M",
Dante seems to spell out the superiority and ultimate triumph
of the true, historical, imperial ideal over that of either

Guelfism, Ghibellinism or French 'imperialism' (Dante's condemnation of the latter is to be found developed at length in *Purgatorio* XX).

116–17 The implication is that the office of emperor, and his authority, are sanctioned directly by God, and are not dependent on, or subordinate to, the Church's authority. This is an important conclusion in Dante's *De Monarchia*. See note to l. 94 above.

118 "the mind": God.

120 "The source": the papal Curia in Rome.

121–3 See Matthew 21.12–13, and cf. the terms of St Peter's denunciation of the Church's corruption in *Paradiso* XXVII.40 f. See Dante's own denunciation in *Inferno* XIX.90 f.

126 "bad example": similar to the terms of Marco Lombardo's reproach of the popes in *Purgatorio* XVI.97 f.

128–9 i.e. by witholding the privilege of the Holy Mass in the ban of excommunication. This weapon was used notably against Emperor Frederick II in his territorial conflicts with the papacy in 1239, by Boniface VIII against Philip IV of France in 1303, and by John XXII against Can Grande della Scala, Captain-General of the Ghibelline League in 1318.

130 The bans of excommunication were, it is implied, quickly lifted once the transgressor had come to heel.

131–2 St Peter and St Paul were both martyred after labouring in the "vineyard" of the Church.

134 John the Baptist, who preached in the 'wilderness of Judaea', was beheaded by Herod as a reward for his niece Salome who had danced for him (Matthew 3.1, 14.1–12). The periphrasis refers not to John as such, but to the florin, stamped with the head of the Baptist, patron saint of Florence.

136 "the Fisherman": St Peter.

PARADISO XIX

In the Sphere of Jupiter, the souls forming the symbolic eagle of Empire speak out in unison on the subject of justice: the question of the fate of good heathen, the inscrutability but perfection of Divine Justice, and the shortcomings of the rulers of Christendom.

2 "The beautiful image": that of the imperial eagle. See note to *Paradiso* XVIII.107.

11–12 The underlying universal and indestructible unity of the concept of justice is suggested in these lines.

13 The two 'ways' of God are justice and mercy (see *Paradiso* VII.103–5 and note), which the emperor in his exercise of power should seek to imitate, since his authority comes directly from God (see notes to *Purgatorio* XVI.98–9, 107–8).

29 "Divine justice mirrors itself": the mirrors are specifically the angelic order of Thrones, attaching to the heaven of Saturn. See *Paradiso* IX.61–2.

30 "Yours": i.e. the 'realm' or heaven of Jupiter.

32 "that question": formulated in ll. 70–78, the problem questions God's justice in condemning as sinners those who are born beyond the reach of the Christian gospel. Dante's Limbo (*Inferno* IV) is a partially unorthodox answer to this perplexing question.

40 "He who drew with compasses": God, who frequently appears in medieval iconography as holding compasses, measuring out the universe ('God the Geometer'). See AV Proverbs 8.27.

46 "the first of the proud": Lucifer (see Isaiah 14.12 f.).

58–63 Cf. 'thy judgements are like the great abyss [AV 'a great deep']', Psalms 36.6.

74 "As far as human reason sees": these words reflect the 'light of nature' in St Paul's discussion of the same problem (Romans 2.11–6). See also *Purgatorio* XVIII.46–8 and note.

86 "The primal will": the will of God.

88 This line contains the essential argument in answer to Dante's problem; God, being perfectly just and loving, is the only measure of justice and good. See Romans 9.14: 'Is God to be charged with injustice? By no means', and following to ib. v. 23; see also *Inferno* XX.29–30.

106–8 Cf. Matthew 7.22–3.

110–11 Cf. Matthew 25.31 f.

113 "the volume": the record of the deeds of the dead, Revelation 20.11–15. Dante's invective against the unjust rulers of Christendom follows from l. 115. In the Italian text, the initial letters of the first lines of the *terzine* from l. 115 to l. 141 (in three groups of three) spell out the word 'LVE' i.e. 'LUE': 'pestilence'; the acrostic appears (it was intended) to arise mysteriously from the text, lending Dante's condemnation of corrupt Christian kings a seemingly supernatural authority.

115 Albert of Hapsburg, king of Austria, Emperor of the Holy

Roman Empire 1298–1308, invaded and devastated Bohemia ("the kingdom of Prague". l. 117), the territory of his brother-in-law Wenceslaus II (see notes to *Purgatorio* VI.97 f. and VII.97–102).

118–20 Philip IV, the Fair, king of France (see note to *Purgatorio* VII.109), financed his disastrous Flemish campaigns of 1297–1304 with debased coinage. He met an accidental death in a boar hunt in 1314 (cf. G. Villani, *Cronica* VIII.58, IX.66).

121–3 The references are to the Scottish wars of Edward I ('Hammer of the Scots') against William Wallace (hanged 1305) and Robert Bruce, and Edward II against Bruce (Bannockburn, 1314).

125–6 "him of Spain": Ferdinand IV, king of Castile and León 1295–1312. After taking Gibraltar from the Saracens in 1296 with Aragonese help, Ferdinand took little further active part in the wider events of Christendom; "that other of Bohemia": Wencelaus II, whose ultimately futile resistance to the invasion of his country by Albert I of Austria in 1304 marked for Dante the height of his achievement as a monarch.

127 "the lame man of Jerusalem": the handicapped Charles II of Anjou and Provence, king of Naples 1285–1309, assumed the crown of Jerusalem from his father Charles I of Anjou. See *Purgatorio* VII.126 and note, XX.79–81 and note.

131 Frederick II of the royal house of Aragon, king of Sicily 1296–1337. His marriage into the family of Charles II of Anjou and Naples, figurehead of the Guelfs in Italy, was a prelude to his final desertion of the Ghibellines after the death of Emperor Henry VII in 1313; hence Dante's disapproval of an otherwise brave and popular monarch. See note to *Purgatorio* VII.119.

131–2 Sicily, where Anchises the father of Aeneas died, is volcanic. See *Aeneid* III.708 f.

136 "His brother": James II, king of Aragon 1291–1327, an able and cultured monarch (he was called 'the Just'). He perhaps earned Dante's disapproval for waging war in 1297, at the insistence of Pope Boniface VIII, against his brother Frederick II to whom he had entrusted the rule of Sicily the year before. See note to l. 131 above, and *Purgatorio* VII.115–19 and note; "his uncle": James, king of Majorca and the Balearics 1276–1311, brother of Peter III of Aragon, waged war in 1284 on the latter, in league with Philip III of France.

138 "two crowns": Aragon and Majorca.

139 "he of Portugal": Diniz 'the Farmer', king of Portugal 1279–1325. The grounds for Dante's condemnation are not clear, as Diniz was an energetic monarch, promoter of farming, commerce, education and the Portuguese navy. Both his all-consuming interest in practicalities and his alleged infidelities towards his wife, St Isabel, have been adduced by commentators as causing Dante's disgust; "he of Norway": probably Haakon V, king 1299–1319, whose reign was marked by wars against Denmark; the sort of squabbles between monarchs of Christendom that Dante especially deplored.

140 "he of Rascia": Stephen Urosh II, king of Rascia (old Serbia) 1275–1321, issued debased coin very similar in appearance to the Venetian *matapan* or *grosso*, causing problems of exchange in Venice and Bologna. The "fatal consequences" (l. 141) may refer more to the damage done to Stephen's reputation than that done to the Venetian economy.

142–3 "O happy Hungary": Hungary lapsed once more into the hands of the Angevins (into the sphere of influence, therefore, of the French monarch, Philip IV, detested by Dante) in 1301 after the death of Andrew III. Charles Robert of Anjou, the monarch in question, son of Charles Martel (titular king of Hungary), was confirmed in the title in 1309 by Clement V, thus guaranteeing, for Dante, "Further mishandling"; "happy Navarre": unable in the event to "arm herself with her mountains" (the Pyrenees), Navarre was united with the Kingdom of France in 1305, under Louis I (later Louis X of France), when his mother Joanna of Navarre (wife of the hated Philip IV of France) died.

145–8 Nicosia and Famagusta, in Cyprus, were in 1300 suffering from misgovernment by the unstable Henry II of Lusignan (d. 1324), who was related to the royal house of France, the Capetians. The troubles in Cyprus in 1300, the fictive date of the events of *The Divine Comedy*, were thus a foretaste of those that would later strike Hungary and Navarre under their French rulers.

PARADISO XX

The souls forming the symbolic imperial eagle in Jupiter disclose the identities of those that compose its eye. The mention of the Emperor Trajan and Ripheus precedes a disquisition on Heaven's tractability and the mystery of divine providence.

1 "he": the sun, which was believed to light up, by reflection, all the heavenly bodies, stars and planets.

2–3 i.e. at sunset.

6 "many lights": the stars and planets; "the one": the sun.

37–42 David, king of Israel, who brought the Ark of the Covenant to Jerusalem (see *Purgatorio* X.55 f. and note), was the author of the book of Psalms ("his song", l. 40). The inspiration of the Holy Spirit (an act of divine grace, rather than his own "counsel") accounts for his reward in Paradise.

44–8 The Emperor Trajan: see notes to *Purgatorio* X.73–5.

49–54 Hezekiah, king of Judah, obtained from God a remission of fifteen years after Isaiah has foretold his imminent death (2 Kings 20.1–6).

55–7 The Emperor Constantine. See *Inferno* XIX.115–17 and note.

55 "the shepherd": the pope, Sylvester I.

56 "a good intention": the Donation of Constantine.

61–6 "the William": the Norman William II of Hauteville, 'the Good', king of Naples (Apulia) and Sicily 1169–89, whose reign was marked equally by acts of justice and piety.

63. Charles II of Anjou and Provence, king of Naples (Apulia), and the Aragonese Frederick II, king of Sicily both reigning in 1300 ("now", l. 63), whom Dante condemns in *Paradiso* XIX.127–35 (see notes).

67–72 Ripheus, 'the most just of all Trojans, who never wavered from the right; yet the gods regarded not his righteousness' (Virgil, *Aeneid* II.426–8). A minor warrior in the Trojan ranks of heroes, Ripheus merits no fuller description than this in the *Aeneid*; yet these are sufficient credentials for Dante to raise him (exceptionally amongst the heroes of ancient Troy, forebears of the Roman race) to Paradise in the Christian hereafter. Ripheus, wholly virtuous but unsung, must have suggested himself to Dante as a perfect case for such extraordinary promotion in order to illustrate the unlimited scope and inscrutability of the ways of Christian providence; and doubtless also the line of Virgil 'yet the gods regarded not his righteousness' must, by its solemn pagan negativity, have tempted Dante to give it the lie, vindicating a new dimension of divine love that antiquity could not have conceived.

94 'Ever since the coming of John the Baptist the Kingdom of Heaven has been subjected to violence and violent men are seizing it' (Matthew 11.12).

100 The Emperor Trajan (ll. 44–8) and Ripheus (ll. 67–72) respect-
ively.
127 "The three ladies": the symbolic figures representing the
Christian virtues of faith, hope and love. These Dante saw
processing in the pageant of Revelation in Earthly Paradise, by
the right wheel of the chariot of the Church (see *Purgatorio*
XXIX.121–9 and note).

PARADISO XXI

*In the Sphere of Saturn, in the Seventh Heaven, a golden ladder
rises upwards, upon the rungs of which the souls of the
contemplatives gather. One of them, St Peter Damian, answers
Dante's questions, and then addresses him on the subject of
declining standards in monastic life.*

6 Semele, daughter of Cadmus of Thebes, was reduced to ashes
when, persuaded by the jealous Juno, she insisted on seeing
Jupiter her lover in his full glory as king of the gods. Only the
child she was carrying, Bacchus, was saved. See Ovid,
Metamorphoses III.253 f.; *Inferno* XXX.1–12 and note.
13 "the seventh splendour": the heaven and planet (sphere) of
Saturn.
14–15 The 'cold and dry' planet of Saturn lay in the 'house' or
constellation of Leo ('hot and dry' in nature) in the April of
1300 ("Now", l. 15), the month of the journey recorded in *The
Divine Comedy*. Cf. *Convivio* II.XIII.25.
18 "this mirror": Saturn.
26–7 "the name": Saturn, the father of Jupiter, ruled as king of
Crete during the Golden Age before crime ("malice", l. 27)
was committed by mankind. See Ovid, *Metamorphoses* I.89 f.:
'In the beginning was the Golden Age, when men of their own
accord without threat of punishment, without laws, maintained
good faith and did what was right.'
29 "a ladder": stretching upwards out of sight, the ladder aptly
symbolises contemplation. Its origin is the ladder of Jacob's
dream in Beth-El, Genesis 28.12, but its use in Platonic
literature may also have been known to Dante.
50 "the sight of him": i.e. the sight of God.
62 "He": Saint Peter Damian; see note to l. 121 below.
91–102 The will of God may be known, but his motives are
impenetrable even to the angels closest to him ("That seraph",
l. 92). See *Paradiso* XIX.52–7, 79–85, XX.130–34.

106 The line refers to the Apennines, the mountainous spine of Italy.

107 "your own country": Florence.

109 Catria: Monte Catria, in the Apennines, north of Gubbio.

110 "a retreat": the Benedictine monastery of Santa Croce di Fonte Avellana.

121 St Peter Damian, born c.1007 in Ravenna of poor parents, died 1072, a doctor of the Church. As abbot (1043) of the monastery of Fonte Avellana and later a cardinal (1057) he wrote several works of a doctrinal and pious nature, amongst which an extended invective against decadence and materialism in the Church (the *Gomorrhianus*). He maintained the absolute power of God over the realm of nature, and refuted the possibility of rationalising faith. Damian signed many of his works "Peter the sinner" (l. 122) and some at least of these he would have written when in the convent of Santa Maria ("Our Lady", l. 123) in Fossella, near Ravenna, "by the shore of the Adriatic".

125 "those hats": i.e. cardinals' hats; but this is an anachronism, as they were only introduced in the thirteenth century.

127 Cephas: St Peter; see John 1.42; "the great vessel": St Paul; see note to *Inferno* II.28–30.

PARADISO XXII

Dante is addressed, from amongst the contemplatives, by St Benedict on the subject of the decline of the Benedictine Order, then, together with Beatrice, ascends the mystical ladder from Saturn to the Eighth Heaven of the Constellations.

10–11 "that song . . . my smiling": see *Paradiso* XXI.4–12, 58–63.

14–15 "the vengeance": it is impossible to specify what form this vengeance on the corrupt monasticism of Dante's day actually took, if indeed it was ever taken. Dante may have intended it to be understood as part of a general purging of Christendom following the advent of the promised champion or saviour (the Greyhound or 'DXV', of *Inferno* I, *Purgatorio* XXXIII respectively), fulfilling also the dark prophecies of *Purgatorio* XXIII.106–11, *Paradiso* IX.139–42, XVII.97–9.

31 f. The voice is of St Benedict. Born in Umbria in 480, Benedict fled from the corrupt life of Rome, where he was educated, to a remote hermitage. In c.529 he founded the monastery of Monte Cassino (built on the site of a pagan sanctuary) and

drew up the general rules of worship, labour and service which have regulated the life of western monasticism ever since.

49 St Maccarius (Macarius): of the two saints of this name, Dante probably intends the Younger of Alexandria, who died in 404, the virtual founder of eastern monasticism. St Romoaldus degli Onesti of Ravenna founded c.1018 the monastery of Camaldoli, in the Casentino, and a reformed Benedictine order of that name.

60 "without concealment": i.e. not concealed by the brightness of the light which the souls of the blessed radiate.

62 "the final sphere": the Empyrean, true Paradise (Canto XXX f.).

70 Jacob: see note to *Paradiso* XXI.29.

77 "a den of thieves": see AV Matthew 21.13.

80 "that fruit": Church revenues. See *Dë Monarchia* III.X.17.

88 Peter: the first of the Apostles. See Acts 3.6: 'And Peter said, "I have no silver or gold; but what I have I give you." '

90 Francis: St Francis of Assisi. See *Paradiso* XI.43 f. and notes.

94–5 The dividing of the Red Sea, and the passage of the children of Israel, is found in Exodus 14.21–2. For the dividing of the waters of Jordan, see Joshua 3.13 f.

111–17 "the sign after Taurus": Gemini (the Twins), the constellation under which Dante was born. The sun ("he", l. 116) is in conjunction with Gemini from 21 May to 21 June. Gemini was believed to dispense intellectual and literary gifts. Dante clearly accepted the notion that stellar influences determined qualities of mind or personality and also initiated one's impulses; however, he refuted astral determinism, and always vigorously vindicated the notion of the freedom of the human will in all cases to exercise choice (see *Purgatorio* XVI.73–81). Dante's 'return' to his constellation supports in part the Platonic notion discussed in *Paradiso* IV.49–60 (see notes).

134 "the globe": the earth, at the centre of the heavenly system.

139–41 The moon, whose dark patches are only visible on the side turned towards the earth. See *Paradiso* II.49 f. and notes.

143 "your son": the sun.

143–4 "the movement/About and near him": i.e. the movement of Mercury and Venus, children of Maia and Dione respectively.

145–6 Jove: the planet Jupiter; "father": Saturn; "son": Mars. See note to *Paradiso* XVIII.68.

PARADISO XXIII

In the Eighth Heaven of the Fixed Stars, Dante witnesses a symbolic spectacle of the Church Triumphant, a moment of vision in which the effulgent forms of Christ and the Virgin Mary appear together with the souls of the redeemed.

11 "that quarter of the sky": i.e. the middle part of the sky, the zenith.

19–21 "the hosts/Of Christ's triumph": the souls of the redeemed in Paradise form the Church Triumphant, those who in life turned the stellar and planetary influences on their characters and minds to good effect (see note to *Paradiso* XXII.111–17). The Eighth Heaven of the Fixed Stars is the celestial counterpart of Earthly Paradise (*Purgatorio* XXIX f.), and the symbolic vision here of the Church in Triumph is the counterpart to the symbolic procession of Divine Revelation and the Church Militant there.

26 Trivia: i.e. Diana, the moon; "the eternal nymphs": the stars.

29 "A sun": Christ.

30 See note to *Paradiso* XX.1.

32 "The substance of light": cf. John 8.12: [Jesus said] 'I am the light of the world.'

37 Cf. 1 Corinthians 1.24: 'he [Christ] is the power of God and the wisdom of God'.

38 Cf. '*Te Deum*': 'thou didst open the kingdom of heaven to all believers'.

40–42 "fire": lightning, which was believed to result from the explosive escape of igneous vapour from enveloping watery vapour.

43–5 The sight of Christ brings Dante a moment of ecstatic oblivion in a profoundly mystical experience.

54 "the book which holds the past": the memory, as in 'the book of my memory', in Dante, *Vita Nuova* I.

56 "Polyhymnia and her sisters": the Muse of sacred song, and her sister Muses.

55–69 The *locus communis* of the inadequacy of art to express divine experience is exploited widely by Dante (e.g. *Paradiso* X.43–5, XXIV.25, XXXIII.55–7), but with a fine subtlety and range. In such passages the traditional *topos* of inexpressibility frequently finds a place (ll.58–9; see Bibliography, E. R. Curtius, p. 159 f.).

62 "The sacred poem": '*lo sacrato poema*', so-called by Dante. The epithet in the modern title *The Divine Comedy* is a sixteenth-century interpolation in one of the Venetian editions. Cf. *Paradiso* XXV.1 ("the sacred poem"), *Inferno* XVI.128 ("comedy").

67–9 See *Paradiso* II.1–6 and note.

70–75 Beatrice here urges Dante to turn from the loving contemplation of herself to veneration of the Virgin Mary. Dante is always careful to insist on the proper order of his affections wherever Beatrice and the Virgin Mary are together at issue in *The Divine Comedy*. Dante's veneration of Beatrice in his lyric poetry of the *Vita Nuova*, and here in his greatest work, may well have laid him open to charges of unorthodoxy, if not heresy; at the culmination of *The Divine Comedy* a similar subordination is effected (see *Paradiso* XXXIII.38 and note).

73–4 "the rose": the Virgin Mary (see Liturgy); "the divine word": Christ (John 1.14); "the lilies": the saints of the Church (Song of Songs 2.1).

86 The effulgent form of Christ's glorified body has ascended towards the Empyrean, allowing Dante use once more of his dazzled sight.

88, 92 "the fair flower", "the living star": the Virgin Mary (see Liturgy).

94 "another light": the archangel Gabriel.

107 "the supreme sphere": the Empyrean, true Paradise.

112 "The royal mantle": the Primum Mobile, or Crystalline Sphere. This is the ninth material, but translucent, heaven, whose swift spinning imparts motion to all the heavens below and within it, and whose location is in the mind of God (see *Paradiso* XXVII.99, 106–20 and notes).

128 "*Regina coeli*": 'O queen of Heaven', the antiphon sung in church in the Easter period.

132 "the good seed": see Matthew 13.4 f., Galatians 6.7–9.

134–5 "in Babylonian/Exile": i.e. in their life on earth, when their souls are 'exiles' from their true home, heaven. The Israelites lived in captivity in Babylon under Nebuchadnezzar (Jeremiah 52).

138 The just of Old and New Testament times.

139 St Peter, the 'rock' of the Church, and holder of the keys of heaven (Matthew 16.19).

PARADISO XXIV

St Peter, in the Eighth Heaven of the Fixed Stars, puts Dante to an examination on Christian faith.

1 "great supper": cf. 'Happy are those who are invited to the wedding-supper of the Lamb', Revelation 19.9.

2–3 "the blessed lamb": Christ; cf. John 1.29. 'I am the bread of life. Whoever comes to me shall never be hungry, and whoever believes in me shall never be thirsty', John 6.35.

8 "dew": see note to *Purgatorio* 1.95.

9 "spring": cf. Revelation 7.17.

13–15 "the interdependent wheels in clocks": see note to *Paradiso* X.142.

20 f. "so exultant a flame": the soul of St Peter, the first of the Apostles, the founder of the Christian church; 'You are Peter, the Rock, and on this rock I will build my Church, and the powers of death shall never conquer it. I will give you the keys of the Kingdom of Heaven' (Matthew 16.18–19).

26–7 i.e human speech and imagination are inadequate to frame and convey an impression of the song's divine quality, in the same way that the colours of an artist cannot convey a brightness that is beyond the brightest of the pigments at his disposal.

38–9 Peter's walking on the water, sustained by his faith in Christ, is recorded in Matthew 14.28–9.

48 "not a definition": in the degree examination for master or doctor the medieval student-candidate (a 'bachelor') was required to offer 'proofs' by argument in the development of a question posed by the examiner. He was not expected to offer a "definition", i.e. a decisive judgement in answer to a question. This was the task of the examiner in his summary.

57 "my internal spring": cf. 'whoever believes in me . . . streams of living water shall flow out from within him', John 7.38.

59 "old commander": St Peter. The Italian text has *'primopilo'* (Latin *primopilus*), the senior centurion of a Roman legion.

62 "your dear brother": these words are used by St Peter himself in his second general letter (AV 2 Peter 3.15) in reference to St Paul.

64–5 The definition of faith in St Paul's letter to the Hebrews: 'Now faith is the substance of things hoped for, the evidence

[Vulgate: 'argumentum'] of things not seen', AV Hebrews 11.1; or as the *NEB* translates: 'Faith gives substance [foundation] to our hopes, and makes us certain [i.e. provides evidence, or "argument"] of realities we do not see.'

72 "there below": on earth.

76 "to syllogise": i.e. to reason, or argue, in order to produce proof or evidence. The syllogism, a mode of argument used extensively in the medieval schools, consisted of three propositions: a major premise or general statement, a minor premise or instance, and a third proposition, the conclusion, deduced from these.

93 The books of the Old and New Testament constitute the Holy Bible.

101–2 "the works which followed": the miracles performed by Christ, his disciples and apostles; 'the main foundation of our faith is the miracles performed by him who was crucified . . . and, in his name, by his saints', Dante, *Convivio* III.VII.16.

104–5 St Peter warns Dante that his arguments, based on evidence from the Bible itself, are tending to become circular. Dante takes the hint, and in ll. 106–11 adduces as evidence the miraculous conversion of the whole western world to Christianity, an argument found in St Augustine and others.

109 Cf. Christ's commission to his disciples, to heal and preach in total poverty, Matthew 10.9–10.

110–11 For the biblical metaphors, see Matthew 13.3 f., 20.1 f.

113 "We praise God": the 'Te Deum laudamus', one of the earliest hymns of the Church, in use since the fourth century.

125–6 Peter entered the empty tomb of Christ before the younger apostle John; see John 20.1–8.

130–32 Dante proceeds to paraphrase freely the initial proposition of the Nicene Creed, which he then develops in terms of the Aristotelian proposition of God as the Unmoved Mover.

133–4 "proofs,/Physical and metaphysical": as those adduced in Aquinas, *Summa Theologica* I, q. II, art. 3, based on Aristotle.

135 "Also the truth": divine revelation by the illuminating grace of God.

137 "you": the plural ('*voi*') indicates not only St Peter, author of two general letters, but also the authors of the Acts of the Apostles, the other Letters (Epistles), and Revelation, which follow the Gospels (the Evangelists) in the New Testament.

138 "the burning spirit": the Holy Spirit at his Pentecostal appearance (Acts 2.1 f.).

139 "three eternal persons": God as Father, Son and Holy Spirit.

144 See Matthew 28.19, 2 Corinthians 13.14, AV 1 John 5.7.

PARADISO XXV

In the Heaven of the Fixed Stars, St James examines Dante on the doctrines of hope. St John then presents himself to Dante, and clarifies the mystery of his presumed assumption into Heaven.

1–3 "the sacred poem": see note to *Paradiso* XXIII.62. Dante's claim (l. 2) for the divine inspiration of his great work is not merely a literary convention of the same order as his invocations to the Muses or Apollo in the prologues of his *cantiche*. In his dedicatory *Letters* X to Can Grande della Scala (the authenticity of which seems beyond dispute), Dante makes an earnest claim for the reality of his experience in Paradise (which might, presumably, hold good also for that related in Hell and Purgatory), urging his doubting critics to consider scriptural authority which authenticates the possibility of such experiences, and also less exalted sources such as the mystical literature of Richard of St Victor, St Bernard and St Augustine. Dante anticipates the criticism that he might have been soo sinful for a similar favour, by alluding to Nebuchadnezzar, whom God enlightened in visions, although a sinner.

5 "that lovely fold": Florence, from which Dante had been banished in 1302 in the political purges mounted by the Black Guelfs. See notes to *Inferno* VI.64–9. Dante may have been writing these lines c.1319, a year or so before the completion of *The Divine Comedy*.

8–9 Dante was baptised in the font of the Baptistry of St John in Florence (see *Inferno* XIX.16–18 and note), where he hoped he might receive the poet's crown on completion of *The Divine Comedy*, in a ceremony that would mark a reconciliation with his much loved, but erring, city. It was destined not to be so. See also Dante's *Eclogues* I (of early 1319) addressed to Giovanni del Virgilio, professor of Latin literature at the University of Bologna.

13 "a light": St James the Great, the apostle and brother of St John, who was killed by order of Herod Agrippa (Acts 12.2). St James was believed to have preached the Christian gospel in Spain, and his body to have been transported miraculously to Galicia (l. 18), to what was to become Santiago de Compostela, a centre of pilgrimage second only in importance to Rome in the medieval world.

19–24 The image of the doves here recalls its usage also in *Inferno* V.82–4, in the very different context of carnal love. Here, uniting the souls of Peter and James in perfect amity, is their "ardent love" (l. 108) of Christ.

26 "before me": Dante employs the latin '*coram me*' in the original text, to elevate the style at this sacred moment when the two apostles descend to speak to him. Dante sometimes attributes Latin phrases to his worthiest interlocuters (Virgil, *Inferno* I), and even whole sentences (Pope Adrian V, *Purgatorio* XIX; Cacciaguida, *Paradiso* XV) whilst he himself more often, and less obtrusively, uses Latinisms to which Italian easily lends itself.

29 Beatrice now addresses St James, whose brief letter amongst the other epistles of the New Testament emphasises more than once the generosity of God's love, thus sharpening the hope and expectation of the believer.

33 "the three": Peter, James and John, who were present at all the significant moments of Christ's ministry on earth, including the Transfiguration (Mark 9.2), and Gethsemane (Mark 14.33).

37 "the second flame": St James.

38 The well-known metaphor is from Psalms 121.1.

52 "the church militant": the Church of all believers on earth.

54 "the sun": the mind of God; "our host": the Church Triumphant; see note to *Paradiso* XXIII.19–21.

56 i.e. from the world, where man is a captive of the flesh and his sinfulness, to heaven, where, released from his sins and tendency to sin, he is truly free. See *Purgatorio* II.46 and note, and Hebrews 12.22.

67–9 Dante defines hope closely following Peter Lombard, *Sentences* III.26.1, since no definition is afforded by either St James (who does not mention the word hope) or other authors of the New Testament. See also Aquinas, *Summa Theologica* I.II, q. 62, art. 1 f., II.II, q. 17, art. 1 f.

70 "many stars": Dante's use is metaphorical here, to denote scriptural and patristic writers; cf. the imagery of Daniel 12.3.

72 King David, author of the Psalms, "the singer of the Holy Spirit" (*Paradiso* XX.38).

73–4 See Psalms 9.10.

78 "your shower": the Italian indicates here both St James and David.

79–81 Dante here uses an apt image, in view of Mark 3.17, where James and his brother John are nicknamed by Christ the 'Sons of Thunder'.

91–3 See Isaiah 61.7 and 10. There the "double garment" is salvation and integrity, but here in "this delightful life" (Paradise) it will be made of the soul and the glorified, resurrected body (see note to *Inferno* VI.106 f.).

96 See Revelation 3.5, and 9.11.

98 "*Sperent in te*": 'they will trust in thee'; see ll. 73–4 and note above.

100 "a light": St John.

101–2 St John's presence is like that of the sun, turning night into day. The constellation of Cancer, in the night sky of midwinter (from 21 December to 21 January) rises at sunset and sets at sunrise.

112–14 St John, Jesus' favourite disciple, reclined on Christ's breast at the Last Supper (John 13.23). Here Christ is seen as a "pelican in the wilderness" (AV Psalms 102.6), redeeming mankind with his blood, as the pelican, according to medieval legend, was believed to succour its young with blood pecked from its own breast. St John was requested by Christ, from the Cross, to take care of his mother Mary after his death (John 19.26–7).

123 Dante somewhat impertinently (the humour of the situation is not to be ignored) attempts to see whether in the glowing form of St John, he can descry his glorified body, and thus resolve the puzzle dear to certain medieval theologians, as to whether the apostle had in fact been assumed into heaven before his death (see John 21.22–3).

125 "the day": the Day of Judgement. See notes to *Inferno* VI.95–106 f.

127 "two robes": see note to ll. 91–3 above.

128 "only those two lights": Christ and the Virgin Mary. St John, Enoch and Elijah, about whom theologians speculated, are therefore all excluded.

PARADISO XXVI

St John examines Dante on love. Adam then answers Dante's questions on the circumstances of his life in Eden and after.

4–5 Dante has been temporarily blinded by the light emanating from the soul of St John (see previous canto, ll. 118–23, 138), and it is in this condition that he is examined by the apostle on love. The blindness is symbolic above all of the occlusion of the intellect (in the allegorical semantics of *The Divine Comedy* 'sight' means understanding), for love is essentially an operation of the will. Faith and hope, on the other hand, belong to the province of the intellect: faith is 'argument from belief', and hope (the "expectation of future glory") has faith as its 'substance' (see *Paradiso* XXIV.64 f., XXV.67 f.). Love, grounded in the will (which is the "spiritual motion" of the desires, see *Purgatorio* XVIII.31–3), and directed towards its fulfilment in harmony with the will of God, is the supreme virtue of the Christian life: 'In a word, there are three things that last for ever: faith, hope, and love; but the greatest of them all is love' (1 Corinthians 13.13; see also St Paul, ib. 1–12 for the characteristics of love). See Singleton.

12 Ananias cured St Paul's blindness, which had been laid on him by Christ at his conversion on the road to Damascus. See Acts 9.1–19.

14–15 These lines, in concept and style, are redolent of the world of the courtly love lyric, proper to the time of the *Vita Nuova*, when Dante first knew and fell in love with Beatrice. See also *Purgatorio* XXX.40–42.

16–17 "The good": i.e. God, as beginning and end of all things (see Revelation 22.13).

25–6 i.e. Dante's love of God, as the "target" (l. 24) of his affection, derives from the speculative reason (see ll. 25, 37–9) and from the revelation of Holy Scripture (l. 26).

31–6 i.e. the soul of man, by its very nature, loves what is or seems good, therefore it is bound to love God above all, since he is the very "Essence" (l. 31) of all things, and *ipso facto* source of all the good that man knows or can know. See *Paradiso* XXIV.130–34 and notes.

38 "him": either Aristotle himself, or St Thomas Aquinas, whose sources in turn range from Aristotle to Albertus Magnus.

39 i.e. the instinctive love of the angels and of men (whose soul is immortal) for God, an aspect of the soul's "natural love" or "primary desire" (see *Purgatorio* XVII.91 f., XVIII.49 f. and notes, *Paradiso* I.109 f. and note).

42 God's words to Moses in Exodus 33.18.

44 The Gospel of St John is probably intended, the fullest exposition amongst the four gospels of the nature and purpose of Christ as life, light and love.

52 "the eagle of Christ": St John.

57 "charity": i.e. Dante's Christian love of God.

59–60 "the death which he sustained": Christ's crucifixion, by which man is redeemed and saved for eternal life, the Christian's hope.

65 "the eternal gardener": cf. 'I [Jesus] am the real vine, and my Father is the gardener', John 15.1.

83 "The first soul": Adam.

106 "the true mirror": God, who mirrors all things, but whom no created thing can fully mirror. Cf. *Paradiso* XIX.49–51.

110 The Garden of Eden, or Terrestrial Paradise, located by Dante on the summit of Mount Purgatory (*Purgatorio* XXVIII f.).

111 "the long stairway": the ascent to heaven.

115–17 "the tasting of the tree": see note to *Purgatorio* XXIV.116.

117 Adam's sin was not gluttony, but disobedience caused by presumption. By eating the fruit of the forbidden tree, Adam directly disobeyed God's word, thus "going beyond the bounds". Cf. note to *Purgatorio* XXIX.24.

118 "that place": Limbo, in the first circle of Hell. See *Inferno* II.52 f., and IV.55.

118–23 Adam, created according to Eusebius in 5198BC, died aged 930 (l. 122; and see Genesis 5.5), and was released by Christ from Hell in 34AD (see *Inferno* IV.55) after a period of 4,302 years.

125–6 Dante's earlier view, in *De Vulgari Eloquentia* I.VI.4 f., was that Adam's language had been spoken by all mankind until the destruction of the Tower of Babel (see note to l. 126 below) and thereafter by the Hebrews alone.

126 Nimrod: see note to *Purgatorio* XII.34.

128 "Following the stars": i.e. in the realm of the natural world. See note to *Purgatorio* XVI.73.

134 "*YAH*": God's name, from the initial of Jehovah; see AV Psalms 68.4.

136 "*EL*": God's name as it frequently appears in Hebrew texts.

137–8 Cf. Horace, *Ars poetica* 60 f.; Dante, *De Vulgari Eloquentia* I.IX.6 f.

139 "On the mountain": i.e. in Eden, before and just after the Fall, and before his expulsion.

141–2 i.e. from 6 a.m. to about 1 p.m.

PARADISO XXVII

In the Heaven of the Fixed Constellations, St Peter pronounces sentence on the materialism of the contemporary Church. Dante and Beatrice then ascend to the ninth and highest of the material heavens, the Primum Mobile.

1–2 The assembled souls of the Church Triumphant burst out in a song of glory to God, in the words of the ancient 'Gloria' of the Church's liturgy.

10 "the four torches": the soul of Adam, and of the saints Peter, James and John.

11 "the one": St Peter, the Rock and founder of the Church. See note to *Paradiso* XXIV.20 f.

14–15 i.e. Jupiter would take on the colour of Mars (a hot, red glow), and Mars that of Jupiter (the white of coldness). See *Convivio* II.XIII.25.

16 "The providence": i.e. the will of God.

22 f. "The man": Boniface VIII, the pope reigning in 1300. See *Inferno* XIX.52–7 and note, XXVII.85 f. and note.

25 "my burial place": in St Peter's Basilica, Rome.

35–6 The convulsion of nature at Christ's crucifixion and death is recorded in Matthew 27.45 f.

40 "The spouse of Christ": the Church. See Ephesians 5.22 f.

41 St Peter and his two successors, the popes St Linus and St Cletus, were all martyred for their faith, in c.67, c.79, and c.90AD respectively.

44 Sixtus I (d. 125), Pius I (d. c.155), Calixtus I (d. 222) and Urban I (d. 230) were popes who died for their faith.

46 "one party": the Guelfs, militant supporters of the papacy in Italy throughout the thirteenth and early fourteenth centuries. See *Paradiso* VI.100 f. and notes.

47 "Upon the right hand": i.e. upon the favoured side. Cf. Mark 16.19 and *passim*.

48 "the rest": including the Ghibellines, supporters of the Empire and the imperial cause, adversaries of the Guelfs.

49 "the keys": the emblem of the papacy (see note to *Purgatorio* IX.117–27), borne in battle by papal troops.

50–51 The papacy conducted lengthy campaigns against Emperor Frederick II and his successors in the course of the thirteenth century, against the Ghibellines in the Romagna and elsewhere, and against rival dynasts in Rome under Boniface VIII (see *Inferno* XXVII.85–90 and notes).

56 "Ravening wolves": see Matthew 7.15.

57 "Up, Lord": cf. Psalms 44.23: 'Bestir thyself Lord!'

·58 "Men from Cahors": John XXII, pope from 1316 to beyond the death of Dante in 1321, was from Cahors, a city noted also for its extortionate bankers (see *Inferno* XI.50 and note). Gascony: Clement V, pope 1305–14, "the lawless shepherd", was a Gascon. See *Inferno* XIX.83 f. and notes, *Paradiso* XVII.82 and note.

61–3 See also ll. 142–8 below. Dante's prophecy of a champion to cleanse and save Christendom is purposely delphic (see also *Paradiso* IX.139 f., XXII.14–15). A fuller identity is hinted at in *Inferno* I.101 f. (the Greyhound) and *Purgatorio* XXXIII.43 f. (the 'DXV'), but nothing definite can be deduced. See notes to the line references above. A constant in all these oracular utterances is Dante's unshakeable faith in the care and providence of God to provide for his people in their need. See note to l. 148 below.

61–2 Scipio Africanus the Elder (d. 183BC) finally defeated the Carthaginians under Hannibal at the battle of Zama (202BC), and ensured the survival of Rome as a Mediterranean power.

64 "heavy with mortality": see note to *Paradiso* I.73–5, XXXII.139.

64–6 Dante is specifically commissioned at only a few points in his narrative to record for mankind what he has seen and learned on his journey through the Afterlife: by Beatrice in *Purgatorio* XXXIII.52 f., by Cacciaguida in *Paradiso* XVII.127 f., and by St Peter in this canto.

68–9 "at the season": i.e. in midwinter, between 21 December and 21 January, when the sun is in conjunction with the constellation of Capricorn ("the celestial goat").

79–84 "when I had first looked down": Dante had first observed the universe beneath him as he paused in his ascent of the celestial ladder from Saturn to the Eighth Heaven of the Constellations (*Paradiso* XXII.133 f.). The first observation had taken place directly over the meridian of Jerusalem; this second observation takes place over the meridian of Cadiz, ninety degrees (l. 80) west of Jerusalem, i.e. six hours later. The "first zone" or "clime" was the first of seven horizontal zones in medieval geography. It embraced the eastern and western extremities of the known land-mass in the Northern Hemisphere, from the Ganges to Spain, with Jerusalem in the middle, an arc of 180 degrees. This new vantage point allows Dante an unprecedented view westwards, into the Atlantic, enabling him to trace the course of Ulysses' last voyage (ll. 82–3; see *Inferno* XXVI.90 f. and notes); his view eastwards, limited by the encroaching dusk, extends almost to the shore of Phoenicia, where Jupiter, disguised as a bull, had abducted Europa (l. 84; see Ovid, *Metamorphoses* II.833 f.). Dante's recall of Ulysses at this point underscores the epic foolishness of the Greek hero and his tragic end, in contrast to the truly moral and heroic journey that Dante is undertaking under the guidance of Providence towards the sublime objective of the vision of God.

87 "a whole sign and more": i.e. in the constellation of the Ram, thirty degrees or more west of Dante, who is in the constellation of Gemini (see *Paradiso* XXII.111–17 and note).

98 "the lovely nest of Leda": i.e. the constellation of Gemini, so named from the twins Castor and Pollux, born from eggs sired on Leda by Jupiter in the guise of a swan (see Ovid, *Heroides* XVII.55–6).

99 f. "the swiftest of the heavens": the Primum Mobile, or Crystalline, the ninth and final material heaven (see *Paradiso* XXIII.112 f. and note). The Primum Mobile is translucent and its matter therefore is "so uniform" (l. 101) that it is not possible to orientate oneself within it. In this heaven time and space ("The nature of the universe", l. 106) have their origin.

106–7 The centre of this Ptolemaic system is the motionless earth, around which the heavens wheel.

111 "the power it rains down": see *Paradiso* II.113 f. and notes.

121 f. "Cupidity!": Beatrice's brief but exalted exposition in the preceding verses, beginning with the nature of the universe and its overall envelopment by "Light and love" (l. 112), and concluding with a reference to the origin of time, leads to a consideration of how humanity, in the midst of the majesty and order of the Creator's handiwork, uses the time granted to it. Man, far from contemplating the things of God, has his eyes "not raised/To things above, but fixed on earthly things", as Pope Adrian on the Cornice of Avarice frankly confesses (*Purgatorio* XIX.118–19, and see ib. XV.49–54). Brutish materialism, rather than loving spirituality, rapidly begins to characterise man as he moves from childhood to maturity (ll. 127–35); and much of the fault must lie with the negligent or corrupt rulers of Christendom in Church and State (ll. 140–41; and see *Purgatorio* VI.97 f., XVI.97–112; *Paradiso* XXVII.22 f.).

136 "the daughter": probably the moon as Proserpine (Diana), daughter of Zeus (Jupiter), who as Lucetius is god of the light of day (l. 137). The moon's full face is largely blacked out in its first phase as new moon (l. 138).

142–3 i.e. 'before long' (by antiphrasis). The inaccurate Julian calendar, in use in Dante's time, which did not take into account the "fractional days" (it lengthened the year by one hour every five years), would eventually after many centuries have pushed January into spring. See ll. 61–3 above and note.

148 "the flower": (Ital. *fiore*) some commentators have taken this to be a veiled reference to the mystic Joachim of Flora (Gioacchino da Fiore) and his predicted Reign of the Holy Spirit, a notion regarded as heretical by the Church, but probably very influential for Dante. See notes to *Paradiso* XII.140–41, *Purgatorio* XXXIII.43.

PARADISO XXVIII

From the vantage point of the highest of the material heavens, the Primum Mobile, Dante experiences a symbolic vision of God surrounded by his angels, which is then explained at length by Beatrice in terms of the reality of the angelic hierarchy and its relation both to God and to the material heavens.

10 Dante's vision of God and his angels begins as a mysterious reflection in Beatrice's eyes, similar in kind to the episode in Earthly Paradise where the mystery of the dual nature of the griffin (Christ) is revealed (see *Purgatorio* XXXI.118–23). Here the partial vision begun in Beatrice's eyes is verified and completed by Dante's own visionary experience, as he turns away from Beatrice in an independent act of contemplation.

16 "a point": the symbolic representation of God, as the motionless and indivisible first cause.

25 "a circle of fire": the symbolic representation of the Seraphim, the first and highest order of angels, who, closest to God, see most of him and therefore love him most.

27 i.e. the Primum Mobile (where Dante and Beatrice now are), the ninth, highest and swiftest of the material heavens in the cosmic system of Ptolemy (see *Paradiso* XXVII.99 f. and note).

32 "Juno's rainbow": see note to *Paradiso* XII.12.

51 "the centre": the earth, centre of the cosmic system of the nine

encircling heavens ("the sensible universe", l. 49) as understood
by Ptolemy.

53–4 i.e. the Primum Mobile, the heaven of the angels, surrounded
by the Empyrean. Dante is still seeing things from a geocentric
viewpoint, whence derives his lack of comprehension.

55 "the model": the vision, still in Dante's mind's eye, of the
concentric system of circles of fire, with God at the centre.

56 "the image of it": the "sensible universe" (l. 49), surrounded
by the Empyrean with the earth at its centre. (See note to l. 51
above.)

64 f. Beatrice now proceeds to explain the relationship between
Dante's geocentric conception of the heavens and the heavens'
true relationship to the Empyrean (essential Paradise) which
lies beyond space and time, "bound only by light and love".
Here the heavens are understood in terms of the angelic orders
which govern them, and which Dante sees in his vision as
circles of fire centred upon God.

64 "The material circles": the nine heavens of the Ptolemaic
system. See *Paradiso* II.112–38 and notes.

70 "the one": the Primum Mobile.

72 "the circle": see note to l. 25 above.

74 "the substances": the circle of fire in Dante's vision of the
angelic orders (ll. 25–39).

75 "the virtue": i.e. the quantum of love and knowledge
appropriate to each of the angelic orders.

78 "intelligence": i.e. angel, or angelic order (angels are 'pure
intelligence', unrelated to matter).

80 Boreas: the god of the northerly winds.

91 "the fire": i.e. the circle of fire revealed in Dante's vision.

95 "the *where*": *ubi* in the Italian text; a Latin term of scholastic
philosophy, used as a substantive.

98 f. Beatrice now enumerates the nine angelic orders, which
appear as in the system of the Pseudo-Dionysius' *De Coelesti
Hierarchia*.

108 "the truth in which every intellect rests": God (see also
Inferno III.18 and note).

109–11 With this tercet, Dante takes a clear stand on an issue of
theological and scholastic dispute in his day, whether beatitude
depended primarily on love (an act of the will) or understanding
("sight", l. 110), or intellection. Dante here sides with Aquinas
and the Dominicans against the position generally adopted by
the Franciscans. See also *Paradiso* XIV.40–41.

116 "that everlasting spring": i.e. in the sight of God as creator and giver of life.

116–17 Aries: the constellation of the Ram, which rises with the night in autumn, but with the sun in spring.

130–32 Dionysius: known as the first bishop of Athens, he is mentioned in Acts 17.34 as having been converted by St Paul, and died c.95AD. He was believed in the Middle Ages to have been the author of a widely known treatise on the angelic orders, amongst several other works. Later scholarship disproved his authorship. See note to l. 98 f. above, and *Paradiso* X.115–17.

133–5 St Gregory the Great, pope 590–604, in one of his works arranges the hierarchy of angels slightly differently from Pseudo-Dionysius, an error followed by Dante himself in the earlier *Convivio* II.V.6.

137 "a mortal": Dionysius.

138–9 St Paul. See note to *Inferno* II.28–30; and Colossians 1.16, Ephesians 1.21.

PARADISO XXIX

Beatrice continues her disquisition on celestial order, begun in the previous canto, discussing the creation of angels, and the fall of Lucifer. She concludes by condemning the excesses of speculative theologians and preachers on the subject.

1–6 The astronomical simile (of sun and moon in precise balance at opposite points on the horizon) is intended to convey the sublime moment of seemingly suspended time between the two parts of Beatrice's discourse.

1 "the children of Latona": Apollo (the sun) and Diana (the moon).

2–3 At the spring equinox, the sun is in the constellation of the Ram, opposite the moon, which is in that of Libra (the Scales). For a fraction of time they are bisected by the horizon ("the girdle", l. 5), before the moment of precise balance is lost.

12 i.e. in the mind of God.

13–18 The motive of all Creation, summarised here, and based on the orthodox theology of Aquinas, is seen as God's desire to share his own goodness by conferring his likeness (a reflection of his essence) on other things, a likeness which is existence and knowledge (see *Summa contra Gentiles* II.46, *Summa Theologica* I. q. 50, art. 1).

21 "the face of the waters": cf. Genesis 1.2. The Italian text, however, may refer more especially to the 'waters above the heavens' (Psalms 148.4), i.e. the Primum Mobile itself, which is translucent and known also as the 'aqueous heaven'.

22 "Form and matter, joined together": the heavens and heavenly bodies. "Form and matter . . . simple": (i) simple form, i.e. the Intelligences (angels); (ii) simple matter, i.e. the primal, undifferentiated stuff of creation. These three things are direct and primary creations of God, and as such are incorruptible. For the place of the human soul in the creative act, and the concept of indirect or secondary creation, see *Paradiso* VII.64–78, 124 f. 'Form', a term of scholastic philosophy, denotes the essential character of something, which here is spirit as 'pure act' (see l. 33 and note).

31 "Order": behind Beatrice's disquisition on angels and the angelic hierarchies lies Dante's larger didactic theme in the *Paradiso*, order itself, as sublimely witnessed in the divine order of things explained here, and as seen woefully lacking in the affairs of men, which sin (pride, envy and ambition especially) has totally undermined; "co-created": order, as the characteristic of a thing ('accident') and not a thing in itself, cannot be created, only co-created with and through a 'substance' (see note to l. 32).

32 "In substance": i.e. in and with the angels themselves, which are 'substance' (Dante uses a term of scholastic philosophy) because they possess independent existence.

33 "pure act": a term of scholastic philosophy denoting constant and eternal spiritual activity or dynamic, unimpeded by matter.

34 "Pure potentiality": the characteristic of primal matter, which is incapable of act (defined in note to l. 33), but has the potential to become something.

35–6 "potentiality and act": the heavens and heavenly bodies ("Form and matter, joined together", l. 22).

37–45 Jerome: St Jerome's position (ll. 37–9) was widely discussed by later theologians. Aquinas (as Dante) found the opposite view more probable, that the angels were created simultaneously with the heavenly bodies and primal matter.

41 "what the Holy Spirit dictated": e.g. as in Genesis 1.1, Ecclesiasticus 18.1, where simultaneous creation is implied.

44–5 "motive powers": those angels whose essential function is to be movers or controllers of the nine material heavens. Dante reasons that such angels, as perfect creations of God, must have functioned perfectly from the moment of their creation as movers of the heavens, and so the heavens (the cosmos) must have been created simultaneously with them.

50 "A party of the angels": Satan and the rebellious angels. See Luke 10.18, Revelation 12.7–9.

51 Earth. See note to *Inferno* XXXIV.112.

56 "Pride": see Isaiah 14.12–15, particularly v. 14, and *Paradiso* XIX.46–8.

56–7 "in constraint": see *Inferno* XXXIV.28 f.

61–3 The good angels by virtue of grace received (elevating grace) were content in their humility and gratitude to await the full light of the glory of God (illuminating grace), by which they could see God as he sees himself, in direct vision. Satan, on the other hand, who "could not wait for that light" (*Paradiso* XIX.48), presumed to raise himself towards God by his own natural light, and thereby sinned and fell. Seeing God in his full light as the supreme Good, the remaining angels, disposed as all creatures to love what of the good they perceive, cannot but will and act in accordance with it. This constitutes their beatitude. See Aquinas, *Summa Theologica* I, q. 62, art. 8.

65–6 Beatrice makes the further important point that merit (l. 62) is the reward of grace, not vice-versa, and that grace is given in proportion to the disposition to love (which is an operation of the will). Satan and his companions fell because they willed not to love God in humility and gratitude, but rather aspired to the rewards of full vision of him before receiving the grace which merited it.

76 "These substances": the angels.

79–81 The faculty of memory is only required in order to return to a past or interrupted impression or concept. If the sight of angels in eternity is directed only upon God, with whom all things are *now*, then recall is superfluous.

97 The sudden darkness at the Crucifixion 'over the whole land' (Matthew 27.45) was explained by some medieval commentators of the Bible as an eclipse of the sun by an aberrant moon. Dante is happy to ascribe it to a miracle; for if it were an eclipse then it would have been apparent only locally, and not (as the Bible states) universally.

110 Cf. Mark 16.15: 'Go forth to every part of the world, and proclaim the Good News to the whole creation.'

111 Cf. 1 Corinthians 3.11: 'There can be no other foundation

beyond that which is already laid; I mean Jesus Christ himself.'

118 "the bird": the devil, who in the popular imagination frequently took the shape of a rook, crow or woodpecker.

120 Pardons or indulgences were sold by friars normally licensed so to do in the Middle Ages. Cf. the Pardoner of Chaucer's *Canterbury Tales*, a paradigm of his type.

124 The monks of the Order of St Anthony the Great were renowned in the Middle Ages for their abuse of privilege (see Boccaccio, *Decameron* VI.10). The symbol of St Anthony was a hog, depicted lying at his feet, perhaps representing the devil in subjection. The monks of this Order, who normally kept herds of hogs, paid for their pasture with (Dante states) unauthorised indulgences (l. 126).

130 "This nature": the angels.

134 See Daniel 7.9–10, where angels are in their 'thousands upon thousands . . . and myriads upon myriads'.

136 "The primal light": the light of God's glory.

139–40 For Dante perception or intellection must precede love (see *Paradiso* XXVIII.109–11 and note).

145 Once more, Dante insists on the indivisible unity of the Godhead. See also *Paradiso* XIII.55–60.

PARADISO XXX

From the last of the material heavens, Dante and Beatrice ascend to the Empyrean, essential Paradise. As Dante's sight becomes adjusted to the light he descries the court of heaven in the form of a rose. An empty throne awaits the imminent arrival of Emperor Henry VII.

1–15 Dante's symbolic vision of God as a point of light surrounded by his angels as concentric circles of light (see *Paradiso* XXVIII.16 f.) begins to fade, an experience he likens in these verses to the fading of the stars before the dawn, on earth.

1–3 To an observer at any point on the earth, about an hour before sunrise, the sun itself is at the noonday point some six thousand miles to the east, below the horizon. The apex of the conical shadow of the earth, projected to the back of the east-facing observer, will at the same time be close to, and slightly above, the western horizon line (the "level bed", l. 3).

7 "the brightest handmaid of the sun": Aurora, the dawn.

12 God is, in reality , "Uncircumscribed, and circumscribing all" (*Paradiso* XIV.30).

23 Following the definition of styles in the *Magnae Derivationes* of Uguccione da Pisa (d. 1210), Dante designated his great poem a 'comedy' (see *Inferno* XVI.128) because it begins badly (in Hell), but ends well (in Paradise); and the style 'comic' (i.e. familiar) because considered appropriate to the matter (see Introduction). Dante expands on the terms comedy and comic, tragedy and tragic (the latter he applies to Virgil's *Aeneid*, see *Inferno* XX.113) in his *Letters* X, to Can Grande della Scala.

16–36 This extended encomium of Beatrice, employing many of the devices of the contemporary lyric poetry in praise of the *donna angelo* (*impossibilia*, *topoi* of inadequacy, hyperbole), is appropriate here in the Empyrean, where her beauty, which has steadily increased from heaven to heaven (see *Paradiso* VIII.13–15), is seen now at its fullest.

39 i.e. from the Primum Mobile to the Empyrean, essential Paradise. Beyond space and time, the Empyrean is the true home of God, his angels and his elect ("both the battalions", l. 43), illuminated by the eternal light of God as mind (understanding), love and joy (ll. 40–42).

44–5 Dante will see the souls of the elect in the Empyrean clothed in their glorified or resurrected bodies, such as they will receive on the Last Day (see 1 Corinthians 15.51 f.), whereas so far they have appeared to him largely as refulgences, without recognisable features. (See *Paradiso* XXII.58–69).

52 The Empyrean 'receives most of the light of the primal being, which is God'; it has therefore 'everything which it is capable of having, so that it needs no motion for its perfecting' (*Letters* X.26).

61 "light in the form of a stream": cf. Daniel 7.10; Revelation 22.1.

73–81 "to drink of this water": the stream of light is also the water of grace that Dante must 'drink' in order to strengthen his spiritual sight for the next stage of his experience, the sempiternal rose of the courts of Paradise.

74 "this thirst of yours": see *Purgatorio* XXI.1–3.

90 Dante is now passing in vision 'from time to eternity . . . since the downpouring light becomes, by reflection, a great circle: a river is a familiar symbol of time, whereas the circle is the symbol of eternity' (Singleton).

96 "Both of the courts of heaven": the angels and the souls of the elect.

97 Dante's invocation is addressed no longer to the Muses, or Apollo, but to the light of the grace of God (cf. *Inferno* II.7, *Purgatorio* I.8, *Paradiso* I.13).

100 f. "light up there": the direct light of God's glory, his true essence, is reflected in "one radiance" (l. 106) from the outer surface of the Primum Mobile. In this circular 'lake' or 'sea' of light (cf. Revelation 4.6) Dante firstly sees reflected "Both of the courts of heaven" (ll. 96, 113); then looking up (l. 118 f.) he sees them directly, encircling the gleaming lake.

108 See *Paradiso* XXVII.106–14.

127 "Beatrice drew me": so begin Beatrice's last words to Dante, drawing his attention to the tranquil order and love of the City of God, and the strife, disorder and avarice of the City of Man.

132 Dante held that the world was in its final age in *Convivio* II.XIV.13, but here he suggests its very imminent conclusion, in harmony perhaps with the eschatological theories of his times (see note to *Purgatorio* XXXIII.43).

135 i.e. before Dante achieves entry to Paradise, after his bodily death.

137 "the great Henry": Henry VII of Luxemburg, Emperor of the Holy Roman Empire 1308–13, on whom Dante placed great hopes of bringing Christendom to a state of order and peace (see note to *Purgatorio* XXXIII.43). Henry died prematurely in 1313, campaigning in a recalcitrant Italy, before the composition of the *Paradiso*.

139 "blind cupidity": an invective similar in terms and intention to that in *Paradiso* XVII.121 f., 139–41, and in *Letters* VI 'To the most iniquitous Florentines', who stubbornly resisted the claims of Henry in Italy.

142–4 Clement V, pope 1305–14 (see note to *Inferno* XIX.83), at first warmly supported the election and progress of Emperor Henry VII and issued encyclicals (1309, 1310) to encourage allegiance to him. Upon Henry's arrival in Italy, however, Clement adopted an equivocal position probably as a result of political pressure applied by the French monarch Philip IV; then in 1312 he switched his support to Henry's opponents in Italy, the Angevin king Robert of Naples and the league of cities (including most notably Florence) which united behind him. Dante's rage as he recalls this betrayal swells his keen contempt for Clement already expressed in several places in *The Divine Comedy: Inferno* XIX.82 f., *Purgatorio* XXXII.148 f., *Paradiso* XVII.82, XXVII.58–9.

145–8 Clement V died in 1314, a year after Henry's death. Dante predicts his fate to be damnation in Hell, in the third valley of Malebolge, amongst the simoniacal popes (see *Inferno* XIX.82 f. and note).

147 Simon Magus: see note to *Inferno* XIX.1.

148 "the Anagni man": Boniface VIII, pope 1294–1303. See *Inferno* XIX.52–7 and note, *Purgatorio* XX.85–90 and note.

PARADISO XXXI

Dante contemplates the angels and the elect in the Empyrean, the sempiternal rose of Paradise. Beatrice returns to her place amongst the elect, leaving Dante (who addresses to her a final encomium) in the care of St Bernard of Clairvaux. The saint and mystic points out to Dante the throne in Paradise of the Blessed Virgin Mary.

2 "The holy army": the glorified souls of those elected and justified by God through faith in Jesus Christ, his Church in Triumph and mystical spouse (see Ephesians 5.22 f.).

4 "the other army": that of the angels.

13 For the aspects of angels described here by Dante, see Ezekiel 1.13, Matthew 28.3.

26 "dispensations": Testaments. The souls are those of believers of the Judaic and Christian faiths: those born before Christ under the old dispensation of the Law of God, and those born after Christ under the new dispensation of the Love of God.

28 "threefold light": the glory of the triune God, Father, Son and Holy Spirit.

31–2 i.e. from the north, in which horizon the constellations of the Great and Little Bear belong. For the story of Helice and Arcas, see note to *Purgatorio* XXV.131–2.

35 "the Lateran": the papal palace in Rome in Dante's time, formerly a residence of the Emperors of Rome until the time of Constantine the Great (see note to *Paradiso* VI.1–3).

39 "From Florence": this is Dante's last remark about his native city, for whose past virtues and achievements he entertained a lasting love (see *Paradiso* XV), but for whose current material-ism, political opportunism and arrogance he felt deep revulsion (see *Paradiso* XVI and notes; *Inferno* XXVI.1 f., and elsewhere).

49 "charity": Christian love (*caritas*), the greatest of the Christian virtues of faith, hope and charity. See 1 Corinthians 13.1–13.

59 "an old man": St Bernard of Clairvaux (l. 102), 1091–1153, of the Cistercian Order of monks. As reformer, preacher and moving spirit of the Second Crusade, his practical influence in Church affairs of the twelfth century was considerable, but he was also a writer of devotional works of a mystical character, and ardently devoted to the cult of the Virgin Mary. Dante refers to one of his important mystical works, the *De Consideratione*, in *Letters* X.80.

72 Again Dante emphasises Beatrice's main allegorical role as she "who lights the intellect to truth" (*Purgatorio* VI.45), i.e. Wisdom, 'the flawless mirror of the active power of God' (Wisdom of Solomon 7.26).

81 Beatrice descended from Paradise into the Limbo of Hell in order to solicit Virgil's help as Dante's guide through Hell and Purgatory (see *Inferno* II.52 f.).

85–6 "from servitude/To liberty": i.e. from the slavery of sin to the freedom of God's service (see Romans 6.20–23), or from the slavery of the Law to the freedom of Love (Galatians 3.13, 23). Dante's claims for Beatrice's extraordinary "power and . . . goodness" (l. 84) may well seem to exceed the bounds of Christian orthodoxy (see also l. 89). But Dante's emphasis is carefully placed, in the body of *The Divine Comedy*, on her intermediary role, in both the literal and allegorical senses. She is the one who led Dante to God by virtue of her beauty and goodness (*Purgatorio* XXXI.22–4), a reflection (l. 72) of those attributes of God (and therefore, she is a channel not a source of grace; cf. l. 83). For the reflexive or intermediary quality of her allegorical sense, see note to l. 72 above and note to *Purgatorio* XXVIII.40.

93 "the eternal fountain": God (see Psalms 36.8–9, esp. v. 9: 'for with thee is the fountain of life').

95 "the path": i.e. the path towards beatitude, which is the direct vision of God (the 'beatific vision'), the path upon which, unconsciously, Dante set his feet in 1274 when he saw Beatrice (the 'bringer of blessing') for the first time (see *Vita Nuova* II).

100 "the queen of Heaven": the Virgin Mary.

104 "our Veronica": the alleged image of Christ left on the towel which had been used by St Veronica to wipe his face on the way to his crucifixion. It was displayed in St Peter's, Rome, on 8 March.

118 "I raised my eyes": Dante with this brief phrasing clearly had

in mind here Psalms 121.1: 'I will lift up mine eyes unto the hills, from whence cometh my help.' The process of Dante's rescue had begun with the concern of the Virgin Mary ("a gentle lady in heaven", *Inferno* II.94).

124–5 "the chariot/Which Phaeton drove": the sun (see note to *Inferno* XVII.107–8).

127 "oriflamme": the red and gold standard of the kings of France, carried in battle from 1152, and last used at Agincourt (1415).

132 Each angel was accredited with a different species.

PARADISO XXXII

St Bernard identifies for Dante the elect from those born before and after Christ who, redeemed, are seated in glory in the rose-shaped court of the Empyrean, true Paradise, and explains to him the presence there of unbaptised children.

1 For St Bernard, see note to *Paradiso* XXXI.59.

4 "The wound": that of Original Sin, caused by Adam's disobedience to the law of God, an act initiated by Eve although completed, ratified and transmitted by Adam (see Genesis 3.1–6, and note to *Purgatorio* XXIX.24). Cf. 'It was through one man [Adam] that sin entered the world, and through sin, death ... through the disobedience of the one man the many were made sinners' (Romans 5.12, 19). The wound, Aquinas specifies, is in man's nature, in which the powers of the soul have since Adam's fault been 'deprived of their proper order whereby they are naturally directed to virtue' (see *Summa Theologica* I.II, q. 85, art. 3, resp.). The Virgin Mary's obedience to God's will in bearing Christ, whose obedience to his Father's will led to the atonement and redemption of man, "closed up and anointed" that wound.

8–12 Rachel: see note to *Purgatorio* XXVII.97; Beatrice: see *Paradiso* XXXI.58–93; Sarah: Abraham's wife, the mother of Isaac; Rebecca: Isaac's wife, mother of Esau and Jacob; Judith: Jewish heroine of the time of Nebuchadnezzar, in the Apocryphal book of Judith; "the woman": Ruth, grandmother of King David, "that singer". David's "fault" was sending his general Uriah to his death, in order to possess his wife Bathsheba (2 Samuel 11–12).

29 "the lady of heaven": the Virgin Mary.

31 "the great John": St John the Baptist, cousin and herald of

Jesus Christ, the prophet of the Judaean desert (Matthew 3.1 f.), who was summarily executed by Herod on the whim of his niece Salome (Matthew 14.3–12) some two years before Christ's crucifixion. St John thus remained two years "in hell" (Limbo; the first circle in Dante's *Inferno*) before Christ's death, his Harrowing of Hell, and his raising of the prophets and patriarchs to Paradise.

34 Francis: St Francis of Assisi (see *Paradiso* XI.28 f. and notes). Benedict: see *Paradiso* XXII.31 f. and note. Augustine: St Augustine (354–430), mystic and scholar, whose works on the Holy Trinity, free will, and the soul form the foundation of Christian theology. In spite of St Augustine's intellectual and spiritual stature, Dante accords him only brief recognition in *The Divine Comedy* (see *Paradiso* X.120).

49 f. Dante's perplexity arises from the fact that some children in the tiers of Paradise occupy higher seats than others. He will learn by what follows that their differing elevation or beatitude is the result not of merit but of their differing capacity for grace, to which they are predestined (ll. 65–6).

53–4 Chance is embraced by the Providence of God and therefore has no real significance; "sadness or thirst or hunger": see Revelation 7.13–17.

68 "those twins": Jacob and Esau, twin sons of Rebecca and Isaac (see Genesis 25.21 f.). Of the two, God chose and favoured Jacob in his providential purpose, rejecting Esau.

72 The metaphor might be construed: 'Shall depend on the capacity for grace with which each has been providentially endowed'.

76 "In the earliest centuries": i.e. from the time of Adam to Abraham.

80 i.e. from the time of Abraham, with whom circumcision was instituted as a profession of faith. Circumcision was not considered by Aquinas, however, as 'the perfection of salvation'.

84 "down below": in Limbo (the first circle of Dante's Hell; see note to *Inferno* IV.24).

85 "the face": that of the Virgin Mary.

89 "those holy intelligences": the angels, whose immaterial 'form' is pure mind; but Dante seems to allow them a translucent body.

94–5 The angel Gabriel is "that love". See AV Luke 1.28: 'Hail [Mary] thou that art highly favoured.'

97 "answer": this would come in the form of the completion of

Gabriel's salutation at the Annunciation, 'The Lord is with thee; blessed art thou amongst women.'

121 "He": Adam (see note to l. 4 above and *Paradiso* XXVI.82 f.).

124–6 "that ancient father": St Peter. See Matthew 16.18–19.

127–9 St John the Evangelist, to whom was attributed the authorship of Revelation, which prophesies the calamities which the early Church ("that lovely spouse") suffered.

131 "the leader": Moses, who led the tribes of Israel through the wilderness to within sight of the Promised Land (see Old Testament, Exodus to Deuteronomy).

133 Anna: the mother of the Virgin Mary.

137 Lucy: St Lucy sits opposite Adam ("paterfamilias"). For her role in Dante's journey of salvation, see *Inferno* II.97 f. and note, *Purgatorio* IX.52 f., and ib. note to l. 20 f.

139 "the time of your vision": Dante everywhere insists that his experience in the Afterlife was a journey, not merely a dream or mystical vision as such. St Paul (not Isaiah, Ezekiel or St John of Revelation) is his illustrious predecessor and model in the Judaeo-Christian tradition. His experience of Paradise is of a journey in which he is "heavy with mortality", as St Peter remarks to Dante (*Paradiso* XXVII.64); and even in the Empyrean, essential Paradise beyond space and time, Dante claims he was actually present: "I have been in the heaven which takes most of his [God's] light" (*Paradiso* I.4). St Bernard's words here to Dante refer therefore not to the journey but to sight, and to the limited time that mortal eyes can bear the refulgence of the courts of heaven, where the souls of the elect appear to him in their glorified bodies and where the light of God's glory is everywhere apparent.

142 "the primal love": God.

148 "Grace from her": from the Virgin Mary.

PARADISO XXXIII

St Bernard's invocation to the Virgin Mary. Dante's vision of God.

1–39 St Bernard's prayer to the Virgin, on which Chaucer freely based the 'Invocacio ad Mariam' in the Prologue of the *Second Nun's Tale*, is itself an effortless synthesis of Marian *topoi* bearing traces and reflections of biblical, patristic, mystical and liturgical writing. Motivated nevertheless by something of the reverence and ardour of Dante's early love poetry in praise of Beatrice, the prayer carefully places her (it is the last mention of Beatrice) in the proper perspective of orthodoxy, and hence in the proper order of Dante's affections (l. 38). See note to *Paradiso* XXXI.85–6.

48 Following Dante's choice of words (*finii*), the translator properly uses "finished" here in the old sense of 'perfected' (see AV Hebrews 12.2: 'Jesus the author and finisher of our faith').

54 The "profound light" of God is the 'true light' (AV John I.9) of understanding, love and power, which is the source of the divine spark in mankind ('the light that lighteth every man that cometh into the world', ib.) and by which all human activity and aspiration is to be judged ('in thy light shall we see light', AV Psalms 36.9).

61 "vision": see note to *Paradiso* XXXII.139.

65 The Sibyl of Cumae (Cuma, near Naples) was one of the prophetesses of the cult of Apollo, whose prophecies were written on the leaves of trees, to be scattered inexorably by the wind (Virgil, *Aeneid* III.441 f.).

76–8 Divine light is unlike intense natural light, from which the eye must turn in order to recover. For Aquinas, divine light must lend power to the inner eye of the contemplative to bear it (*Contra Gentiles* III.54). Cf. ll. 112–13.

85 f. Dante's vision of God is a remarkable *tour de force* of poetry, perhaps unequalled in any literature. The subject is properly speaking inexpressible, since the experience is ineffable ('unspeakable words which it is not lawful for a man to utter', St Paul in AV 2 Corinthians 12.4). Dante's antecedents in apocalyptical and mystical literature (Isaiah, Ezekiel, St Paul, St John, Richard of St Victor, St Bernard, St Bonaventure) resort perhaps more confidently to the requisite analogies than Dante himself, whose approach is conditioned in part by an awareness of the philosophical difficulties inherent in the unique experience. But out of the difficulties arises magnificent poetry, shot through with pathos, since even his powers must logically be unequal to the challenge. For pure understanding, such as Dante begins here to experience in the Beatific Vision, does not require for its acquisition the intermediary of the organic mind (*fantasia*) with its 'material phantasms' (cf. *Convivio* III.IV.9), hence recall must operate in a void, and fail. The point at which the canto ends is the point at which "high imagination" ('*alta fantasia*', l. 142) is starved of material analogues. Dante's vision is perfected in three ascending stages, moving from a perception of the "light" of love which binds the "leaves" of material creation (phenomena represented in scholastic terms as "substances", "accidents" and their mutual relationships) into one unifying principle (a "single volume", l. 86), to a yet deeper vision of the triadic nature of the Godhead (l. 115 f., "three circles/Of three colours"), and finally (l. 127 f.) to a perception within the Trinity of the human contours of the Son of God. Yet even here the philosopher in Dante is not fully appeased, for there remains the deep intellectual problem of the principle that relates the Creator to humanity in the Incarnate Person of the Son: it is a mystery that lies deepest of all, and is revealed to Dante in a properly ineffable moment of illumination (l. 137 f.). See Dante, *Letters* X.28, to Can Grande.

88 Aristotelian terms employed in scholastic philosophy: *substances*, things in themselves possessing independent existence; *accidents*, the inherent, differentiating qualities of things.

91 "form": a scholastic term, signifying the essential character of a thing.

93 The soul is an intellective entity, finding its fulfilment ("gladness") in perfect knowledge of the Truth, which is the Wisdom, the Love and Power of God.

94–6 Normally the memory fails through the passing of time, but Dante's memory here fails instantaneously because of the unmediated fusion of his understanding with infinite reality (see note to l. 85 f. above). Lines which delighted T. S. Eliot ('it is the real, right thing, the power of establishing relation between beauty of the most diverse sorts: it is the utmost *power* of the poet', *Dante*, 1929), they contain an intriguing parallelism of roles, since Dante and a god, Neptune, are linked by their marvelling at something beyond their comprehension; the former at the majesty and mystery of the Godhead, the latter at the ingenuity and presumption of man in the invention of a ship.

96 Neptune: the sea god. The *Argo* carried Jason and his companions, the Argonauts in search of the Golden Fleece at Colchis at a date precisely computed by medieval historians. See *Paradiso* II.16 f. and note, *Inferno* XVIII.83 f. and note.

103–5 cf. Aquinas: 'But the sight of the Divine Essence fills the entire human soul with Its good . . . Therefore it is clear that the soul so beatified cannot of its own will forgo its beatitude' (*Summa Theologica* I.II, q. 5, art. 4, resp.).

106–11 As Dante's perception sharpens so as to descry the

Trinity of the Godhead, he insists firstly on the inevitable puerility of his efforts to match words to his experience, and secondly stresses the notion of the Unity of the Godhead as of equal importance to that of His triadic being ('Three Persons in One God': Nicene Creed).

116–20 God the Son is represented as a reflection of God the Father ('Light from Light, Very God of Very God, begotten not made, being of one Substance with the Father', Nicene Creed), the Holy Spirit is the flame that is "breathed equally from both" (cf. the Pentecostal appearance of the Holy Spirit as 'tongues like flames of fire', Acts 2.3).

124–6 Marvellously synthesised into poetry, this tercet is based on several theological propositions: 'God is light' (1 John 1.5); 'As the Father knoweth me, even so know I the Father' (AV John 10.15); and the related propositions that God the Father has entire knowledge of Himself, God the Son who shares this knowledge is understood alone by Him, and God the Holy Spirit, as knowing and known, reflects love of, and joy in, this fulness of knowledge.

131 The human profile of the Godhead as God the Son Incarnate.

133–5 "To square the circle" is the mathematically impossible task of discovering the formula that exactly relates the side of a square to the diameter of a circle of equal area.

143–5 Dante's soul, replete with the knowledge and love afforded by a momentary revelation of the deepest mysteries of God, has achieved total freedom to be and enjoy what is its true nature and inheritance. In harmony with the spheres, which respond fully and freely to God's loving order, Dante's soul is one of balanced forces: desire and will are no longer at variance, as Dante wills what he most deeply desires, and desires what his soul most deeply needs.

SELECTED BIBLIOGRAPHY

DANTE'S WORKS IN TRANSLATION

Vita Nuova and Canzoniere, translated by T. Okey and P. H.
Wicksteed, Temple Classics, London, 1911

Dante's Lyric Poetry, translated by K. Foster and P. Boyde,
Oxford University Press, 1967

The Latin Works of Dante, including 'De Vulgari Eloquentia',
translated by A. G. Ferrers Howell; 'De Monarchia', 'Epistolae',
'Eclogues', 'Quaestio de Aqua et Terra', translated by P. H.
Wicksteed, Temple Classics, London, 1904

Dante's Epistolae, ed. P. Toynbee, second edition with bibliography
by C. G. Hardie, Oxford University Press, 1966

Convivio, translated by E. Moore and P. H. Wicksteed, Temple
Classics, London, 1903

Monarchy [De Monarchia] and Three Political Letters, translated
by D. Nicholl, and chronological note by C. G. Hardie,
Weidenfeld and Nicolson, 1954

The Divine Comedy, ed. J. Sinclair, Bodley Head, 1948

The Divine Comedy, ed. C. S. Singleton, Princeton University
Press, 1970–75

DANTE: LIFE, BACKGROUND, GENERAL

Anderson, W., *Dante the Maker*, Routledge & Kegan Paul, 1980

Barbi, M., *Life of Dante*, translated by P. G. Ruggiers, Berkeley
and Los Angeles, 1954

Barraclough, G., *The Medieval Papacy*, Thames and Hudson,
1972

Bergin, T. G., *Dante's Divine Comedy*, New Jersey, 1971

Boccaccio, G., 'Life of Dante', in *The Early Lives of Dante*,
translated by P. H. Wicksteed, Gollancz, 1904

Cosmo, U., *A Handbook to Dante Studies*, translated by D.
Moore, Blackwell, 1950

Curtius, E. R., *European Literature and the Latin Middle Ages*,
translated by W. R. Trask, Pantheon Books, New York, 1953

Eliot, T. S., *Dante*, Faber, 1929

Fergusson, F., *Dante*, Weidenfeld and Nicolson, 1966

Gardner, E. G., *Dante*, Temple Primers, London, 1900

Haskins, C. H., *Studies in Medieval Culture*, Oxford University Press, 1929

Higgins, D. H., ' "The Power of the Master": Eliot's Relation to Dante', p. 129 f., *Dante Studies*, LXXXVIII, 1970

Holmes, G., *Dante*, Past Masters series, Oxford University Press, 1980

Hyde, J. K., *Society and Politics in Medieval Italy*, Macmillan, 1973

Keen, M., *The Pelican History of Medieval Europe*, Penguin, 1969

Larner, J., *Italy in the Age of Dante and Petrarch*, Longman, 1980

Leff, G., *Medieval Thought*, Penguin, 1958

Villani, G., *Chronicle [Cronica]*, translated by R. E. Selfe, ed. P. H. Wicksteed, London, 1906

Vossler, K., *Medieval Culture. An Introduction to Dante and his Times*, translated by W. C. Lawton, Constable, 1929

Wieruszowski, H., *Politics and Culture in Medieval Spain and Italy*, Edizioni di Storia e Letteratura, Rome, 1971

THE DIVINE COMEDY

Dante's Sources (a selected list)

Aquinas, St Thomas, *Summa Theologiae [Theologica]*, Latin text and English translation, eds T. Gilby, P. K. Meagher, T. C. O'Brien, Eyre and Spottiswoode, 1964–76

Aristotle, *Ethics*, translated by J. A. K. Thomson, revised by H. Tredennick, Penguin, 1976; *Politics*, translated by T. A. Sinclair, Penguin, 1962

The Bible (Vulgate version)

Boethius, *The Consolation of Philosophy*, translated by 'I. T.' (1609) and revised by H. F. Stewart, Heinemann, 1918

Cicero, 'On Duties', 'On Friendship', 'On Old Age', 'The Dream of Scipio', in *Selected Works*, *On the Good Life*, both translated by M. Grant, Penguin, 1971

Horace, 'On the Art of Poetry', in *Classical Literary Criticism*, translated by T. S. Dorsch, Penguin, 1965

Livy, *The Early History of Rome*, translated by A. De Sélincourt, Penguin, 1960

Ovid, *Metamorphoses*, translated by M. M. Innes, Penguin, 1955

Plato, *Timaeus*, translated by D. Lee, Penguin, 1965

Richard of St Victor, 'Benjamin Minor', in *Selected Writings on Contemplation*, translated by C. Kirchberger, Faber, 1957

St Augustine, *The City of God*, translated by D. Knowles, Pelican Books, 1972; *Confessions*, translated by R. S. Pine-Coffin, Penguin Books, 1961

St Bernard, *On Consideration*, translated by G. Lewis, Clarendon, 1908

St Bonaventure, *The Soul's Journey into God*, translated by E. Cousins, SPCK, 1978

Statius, *Thebaid, Achilleid*, translated by J. H. Mozley, Heinemann, 1928

Virgil, *Aeneid*, translated by W. F. Jackson Knight, Penguin, 1956

Virgil, *The Pastoral Poems [Eclogues]*, translated by E. V. Rieu, Penguin, 1967

Reference Works

Enciclopedia Dantesca, 5 vols, Rome, Istituto della Enciclopedia Italiana, 1970–76

Siebzehner-Vivanti, G., *Dizionario della Divina Commedia*, Olschki, Florence, 1954

Toynbee, P., *Dictionary of Proper Names and Notable Matters in the Works of Dante*, revised by C. S. Singleton, Oxford University Press, 1968

Studies

Armour, P., *The Door of Purgatory: A Study of Multiple Symbolism*, Oxford, 1986

Auerbach, E., *Dante, Poet of the Secular World*, translated by R. Mannheim, University of Chicago Press, 1961

Auerbach, E., *Mimesis*, translated by W. Trask, Oxford University Press, 1953

Bergin, T. G., ed., *From Time to Eternity*, York 1967

Boyde, P., *Dante: Philomythes and Philosopher*, Cambridge, 1981

Brandeis, I., *The Ladder of Vision*, Chatto and Windus, 1960

Caesar, M., ed., *Dante: The Critical Heritage*, Routledge, 1989

Charity, A. C., *Events and Their Afterlife: The Dialectics of Christian Typology in the Bible and Dante*, Cambridge University Press, 1966

Croce, Benedetto, *The Poetry of Dante*, translated by D. Ainslie, Allen and Unwin, London, 1922

Davis, C. T., *Dante and the Idea of Rome*, Oxford University

Press, 1957; 'Dante's Vision of History', p. 143 f., *Dante Studies*, XCIII, 1975

D'Entrèves, A. P., *Dante as a Political Thinker*, Oxford University Press, 1952

Fergusson, F., *Dante's Drama of the Mind, A Modern Reading of the Purgatorio*, Princeton, 1968

Ferrante, J. M., *The Political Vision of the 'Divine Comedy'*, Princeton, 1984

Foster, K., *The Two Dantes*, Dalton, Longman and Todd, 1977; 'Dante's Idea of Love', see Bergin, T. G., ed.; 'Religion and Philosophy in Dante', see Limentani, U., ed.

Freccero, J., ed., *Dante: A Collection of Critical Essays*, New Jersey, 1965

Gilson, E., *Dante the Philosopher*, translated by D. Moore, Sheed and Ward, 1948

Grayson, C., ed., *The World of Dante*, Clarendon, 1980

Higgins, D. H., *Dante and the Bible: An Introduction*, University of Bristol Press, 1992.

Kaske, R. E., 'Dante's DXV', see Freccero, J., ed.

Kirkpatrick, R., *Dante's Paradiso and the Limitations of Modern Criticism*, Cambridge University Press, 1978; *Dante 'The Divine Comedy'*, Cambridge University Press, 1987

Lewis, C. S., 'Dante and Statius', *Medium Aevum*, XXV, n. 3, 1956

Limentani, U., ed., *The Mind of Dante*, Cambridge University Press, 1965

Mazzotta, G., *Dante, Poet of the Desert*, Princeton, 1979

Moore, E. H., *Studies in Dante*, 4 vols, Clarendon, 1896–1917, reprinted 1968

Orr, M. A., *Dante and the Early Astronomers*, second edition revised by B. Reynolds, Allan Wingate, 1956

Ralphs, S., *Dante's Journey to the Centre*, Manchester University Press, 1972

Reeves, M., 'Dante and the Prophetic View of History', see Grayson C., ed.

Reynolds, B., '*Inferno* XXVI, Dante's Ulysses', p. 145 f., *Lettere Italiane*, XXIII, n. 2, 1971

Scott, J. A., 'Politics and *Inferno* X', p. 1 f., *Italian Studies*, XIX, 1964

Singleton, C. S., *Dante's Commedia. Elements of Structure*, Baltimore, 1977; *Journey to Beatrice*, Cambridge, Massachusetts, 1958

Stanford, W. B., *The Ulysses Theme*, Blackwell, 1963
Whitfield, J. H., *Dante and Virgil*, Blackwell, 1949; 'Dante and the Roman World', p. 1 f., *Italian Studies*, XXXIII, 1978

American Literature

British and Irish Literature

Children's Literature

Classics and Ancient Literature

Colonial Literature

Eastern Literature

European Literature

Gothic Literature

History

Medieval Literature

Oxford English Drama

Poetry

Philosophy

Politics

Religion

The Oxford Shakespeare

A complete list of Oxford World's Classics, including Authors in Context, Oxford English Drama, and the Oxford Shakespeare, is available in the UK from the Marketing Services Department, Oxford University Press, Great Clarendon Street, Oxford OX2 6DP, or visit the website at www.oup.com/uk/worldsclassics.

In the USA, visit www.oup.com/us/owc for a complete title list.

Oxford World's Classics are available from all good bookshops. In case of difficulty, customers in the UK should contact Oxford University Press Bookshop, 116 High Street, Oxford OX1 4BR.

SERGEI AKSAKOV	**A Russian Gentleman**
ANTON CHEKHOV	**Early Stories** **Five Plays** **The Princess and Other Stories** **The Russian Master and Other Stories** **The Steppe and Other Stories** **Twelve Plays** **Ward Number Six and Other Stories** **A Woman's Kingdom and Other Stories**
FYODOR DOSTOEVSKY	**An Accidental Family** **Crime and Punishment** **Devils** **A Gentle Creature and Other Stories** **The Idiot** **The Karamazov Brothers** **Memoirs from the House of the Dead** **Notes from the Underground** and **The Gambler**
NIKOLAI GOGOL	**Village Evenings Near Dikanka** and **Mirgorod** **Plays and Petersburg**
ALEXANDER HERZEN	**Childhood, Youth, and Exile**
MIKHAIL LERMONTOV	**A Hero of our Time**
ALEXANDER PUSHKIN	**Eugene Onegin** **The Queen of Spades and Other Stories**
LEO TOLSTOY	**Anna Karenina** **The Kreutzer Sonata and Other Stories** **The Raid and Other Stories** **Resurrection** **War and Peace**
IVAN TURGENEV	**Fathers and Sons** **First Love and Other Stories** **A Month in the Country**

A SELECTION OF OXFORD WORLD'S CLASSICS